A Sparkle of Silver

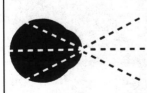

This Large Print Book carries the
Seal of Approval of N.A.V.H.

GEORGIA COAST ROMANCE, BOOK 1

A SPARKLE OF SILVER

LIZ JOHNSON

THORNDIKE PRESS
A part of Gale, a Cengage Company

Farmington Hills, Mich • San Francisco • New York • Waterville, Maine
Meriden, Conn • Mason, Ohio • Chicago

Copyright © 2018 by Liz Johnson.
Scripture quotations are from the Holy Bible, New International
Version®. NIV®. Copyright© 1973, 1978, 1984, 2011 by Biblica, Inc.™
Used by permission of Zondervan. All rights reserved worldwide,
www.zondervan.com
Thorndike Press, a part of Gale, a Cengage Company.

Thorndike Press® Large Print Christian Fiction.
The text of this Large Print edition is unabridged.
Other aspects of the book may vary from the original edition.
Set in 16 pt. Plantin.

LIBRARY OF CONGRESS CIP DATA ON FILE.
CATALOGUING IN PUBLICATION FOR THIS BOOK
IS AVAILABLE FROM THE LIBRARY OF CONGRESS

ISBN-13: 978-1-4328-5853-7 (hardcover)

Published in 2018 by arrangement with Revell Books, a division of
Baker Publishing Group

Printed in Mexico
1 2 3 4 5 6 7 22 21 20 19 18

For Aunt Chris,
who invited me to fall in love with
books when I was a child
and to visit her on St. Simons Island
when I was an adult.
You are a brilliant cheerleader and an
incredible woman.
I'm so thankful you're my aunt.

The greedy stir up conflict but those who trust in the LORD will prosper.

Proverbs 28:25

ONE

There were some things Millie Sullivan would rather forget. The long gravel lane up to this home. The drab interior walls that melted into sticky carpet and stained tile floors. The fact that she could afford nothing better for the woman she loved most.

But every time she stepped into her Grandma Joy's room, Millie tried to be thankful her grandmother could remember anything at all.

"Who are you?" Grandma Joy squinted from across the small studio apartment, her hooded eyes suspicious and the wrinkles at the corners of her mouth growing deeper. "I don't know you. What are you doing here? What do you want?"

Her breath caught in the back of her throat, and Millie tried to recall what she'd done last time. What had the doctor said? *Speak in low tones, calming words.*

"It's all right." She held out her hands,

palms up, an invitation. Taking two slow steps, she dipped her chin and lowered her voice another half an octave. "You're safe. You're in your home."

"I know that. What do you take me for?" Grandma Joy looked like she had half a mind to hop out of her overstuffed rocker at such an offense. "I want to know who you are and what you're doing here."

Fair question.

Try to use familiar words and phrases.

"I'm Mil— Camilla."

Grandma Joy's eyes narrowed further, nearly disappearing beneath loose skin. "Camilla?" Her tone held a hint of recognition.

Millie's chin hitched, a smile already spreading into place. "Yes, Camilla. I'm Robert's daughter."

"Robert?" Any sign of clarity vanished, and her too-pink lips smacked together. "Never heard of him."

Wrapping her arms across her stomach, Millie nodded. "Okay." But it wasn't, not even a little bit. Nearly everything she knew about her dad, she'd learned from his mother. And today Grandma Joy couldn't even remember him.

Her stomach heaved like a boat on stormy waves. What if last time was the last time

Grandma Joy remembered her? What if last time was the last time she heard Grandma Joy's laugh? What if last time was the last time Grandma Joy kissed her forehead and promised that all was well?

The back of her eyes burned, and Millie pressed her hands over her face. Holding every muscle as tight as she could, she forced a smile in place and held it there for three seconds before meeting her grandma's gaze again.

Yes, a smile. That's what she needed. Even if she didn't feel it, Grandma Joy would see it. And even if she didn't recognize Millie's smile specifically, well . . . everyone appreciated a smile. Right?

The smile in question trembled behind the cover of her hands, and Millie sucked in a quick breath between pinched lips.

Remember. She just had to remember. This woman — the one in the faded purple rocking chair — wasn't the one who had raised Millie. She wasn't the one who had taken in her only grandchild and provided for her every need. At best she was a facsimile.

But the only thing Millie could do about it was paste a smile on her face and try to help her remember. And pray that Grandma Joy would come back to her.

Please, God. Let me have her a little longer.
"Miss Sullivan?"

Millie jumped, a shiver racing down her spine. She knew that voice, and it never brought good news. But she was paid up. She was. Her last check hadn't bounced, and Golden Isles had cashed it immediately.

Turning toward the woman at the open door, Millie bestowed the smile she'd been saving for her grandma on Virginia Baker.

The woman's sleek bob wobbled in greeting, but she didn't bother returning the grin. "May I have a word?"

A word, sure. It was imagining the second, third, fourth, and fifth that sent her stomach into a nosedive. Still, Millie turned her back on Grandma Joy and walked toward the door.

Virginia held out her hand in a silent invitation for Millie to step into the hallway. Millie tried to take a steadying breath. The rumble in her stomach was far too much like that time she'd been called into the principal's office for falling asleep in class during high school. She hung her head the same way she had all those years ago as she stepped past Virginia from the warm tones of Grandma Joy's room into the garish lights of the hallway.

"Miss Sullivan, there's just no easy way to

say this."

Suddenly it was hard to breathe. She pressed a hand to her throat and tried to gasp a thread of air, but it didn't help. Neither did Virginia's unforgiving monologue.

"She's getting worse." When Millie opened her mouth to offer an argument, Virginia shook her head. "I'm not telling you anything that you don't already know."

Millie risked a glance toward Grandma Joy, who had closed her eyes and let her mouth drop open. The even creaking of her chair had ceased, and she looked at peace. No longer disturbed by the arrival of a woman she couldn't recognize.

With a sigh Millie nodded. She knew. And no matter how much she wanted to deny it, there had been no evidence to indicate otherwise.

Grandma Joy wasn't going to get better. Her memories weren't going to come back — at least not for longer than a few minutes. But they were in there, and every so often one surfaced, only to nosedive back into oblivion before Millie could use it to pull her grandma closer.

"Your grandmother needs better care. More personalized. She needs someone to look after her one-on-one. All day. And night."

"I know, but —"

Virginia held up her hand. "I know money is a concern."

That was the understatement of the century. Money wasn't just *a* concern. It was the only one. It was all that was holding Millie back from giving Grandma Joy the finest room in the best memory-care facility.

But she couldn't make money where there was none. As far as she knew, it was still illegal to print her own. Besides, she'd need a printer for that, and she highly doubted the library would let her use theirs. Not that she would do such a thing even if she could, of course.

"There is government help available."

"I know. I've applied for all of it. But they've turned her down. Her diagnosis isn't severe enough or something."

Virginia rubbed her chin, a frown tugging at the corners of her lips. "Then you have to appeal. Get a lawyer and take it to court."

Millie held back a snort, but only just. That required money too — a lot of it. And time, which was hard to come by when she was working two jobs just to make ends meet. And even then she'd been late with

14

her own rent again last month.

Maybe Virginia read her face, because she moved on to another option with a hopeful lilt in her tone. "Well then, what about her Social Security?"

"What about it? It doesn't even cover half of your fine establishment's fee every month." As if on cue, the fluorescent light above them flickered, and Virginia's shoulders drooped.

"I'm sorry," Millie said, forcing her sarcasm to stay in check. It wasn't Virginia's fault. None of it. And she couldn't afford to alienate the home's administrator. "I've tried everything I can think of, but we're out of options. Golden Isles is our only choice."

Chewing on her lower lip, Virginia shook her head. "We have a list of people who belong here waiting to get in. I'll give you ninety days. And then you're going to need to find her other arrangements."

"Three months? You can't be serious." Millie's voice rose with each word, her heart skipping every other beat until the chair in her grandma's apartment resumed squeaking. She couldn't look across the room and could barely breathe. "What am I supposed to do?"

Well, that was a silly question. And Virginia

seemed to have only a silly answer.

"Some people find in-home care to be a better choice."

Millie's chin fell against her chest, and she wrapped her arms around her middle as a chill swept down her spine. She'd tried caring for Grandma Joy at home, but the first time she'd been called home from her job at the diner to find her grandma wandering down the road in little more than a threadbare robe, she'd known that they needed help.

That's where Golden Isles Assisted Living had come in. They were desperately understaffed and in a building older than any of their residents, but bless their hearts, they tried. That was all Millie asked for. A safe place with people who genuinely cared for Grandma Joy.

But now they were kicking her out. And leaving Millie in a pickle too big to swallow.

"Please." She hated the way the word came out — desperate, strangled. Taking a deep breath, she tried again. "There has to be another option. I could . . . I could pay you more. I could pay for an extra night nurse."

Yeah, right. She didn't have that kind of money, and she didn't have a clue how to get it. Maybe she could get an extra shift at the diner. That would get her approximately one percent of the way there. The truth was, there weren't enough shifts at the Hermit Crab Café to cover that kind of offer. Not that Virginia Baker was inclined to accept it anyway.

"This isn't a negotiation, Miss Sullivan. She has to move." Virginia dropped her voice on the last sentence, a small consolation to the complete rejection in her words. "I'll begin preparing her paperwork. Let me know if you need some recommendations. I have some literature in my office." She didn't wait for Millie to respond before patting her shoulder and walking away, head high.

Millie slumped against the wall and stared hard at the gray laces of her tennis shoes. She was pretty sure they'd only had one previous owner, the best pair she'd ever found at the thrift store. She pressed her toe into the carpet, wishing there was some sort of pedal she could push that would reveal a solution, but it wasn't that easy.

It never was.

"You're just like your dad."

Her chin snapped up, and she peeked into the room. Grandma Joy's eyes were still closed, but there was a tension in her features that suggested she was awake and

17

— dare Millie even hope? — lucid.

"He never knew what to say to bad news either."

"My dad?"

"My Robert." Grandma Joy readjusted her folded hands over her middle and sighed. "He was so smart, but sometimes he couldn't find the words. He said he always wanted to go to college. Then he up and met your mama, and he couldn't tear his eyes away from her."

Millie took a tentative step into the room, careful to avoid the groans in the old floor, careful not to spook her grandma out of this bout of memory.

"He made mistakes, but he loved me. Just like I know you do."

Millie pressed her lips together and tried to form a picture in her mind of the man she'd last seen when she was four. But the memories were too faded. Maybe that was what it felt like for Grandma Joy, looking for the past that remained elusive.

"Yep. You're so much like your father."

She wanted to ask if that was a compliment. Even though the memories were thin, her perception of her father was anything but. Everything she knew about him was tainted with a thick layer of cynicism based on his selfishness.

But before she could ask, Grandma Joy kept going. "You are your father's daughter. But I'm not."

Millie's eyebrows rose, and she met Grandma Joy's gaze. "You're not what? Not your father's daughter?" That couldn't be. Grandma Joy's dad, Henry, was a good man. There had been pictures of him all over the farmhouse where Millie had grown up.

Grandma Joy's lips twitched, a sparkle in her eyes promising a good secret.

"You're joking, right?" Millie couldn't hold it back.

"My mother, Ruth, was a guest at the Chateau. Before she married Henry."

"Chateau Dawkins?"

Grandma Joy chuckled. "Is there another one?"

A picture of the grand estate on the coast, built by Howard Dawkins, flashed across her mind. Three stories of gleaming white glory reached by curving white staircases and rich archways, surrounded by lush lawns and waving palms. They said at night the lights could be seen half a mile across the ocean, glowing like a beacon, brighter than the island's famous lighthouse. The Chateau adorned postcards in every St. Simons Island gift shop, and the library carried a whole shelf of books about the mansion and its short-lived golden era.

"I just . . ." Millie shook her head, trying to find her words. "You never said."

"Oh, Mama mentioned it a time or two. I think she fell in love there."

Her stomach lurched as Grandma Joy's ramblings suddenly began to make sense. Ruth — Great-Grandma Ruth — had stayed at the wealthiest estate in Georgia during the late 1920s and fell in love there. And Grandma Joy wasn't her father's daughter, which meant . . .

Millie gasped and dropped to her grandma's bed, perching on the edge.

Grandma Joy was the illegitimate child of one of the wealthy guests. Oil and newspapers, real estate and coal — Dawkins had been connected to millionaires of every ilk.

And even an illegitimate heir deserved something from the estate of her father. Right?

"Who was it?" Millie clapped a hand over her mouth. "I'm sorry," she whispered between her fingers. "That was crass. I just meant . . . do you know who your father is?"

That twinkle in Grandma Joy's eyes returned, mischief personified. "She would never say. She didn't put his name on my

20

birth certificate. After all, she was married to Henry before I was born. She said it was between her and her diary. And she hid that away at the estate. After all, she didn't want the treasure map in it to get into the wrong hands."

Ben Thornton scribbled another name on the list. Judith Tulley. That made twenty-three. Twenty-three people identified. Twenty-three lines in his notebook. Each one a ruined life.

"You hear me, Ben?"

He glared at the phone on his desk, faceup and glowing. The thick Southern drawl on the other end echoed in his empty classroom but still managed to make his skin shiver.

"Judith Tulley from Augusta. Ninety-one."

"I heard you, Owen. Why wasn't she in the case?"

Owen shuffled some papers on the other end. "I don't know. Maybe they couldn't find her. Maybe she didn't . . . Well, you know. She's old. Maybe she just didn't want to bother."

"With justice?"

Owen sighed, and Ben could picture the young lawyer running a hand through his too-long hair. "With the hassle," Owen said. "It's not easy. It takes time. A lot of it. Y'all know that."

Yes, Ben knew that litigation had a tendency to drag on. And maybe Judith didn't want to spend what was left of her time on earth trying to see a woman pay for her crimes.

But Ben was young. And he would see that her crimes were paid for and her victims compensated.

"Ben, there's something else." Owen's voice took a decidedly deep turn.

Ben leaned an elbow against the desktop, pushed an essay he'd been grading out of his way, and rested his forehead against his open palm. "What is it?"

"She's filed for bankruptcy."

His groan was entirely involuntary, and he doubled all the way over, face against his desk. "She's going to get away with it." There was no question involved, just a dull certainty that throbbed at the base of his skull.

"If she has no assets, she can't repay the claimants."

That sounded about right. Maybe it had been her plan all along. If she lived lavishly off other people's money, she'd never have to repay all that she'd stolen. And without another mark, she had no source of income.

"I guess that's all we can do." Owen

sounded defeated. Even after he'd won the trial and put a swindler behind bars.

But jail time wasn't restitution. It wouldn't give those people back their savings. It wouldn't make their lives any easier. And if she was claiming bankruptcy, then there was no one to pay them back, no one to make things right.

No one but him.

"Have a good day," Owen said before hanging up the phone.

Standing, Ben took a deep breath of the stale classroom air. He strolled through the rows of empty desks, stooping to pick up a crumpled piece of paper.

He wasn't exactly responsible for cleaning up the classroom. It was only his for three classes a week, after all. Still, the sparse furniture made it easy to tell if the room had been picked up or not. He wasn't about to leave a mess for the tenured professor who would teach the next course here.

Bending over, he snagged a pen that a student had dropped before tossing it into the cup on his desk for anyone who showed up to class without a writing utensil. If only it were as easy to clean up after the mess his mom had made.

And he would have to. It wasn't even a question.

As he slid back into his desk chair and straightened the pile of essays that had been turned in, he gave another hard look at the list in his notebook. There were a lot of names there and few dollars in his checking account. He needed another job. Maybe two.

TWO

A scuffle down the hallway made her gasp, and Millie flung herself against the bookcase behind the door. Holding her breath, she pressed her eye to the crack above a hinge, searching the corridor beyond for the source of the commotion and praying that the pounding of her heart was only audible to her own ears.

If she was caught, her grand plan — her only plan — would be ruined. It had taken her three weeks to cook up the scheme, land a job at the Chateau, and begin searching for her great-grandmother's diary. And as long as she was here, there was hope. At least an inkling that she could find a treasure that would save Grandma Joy.

Whether the treasure was marked on the map in the journal with a big red *X* or Ruth's words revealed the identity of Grandma Joy's father, the Chateau was her only hope. She couldn't afford to be found out of place on her third night at work, or she'd certainly be fired.

Peeking into the hallway, she could only see the pale yellow lines of the wallpaper through the opening.

Until a small child pressed his chubby face into the crack. "What are you doing in there?"

Her pulse galloped as she blinked at the little intruder. She tried to find her breath and her words. "Shh." Adjusting her dress to lower herself to his level, she pressed her finger to her lips. "I'm playing a game. We have to be silent."

"Can I play?" He clearly didn't understand the definition of silent, his voice bouncing down the generous corridor and probably down the spiral stone staircase at the end of it.

"Your mom and dad will miss you. You should go find them."

He wiped the back of his hand across his mouth, and in the flickering light from the antique sconces, she could make out a trickle of green from the corner of his lips to his chin. Apparently he'd indulged in some mint ice cream at the gift shop by the front gate. And now his sticky fingers were pressed against a wooden door older than his great-great-grandparents.

"No. I don't want to. This house is boring."

Boring? For a five-year-old, maybe. For all of the other tourists who paid the entrance fee, Chateau Dawkins was an entry to the past. A window into what had once been. And it held more than enough secrets to keep her interested. But arguing the point wasn't going to get her little visitor to leave her alone. And letting him stay would only alert others to her location.

She patted her hips as though the sleek silk gown would magically grow pockets and a stash of candy in them. But she had nothing to distract him. Nothing she could even use to bribe him.

And all the motion did was remind her how strange the dress felt, even on her third shift. Her simple cotton wardrobe didn't include anything half as luxurious as the knee-length evening gown with its feather embellishments at the shoulder. It was a few decades out of style, but exactly what her Great-Grandma Ruth might have worn when she visited this estate.

But if she wasn't careful, Millie might never find out anything more about Ruth.

Her gaze darted around the room on this side of the door. Cloth-covered books in faded blues and greens and burgundies lined every inch of the deep cherry shelves. Like china in a cabinet, many of them were hemmed in by locked doors, the windows replaced with chicken wire so trapped humidity wouldn't ruin the precious tomes. A turn-of-the-century sofa took up the majority of the center of the room. The matching gray wingback chair in front of the empty fireplace looked perfect for curling up with one of the thousands of stories on these shelves. On any other night, in any other situation, she might have done just that. But none of this would distract her young visitor.

The red velvet rope across the doorway hadn't stopped her from entering. And it wasn't likely to keep out someone who could so easily go under the barrier.

The little guy made a move to duck under it, his eyes bright with mischief, and she lunged around the door, blocking his entry before slinking into the shadows on the opposite side.

"You have to go back to your family. Please."

Perfect. Now she was begging a five-year-old. She might not have had a lot of experience with kids, but even she knew that showing her desperation was bound to end poorly.

"But I don't want to. I want to play the game."

The game? Right. The one where they were silent.

Except it would be anything but when the kid's parents noticed he was missing. Every flickering light in the house would be turned on, every employee — from security all the way to reenactors like her — would be sent out to find him.

Maybe she could convince him to go back with a different tactic. "Where did you last see your parents?"

He waved a finger past the room that had once served as Howard Dawkins's study and toward the stairwell at the end of the hall. "Over there."

"What did the room look like?"

His eyebrows, so fair that they nearly disappeared into his pale skin, rose halfway up his forehead. "There was a big table."

"The dining room?" Oh dear. That was on the far side of the house. How had he wandered so far?

He shook his head. "It was for playing a game."

She let out a quick breath and offered a soft smile. "The billiard room?"

He shrugged. "Maybe."

Well, as far as confirmations went,

"maybe" was pretty weak. But it would have to suffice. The game room was at the foot of the stairs, and she couldn't think of another room in the house with a big table.

Glancing behind her once more at the rows of unsearched books, she sighed. They would have to wait for another night.

She unlatched the velvet rope from its gold post, slipped past him, and held out her hand. "Let's go for a walk."

"Is this part of the game?"

"Um, yes."

With a nod and a skip, he led the way down the corridor, the sound of his little feet echoing off the arched ceilings. At the top of the stairs, he turned back to her. "What do we do next?"

Sure, he'd ask her about the rules of a game she'd only made up to distract him.

"Well . . ."

"Jamie! Jamie, where are you? Come here now."

Saved by the call of a frantic mom. Millie heaved a sigh of relief, and Jamie must have recognized a tone that meant business. Grabbing onto the relatively recently in-stalled handrail, he disappeared down the spiral staircase. Within moments his moth-er's audible relief reached the upper hallway.

"I was so worried about you. Where did

you go?"

"I was playing a game with the lady."

"What lady?"

There was a long pause, and Millie's heart jumped to her throat. This was it. The moment they rushed up the stairs and she was discovered at the very last place she should be — in the room she most needed to search.

"That lady with all the books."

"Don't be silly. There's no one up there. Now, come along."

"But there is, Mama. There's a woman in red."

Jamie's mother must have dragged him back to join the rest of the tour group, his voice disappearing but remaining adamant.

Millie smoothed down the front of her red evening gown, and even through her white gloves the silk was cool beneath her suddenly trembling fingers. Too close. This was all too close.

And it might all be for nothing.

There was no telling how much of Grandma Joy's story had been true. Probably less than was false. Still, she had seemed so certain. There had been something about the fragile old woman's eyes that gleamed with excitement and hope. *"It's* in the room with the books. Find it. It's in there."

"Find it," Millie muttered to herself as she slipped across the hallway and let herself back into the library. "No problem. Find a book in a library." It was like finding a particular piece of hay in a haystack. Every single binding could be the journal she hunted for.

But after two tries, she wasn't sure any of them really were.

Running a finger down the blue spine of a classic by Jules Verne, she sighed. The three cases to her left had all been history and architecture. Then there were several rows of poetry. Where the dust was too thick to read the gilded titles, she brushed it away, whispering every name to herself, lest she skip the only book she really wanted to find.

"Leaves of Grass. Poems by Emily Dickinson. The Road Not Taken and Other Poems."

No. No. No. Not what she needed.

The clock on the mantel above the fireplace chimed a tinny, hollow sound, its bells long since coated with the same film that covered every other surface of the room. But it couldn't be ignored. Nine o'clock. The last tour would be wrapping up in fifteen minutes. If she wasn't in her place in the theater room in ten, she'd be missed.

And then she'd be fired.

But she was so close. There was only one more bookcase. She hurried over to it, her finger almost but not quite touching every cover as she moved from poetry to prose.

"Poe. Hawthorne. Melville. Alcott."

Whoever had organized this library was a fan of neither Mr. Dewey nor the English alphabet. But she couldn't very well argue with them, as they'd likely been gone for as long as her Great-Grandma Ruth. Longer than Millie had been alive.

A shiver raced down her spine at the very thought. Ruth had been in this room, maybe perused these same tomes searching for a summer read to indulge in on the beach or on the deck of the estate's swimming pool.

Ruth had been here. At least according to Grandma Joy. Though nearly ninety years apart, great-grandmother and great-granddaughter had found their way to the same place.

If only Millie could find Ruth's journal and the map Grandma Joy had promised would be in it.

The ever-present ticking of the clock reminded her that she had to hurry. If she wanted another chance at searching this room, she'd have to stay on the payroll.

She sighed, her shoulders slumping as she

rested her hand on the final volume in the third row from the bottom. Tucked between the wooden column built into the wall and Edith Wharton's *The Age of Innocence* was a slender volume. Its dark brown cover wasn't the same quality leather as its compatriots, but that wasn't the most interesting thing about it. It didn't have either a title or an author printed on it.

Holding her breath, she gave it a gentle tug. The book and a tumble of cobwebs pulled loose. Heart thudding harder than it had when Jamie's mother had come after him, she gingerly opened the front cover.

In perfect script someone had written *Ruthie Holiday — 1929.*

"Oh." It was more breath than actual word, but the moment seemed to require something to recognize its importance.

Then, because she did the same with every book she'd ever read, she turned it over and opened to the last page to read the last line.

Let it be there. Please, let it be right there.

"Come on, come on," she whispered.

"Come on out of there."

The deep voice made her drop the journal.

Ben stared hard at the woman in the shadows on the far side of the room. Partly because she'd pulled him from a warm cup of coffee in the security office. And partly because he couldn't believe that little Jamie Grammer had been right.

There really was a woman in red in the room with all the books. But she didn't look anything like the other visitors finishing up the final tour of the night.

He let his gaze sweep over her costume. The shimmering red fabric of her dress skimmed her thin frame and swished as she turned toward him. With wide eyes she stared back, the angle of her chin both certain and stubborn.

He couldn't make out her coloring under the too-yellow lights of the library, but her fair hair was held in place by a red headband that sparkled with every hitch of her breath. All of the actresses on the property had costumes covered with too many ornaments, and sometimes it seemed the outfits from the twenties wore the women.

Not the case with this one. Her firm shoulders and staunch posture could have easily placed her in the Chateau's heyday. But she wasn't an apparition. She was an actress. And she had broken at least half the rules in the relatively short employee handbook.

"Come on out," he said again.

She froze, her gloved hands fixed behind her.

"What's your name?"

She still didn't respond, but neither did she drop her gaze.

The clock on the wall to his right chimed the quarter hour, and they both turned toward it. Her shoulders slumped. No doubt she'd missed her last post of the night. She would have lost her job even if he hadn't found her beyond the red velvet rope. "Where are you supposed to be?"

"The theater."

He nodded. "Are you ready to go?"

As she stepped into the beam of light from the hallway, she shook her head. The feather tucked into the band around her head dipped and brushed her cheek, only emphasizing her impossibly smooth skin.

He had no business noticing that. He had a job to do, and two weeks into his new job at the Chateau, he didn't intend to lose it for a pretty face. After all, there were twenty-three other faces counting on him. Sure, he hadn't seen them. That didn't mean he didn't owe them.

Squaring his shoulders, he cleared his throat and pulled himself up to his full height. "Let's go, theater girl."

"It's Millie — Camilla, actually. Please.

36

Plea—"

"You know the rules." His tone carried a hint of bitterness, and he tried to dial it back. "We'll both be here late enough filling out paperwork."

"But I . . ." Her voice trailed off as her eyebrows bunched above her nose. "You don't have to turn me in."

If he'd expected her to beg for a reprieve, he was disappointed. While distress was scripted across her features, her voice never wavered.

"I was looking for something. It belonged to my family."

"Ha!" He couldn't help but bark out the laugh. "Are you a Dawkins?"

Her pale features turned even more wan in the dim light, and she opened her mouth, only to close it again without a peep.

"I'll take that as a no."

Still she made no motion to step out of history and into the present. Into the hallway with him. So he unclipped the rope from its gold stand.

"Let's go, Camilla."

"It's Millie." The knot in her jaw suddenly relaxed, and she pressed her shoulders back. When she spoke again, her voice was stronger. Certain. "My name is Millie Sullivan, and my great-grandmother was a guest here. She left behind a journal. It's — it has some family history. I need it."

As she spoke, he couldn't tear his gaze away from the red line of her lips — the same shocking shade as her dress. There was a firmness to their set, a quiet line at each side that seemed to swear to the truth of her words.

Oh, if they were true. How incredible it would be to find family history in this great castle looming along the Georgia shore.

And how very unlikely.

He had an early class in the morning and no time for fairy tales. "Come on." He grabbed her arm right above her elbow at the top of her white evening glove. "Let's get going."

"Wait! Wait!" She tugged on her elbow, trying to free it from his grip, but he refused to let go. Whatever other wild stories she might concoct, he wasn't interested. At more than fifteen bucks an hour, this was the best part-time job he'd been able to find on short notice. That it happened to be at the island's most famous historical locale was just a perk.

Fear and hope flashed in her blue eyes, promising that whatever she was about to claim would almost certainly land him minus one job. And he didn't have any to spare.

"I don't think so. Let's go."

Beneath his fingers, her muscles flexed. "There's a lost treasure."

His eyebrows pulled together, his forehead wrinkling.

"In my great-grandmother's journal." She took a ragged breath and struggled again, but he shook his head hard. Best to put a stop to this and get her to the office, where her manager could take care of the situation.

But she was still going, as though more words would somehow convince him. "It's on the property. Here. At the estate. Don't you see?"

"I understand what you're saying." He let his gaze narrow in on her front teeth, which bit into her full lower lip, picking up a tint of the red there. "Doesn't mean I think it's true."

The way her eyes widened, it was clear she did. Whoever had sold her a tall tale about some riches hidden at the Chateau had fully convinced her. That didn't mean he needed to be as gullible. He'd read nearly every book about this old property, and then he'd taught a class about it. History 103: "Georgia's Past to the Present."

Sure, every now and then a rumor emerged about lost treasure in the area. There were even a few rumors of buried treasures dating back as far as the heyday of pirates, but every single one of them had been debunked. There was no treasure here except fifteen bucks an hour. And he wasn't about to give that up.

"Look, lady."

Her eyebrows darted together, a storm cloud rising.

He quickly modified his comment. "Millie, I'm sorry. There's nothing I can do. You're clearly not where you're supposed to be, and that's grounds for termination. You know that."

Gaze darting toward the floor, she nodded. The landmark's supervisors were pretty clear about actors only going where they were assigned — the parlor and pool deck mostly. It was about preserving the historical integrity of the old house as long as possible. Even without extra foot traffic, the carpets had begun to wear in strange patterns. And peeling patches of fabric wallpaper would soon require repairs, another piece of history gone.

"I know. But can't you make an exception?"

"No."

He sounded like a jerk. Maybe he was a jerk. But what if he let her go and someone found out? He couldn't risk that.

Trying to keep his grip firm but gentle, he gave her a small tug. "Come on. We'll get this sorted out at the office."

"Please." There was a tremor in her voice, as though more than a fictional gold chest was at stake, but her spine remained straight, her chin at a stubborn angle.

"Let's go."

Her feet slid along the rug, its maroon and gold thread already thin in patches, and he almost stopped so she wouldn't damage the original carpet. Almost. With a quick glance over her shoulder, she let out a faint sob and pointed toward a book on the floor. "It's all in there. In the diary."

A boulder dropped in his stomach.

"And I'll split it with you."

Well, that was interesting.

THREE

"So what happened? Did you get sick or something? You missed your whole last act!"

Ben risked a slow look out of the side of his eye at Millie as she took her manager's scolding, the older woman clearly doubtful about her subordinate's claim. Millie's long arms were wrapped around her middle, her eyes glistening with something that certainly looked like tears. They had the strangely unfocused look of someone truly ill, although she'd never even hinted that she wasn't feeling well. And her shoulders twitched with the uneven rhythm of shivers. Or maybe she was just nervous under the firm eye of her boss. If he hadn't known better, he'd have guessed she really had the flu rather than a case of the nerves.

Juliet Covington, the manager of all the talent at the Chateau, sucked on her front tooth, her dark gaze moving from Millie to him and back again. "And *you* just so happened to find her." Skepticism dripped from her words.

"Yes. I was looking for the woman the little boy saw. It must have been Millie." His voice nearly cracked on the last word, and he could have shot his own foot. He was botching this performance. Juliet didn't believe them. Or rather, she didn't believe him. Millie could have convinced the world she was Princess Anastasia — a century late and blonde to boot.

What had he been thinking? He never should have agreed to any of this. It was a ridiculous plan. And the chances of there actually being any treasure on this property — besides the gold-plated tiles in the swimming pool and other adornments — were beyond slim.

Stupid. Foolhardy. Reckless.

He was banking everything — his job, his reputation, and maybe even his position at the college — on a silly story from Millie's grandmother and the evidence in an old journal. And all for what?

A chance to repay the people he owed.

The truth struck him like a punch to the gut. It didn't matter how many times he reminded himself of what he owed them. It always hurt. It always stole his breath.

Paying back those people was worth it. It

had to be. And at least if he was along for the ride, he could keep an eye on Millie and make sure she didn't walk away with anything that didn't belong to her.

He sucked in a quick breath as Juliet's gaze traveled from him to Millie and back again. He should just give the journal to Juliet. His hands itched to reach for the book carefully tucked into the back of his waistband, covered by his black security jacket, but he fisted them at his sides instead.

"Uh-huh." Juliet huffed and leaned back in the chair behind her desk, which was twice as large as it should have been for an office so small. "You two just *happened* to be in the same place. And you lost track of time."

The way her gaze volleyed back and forth left little room to wonder what Juliet was thinking. She assumed that when single coworkers disappeared, they were taking advantage of one of the hundreds of dim corners or shadowed alcoves. She assumed they'd been up to something.

And they definitely had been — just not what she assumed.

"Well, I knew what time it was," Millie said. "But I was answering Mr. Thornton's questions."

He shot her a hard stare. She made him

sound like he was eighty. Well, he wasn't. Just because he liked to follow the rules — *normally* — well, that didn't mean he was an old fuddy-duddy.

He caught another glimpse of her profile, all smooth lines and porcelain skin. But she wasn't as young as she looked. There was an understanding in her eyes that reminded him of the pleading in her voice when they'd met in the library. She needed that treasure for some reason. She needed it badly enough that she was willing to share what she found. And she needed help to find it — his help.

Millie lifted her chin under Juliet's scrutiny, firmly setting her jaw. Most girls would have blabbered on, but Millie handled the weighty gaze with quiet solemnity.

Maybe it was because she knew that the journal was safely tucked away. But if she was fired, she wouldn't be free to search the grounds. Then it would be up to him to . . . what? Find a treasure that never existed?

He cringed at the thought. This was all a mess, and he'd gone and gotten himself wrapped up in it like a fool. If he ended up on the wrong side of the law, he wouldn't be in a position to repay all those names on his list.

Juliet squinted at him. "What are you two up to?"

Millie bit her lips until they disappeared, and Ben crossed his arms over his chest. Then dropped them to his side. Then crossed them again. Juliet's eyes followed every movement.

With a tap of the wooden desktop, Juliet said, "I should have you both fired."

Millie let out a little peep of anguish, and he had a sudden urge to put his hand on her shoulder. Of course, that was crazy. He didn't console women he didn't know. And he didn't have time to know many women. Besides, Juliet was threatening his job too.

"But . . ."

He let out a little sigh.

"I've barely gotten you trained, and I don't like to waste my time." Juliet stood to her full height, nearly as tall as Ben, and waved one finger at them both. "This is your only warning. Do you understand me? Next time you're not where you're supposed to be, I'll personally kick you off the property — both of you."

A knot in his chest that he hadn't even realized was there suddenly unraveled, and he gulped a deep breath.

"Yes, ma'am." Millie's voice dipped into a thicker, deeper accent in those words that

46

every Southern child knew. Ben could only nod.

Juliet dismissed them both. Her mouth said, "I'll see you for your next shift." Her tone said, "I'll be watching you."

No doubt that would be true, which would not make searching for a treasure on the grounds easy. That is, if there even was one.

He backed out of the office and followed Millie toward the women's locker room. "I need to change and get my purse," she said. Her sapphire gaze was sharper than he'd ever seen it in the exactly thirty two minutes he'd known her, and it was rather unnerving.

Actually, everything from this night was a little bit out of his norm and a whole lot out of his comfort zone.

"Do you know Coastal Coffee by the pier?"

He nodded.

"Let's meet there in about twenty minutes."

His forehead wrinkled so hard he could feel it, but her gaze never wavered from his.

She glanced toward his side, and after a brief moment, she gave a decisive nod. "You can keep the journal until then if that makes you feel better."

It didn't. Taking an antique book — even a handwritten one — off the property made his stomach feel like it had taken too many loops on a roller coaster.

The slow traffic across St. Simons Island didn't help the matter. By the time he pulled his car into the almost empty parking lot of the island's coffeehouse, loved by locals and generally missed by tourists, he'd decided this had all been a terrible mistake.

Millie had nearly gotten him fired, and he didn't hold out much hope that he'd be able to hang on to the job as long as he was running around with her. He couldn't work with her. But if he didn't, she was going to hunt on her own. What kind of trouble would she get into then?

Besides, if the diary did belong to her great-grandmother, then she was entitled to it. Right? He didn't exactly know the rules for these things — forgotten treasure and all that.

This was a bad idea. Terrible. The very worst. Maybe it wasn't too late to back out now.

Yet his hand had no problem resting on the journal riding shotgun in his coupe. There was no telling the mysteries this book might reveal. It was a window into the Chateau at its most luxurious. It was an important piece of history.

And he wanted it for a stupid treasure map.

He pressed his forehead to the cracked steering wheel and took a deep breath. The cool summer air carried the scents of the sea, water, and fish. And home. But it did little to calm the speeding train threatening to run off his mind's track.

God, I think I'm in over my head here. I have no idea what to do now.

Two sharp raps on his window jerked him upright, and he stared into that blue gaze.

Whether Millie was an answer to prayer or just had uncanny timing, he'd never know.

Millie picked up her small black coffee and slipped into the corner booth. The blue vinyl cushion stuck to the back of her legs, and she suddenly missed the sleekness of silk. Her costumes all made her feel like she could slide through the eye of a needle. Should she ever need to.

But she'd left her silks at the Chateau, and apparently she'd deserted her good sense long before that. Whatever had convinced her to offer to split the reward they found had left behind only regret in its wake. What had she been thinking?

Oh, that's right. She hadn't been. She'd let her mouth run away with her because she'd been backed into a corner and couldn't see any other way out. But that didn't excuse her behavior. And now she was stuck. Stuck with a partner she didn't know. Stuck with a journal she had barely touched. Stuck with a clock that wouldn't stop counting down.

Sixty-three days. That's all she had left to find a miracle.

As Ben slid into the seat across from her, he laid the brown journal onto the table between them. It took everything inside her not to snatch it up and begin reading her great-grandmother's story and searching for the map Grandma Joy had said it contained. But the heavy weight of Ben's gaze kept her hands wrapped around her paper cup.

"So . . ." he began.

Back in the library she'd promised him the truth, but now that the moment was here, she wasn't quite sure it wouldn't sound a bit ridiculous. Actually, she was absolutely sure she would sound ridiculous. There just wasn't any other way around it.

"You see, it all started with my grandma."

His eyes shot toward the journal. "I thought you said she was your great-grandma."

"No. Yes." Millie rubbed her forehead, trying to figure out how to explain only the parts he needed to know — and there were certainly plenty of those — in a way that would make any sort of sense.

But there was also information he didn't need. Like the conversation she'd had with Grandma Joy. The news that Henry wasn't Grandma Joy's biological father. The realization that they might be heirs of a wealthy guest at the Chateau.

Ben, with his gaze that seemed to see straight through her, did not need to know about all of that. And he definitely didn't need to know that the most famous guest of the Chateau the summer of 1929 had been Claude Devereaux.

As Ben stared at her with unmoving eyes, every line of his face turned tight and expectant.

He'd said he was in. But somehow she knew if she didn't impress him right now, she was going to lose everything he could offer her search — the protection of a security guard on the grounds and the help of another set of eyes. Maybe it wouldn't be the worst thing to lose his help. But if she didn't know he was on her side, she couldn't be sure he wouldn't spill her secrets.

Under Juliet's watchful gaze, Millie would

have to be extra careful not to be found out. And that's where Ben could help. A lot. Even if working with him meant sharing the money, there was more at stake here.

Her gut twisted as she thought about the secrecy it would take to search the estate. Grandma Joy would be appalled. Millie was nearly there herself. Sneaking around places she knew she wasn't supposed to be in wasn't how she would have chosen to find the treasure. But she hadn't been given a choice.

Grandma Joy needed a safe home — a permanent one. And she'd do whatever she needed to make that happen.

"My Grandma Joy was telling me stories about her mom — my Great-Grandma Ruth — a few weeks ago."

He nodded, scratching at his chin with his thumb.

"She — I mean Ruth — was a guest at the Chateau the summer of 1929."

His lips pursed, and he let out a low whistle just as his coffee reached his mouth. He tilted the cup up but never looked away, and her skin broke out in goose bumps under his scrutiny. But he said nothing else.

He clearly didn't need to be reminded that that was the last summer before the stock market crashed and the Great Depression settled over the country. He didn't need to be reminded that the guests had enjoyed every luxury money could buy. And he definitely didn't need to be reminded that the Chateau had never been the same after that summer.

"Grandma Joy said that her mom had mentioned a lost treasure at Howard Dawkins's home. Jewelry and diamonds and such."

His jaw locked, and he shook his head. "I've been studying the history of the barrier islands for more than a decade, and those are only rumors, old stories that have been tossed about for years. No one's ever proved there was anything on the property. What makes you think your grandma is telling the truth?"

Millie chewed on her lip and spun her coffee in a slow circle. What did make her think Grandma Joy was telling the truth? Especially given her diagnosis.

Sure, it was easier to believe that this was just another story concocted after a sleepless night or one too many prescriptions. But that didn't explain the most important element.

"She knew about the diary. It stands to reason she could be telling the truth about its contents too."

His blue eyes darted toward the book as his dark eyebrows pinched together. Three little furrows appeared above his nose, but he didn't speak for several long seconds. Finally he said, "You really think there's a map in there?"

"Only one way to find out." Inordinately proud of how confident she sounded, she reached for the diary.

He pressed his hand over hers to stop the movement. "Be careful."

"I know." Her voice had picked up a little tremor in the previous minute, and she clamped her lips closed to keep anything else from coming out. To keep anything else from giving away how very unsure she was about everything that had happened in the last two hours.

She'd discovered the journal, and now she had an accomplice on her mission. But she still hadn't read even one line of the book. Only God knew what she'd find in it.

With a steadying breath, she slipped her hand from under the heavy weight of his and eased the diary across the table. The supple brown leather glided over the wooden tabletop, and she slowly flipped the cover open. Page after page revealed only the narrow script of Ruth Holiday's penmanship. There were no drawings, no "X marks the spot" indicators.

With each turn of the page, her heart sank a little lower. It was in her shoes by the time she reached the last page.

Nothing. It wasn't a treasure map after all.

Grandma Joy had been wrong, and this had all been for nothing.

Her dejection must have shown across her face, because Ben reached toward her hand again, stopped short, and then drummed his fingertips next to his cup. "Maybe it's in there." He tried — and failed — to keep his tone light, and his words hit almost as hard as the truth had.

She shook her head, her chin bowing and her hair falling over her shoulders and across her face. Something deep in her chest longed to deny the truth. But it was like she'd woken from a dream right in the middle of it. Now she could only imagine how it might have ended. But she'd never know for sure.

Always a dream. Always past the tips of her fingers.

This diary had meant hope. And now . . . Now she was exactly where she'd been when the doctor had said there was no cure.

"Maybe she wrote out the directions to the treasure." Ben shrugged. "She could have been a terrible artist."

Her head snapped up, the weight on her shoulders instantly lifting. "In the words. Of course!"

He grinned, his smile a little lopsided but filled with satisfaction.

"Why didn't I think of that?" Because she had a lot more on the line than he did, and the absence of a drawn map didn't define him.

"Hey, I've got a stake in this now too." He winked, and she laughed. "You can't be the only one coming up with ideas."

"Fair enough." She glanced back down at the diary. If — and that was still a big *if* — there was a treasure map in these pages, it was hidden in the words, somewhere in Ruth's memories. And someone was going to have to ferret it out.

Before she suggested that she take the diary home, Ben scooted across his bench seat and glanced at his watch with a shake of his head. "It's late. I have to be up for work in five hours."

"You work the day shift too?" The question popped out even before she fully formed the reason behind it. If he was at the Chateau during the day, maybe he could uncover information that she didn't have access to during her night shifts.

But he didn't give an affirmative reply. "No. I teach a couple classes at the Georgia Coast College in Brunswick on Tuesdays and Thursdays while I'm working on my PhD."

"Oh. That sounds nice." She sounded lame. And it sounded like he had to work two jobs and go to school. No wonder he was interested in the money.

With a shrug and a hand covering his yawn, he said, "It's not bad. Except the eight a.m. class is filled with a bunch of sleepers." The corner of his mouth ticked up a notch. "But that might not be a bad thing tomorrow. They won't mind if I cut class a little short."

"So what are we going to do?"

"I'm going to go home and get some sleep. And then we're going to find that treasure."

"You really think it's there?" Again her tongue got ahead of her, and she hated the uncertainty she'd just displayed. She wanted — maybe even *needed* — his help.

He lifted a shoulder. "I think your grandma knows something, like you said. That diary was just where she said it would be. So you better start reading."

"You're going to let me take it home?"

"Well, we can't read it at the same time,

so one of us is going to have to go first. I figured since it's your family history, you should do it."

June 15, 1929

Dear Diary,

The Chateau is beyond anything I could have dreamed. I had heard of the opulence and luxury, of course. The stories reached clear to Madison and certainly into the heart of Atlanta. They likely go much farther. How could they not?

Mr. Dawkins's gilded roof must be visible from a mile out to sea. Three stories tall and more than enough lighted windows to guide a ship to safety. Now that I am here, I can hardly believe my good fortune.

Our party is quite diverse. Jane and I are first-time visitors, of course, but Mr. Dawkins has made us feel especially welcome as guests of his particular friend, Miss Lucille Globe. We met her at the bank and were too eager to hear her stories about being on the radio. Can you imagine? Her life is ever so glamorous. She spends her days on the studio stage and her evenings on the arm of one of the richest men in America. We could hardly believe that she would invite us to spend the summer with her on St. Simons Island. How could we decline?

The rest of our party is nearly as glamorous as Lucille. Angelique, a singer who nightly entertains us in the parlor, has been here often, accompanying her brother, Mr. Claude Devereaux. He is the most dashing radio producer, and I was seated next to him at dinner last evening. He spoke endlessly of his travels through Europe, visiting family in France and London.

I confess that I could not follow all of Mr. Devereaux's conversation for his most distracting mustache. It is sleek and trimmed and ever so handsome. I could not look away. His eyes are rich like warm chocolate before bed, and they seemed to look right into me.

He invited me to go swimming this morning, and I accepted, perhaps faster than Mama would think proper. But what is the purpose of being at such a place without having some fun this summer?

I must prepare. We're to meet shortly.

June 16, 1929

Oh my! I can hardly breathe for recalling yesterday's ordeal.

I had planned to meet Mr. Devereaux at the agreed-upon time, and Jane had promised to accompany me. However, she awoke late and was still at breakfast when I went down to the pool.

There wasn't a soul around, but Mr. Devereaux had assured me he would meet me. So when I found the deck empty, I peeked around the Grecian columns to be sure he wasn't hiding. But they are too narrow to conceal a man of Mr. Devereaux's stature. His shoulders are so broad, and when he and his sister played lawn tennis, he rolled up his shirt sleeves enough to reveal rather sculpted forearms. He puts the statues in Mr. Dawkins's gallery to shame. He must do more than sit behind a desk at the radio network, or he could not possibly look as he does. And Mama would approve of a man who works hard, like the farm-hands back home.

After several minutes, I decided to slip into the water. The sun was so warm, and I looked up as I stepped in. My foot landed on something slick on the top step. Perhaps it was one of the gold tiles Mr. Dawkins had installed along the bottom of the pool. I flung my arms about and screamed as I splashed into the water, but I hit my head on the edge of the deck, and then all went black.

I remember nothing until I woke up coughing and choking. It felt like my throat was on fire as my stomach writhed to release all I had swallowed. And then a face appeared right above me, the unforgiving deck to my back. The face was familiar, but I could not quite place it.

"Miss Holiday? Miss Holiday, are you well?" His voice was gentle and kind, his eyes even more so. They were so soft, like pasture grass warmed beneath the summer sun, but worry and concern filled them too. His skin held the deep tan of a man who worked outdoors.

Only after assessing all of that did I realize that his dark brown hair was dripping down his face. His pale blue shirt clung to his chest and around his arms as though he'd gone swimming in it.

"Miss Holiday, I'm going to go for help. Will you be all right here?"

His words did not immediately make any sense to me. Perhaps he read my confusion on my face, for he brushed a wet strand of hair off my forehead. His fingers were infinitely gentle, but my head suddenly felt like a melon crushed by a hammer. Mama would have been so embarrassed, but I could not help it. I began to cry.

He did not seem to mind, merely scooping me into his arms and carrying me like a child. He moved quickly but never jarred my still throbbing head, and quickly we arrived in the dining room.

Jane gasped and Lucille scrambled toward us, demanding to know what on earth had happened. Her high-pitched squeal only made the pounding at my temple increase, but her hands quickly guided the man to the sofa. As he laid me down, he told them what had happened, then stepped away. I could only see him from the corner of my eye, his hands in front of him as though holding a hat.

Lucille asked if he had gone in after me, her gaze darting between us as though pursuing another story. As though there could possibly be any explanation other than the one he gave.

He looked up, and our gazes met. His was so warm that I nearly forgot to shiver in the cool house, my skin still damp and my hair soaked through. He gave her a "yes, ma'am" that was as sweet as peach preserves.

And then suddenly Jane was there, wrapping a blanket around me and holding me close. She apologized profusely for letting me go alone and begged to know if I was terribly hurt.

I tried to give her a small smile. But then Mr. Devereaux descended on the room, his apologies overflowing and rattling around my head.

Finally it was Mr. Dawkins who arrived, stilling the room with his quiet words. Shaking hands with the man who rescued me, he called him George and thanked him for his service before sending him to go clean up.

George looked at me again and gave a small nod, and I tried to thank him with my eyes. I would have surely drowned if not for his quick action. And I don't even know his last name.

Mr. Devereaux stayed nearby me for the rest of the day, ever watchful until he saw me to my room. I decided to eat upstairs, as I could not manage to dress myself for dinner.

When we first arrived, Jane and I were assigned one of the cottages near the pool. However, after the ordeal, Lucille insisted we be in a room in the house, near her and Angelique and the two actresses from Mr. Devereaux's latest soap opera. It was quite kind of her, and I slept very well.

I am ashamed to admit it even here, but I dreamed about a blue cotton shirt stretched across a broad chest last night.

FOUR

Millie looked over her shoulder down the empty corridor, expecting someone to tell her to go back where she belonged. But the hall was empty, the only noise trickling from behind closed classroom doors. Well, that and the squeaking of the rubber soles of her shoes on the tile floor. No one peeked around the sterile corner at the end of the hall and told her to leave, so she took several more steps, swallowing the strange sensation that made the back of her throat itch.

Checking the scrap of paper in her hand, she confirmed the room number: 122. Ben had scratched it onto the back of her receipt from the coffee shop, along with directions to the history building at the college, before leaving the night before. She'd thanked him, mostly grateful that she didn't have to pay for another cup of coffee when they met up again. Such frivolities weren't in her budget.

The second-to-last door in the hallway

was marked with a tan plaque identifying it. But this one was closed too.

That bothersome itch returned to her throat, and she scratched at her neck. Maybe this was an indicator that she shouldn't be here. She'd never even been on a college campus before.

But it wasn't her fault that she'd landed herself a partner. Or that he happened to be something of a smarty-pants.

She pressed her ear to the door just as a chorus of laughter broke out.

Was it possible he was funny too? There was only one way to find out. She turned the latch as silently as possible and opened the door a crack.

"Not quite, Mr. Thurber. The American Revolution wasn't started by a bunch of farmers with muskets looking for free tea." It was definitely Ben's voice, but there was a lightness to it, a bit of humor woven into every phrase, and she stepped toward it. "These men — Revere, Adams, Jefferson, Washington — they were facing the greatest military of the time, so they'd better believe in more than their right to drink tea."

Suddenly Ben looked directly at Millie, and his voice trailed off. She froze. Oh dear. She'd stepped all the way inside the room behind a dozen rows of desks. A push at the door behind her proved that it had shut all the way, and she tried for an apologetic smile. It felt more like a grimace.

But Ben didn't seem to mind. The corner of his mouth quirked up, and he raised his eyebrows as he nodded to an empty seat three rows down.

Sit. Right. That would be less conspicuous.

She slid into the chair, and the girl in the next seat glanced at her questioningly. But before Millie could respond, the other girl grinned. "I'd sneak into this class to see him too."

Millie almost swallowed her tongue.

At least she didn't have to respond. The girl turned back toward the front of the room, propping her chin in her hand, a dreamy look settling across her features.

Millie tried to follow the exact path of her stare, which seemed to land on Ben as he paced before a large whiteboard. The student was clearly enamored. But Millie couldn't tell exactly why.

Tracing his movements, she stared hard. He wasn't particularly striking — certainly not the hero type in the books she loved to read. He couldn't serve as a stand-in for Sir Robert, the medieval knight in her current read. Tall and a little lanky, Ben wore a corduroy jacket that was a bit too big across his shoulders. The leather patches on the elbows made him look like a man lost in time, one who belonged two or three generations before.

A student in the second row raised her hand, and Ben pointed at her. "So what is it they believed in?" she asked.

Ben ran his fingers through his hair, ruffling his dark waves, and a broad smile broke free. "That's what I want to know." He turned his back to the room and picked up a black marker. "Three pages answering the question, Which of the Founding Fathers' beliefs would have prompted *you* to join them in the war with England?"

"All of them?"

He glanced over his shoulder at the boy who had interrupted. "Well, who'd you have in mind?" There was a long pause before Ben gave him a knowing smile. "Sam Adams, I suppose."

A wave of red crept up the boy's neck until his cheeks flamed.

"Yes, he brewed his own beer. No, you may not write an essay on his belief in good alcohol."

The whole class giggled as Ben finished outlining the assignment on the whiteboard. "Might I suggest choosing one or two key

topics and unpacking why those who supported them did so and why you agree?
Don't try to cram all of them into one
paper. I'm looking for a thoughtful consideration rather than a regurgitation of the
Declaration of Independence. That's why
I'm giving you a week." His eyebrows went
up again. "Questions?"

When there were none, he dismissed the
class.

Millie was glued to her seat. Her first college class. She'd just survived her first —
and only. Okay, so it was more like the last
seven minutes of the class. But still. It had
been fun.

She frowned. Classes had never included
laughter and teasing during her school
years. They'd been focused and demanding
and utterly boring. Somehow her teachers
had even managed to make literature a
yawn.

Could a good teacher make that much of
a difference? Given the smiles and chatter
of the students filing down the aisle and out
of the classroom, apparently so.

She was so wrapped up in watching the
interaction of the young students that she
didn't notice she had an audience until his
shadow fell across her desk. Glancing way
up, she met Ben's deep blue gaze as he

crossed his arms.

"I'm sorry. I didn't know you were going to be in the middle of class. I'd have waited outside."

The corner of his mouth tipped up. "No problem." There was an unspoken question in the squint of his eyes, but she couldn't quite make it out.

"I . . ." Searching for a response, she dropped her gaze to the line at the corner of his mouth.

Lips pinched together, he seemed to lean forward, waiting. On her.

"Um . . . I've never seen such a fun class." His grin returned, so she spit out another compliment. "I really enjoyed it."

Ben nodded, dropped his arms to his sides, and tilted his head toward the desk at the front of the room. "I'm glad. I had fun teaching it."

There was nothing to do but follow him, so she ambled a few paces behind him. "Is this . . . what class is it?"

"History 120 — A Survey of American History."

"Summer school?"

He glanced up from where he straightened a stack of papers, his lips pursed to the side.

Stupid. Stupid. Stupid. Of course it was summer school. It was the middle of June.

But the only thing she knew about school at this time of year was related to making up a geometry class that she'd bombed during the regular semester. Worst summer of her life.

"I mean, are they making up a class that they failed?" He probably thought she was an idiot.

His gaze darted to the closed door as a snort escaped the back of his throat. "Um, no."

"Oh." Perfect. Now he *knew* she was an idiot.

"Most of them are trying to get ahead so they can graduate early. Some of them are nontraditional students." He must have read the confusion on her face, and he quickly defined the unfamiliar term. "They have full-time jobs or families and can't take a full course load, so they take whatever classes they can squeeze into their schedules."

She pressed her hands together and frowned. That was an option — fitting in the classes you could manage? It hadn't been when she'd been in high school, which was why she'd ended up in summer school in the first place.

But there wasn't anything to do about it now. That summer was gone. And this one promised so much more. An extra job. A treasure hunt. Riches beyond anything even in her favorite novels.

And maybe even a new family name. Claude Devereaux might be her great-grandfather. Or he might not be. But it was clear even in the first few pages of Ruth's diary that she was smitten. And if the summer of 1929 played out as Millie hoped, she could be part of a family that had never had to pinch pennies. She closed her eyes and sighed, lost in the possibilities of that what-if until Ben cleared his throat, a question seeming to punctuate the sound.

Shaking off her daydream, Millie snapped her gaze to meet his. "Sorry. I must have . . ." Spaced out. Like the idiot he already knew she was. "You're pretty good at this." She waved at the whiteboard still covered in his neat block letters. "Why not do it full-time?"

Something close to a scowl flickered across his features. It was there only a moment and then vanished, but his eyes remained narrowed for a long second, and she was beyond thankful that the weight of his gaze fell on the loose pages in his hands.

"You know. Between working on my PhD and life. I guess there are extenuating circumstances."

"Like what?"

His eyes flashed in her direction, and she immediately looked around for a place to hide. No such luck, unless she crawled under one of the desks. "Never mind."

He stabbed his fingers through his hair, sending his hair into even more disarray. "It's been . . . these last few years have been tough."

Like Ramen noodles seven days a week, tough? Like splurging on a bike only because it meant not having to pay for gas? Like running the air-conditioning once a week as a special treat? He didn't confirm as much, but she knew a thing or two about those. Maybe that's why he didn't have to spell it all the way out. Sometimes she could just tell with people who shared the same struggles. It wasn't quite a secret handshake, but it might as well be. Theirs was a club no one wanted to join.

But if he was really a member, how had he reached this point? Not only a graduate of college but *teaching* at one.

She couldn't ask another impertinent question. And that was all she had.

Thankfully he saved her from testing the size of her mouth with her foot. "So, did you discover a map in the diary last night?" His scowl disappeared, replaced by the hint of a smile.

"No." She swung her bag onto a desk in the front row and cringed when it settled with a loud thunk. She shot a side glance at Ben, who paused as he put his stack of papers into his beaten-up messenger bag.

His look seemed to suggest that perhaps she ought to have a little more respect for a treasured artifact that, at the least, carried her family's history. At the most, it was the key to wealth that would change both of their lives. Forever.

"Sorry." She mouthed the word as she pulled out the brown paper bag–wrapped package, the diary just as she'd found it the night before — minus some dust that she'd blown off. Flipping open the first page, she paused, then glanced up from beneath her lashes.

His bag now packed, Ben had repositioned himself. Sitting on the edge of his desk, his long, khaki-covered legs stretched out before him, he crossed his arms. "So what did you find?"

"Um . . ." She tried not to look guilty, but the glint in his eyes was either humor or accusation. While she hoped it was the first, the rope around her chest suggested that it very well might be the second.

"I read the last line. First."

His eyebrows went up, but other than that he remained still.

"It's just a thing I do."

Those deep brown arches rose nearly to the matching wave sweeping across his forehead, and her neck immediately burned under his scrutiny.

Pressing a hand to her throat, she dropped her gaze to the diary. "I always read the last line of a book first." He opened his mouth to ask the same question that everyone else did, but she beat him with the response. "Of course, not mysteries. I'm not trying to ruin the book, but if I know where I'm going, I know if the journey is going to be worth it."

She glanced down at her feet, pressing one hand to the desk at her side and clutching the journal in the other. They were maybe three feet apart, but in his current pose, they could have been eye to eye if she'd looked up. Which she didn't.

She could only bring her gaze as far as his feet. The look of censure she was sure would be on his face kept her from lifting her eyes. She wasn't educated like he was. She didn't do things the way she was supposed to like he did. And she'd found herself in a position he could never understand.

He uncrossed his ankles, then crossed

them again. "Isn't this a mystery?"

Her stomach seeped toward her toes. "I-I suppose." And it wasn't just any mystery. It was *the* mystery. Her past and present swept into one big question.

"So what does the last line say?"

She cringed. "There's another journal."

"What?" He grabbed for the book, his hands gentle but nothing less than intent. Flipping to the end, he scanned the last lines. Ones she'd memorized in a single read.

This summer is so different than I antioi pated. There is more to share. It is a good thing Mama thought to pack a second journal, for I shall have no difficulty filling it.

"This is only the first volume?" The disbelief evident in his voice was just like hers had been the night before, and he smoothly flipped the pages before him, his eyes scanning them, clearly searching for a clue that had been missed.

But the only missing piece was from Grandma Joy, who had said the map would be here. She'd known about the diary, so how had she missed that there was a second one? Had she not known about it at all? Or, more likely, had she forgotten?

"What else did you find out?"

"Ruth was invited to the Chateau by Lucille Globe, who was" — she held up her fingers in air quotes — " 'the particular friend of Howard Dawkins.' "

Ben's chuckle wasn't really humorous but spoke to the absurdity of the phrase.

"I know. It's amazing how they flaunted their inappropriate relationships."

He nodded. "But labeled them with the most unassuming titles."

"And everyone knew." She pointed at the journal. "Ruth wrote about it so matter-of-factly. It wasn't even questioned. Lucille was the mistress of the Chateau — at least for the summer."

That scowl he'd worn before made its way back into place, the tip of his nose twitching. "Even though Dawkins had a wife and a son back in Chicago."

Her stomach did a full flip. "He did?"

"Sure." Ben shifted his weight against the desk beneath him, but he didn't attempt to make eye contact. "His son passed away about ten years ago. It was big news because it was on the eightieth anniversary of the stock market crash, and of course his dad had been hit hard by it."

Her insides shivered, and she wrapped her

arms around her middle, not sure how to make sense of this bit of information or if it mattered at all. "I guess I assumed . . . Wasn't the Chateau passed down to his nephew or something?"

Ben nodded. "Maybe his son didn't want it. Maybe his wife didn't. There must have been a lot of bad memories wrapped up in the old place."

Millie had just assumed he'd been single. She wasn't naive enough to believe that married men were always faithful, but . . . In her first entries, Ruth had made it seem as though everyone liked Dawkins, that he was a man worthy of their respect.

But if Dawkins wasn't the man Millie had assumed him to be, then was Ruth a reliable narrator? Or was Millie missing the truth on the pages?

She hated those novels — the ones where she couldn't tell if the main character was lying to her. And now she had to wonder if her great-grandmother was doing the same. Was this all a wild goose chase or an elaborate hoax? Or was it possible that there was *some* truth — hidden though it might be — in what Ruth had written?

"Did the diary mention anyone else? Besides Dawkins and his girlfriend?"

Ben's question made her jump, and she

jerked herself away from her own troubling inquiries. "Yes. A few. There was a gardener and her friend Jane. And Claude Devereaux." She stumbled on the name, but he didn't seem to notice, his jaw dropping and his eyes narrowing in on the leather volume dwarfed by his long fingers.

"Claude Devereaux? As in . . ." He found her gaze and held it for a long moment. "*The* Devereaux family? As in Henri Devereaux? As in the Louisiana Vanderbilts?"

Millie swallowed the lump that had suddenly formed in her throat, but it refused to fully dislodge, and she had to resort to a simple nod of response. Which felt rather pathetic given the incredulity of his tone.

She hadn't been surprised to see the name of one of the wealthiest families in the country written in her great-grandmother's handwriting. As soon as she'd learned that Ruth had spent time there, she'd begun to research that summer on the shore, and the Devereaux name had been mentioned. Perhaps not effusively, but it wasn't hidden either.

But Ben didn't need to know what that meant. After all, that information had zero effect on him. It wasn't tied to the treasure. Not really.

No. Not at all. They were definitely two

very different searches.

"Henri was the oldest brother and inherited the majority of their father's estate," Ben said, "but Claude was no slouch. Wasn't he interested in radio?"

Millie nodded quickly, and Ben opened his mouth like he was going to explain, but she jumped in. She didn't have to read it in a textbook. She'd read about the prevalence of personal radios in a Depression-era novel. "Because television wasn't really around yet. Radio was the way most people kept in touch with the rest of the country. It was also a key source of entertainment."

Ben smiled. "Exactly."

"And of course Dawkins invested heavily in radio."

"Ha!" Ben's laugh was like a chocolate-covered caramel, all things pleasant and soothing. "How'd you know that?"

Pressing her hands to her hips, she cocked her head and shot him her best fake scowl. "You think I don't listen when the tour guides come through the Chateau?"

He crossed his arms and leaned back, but his lips twitched like they were fighting back a smile. "I would never presume such a thing."

"Good."

"But this isn't going to help us figure out

where the treasure is hidden or the location of the second diary."

Fair point. But not really helpful. "So . . . I guess we go back to the start? It stands to reason that the second journal would be near the first."

Ben scrubbed his cheek with a flat hand and stared at a spot over her shoulder, but it was clear he wasn't really focused on it. Finally he gave a curt nod of his head. "Back to the library, then?"

"Unless you have a better idea."

June 19, 1929

I am glad to be fully recovered from the ordeal at the pool. The ache in my temple has finally subsided. However, Mr. Devereaux took it upon himself to inspect the injury. No man has ever asked if he could touch me so, but his fingers were terribly gentle, and it was all very decent in the company of his sister and Jane.

What was happening in my nerves was rather lacking in decency. He is a very handsome man, and I could not help but lean in toward him ever so slightly.

Willa and Betsy arrived in the midst of his examination, and they scowled at me as though I'd stolen their spots in his next production. Of course, I have not. He has said nothing about his work except in passing. Perhaps he does not realize that I long to pursue a career in radio. I have no desire to work as a bank teller forever, even if banking has made Mr. Dawkins sinfully rich.

Although I see Mr. Devereaux watching me, I am afraid I have missed several chances to spend time with him. Yesterday the whole of the house party took advantage of the stables, and I stayed in my room.

By the afternoon, the light through the window was too bright for me to keep my eyes closed. I wandered the house for a while and ended up thoroughly lost. I walked the hallways for an hour, trying to locate a familiar room or stairwell, but they all seemed to blend together. Just when I had decided to sit a spell on the floor, I discovered a small spiral staircase. I followed it down and found myself by the kitchen. It smelled of wonderful roasted duck and sautéed onions.

Everyone here has been so kind to me, but I could not bring myself to ask for assistance. Instead I found a back door and snuck through it, successful in avoiding detection by any of the household staff.

That is, until I rounded the corner of the outside of the house. The sun nearly blinded me as it peeked around the column of one of the towers and through the Spanish moss hanging from the enormous oak trees. I promptly ran into what I thought was a brick wall. Then it grunted. Or rather, he grunted. When he spun around, he put his hand to my elbow, as I was dangerously close to toppling over after our collision. And that is when I realized who he was. It was George, the man who rescued me from the pool.

He dropped his hand, leaving behind a coolness in its absence, but his eyes were as warm as any I have ever seen.

He tugged on the corner of his brown cap before wiping his forehead with the back of his hand and called me Miss Holiday. The farmhands often made a similar movement when the sun burned so brightly. But here, so close to the coast, the breeze off the water keeps us cool beneath the ever-present summer sunshine.

He made no other movement, only holding a rake steady at his side. I held out my hand, and he stared at it for a long moment, making no motion to shake it. I told him that I owed him my gratitude, but when I went to call him by name, I trailed off, my face flushing. We hadn't been introduced, and I did not know his last name. The man had pulled me to safety and carried me through the house, and I knew absolutely nothing about him. Except that his eyes were the color of grass and his embrace was as gentle as a newborn kitten.

As his gaze rose to meet mine, he transferred his rake from his right hand to his left. After a swipe of his fingers against his brown trousers, he shook my hand and supplied his name. Whitman. George Whitman. But he said everyone here just calls him George.

I tried to smile, but it wasn't easy given the strange tumult inside me that seemed to be tied to his grin. It was slightly lopsided. His front teeth are the slightest bit crooked, but it is endearing rather than off-putting.

"Ruth Holiday," I said. And then I nearly bit off my tongue. What on earth was wrong with me? He knew my name. He had called me by it many times by the side of the pool. I sputtered on, trying not to be even more inane, but there is no way to be certain if I succeeded. I bumbled on with my thank-yous, even specifying where he'd rescued me, though he certainly remembered the ordeal.

His chin dipped, but his gaze stayed locked on me. He said nothing else, so I was forced to continue.

I said that I hoped his clothes were not

ruined. He responded only that they had already dried. Then I tried to ask him if he'd had someone wash them for him, but oh dear, I botched it terribly. Because suddenly it was the most important thing to know if there was a woman in his life who would take care of such things.

I felt a strange sensation in my stomach as he paused. Oh my. I've never experienced anything like that in all of my nineteen years. It was the oddest feeling.

Before I could fully analyze it, the corners of his eyes crinkled. There was no accompanying smile, but the planes of his face transformed with a humor that had not been there before.

He said he had managed, and he sounded fully capable. However, it was not an answer to my question. And I think he knew it.

Before I could push further, he asked me what I was doing outside alone. And I was forced to tell the truth. George laughed so hard at my silly story of getting lost and wandering for an hour, pressing a hand to his side and leaning heavily on his rake.

When his humor finally abated, he agreed to show me the way. Mama would have said I was too forward asking for his help. But he had already saved my life once. How could a short stroll around the Chateau be wrong? No one was around to see us anyway.

It was a lovely walk.

June 20, 1929

The strangest thing has happened at the Chateau. Last night after dinner, we retired to the parlor and the men poured themselves drinks. Mr. Dawkins says that no matter what the government says, certain men will always have access to the best liquor. He is one of those men.

Some men indulge in their drink among friends. Some in private. But aren't all breaking the law?

I must say that Mr. Devereaux abstained from a drink last evening. When the butler offered him the highball glass filled with amber liquid, he caught my eye, waved the drink off, and winked at me from his place on the far sofa.

It was rather forward of him, but I smiled nonetheless. He is a handsome man and has been terribly attentive since my ordeal. I believe he blames himself for not being at the pool when he had said he would meet me there.

He stood then and walked toward me. But before he could even make it halfway around the circle of women playing cards at the center table, Angelique spoke loudly, declaring that Willa must be mistaken.

Every eye in the room, including mine and Jane's beside me, turned toward the four women.

Willa, the actress with deep chestnut hair, said she could see no other way around it. Her silver sapphire necklace and earrings were missing, and only the maid had been in her room. Lucille looked aghast and pleaded with Mr. Dawkins to tell Willa that she was mistaken.

Mr. Dawkins only reclined further in his chair and mumbled something about how it must have been misplaced. Willa seemed disinclined to agree, but she said that she would look again in the morning in fresh light.

But I thought it very strange, as Jane had lost a brooch just that morning.

FIVE

"There's something strange going on."

Ben snapped his head toward Millie, still hunched over a low shelf, then in the direction of the library door, looking for any sign that they'd been caught beyond the burgundy velvet rope by his supervisor or hers. But the only thing there was the faint smell of summer rain wafting through the screened windows on the other side of the third-story corridor.

"What?" He kept his voice low, but an inch of frustration seeped into it. He didn't have any desire to identify the source of that irritation, but he took a deep breath anyway. Forcing his hands to unclench, he tried again. Gentler. Softer. "What do you mean?"

She didn't even bother to look up from where her finger scrolled below every leather-bound title on the shelf before her. Just as it had for the last forty-five minutes.

And they'd found nothing.

Frustration, meet your maker.

Rubbing his hands on the front of his navy-blue uniform pants, he tried not to focus on their wasted time, their blatant rule breaking, and the little voice in the back of his head that kept chiding him. *This is all for nothing. You're never going to find that money. Your life isn't going to change unless you change it.*

Yes, if he wanted a different future than the one he'd been handed, he was going to have to make it happen. There were debts to pay and he was going to have to pay them. And this sneaking around — even if it went against everything he believed — might be his only chance to pay them back before there was no one left to pay back.

There was another voice too, this one sweet and promising. And it tempted him with a future where he'd only have to work one job — one he loved. A future where the bills could be settled as soon as they arrived. A future where he didn't drive a coupe that only started when it felt like it. A future that wasn't cloaked in his mother's sins.

And he wanted that future. He'd worked for that future. He'd prayed for that future. Maybe this — meeting Millie and agreeing to help her search for her treasure — was some sort of answer to that request.

Or maybe he was ignoring the still small voice of God telling him to run.

"I said there was something going on at the Chateau."

"What? When?"

Stupid questions. He knew when. When it came to the two of them, there was only one *when*.

But she didn't harp on it. "In the diary. Ruth said that one of the guests lost a sapphire and silver necklace."

Looking up from where he'd knelt before the bottom shelf, he shot her a look that he hoped conveyed just how much he didn't care about a rich woman misplacing a necklace that could more than cover the down payment on the townhouse he'd been dreaming of for the last nine months. "So what?"

Her eyebrows rose, and he immediately regretted the sharp words. "I'm sorry." Scrubbing his hand down his face, he shook his head. "I'm just tired. I didn't mean to snap at you."

She glanced back down toward the shelf she'd been checking, her shoulders slumping beneath the gauzy weight of the navy-blue straps that crisscrossed below her neck. She had to be as exhausted as he was after a long shift at the Chateau, and it wasn't her fault that there was a second diary or that she hadn't known about it.

Taking a shallow breath, he tried for a softer tone. "What do you think was going on?"

Her gaze remained trained on the leather casings at her knee, and her volume stayed just as low. But there was a certainty in her tone when she finally spoke. "Someone stole them."

"Them?"

"Ruth's friend lost a brooch too. The same day."

"You think there was a thief?" He couldn't help the way his voice rose in astonishment, and he clapped a hand over his mouth at her startled glance. At least, he thought she was startled. The yellow and pink shadows from the low lamps played across her face, hiding some of her features. The big window in the wall adjacent to the empty fireplace didn't even let in the moonlight, a blanket of clouds covering the sky.

But there was no anger or palpable tension flowing from her, so he made his move. Tiptoeing to the door and ducking his head around to stare down the hallway, he held his breath, only releasing it when he'd confirmed that it was empty. "Coast is still clear."

"Lucky you. Unless you're *trying* to get us caught and banned from the premises."

He wrinkled his nose, and she giggled behind the fingers of an elbow-length white glove.

It wasn't surprising that she was teasing him. What was surprising was his laugh joining hers. It snuck up on him and popped out before he even realized it was coming. Or how much he liked the sound of their mingled laughter. He couldn't remember the last time he'd let himself enjoy a moment of humor with someone else.

Probably not since before his mother's arraignment.

A memory flashed against the back of his eyelids. The courtroom. The stern scowl on the judge's face. His mom's cold gaze. Her crisp black suit — most likely purchased with someone else's hard-earned money.

The images reached into his chest like spindly fingers and then clenched into a fist that had him doubling over before he knew it.

"You okay?"

He nodded quickly, rubbing at the spot over his heart and praying that the memories would subside.

Someday.

Someday he'd forget. When the debts were repaid.

And the treasure could take care of that. It could make at least half of his problems disappear. Redoubling his efforts to find that elusive second diary, he returned to his spot on the shelf and ignored the way her gaze stayed heavy on his back. He needed something to distract her.

"So how'd you say you knew about the first diary?" His question popped out without much thought, and as soon as it did, he remembered that she'd already told him the answer.

"Um . . . my grandmother." The lilt at the end of her response made it sound more like a question, but he kept his back to her and his finger nearly tracing the outline of the books at hand.

"Any chance she could help us find the second? I mean, how did you know where to find it exactly?"

Millie cleared her throat, and it seemed more like an excuse to delay her response than a necessity. "Well . . . I'm pretty sure she told me everything she knows."

Looking over his shoulder, he squinted at her. "What exactly did she tell you?"

Tilting her head back and closing her eyes,

she seemed to stretch for the words. "She said that her mom had often wished she had her journal from that summer."

"Single?"

"Yes. Just the one." Millie cracked an eye open at him as she smoothed her hand down the front of her dress. In the dim glow its fabric swished and shimmered like the sky in a midnight thunderstorm, but he kept his gaze on her face.

"She never said anything about there being two," she continued.

"So how'd you know where to find it?"

The look in her eyes shifted from seeing into the past to a very curious direct stare into the present. "She said, 'It's in the room with the books.' Why?"

He met her gaze with the same fortitude. "Maybe she could help us find the second. I think we should ask her."

Millie's lips — still outrageously red from her role that evening — nearly disappeared as she bit them together. Tugging up her gloves, she dropped her gaze to her fingers. "Sure. I'll ask her."

Ben frowned. That wasn't what he'd been proposing. And he had a gut feeling she knew it. She was keeping him away from something. Maybe it was a bit of key information. Or maybe it was . . . more.

He didn't have a clue what he was missing, but the longer she hemmed and hawed about it, the more he was going to press. And he'd get there. He'd figure it out. Digging up the past was his job. All three of his jobs, actually. He'd uncover the truth, whether she wanted to tell him or not.

"I meant *we* should talk to her. Together. What are you doing tomorrow?"

If Millie had been chewing gum, she'd have swallowed it. As it was, she choked on an otherwise typical breath, coughing and wheezing until Ben marched across the room and ushered her to the antique settee centered between the four book-lined walls.

"I'm fine." She held up a hand even as he nearly pushed her to the sofa. Its burgundy upholstery let out a little puff of dust, which only made her cough harder.

"Sure you are." He lowered himself to her side but refrained from the standard thump on the back, for which she was incredibly grateful. It was hard enough to catch her breath without being pounded into the lumpy cushion.

Ben pressed his hands to his thighs but didn't say a word for several long seconds as she tried to quell the tickle in the back of her throat that had turned into a forest fire.

"I'm okay. Good. Fine." And apparently a liar too.

An errant cough was the least of her worries. She closed her eyes, hoping that the truth hadn't spilled down her face as easily as the tears streaming there. After tugging off a glove, she swiped at them with her fingernail and managed to keep from adding a saltwater spot to her silk gown. Finally she sucked in a breath, the tension in her chest easing ever so slightly.

When she snuck a glance at Ben, he raised his eyebrows in an unspoken question.

"Yes. I'm okay." She gulped and swallowed the air with an extra measure of caution. "Sorry about that."

He nodded an acknowledgment, but there was something in his eyes that said her unplanned distraction hadn't distracted him at all. It promised that he wasn't going to let go of his idea.

That wouldn't — *couldn't* — happen. She couldn't take him to meet Grandma Joy for at least one very important reason, so she scrambled for another focus. "I can't believe you let me sit on this couch."

He looked down, and his face twisted like he'd suddenly realized he was sitting on a shark. Jumping up, he stared back at the furniture, shaking his head.

"And that's probably not great for the carpet," she said.

His gaze darted in the direction of his black work boots, his eyes bright and round. But it was his tiptoeing to the wooden floor that made her burst out laughing. Immediately she clamped her hand over her mouth. The tears that had been loosened before weren't so easily stemmed. Two big ones raced down her cheeks under his watchful glare.

"It really isn't good for the antiques, you know. And what if the sofa was damaged? They'd know we were in here."

"They'd know *someone* was in here." Her correction was cautious, thoughtful. They couldn't risk alerting the other private security personnel that there was anyone slinking through the shadows. If the historical preservation society thought that someone was sneaking around the property, they'd amp up security faster than Millie could fill a cup of coffee — which was quicker than any other waitress at the Hermit Crab Café.

That meant they had to leave everything precisely as they found it.

Slowly she rose from the hundred-year-old sofa, brushing at the dust she'd undoubtedly picked up and praying that it hadn't stuck to unmentionable areas. Twisting to check her backside, she nearly missed the set in his jaw, which should have tipped her off to what was to come.

"Do you really think the second journal is in here?"

No. But she wasn't about to give in that easily. "Why wouldn't it be?"

"Because we've searched every shelf — three times — and there's no sign of it."

"Okay . . ." As far as concessions went, it wasn't one. But she didn't have another comeback, so she stared at him. Hard. Maybe he'd back down.

He blinked, a slow smirk rolling across his lips.

All right. Back down unlikely.

"It's not in this room, Millie." He waved a hand toward the window. "Maybe it's somewhere else on the property. Maybe it's not at the Chateau at all. But one thing I know for sure. We need more information."

Ack. He was right back to where she didn't want him.

"We just need to read the diary." That sounded like a valid point. It *was* a valid point. They had no idea the secrets that slim volume might hold, and the only way they'd find them is if they read the book.

If only she didn't have to get some sleep

between her jobs.

She'd dozed off after just two short entries the night before. She'd wanted to keep reading, but her eyes refused to cooperate, drooping and closing without permission. One minute she'd been about to flip the page, and the next her alarm clock insisted she roll out of bed and race to the diner, or she'd be late. And late meant fired. She couldn't afford that until she — they — found whatever had been hidden on this estate.

"Sure, the book is important, but what if there's something in there that we don't know because we're missing the details?" He crossed his arms again, the shoulders of his jacket pulling almost as tight as the lines around his mouth. The faint wrinkles at the corners of his eyes deepened.

He'd make a good lawyer. She felt like she was on trial and he was about to act as judge and jury too.

"Of course. I'll ask her."

He began to shake his head slowly and then stopped in mid-motion. "I'll go with you."

"No —" It popped out like a firecracker, unexpected and loud, and she slapped a hand over her mouth, remembering too late that her lipstick would likely leave a mark against the white fabric. But that was the least of her worries if Ben's squinted glare was any indication.

"Is there a reason you don't want me to meet your grandmother?"

"Of course not."

Liar, liar. You know better.

Her conscience chided her, reminding her of the sermon her pastor had preached a few weeks before. *"Do not lie to each other."* It was somewhere in Colossians, but she couldn't remember exactly where. It didn't matter. She didn't need to know the reference to know lying was wrong. Even if her reasons were . . . mostly honorable.

He opened his mouth to respond, but she shook her head quickly, cutting him off. She could do better. She *would* do better.

"Grandma Joy is a wealth of knowledge, but . . . um . . . sometimes she requires a delicate touch. New people can overwhelm her." She closed her eyes and prayed for the words she needed, ones that made sense. "And her mom — Ruth — died when she was fairly young. The stories, the memories, are pretty old."

Ben stood a little taller and relaxed his arms a fraction. "She doesn't always remember?"

Well, that was a benign way of putting it.

Millie grimaced but leaned into the truth, hunting for words that were accurate but gentle. Because, while she'd wished at least once that she'd never even met him, she needed his help. And the truth — all of it — was more likely to make him run than stick around for the hard stuff.

"You could put it that way. Her memories aren't always particularly . . . crisp."

Oh, man. That was a stretch. Sometimes Grandma Joy's memory was sharper than a new knife. But sometimes — more often than either of them wanted to admit — her mind wouldn't cut through the mashed potatoes they served at the home.

When she looked up at Ben, his thick brows had dipped until they met in the middle. The rest of his features pulled tight. "I'm sorry." He sounded like he actually meant it, and it surprised her how much those two little words warmed that spot in her chest that had to grow a little bit cold every time she saw Grandma Joy.

"Thank you." She sounded stupid, but really, what else was there to say?

Except, of course, a rapid reassurance that this wasn't all a waste of their time.

"She has good days. And she knew about the first journal. She knew — she knows. She's just —"

This time Ben stopped her, raising his hand with a sad grin. "I get it. My grandpa was forgetful too."

Forgetful? Sure. They could go with that. For a while.

Maybe Grandma Joy could even pull it off. For a while. But then what? What would she do if Ben witnessed one of Grandma Joy's more painful moments? What if he freaked out and took off and left Millie to do this all on her own?

That was where she had started anyway. But now it felt different.

She frowned and pressed a hand to her forehead. It wasn't different. It was just new. She'd been on her own most of her adult life. After her grandpa died, it had been just her and Grandma Joy. Those had been a good two years. Fun even. Until Grandma Joy started forgetting. Until the house had been sold.

Her lungs ached for a breath, but it was too painful to remember how everything had changed so suddenly. One moment Grandma Joy had been taking care of her. The next, Millie had to take care of Grandma Joy.

"I still think she's our best resource."

Millie tiptoed off the rug and then paced the narrow confines of the available hardwood floor, trying to rid herself of both the memories and Ben's suggestion. She couldn't take him to meet her grandmother. She just couldn't.

Except he was right. Grandma Joy knew more about Ruth's story than anyone else alive.

A question wiggled its way into the back of her brain, refusing to leave. What if Ben could do more than keep her out of hot water with Chateau security?

He'd already proven to be helpful. And he was an unabashed history nerd — from the leather patches on his tweed jacket to the way he riled up a classroom full of college students over the American Revolution. While he'd never said as much, she had a feeling that he hadn't picked up a part-time job at the Chateau because he loved being a security guard or because it paid particularly well. He loved the area and its history as much as anyone else. He knew things she'd never had the opportunity to learn.

Not that she would have chosen to learn what he had. But it would have been nice to have the option.

She swung a glance in his direction as she spun to make another trek over the open boards. He'd crossed his arms again, and his gaze had turned intense. But he didn't seem in a rush for her response.

Maybe he understood that introducing him to her grandmother was so much bigger than a lost treasure. It meant taking this from the page to real life. And her life didn't look like silk gowns, white gloves, and diamond necklaces.

There was more at stake than what once was lost on this estate.

"I'll see if she's up for a visitor."

June 25, 1929

Claude took me on a walk today, only the two of us. He insists that I call him Claude instead of Mr. Devereaux, and I have agreed. We have two more months together, and we must be friendly, so I have given him leave to call me Ruth. When he does, my entire spine tingles.

We strolled along the beach, and I didn't even mind that the breeze off the water whipped my hair about my face. Who needs to be able to see when such a strong, handsome man is walking at your side, the crook of his elbow a sure guide?

Oh, but he is a fascinating man. He's seen so much of the world and has such incredible stories to tell. He's even been to Africa and seen elephants and lions and something called a gazelle, which sounds like a deer. I could have listened to him talk all day about his adventures and his life. It's so foreign to me. The ships he sails on are nearly as luxurious as the Chateau, although that is hard to comprehend.

His life is so unlike anything I knew on the farm. There are no children running about his legs. I suppose that could be because all of his siblings are older. But even those he does not speak of, except Angelique, of course. They rarely have more than a casual greeting in the evenings before dinner, a simple kiss on the cheek or a mild embrace.

I cannot help but remember when I returned to the farm after my first month away. Jimmy, Sarah, Abraham, and Shirley raced to me, tangling in my skirts until I nearly fell to the yard, the air filled with their screams of delight. The farm is never quiet, but it is also never lonely.

Perhaps he has never known such a life.

We had walked nearly half a mile along the water before he stopped. There was no one else on the sand as far as I could see in either direction, so I let him take my hands in his. They were gentle and soft, not at all like George's hands with their rough calluses. Not that I have been thinking about him. I certainly have not.

Claude told me I am beautiful. When he looked into my eyes and said those words, my insides melted like butter over hot bread. I could only stare at him, and I do not think I even blinked.

Oh my, but he is handsome. His narrow mustache is so refined and elegant, and his smile makes me want to fall into his arms. Mama has always warned me away from men. "There ain't near enough good ones," she says. But surely Claude is one of the good ones. Certainly he's always been kind to me. And whatever his shortcomings may be, life with him would never be boring. There would be so many adventures, enough money to buy a house on the beach beside the Chateau. Perhaps near the creek to the south. I love the sound of it as it bubbles and gurgles its way to the ocean. The water is so clear that you can see right to the bottom of it.

On the beach, Claude lifted my hand and pressed his lips to my palm. If I had been wearing gloves, it would have been nothing but innocent.

I was not. But I could not make myself chastise him for any impropriety. Not even when he kissed the inside of my arm. All the way up to my elbow. Below the sleeve of my dress, his mustache tickling my arm, his breath warm against my skin, he stopped.

I did not want him to.

Am I so very wicked?

He sighed when he stopped, and I

think he wanted to keep going as well. But he said only that I was truly beautiful and that I could be in the moving pictures, except then he would not get to work with me. I think that made him sad.

I managed a strangled giggle and tried to tell him how much I long to work with him. I could only focus on the shiver that ran across my arms and had absolutely nothing to do with the breeze off the water. Somehow the rolling waves and endless blue expanse had disappeared. There was only he and I. Together.

And when he raised his head, I let him kiss me.

June 26, 1929

My maid is gone. Jenny was not mine exactly, but she was one of the housemaids on loan to the guests each morning. She always brought fresh towels piled to the ceiling. They were so soft and fluffy and smelled of sunshine and gardenias. And she often laid out our clothes for the day, taking care of any wrinkles.

This morning she did not appear. My

dress still hung in the armoire, simple cotton and decorated with all the wrinkles my trunk could give it. Jane's as well.

We did our best, taking special care with our hair. But when Jane stabbed herself for the third time while pinning up her great chestnut waves, she gave up and declared that she would much rather have one of those new short hairstyles. I almost think she is serious.

When we did finally make it to breakfast, Angelique and Willa and Betsy were whispering unabashedly just inside the dining room. I could not make out their words, but the tension was absolutely palpable. It drew us to them. We were merely moths and they the lamp. As we approached, their voices rose, and I could not help but wonder if this was a performance, and Jane and I the audience.

Willa squealed that we would never believe what had happened. Mr. Dawkins had fired her.

Jane and I looked at each other, both terribly confused. Angelique was quick to tell us that Jenny had been caught stealing from Betsy's room the night before. Betsy nodded right along, holding up the gold bracelet that had nearly been taken from her.

It is stunning. Truly. The golden band glistened in the light, the intricate design work as delicate as Betsy's wrist. Rubies and emeralds make it look like a Christmas decoration — one that costs more than Papa will earn in his entire life.

But I cannot begin to imagine why Jenny would want to take it. She would never be able to wear such a thing. It is so easy to recognize, especially on such a small island. And if she tried to sell it, she would have the same trouble.

Why on earth would Jenny try to take something so noticeable? If I were to steal something — not that I would ever ponder such an unlawful act — I would choose Angelique's string of pearls. So beautiful and as fresh as the oysters they came from. But they are common. Well, they are not common on a Georgia farm, but Mr. Dawkins gave Lucille a long string of them only a few nights ago. She tittered like they had come off of Mr. Ford's motorcar assembly line. They are stunning against the flawless skin at her neck.

None of this explains why Jenny is gone. Angelique said Mr. Dawkins had to release her. There was no other way. He cannot have a thief in his employ, under his roof. I suppose she is right.

The whole situation bothered me so much that I snuck away from the rest of the party as they ventured out for another excursion. When Jane asked why I wasn't going to see the lighthouse, I begged another ache in my head. She wanted to know if it was from my accident. Of course not. But I was instantly reminded of George, and I wondered if I could find him somewhere beneath the shade of a tree. That would have been terribly inappropriate. Especially after my walk with Claude yesterday.

Instead I snuck up to the library to continue the novel I began last week. This is one by Jane Austen about a man and a woman who despise each other upon first meeting. I am thankful that Claude and I had quite a different introduction.

I fully enjoyed the book, but my mind kept wandering to Jenny. If she had indeed tried to steal the bracelet, had she also taken Jane's missing brooch? And what about the misplaced necklace? Where would she have hidden them in her little room?

SIX

"Meet me in the maids' quarters."

Ben jumped as the hair on the back of his neck stood on end. The whisper in his ear traveled across his shoulders and down his arms, causing an uncontrollable shiver.

The voice was familiar, but the urgency was new since they'd searched the library three days before. There was no time to stop Millie as she brushed past him on her way into the parlor. She didn't even acknowledge him beyond that barely-there command, her gloved hand hooked into the elbow of a man in a black tux. She followed the man through the giant doorway and beneath the arch of carved wood showing ducks and dolphins and a turtle making its way down what was clearly a beach. Even after nearly ninety years, the animals were unmistakable.

Less clear was why she'd whispered so urgently in his ear. And the reason it still echoed inside him.

A herd of tourists thundered down the hallway, their stomps on the original wood floors dragging him from his wonderings. He looked up just in time to step out of the way of the guide, who strolled backward without a glance over her shoulder.

"Howard Dawkins loved to throw parties, but they weren't your typical evening soirees. He filled his home with guests all summer long, and his Chicago colleagues sometimes visited around the holidays to take advantage of the Georgia winters." The docent — he thought her name was Felicity, but he couldn't remember for sure — flicked her wrist in a wave toward the parlor behind her and offered each of the children a mischievous grin. "After dinner, Mr. Dawkins and his guests retired to the drawing room to play games and enjoy a drink. Let's see what they're doing this evening."

Like every one of the paid ticket holders, Ben leaned toward the entrance, Felicity's tone an undeniable invitation to peer into the past.

Taller than most, as he had been at nearly every stage of life, he had no problem looking over the heads of the group. They shuffled to the edge of the red carpet, breath held and eyes wide.

And that's when Millie made his heart stop.

Looking up from her hand of cards, her lashes long and black, she winked at her audience. "I suppose I'd better *let* him win tonight."

A burst of giggles followed, every eye in the group looking across the gaming table to the sleekly mustached man Millie had clung to on her way into the room. Everyone except Ben. He couldn't seem to look away from her cheeky smile and knowing eyes. Despite her scarlet evening gown and redder lipstick, this was the same Millie who had worn shorts to get coffee and nearly caused a scene in his class. This vision with a halo of golden curls pinned at the nape of her long, slender neck. They were one and the same, two parts of the whole.

Just like his mother, who had two sides.

His stomach took a leap, but Millie's laughter shook him free of his sudden plunge. So deep, so joyful. The sound trickled over him like the lightest summer rain, soothing and welcome. And the absolute opposite of Patty Thornton.

Millie wasn't like his mom. At least, he didn't want to believe she was.

But reasoning out the truth in his mind and knowing it in his heart when he looked at his partner were very different things. Millie played a role. And she'd been doing it since the night he met her. She put on a dress and performed her part for an audience. Then she changed into her cutoff jean shorts and played an entirely new part for him.

Patty had done the same. She'd doted on him, seeming the concerned parent. His lunches were packed for school every day. His clothes were clean and folded and on the foot of his bed every afternoon. His car had gas in it, and his wallet wasn't empty. From his perspective, she'd looked like the perfect mom. Most of the time.

The problem was the side he hadn't seen, the side that had been busy convincing near-retirees to let her invest their money. That was the side that had pocketed every dime. That was the side that had sat in a courtroom, so cold, so detached. That was the side that hadn't even apologized when the judge gave her the opportunity to do so.

That was the side she had hidden.

Or the side you refused to see.

He cringed at the memory. He'd been barely twenty at the time, but he'd been certain he knew his own mother. It had been just the two of them for so long that he'd convinced himself she was just what she appeared.

But he knew the truth. He'd been afraid to ask the hard questions, even the obvious ones.

Patty had never held down a job, so where did the money come from to pay the rent, keep the lights on, and buy him a car? He'd wanted to believe it could have come from his dad, but that lout hadn't even bothered with a wave as he walked out the door and never looked back.

His mom had straight-up swindled him right along with every one of her victims.

But Millie wasn't the same type of woman. Millie had been up-front from the beginning, hadn't she? She'd told him what she was looking for. He hadn't asked a lot of questions in that first conversation, and she'd told him just enough. There was a treasure, and at least some of it had belonged to Ruth. Millie was looking for what was rightfully hers. Right?

A tiny prick at the back of his skull jabbed him a few times.

Right?

Ugh.

The dull nudge turned into a sharp ache as most-likely-Felicity led her group away, leaving Ben and the thunder at his temples to focus on Millie, who had never once confirmed that Ruth held any claim on the treasure. Of course, she couldn't have confirmed his assumption because he'd never asked.

Brilliant.

Millie giggled at something her costar said, and she was back. No longer the sultry eyes and throaty laugh, she was the Millie he was coming to know, the Millie who read the last page of a book first. Who teased him for walking on carpet he'd never have considered treading on before. Who whispered to meet her in the maids' quarters.

But that was after his shift, which wasn't over yet, despite his wandering mind. Scrambling after the tour group, he gave her a little wave and caught the nod of her head just as he turned a red-carpeted corner.

"This isn't the maids' quarters."

"Of course it is." Millie fumbled for a folded sheet of paper that she'd procured at the front entrance, pulling it from the pocket of her shorts. "It says so right on the map." She pointed to the room on the second-floor blueprint.

Ben shrugged, a slow smile worming its way across his lips. A dimple appeared in each cheek, but she refused to let her scowl fade.

"Besides," she said, "you're the one who's late."

"I'm not late." He held up his hands, his smile growing more generous with each passing tick of the grandfather clock at the end of the hallway. It echoed in their pause. "I was right on time. *At the maids' quarters.*"

He leaned heavily on those words, and it made her stomach drop. "This *is* the maids' quarters, as previously established." She flapped her paper map again, but the impotent flop of her wrist did little to convince even her. Clearing her throat, she tried again. "See the beds and the dressers? And there's no running water."

Ben followed her command, ducking his head into the simple square of a room. Matching twin beds covered in unremarkable brown blankets abutted the far wall, and a simple wooden dresser along the adjacent wall clearly held two sets of toiletries.

He simply shook his head.

"But . . . the guide said so?" She hated the way she sounded so deflated, hated how he might be right. "How do you know? They always point this room out, and . . ." Again she flapped the map in his direction.

120

"And you believe everything they say on the tours?"

"No-o." She knew that some of the furniture passed off as antique was really a recreation of pieces that had been destroyed during a fire in the fifties. She knew that the wallpaper in the dining room had been ripped and repatched with a mere fabrication. But those were important parts of the home's history. Surely they wouldn't have fabricated a maids' room.

"How do you know?" she asked again.

He shrugged, but his eyes never wavered from hers. "I just do."

"Have you been searching the house? Are you looking for the treasure yourself?" She clamped her mouth shut as his eyes grew to the size of the estate's gold-rimmed dinner plates, and he jerked back as if she'd smacked his shoulder. But when he opened his mouth, nothing came out.

"I'm sorry." Whispering through her fingers, she tried to find better words. But they weren't there. There was nothing to say after she'd accused him of double-crossing him — in so many words. She hadn't meant to. She hadn't even considered the possibility until that very moment. "I'm sorry. I don't think you're trying to . . ."

"Steal your treasure?" The words came

out like they were being dragged over a gravel driveway.

She nodded. And then shook her head. "Are you?" This time it was her eyes that went wide, and she scrambled for an explanation. "I'm so sorry. I didn't realize I was . . ." Worried? Anxious? Uncertain of him?

Ben crossed his arms, his lean shoulders still broad enough to stretch the fabric of his knit T-shirt. Not that she'd noticed. But the heroine in the novel she was reading — Genevieve — had spent three pages thinking about her Sir Robert's shoulders.

Not that Ben was like the hero in her story. She didn't need a hero. She needed a fortune. She did not need broad shoulders and expressive blue eyes and a generous smile.

Nope. She didn't need or have time for any of that.

"Listen, I know we don't know each other very well. I totally get that. And you're trusting me with a lot."

That was it. He stopped right where he should have gone on. He offered no promise that she could trust him. He didn't assure her that he was a good guy or that he'd never take off with her money. He simply offered an unwavering gaze.

That was better than most promises. It was real.

When he did continue, he said only, "We both have something to bring to this partnership."

She didn't want to seem too eager, but her question came out before he even finished speaking. "Like what?"

"You have the journal and access to the only person who heard those stories firsthand."

She nodded slowly, and his arms relaxed to his sides before he went on. "I know the real history of this property and the location of the actual maids' rooms."

"Looks like I'm bringing more to this partnership than you are."

Lifting his eyebrows, he seemed to consider her argument for a long moment. Finally he said, "And I promised not to get you fired for sneaking around the estate at night."

Her giggle wouldn't be subdued even as she pressed the back of her hand to her mouth. "Fair enough. Partners?"

He looked down at her outstretched hand. "I thought we already were."

"Let's make it official. I'll trust you and you'll trust me. And neither of us will run off with the other's share."

A dark shadow slithered across his face. It was there and gone in an instant, but it left her cold, and she almost pulled her hand back. But he grabbed it before she could.

"Partners," he said.

"Partners who —"

He cut her off with a quick wave of his hand. "Sneak around the house and find the treasure."

Something deep in her stomach still rumbled with an uncertainty she couldn't name. He had said the right words, looked her directly in the eye. She could trust him. She had to, or she had to cut ties now. And that wasn't really an option. So she pushed down the uncertainty and moved forward.

"To the maids' room, then." Turning around, she began marching. He cleared his throat and she stopped midstep.

Peeking over her shoulder, she squinted in his direction. Ben said nothing. He just pointed over his shoulder with his thumb.

Spinning around again, she muttered under her breath, "Well, how was I supposed to know that?"

His grin set her insides to rolling as she tiptoed along. She couldn't afford to let an errant step on a squeaking floorboard announce their location to anyone in the area.

The thought made her slam on her brakes,

and Ben ran smack into the middle of her back. They both wobbled for a precarious moment. Grasping her shoulders, he kept them standing by sheer force of will and firm footing.

"What is it?"

His breath at her ear sent shivers down her arms, and she couldn't help but wrap them around her middle. "We've been too cavalier, haven't we?"

"What do you mean? Do you think security is onto us?"

"They might be. Or Juliet." She lifted a shoulder, brushing against his arm. Which was warm and solid. That was just what the heroine in her book would think. And this was not like that. Not even a little bit. "We just haven't been very careful."

With a slow nod, he caught her hair against the whiskers on his cheek, tugging it gently. "Sure. But who do we have to hide from right now? The cameras are turned off after the last tour."

"Are you sure?"

"I did it myself tonight."

With a slow sigh, she let herself breathe again. She'd somehow forgotten to do just that for the last minute, and the air, warm and thick with humidity, was still somehow refreshing. "And the night guards?"

"Night guards?"

"You know, the ones who patrol the grounds at night?"

When he shook his head, she leaned away from him. Coolness washed down her back in his absence, and she subdued the shiver so eager to betray her. Glancing over her shoulder, she tried to read his face, but his smile was easy, indecipherable. "No night guards?"

"I think that you're giving far too much credit to the Chateau's security system, which generally consists of trying to keep riffraff off the lawns." He nodded toward the open window and the paved driveway beyond. "In its day, that gate was state-of-the-art. But that day was thirty years ago. Now . . . well, not so much."

She looked in the direction he'd indicated and could see only darkness.

"The historical preservation society doesn't have money to waste on overnight security — cameras or otherwise — when the estate is supposed to be closed. They figure once it's locked up for the night, it's safe."

"And let me guess, you're the locker-upper."

"You know that's right." He hooked his thumbs behind imaginary suspenders. "And here you thought I wouldn't come in handy."

"I never said . . ." Okay, she'd had her doubts, but that was neither here nor there.

They were alone inside the Chateau, alone on five acres of prime shoreline and surrounded by a ten-foot stone wall. She couldn't make out the stones or the gate she entered through in the barest hint of their neighbor's lights, which stretched through the Spanish moss hanging in the old sycamores. Draped in their finest, the trees masked the wall that surrounded the property from the shore to the entrance. Its imposing façade had been Howard Dawkins's idea — if the tour guides could be believed at least in that area.

Dawkins had been vigilant about protecting his guests and their privacy. And if he'd spent thousands of dollars — in the twenties, no less — to keep interlopers off his property, how much more vigilant was he about the ones he let in? Wouldn't he have interviewed Jenny the maid? There would have been letters of reference from her previous employers, right?

He wouldn't have been careless. He never would have hired Jenny if he didn't trust her. But he hadn't hesitated to fire her.

"We have to get to Jenny's room." She

grabbed at his wrist and tugged.

He tripped on the sudden step but followed closely behind her. "Who's Jenny?"

"Ruth's maid. Well, not really Ruth's. She was a housemaid here, and she helped Ruth get dressed. She probably turned down their beds."

At a T in the hall, he pointed her to the left through an open archway that led to an exterior hall. She ran her fingers along the stucco wall, its open windows inviting in the night winds off the water. "She was sacked."

When they reached the top of a set of stone steps, Ben stopped. The humor in his features had disappeared, replaced by a mix of concern and curiosity. "For stealing?"

Millie paused too, able only to offer a slow nod. Then because it was clear he was waiting for even more clarification, she added, "From the guests."

"That's great."

Mouth dropping open, she paused, but he didn't expound on his thought. Stepping around her, he took the first three stairs in quick succession before turning around and offering his hand. There was no handrail inside the tightly spiraled stairwell, so she slipped her fingers into his grasp. And instantly regretted it.

It wasn't like that boy in junior high school who'd had sweaty palms. She'd pulled away from his damp grip immediately. And it wasn't like her high school boyfriend, who had used their linked hands to steer her wherever he pleased.

Ben's large fingers surrounded hers. Cool. Firm. Secure. Competent. He held on to her like he knew what he was doing. Like he was as concerned for her well-being as he was his own. Like the heroes in her books.

Nope. Not that again. You are not going down that path.

Her life wasn't a romance novel. But his touch did make her wonder what she'd been missing out on all these years, confining love between the covers of her favorite paperbacks.

She pulled her hand from his, and he looked back at her, a question flitting across his face. At least that's what she assumed. It was hard to tell for sure. The moon's light couldn't reach within the narrow confines of the stone walls, and a faint glow from the bottom kept him mostly in shadow.

Suddenly the silence felt heavier than the dark, and she stretched for anything to fill it. "I guess how great it is depends on who you are. Jenny probably didn't think it was very great."

He grunted something that sounded like agreement. "Did they search her room back then?"

"I'm not sure. Ruth didn't say anything about it, but I assume they would have checked. Wouldn't they?"

Pausing on the bottom step, he poked his head into the crossing hallway, looking each way. "Almost there," he said, leading her into what she'd assumed was a hallway. But the vast room was filled with an antique icebox, a cast-iron stove, and the largest island she'd ever seen. It was laid with wax fruits and faux meat that sat in a pool of moonlight shining through a row of windows to her left. To the right an open door showed a clear path to the butler's pantry. The opening was roped off with the telltale crimson velvet.

She stepped in that direction, but he tugged on her arm and ticked his head toward a barely-there panel hidden between the icebox and a sugar chest.

Millie tripped over her own feet and caught herself on the corner of the island. Her hand immediately burned, but not from the impact. Yanking it back, she clutched both hands to her chest, giving the exit a quick glance over her shoulder.

"There's a whole other hallway back here," Ben said.

"But . . . the house was built after the war. Didn't live-in help go out of style in the twenties?" She was blabbering, her thoughts suddenly jumbled and unclear, but a cleansing breath did absolutely nothing to help. Her skin tingled where she'd slapped the oak countertop.

She wanted to get to Jenny's old room. She wanted to know what was back there. The money, the jewelry, the evidence of who she really was. It could all be behind that thin door, painted green to blend into the surrounding wall.

Her heart gave a hard thump, then another, until she could feel it pounding at the base of her throat. "We aren't supposed to be here."

"What do you mean? This is where Jenny's room would have been."

Yes. She understood that. But there was something like a hook around her middle pulling her from the room. Something like fear that kept her from wanting to find what might actually be hidden nearby.

She wasn't doing this just for the sake of breaking the rules. There was more at stake than protecting the past, like freeing the truth. After all, the Bible said that if she found the truth it would set her free.

But what if she didn't like the truth she found?

"Are you all right?" He closed the distance between them, his grip on her elbow firm but understanding.

"I-I think so."

"Millie, what's your —" He let go of her and stabbed his fingers through his hair, his gaze trained on the floor.

His hesitation made her stomach do a couple flips, and she tried to step back from his warmth. The kitchen stayed relatively cool since the air-conditioning unit had been installed in the eighties, but within an arm's length of Ben, she suddenly wondered if she was suffering from the hot flashes that Grandma Joy complained about.

Letting out a slow breath angled toward her forehead, she tried to keep her face from turning red or her upper lip from breaking out in a stiff sweat.

He couldn't possibly know about Devereaux. He just couldn't. He hadn't read more than a handful of words in Ruth's diary, and Millie had been so careful. Of course, he knew that Devereaux had been a guest at the house that summer. They'd talked about that. But he didn't know about Ruth and the millionaire. He didn't know about walks along the beach or liberties taken beneath the afternoon sun or Ruth's dreams of being a radio actress. He knew nothing.

So why did she feel like she was about to be sick?

Would it be so bad if he knew?

Fair question. Just not one she knew the answer to. He might not care. Or he might insist she cough up half of whatever a Devereaux family connection might afford her. After all, she'd promised to share the treasure. Only she had no idea how much that might be. If it wasn't enough, she'd be right back where she started — without a fortune or a hope or any way of helping Grandma Joy.

She should tell him anyway.

"Ben . . . the thing is . . ."

When he finally looked up, his eyes were filled with determination. "Millie, what's your claim on this treasure?"

SEVEN

"Finders keepers?"

Ben let out a full-bellied laugh, bending at his waist and leaning a hand on his knee just to stay mostly upright. She put her hands on her hips and stuck out her bottom lip like she couldn't believe he was actually laughing at her.

He wasn't sure what he'd been anticipating, but "finders keepers" wasn't it, and the absurdity of it kept bubbling out of him on each guffaw.

"Hey now, mister." She straightened, and the look of disbelief turned into one of mock indignation. "There's no need to laugh. I mean, if someone just left it behind, we can keep it."

That was enough to swipe away all humor. It was too close to his mother's justification. *"If someone is stupid enough to give me their money, then I'll keep it."* And she'd done just that. She'd found more than a hundred marks willing to hand over their hard-earned savings. And while he only knew the names of the twenty-three on his list, the truth still applied. He wasn't going to begin stealing because it was a family trait. He wouldn't take money from the rightful owner of the Chateau's treasure. Whoever that might be.

"I'm not taking someone else's money."

Millie wiped the teasing look from her face. "What do you mean?"

"Just what I said. You said you'd share it with me, but who says it's yours to share?"

She looked at her empty hands as though expecting the journal to be there. "I mean, my great-grandmother knew about it. She had to tell my Grandma Joy. And she wrote about it."

"We think." He didn't know why he interrupted her. He didn't doubt that Ruth had been there and told Joy something that had sent her granddaughter on a chase. But if he and Millie never found a map, they'd never know for sure.

"She did." Millie looked on the verge of stomping her foot, her hand flapping behind her in the general direction of the icebox. "She wrote about the pieces of jewelry that were stolen."

"But none of them were hers, right?"

Her shoulders slumped like a deflated balloon. She took a deep breath, reinflating her stance. "Probably not." She paused for a moment, and then the truth just spilled out. "It was a feat for Georgia farmers to send their daughters to the city at all. There's no way Ruth's father could have bought her diamond bracelets or" — she twirled her finger at her throat as though looping it around the necklace she'd worn earlier — "pearls."

He scrubbed his hand down his face, something not far from disappointment swirling in his middle. "So what makes you so sure that what was taken belonged to her — belongs to you?"

Millie looked at the floor for far too long. "I'm not."

Her quiet honesty disarmed him, sending him stumbling back a few steps. He'd expected bravado and anger and insistence that she could do and take whatever she wanted. Instead, she looked up through lashes too long to be her own, her lips pulled tight and hands folded before her.

"It belongs to the owners of the estate at this point. At least that's the legal precedence here in Georgia. Dawkins's great-nephew still owns the property. He just contracted with the local historical preservation society to run it as a museum."

"You bothered to look that up, but you didn't bother to tell me as much?"

She nodded slowly, her face collapsing.

He couldn't hold back a scowl, hating the rising anger that churned in his stomach and took off along a fiery trail up his esophagus. "So you promised me half of something that isn't yours. That's very generous of you."

She blinked quickly, remaining otherwise still for a long second. But then she hurried forward two steps. "Yes, I was going to turn over what I found to the authorities so they could return it to the rightful owners. But what about a finder's fee? It's not unheard of for people to show their appreciation."

Good. They were on the same page at least. They weren't keeping someone else's money. But that didn't leave much. "What is it you think Dawkins's heirs are going to offer?"

"Maybe ten percent of whatever we find." The last word ended on an uptick, a question more than a statement. Uncertain. Hopeful. And probably utterly ridiculous.

He grunted and crossed his arms over his chest, the urge to reassure her battling with the one to storm away. He wanted a treasure. Or half of one. It wouldn't come close to covering what he needed it to, but he'd pay off at least a few of those debts.

Half of a finder's fee wasn't what he'd signed up for.

"And how much do you think we'll find?"

She shrugged a shoulder, maybe a little too nonchalant about the whole situation. Sure, she'd had time to consider the rightful owners, and she'd known about this a lot longer than he had. But the difference between ten percent and a hundred barely seemed to register on her face.

"I don't have any idea. But I know it's worth something."

"Worth risking your job?"

He already knew the answer to that because she'd put her job on the line every day since he'd met her, and at least a few times before that.

Her chin tipped up as her eyes narrowed. "It's worth everything."

A shiver raced down his spine at the urgency in her voice, and the drop of her jaw revealed that she'd said more than she'd planned on. There was something more than money on the line for her. But he wasn't sure he wanted to be mixed up in it for a twenty-dollar payout.

You can't leave her on her own.

He wanted to punch whatever whispered

that into his ear. But he couldn't argue the point. He'd promised to help her. Before he ever truly believed that there was even something to find, he'd promised.

"Aren't you at all curious about what's been hidden for so many years?" She closed one eye and raised the other eyebrow. "Imagine the history we could uncover. Imagine what it will tell us about the people who stayed here, the man who built it, the surrounding area."

That was clearly bait. The good kind too. But he hoped his glare told her he was onto her schemes.

Millie stepped closer before tipping her head toward the invisible hall behind her. "Have you been inside? Haven't you ever wondered what it looks like?"

He added a scowl to his glare, but her puppy-dog eyes never backed down. Innocent and compelling, she nudged him toward the nearly invisible door. "When you teach about the history of St. Simons Island, don't you wish you could see what the people back then saw? Don't you wish you could tell your students firsthand?"

He almost nodded, almost gave in. A flicker of a smile across her pert pink lips made him pause.

"When I teach about the history of the

island, I spend about a minute on the Chateau." That was an understatement. He spent at least a couple sessions of his local history class talking about the Roaring Twenties. Men like Rockefeller, Ford, and Dawkins had made a name for themselves. Some of those men had reached the shores of St. Simons and changed it forever.

He'd give just about anything to see what the world had looked like through their eyes.

With that thought, he knew he was hooked. He was a bass and she a fisherman, and she had reeled him in with an expert hand. But he could put up one last fight.

"If you had a treasure at Christ Church of Frederica, we could talk."

She crossed her arms and turned her head in the direction of the small white church building. It wasn't visible from anywhere on the Chateau's first floor, but she looked like she could almost see its charcoal-gray pitched roof and jutting steeple beneath a shower of thick moss and surrounded by sentinels twice as tall.

Shaking her head, she took a step backward, then another. Skirting the corner of the kitchen island, she made steady progress across the room. "I can't help you there. But tonight I'm going into Jenny's room, and I'm going to dig until I find what I'm

140

looking for."

Her determination made him grin, and he hurried in her direction. "What do you think you're going to find in there? Don't you think they searched it?"

He hadn't been trying to deflate her, but it sure looked like he had. Her shoulders slumped, and her face puckered with concern. "Of course. Yes." There was an unspoken "duh" in there somewhere, and she paused for a long second. "But maybe they missed something. If they had found the stolen jewelry well, then there wouldn't be a lost treasure, right? Maybe there's a clue or something." She picked up speed as she crossed the room to the door, and he followed right behind her.

The flash of her teeth in the darkened room was nearly blinding, but he couldn't look away. The hidden door opened with a creak, letting loose an avalanche of dust, and Millie jumped back, straight into his arms.

He'd been aware of her before. Her hair smelled of citrus, and her laughter was contagious. He'd felt her presence somewhere deep inside him. Now he fully enjoyed it.

She was filled with life and verve that made his heart slam against his ribs. And she hadn't lied to him. She hadn't tried to convince him that the money belonged to her. She'd owned up to it. Even if something deep inside him whispered that she wasn't telling the whole truth. For now it would be enough.

Brushing his hands from her shoulders to her elbows, he leaned into her ear. "Okay?"

She wrinkled her nose. "I have to pay for my own dry cleaning if I make a mess of my costume." They both looked down at her black tank top and blue jean shorts. Then she shot him a guilty grin. "Force of habit, I guess."

As soon as the dust settled, she wiggled free, and he tried not to think about how empty his arms felt in that moment. There were more important things to consider. Like a hallway with four doors off of it. Millie shrugged and reached for the nearest brass knob. It turned and must have released faster than she'd expected as she sailed into the room.

Ben was right behind her, suddenly inside an empty space, the white paint on the four walls peeling in each corner and around the small window. The planks of the floor had obviously not been treated to the same restoration efforts as the rest of the house, and the room had never been anything more than what it was now. A strange juxtaposition to the rest of the house and its over-the-top grandeur.

Millie made a slow turn, her arms outstretched as though she'd like to see if she could reach from wall to wall. Almost.

"So if you lived in this room, where would you stash something?" She spun again, her gaze darting from corner to corner.

"Not just something — the most valuable things you'd ever seen."

She nodded, lips pursed and eyes narrowed.

"I guess I'd start with the last place anyone would look."

"Or the place they didn't know to."

Immediately they took off in different directions. He dropped to the floor, running his hands along the seams of the hardwood. Millie rushed toward an iron grate in the corner.

His fingers searched out any inconsistencies, any mismatched joints, for a hidden compartment beneath the floorboards. He rapped his middle knuckle against a soft spot, but the floor echoed like it should. It was solid and steady. He moved onto the next board, shuffling on his knees, but was quickly interrupted.

"Do you have a screwdriver?"

He shot her a lifted eyebrow and half frown. She was bent over the metal grate in the floor, her fingertips prying at the corner of it. "I must have forgotten it in my other tool belt."

She rolled her eyes and turned back to her pursuit. "There are a couple of screws on here, and if I could just. Get. Them. Out." She was nearly grunting by the end, her fingers twisting.

She was going to break a nail. Or worse.

Suddenly she sucked in a sharp breath and popped her finger into her mouth. But she didn't look over at him or wail her complaint. She simply went at the stubborn screw with her thumb instead.

Taking his turn with the eye roll, he dug into his pocket and pulled out the Swiss Army knife his mom's then-boyfriend had given him in the seventh grade. *"A man should always carry one of these. You never know when you're going to need a screwdriver or toothpick."* Tim had put it in his hand, patted his shoulder, and set the table for dinner.

Patty had packed up their car and moved them three states away the next week. Ben had never seen Tim again. But Tim's face was as clear as a picture in the deepest recesses of his mind. And he had been right.

You never knew when you'd need a Swiss Army knife.

"Heads up." He waited for Millie to look at him before lobbing the knife in her direction.

She reached up with both hands and snagged it out of the air. "Thanks," she mumbled into her hands, then began pulling out and putting away the various tools until she found the blunt-tipped one that would work best.

He was so busy watching her work with hunched shoulders and purposeful movements that he almost forgot his own job. Even as he crawled along the floor, his hands running the length of the joints, his gaze kept wandering back to Millie, who had managed to get three screws out. But she was stuck on the last. She grunted once, pinched her eyes closed, and torqued it for all she was worth. The muscles in her arms shook, hands clasped together in front of her, and for a brief moment he worried about the safety of his knife.

"Let me." He was across the room before he even realized it.

"I've got it," she said between clenched teeth. "I'm almost —"

Suddenly her hand slipped, and she flew back on her rear end, slamming into the wall with a crash that almost brought the roof down.

"Ow." She moaned and rubbed the back of her head.

He squatted by her side, eye to eye. "You okay?"

She looked at him like she might enjoy seeing the roof come down on him. "Fine." But when she moved again, she cringed.

He reached for the back of her head, although he didn't know precisely what he planned to do. He never got the chance to find out because she swung her arm up to stop him. "I'm fine. Really." The way she squeezed her eyes closed suggested that her head felt anything but.

Picking up the knife from where it had fallen, he took his turn at the remaining screw. Gritting his teeth, he gave it the full force of his strength. It wouldn't budge.

"Thought you could help, huh."

He glanced up just fast enough to catch her smirk before the knife twisted in his hand and the whole grate came free. "You were saying?"

She humphed and mumbled something under her breath about loosening it for him, but there was laughter in her voice, and he chuckled too.

"I'm sure you did."

But when they looked into the black hole of the vent, it didn't matter. Illuminated by the light on her phone, it wasn't any better.

The vent was clearly empty. No stash. No chest. No glittering diamonds.

The room was empty. So were the other three in the same hall. No secret holes or any evidence that there had ever been a treasure. No trace of even a secret hiding hole.

It was well after midnight by the time they slid the last grate back into place and examined the last section of flooring. Millie leaned a shoulder against the doorjamb, her head low and her other hand protecting the back of her head. "I was sure there would be something here."

Ben racked his brain for a piece of encouragement, but the only words that came to mind felt more like a slap than a boost. "Maybe there used to be."

Her long lashes blinked rapidly, but her gaze never strayed from the spot between her knockoff Converse sneakers. "You think someone beat us to it?"

He hadn't said that, but . . . "Could be. Maybe. I don't know."

"It would explain the missing second diary."

That felt like a punch to the gut. It was

too true to ignore. "Ye-es . . ." He used every second of the dragged-out word to formulate his thoughts and then took an extra breath. "If someone else knew about the journal and took it, they might have already searched these rooms."

"But the dust and the cobwebs." She waved a hand toward the footprints they'd left behind.

"It could have been years — decades — ago."

Finally looking up at him, she gave him a pinched smile. "So we're looking for a treasure that was found years ago."

There was that jab to the gut again. Why? Because he wanted half of whatever that finder's fee might be. And because no matter how sarcastic she got, he hated to see her disappointed. At all.

Well, that was inconvenient.

"Did anyone else know about the diary? About the treasure?"

"I don't know. I don't think so."

"Your parents maybe?"

She whipped her head back and forth so fast that it jerked him to another realization. He didn't know a thing about her family situation. It was a blank beyond Ruth and Grandma Joy. And the fire in her eyes promised that pushing wasn't going to get her to give up any of that information. Not now and maybe not ever.

He knew a thing or two about that. He'd never told a soul about his mom.

"Then we better ask Grandma Joy."

She countered his argument in a voice suggesting she hoped he didn't notice that was exactly what she was doing. "There has to be a way to find out if a treasure was ever found at the Chateau."

"Of course there is." And he was such an idiot for not looking into it from the first.

"Whatcha lookin' at?"

Ben shrank away from the question and the man who asked it, shifting his shoulders in a vain attempt to cover the computer screen on the desk before him. "Nothing."

"Uh-huh." Carl Ingram crossed his arms over his chest and pursed his thin lips. If it was possible, his squinty eyes narrowed even more, trapping Ben into his small corner.

Ben could shrug the questioning gaze off, but he knew that was a bad idea for two reasons. One, Carl wasn't likely to let it go. He hadn't become the lead historical archivist at the Glynn County Library because he gave up on tracking down the details. Carl would pester him until he got to the truth. And two, Carl was his boss.

At least Carl was his boss at the library —
his third job. Ben picked up a handful of
hours every week helping Carl document
and track the county's historical archives to
bring in a few extra dollars — dollars that
went out just as fast. And it was the kind of
thing he enjoyed.

Leaning back in his chair and crossing his
arms, Ben took a deep breath and revealed
the screen he'd been hovering over for half
an hour. The site specialized in detailing
rumors and discoveries of treasure in the
South, but at the moment, its flashing ads
and blinking screen just made Carl recoil.

"How do you kids stare at that junk? It's
enough to make a donkey run."

Ben chuckled. He wasn't familiar with the
phrase, but that wasn't too surprising. Carl
had a habit of making up words when he
didn't know what to say.

"I was wondering about something. You
ever hear about a lost treasure on St. Simons?"

Carl's bushy eyebrows did a little bop of
surprise. "Sounds about the opposite of
nothin'." His Southern drawl dragged the
words out to twice their length.

Ben nodded. "Could be. But maybe not."

Carl peered at the screen before shaking
his head and pulling his glasses out of the

front pocket of his short-sleeve button-up, which was tucked into pants way too close to his armpits and much too far from the floor. Shoving the enormous frames farther up his face with one finger, he wrinkled his nose.

"Pirate treasure?" He waved at the webpage that still displayed the only St. Simons treasure Ben had been able to find.

"No."

Carl grunted and squinted again, this time directly at Ben. "What kind of treasure you looking for?"

Ben looked around Carl, giving the long room a careful survey. The far wall was lined with cabinets that housed many of Glynn County's and the island's historic documents, preserved and protected. A table in the center of the room held the project that Carl had been working on for two weeks, a series of letters donated to the county by one of St. Simons's wealthiest families.

Carl's desk in the opposite corner was pristine as always. Also per usual, he hadn't bothered to turn on his computer.

The room was empty, nothing out of place, so Ben took a deep breath. He wasn't quite sure why he had to steel himself for this conversation. Sure, he'd promised Millie that he wouldn't tell anyone else about Ruth's journal and the treasure. But picking the brain of the most knowledgeable historian in the area wasn't the same as announcing their search for treasure on the website he'd just been exploring.

"What about at the Chateau?"

Carl sniffed. "You mean other than the gold on the bottom of that ridiculous pool?"

With a low laugh Ben shook his head. "No. Not that gold. Something else. Something better, maybe."

Carl hitched up the leg of his polyester pants as he gazed toward the ceiling. When he looked back down, he seemed to be able to see through walls, his focus somewhere in the far distance. "You see something over there?"

Well, that wasn't an answer. And it certainly wasn't the response that he'd expected.

Maybe — *maybe* — Carl would have mentioned the rumors that sometimes surfaced around the great house. But Ben had really anticipated a flat-out denial.

He sat up straighter so he didn't have to tilt his head back quite so far to get a good view of Carl's expression. "No." The word came out about three times too long and couldn't even convince him.

"What'd you find?" Carl leaned forward,

shoving his glasses up from the tip of his nose as he drew eye to eye with Ben.

"Nothing." Except Ruth's journal. And no one really knew what it held. Millie had been working her way through it, filling him in as she went, but she wasn't nearly finished yet. It was quite a bit longer than the thin tome had suggested, and the sometimes fading handwriting could take a while to decipher. She'd apologized for not reading faster, but he couldn't blame her. It wasn't easy juggling multiple jobs and needing to catch at least few hours of shut-eye at night.

The one thing they knew for sure was that there was a whole journal more to the story. But telling Carl about that meant breaking his promise to Millie, which he wasn't interested in doing.

A burst of fire shot up from his stomach, and he pressed a fist against his chest. Not that it was going to stop the heartburn. He had an antacid in his desk drawer, an arm's length away. But reaching for that would surely clue Carl in that he hadn't disclosed all he knew.

With a snort, Carl shook his head. "You know something, don't you? Might be better than the crumbs I've heard. Take your chalk, young man." He reached for another chair on wheels, rolling it over before falling

153

into it. "Then we'll compare notes."

Apparently Carl could read his mind. Not helpful. Unless, of course, it meant Ben didn't have to say a word about Millie and Ruth and a treasure that had been lost for nearly a century.

He snatched the bottle from his drawer, popped three of the chalky disks into his mouth, and chewed them quickly. They tasted like fake oranges and regret. And they did absolutely nothing to stem the acid churning in his stomach.

"Tell me everything you've heard."

Ben rubbed his chest and swallowed thickly. "Why don't you start?"

"Because I fought in Korea, I raised four children, and I'm your boss."

He rolled his eyes but nodded. He wasn't sure why the first two mattered in this argument, but the third was enough. "I heard about . . ." He took another deep breath as he tried to sort his thoughts into something that would make sense. "I heard that someone was stealing from some of the guests that last summer before the crash."

Carl nodded appreciatively. "Jenny Russell. She was barely twenty when they ran her out of the house and off the island."

Jenny. The maid whose room showed exactly no evidence that she'd ever hidden anything there — or in any of the maids' rooms. "How do you know about that?"

"Oh, her firing made all the local papers. She was forced to move to Augusta just to find work, and her family was none too happy about it. That reputation followed her for the rest of her life."

Whether from the acid in his stomach or the certainty that Jenny hadn't committed the crimes she'd been accused of, his insides twisted. He didn't know who had stolen from the Chateau's guests, only that the wrong woman had been accused.

" 'Course, none of those accusations amounted to a hill of beans," Carl said.

"You don't think she did it?"

"Oh, I doubt anyone — least of all Howard Dawkins — really thought she did it."

"Then why'd they . . . ?" Ben wasn't quite sure what he was asking. Or maybe he already knew the answer and didn't want to confirm it.

Carl answered anyway. "People with power, my boy. People with power will do anything to protect that privilege."

"So what happened to the things that were stolen? Were they ever found?"

Leaning his forearms on his knees, Carl licked his lips, his gaze again focusing on something too distant to see or too long ago.

"Far as I know, no one ever went looking for them."

"But how does an entire island just forget about something like that? Especially the ones who were stolen from."

"I'm not sure anyone knows just what was taken. There's no record of it."

Except Ruth's diary.

"There was a fire in the police records office around 1932. After that, no one cared enough to keep looking," Carl said. "Truth was, by that point, no one had cared for almost three years. Whatever was taken couldn't make up for all that was lost."

"You mean Dawkins?"

Carl tugged on his earlobe. "I suppose it's hard for a man to face something like that. To lose all of your money in an instant and to realize that everything you've worked for is suddenly worthless. The crash hit a lot of people hard."

"But the Vanderbilt and Rockefeller and Devereaux families all survived the Depression, wealth and name intact."

With a sigh and a sad shake of his head, Carl continued his train of thought as though Ben had never spoken. "Dawkins poured everything he had — and a whole lot of what he didn't — into building the Chateau. It was his masterpiece, his *Mona*

Lisa. He never had the money of those other families, but he knew that the Chateau would give him the credibility to run in those crowds. And that's really all he ever wanted. So when the market crashed and his fancy furnishings were worth pennies on the dollar, he did what he thought was honorable."

Ben knew that part of the story and the rest. Dawkins, sure he would never recover his losses, had ended his own life. The house had been willed to his nephew instead of his wife, who probably didn't want a thing to do with it and the reminders of his life without her that it contained. But by the seventies it had fallen into disrepair, so Phillip Dawkins had partnered with the historical preservation society to return it to its old glory and turn it into a privately owned museum.

"Everybody gave up on it after Dawkins died. Funny how something so big can be so quickly forgotten."

Ben responded with a humorless laugh, more to fill the silence than because he felt like laughing. But there was something in Carl's pale gaze that didn't quite fit with the rest of their conversation. "You mean the Chateau?"

Carl patted his knee. "That too."

July 1, 1929

George invited me on a picnic today. I was supposed to go to the beach with Jane and Angelique, as Claude is still out of town on his secret mission, but George slipped me a note this morning as we left the house for a walk.

I should not have agreed. It is highly improper. But how could I not when he said he would like to take me to his favorite spot on St. Simons?

I told Jane I wanted to stay near the house. She was concerned about my health, but I assured her I only wanted to stay out of the sun.

God, forgive me these fibs. And my impropriety.

There is just something about George that makes me . . . well, I don't exactly know how to explain it. Sometimes when I catch a glimpse of him in the yard, my heart begins to beat faster, and my head spins. And I think it quite likely that I will swoon, even though I have never done such a thing in my life.

I snuck to the gardener's shed a little before noon, making sure that Jane and Angelique were long gone. Lucille and Mr. Dawkins were nowhere to be found, so I tiptoed down the long corridor and past his study. There was no sound coming from behind the closed door, so I hurried along, remaining as silent as I could.

George was right where he said he would be, a wicker basket in his hand and a shy smile on his face. And my heart responded immediately.

He called me Miss Holiday again, despite my insistence that he call me Ruth. He dipped his chin and probably missed the way I rolled my eyes at his insistence on propriety.

Maddening man. But I could not stay angry as he held out his hand. I stared at it for a very long second — all long, lean fingers and calluses across his palm — and I wanted to reach out and grab it and let it swallow mine. But when I glanced up for a moment, I saw a look of horror in his eyes. It was there only for a flash, as though perhaps he could not believe he had just made such a gesture. Before I could grab him and tell him how I was the opposite of repulsed, he shifted his arm, poking his elbow in my direction as he turned.

I blinked and tried not to let my disappointment show. When I tucked my fingers into the crook of his arm, he set off in the opposite direction of the beach.

I asked him where we were going, and he chuckled. (He has such a nice laugh.) But he said only to his favorite spot on all of St. Simons Island. I nodded like I knew where that was or even generally what direction we were headed. I had not an inkling.

We walked for approximately twenty minutes, all beneath the shade of the moss-covered oak trees. They hung over a path, the grass worn thin from frequent trips. Had George made all of those? There was no time to ask, for just as soon as I opened my mouth, we came upon a clearing. Truly, it was much larger than a clearing. But the break in the hanging branches left room for the sun to shine directly on a small white cross atop a steeple adorning a dark gray roof.

Oh my. It took my breath away.

It was a simple church, having the standard four walls and a wooden door. It sat on a patch of lawn nearly as green as George's eyes. But the spot of sun illuminating it all made it look nearly angelic. Somehow holy.

I could only put my hand to my throat,

but George seemed to understand. I tried to find the words to describe just how beautiful it was, but I lost them all as he led me into the open, into the warmth of the sunshine and the coolness of the breeze. It tugged at my hair, and before I could push it into place, George reached for it, tucking it behind my ear.

I must have frozen. He certainly did. Only his eyes changed, growing larger and filling with shock. Twice in the span of half an hour I had caused him to do something he found to be dreadfully scandalous. I barely know this man. What was I doing alone with him, letting him touch my hair and my ear and my cheek?

But if I had not agreed to this walk, I would have missed this church. I'd have missed this moment. I'd have missed him.

A bird sang loud and long, and it must have pulled him from his reverie. George jumped into action, telling me all about Christ Church of Frederica. Nearly 200 years old, it was started by the renowned preacher John Wesley and his brother Charles.

There is so much history in this little

slice of heaven, and I wanted to focus on what George said. I really did. But I got lost just past the history of the building in the tenor of his voice, the way it rose and fell with excitement and joy. I think he went on to talk about the graveyard and the grounds. I heard none of it.

By the time he had laid a blanket down to cover the grass and pulled paper-wrapped sandwiches from his basket, I realized my eyes were closed and my face turned up to capture all of the sunny warmth as he told his tale. When he asked if I was well, I jumped, startling us both. I reassured him that I was only enjoying the scenery. I could not very well admit to having been enjoying the sound of his voice. He deserves to be on the radio if anyone does.

One of his eyebrows arched, but he did not point out that I had been looking at exactly nothing. So I attempted to change the subject as quickly as I could, and asked him why this was his favorite place. He looked surprised for a moment but then said the church lawn has everything he needs for peace. Sunshine, roses, and the gospel.

He made it all sound so personal. I had

never heard anyone but a preacher talk about the gospel like that, but I could not bring myself to ask another intrusive question, so I took the sandwich he offered and nibbled at the corner.

We barely spoke after that, reclining lazily in the sun until it was time to go back. All I could think about was how glad I was that I had not gone to the beach.

I love the gazebo with all my heart. It is so quiet and calm in the early mornings and still my favorite spot at the Chateau. But George's favorite spot on St. Simons might become mine as well.

July 17, 1929

Claude pulled me into an alcove and kissed me today just as I left my room. I do not know how else to describe it. There were no romantic words or gentle kisses to my wrist beforehand. One moment I was hurrying to meet Jane and Betsy for a swim, and then something grabbed my arm and pulled me right off my feet.

Of course it was Claude. But before I could even realize that, his hands were on my face and he was kissing me. Thoroughly.

This was nothing like the sweet, chaste kiss of the beach. It was not like the playful kisses that Mama and Papa share when they think no one is looking.

Just when I thought I would never have the opportunity to breathe again, he stopped abruptly to tell me that he had missed me. He nearly growled those words. I didn't even know a man could make that sound.

I hoped that his surprise kiss would make my insides take flight yet again, but instead I wanted to flee. I only wanted to find Jane and sit near her or have her put her arm around me.

No, that was not entirely true. I most wanted to be in that patch of sunshine on the lawn of the church. With George.

There was barely space in that tiny little room off the upper hallway for the two of us to stand. There certainly was not room for me to think about George too. Claude tilted my head up, and I tried to smile. All I could focus on was the strange little curve of his mustache. It sent shivers down my spine, but not the kind I so wanted.

When I finally registered his initial

greeting and responded that he had just seen me at breakfast, he assured me that two hours was far too long. And then he called me "my dear."

He was so suave, so debonair. The type of man I have always dreamed of. And the man who could make my dreams come true.

I fled anyway. I am sure I must have given him some sort of excuse or apology, but I can only recall running. The sunlight through the windows was warm, and my skin felt flushed. By the time I burst through a door on the first floor, I had lost track of where I was. I only truly recognized that I had exited the house because the steady slap of my feet against the hard floors disappeared when I reached the grass.

Free of the house and with no further sign of Claude, I tried to orient myself. Useless.

And that is when I heard a familiar chuckle from behind me. I turned to find George leaning on his rake and grinning like he had won a prize. He presumed I had lost my way and insisted on calling me Miss Holiday.

I insisted on Ruth.

He nodded and promptly called me

Miss Holiday.

This again. I was already disoriented, uncertain, and . . . frightened? I was not scared of Claude. He would never hurt me. But I was in turmoil. My insides were scrambled like a batch of eggs. And before I could help it, I burst into tears. I put my head into my hands and tried to muffle the sobs, but I am afraid there was no helping them.

Suddenly something clattered to the ground — it must have been the rake — and two strong arms wrapped around me. They were gentle and warm, and I leaned into them, resting my forehead against George's chest. He rubbed a small circle on my back and offered to help me find my way back.

I wanted to scream. I was not lost, and I assured him so.

His hand stopped moving, and his entire body grew stiff. He said, "Are you injured? Has someone hurt you?"

I believe I will remember those words for the rest of my life. They were so simple but seemed to mask a fierceness, a promise of protection. I pulled back but immediately felt the loss of his arms, so I took a tiny step back into his embrace. I told him I had not been injured.

Not really. I am not sure why I added that caveat — I just had to. Truly I had not been harmed, simply shaken up. Surprised. Terribly upset by my response to the man I care for.

And I do care for him — Claude, that is. However, I did not mention such a thing to George. He simply looked at me intently, as though he could see right into my heart. It is not the first time he has done that. But I had to look away.

He kept asking if I was certain I was unharmed. Although I spoke my assurances to him, tears still slipped down my cheeks. I tried to wipe them away, but he beat me to it. His thumbs were large and coarse and as gentle as they had been that day he rescued me from the pool.

He did not quite meet my eyes when next he spoke. But again his words were filled with such depth. "I can take you away from here."

I smiled at that. What a sweet gesture.

As I pulled back all the way, I sniffed but kept my eyes lowered. I looked a mess, surely, and probably a fool too. Mama always says that the tip of my nose turns red when I have been crying. But somehow the weight of George's gaze on me made me feel beautiful, cherished.

I could not help but compare the way he held me with the way Claude had only a few moments before. There was no comparison. And I hate myself for feeling those things with George. It is not right. I have kissed Claude. I am certain that he cares for me, and I for him.

So why did I run into George's arms like a ninny?

I ran away from George just as fast. I am sure I gave some sort of excuse to him as well, but honestly my throat closed right up, and I could barely breathe as I raced for the outdoor pool.

I was so distracted that I nearly missed the breeze off the ocean and the way the palm trees dipped under the weight of the wind. The air felt thick, wetter than usual, and I looked up into the sky. The clouds unfurled, dark and foreboding. As I reached Jane on the pool deck, they opened up and poured out everything they had inside.

We spent the rest of the day in the parlor playing card games. I lost them all. Every time someone passed the door, I jumped, afraid that I would be forced to face Claude. I was not ready to see him again. At least not yet.

I was much calmer by the time dinner came around. "Much" may be too great of a word. But I was at least able to greet Claude with a quiet smile. He took my hand and kissed it as he helped me into my seat. Betsy and Willa scowled at me, but Lucille tittered to Angelique.

Later, after dinner, Jane said that Claude could not take his eyes off me all through the meal. He even missed a bite of his food for staring too intently. I did not dare let my focus waver, even when the conversation turned to more missing pieces of jewelry. I caught a peek of Mr. Dawkins looking rather troubled, and I cannot blame him. He sent Jenny away, almost certainly without a reference, and items are still disappearing. He said even some valuable papers, something to do with the stock market, have disappeared from his study.

If it was Jenny, she had an accomplice. Someone is still at the Chateau.

And yet I am sitting at my vanity scribbling in this journal while Jane sleeps, and thinking only of George.

I cannot help but think he was offering me more than a drive down the lane or a diverting trip to Christ Church of Frederica again. There was something in his eyes. They are so terribly green and expressive, and I almost thought that he might . . . well, it is too embarrassing to even write down. But could he have meant more? Could he have been offering to take me away? Far away? For good?

But how? How could he ever manage that on a groundskeeper's salary? And he would have no salary at all if he left the Chateau. It makes no sense.

Yet I am rather sad that the prospect is mere fancy. I am a silly girl.

I would never go with him even if he had the means, which he never could. Unless . . .

Oh my. I have the most painful knot in my stomach.

Is it possible? Could George be Jenny's accomplice? Or could he be working on his own to steal from the guests?

What a ridiculous idea.

I'll never sleep now.

EIGHT

Millie slammed the journal closed and glared at the giant red numbers of her alarm clock. Stupid alarm clock. Stupid job. Stupid story.

Stupid Great-Grandma Ruth. She was a ninny. Through and through. She'd had one of the wealthiest men in America at her beck and call, and she'd been playing around with the gardener.

Who was rather dashing.

He was not. He was a landscaper with absolutely nothing to offer Ruth. And he could be the thief. Even Ruth had suggested it. Yet she seemed to have some sort of *feelings* for him.

You would have too.

She set the journal — much gentler with it than she'd been before — on the folding tray that served as her nightstand before flopping to her side and smashing a pillow over her ear. Punching it into place, she

171

tried to ignore the little voice still whispering to her.

Admit it. He was a good man. He understood Ruth in a way that Claude never could.

She would admit no such thing. Okay, maybe he was a good man — not the dashing heroes on the covers of the other books by her bed, but still kind. He'd rescued Ruth from the pool, after all. He'd taken her to the church and spoken of the gospel. But that didn't mean Claude didn't care for Ruth in the same way. It wasn't that Claude didn't understand her. It was that Ruth didn't understand her own emotions.

That had to be it.

Yes, she could rest in that knowledge. And she needed to rest.

She flopped to her back, arms and legs splayed, and stared at the ceiling, muttering under her breath at the tick-tick-tick of the fan. It just kept going, ticking along at its uneven pace.

Ugh.

Rolling over to her stomach, she burrowed her head beneath her pillow, but her sleeping shorts had twisted around her legs. She kicked to straighten them out. No luck. Another try. Same result.

Flopping to her back, she caught a glimpse of the alarm clock yet again. That was ten minutes of sleep she wasn't going to get.

He's not a thief and you know it.

She didn't care. She really didn't. He could have stolen the London Bridge for all it would matter to her. Just as long as George wasn't her great-grandfather.

He couldn't be. He wouldn't be. Ruth had bigger plans than a laborer. She'd wanted to be a voice actress in the radio dramas of the day. She'd dreamed of the big city far from the Georgia farm where she'd grown up. She wouldn't have gotten in trouble with George.

Millie nodded her head firmly.

With that settled, she could go to sleep. Because she had to be up in . . . She flicked off the hours on her fingers. Six hours. Well, five hours and forty-eight minutes.

"Go to sleep, Millie."

Closing her eyes, she held herself as motionless as possible. But her shorts were still twisted, and the fan still clicked along its merry way.

Stupid fan.

Sweat trickled down her back and across her upper lip. There was no way she could turn it off. Not when the window AC unit had been struggling to keep up with the humidity. Especially when the apartment below her was the center of the sun.

Rolling onto a cool spot of the sheet, she kicked at the covers until they tumbled off the end of the bed.

There. Now she could sleep.

Maybe not. Another fifteen minutes of the ticking fan and coughing AC, and she was no closer to falling asleep. She was only closer to throwing the nearest book across the room. But it was a loaner from the library, and she had no idea where she'd come up with the money to replace a hard-cover with a broken spine.

Not an option. She just had to go to sleep.

If she fell asleep right that minute, she'd still have five hours and twenty-nine minutes before her alarm went off. Six hours and twenty-nine minutes before she had to serve coffee to a roomful of grumpy diners in desperate need of the sweet elixir. They were all irritated before their first cup. But she couldn't be grumpy back.

Fall asleep. Fall asleep. Fall —

You know he was good to her.

So what if he was? It didn't matter.

You know he didn't steal anything.

Again, it didn't matter.

Maybe it does.

It did not. It only mattered that she was functional enough to work in the morning. If she wasn't, she'd have to move into her car, and then what would become of Grandma Joy? As it was, Millie only had fifty-three days to find a miracle source of income and a new home for Grandma Joy. Right now it only mattered that she was functional enough to find Ruth's other journal. It only mattered that there was a map in it.

That's what mattered.

No, it's not. And you know it.

She flopped over again, pressing her mouth into her pillow and screaming for all she was worth. She could still hear the clicking of the fan.

When her breath ended and her head thumped in time with the rotating blades, she rolled onto her back and sighed. The moon's light filled the gaps in the blinds, covering her room with shadows as clouds rolled across the sky.

It had rained when Ruth was on St. Simons too.

But that and a bit of DNA were all they shared. Ruth had had two loving parents, a chance for success, and the eye of the richest man in Georgia at the time. Millie had two exhausting jobs, a chance that her electricity would be turned off, and a partner she'd never expected.

Ben's face flashed through her mind, and

she tried to forget the way he'd looked the last time she'd seen him, when they searched the maids' rooms. He'd swiped his dirt-covered hands across his face at some point, and there was a swath of black from his forehead around his eye to his chin. It hadn't dampened his grin at all or the twinkle in his eyes. Or maybe that had been her imagination. It had been relatively dark, after all. And she hadn't been staring all that hard.

Liar.

Sticking her tongue out, she blew a raspberry. That's what she thought of that voice in her head. It insisted on keeping her up and calling her names.

She did not need that kind of negativity in her life. Not now. Not when she had a mission to complete. Not when Ben seemed intent on distracting her at every curve.

He wasn't. At least not on purpose.

It wasn't his fault that she still felt his firm grip on her hand as he led her down the stairs. It wasn't his fault that his hair fell across his forehead and he just *had* to brush it out of the way. And that made her insides wiggle like unset Jell-O.

She didn't have time to think about him — or any man, for that matter. She never had. Not since Grandma Joy had needed her help and her care, anyway.

That didn't stop his too-blue eyes from flashing before her. Or that little voice in her head from wondering what it might be like to be the heroine of one of the novels stacked on her floor. Somehow those women found a way to make it work. All of them. They found a way to balance the responsibilities they carried with the men they fell in love with.

But that was fiction. This was real life.

Of course nothing could keep the girl from falling in love with the guy. She didn't have actual bills to pay. She didn't have an actual grandma who needed to be cared for. She didn't have to actually find a safe place where her grandma could be cared for.

Of course it was all going to work out in the books. At least the ones that she chose to read. She made sure of it. A quick peek at the last page was all she needed in order to know if the story would have a happy ending.

Real life didn't come with the same guarantees. And neither did Ruth's story.

Millie flopped over one more time, hunting for a cooler spot free of the stickiness that caked her limbs. There wasn't one. Her bed had turned into a radiator.

Finally she dripped out of bed, crawling

across the floor of the semi-enclosed bedroom toward the bathroom. Turning on the cold water, she splashed some on her face. Then a little more. Then she held a washcloth below the cool water — *cold* was far too generous a description. It felt good pressed against the back of her neck. And down her arms, right where Ben had touched her.

Flinging herself back into bed, she tried to wipe that memory away. But it would take a full scrubbing, maybe more.

Maybe Ruth had felt the same. About George, that is.

Maybe she wouldn't think about this right now.

Sure. That was a logical plan. But logical and actionable were very different things. Despite the alarm clock reminding her that she had to be awake in a little more than four hours, she couldn't stop thinking about it all. About Ruth and George. And Ruth and Claude. About why she herself had hesitated to enter the maids' quarters a few nights ago. About whatever Ruth's second journal would reveal.

Millie knew what was keeping her awake. She just didn't want to put it into words. It was easy to look for a treasure. It was so much harder to look for family.

Whether George was a thief wasn't the question. If he was, her great-grandfather was.

And she desperately needed it to be the other man in Ruth's life.

"Are you all right?"

Millie nearly jumped out of her skin at the breath in her ear, and her hands flew to her throat as she stumbled backward. Right into the arms that seemed to be ever-present lately.

"Whoa there." His voice sounded like it had been raked over gravel. "It's just me."

No *just* about it.

"Yes. I'm fine." Her words were barely more than a breath, and she had no doubt that gravel could take her down in a heartbeat. Especially after the night before.

Isabelle Calhoun, the aptly named actress who played the Southern belle of the house party, glanced their way. She seemed quick to dismiss the way Ben held Millie upright and how close his lips were to her ear. Until she zeroed in on Ben.

Who wouldn't? Millie hadn't at first, true, even when Ben's student had pointed it out. But after a sleepless night that involved way too much thinking about Ben on the cover of one of her library books, she understood why women might take another look.

Millie immediately recognized his absence as he stepped away. Probably because he'd noticed that they'd been spotted. Thus far they'd managed to keep from arousing Juliet's suspicions of an inappropriate relationship any more than they had on that first night.

Isabelle, however, wasn't known for her discretion. And if she thought she'd spotted something between tours, it wouldn't take long for the entire cast — and management — to hear about it.

Millie did a quick sidestep, tugging on her gloves and straightening her necklace. Forcing her face into a mild look of surprise, she took a quick breath before diving in. "Ben. How are you? It's been ages."

Oh dear. She sounded like an idiot. Probably because she was one.

The angle of Ben's lips seemed to ask what game she was playing. She didn't know what it was called. She just needed him to play along.

Please. *Please.*

She tried to convey everything flying through her mind in a single glance.

"Hi?" His response was definitely a question rather than a statement. He might not have gotten everything she was trying to send him. So she tried again with a harder look filled with all the things at stake.

"You look great. How is everything?"

Isabelle was still staring at them, leaning toward them, ignoring her partner for the night, Duncan. He was probably rambling on about his new car. It was always about his car or his clothes or some exorbitantly priced steak he'd eaten. Sort of the opposite of Ben, who seemed to always be working and never spending his money.

"Good?" The tilt of Ben's head and furrowed eyebrows said he still wasn't sure what she was up to.

"Great." Now what? She searched for anything that would sound normal. Natural. But she'd forgotten how to have a conversation. "Um . . . You seem . . . How's work?"

Ben's voice dropped a full octave and more than a few decibels. "Did you hit your head?"

Spinning so her back was fully to Isabelle and — she hoped — blocking their conversation, she whispered, "We have to be careful. She's watching us." She hoped her nod toward the redhead across the room was imperceptible from the back. And that Ben would understand.

"You don't look very well."

Wrinkling up her face as much as she

181

could, she scowled at him. "Well, you're too tall."

He laughed right into her face, and for a minute she forgot that she was supposed to be playing this cool and giggled back at him.

"Your gloves keep falling down."

"I know." She jerked them back up again and let her gaze sweep over him, hunting for anything to criticize. It wasn't easy. He *was* tall. Probably three inches over six feet. And a little on the lanky side. But there was nothing wrong with his dark hair, pale eyes, regal nose, and steeply angled jaw. Or the five o'clock shadow growing on it.

"Well . . . well . . ." Argh. Why couldn't she be quicker on her feet? Maybe if she'd gotten more than three hours of sleep the night before, she could be. "Your . . . your . . . eyes . . ."

Their gazes locked, and the bottom dropped out of her stomach.

Those eyes. Looked. Right. Through. Her. And the teasing light that had filled them just a moment before disappeared.

"Seriously, are you all right?" He waved toward her face, and she leaned away on reflex. "You're looking a little tired."

"Is that a subtle way of saying that I have dark circles under my eyes?"

He didn't really have to point it out. She

already knew they were there. They had been since she'd dragged herself out of bed, brushed her teeth, looked in the mirror, and groaned.

Ben shrugged.

"I didn't get much sleep last night." She glanced over her shoulder at Isabelle, who had turned her attention back to Duncan and followed him across the room. At least for the moment they had a bit of privacy, and she could be honest. "I was thinking about Ruth."

He squinted, "Something new?"

"The thefts didn't stop after the maid was fired."

He scratched at his chin, his whiskers rustling beneath his fingernails. "It wasn't her." There was a certainty in his voice that made her lean in closer.

"You seem pretty sure for someone who hasn't even read the diary."

"I have my sources."

"You do?" Her voice rose in volume and pitch, and she quickly pinched her lips together.

"Don't look so surprised." A smug smile crossed his lips as the antique clock on the mantel rang the half hour. They both looked toward it and recognized it as their warning bell. Five minutes until the next tour arrived at the parlor.

He turned to find his spot in the hallway, but she grabbed his arm. "Ruth said her room was near a small alcove on the second floor."

His gaze turned distant, like he could see the blueprints rolled out before him. "She said the second floor? There isn't an alcove on the second floor."

Millie mentally ran back through the words she'd read. "Upper hallway maybe? Could there be something on the upper hallway?"

A slow smile made its way across his face until the corners of his eyes crinkled. "I'll meet you outside the women's locker room after your shift." With that, he disappeared between two ficus trees, removing his modern self from the old-time elegance of the parlor. She glanced down at her dress — silk and satin except for the beaded chain at the low waistline — and then at the knit cotton covering Ben's retreating form. He certainly didn't fit into the world created for the guests.

But he was beginning to fit into her life.

He also knew more about this old house than anyone she'd ever met. He could be the difference between finding the truth about her past or losing her future entirely.

NINE

Ben stayed in the shadow of a large sycamore tree for several long seconds after Millie made her exit from the locker room. She looked around quickly, then down at the phone in her hand. He almost texted her his location, but he waited another second.

Right on time, Felicity, the tour guide, walked out behind Millie. She said something that sounded like "good night" and then stalked toward the employee parking lot.

Then the redhead who had stared at them earlier that night joined Millie, her costume traded for jeans and a tank top. Spinning her keys around her finger, she stopped to say something.

He couldn't hear the words, but he could see Millie's profile. First she plastered a fake smile on her face. Then it dipped. She fought to get it back into place, but it was a losing battle. Millie looked like she couldn't be any more uncomfortable if she'd come face-to-face with a rattlesnake.

Maybe she had. And from the flip of the redhead's hand through her hair, she knew what she was doing.

Before he even knew his plan, he stepped forward. The Chateau's lights had been turned low and clouds covered the moon, so he had about a second and a half before he was visible.

Millie's voice rang out clear. "I don't know what you think you saw, Isabelle."

The redhead only leaned in closer, but if she spoke, Millie cut her off. Ben shuffled back into the safety of the shadows.

"Ben and I are acquaintances. That's all. And he noticed that I wasn't looking my best tonight and wanted to make sure I wasn't sick. End of story."

"Hmm." Isabelle seemed to take her time digesting the information. "Then, you know him?"

"I guess." Millie's eyes darted in his direction, but he was still hidden. He hoped.

"Because I've seen him around. Some of the other girls were asking about him, you know. Is he single?"

He crossed his arms and flexed his muscles. Because what else could a guy do when he knew women were talking about him?

Not that he was interested. He certainly didn't have time for anything like that — love and marriage and the whole thing. He'd thought about it, sure. But always down the road.

Still, it was a boon to hear that someone found him attractive. Too bad it wasn't Millie.

He gasped at the thought, hunting for its root and determined to rip it free. He had no business thinking things like that, given their current arrangement. He did not need her to think he was handsome. Even if he thought she was just as stunning in cutoff jean shorts as she was in her costumes.

Millie looked like she'd swallowed her tongue for a split second before answering Isabelle's question. "I have no idea."

He couldn't tell if Millie was still performing or if she really had no idea about his relationship status.

Isabelle shrugged. "Either way." There was a looseness in her words — so cavalier — that made his stomach churn. She either had no respect for him or had no respect for herself. In any case, he wasn't interested in that.

"He doesn't date co-workers," Millie said through clenched teeth.

Had he said that to Juliet? Or was Millie taking license with their friendship? Or did she already know that about him with certainty?

With a "we'll see," Isabelle spun and sashayed across the paving stones, leaving a scowling Millie to stare after her.

When she was gone and the echo of her footsteps had long since vanished, Ben whistled low. Immediately Millie's head snapped in his direction. He could tell the exact moment she saw him. Her eyes went wide, then narrowed, and she marched toward him like a soldier on a warpath.

"How long have you been there?"

Stuffing his hands into the pockets of his navy pants, he shrugged. "Long enough."

Despite the shadows hanging low over them, the pink on her cheeks was undeniable, and she dipped her chin quickly.

"You were right."

Closing one eye and glaring at him through the other, she said, "You're not all that handsome?"

He shook his head. "I don't date co-workers."

With a playful slug to his arm, she walked toward the Chateau's main entrance. "So where are we going?"

He led the way to the front stairwell, opposite the one they'd taken to the kitchen a few nights before. She stayed close, but he could tell when she paused to look behind them. "Don't worry, I shut off the cameras."

She didn't budge for a long second, so he reached for her hand, only to find hers halfway there. "Come on." Pulling her up the stairs, he rushed for the alcove she'd mentioned, the only one on the upper hallway. It was a few dozen winding yards from the master suite, Dawkins's private rooms.

"How'd you remember this was here?" She spun around in the little offshoot just large enough for two people to stand in.

Tapping a finger to his temple, he smirked. "Same way I knew where the real maids' quarters are."

"You're a big geek and spend all your time studying ancient blueprints."

Shrugging, he nodded. "Basically."

She smiled at that, flashing her white teeth and crinkling her nose. "Ruth said in her journal that she was leaving her room, heading for the swimming pool — the outdoor one — when she got pulled into the alcove."

Ben turned and played out Ruth's movements in his mind, then stopped short. "Got pulled in?"

"Oh, um . . ." The moonlight through the

windows made the flames of her cheeks gentler, but there was no mistaking that she'd revealed something she hadn't wanted him to know. "She was kind of seeing one of the other guests. He pulled her in for a . . . private moment."

"To kiss her."

She nodded.

"Was their relationship a secret?"

She stared at the ornate brass designs on the ceiling for a moment before shaking her head. "No. I think it was common knowledge among all the guests."

That wasn't the full truth — he'd bet every penny his mother had stolen on it. And if she was telling him partial truths about this, what else in that book wasn't she telling him?

He wanted to push, but this wasn't the time or the place. They were already pushing their chances that they'd be caught. A burst of acid reflux reminded him how much he wished he could change the circumstances. Two wrongs did not make a right. But he prayed that what they found might begin to make right some of his mother's many, many wrongs.

Dawdling because he had questions wouldn't help. Later he'd push Millie to explain what she was hiding. Right now he'd find Ruth's old room and pray that she'd hidden her second journal there.

"Well, if she was going to the pool and had to pass in front of this alcove . . ." He pointed to the right, to the only door there.

"Makes sense, I guess." Millie strode in that direction. "After her accident, Ruth said that Lucille had moved her and Jane from one of the bungalows to be closer to her and Dawkins."

Close was a relative word, but in this case, they couldn't get much closer to the banker and his particular friend

As they stepped into the room, he tried to see it through Millie's eyes. The furniture most likely wasn't original to the room, which sported two twin beds, each with four posters and a blue bedspread. Still, her great-grandmother had fallen asleep in this room to the rhythmic crashing on the beach below. She had stood at that window, over-looking the sand and water, and watched the people strolling along the shore.

Even he — no relation whatsoever to Ruth — felt the physical weight of stepping back in time. It was hard to breathe and hard to think about anything but what Ruth might have felt in this room.

Millie immediately went to the window and rested her hand on the white sill. The glass was foggy, but she stared through the panels like she could see forever.

"She loved being here."

"What's not to love?"

Looking up and focusing her eyes on the present, she smiled. The makeup she'd worn earlier that night was gone, and in its place was the natural glow of her cheeks. "Good point."

Maybe it was the smooth line of her cheek or the way she wrinkled her nose or the way she was lost in the past, but he took a step forward. Then another. Until the space between them vanished.

Something had knotted in his chest, and it refused to let go. Especially when she tilted her head and stared back at him with narrowed eyes. Could she see right through him?

He didn't have even a second to answer that question before she slid around him, strolling across the room. "Let's find out if she stashed that other journal in here."

If it was possible, he was both relieved and disappointed that whatever might have happened didn't. But he refused to focus on it, instead pulling out his knife and setting to work on the grate in the corner.

Unlike the maids' rooms, this one had a closet, and Millie stepped into it. "Ouch!"

"You okay in there?"

She poked her head out, holding up a finger in front of her face. "Splinter. I'll survive."

"Glad to hear it."

The screws in the grate came out without much effort. They twisted with ease, and he almost didn't even need to use his knife.

Because maybe they had been replaced by someone using her fingers?

The thought made his heart stop, then slam back into his breastbone. It could be in here. It *was* in here.

He almost called Millie over to see, but something made him stop. He should find it first. Definitive proof and all that.

Pulling the grate out, he shined the light on his phone into the darkness, giving it a few quick swipes. All was black. Empty.

His stomach sank and he leaned his head into the corner.

Lord, are we even supposed to find this journal? This treasure?

Still hovering somewhere near his toes, his stomach gave a lurch, and he pressed his hand over his eyes as regret washed over him. This was the first time since he'd met Millie that he'd stopped to talk to God about this. Any of it. Of course, it shouldn't have been. But knowing what he should do and actually doing it were two very different things.

Why hadn't he spent every day since he'd met Millie asking God for direction and clarity and wisdom? Maybe then he wouldn't have ended up with a partner who traded in half-truths and was far too pretty for him to ignore.

"Well, the closet's empty. You find anything?"

He shook his head as he lifted the grate back into place. "Empty. Is your finger okay?"

"Yes. Just a loose baseboard." Her voice stopped suddenly, and he launched himself across the room before he even knew what he was hoping for. Millie had fallen to her knees, her fingers pinching the pale wooden baseboard. It was only about three inches tall, but there was a definite movement to it. Even more, there were notches in the top of the board, as though someone had wedged a screwdriver or other tool between it and the wall.

"Here. Let me help." He dropped to her side and used the blade on his Swiss Army knife to lever the board away from the wall.

Suddenly Millie's fingers vanished and were replaced by the bright flashlight of her phone. "Is that better?"

He nodded just as the board popped loose. They both gasped, and Millie angled her light into the darkness beyond.

Ben stretched out across the floor of the closet, his legs reaching into the bedroom. Pressing his head against the floor, he tried to see into the hole they'd discovered. But it was mostly cobwebs.

He shivered. "I think the spiders beat us to it."

She gasped and jumped back, the light flickering. "Are they still in there?"

"I'm doing my best not to think about it." He closed his eyes and reached into the opening. It wasn't much wider than his hand. Not much deeper either. But suddenly his finger brushed something.

He couldn't help the yelp that escaped as he jerked back, his hand caked with spiderwebs. Pressing the baseboard back into place, he hoped the spiders would stay behind it.

"What? What is it?" Millie shined her light on his outstretched arm and the gossamer threads clinging to his skin.

He pinched a yellow piece of paper between his fingers.

Millie sucked in an audible rush of air, and his jaw hung slack. "Read it," she whispered.

He wanted to take the moment to point out that she wasn't reaching for the spiderweb-covered clue. But this wasn't the time. This was the time to find the next step.

With his clean hand, he plucked the scrap of paper from its sticky prison and turned it over. Before he could even make out the faded script, Millie leaned over his shoulder and read it herself.

" 'I've found a better hiding place. R.' "

"What's that supposed to mean?"

"Um . . ." Her eyes shifted back and forth, reading and rereading. "It's probably . . ."

Ignoring the long thread hanging from the end of his shirt sleeve, she hovered over his arm.

The note had been written in pencil and the charcoal had faded, now barely distinguishable from the yellowed paper. But the words were all there. Just as Millie had spoken them.

"Well, there was definitely something hidden here."

She nodded. Then she swallowed so loudly that he could hear it. "You don't think . . . Was she hiding the . . ."

"The treasure? No way."

Her eyes glimmered with something resembling hope, but doubt seeped in like a shroud.

"Why would she leave a note telling someone that she'd moved a stolen treasure? If you think someone knows where it is, then you move it. If someone had suspected her and searched the room, this note would have been evidence against her. No way would she have risked that."

Millie let out a low sigh. "You're right. But then what —" She bit her lip. "The journal. Someone was reading her journal."

Millie expressed no question about it, and he had a hunch she was right.

"But who?" she asked.

"If she hasn't said anything in her journal . . ." He dragged out the words, wishing she'd say there had been some clue, but with a quick shake of her head, she dashed his hopes. "Then we have to get more details — from someone who was there. Or at least the next best thing."

"But no one who was there is still —"

He knew the moment she realized what he was suggesting. Her eyes flashed and she opened her mouth, but no sound came out. A quick jerk of her head in a decidedly negative direction was all she needed to communicate.

He narrowed his gaze directly to hers. Her sapphire eyes turned to ice, and she crossed her arms over her chest.

"No."

He hadn't even asked a question yet. But she was as smart as she was pretty, and she could probably read his mind.

"We need to know what she does. You know we do."

Her lips puckered, but her gaze never wavered. "We can't. It's not . . . it's not as easy as all that."

"Right." What had Millie called her grandma before? Forgetful? "She might not remember?"

Millie's lashes dropped to her cheeks as her gaze dropped. Her hands shifted from fists under her arms to embrace herself.

A sudden urge to pull her into his own arms washed over him. He wasn't a hugger. His mom hadn't been. Neither had the parade of men who came and went. He didn't really know *how* to be. But when Millie released a pained hiccup that sounded far too much like a sob, Ben couldn't remain still. Grabbing her shoulder with his free hand, he did what his instincts said he should. He pulled her to his chest.

She was stiff as a board for a long moment as he clumsily crossed his untainted arm over her back. Suddenly she let out a breath with a loud whoosh, and her arms went around his waist. Tight.

Tucking her head under his chin, she pressed her face into his shirt. Her breath was warm through the cotton, and his skin erupted in goose bumps under the contrasting air-conditioning. Yes, it was definitely the AC that made his whole body feel like he was on high alert.

The cedar smell that had clung to the inside of the closet faded, and she was all sweet citrus and warmth in his arms. She melted like chocolate in the sun, and he could do nothing but hold on and pray she didn't slip through his fingers.

"Millie?"

She sniffled, and he had never been so grateful that he couldn't see her face and the tears he could feel through his shirt.

Say something. Say something. Say something.

But the mantra did nothing to bring comforting words to mind as the truth seeped through him. Its icy fingers wrapped around his spine until he shivered. Only one word repeated through his mind. *Alzheimer's.*

"Is she . . . worse than forgetful?"

She didn't say anything. Her body trembled like she was trying to regain her solid state, which came in fits and starts. With her backbone back in place, she shook her head fiercely. Then she stopped. And nodded.

He waited a brief moment to make sure that was her final answer, and it wasn't until she wheezed against him that he realized how hard he'd been squeezing. Quickly relaxing his hold, he thought about dropping his arm. But she wasn't ready for that. He could feel it in her arms still around his waist.

When it became clear that she wasn't going to add any more to her response, he asked another question. "How much worse?"

"Much." Millie sounded like a bullfrog, but no amount of clearing her throat was enough. "It's been diagnosed as dementia."

"Alzheimer's?"

Her head wiggled against his chest in a decidedly negative motion. "The doctors say it's only dementia. She doesn't have the other symptoms associated with Alzheimer's." Her breath was audible, and she cleared her throat again. "But she can't take care of herself anymore. She forgets things she's known her whole life."

Millie held her breath for a quick second before letting it out in a quick rush. "But she was lucid when she told me about the treasure. I promise. Otherwise she wouldn't have known about —"

"The journal," he finished for her.

She nodded but didn't pull back just yet. She probably didn't want to watch him process this particular kick in the pants. He didn't blame her. But he was surprised at how little it actually affected him. They were right where they had been ten minutes before. Nothing had changed, and at least some of Grandma Joy's story had been true.

He wouldn't back out now.

Maybe he should pat Millie's back and promise that it would all be okay. But that was a lie. It was probably going to get worse. A whole lot worse.

At least now he knew what secrets she'd been keeping and why she was after the money. Caring for Grandma Joy would cost a pirate's treasure. Whatever gold the Chateau held might only make a dent. But at least it was a dent.

"Does she live with you?"

"No. I had to . . . I just couldn't watch out for her like she needed. I had to move her into a care facility." She looked away, finally dropping her arms and trying to pull away.

But he kept her close for another moment, rubbing a gentle circle on her back. It was awkward but the only thing he could think to do in the face of her regrets.

When she pulled fully free, her hands folded in front of her and her chin hanging low, she looked about fifteen years old, buckled by the weight of decisions she wasn't ready to make and responsibility that shouldn't have been hers. He wanted to ask about her parents. He wanted to know why she'd had to be the one to decide to put Grandma Joy into a home.

There were so many questions, but only one thing he knew to say. "Let's go see her."

She looked up, a furrow already worming its way between her eyebrows.

"Together."

TEN

Millie cringed as Ben pulled his rattling coupe into the long drive. A faded blue sign at the beginning of the lane claimed this was the Golden Isles Assisted Living Home, but there wasn't anything golden about it as far as she could see. At first glance the row of oaks adorned in Spanish moss seemed a regal welcome, an invitation to visit one of the South's most luxurious plantation homes. And maybe once upon a time it had been. Before the war. Before Reconstruction.

Now it just looked like no one had bothered to bring a hammer to it since. White paint flaked off the two-story columns before twin oak doors that hung at wrong angles, and the red bricks of the front wall had been bleached by years in the hot summer sun.

But Ben didn't seem to notice. He continued to drive in silence, taking the rutted gravel road with its due reverence. That gave her plenty of time to second-guess this plan. It was a terrible one.

Grandma Joy didn't do well with new people. When a new nurse was assigned to her wing, Grandma Joy had screamed through half the night, calling for Grandpa Zeke. But he had been gone for nearly ten years.

Millie shuddered now with the same trepidation she'd had when her phone had rung at two that morning, insistent and nearly as loud as her thundering heart as she raced for the home. It had taken an hour of sitting with Grandma Joy, squeezing her hand and whispering in her ear, to calm the frightened woman down. Nothing worked until she sang Grandma Joy's favorite hymn. No instruments and barely a tune. But the words seeped through a consciousness clouded by time and disease.

When peace, like a river, attendeth my way,
When sorrows like sea billows roll,
Whatever my lot, Thou hast taught me to
 say,
It is well, it is well with my soul.

Millie had spent the night with her, sleeping in the recliner by her bed, always an arm's reach away. But while the words two generations older than Grandma Joy had held a comfort for her, Millie couldn't muster much hope in them.

Whatever my lot . . .

She didn't know what kind of lot the guy who wrote that song had had. Maybe he did have sorrows. Shoot, maybe he was on a ship in the middle of a storm and praying he didn't fall out. Maybe he was in full-on Job mode.

But one thing was for sure. He hadn't had to send his grandmother to a care facility. He hadn't counted every nickel of every tip, simultaneously hoping it would be enough to pay for another month and feeling shame over having to send her there at all. He hadn't driven down this road, his insides a knot because seeing Grandma Joy was both the best thing in his life and a reminder of his worst failing. He'd never lain awake at night wondering where his grandma would go when Virginia Baker kicked her out. He'd never felt the days ticking by like the clock on a bomb and known that whatever he did probably wouldn't be enough to care for the person he loved most in the world.

Maybe he'd learned to be happy with whatever his lot was. But he hadn't been the granddaughter of the most wonderful grandmother in the world.

Ben kept his gaze straight ahead as he pulled into one of seven empty spots in the ten-car parking area. When he spoke, it was clear he'd noticed something was going on.

"Have you changed your mind?"

Yes.

No.

"I'm not sure." She pinched her lips together, crossed her arms over her stomach, and then uncrossed them just as fast.

"What's worrying you?"

Her laugh was more of a huff of disbelief. "What's not?"

He cracked a smile, turning toward her. His knees banged against the steering wheel, his legs too long for the little car. Readjusting his position, he pressed his hand to her forearm. "We're on the same team, right? We agreed from the beginning. We'd do this together."

She nodded slowly, knowing where he was going with this and at the same time needing him to spell it out.

"We're looking for something that could change both of our lives, and maybe your grandma can help us find it. But we would never do anything to hurt her. Right?"

She nodded, the rope around her chest loosening its hold.

"If today's not a good day, then we'll wait until there is one."

That rope slipped a little lower. If Grandma Joy wasn't up for meeting someone new today, they could wait until tomorrow or the next day, but time was running out. She had to move in six weeks.

She gazed at him for several long seconds, staring into his eyes, reading his face, searching for the truth. And it was in there. The crinkles at the corners of his eyes told her what she needed to know. She could trust him. Even with this.

Then why can't you trust him with the truth?

The question barreled through her, and she had to look down for fear that he'd see it scribbled across her features.

With a quick nod, she opened the car door. "We can only try."

As they walked up the front stone steps, Ben put his hand on the rail and it wobbled wildly. "Guess this old home could use a few new nails."

He'd clearly tried to make a joke, but Millie cringed. "I mean, it wasn't the best, but it was the one . . ."

She could afford.

She didn't have to say it aloud. She knew he knew.

"She doesn't like to be alone." Millie

didn't direct her statement toward him exactly, and he didn't seem to think he needed to respond, so she kept going. "She gets scared when she doesn't see a familiar face or the doorbell rings. I tried to keep her with me, but I couldn't be there all the time."

Even she thought she sounded like she was trying to rationalize her decision, although Ben had said exactly nothing accusatory. It didn't matter.

"Sure. I mean, you have to work." As he stepped back to hold the door open for her, the side of his foot caught on a crack that stretched the width of the cement porch, and he nearly took a tumble.

Millie scrambled for his arm. "I'm sorry!"

Before she could even reach him, he'd righted himself and laughed. "I never was light on my feet. My ballet teacher yelled at me about it all the time."

Her chuckle came out as half surprise and half humor. "You took ballet?"

Shrugging one shoulder, he followed her. "I could have."

"But you didn't."

"No. We moved around a lot when I was a kid. I didn't really get to participate in extracurriculars."

This was maybe the first time he'd ever

spoken about his childhood. Or at least opened more than a window. She wanted to dig in. He'd learned more about her life in the last two weeks than she'd ever wanted to share with anyone.

But there wasn't time. Not as they approached the front desk under the watchful eye of a new attendant. Her brown eyes followed their every move, and Millie tried to ease into their visit with a gentle smile.

"We're here to see Joy Sullivan."

Without a word, the woman slapped a clipboard against the Formica countertop, her gaze never leaving Ben.

"Is that Millie?" The disembodied voice from the back room flew out to them, clear and confident.

"Yes," Millie said, but it sounded more like a question than she'd like.

The front desk attendant checked the clipboard, then called out her agreement like Millie needed to be verified.

"Hold on a sec!" It could only be Virginia Baker. What more bad news could she have? When she appeared at the door to her office, her short brown hair was sleek and flowy, like she didn't even know the definition of humidity. Millie ran a hand over her own curls, which had taken on a life of their own in the misty morning air.

"Millie, I need to speak with you."

She looked at Ben, who nodded quickly and said, "I'll wait right here with my new friend."

The attendant looked like she'd never had a friend in her life and she wasn't currently shopping for one. Ben was undeterred, his smile nearly blinding.

Millie slipped behind the counter and followed Virginia into her cramped office. Stacks of files filled every corner of her desk, and a computer screen was barely visible behind the central pile. The only chair for guests was also covered in red folders, so she stood at the doorway and smoothed her hands down the front of her cotton Bermuda shorts.

"Have you had any luck finding a new place for your grandmother to stay?"

Millie pressed a hand to her stomach as it gave a sharp twist, and she squeezed her eyes shut. She'd considered every other possibility within driving distance when choosing this facility. But without an influx of money, she was still without options. "Have you found a pot of gold at the end of a rainbow?"

Virginia clucked her tongue. "I know this is difficult, but we have another resident waiting for the space."

Her eyes flew open, and she stared at Virginia. The woman looked unassuming, but her words had the power to blow up Millie's entire life.

"What are you saying?" Millie tried to keep her voice down, but it rose with each word.

Virginia made a motion with her hands to indicate they should stay calm, but Millie didn't feel calm. Her insides were a hurricane of uncertainty, every piece of her tossed about at the whim of the administrator.

"We're going to need your grandmother's room in thirty days." With a sad smile, Virginia held out a single sheet of paper, but the black print on it blurred as Millie stared.

Her spine tingled, and she fisted her hands at her sides, unable to accept whatever document Virginia had prepared — probably a notice of eviction. "You said we had ninety days. It's only been forty."

"Well, technically, it's been forty-four. But we need her to move out by the end of the month." She turned and picked up a few fliers from her desk, the colorful brochures featuring enormous estates and pictures of smiling seniors. "Maybe one of these will help."

Virginia thrust them at her, and Millie had no choice but to take them and stuff them in her purse. She'd seen these before. And seen the hefty price tags placed on the rooms. Still not an option. And now the clock on the bomb had sped up. She'd lost more than two weeks. And she was no closer to finding a connection to the Devereaux family.

She'd never wanted to crawl into the pages of her books more than she did in that instant. Deep in those stories the heroines never faced more than they could handle. This was so much more than Millie could handle.

Unless . . . Unless Grandma Joy had been telling the truth. Unless she was from the wealthiest family in the South. Unless she was heir to something so grand she couldn't even imagine.

Unless that was all a pipe dream, a wish too good to be true. Heroes swooped in to save the day in the fairy tales. But her life was all cinders and none of the belle of the ball. Not that she was going to complain about it. It was her lot. Just don't expect her to say it was well with her soul in the midst of it.

"I really am sorry," Virginia said.

Not sorry enough. Millie trudged out of

the office, her eyes burning and her hands still shaking. This had to work. It just had to, because *sorry* didn't give Grandma Joy a safe place to stay with staff who actually cared about her.

She didn't even motion to Ben as she slipped out from behind the counter and shuffled down the hall. Natural light seemed to have been banned, but she didn't mind. Not when she'd much rather cover her face and hide the red tip of her nose that she knew was already there.

"Hey." Running footfalls behind her drew closer. "What was that all about?"

"Nothing. Just . . . nothing." She shook her head and stared at the wallpaper that might have been white at some point in the distant past. But the curling edges had lost their brilliance a few decades before.

This was all she could provide for her grandmother. And not for much longer.

A fist squeezed around her heart, and she slowed her walk just to catch her breath. It was broken by a silent sob, and she pinched her eyes closed, turning away from Ben's inquisitive gaze. Hunching her shoulders, she tried to create a wall between them. But he was so much taller than her that it was useless.

He said nothing, but he didn't walk away.

There was a strength radiating from him. It was subtle but stable, low-key and constant.

She hated how much she wanted to turn into his embrace and enjoy the warmth she knew was there. She couldn't. Not here. Not now. She scrubbed her hands over her face and tried to find that steel backbone that Grandma Joy had always modeled. It was in her, somewhere deep. She needed only to find the courage to use it.

Letting out a slow breath, she lowered her shoulders from where they nearly reached her ears and forced her hands to her sides. She shot him a glance out of the corner of her eye. "I need to find that treasure."

His dark brows lowered over his eyes, but he nodded slowly, following her down the hall to room 22. The nondescript wooden door was like every other one in the building, but she knew it as if it had a giant X marking the spot. The door was open a crack, but all was silent inside.

Until it wasn't.

Suddenly a loud bang sounded against the door, shaking it hard. "Blasted shoes!"

"Grandma Joy!" There was no time to even consider Ben as she flung open the door, scooped up the sneaker that had clearly been thrown across the width of the room, and raced toward the purple recliner.

The petite woman sitting in the seat had a face redder than a beet, and she glared at the other shoe on her foot. Bending lower, she gripped the white laces between trembling fingers, her hoarse mutters filling the room and certainly spilling out the open door into the hallway.

"Over, then under. No. No." She shook her head hard, her fluff of white curls bouncing with agitation. "Under, then over, then loop and loop and . . ." Her voice petered out, and she looked up, confusion filling the wrinkles of her face. "You changed it on me again. I could tie them this morning. I could."

Millie's mouth went dry, her fingers forgetting how to function. She could only hold the shoe by its laces as understanding dawned. And with it an ache so deep that it threatened to tear her in half.

"It goes over first, right?"

Dropping to her knees, Millie gave her grandmother a soft smile. "Yes. It goes over first. Then loops."

Grandma Joy gave a firm nod and followed the motions with her knobby hands, stiff and uncertain. "I could do it this morning."

"I know." Millie tried to find some other words of comfort but knew they'd be quickly forgotten too, so she let herself off the hook and simply reached for her grandmother's hand. She pressed the paper-thin skin firmly but gently until Grandma Joy looked at her, really looked at her. "Let me help you."

"Camilla?"

Dear Lord.

It was the only prayer she could muster as the hope she so desperately needed was washed away.

How did she not remember? How could she have forgotten the thirteen years they'd spent together with Grandpa Zeke? How had she forgotten the little kitchen table where they'd eaten their meals and put together puzzles? How had she forgotten teaching Millie to drive in the back pasture and the little tree Millie had run over? It never did recover. But they'd been a family, the only one Millie had.

And now Grandma Joy didn't even know her.

"Yes. It's me."

The gold in her grandma's eyes became less fire and more relief as a gentle smile tugged at the corners of her mouth, her pink lipstick seeping into the deep crevices of her skin. "Camilla." This time it wasn't a question as much as the simple enjoyment of saying a familiar name, and Millie tried to let that be enough. "Why — why are you here? How long have you been here?"

"I just got here. I'm going to help you tie your shoes."

"Oh." Grandma Joy patted her bent head. "You're such a good girl. You always take such good care of me."

She had to close her eyes as tears once again threatened to break loose.

Ben clutched at his chest, trying to reel in the top that spun somewhere deep inside. It didn't help.

Watching Millie slide her grandmother's foot into the shoe that she'd thrown across the room and tie it snugly made him want to laugh and cry. It was so sweet and utterly painful at the same time.

But he mostly wanted to run.

This little woman could hold the answers to everything they were hunting for. Yet getting to those answers wouldn't be easy.

"See?" Millie patted the top of the shoes. "All set now."

Despite her perky tone, there was a hesitancy in Joy's responding smile. It seemed to be searching for the true emotion inside, like she was sure the smile was required but not sure why.

Oh, Lord, why do some people have to suffer through this? It wasn't fair.

Then again, life wasn't fair.

It wasn't fair for people who lost their memories. It wasn't fair for people who lost their loved ones. It wasn't fair for people who lost their money. And it sure wasn't fair that someone he loved had caused at least two of those three.

The reminder was enough to turn the pulsing in his sinuses into a full-blown throbbing, and he pinched the bridge of his nose in an attempt to stem the headache where it started. Useless.

So he pushed through, trying to focus on the exchange between grandmother and granddaughter and whatever that might reveal. Despite Millie's assurance to Joy, she wasn't there to help her tie her shoes. This visit was about a book with a map that was still missing. No one was going to hand it to them. They'd have to find it themselves with whatever help was available.

"Camilla?" Joy patted Millie's shoulder, seeming to need a third confirmation.

Millie nodded, and Joy looked across the room. "Do I know you?"

She was obviously speaking to him, but he still pressed a finger to his chest in an unspoken question before barreling on.

"No, ma'am. I'm Ben Thornton."

Joy's gaze meandered from him to Millie and back again before settling on her granddaughter. "You know him?" Her Southern drawl became more pronounced, and the blank stare in her eyes was replaced by something that resembled humor. "Or did he follow you in?"

Millie laughed. It was almost sweet enough to overpower the weighty smell of cleaning products and confinement.

"He's a friend of mine."

"Friend?" There was a lingering undertone in the word that danced with romantic suggestion. It was only missing waggling eyebrows to be the stereotypical setup. Meanwhile Ben was still wondering if what they shared could really be called *friendship.*

Acquaintances. Co-workers. Treasure sharers. Yes to all. But *friends*?

Maybe.

He had hugged her. No, that wasn't right. He'd *held* her. He'd let her cry all over his shirt as he'd tried to comfort her. He'd done an extra load of laundry for her. He didn't do that for just anyone. And he hadn't minded a bit.

She'd become a staple in his life. Someone he looked forward to seeing. Someone he wanted to . . .

Well, he'd stick with *friend*. She was definitely a friend.

"My, but you are a handsome man." She motioned for him to step farther into the room. "Like my Zeke. He's tall too."

"My grandpa," Millie said.

He nodded as he took another couple steps into the studio apartment. He'd figured as much. He also had a feeling that Zeke was long gone. If he was still around, the responsibility for Joy wouldn't have been solely on her granddaughter's shoulders. Or Millie would have been taking care of him too.

"Zeke. He's a handsome man."

"You said that already, Grandma."

Those blue eyes laser-focused on Millie. "Some things are worth repeating."

Millie chuckled. "Fair enough."

"Are you from these parts?"

Ben almost missed that Joy's focus was back on him, and he scrambled for the right answer. The one that was true but not too true. "Um . . . no, ma'am. I'm . . . I moved here for graduate school." And to get away from a town where everyone knew his name and what his mother had done. Technically they had lived in Brunswick — just on the other side of the bridge — for a short time years before. But St. Simons had felt like a safe place to mostly disappear. A safe place to forget.

"An academic, then?"

"Ben is a history professor."

"Adjunct professor," he quickly amended. It might not mean much to Millie, but it was the difference between working one job and three.

"At the college?" Joy didn't wait for anyone to confirm. "You know, we all said that Millie could have gone to college. She was smart enough. She just never liked going to class."

Out of the corner of his eye, he saw Millie's cheeks go bright red. He tried to catch her eye with an encouraging grin, but her gaze had fallen to the floor, intently focused anywhere but on him.

"She's smart as a whip, really. Loves those books. She was always up until the wee hours of the morning. I couldn't get her to go to bed, bless her heart."

"That's okay, Grandma. Ben doesn't —"

He held up a hand. "Of course I want to know."

When Millie did finally look in his direction, it was accompanied by pursed lips and a cute little wrinkled nose. He could barely keep in a burst of laughter. Grandma Joy's memories of Millie's childhood seemed more than adequate to annoy her grand-daughter. But would she remember the things they really needed to know?

"She insisted on being called Millie." Joy harrumphed, folding her arms, which were only just long enough to cross her body. As she leaned back in the chair, Ben suddenly realized just how petite she was. Her feet dangled above the floor, and he decided she might not even be five feet tall. But spitfire didn't require a size.

"She wanted everyone to call her Millie, even though her mama named her Camilla."

"Yes, yes. I've always preferred Millie. Not that you ever called me that."

"And she back talked like no child I'd ever seen." But there was a lilt in Joy's tone that revealed even she didn't believe what she was saying.

Millie swatted at Joy's arm with a laugh. "I did not. I was perfect."

"If you call staying up until all hours of the morning *perfect.*" Turning back to him, Joy whispered, "She wouldn't close those books. Stayed up all night reading them. I couldn't get her to stop. And if I couldn't find her, I knew where she was."

She didn't have to say it. Somehow he just knew. "The library."

"Yep."

"Well, I'm reading something else interesting right now," Millie said.

Joy pushed herself to the edge of her seat and rested her arms on her knees. "The journal? You found it?" With a tilt of her head, she motioned to him. "He knows about it?"

"I had to tell him. He caught me snooping around."

"So, what's it say? Does it have the map?"

Millie dug into her bag — the substitute suitcase always hanging over her shoulder — and retrieved the carefully wrapped book. Unwinding it from the cloth protector, she slowly shook her head. "There's nothing in here about a treasure. There's no map."

Joy had been reaching for the journal but dropped her hand as soon as Millie confirmed the worst. "No map? But there has to be. She said. She always said." The clouds in her eyes that had blown away flew back in on the winds of a hurricane.

Ben stepped forward, wanting to help her understand but powerless to do anything more than shake his head. It was Millie's comforting hand that settled onto Joy's knee. "But it says there's a second journal. Do you know where it might be?"

Joy's gaze turned distant even as she

clasped Millie's fingers in her own gnarled ones. "Another book?"

"Yes. Grandma, it was right where you said it would be. The journal was there. But there's another one."

"The journal? I never wrote a journal."

Millie clutched the diary in her free hand and held it out. "Your mama's. Ruth Holiday's. You told me she left it at the Chateau. In the library. It was there." There was an urgency to Millie's words. They didn't rush but rather came out in waves, imploring Joy to understand, to remember, trying to sweep her back into the land of the present.

Joy's eyes reflected only confusion. Patting her white curls, she frowned. "I don't — that's not right. My mama is — she lives on the farm. Not the Chateau. She loved the farm. Said all the best things were there." She rocked in her chair, her breathing picking up speed.

Millie looked up at him, her eyes wide and fear stamped across her face.

This wasn't something he could fix. There wasn't something he could do to make it better. This felt like when Millie had broken down, and he'd gone on instinct, knowing nothing except that he could hold her.

Dropping to his knees beside the rocking chair, he put his hand on the armrest right next to Joy's elbow. "Tell us about the farm."

"The Chateau?" A childlike smile fell across Joy's face. "It's so pretty at night. All lit up with the electric lights. Mama takes me to see it sometimes."

Just as quickly as it had arrived, hope seeped out of him on a long breath. And something inside his chest split like the *Titanic.*

"What about the farm? Did you live there?"

"Mama said all the best things are at the farm."

Millie looked up at him through long lashes, jaw clenched and lips tight. Silence dragged between them as Joy mumbled on about the farm, her words making only minimal sense.

Finally Millie mouthed two simple words that made perfect sense, "I'm sorry."

He could only nod. There were no words for moments like this, so he simply waited with the two women as one fought for every memory and the other grieved the ones forever gone.

The minutes ticked by. A quarter hour. Then half. The steady squeak of the rocker counted down every second. Until it stopped.

He looked up to see that Joy's eyes had

225

drooped, her chest rising and falling in a smooth rhythm beneath her folded hands.

Millie seemed to have noticed as well. Leaning forward, she kissed Joy's forehead. "Love you, Grandma." With a pat of her hand, she turned toward the hall and led the way. Outside she closed the door with an almost imperceptible snick.

She didn't move, her head still hanging low and her gaze somewhere near her blue sneakers. "I'm sorry."

He wanted to tell her not to be. He wanted to promise that it was all right. But mostly he wanted to fix this, to do something worth doing. To pursue a lead worth chasing. So he said the first thing that jumped to mind. "All the best things are at the farm."

August 1, 1929

I feel certain that I have ruined any friendship I might have had with George. It should not feel so terrible, but it does. I am sure he will be fine. What is less certain is if I will fully recover.

But I had no other choice. Not after the evening that Claude and I spent together. He has been so concerned about me since he startled me in the little alcove. He is forever checking on me to make sure I am well and that he is not pushing me beyond where I feel comfortable. And the truth is that I feel much more than comfortable in his arms. I like it more than I probably should.

It began two evenings ago. After dinner, Claude invited me for a walk on the beach, and when I suggested that Jane join us, he was insistent that it be just the two of us. I could hardly refuse him. Of course, I did not want to.

He led me by the hand through the parlor and through a side door. Lucille gave me a highly knowing look as we walked by, but I have no idea why. I suppose she assumed that I might be free with my attentions, but she does not know Claude as I do. He is a gentleman through and through. Or, I thought he was.

No, I am sure of it. That evening was simply an anomaly.

We walked along the beach for what felt like hours. The moon was twice as large as normal, and as it cast its great shadow across the rippling waters, it also cast a spell of some sort. I am not entirely sure how to describe it, except to say that I was drawn to Claude in a way that I did not expect. Walking by his side, hearing him speak of traveling across Europe, made me long for a life I have only ever dreamed might be possible. What would it be like to see the great wonders of the world? Paris adorned in her beautiful lights? England's ancient castles? Rome's Colosseum? I have only ever seen pictures in books at the library at Miss Truway's School. Claude describes them with such tenderness that I cannot only picture them, but I can imagine myself there.

He asked me if I would like to travel. I almost responded that I would like to go someday. But Mama says that someday is today. So I simply told him that I would.

He squeezed my hand and said he would take me. I wished I had thought to remove my gloves. Without the silk barrier, I am sure that I could have felt his pulse at his wrist. I wished too that I had worn other shoes. The heels of my shoes sank into the beach, and grains of sand slipped inside, rubbing at my toes through my stockings.

The sand gave way under each of our steps, and he suddenly stopped. Pulling off his shoes, he said we should go barefoot. His shoes and socks were discarded before I could even blink, and he bent over to roll up the hem of his pants.

I have seen a man's ankle before, but this felt oddly personal, strangely intimate outside the context of the swimming pool. His feet are wide and strong, and the dark hair on the lower part of his leg made me realize he is very much a man. I knew that before, of course. But it was a strange realization that I was alone with a man on a beach.

When he looked up, he laughed at me and asked if I had never seen a man's toes before. I assured him I had, and he insisted that he should have the same pleasure. He winked as his fingers cradled the back of my foot and slipped off my shoe.

He wanted to see my feet, and then he said he wanted to see so much more than that.

I should have walked away. Willa or Jane might have slapped him. But I stood frozen. How could I move when my whole body felt afire?

The moon and the lights from the Chateau were plenty bright to see his face, and in his eyes I saw a longing that I'd never witnessed before.

I melted in that instant. My better angels did not try to make their case. There was only Claude and me and the Chateau.

We walked back to the house much later, our feet bare and our hearts full. He stopped me near one of the large trees, cupping my face with his hand and whispering to me of his feelings, calling me "sweet Ruthie."

I thought I should perhaps tell him that I love him, but before I could fully respond, he kissed me well and good. The crashing of a clay pot broke us from our reverie.

Claude stepped back as a knot formed in my stomach. I knew without looking who was there.

Oh, George. His words spouted apologies, but his eyes were luminous and unrepentant. I wanted to run. I wish he had never seen us. He, of all people, must think me a terrible person. But as Mama would say, there's no use crying over spilled milk.

Still, the next morning I woke with a peach pit in my stomach. Why do I feel as though I have treated George poorly when there is nothing between us? Certainly there has been no agreement or even mention of an interest beyond friendship from him. And I have not led him on. Not when Claude's attentions have been so clear.

George did offer to take me away from this place, but I cannot believe he truly meant it. At least, he could not have meant it in the way I thought. He had not offered me a life and a future. He had no means to do so. Even if he did have money, he had no desire to marry me.

Oh my. My mind has conjured far too many unfounded things. I refuse to even wonder about George in such terms.

However, I knew that I must speak to him. But I am a coward, so I wrote him a letter. I thought to have a maid deliver it, but Jenny is long gone, and I realized there was no one I trusted with something so precious. While the rest of the house enjoyed a lounging afternoon around gaming tables, I ducked outside. I even managed to find the same exit I have taken twice, where I have run into George. He was not there.

I walked all the way around the house, past the main entrance and between the rows of sycamores. The air is spicier out there, sweeter somehow. It's as though a few more yards from the ocean, the air is free to highlight the fragrance of all of George's beautiful flowers. Roses. Gardenias. Honeysuckles.

My nose was still pressed into the delights of one of the flower beds when George spoke, addressing me as always as Miss Holiday. I snapped to attention, the silly letter falling right to the muddy earth. I picked it up quickly and shoved it toward him.

He turned it over, looking at the front and back of the blank envelope, and then asked what it said. I almost blurted it out, but how could I say such things face-to-face? So I told him to read it himself.

He stared at the paper again and said only that he would rather hear it from me. He was so unassuming, rather undemanding, and he acted as though nothing had changed. As though he had not seen me just the night before in a rather compromising situation. I so wanted to punch him, as my brothers have done to each other a hundred times. I wanted to sock him right in the eye for being so . . . so . . . George.

Instead I yelled at him, waving my arms about like a madwoman, insisting that he knew very well what was in the letter. He assured me that he did not, but I still don't believe him.

I waved my finger between us, my voice rising with each word, and told him that what was between us was terribly inappropriate and must end.

He looked at me through one narrowed eye. "Is it now?" he asked.

Oh, I was so bothered. I screamed at him not to play coy with me. I tried to punctuate my words by calling him by his surname, but I could not remember it. And when I called him George, I lost a bit of my steam. Not all of it, mind you. I was still worked up, but not angry exactly. Unsettled.

He insisted that he was not playing coy and that we had indeed done nothing improper. Walks. A picnic. Always in full view of anyone who might like to watch. He said we had nothing to hide.

Oh, that infuriating man, making so much sense. He thought I had exhausted my arguments, but I still had the truth on my side.

I reminded him that he knew very well that Mr. Dawkins would not like it if he was mingling with guests. George said he would have liked it less if I had drowned on his property. I could not help but touch the spot on my head that had ached for weeks after my accident.

He nodded and held up the envelope. He had been planning to invite me to join him for church on Sunday, but we agreed it would be best for me not to go.

I did think that. I really did. Until his chin dropped, his shoulders slumped, and he walked away.

And I felt as though I had kicked a puppy.

I did the right thing. I know I did. But I am heartsick over George. How can I be so near to pure bliss with Claude and still regret sending George away with every fiber of my being?

August 5, 1929

Things have become quite serious. I do not mean to imply that stolen jewelry is not a serious matter. Obviously Mr. Dawkins believes it to be so or he would not have sent Jenny away.

However, the absolute worst thing has happened. It all began this morning when I slipped out of the house to see George.

That is not quite right. It started before that, and I was not intentionally going to see George. I happened to see him as I walked past the gardener's shed. Actually, it might have been on my second or third time past the open window that he called out to me.

He always sounds so formal, calling me Miss Holiday, and I wonder what his education must have been like. But in that moment, I could only peer through the cloudy glass. He stood beside the big table in the center of the room. A very large pot sat in the middle, and from its rich black earth grew the most beautiful rosebush I have ever seen.

I asked him where it was going to go, and he turned back to his work, snipping at the wayward branches before telling me he thought this might be an improper conversation . . . "Miss Holiday."

Oh, I felt awful. How could I explain that Claude had all but stated his intentions? I am certain that we are close to an understanding. He has kissed me many times now. And I have allowed him to do more. I know that Mama would certainly disapprove, but he can provide for me in a way that I could never have dreamed before. And I do care for him. He is a good man, wise and worldly.

I never meant for George to have feelings for me. But when I told him that I should not, could not, see him anymore and that our letters must stop, I felt as though I might have truly hurt him. His eyes, usually so green, turned to brown, deep and soulful. While he said he understood, how could he, when I can hardly believe what I said to him?

I needed another opportunity to explain myself. I had to.

That is why I went to the gardening shed. Except I could barely find any words. It is not an easy thing to do, breaking a man's heart.

"George. Please," I said. I sounded like I was begging. I probably was, even though I had no idea what I was begging for.

He looked at me then, through the glass that still carried the splatters from the last rain. He did not smile. Neither did he frown. He only stared, and I could feel it like a caress across my skin, deeper than anything that Claude had ever made me feel.

Feelings are foolishness. Mama has told me that a hundred times. I must be practical. I must think about my future. I must think about the opportunities that Claude can provide for me.

I tried to brush George's gaze off, but he didn't waver. So I looked to the side, and that is when I saw it. A piece of pink fabric poked out from behind one of the tall sycamores. The tree's base was so wide that I could not see what was on the other side, but that cloth was familiar. A rock too big to move sat in my stomach.

I looked back at George, who must have immediately read my face. He asked what it was but was already running from his shed.

He told me to wait where I was while he went to investigate, but I did not listen. I followed right behind him, clutching the back of his shirt. Suddenly his hand was over mine, sliding his fingers through mine. I did not mind a bit, as my heart was beating in my throat. It was so loud I imagine the whole beach could have heard it.

As we approached the tree, I could see that it was more than a scrap of fabric. It was a full skirt. And a woman was still wearing it.

I cried out, and George pulled me into his arms. He held me tight as I covered my eyes and tried desperately to erase the image that had been seared into my mind. Willa — talkative, vibrant Willa — lay at the foot of the tree, blood running from her hairline to the corner of her mouth.

George did not hold me nearly long enough. He let me go and dropped to his knees. Pressing his hands to Willa's face, he called her name. She did not respond. Then he touched her arm and shook his head.

I turned and vomited on the spot. I had never seen a dead body before. At least not a person. And dead animals cannot compare.

George hurried me back to the house, leaving me in the parlor, where I sank into the nearest sofa. Before I knew it, Jane was by my side with a glass of water. I drank it empty in one try and then just stared at the crystal bottom as the rest of the house came to life.

It was early and Mr. Dawkins was still pulling on his jacket as he raced down the hallway, hollering for Lucille to telephone the police chief.

The rest of the morning is a bit of a blur for me. I spoke to at least six police officers and told them my story over and over. At some point Claude slipped to the couch beside me, put one arm around me, and held my hand in his.

The day turned rainy just as they drove Willa away. It seemed fitting.

We have all been stuck inside for hours, mostly silent. Except for Angelique. She is beside herself, swearing that she and Willa were to take a walk along the beach this morning. Angelique was running late and blames herself for not being there. Claude and I tried to assure her that certainly if she had been there, they both would have been injured. Or worse.

The worst part of it all is that no one knows why she might have been attacked. Was it an accident? A fluke? Or is it somehow tied to the thefts that have happened here?

This summer is so different than I anticipated. There is more to share. It is a good thing Mama thought to pack a second journal, for I shall have no difficulty filling it.

ELEVEN

How much more?

The question had haunted Millie all night and the one before that, ever since she finished reading the diary.

Ruth had allowed Claude Devereaux certain liberties beyond a chaste kiss, but there was no telling just how far they'd gone on the beach. Or anywhere else, for that matter. It was clear that Ruth had assumed a proposal was imminent. So had she given herself fully to Claude?

If Ruth's story had been a modern one, there'd have been little room for doubt. But ninety years ago? Howard Dawkins had had no shame in bringing his "particular friend" to the Chateau while his wife and child remained in Chicago, but Ruth wasn't afforded the same social freedoms. Her station wasn't even on the same map as Dawkins. How could a farm girl expect to be treated as well as a wealthy banker

Grandma Joy had once said that Ruth's aunt had paid for her niece's education at a girls' academy. But it wasn't enough to set her among the elite.

Millie needed to know where she'd landed. Had Ruth succumbed to Devereaux's charms? Or had she held fast in the face of temptation? Given their escapades on the beach, Millie wasn't so sure she knew the answer.

And what of George? He was a fine man. She'd conceded that point. Sometimes Ruth's descriptions of him made him sound like he belonged on the pages of her latest library read. Ruth had let him hold her. But Millie had let Ben hold *her*. No big deal.

Except sometimes it felt like a big deal. No, not a *big* deal. But a deal. A situation. A thing.

If that was the best she could do in describing it, then it really wasn't any of those. But that didn't —

"Millie? *Millie!*"

She jerked around, almost toppling the tray in her friend's hand. "Ella!"

"Where were you? Cook's been calling your order for ten minutes."

Millie blinked quickly, trying to erase a vision of grass-green eyes and a warm smile beneath a sunny summer sky. "I'm here.

Sorry. I'm here." At least, she was here for another twenty minutes before Ben picked her up for what would probably turn out to be another wild goose chase.

Scooping up the plates at the window, she dodged Cook's salty glare and headed for the end of the counter. All but two of the red padded stools were filled, and the four teenagers on the end scowled as she approached. The only girl in the group said something, but the clanging of Cook's spatula against his griddle mixed with Elvis on the jukebox drowned her out.

"Sorry about that wait. Here you go." She slid each plate into place across the narrow Formica counter and pulled a bottle of syrup from her apron pocket. "Can I get you anything else right now?"

The girl huffed and rolled her eyes as she squeezed out enough ketchup to drown her hash browns. "I'm out of water."

"Of course. Anything else?"

The three boys were already neck-deep in their breakfasts, rich maple syrup drenching their pancakes. They shook their heads, so she reached for the pitcher of ice water.

Just as Millie began to refill the glass around a dancing straw, the girl shrieked. "Ugh! This is cold." And then she shoved her plate.

In an instant Millie dropped the water, the pitcher cracking against the black and white tiles of the floor, and grabbed for the plate, which flew over the counter's edge. She kept it from hitting the floor only by scooping it into her arms. Right against her middle.

The ketchup was cool and wet through her uniform dress, and she froze as it began leaking toward her waist. It didn't pool like the water from the pitcher did in her white tennis shoes, but it globbed against her skin, leaving sticky trails all down her front.

The whole room seemed to freeze. Even Cook's spatula paused. Only Elvis, begging for his girl to love him tender and true, continued.

And every single gaze zeroed in on her.

She tried to find a smile or a chuckle or something. Anything to detract from the fiasco. But before she could break the tension, the rude girl brayed like a donkey. Her laughter was as coarse as her manners, and every other face in the room seemed unsure how to respond. Even the girl's three companions struggled to follow her lead. Each of the teenage boys, all clean-cut and polished enough for Sunday morning, blinked in slow motion as strained smiles pulled at their faces.

Easy for them — they didn't have a mid-section full of ketchup, fried potatoes, and runny eggs that had made it to the bottom of her skirt and oozed past her knee.

"Idiot." The girl glared at her, daring her to speak up against the injustice, knowing somehow that she wouldn't. Couldn't. There were unspoken rules about these things. The customer was always right. Treat others as you'd like to be treated. She needed this job.

It was the last that made her clamp her mouth closed and ease the plate away from her. Looking down, she surveyed the damage. She looked like she'd been in a knife fight. More specifically, she looked like she'd taken a plate to a knife fight, and she'd lost. Badly.

The ketchup was still spreading, but there were three distinct splotches in the region of her belly button.

"Millie? Are you all right?"

His voice was both wonderfully familiar and terribly jarring. And it seemed to pull everyone else from their stupor, the whole place erupting with sound and activity at once.

Buddy, the café's manager, lunged for her, holding out a wet towel that had probably wiped down a thousand greasy tables. She deflected it with her free hand, trying to find the face she hadn't seen but knew was there.

Not at the counter. Not in a booth. There, at the hostess stand. Ben in his wrinkle-free shirt. Ben, his damp hair a testament that he'd recently showered. Ben, his eyes wide with concern.

She could only meet his gaze, hold up the plate, and shrug.

He seemed to understand. At least enough to realize that she wasn't gravely wounded and that the attack had been more emotional than anything else. So he offered her a gentle smile, crinkled eyes and all.

That's when her insides, which had been frozen in shock, suddenly twisted with the force of a tornado. Her head spun and her eyes went blurry, and for a moment she thought she'd lost her ever-lovin' mind. Maybe she had. Maybe Grandma Joy and Ruth and Claude Devereaux — or maybe George — had gotten to be too much.

All she wanted to do was curl up in her bed and disappear into the pages of a book. Not forever, but for a while. A long while. Only that wasn't really an option at the moment. Every single one of her worries wasn't going away. Not anytime soon.

So she stared at Ben and sucked every bit

of strength she could from his stable, solid stance as three other waitresses fluttered around her. One pulled the plate away while another wiped her hands with a napkin, and the third glared at the nasty girl.

"Come on, guys," the girl said. "We're leaving. This place smells like rotten fish."

Two of the boys followed her across the diner floor, but the last one dug into the pocket of his jeans. "Man, I'm sorry about your dress." He pulled out two twenties, which would barely cover the four breakfasts, and tossed them on the counter. Then he followed his buddies, and they disappeared to the sound of the jingling bell on the door.

"Are you all right, Millie?"

"That girl's the worst. She sat at my table last week."

"I'll ask Buddy to comp their meals so you can use the money to get your uniform cleaned."

All three women spoke at the same time. She just couldn't seem to look at them. Not when Ben was making his way over.

"You want me to go take care of them?" His voice was lower than usual, and it sounded like he hadn't used it in days. But his words made her laugh.

"And how exactly would you take care of

them?" Foot sloshing in her shoe, she took a step toward the counter.

His brows furrowed and his lips pursed as he looked over his shoulder at the place where they'd exited the diner. "Um . . . well . . . you know. I'd take care of them." He held up a fist and waved it around.

She laughed again. He was one hundred percent history professor in his dark jeans and green button-up shirt. Even with the sleeves rolled up to his elbows, he looked about as capable of "taking care" of those kids as she was able to snap her fingers and make her uniform spotless.

Shaking her head, she managed a genuine smile. "Thank you, though. I'm glad you offered."

Strangely, she was. She didn't want him to beat them up. She didn't think he'd even meant that in his offer. But even if he'd said it only to make her laugh, it had been exactly what she needed. And the spectacle she'd been had suddenly become a lot less interesting to every other patron in the Hermit Crab Café.

"Who's this guy?"

Suddenly Millie realized that she and Ben weren't alone. At the counter between them still sat a dozen other well-behaved diners. And Courtney, Priscilla, and Ella — the other waitresses on the morning shift — were still by her side.

"Um, this is Ben. He's . . . um . . ." She hadn't even had as much trouble introducing him to Grandma Joy. So why was this so hard? But as she looked into the expectant faces of her co-workers and gossip queens, she cringed. "He's a friend of mine."

Lamer words had never been spoken.

"A friend, huh?" Ella eyed him like a medium-rare steak, just the way she liked it.

Ben nodded slowly and spoke like Ella might need him to spell it out. "Yes. A friend. We work together."

Courtney's nose wrinkled. "You don't work here."

Maybe these girls did need Ben to speak slowly.

"We work together at my other job," Millie said. "At the Chateau."

"Oh." Priscilla eyed him up and down, twirling a platinum-blonde corkscrew curl around her finger. "You a tour guide there too?"

"She's not a —" He was halfway to explaining her job to them when she held up a quick hand. She'd already told them a thousand times what she did there. How three women who could remember every "hold the pickle" and "add mayo" for a buzzing party of ten couldn't remember that she played dress-up six nights a week, she'd never understand.

"You girls going to serve some of this food?" Buddy yelled right in her ear.

The others hopped up and took off to deliver the plates stacking up at the window. Millie just turned around and motioned to her dress. "My shift is over in ten. Mind if I go home?"

Buddy rubbed his hands together in front of his too-short tie. Patting his greasy bald spot, he gave her a once-over and then went back for seconds and thirds. His gaze made her skin crawl, but she tried to keep her smile from slipping away.

"Okay. Ella, cover Millie's tables."

She didn't need a written invitation. Sliding around the counter, she ducked into the back room, grabbed her purse and the bag of clothes she'd been planning to change into, and met up with Ben just inside the front door.

As he held it open for her to exit first, he said, "You want to go home?" His tone took a decidedly disappointed dip.

She took another good look at the front of her uniform and sighed. "I don't have much of a choice."

She'd planned to change her clothes at the diner and leave straight from there with Ben. But that was before ketchup started pooling at the waistband of her underwear. Not that she was going to explain that particular discomfort to him. Still, she gave him a hint as she wiggled against her damp underthings, praying that she wouldn't leave stains all over the seat of her car.

Except she hadn't driven that morning. Her car had refused to start. At least she wouldn't have to worry about making a mess.

"Can we go another day?"

He looked toward the far side of the road, over the passing vehicles, like he could see something more than the threadbare clouds. "Today's my only day off for another couple weeks. I'm working a few extra shifts."

"At the Chateau?"

Squinting, he looked back at her. "At the library."

Just how many jobs did this guy have? By her count that made three. Three and a half if treasure hunting took up any more of their time.

She was busy — but Ben was crazy.

Opening her mouth, she started some sort of casual dismissal. She could go on her own. He didn't need to go with her. She probably wouldn't find anything anyway.

But even as she began to form the words, she shook her head at her own arguments. She didn't want to go alone. And she sure didn't want to dwell on why she felt that way.

Maybe Great-Grandma Ruth was right and feelings were foolishness. But they were still feelings. It was that simple. That complex. Sometimes they required untangling, and sometimes she could ignore whatever knotted mess they held.

She'd go with the latter today.

"I do need to run home."

His eyes dropped.

"But I can be fast. I live close by."

As soon as his lips parted in a grin, her ketchup-covered stomach dropped. Why oh why had she said that? Stupid. Stupid. Stupid.

"Okay. I'll drive." There was no question in his words, only a logical plan he expected them to follow. Except his plan included him seeing where she lived. And worse, maybe coming inside.

Her left eyelid began to twitch, and she rubbed her fist against it. It didn't stop.

He walked to the passenger-side door of his coupe and pulled it open. In his best impression of a fairy-tale prince, he motioned for her to enter. Well, a prince with a twenty-year-old two-door carriage that probably had the actual horsepower of a couple of geldings. But the car was impeccable, inside and out. There were no residual water spots from the last rain marring its faded finish. No fast-food wrappers littering the floorboards. Not even the little mulberries tracked in on the rugs.

His car was pristine. She was not.

Holding out her arms, she did a little shimmy. "I'm a mess." Perhaps an unnecessary reminder since he was looking at her, but he seemed to have temporarily lost his good sense.

"Don't worry about it. I have seat protectors."

She'd barely noticed those in her previous trip in his car. She hadn't needed them. But now they were just one more reason he could take her to her home. She needed a new plan. But knowing she needed one and coming up with one were apparently two different things.

He just kept staring at her and gave her another little wave into the car while ketchup baked onto her skin, which promptly started sweating and sent the ketchup rolling once again.

You could have been home and changed by

now. Why are you holding this up?

Because . . . because . . .

Great. Now she couldn't even answer her own questions.

Because you don't want him to know that you live in an apartment the size of a postage stamp above someone else's converted garage.

It was possible. Okay, probable.

Get over yourself.

"Are we going to stand outside and melt, or are we going to do this?" Ben asked.

She slid onto the fabric seat protector and immediately began to cook as he walked around and got in behind the steering wheel. No matter how hard the AC blasted, it couldn't cut through air thicker than water, and she held herself as still as possible to keep whatever was oozing down her skin from spreading.

Somehow she managed to give him directions to the house three blocks away, and he let out a low whistle as she pointed to it. It must have looked impressive to an outsider. The two-story main house had been repainted in dazzling blue in the last year. It nearly glowed with bright white shutters and gingerbread over a quaint veranda. A quintessential wooden porch swing squeaked in the wind as they got out of the car. Even among the other impressive homes in the neighborhood, this one stood out.

Ben moved toward the big house, and Millie cleared her throat, heat already making its way up her neck. "My place is over here."

He mumbled something and followed her around to the back of the house toward the two-story structure that had once been a garage and storage. And that was being generous. Where the house was updated and upgraded, the garage had received only just enough attention to call it habitable. Anything beyond that was up to the tenants. And she had exactly no skills in that vein and no money to put into it even if she did.

But at least the rent wasn't bad. And when her car refused to start, she could walk to the diner.

Again Ben walked toward the door on the first floor, and she nodded around the side of the structure. "I'm up there."

She hadn't noticed just how flimsy the wooden stairs were until there were two people on them. Suddenly she worried that a little pressure on the railing might send them both right over.

When they reached the landing, she quickly let them in and looked anywhere but at Ben as he surveyed her home for the first time. It took him all of three seconds to spin around the single room — complete with a bed, kitchen, and table — and she hated herself for sneaking a peek at his reaction. At his smile.

"This looks like you."

"What? Small and a little grimy?"

He laughed but immediately pointed to a framed picture on the wall. "That must be Grandma Joy and Grandpa Zeke." She nodded, and he continued, "And the note on the fridge." He pointed to a white sheet of paper held up by a magnet. It said only, *It's all for Grandma.*

He leaned into her kitchen, looking at the stacks of mismatched plates and cups, which were visible on the shelves that were stand-ins for cabinets. "And the dishes are so eclectic." He sounded wowed.

But he likely wouldn't feel the same if he knew she'd gotten them all at the thrift store for fifty cents apiece. If he'd known that was her only option. Even saving and reusing paper plates had become too expensive.

"Well, let me just get cleaned up."

She grabbed some clothes from her closet and hurried to the bathroom. It was a bit of a tight squeeze, but she managed to slip out of her uniform, clean herself up, and put on fresh everything. She emerged from behind the accordion door to find Ben reading one of the books that were piled on the table.

Oh no.

"There's got to be something more interesting for you there." She tried to laugh it off, all the while praying he wouldn't realize just how fluffy and fairy tale-y the book in his hands really was.

She'd never gone for the bodice-ripper books. She much preferred leaving some things unread. There really wasn't anything to be embarrassed about

Except that he — an academic and a lifelong student — would likely discover that she was a silly romantic through and through. And while she liked being a romantic, the thought of him thinking less of her made her stomach ache.

He looked up from the pages in his open hand and smiled. "I was just skimming. Seems like a fun story. Pirates and buried treasure and all that." Setting it back down on its stack, he motioned to the others. "So, I guess you like to read."

Pulling her hair back and fastening it with a rubber band, she nodded slowly. "Mostly just fiction." Since she didn't want to have to explain about the particular kinds of books she loved, she pointed toward the door. "Ready?"

He nodded and led the way, and they were soon on the road headed inland.

"Have you been to this house before?"

Millie's mind had been somewhere out the window and across the green fields, and she jumped at his question. "The house? To my grandma's house? Yes, I've been there. I grew up there."

The car swerved a little before Ben righted it. He worried his lip with his upper teeth for a long moment, and she could almost see the gears in his mind trying to parse her story.

There was no use hiding it — no reason to. "My parents took off when I was a toddler. They decided they didn't like being parents. It was too hard. Too exhausting. Too much." A lump formed in her throat, and she tried to swallow it away. But it refused to budge, so she cleared her throat and tried to speak around it. "They left me with Grandma Joy one day and never came back for me."

Okay, it was out there now. No taking it back. It just hung like a funeral shroud in his car, like she'd killed any chance of a normal conversation.

She opened her mouth to apologize for dropping a bomb on their road trip, but his question beat her to it. "You haven't seen them since?"

"Once, when I was seven or eight, I thought I saw my mom outside my school." She shrugged and tried to conjure up that memory and the hope it had carried for so many years. If it had really been her mother, then maybe she had wanted Millie. Maybe she had realized what a terrible mistake she'd made. Maybe she'd loved her.

But the memory was faded, like a book read too many times, its pages smeared and unclear. Maybe Millie's young eyes had seen what she so desperately hoped to.

"Wow."

She'd almost forgotten she wasn't alone, that she wasn't drumming up those old memories for her own private torture, as she usually did. "You probably had great parents, huh? Packed up your car and sent you off to college with a box of cookies and a tank of gas."

Ben snorted. "Hardly. My mom was a different sort. She was a bit of a hippie, and she never gave it up. We lived in communes and were always moving. She never seemed to have a job, and there was always a parade of guys staying with us." His knuckles on the steering wheel turned white and then relaxed as he took a deep breath.

Millie didn't want to ask. She didn't have

any right to. But she did anyway. "Were you close with her?"

Ben licked his lips, which were working hard to fight a frown. He was silent so long that she thought he might not answer the question. Finally he shrugged. "My mom has a lot of problems. She made a lot of mistakes."

She nodded, giving him a silent nudge to keep going.

"When I was a kid, I thought she was the best. She always cut the crust off my PB&J sandwiches. Our house was mostly clean, and she pretty much let me do whatever I wanted."

"Where is she now?"

He didn't say anything, and his gaze never left the road.

"Do you know where she is?"

He gave a quick nod but didn't expound.

"Do you spend much time with her?"

"She's otherwise engaged. And she will be for another seven to ten." His words carried the tiniest hint of bitterness, and Millie's stomach fell to the floorboard.

There was no doubt what he meant. His mom was in prison. And he seemed to think she belonged there. But why?

She wanted to press. She wanted to ask for any teeny detail. But she had no right to do so, so she took a side path and asked something else she had no right to. "What about your dad?"

He narrowed his eyes at the road, and this time his knuckles didn't relax. "I never knew him. I'm not even sure my mom knew who he was."

He said it so matter-of-factly, but it twisted in her chest, tugged at her insides. That was Grandma Joy's story too. At least, that's what she believed.

"I'm sorry," she whispered. If there were other words to say, she didn't know them.

"It's all right." The words were more growl than she expected, and he coughed before continuing. "I made peace with that a long time ago."

She nodded toward a drive off the two-lane country road not even an hour from St. Simons. "Take that one." He did, and they bounced along the gravel toward a square, two-story white house. Its paint was chipped and unfamiliar trucks were parked next to rusted tractors in the yard, but her childhood home had never looked so wonderful.

As he parked the car, she blurted out a thought before it was fully formed. "Do you think that it would have made a difference — knowing your dad? At least knowing who he was?"

"I don't know. Maybe." He crawled out of the car and looked at her over its top. Shadows from the giant oak tree in the yard danced across his face. "Why?"

And then she said the very last thing she'd planned to. The very last thing she should have. "I wonder what difference it would have made if Grandma Joy had known about Claude Devereaux."

TWELVE

Claude Devereaux. Grandma Joy and Claude Devereaux.

Ben stumbled to keep up with Millie, who marched toward the front door of the house. He might have called out to her and demanded to know the connection between her grandmother and the wealthiest family in Louisiana, except for the twitching blinds at the window.

Someone was inside and close. Someone whose help they needed. But all he wanted to do was grab Millie by the arm, spin her around, and insist she tell him the truth. Of course, if the wild look in her eyes right after she had spoken meant anything, she hadn't meant to tell him any of it. Not a single syllable.

He needed to know more than ever. But there wasn't time to uncover the truth when the front door at the top of a short flight of stairs swung open halfway. A young woman with mousy brown hair and a baby on her hip filled the opening. Her glare was enough to send goose bumps down his arms. He wouldn't be surprised if she had a shotgun at the ready.

But Millie wasn't deterred. Gravel crunched under her feet with precise rhythm, and her shoulders squared, as though this home and all of its precious memories belonged to no one else.

"We already believe in Jesus. We don't got nothin' you want. We ain't buyin' nothing you've got." The woman — too young for that moniker, really — poked her chin toward their car. "You best be gettin' on your way. My Danny will be back soon enough."

"Ma'am, my name is Millie Sullivan." She spoke like the other woman hadn't cordially told them to get off her property. With a wave of her hand toward him, she said, "This is my friend Ben Thornton."

Maybe she leaned a little heavily on the word *friend.* Maybe he was reading too much into it, like everyone else seemed to be doing these days.

"I grew up in this house."

Millie was halfway up the stairs, and the woman had closed the door partway. Now only her eyes and scowl were visible through the crack. "We ain't interested in sellin'. We bought it fair and square."

Millie chuckled, and although he couldn't see her face, he could imagine her smile. She didn't have three quarters in her pocket, and this woman thought she wanted to buy the house out from under them. Not likely.

"Of course. You bought the home from my grandmother. Joy Sullivan?"

The door creaked to a stop, held open with the toe of a house shoe, and the scowl turned from distrust to curiosity. "Mrs. Sullivan? This was her family's home."

Millie nodded quickly, eating up the last couple steps to the top and meeting the other woman eye to eye. She reached out a hand and introduced herself again. "My name is Millie."

The woman's gaze dropped to the outstretched hand, her eyes narrowing. Finally she looked back up and toed the door open another six inches. "Samantha. Sam. Williams."

"I'm so happy to meet you." Millie reached out farther until Sam moved her baby to the other hip and opened the door enough to shake her hand.

"I met your grandma. She was a kind woman."

Millie nodded again. "She still is."

"Terrible what happened to her."

He still couldn't see Millie's face from his place at the bottom of the stairs, but he could see her back grow tense and her knees below her shorts lock. She mumbled something that sounded like agreement.

"What're you folks doing out here?" Sam made it sound like they were on top of a distant hill instead of forty miles outside of town among a sea of other family farms.

"I was hoping to ask for a favor."

Sam began to close the door again. "We ain't got much."

"Oh, no. It's nothing like that." Millie looked over her shoulder at him, and for a split second he forgot that she had been hiding something from him. He saw only the kindness in her smile, the warmth in her eyes. The reminder that they were a team — that he was part of a team. For the first time in his life.

The truth hit like a baseball bat to the gut — not that he'd ever swung one. He'd been on his own for so long that he'd forgotten what it meant not to have to do life alone — if he'd ever actually known. And it was nice. No, it was so much better than nice. As he tried to find the word to describe his life after meeting Millie, she offered Sam the barest minimum of their story.

"You see, my great-grandmother built this house with her husband, Henry, and my grandma thinks she may have left something here. Maybe paperwork of some sort. Have you ever found anything like that?"

Sam patted her gurgling baby on the back as he chewed on his own fist. She looked closely at Millie, then at Ben. Her gaze burrowed into them, searching out every half-truth and concealed lie. "What's her name?"

"My great-grandma? Ruth Holiday. Well, Ruth Jefferson after she married."

Sam's mouth dropped open like Millie had given the secret password, and she pushed the door all the way open. "We found a box of letters and such up in the attic. They was all addressed to Ruth. All of 'em."

Millie shot him another look, this one filled with hope. He bounded up the steps to her side as they followed Sam's sweeping arm into the house.

"Can we look at them?" Millie asked.

Sam nodded and closed the door behind them. It wasn't much cooler inside than it had been in the direct sun, and Ben hooked a finger into the collar of his shirt. It was already damp, and air thick enough to cut wasn't helping the situation. He added another roll to his sleeves. It didn't help either.

"You can have 'em if you can find 'em. They're up in the attic, far as I know. But there's some other stuff too."

"Some other stuff" turned out to be a euphemism for a lifetime of junk crammed into a space smaller than Millie's apartment and hotter than an oven. One small vent on the floor didn't do anything to keep air circulating except mock them for every deep breath they tried to secure. After climbing the pull-down ladder and traipsing into the gray unknown, Ben wasn't confident they'd find anything at all, except possibly a stubbed toe.

Millie walked right into an old chest and clapped her hand over her mouth. It didn't do much to muffle the subsequent scream. "Ow!"

"You all right?"

"I'll live. But they might have to take the whole foot." She dug into her pocket and pulled out her phone to turn on its flashlight while mumbling, "That's what I get for wearing flip-flops on a treasure hunt."

He followed her example and held up his light against the darkness. "I thought the treasure was at the Chateau. Aren't we just looking for clues?"

"Who knows at this point?" Her beam illuminated a pile of boxes, and she snaked her way toward it. "Over here."

They opened every lid and peered in every box. They found baby books and baby clothes and little pink baby shoes. They found photo albums and high school yearbooks from the 1950s. They found crayon drawings and pieces of art.

But there were no letters to Ruth.

Kneeling before the bottom box on the stack, Millie leaned back and crossed her arms. Her shoulders slumped, and her chin rested against her chest.

He couldn't blame her. She'd had a long day, and it was only midafternoon. They were both covered in dust and sweat, and he'd give his car for a glass of sweet tea right about then.

Pushing himself off the floor, he followed the beam of his flashlight through the maze of wicker and wooden furniture. For people who claimed not to have much, the Williams family sure did have a lot of junk. But he kept going, searching for anything cardboard. Preferably it would have the name Ruth scrawled along the side. But he'd settle for anything that looked out of place.

Deeper in, he had to duck his head to keep from smashing it against a beam. And that's when he saw it. Covered in dust and buried beneath a mound of old painting tarps was a white box — or at least it had been white at some point in its life.

It scraped along the wooden floor as he pulled it out from its hiding place and flipped the lid open. It was filled with papers yellowed with time. Newspapers and stationery. Envelopes and postcards. And a bundle of them were tied up with blue ribbon.

"Millie. I found it."

Scraping and scratching to move things out of her path, she clawed her way across the narrow room. She didn't have to duck, and she didn't slow down until she reached him, her hands landing on his back. "What is it?"

"Look at all these letters."

She knelt down, the sagging of her shoulders all but gone. Gently she lifted one of the envelopes from the mess below and pulled out the letter. "George." She said his name in hushed reverence, and Ben racked his brain for any memory of the man from what Millie had told him of the diary. Certainly she hadn't told him every little detail, but he knew that George had been important to Ruth.

"The gardener?"

She nodded. "She . . . she broke things off

with him —" Looking up, she shook her head. "No. That's not quite right. They were never seeing each other."

He was listening to her. Mostly. Except when he undid the ribbon bow around the packet of letters and pulled the first note free. His eyes skimmed the contents, and his stomach twisted into a loop tighter than the script on the page.

Millie rambled on. "She told him she couldn't spend time with him anymore because of —"

"Claude Devereaux."

Her eyes went wide, and she nearly dropped the letter in her hand.

The truth seared through him, and he wanted to yell at her that he had a right to know, that he deserved to know. Instead, he took a deep breath in through his nose and let it out through his mouth.

"What exactly is it with Devereaux and your family? What did you mean earlier about if your grandmother had known about him?"

"Nothing." She looked away as though holding his gaze was far too much weight for her to carry. It seemed the pressure of knowing too much and telling him too little covered all of her as she sagged against the box and put her head in her hands. "I don't know what to say." Her fingers muffled her words as the paper crinkled in her fist.

A twinge of heartburn caught him off guard, and he smashed his fist into the spot right below his sternum. It didn't do much to stem the fire, which could have been a product of betrayal.

But that would require him to care about Millie and whatever they had shared. He didn't. He wouldn't. He'd felt sorry for her. He'd been intrigued by her offer. He'd wondered how she was making ends meet caring for Grandma Joy all by herself.

He did not care about her. Not even a little bit.

Yeah, that wasn't true either.

"I'm sorry." When she finally looked his way again, she'd rubbed two sooty black stains around her eyes. "I should have told you before. I meant to. I planned on it. I wanted to. I just thought that . . . that if I did . . ."

"I wouldn't help you." He didn't have to be a great detective or treasure hunter to put those pieces together.

She nodded. "I do need your help. But also" — she took a big breath that filled her shoulders and lifted her chin even higher — "I like your help."

"You have a funny way of showing it." He

could have bitten his own tongue off. He had no business being so outright rude to her. She was obviously about to tell him something important, and he'd just given her every reason to leave him behind. Pressing his forefinger and thumb into his eyes, he sighed. "I'm sorry. Go on."

Biting her lips until they nearly disappeared, she lifted one shoulder. "No. You're right. And if you want to walk away, I won't blame you."

"Just —" He ran his fingers through his hair and pressed his other hand to his waist. He could take her up on her offer and walk away forever. The money wasn't going to be enough to make much of a difference in his life anyway. Okay, sure, it was better than nothing. But it wasn't going to change his course. He was still going to have to work three jobs, still going to have to make right what he could. "Just tell me what's actually happening here. Who is Devereaux to you?"

"I don't know for sure. That's what I'm trying to figure out. That's what I'm hunting for." She held up the letters in her hands. "Claude was at the Chateau the same summer that Ruth was there."

"You already told me that."

"But . . . but . . ." She seemed to be searching for words, and he wanted to throw the pile of envelopes with Devereaux's seal at the wall.

"Just tell me when this all started. Tell me why you took the job at the Chateau. Tell me whatever you want. Just tell me the truth." His voice had risen with each word, and suddenly a dog outside the house barked loudly. He refused to let it distract him from watching her reaction.

Another deep breath. Another long pause. Her gaze wandered to a different time and place. And then she started, presumably at the beginning.

"I was visiting Grandma Joy at the home a couple months ago. She looked at me so closely, like she could see right into my heart. And then she said the strangest thing: 'You are your father's daughter.' I laughed because she'd often said how much I looked like him. Then she got very serious. It was strange, but I knew that she remembered. She was fully lucid in that moment, and she said, 'But I'm not.' "

He sucked in a sharp breath, but Millie didn't give him time to digest the information. This wasn't a performance with perfectly delivered lines.

"I asked her who her dad was, and she laughed a little. It definitely wasn't Henry, the man Ruth married. But Grandma Joy didn't seem to know. She kept saying that there was more than treasure buried at the Chateau. She said the truth would be there too."

"And that's when she told you about the diary." He didn't actually ask a question, but she nodded anyway.

"Grandma Joy was born in April of 1930, so it doesn't take much math to put it together. Ruth must have been with Joy's father that summer, the summer she was at the Chateau."

He crossed his arms and took a step back. "And you hoped it was Devereaux?"

"No!" She shook her head hard. "I mean, I do. But I didn't even know he was there that summer until after Grandma Joy told me about the diary. I had no idea who it might be. But I knew there were wealthy guests at the estate."

"And now that you have letters to her from Claude Devereaux, filled with bad poetry and offering a role in one of his upcoming radio productions?"

"What?" She jumped to her feet and reached for the letter he'd only skimmed. "He was going to give her a job?"

Letting go of the slip of paper, he watched as her eyes devoured every word, every detail. "What does her diary actually say?

How close was their relationship?"

She looked back up, and even in the gray room, he could see the pink flames licking at her neck.

"Close. He . . . he's the one who pulled her into that alcove to kiss her."

Naturally. He knew that had been a romantic rendezvous. He just hadn't guessed that it involved a poor girl from central Georgia and a man whose family could swim in their millions a la Scrooge Mc-Duck.

"That one kiss — that's a pretty thin connection. And a big leap to having a child out of wedlock."

She cringed, but she had to know.

"Devereaux never married a woman named Ruth. He managed to keep his radio empire afloat during the Depression, and then he married a Rockefeller cousin. That's historical fact."

He should punch himself. Not for telling the truth but for enjoying it quite so much. He hated that he took even an ounce of pleasure in watching the light in her eyes dim.

"I know they weren't married." A muscle in her jaw jumped, and she wrapped her arms around her middle, beginning to collapse on herself. "I know I'm not a legitimate heir. Ruth would have clung to that name for her whole life. There's no way Joy would have become a Jefferson if she didn't have to be."

"Then why put everything on the line looking for that connection?"

"Because even being an illegitimate heir might be enough to provide for my grandma."

And there it was. The whole truth. Everything she'd done had been for Joy — just like the note on her fridge said. For Joy, who had put her life on hold to care for a little girl. It was Millie's turn to repay the sacrifice.

And God help him, he wanted to help her. He had plenty of other wrongs to right and no time to waste on a ridiculous chase — first a treasure they had no claim to, and now a heritage that she couldn't rightfully call her own. Apparently it didn't matter.

"Let's get the letters." He snatched them out of her hand and shoved them back in the box. He slammed the lid back on it, not really sure if he was angrier with her for keeping all of this from him for so long, or with himself for so quickly deciding he'd let it go. He wanted to hold on to at least a glimmer of annoyance. After all, he'd managed to despise his mother for years.

So why was Millie so different? She hadn't exactly lied to him. Neither had his mother.

Still, Millie should have told him what she was really after. She should have let him decide if he wanted to be caught up in all of that.

Millie looked from the box in his arms to his face and back again as he stood. "What? What are you doing?"

"Sam said we could take them. They might have information about Ruth and Claude, right?" He nearly spit the words over his shoulder as he marched a winding path through the attic.

"Y'all doing okay up there?"

Speaking of Sam, there she was. Within earshot, and probably curious to boot why two strangers had spent more than an hour in her attic.

"We're on our way down," he called, moving to the top of the ladder. Turning back to Millie, he lowered his voice. "This time we're going to split up the reading responsibilities, and you're going to tell me everything."

"So you're still with me?"

Narrowing his gaze on her, he adjusted the box in his arms before letting out a soft sigh. "I've done some stupid things in my life, and this may be one of them, but I'm with you until we find that treasure."

August 12, 1929

My dearest Ruth,

I have been distraught without you this past week. Atlanta holds no comparison to your beauty, and I long to return to the Chateau, to your side. I yearn to hold you in my arms once again, to press my lips to yours.

I know you would tell me not to say such things, but I must. For I feel them so fully that I fear they will consume me mind, body, and soul. I hope that they do.

As I walked from the studio to my hotel room tonight, I saw a star in the heavens that could only offer a fraction of your beauty. I sat on a park bench to stare at it but managed only to think of you. These lines came to my mind.

How I miss her skin so fair
And silken hair.
She is brighter than the moon,
Her song lovelier than the loon.
I am hers,
Like the cat that purrs.
She has the sweetest kiss,
It is she that I miss.

I am very busy at the studio here. There is much to be done to launch the new production. My friend Orson warned me of such things, but I foolishly thought that I could spend most of my summer at the Chateau and trust my staff to have everything in place. They are working hard, but they do not have my vision. I suppose that is why I am in charge. Also, it is because I have put up the money to get the production begun.

We are nearly ready, and I wish I had a woman of your talents on set. But the others are under contract, and there is nothing to be done until the next production, or until the writers write a new character. She will be lovely and have the sweetest smile in the world. Would you like that, my dear?

I will be back to the Chateau soon, and you will be the first person I seek out. When I do, I hope to have good news and an important question to ask you.

Yours completely,
Claude D.

August 12, 1929

Miss Holiday,

Perhaps my letter is no less improper than taking you on a picnic or walking with you around the house, but I must check on you. Since we discovered Miss Abernathy under that tree, you have not been yourself. Your smile is a mere ghost of what it can be. You seem quite unwell.

It would be an honor to offer my services to you. I know of a distraction that might take your mind off the shock of what you saw. You need only call on me.

George

August 14, 1929

Miss Holiday,

Your thanks is not required. I only wish to see your joy restored, and I knew that a trip to the southern creek and the opportunity to put your feet in the water there might help you find a moment of peace, as it has for me. There is such a restorative quality in the sound of the water bubbling back out to the sea.

I am ever your friend. And as your friend, I must tell you the truth. You asked me on our walk down to the beach what I think of Mr. Devereaux. You must know that we see very different sides of him.

Quite honestly, I neither like nor trust the man. He is too polished among your people and quite the opposite among the staff. The maids talk of him wandering below stairs after having far too much to drink. I have no proof of it, but I believe that Jenny might have been accused and dismissed for reasons completely unrelated to the things stolen in the big house.

This is no indictment on you or anyone else in the house. But I cannot in good conscience encourage you to continue a relationship with him.

I remain ever yours.

G

THIRTEEN

"Jumper! Jumper! He's coming over the south fence. This is not a drill. All hands to the south lawn."

Ben clenched his jaw until he thought his teeth might crack, but he still managed to run. Pressing his walkie-talkie to his cheek, he responded to the call from the security office. "I'm on my way." He was panting already, his chest heaving just to snatch a breath from the evening air. Or maybe it was the sudden thundering in his chest that kept his lungs from doing their job.

He wasn't supposed to do this. He was a historian, a reader of books, a studier of the past. He was not a chaser of kids who thought it would be a good idea to trespass on private museum property ten minutes before closing time.

The house was ablaze in all of its night-time glory, golden lights lending their glow to the monstrous silhouette. The arches of the front portico were filled with potted palm trees, and he fell off the cement path in an attempt to dodge one.

The final tour of the night was just wrapping up, and the entrance had long since been abandoned. If the jumper was headed his way, he hadn't made it very far.

As he rounded the last corner of the building and turned into the south lawn with its palms blowing in the wind, he spotted the lone figure. While he was little more than a shadow, one thing was clear. This wasn't a kid. This was a fully grown man — all five and a half feet of his height and nearly that much around his middle.

The man swung a long metal rod from his hand, and for a moment Ben thought it was a cane. But that would have been some feat to climb the wall — even with the aid of a ladder — and need help to walk. Then the man swooped the rod along the grass in rotating circles, and Ben's stomach clenched.

It was a metal detector. This man was looking for something buried on the grounds.

The man looked up, straight at Ben, and he swore a single word that fully expressed the situation. He looked as surprised to see Ben as he was to be seen.

"Well, I figured you'd all be gone by now." There was a note of disappointment in the man's words, and Ben knew how he felt. He'd taken this job in part because the pay was relatively good and in part because they'd promised him that no one had tried to break into the Chateau in twenty years. It was revered and respected by the locals, and no one was interested in defacing the property or barging into the grounds.

It didn't hurt that most of the locals were senior citizens, their hooligan years long since gone. And the visiting youngsters looking to carouse on their spring breaks could find better bars and more trouble in Brunswick on the mainland.

Even this time of year, the island was filled with tourist families who didn't trouble the locals much. Which made what he was seeing at the moment a little hard to believe.

The man had to be at least sixty, and his hair was more silver than black. It reflected the moon as he hung his head and jammed the toe of his black sandal into the ground.

"I thought your last tour was at eight." His tone suggested that Ben had personally lied to him.

Ben nodded slowly, shining his flashlight toward the man's metal detector, which was still moving in smooth circles. "It is. It begins at eight and lasts an hour."

The man looked at his watch and swore again. The realization of his poor timing visibly dawned on him.

"Can I ask what you're doing here, Mr. . . ."

"Fazetti. Milo Fazetti." He shrugged. "I heard there might be something worth finding here. Thought since I was close by, I might beat the rush."

Ben froze, everything inside him screaming that he had to be mistaken. He had to have misunderstood. There was no way that Milo Fazetti — of the loud Hawaiian print and socks with sandals — knew about the treasure. He couldn't possibly have heard about Ruth's prize. The one that no one had looked for in almost ninety years. Ben had searched the treasure-hunting websites just weeks before. There hadn't even been rumors of sparkling silver at the Chateau.

But what other treasure could it be? Carl knew everything about the history of this island. And even he knew of only one rumored treasure — Ruth's. The truth was that the Chateau had only hosted guests for two summers. It had closed quickly after the stock market crash. And after that there had been no one wealthy enough to leave any treasure of substance behind.

They had to be looking for the same treasure. But how did Milo know about it?

"Well, I'm afraid you beat the rush by a few hours too many. Would you mind coming with me? You're trespassing on private property."

Milo shrugged. "If I buy a ticket, can I walk around the grounds?"

"I'm afraid not. Our last tour of the day is coming to a close, and you're about to be banned from this property for at least a year."

"A *year?*" Milo sounded like he'd been sentenced to life in prison. "Do you know how many yahoos will get here in the next year? I can't wait a year."

Ben's stomach sank, and his shoes suddenly felt heavier than cement. How many treasure-hunting yahoos *could* get there in a year? More than he and the Chateau's crack security team of two retirees and a college kid could keep at bay, that was for sure. And there was no telling how fast the wave would approach. They might not have Ruth's diary, but they would sure have the numbers to unearth something. And do it before he and Millie could.

That would leave him and Millie right where they had been at the start. Broke and in need of at least one small miracle.

God, if you're waiting for me to ask, this is me asking. We could really use a miracle right about now.

Millie paced the length of the corridor, her tennis shoes nearly silent on the concrete. She checked her watch again. Nine twenty-seven. They'd agreed on nine fifteen, and she'd arrived two minutes early.

Ben still wasn't here.

He'd said there had been something interesting in a letter he'd read, one of them from Claude. He thought it pointed to a spot in the house. He thought it was worth checking for the other diary, and she had to agree.

The trouble was, she didn't know what the location was. And Ben was nowhere to be found. She texted him again and was greeted only by the call of an owl from its perch in a nearby tree.

"Not helpful," she mumbled as she traipsed the hall yet again, her insides winding tighter and tighter. The stucco arches gave her a view of the waves, their crests glowing white in the moonlight and orange in the reflection of the house. If only she could be as patient and serene as those waves.

Not likely.

Putting her hands to her hips, she blew her bangs out of her face and tucked a stray curl behind her ear. It was crispy from hair spray, and suddenly her scalp and shoulders itched from the three-inch coating they'd received at the start of the night. Her hair had stayed in place, the knot at her neck both graceful and rigid, and apparently so had her skin.

Twitching for a shower, she looked at her watch again. Nine twenty-nine.

Still no sign of him. Either he'd forgotten or he'd run into trouble or he'd set her up.

But why would he set her up? To send her to a deserted hallway in order to keep her out of his hair? While he did what? Searched the spot where the diary might be?

Her brain was filling in the answers to questions faster than she could ask them, and every single one was the worst possible scenario. Every single one sent her pulse racing and her head throbbing and her heart plummeting.

Stupid treasure. Stupid Ben. Stupid her for trusting him.

But he forgave you when you told him the truth about Devereaux.

Stupid conscience for making sense.

The nonsensical arguments worked much better for her. They kept her safe. Safe from relying on anyone else. Safe from trusting too much. Safe from being let down. Again.

"Millie."

At first she thought the sound of her name had been only a mixture of birdcalls and waves against the beach. And then she heard the slapping of feet against the floor. Hurried and urgent, they raced toward her from behind.

"I'm sorry I'm late."

She spun on him, her fists at her sides and her tongue ready to slice. But something about the wildness of his hair — as though he'd been running his hands through it over and over again — and the wideness of his eyes spoke a different truth. He hadn't stood her up. At least not on purpose.

"We have a problem."

Her heart stopped, her breath vanishing with it. "What happened?" was all she could muster on the tail of her gasp.

"There was a trespasser. Someone jumped the fence."

She shook her head. Why should that matter to them?

"He had a metal detector. He's after a treasure. And he's not alone."

Seconds passed as his words sank in. Her knees gave out, and she slumped to the ground, her back pressed to the wall. Wrapping her arms around her bare legs, she tucked them under her chin and tried to process what he was saying. This wasn't fiction. This was real life.

Someone else knew about the Chateau's secrets.

He sagged down beside her, stretching out his legs and gasping for breath. It looked like he'd run a marathon.

"What did he say — the kid who jumped the fence? How did he know?"

Ben shook his head. "He's no kid. He's old enough to be my dad. And he's not alone. There's an article about the Chateau on a website for amateur treasure hunters. They don't have a clue what they're looking for, but they're looking."

"They?"

Ben shook his head and drummed his fingers against his knees. "He said he was the first."

The first of how many? How had word gotten on that site?

The truth zapped her. She hadn't told a soul. Which meant . . . She straightened up, forcing herself not to wave her finger in his face. "Who did you tell?"

"Me? I didn't tell anyone. Who did you tell?"

"Why would I tell someone?"

"You told me."

She gasped. He had *not* just thrown that at her. "I had to tell you. You were going to get me kicked off the property. Besides, if I hadn't, you wouldn't know about any of this."

"So it stands to reason that if anyone else was threatening your chance to search the property, you'd tell them too."

Squaring her shoulders, she turned to face him full on. "Well, *you're* the only one who's threatened to have me fired."

"And I wouldn't have if you hadn't been in the library on the other side of the velvet ropes."

"So you're saying this is all my fault." Something bubbled in her chest, something she couldn't name and didn't really care to. It was unsettling and a bit annoying. Because they were fighting — and she couldn't remember the last time she'd had such a good time.

Maybe this wasn't really fighting. Maybe it was just a squabble. There was something serious at its root, but all she could focus on was the crinkle at the corner of his eye. It always did that when he was smiling. Or about to smile. Or thinking about smiling. That was something she knew about him.

And also that he'd stayed with her. When

he had every right to walk away, he'd stayed.

And she knew he was a good man, a kind man, a hero. Villains didn't hold your grandma's hand while she had a complete break from reality. Villains didn't hold *you* and tell you they would stay by your side until it all worked out.

If her life were written in the pages of a book, one thing would be abundantly clear. Ben was the hero. Whether she was the heroine was still up for debate.

"What about your friend from the library?" she asked.

"My boss, Carl?"

She nodded and crossed her arms so they landed with a resounding thump.

"Yes, I told him. I'd also trust him with my life. But he already knew about the rumors of hidden treasure anyway. He's known for years. Why would he wait until now to tell someone else? Besides, he wouldn't know how to post in a forum if you paid him."

She hadn't met Carl, and she had absolutely no picture of him in her mind, so it was easy to fabricate him to fit her story. "Maybe he's been waiting for the diary, and now that he knows we have it, he'll be after us both. First he'll cut the brake lines on your car so you go careening off a cliff and die in a fiery crash. But that's okay with him because you didn't have the diary anyway. Then he'll be after me, stalking me at my house, only he'll miss the *C* on the street address and think that I live in the big house too."

Ben's eyes grew bigger with each word, each wildly concocted scenario. He opened his mouth as if planning to refute her story, but instead he laughed. Booming and full, the sound echoed around them, bouncing off palm trees and stone archways alike. "Just what kind of books have you been reading?"

"What?" She pinched her lips together, bracing every ounce of her being against the smile that wanted to escape. True, that brake-line plot had appeared in one of the books she'd borrowed from the library. It had involved embezzled money and an angry lawyer. It hit too close to home to really enjoy, but she'd gotten a giggle out of the ridiculous villain nonetheless. Just as she'd hoped, Ben had too.

"There's one flaw with that plan."

"Oh?"

"If Carl killed me, he'd have to do all the grunt work at the library. No way would he willingly get rid of me before lining up a replacement."

"Oh." No matter how hard she pursed her lips to the side, she could feel the smile breaking loose. "Then maybe not Carl."

"Decidedly not Carl." His grin matched her own.

Resting her head against the wall at her back, she watched the hanging moss play in the wind. Even the leaves got in a good rustle or two between the night birds calling. "But then who? If neither of us have said anything . . ." Suddenly her stomach clenched, and she pressed both hands over her middle.

"Grandma Joy." She could only whisper the words, and Ben leaned closer, his brows knitted together and his features tight.

"Huh?"

"Grandma Joy. What if she told someone? She might not even remember that she did. But it would have been so easy to just . . ." She waved her hand, and his eyes followed it, understanding lighting them.

"It could be anyone. It could be that administrator at the home."

"Virginia Baker."

He nodded quickly. "Or one of the nurses. Or a cleaning person. Or even a guest."

"You think the guy that broke in here tonight has been to the assisted living home?"

With a sharp shake of his head, he rejected her premise. "No. But someone who has been there told the world. Milo — the guy who climbed the fence —"

"How'd he get over the wall?"

"Ladders. A metal one on the outside and a rope one on the inside."

She motioned for him to keep going.

"Milo said he was trying to beat the rush. He thinks there's going to be a rush. In fact, he offered me a fifty-fifty cut if I'd give him unfettered access to the grounds."

She tried to chuckle, but it came out arid and tired. "I might have liked this guy."

He raised his eyebrows. "You certainly have something in common."

"When will the others get here?"

"Soon."

Despite the humidity that made her skin sticky with sweat, she shivered at the very thought. They were about to be inundated by people looking for the same thing they were. And not just anyone. These people might be amateurs. They might be pros. Either way, they knew more about finding treasure than she and Ben combined. And without Ruth's other diary, they were fishermen without lines.

"Speaking of the grounds —"

"Were we?"

"Yes. Before. Whatever." She flapped her hands in front of her to clear away the conversation in her mind. "The security manager knows now."

He nodded.

"Things here are going to get a lot tighter, aren't they?"

He nodded again.

"Like tonight."

One more nod.

"What are you supposed to be doing right now?" she asked

"Officially I'm searching the grounds for any signs of other intruders." He pushed himself off the floor and rose to his feet. "Speaking of which, I guess I should get to that."

"So we're not going to check out Ruth's favorite spot?"

He reached out his hand, and she slipped hers into it. The muscles in his forearm bunched, and suddenly she was standing in front of him. *Right* in front of him. She had to put her free hand up to keep from bumping into his chest, and all of a sudden she could feel the lean muscles there, the ones she'd only glimpsed before.

Glancing up into his face, she could feel his breath in her hair. Slowly — so slowly, as though he was asking permission — he wound a finger into a curl that had escaped that night.

She wanted to lean into his hand, to press her cheek to his fingers and feel his touch. But the only thing she could see was his mouth, his perfect lips, firm and sure and entirely kissable.

She'd gone over the edge. She'd turned into one of those heroines in her books who swooned over a man. But she didn't care one bit.

Or maybe . . . maybe she was more like her great-grandma than she wanted to admit. Ruth had swooned over Claude, without question. Maybe in this very hallway they'd stopped for a short embrace. Maybe they'd kissed and sighed and whispered sweet nothings.

In this moment, that's all she wanted to do with Ben. All she could see were his lips and all she could think about were those lips on hers.

"Millie."

The lips in question said her name. It wasn't so much an inquiry as an urging. She just didn't know what he was urging her to do. She didn't actually care. As long as it meant they could be closer, as long as it closed the distance between them.

Beneath her hand, his heart beat steady,

while her pulse pounded a wild tattoo at her throat. He leaned an inch closer to her. Or maybe she'd pressed into him. It didn't matter. It only mattered that they were there — well, almost there.

"Millie?" This time it was definitely a question, and she managed to raise her gaze to the same emotion reflected in his eyes. He wanted to know that this was okay. That this was all right. That she wanted this as much as he did. That —

"Ben? You still out there?" The walkie talkie on his belt crackled with the call, and Ben froze. Then he leaned back, his smile filled with regret.

"This is Ben."

"You see anything out there?"

"No, sir. The beachfront is clear. I'm on my way to the north wall now."

His supervisor gave him the go-ahead, and he squeezed her hand before dropping it. "Next time we're working together, we'll check Ruth's favorite spot."

"But where is it?"

"Where would Devereaux think it was?"

FOURTEEN

"He's not here today," Millie said.

"Well, I can see that. But he should be. He's such a handsome young man."

Millie rolled her eyes at her grandma's clear matchmaking attempt and leaned back a few inches. Grandma Joy's eyes were bright, her cheeks pink, and her gaze focused today. Too bad Ben wasn't here to see it.

Yeah, that's why you want Ben here.

Oh, be quiet.

Her mind had been telling her all sorts of things, poking and prodding about what might have been, what almost had been.

But that's all it was. An *almost*. Anyway, maybe it would have been terrible. What if there were no sparks?

Oh, there were sparks when you were five feet away from him.

Pipe down.

What if he was a slobbery kisser? What if

she was a slobbery kisser?

You're never going to know if you're a good kisser or not if you don't actually do it.

Seriously. Be quiet.

What if they kissed and it was so bad that they couldn't even look at each other?

Really? You think that kissing him could be bad?

Well, maybe not for her, but what about for him? What if he thought it was so bad that he never wanted to kiss her again, and then they were stuck working together, but it was completely awkward and he felt obligated to keep helping her?

How come the heroines in her books never wondered if they were good kissers? How come they just kissed and it was always perfect and wonderful and magical? How come there were always fireworks in the books? What if there were never fireworks in real life?

Her hands clenched into fists at her stomach, and she fell back against her grandma's pillows, wrinkling the previously made bed.

"What are you thinking about, sweetheart?" Grandma Joy rocked back and forth, her eyes closed but somehow fully seeing.

"Nothing."

Creak. Creak. The chair announced each

movement. "I thought you came here to make me my favorite soup. Sounds like you're just telling me stories instead."

Millie pushed herself up and took a deep breath, hoping it would wipe Ben and whatever had almost happened — good or bad — from her mind. It did not. She tried to fake it anyway.

"Of course I'm here to make you soup." She was there for information too, but Grandma Joy didn't need to know that was the heart of the reason.

Walking over to the kitchenette — the standard two burners and four cupboards in each resident's room — Millie took a long look at her grandma. She still looked lucid and thoughtful.

As she pulled a small cutting board from a cupboard and carrots from her own grocery bag, she took a quick breath. "Grandma, we can't find Ruth's other diary."

"Mama's diary?"

Oh no. Already? Grandma Joy sounded distant, fading into the past — or a murky version of it.

Millie swiped the peeler over the length of the carrots harder than was necessary, already seeing where this conversation was going. Nowhere.

"You found my mama's diary."

"Yes, but there is another one." She wanted to ask if her grandma remembered. She wanted to beg her to recall what they'd already talked about. But it would do no good. With each whack of the knife against the carrot, she imagined dementia could be cut and destroyed just as easily. She wished it was so.

"You told me that already."

Millie jumped and turned around. Grandma Joy's eyes were wide open "Yes. I did tell you that."

"Where do you think it is?" Her features turned thoughtful.

"I don't know. We found a note that makes it sound like Ruth thought someone was reading her diary, so she moved it. But I don't know if it was the first or the second. And I have no clue where she would have moved it to."

With a nod, Grandma Joy asked, "What does your handsome young man think?"

Millie tried not to focus on the reminder of handsome Ben or the implication that he was hers. Instead she thought about what he'd said the night before. "He thinks it might be in her favorite place on the grounds."

"And he knows where that is?"

305

"Well, we found some letters from —" She slammed on the brakes nearly too late. She couldn't very well drop the name Claude Devereaux to her grandmother. Especially not when it was entirely possible that Joy had been the one to leak word about the treasure to the rest of the world. Accidentally, of course. But remembering to keep secrets required remembering. Not Grandma Joy's strong suit.

Her stomach twisted at the thought of not telling the whole truth — or even what she guessed was the truth. But this was too important to do wrong. And letting word slip out to the rest of the world that there might be another heir to Claude Devereaux's fortune was doing it wrong. She needed proof. No court would call for a DNA test if she didn't have probable cause. That family likely received a hundred fake claims on their money every day. She didn't want to be just another huckster begging for a handout.

She wasn't prepared to fight the court of public opinion. Not until she was ready to fight in a court of law. Of course, she hoped it never got to that level. She prayed that the family would see her plight, understand that Claude's own daughter was in need, and offer a lump sum that would care for

Grandma Joy until her dying day.

But first Millie needed more than a scrap of evidence that he had been her great-grandfather, that Ruth hadn't married him but had still given birth to his child.

Millie looked at her grandma and tried to see in her the dark hair and olive complexion of the Devereaux family. But all she could make out were stooped shoulders from a lifetime of hard labor and eyes that, when focused, told of losing the love of her life.

Pouring chicken broth and water into a saucepan, she tried to pick up where she'd left off with fewer details, grateful that her grandma was prone to long silences and hadn't bothered asking a follow-up question. "We found some letters that Ruth had saved. One of them, from another guest at the Chateau that summer, identified her favorite spot on the grounds. We thought we'd check there."

"Oh, I know her favorite spot. She talked of it often. The very southeast corner of the estate, where the ocean meets the creek. She loved to put her feet in the water. It was cold. She said that when she was pregnant with me, she would put her feet in to keep her ankles from swelling and to listen to the sound of the wind through the moss of the trees."

Millie opened her mouth to argue. The estate didn't have a piece of land like that. The southernmost point along the beach was just a typical beach. No inlet. No copse of trees. Maybe the estate had covered more ground back then.

Or maybe Grandma Joy was remembering wrong. That wouldn't be the first — or last — time.

Her soup base boiled, and she dumped her chopped vegetables into it, stirring slowly, watching the bubbles pop and the steam rise.

There was no point in telling Grandma Joy that she was wrong, so instead Millie diced rotisserie chicken and measured rice and tried to think of something encouraging to say. But before she could come up with a full phrase, Grandma Joy dropped a bomb.

"So they're going to make me move."

Millie spun around, the wooden spoon in her hand at the ready. "Who told you that?"

"My nurse. She's a silly little girl, always giggling when she gives me my medication." She sounded completely detached, like she didn't fully comprehend what she was saying, but it didn't stop her from going on.

"She said I'm too much of a handful, but I've been behaving myself. I didn't even point out when that Mrs. Baker had her skirt tucked into her tights."

With a snort and giggle, Millie covered her face. Her shoulders shook until her laughter couldn't be contained and pealed through the room.

"Well, I didn't." Grandma Joy looked nearly offended. "They don't rightly like it when I correct them, so I let her go on out the door with her family flapping in the breeze, bless her heart."

Gasping for breath, Millie said, "Please tell me you didn't."

"I most certainly did." Hands on her hips and rocker still going back and forth, she nodded. "It was either that or get a full tongue lashin' for speaking my piece. Why would I want that?"

When Millie finally got her laughter under control, Grandma Joy looked at her, arms folded across her stomach. "Are they really going to make me move?"

Sometimes the questions were easy to answer. Lately they were hard. All of them.

Lying would be easier than telling the truth. And Grandma Joy might not remember. They might have to have this conversation a hundred times. Did it really matter if she told one little white lie?

Yes. It did.

If she was willing to lie to the woman who had raised her as her own, who wouldn't she lie to? She wouldn't start with Grandma Joy.

"It looks like it. They . . . they say that you deserve more specialized care. And they can't give you that attention here."

"So where am I going to go?"

"I'm not sure." Millie turned back to the simmering soup, anything to keep from admitting that she had exactly zero plans and twenty days to make one happen.

"We have the money for a nicer place. Why not let me move in there?"

Giving her soup another stir, Millie shook her head. "We don't have the money."

"Sure we do. What about the money from the sale of the house? It sold for better than we asked." Grandma sounded so certain that it stabbed Millie through the chest. She leaned against the counter just to keep herself upright.

Taking a deep breath, she reiterated her personal decision. If she was willing to lie to Grandma Joy, she'd lie to anyone. So she wasn't going to start here. It wasn't an option even to stretch the truth. So she took a deep breath and said the most honest thing she could. "That money's gone."

"Well, what happened to it? We just had it."

Millie nearly choked on the lump in her throat. It had all happened before the diagnosis. Before they knew why her memory failed so often. Before Millie had been the responsible one.

She should have stepped in sooner. She should have stopped her. She should have stopped it all. But she hadn't.

"You invested it."

Grandma Joy rubbed her head, as though trying to conjure the memory gave her a raging migraine. "Invested it? Of course not. I would never put my money in the stock market. My mama taught me better than that."

Tears pricked at the corners of Millie's eyes, and she had to keep her back to Grandma Joy. She made a couple listless motions with the wooden spoon in the pan, but even the bright orange carrots bobbing in the broth faded from view. "I'm sorry, Grandma, but you did. You gave it all to Aspire Investments."

As her grandmother muttered that it couldn't be true, Millie could still see the computer screen in her mind, her grandma's savings account showing a giant zero. She could imagine the face of the person willing to target the older generations. He looked a whole lot like Captain Hook from *Peter Pan,* all sinister, twirly mustache. Or that really terrible child catcher from *Chitty Chitty Bang Bang.* Or Honest John from *Pinocchio.*

Probably the latter. Grandma Joy would have taken note of twirling mustaches. She never would have trusted someone like that. But someone came to her, promising to be her friend. Promising to help her double the money from the sale of her house. Promising that Millie would be taken care of for a very long time.

And Grandma Joy had written a check and handed it over.

This wasn't the first time they'd had this conversation, rehashed the past. It probably wouldn't be the last. But somehow this hurt more than it should. For Grandma Joy the truth was new information. For Millie it was a frequent and searing reminder that she'd failed to protect the person she owed everything to. It was a push that she needed to find that treasure. It was a confirmation that she needed to find evidence of exactly who her great-grandfather really was.

Please, Lord, let it be Claude Devereaux. The prayer popped to mind before she could even form it.

Truthfully, those were the only prayers happening these days. Between two jobs, Grandma Joy, a treasure, and a man who kept coming to mind even when he shouldn't, it wasn't easy to think about praying. It was even harder to go to church.

If Grandma Joy knew that, she'd threaten to take a switch to her. Of course, such words had only ever been threats. Millie knew the heart behind them had always been love. Even now — especially now — Grandma Joy wanted her to be safe and loved and to know God loved her. And Millie did.

She did.

Mostly.

But when that piercing pain through her middle reminded her that God had allowed all of it — the dementia, the huckster, the barely making it from paycheck to paycheck — it wasn't always easy to *feel* that she was loved. Feeling and knowing were two different things.

Great-Grandma Ruth's mama had said that feelings were foolishness. But sometimes they felt like more. Sometimes they felt like a stone sitting on her chest, crushing the air from her lungs and making her wish . . . well, she wasn't sure exactly. What did one wish for when she longed for a different life but the same family? She didn't want her parents back or to be someone else's kid. She didn't want to grow up with a silver spoon in her mouth. She didn't want an *easy* life.

She just wanted to be able to say that all was well with her soul. She just wanted to have her grandma — the wise, witty, wonderful woman who raised her — back.

But that was never going to happen.

FIFTEEN

Millie read the last four pages of the hardback in her hands one more time. She'd long since had to crack the door of her car open or suffocate in the direct line of the sun. But she needed this. Just a moment with her book. Just a moment with Genevieve and Sir Robert, who had overcome everything to be together. There had been a war and an evil stepfather, and Sir Robert, who was terrified of the water, even swam across a moat to rescue his beloved Gennie.

Sappy? Terribly.

Did she care? Not even a little bit.

This escape was what she had. And she'd cling to it for as long as it made butterflies swoop in her stomach and love feel like it was within arm's reach. Maybe she'd have to stretch, but all was not lost.

As Sir Robert pulled Gennie into his arms for one final kiss, the image of him in her mind morphed. She had never pictured him as a Fabio knockoff — more like that NFL quarterback who was way too good-looking for his own good, the one in all of those commercials. That was the face of Sir Robert when she'd read this book the first and second time.

But this time he looked different. His hair was shorter, cropped close over his ears but longer in front, a few curls just evident. His eyes were so blue that they rivaled Georgia's summer sky. His chin wasn't square but pointed. And his grin — it was both wry and crooked.

She knew that face. And Ben had absolutely no business showing up in her mind when she was reading about a medieval knight. The two had nothing in common.

Except for brilliant smiles, expressive eyes, and a forgiving heart. There was that.

She tried to keep reading, but suddenly Gennie didn't look a bit like the fierce maiden on the cover. She looked a whole lot like the image Millie saw when she looked in the mirror. And when Sir Robert swept Gennie into his arms . . . well, suddenly Millie was the one being swept away. By Ben. *Her* Ben.

Nope. Not hers. Not at all. Not even a little bit.

Be quiet.

She much preferred to be the one telling the voice in her head to pipe down. And she wasn't comfortable with this shift at all. Not when she was being practical, logical even.

Except there had been that moment, the night of the jumper at the Chateau. It had felt like maybe there was a little something between them. It didn't have a name. It wasn't defined. But it was definitely something.

Told you.

She slammed the book in her lap closed and swiped the back of her hand across her forehead. She needed to drop these books off inside, and with them any reminder that Ben might have played the role of the hero.

Sliding out from behind the steering wheel, she gathered her books to her chest. There were eleven of them in all, and she was halfway across the library parking lot before she began to question the wisdom of this idea.

A gust of wind picked up the front flap of a paperback. It teetered precariously, so she tried to balance her chin on it but only managed to wrinkle the title page.

The hardbacks on the bottom began to slip in her damp palms, and every step bumped them further and further from a secure grasp. She was still at least twenty yards from the library's sliding glass doors, and a quick glance over her shoulder showed that she'd come just as far. There was nothing to do but press on, even as the wind picked up.

Stumbling up a curb, she nearly lost all the books and wondered if she should have just let them go. Then she took another step, and pain shot through her ankle, stabbing like a fire poker fresh from the coals. Her leg buckled and she began to go down. Trying to aim for the grass, she braced herself for the fall.

Suddenly two arms scooped her up from behind. Wrapping big hands under her elbows and around the books clutched to her, he pulled her back against his chest.

"Well, well, well. If it isn't Millie Sullivan, falling all over herself to see me outside of work."

That voice. It was Sir Robert's. Or rather Ben's. How quickly they'd become interchangeable.

"I was not." She tried to straighten away from him to hold herself erect, but the second she put an ounce of weight on her foot, her ankle screamed at her, and she sank back against him. So solid. So firm.

His arms squeezed tight with no indication he was going to let her go again. "You okay?"

"I guess I twisted my ankle. I'll be fine." She rotated it to show that she was all right, but he gave her a doubtful look when she grimaced halfway through.

"Let me give you a hand."

Like Sir Robert gave Gennie, which led to her falling into his arms and being thoroughly kissed?

Yes, please.

Oh, shut up.

"I'm good. Really."

He didn't say a thing. Instead he scooped her books from her hands and stuck out his elbow. Giving her a pointed look and a nod toward his extended arm, he waited.

Grandma Joy would say it was rude not to take a gentleman's arm when it was offered. Sliding her hand into the crook, she leaned on him with every step, each one like fire in her shoe.

"I think Carl has an ice pack in the freezer in the office."

"I'll be fine. Really." She cringed again, and he shook his head.

"You going to run around the Chateau in high heels tomorrow?"

She opened her mouth to argue with him, but the thought of having to walk in even

her costume's kitten heels made her consider lobbing off her whole leg. "All right.
Some ice might be good."

"Good. Now, how did you know I was
working here today?"

"I didn't. I came to return those." As soon
as she pointed out the stack of books in his
arms, her insides gave a wild lurch. Which
was entirely ridiculous. It wasn't like he'd
have any clue that she'd been picturing him
in the pages of one of those sweet romance
novels. Or worse, that she'd been picturing
herself with him.

He nodded. "Anything good here?"

"No." Maybe she'd said it too quickly. The
rise of his eyebrows suggested that might be
the case. She hurried on. "Just filling time
until we find Ruth's other diary."

He didn't say much as they entered the
library. He simply deposited her books into
the return slot and then led her through the
library toward a back room. Brightly colored
books filled every shelf, and the main room
smelled of paper and ink and glue, the
sweetest scents in the world.

The back wall contained a row of glass
doors, which led to individual study rooms.
Millie had never been this far inside. The
fiction titles were housed up front, and
she'd never needed to dig deeper. But Ben

knew where he was going, and he didn't seem to mind that she leaned heavily on him across the patchwork carpet.

Past three rows of tables — all packed with kids at their laptops, earbuds firmly embedded — a single door said *Archivist*. Ben pushed it open, then helped her through. "Carl, this is my friend Millie."

"Friend?" He waggled his bushy eyebrows and patted the top of his balding head, smoothing what little hair remained.

What was with people of a certain age trying to set them up? First Grandma Joy and now Carl.

Ben was quick to the correction. "Just a friend. She's the one I told you about. We found her great-grandmother's diary."

"Oh, that Millie." Carl rushed forward, reaching out both of his hands to shake hers. "It's quite nice to meet you. Sit. Sit."

Ben quickly explained about her twisted ankle, and Carl shuffled off to a back room with promises of comfort to come.

"So, you've been talking about me?" She raised her eyebrows as she lowered herself into the rolling chair Ben pulled from a desk. It wasn't until she fell onto the cushion that she realized there were actually two desks in the room — smallish metal ones. When she'd entered she'd focused mostly on the two large wooden worktables. Carl had been standing at one, yellowish papers scattered before him.

"Absolutely not. I mean, except for that time I asked if he knew anything about a treasure at the Chateau."

Maybe it was the speed with which he'd offered his rebuttal, but something in his response suggested he might not be telling the whole truth. And butterflies doing a little dance in her stomach suggested that she quite liked the idea that he'd been speaking of her to his . . . well, Carl was sort of a friend.

Just as she was trying to formulate something to say in return, Carl bustled back into the room, his button-up shirt and gray sweater vest as rumpled as ever. As promised, he carried something wrapped in a towel. Rolling over another chair, he patted the seat. "Put your foot on up here, young lady."

She nearly snorted. "Young lady?"

He tsked as she stretched her leg out, and then he set the cool compress on her ankle, which made her suddenly shiver all over. "Well now, you're certainly younger than me, and I'm going to give you the benefit of the doubt for that other descriptor."

Laughter rolled out of her, clear and full

and filled with pure joy. A deeper laugh joined hers, and she glanced at Ben just in time to catch him wiping his eyes as he bent low to catch his breath.

Between giggles, she managed to shoot back, "Do you always come to such rash conclusions, Carl?"

" 'Course I do. When y'all get to be my age, you'll see you don't have time to waste on second-guessing."

Ben crossed his arms as he perched on the edge of the nearby desk. "Carl's a smart guy. He rarely gets it wrong."

"Rarely?" she asked.

"Well, I wasn't so sure about this guy when he first started." Carl flippantly waved his hand in Ben's general direction. "Had my doubts he'd be much use, what with his nose in a book nonstop."

"I was working on my thesis." Ben cleared his throat and shifted positions. "And I had a few things on my mind."

There was a strange timbre to Ben's voice. It wasn't entirely different than usual, but there was a gravel to it, a coarseness. It made her sit up and take notice.

He'd said he'd been working at the library a couple of years. What had been going on in his life then? Something with his mother? She used her propped-up ankle to push

herself higher, which of course sent fireworks up her leg and forced her to bite her
lip in order to keep from squeaking in pain.

"Careful there," Carl said, readjusting the
ice pack on her leg.

She nodded, but her gaze held firm on
Ben. She thought she'd been the one with
all the secrets, but he hadn't told her
everything yet either. What exactly was he
not telling her?

Carl kept her from asking. Her questions
felt too personal to ask in front of someone
she'd met exactly six minutes before. So she
tucked them into her mind for later. Later
she'd ask why he'd held back, even after
she'd told him about Devereaux and the
connection she hoped to find.

And after that — much later — she'd be
honest with herself about why it mattered
at all. Because one thing was certain. It did
matter — maybe too much.

"So you're the one with the diary." Carl
didn't really ask it as a question, but Millie
took the opportunity to confirm.

"It was my great-grandmother's. She was
a guest at the Chateau."

"Mm-hmm." Carl nodded and folded his
hands in front of him. He took a couple
sideways steps and then back again, but
always he kept his eyes on her. "How'd she

wrangle an invitation? It was supposed to be the best party in Georgia in those days. Wine and liquor, even though it was the height of Prohibition. Fancy dinners and fancy people. She ran in that set?"

"Not at all." Millie glanced toward the ceiling, trying to remember the details she'd read from Ruth's own pen. "She worked in a bank in Atlanta. She'd grown up on a farm, a small one. But her aunt was rich, and she paid for Ruth to go to school. She's a beautiful writer. She must have learned that at the finishing school. Anyway, she met Ms. Lucille Globe at the bank."

Carl whistled long and low, and she knew she didn't need to explain who Lucille was.

"She invited Ruth and her friend Jane to spend the summer at the Chateau. So of course they went. I don't think many people said no to Howard Dawkins. Or Lucille, for that matter."

Carl chuckled and scratched his chin. "Could you imagine? That big white house lit up at night, filled with music and dancing. It must have been somethin' else."

"It still is."

Carl jerked his head toward her, his eyes wide with surprise.

She shrugged. "I play the part six nights a week."

"Of course you do." He patted her shoulder and ambled back to his table, his gaze lost somewhere between the past and the present. "I almost forgot." After pulling on white cotton gloves, he picked up the pages before him, alone in his world yet again.

Millie shot Ben a look, and he shrugged. Maybe this was normal behavior. But she couldn't help but hope that a man who knew the Chateau and the area's history better than anyone else might be able to help them find Ruth's other journal. Although, why would he know more than Grandma Joy or even Millie? After all, she'd read the diary. She knew Ruth's experiences. Well, she knew a couple months of them.

"Did you . . ." Millie wasn't quite sure what she was asking and lost track of it when he didn't look up. Stumbling to find the right words, she tried again. "Did you ever read about a Ruth Holiday at the Chateau?"

Carl didn't look up. "No. Just the usuals."

Ben grunted. "Usuals? The Chateau was only open for two summers."

"Yes, but there was a crowd. A conglomerate of wealthy families — young men and women who ran around together. Dawkins was a bit of an outsider. He was a little older

326

and never quite as well-known as the Rocke-fellers and the Vanderbilts. His was new money and therefore frowned upon by some of the old-money families. And his Lucille wasn't like the other women in that circle. She was a stage actress who caught his eye, his heart, and apparently his wallet."

Carl had spoken while inspecting and sorting what looked like century-old letters on his table. Finally he looked up. "But there was one family who didn't seem to care too much about Dawkins's past."

"Claude Devereaux."

Carl dipped his head in agreement. "And his sister Angelique. She was as scandalous as Lucille or any of the actresses that ever graced a vaudeville stage."

"Really?" Millie tried to match his description with the one Ruth had given, but the pieces didn't quite fit into place.

"Definitely. She was engaged to at least three men in the two years before the crash. There were rumors that she'd fallen in love with a man who'd lost his fortune to gambling and she was fixin' to marry him, even though her father forbade it. They snuck off to Europe together after the stock market fell."

"What happened to her?" Ben asked.

"Tuberculosis. She died in 1930. Alone

and single."

Ben's eyebrows dipped, and he uncrossed his arms, leaning into the story. "What about her husband?"

"Ah, he divorced her when he found out she'd been disinherited."

Carl's words were stoic. Not cold exactly, just factual. But they pricked at something deep inside. Millie bit her lips. Should she feel more emotion than she did at Angelique's sad life and death — especially if she was her great-great aunt?

But there was no proof of that. Not yet anyway.

She risked a quick glance at Ben, who stared at her with a knowing gaze. He knew exactly what she was going to ask. But Carl didn't, so she tried to play casual. "What about Claude?"

"Oh, he had a good life. There were rumors that he'd planned to wed a poor girl."

Millie's stomach twisted until she thought it might explode. She tried to sit up, but it wasn't easy with her ankle still throbbing. She rolled a little bit in Carl's direction, leaning closer. "Do you know who?"

"That's a family secret that's likely gone to the grave."

Carl hadn't meant to — he probably

hadn't even noticed — but he'd just let the air out of her balloon, and she sagged against the chair.

Ben, on the other hand, had noticed. "Why don't you let me drive you home while you rest your foot?"

She glanced over at him as her eyes began to tingle. She had no reason to be upset. Maybe there was still proof out there. Who knew what was in Ruth's second journal? Certainly Carl didn't.

She didn't need much. She just needed enough to compel the Devercaux family — Claude's three remaining heirs — to give her an audience. Then she could ask for the help she needed. It wasn't much, and it wasn't even for herself.

But it might as well be the world.

Ben reached for her, and she let him help her up. Hopping on her good foot, she leaned against his side, his hands at each of her elbows.

"Thank you for your time and your ice pack, Carl."

He nodded but didn't look in her direction. "Some treasure hunters you two are." His low mumble caught her off guard, and Ben's grip on her arms tightened.

After a long moment, waiting for him to continue, she gave Carl a nudge. "What's that supposed to mean?"

He kept right on reading his papers, sorting them into clear plastic covers with the tenderness of a new mother caring for her child. "Only that every other treasure hunter who's called here in the last two days asked about the actual Chateau."

"Wait —"

"What?"

She and Ben spoke over each other, and she could feel his heart beginning to race against her shoulder. She had no illusions that it had anything to do with her proximity.

The others — the ones Milo Fazetti had promised — were already calling. And they couldn't be far away.

"Oh yes. They want to know about the layout and the best hiding places. And they want to know how to sneak in. Some yahoo asked me if his boat would be noticed parked at the dock behind the house." Carl chuckled. "Bunch of hooligans chasing down some lead on the internets."

Ben nodded. "We know about it. I checked it out after I caught the guy on Chateau grounds, but it's mostly wild speculation. All it says is that there's money — lots of money — to be found on the estate."

"I looked too," Millie said. "There's nothing even remotely backed up with evidence. These treasure hunters are just talking about what might be lost there. Some even think it's an old pirate treasure."

Finally Carl looked up from his work. "I know they're just speculatin'. If they knew what they were looking for, bet they'd stop callin' and askin' for help."

"And what have you been telling them?" Ben said.

"Nothin'. Why would I help them? You two, on the other hand   I like you two."

Millie laughed out loud, and Carl gave her a brilliant smile. "How are you going to help us?" she asked.

"I'll tell you about the secret passage."

SIXTEEN

Ben took off after another tour guest. His legs shouldn't have been tight — not after three other chases that night — but they were. And his boots felt like they had been made out of cement. Every step crashed into the stone pavers along the back of the house, jarring his knees, sending sparks up his back.

He wasn't really old. Thirty was still young. So why did he feel like he'd doubled in age and thrown out his back for good measure?

He let out a groan as his mark tossed away an oddly shaped object — surely something intended to help him find a treasure underground — and zigzagged at the bottom of the twin stairways. The Chateau's spires rose before them, the second-story deck stretching a welcome to guests. The curved staircases on each side were as sleek as the rest of the house in the yellow glow of the night lights.

The guest on the lam couldn't have been much younger than Ben, and he couldn't seem to decide which staircase to take. He bobbed to one side and then darted in the other direction.

Ben didn't know why the other guy was having such a hard time deciding, but he didn't complain, as it gave him a split second to catch up. "You. Stop!"

The guy looked over his shoulder, and Ben realized he was more of a kid than a man. His ruffled blond hair looked like straw, like he'd spent every single one of his few years swimming in the Atlantic. His skin was as light as his fair hair, and his eyes were wide, haunted. He was in over his head, and there was no escape. But he kept running.

"Not up the stairs," Ben grumbled to himself, as he tried in vain to fill his lungs. There wasn't anything to be done about it. He had to push through the stabbing pain in his side. It was far too late to start that gym regimen he'd considered six months ago. There was only time to lament his own stupidity and keep going.

God, please let me catch up to him.

The stairs were tough. Wider than usual stairs, they forced him to adjust his stride.

But the kid didn't know to do that. Halfway up the stairs — while Ben was only on the third step — the kid missed his footing and slammed into the steps. He squealed in pain, and Ben picked up speed. He didn't know where the extra burst of energy came from, only that he was suddenly at the kid's side, reaching out to check on him.

The kid groaned and rolled himself over, his back against the steps and his eyes closed. "Guess I'm busted, huh?"

"Pretty much." Ben squatted next to him, taking a quick visual survey. There wasn't any blood, which was a good sign. But that didn't mean there weren't any broken bones.

Cradling his left arm against his chest, the kid sighed. "I just wanted some of the treasure."

"You and everyone else here tonight." Ben wasn't exaggerating. They were coming out of the intricately carved woodwork. An older woman and a middle-aged man had broken free from their tours and set off to explore the grounds, and a man older than Grandma Joy had tried to enter the grounds from the beach side. And those were just the ones Ben had been sent after. There had also been a family trying to hide a metal detector in the dad's pants and two frat boys carrying shovels who had been turned away by security at the front gate.

"Yeah, well, treasureseekers.com knows its stuff, man. If they say there's something here, it's big. Huge." The kid groaned as he tried to sit up, but he moved like his head weighed more than the rest of him.

"Treasureseekers.com, huh?" Ben shifted to sit on the step below the kid's head. His chest still burned, but at least he could gulp in deep breaths. And the thundering pace of his pulse was beginning to slow down.

"Sure. You know, it's like where people post about tips and stuff they've heard about. Some lady found half a million dollars in Arizona last year just from one post on the forum. Like, she just went to her backyard and dug it up."

Ben nodded. He did know about it. He'd checked it out after Milo first arrived on the scene. But it didn't mean that any of the information on the site was more than speculation. No one had any of the details that he and Millie did.

Besides, all these jokers seemed to think treasure hunting looked like it did in the movies. It didn't. It wasn't quite so frantic or fast-paced. At least not like the action movies he'd seen. Treasure hunting was more like searching for clues and then waiting to see how they fit into place — *if* they fit into place. It was a slow grind. Not that he minded that part of it.

But now . . . now there wasn't time to waste. Not when the Chateau was pretty much under siege and he needed that treasure more than ever.

He was apparently a treasure hunter too. He'd never wanted to be one. Never considered it, not once in his life. Not until he'd met Millie. And now it was pretty much all he thought about. Well, the treasure and that list of names on his desk at home. The list of names of people who were owed as much as he could repay them.

The treasure and the list.

And Millie.

He had to be honest with himself. She was taking up a fair bit of space in his brain of late. He didn't really mind. Not when he thought about that wry smile she sometimes had. Or the way she'd kept her cool with a plate of ketchup-covered potatoes all over her. Or the way she wore her hair all pulled back in a knot at her neck. The costumes were pretty, the jewelry flashy. But they couldn't hold a candle to the line of her neck, so elegant, so graceful. And that was all her. He'd wondered more than once what it would be like to press his lips to that hollow where her neck met her shoulder.

And then he'd promptly given himself a swift kick in the pants.

Millie was beautiful. She was smart. She was funny. And she fit in his arms like she'd been handcrafted to be right there. He rather liked it when she slipped into his brain a third — or half — of the time.

But he didn't have anything to offer her. Not now. Not for a long time. Not until every name on that list had been checked off, every person represented on that sheet of paper given back what had been stolen.

It was too late to save those people from his mother's crimes. But maybe — just maybe — it wasn't too late to give them back some of what had been taken from them. More than money. More than security. This was about dignity.

Ben was so lost in memories and scribbled lists and the smell of sunshine in Millie's hair that he almost missed the kid beside him pushing himself up. Jerking back to the present, Ben stood and held out his hand. The kid took it and pulled himself to his feet.

"Guess you're going to turn me in?" There was a slight question in the statement, a hope for leniency.

Ben nodded. "I have to if I want to keep my job."

The kid shrugged. "Figured something like this might happen."

Ben wanted to tell him that if he was going to give up so easily, he might have saved them both a heart-pounding chase and a stumble up the stairs. But he was just thankful the kid didn't fight him on the way back to the security office.

After the paperwork was completed and Billy Cruze was escorted off the property, his name added to the list of *personae non gratae*, Ben sank into a chair in the security office. Maybe he and Millie had brought this on themselves. No one had talked about this lost treasure for ninety years — until they started snooping. And now it was everyone's favorite target.

Putting his face in his hands and his elbows on his knees, he let out a deep breath. *God, what kind of Pandora's box have we opened? And what if Millie really is a Devereaux?*

There was no audible response. Not that he'd expected one.

"Benji!" The least favorite of all of his nicknames — probably because his mother had called him that — was accompanied by a smack on the shoulder and a low laugh.

338

He didn't need to look up to know who had joined him. "Hi, Theo."

The twenty-one-year-old kid bounced in his chair. "Man, some night, huh? I mean, I knew things were going down and all that when they called me in to work overtime, but . . ." He swore proudly, like he'd just learned the word and wanted to show off that he knew how to use it.

Ben cringed. He'd give his overtime paycheck to have ended up on a shift with Jerome or Richard, two men who'd served in the military, earned the right to say whatever they liked, and respected others enough not to take advantage of that.

"You hear about the new monitors?"

Ben sat up a little straighter and looked Theo right in the eye. "What new monitors?"

"They added some cameras. They're going to keep them on 24-7 — like all the time."

Yes, he knew what *24-7* meant. And the growing ache in his gut told him exactly what it could mean for Millie and him.

"They're installing them now, and they'll be up and running by tomorrow. Gotta get the new monitors installed in the morning. This place is gonna be the business." Theo waved his hand to the desk that currently held three computer monitors.

Ben hunched against the riot in his middle. If cameras were rolling, he and Millie wouldn't be free to explore the grounds. They could kiss the second diary farewell and bid adieu to the treasure. Wherever it was.

His stomach rolled, and for a second he thought he'd be sick.

Theo swore again. "You don't look good, man."

Not surprising. His leg bounced, and he pounded his fist against his knee. He needed to let Millie know. They needed to make good use of this night. Their last night. They needed a plan and a map and . . . and more than a couple secret passages hidden in the old home.

They needed to check out Ruth's favorite place. They needed to find the diary right there, in plain sight, because a million restorers and visitors had failed to see it before. They needed the map to be on the first page and so clear that they couldn't mistake the directions. They needed the treasure to be an inch below the ground.

And if — by some wild miracle — all of that happened, they still needed to prove that Millie was a Devereaux and had some claim to the money they'd discovered.

His head began to pound, and a shooting pain behind his left eye was followed immediately by his ever-present acid reflux.

Perfect.

In that list of all the things he needed, a dysfunctional esophagus wasn't one of them. But it was what he had.

Doubling over, curling against the pain, he pressed his face into his hands and closed his eyes. Taking as deep a breath as he could muster, he tried to still his spirit and quiet his soul.

Lord, we need your help.

Such a simple prayer, yet it seemed to lift something from his shoulders. Some of the weight that had been stacking higher, heavier, with each of their needs.

Could it really be that simple? Not that God was going to automatically give them whatever they asked for. But Ben was reminded that it wasn't all on his shoulders.

It felt like it was. Most of the time anyway. He'd been on his own so long that it was hard to remember he wasn't in this life alone.

Except sometimes — when he was with Millie — it didn't feel like he was doing it all on his own. He had a partner.

He smiled and stood up. If they only had one more night at this thing, then he was going to go find her. They'd make the most of every minute beneath the shadow of darkness.

Millie was hungry and tired and so ready to go home. If her apartment had a bathtub, this would have been the night to fill it with bubbles, sink into it, and wash off the spit-up from the baby during the last tour. The mom had been terribly apologetic. But it didn't change the fact that she was on the hook to get her costume dry-cleaned. Or that she smelled of sour milk.

She gagged as the wind floated the odor past her nose again. Trudging toward the women's locker room, she trailed behind the others, each step like dragging a ball and chain.

"Millie."

The whisper was urgent and so unexpected that she nearly jumped. She really might have if the ball and chain hadn't been so heavy.

Spinning, she saw Ben's face between two of the palmetto trees. He looked around quickly before motioning her toward him.

"What's going on?"

His eyes darted back and forth again, and it made her skin tingle. She looked over her shoulder as well, but the path between the main house and the offices was empty.

"Ben?"

His eyes were intense, and he pressed a finger to his lips. "They're adding twenty-four-hour cameras. Because of the treasure hunters."

"But you're still security, right?"

"Yeah, but I can't protect us from this — new cameras that are recording at night. After tonight, there's no way for us not to be caught."

"So we have tonight?"

He nodded. "Barely."

"So . . ." She began to wring her hands as her insides churned. There wasn't enough time. This wasn't going to work. They weren't going to find what they needed. She wasn't going to be able to prove anything.

He put one of his big hands over both of hers, and she gulped for air. "I know. Let's give it our best shot."

Apparently he'd learned to read her mind in the four weeks they'd known each other. Since she didn't have anything to hide anymore, she didn't mind. She wouldn't have minded being able to read his mind too. But that was a distraction they couldn't afford tonight.

Suddenly his face twisted, and he blinked hard. "What is that?"

She caught a whiff of it again. "Oh, sorry. That's me. Projectile vomit."

He looked like he had to wrestle his smile down to the mat, and even then the corner of his mouth tilted up.

"Let me go change. I'll be right back. Meet you here?"

"Sure. Then we'll go find Ruth's favorite spot."

She took off for the locker room, which was beginning to clear out, and as she stripped out of the foul dress, she thought of everything she knew about Ruth and everything she knew about Devereaux.

Ben had said that in one of the letters, Claude had identified Ruth's favorite spot on the estate. She didn't know where that was, but something about it didn't sit well in her stomach.

She needed Claude to be her great-grandfather. But she was starting to wonder if she *wanted* him to be.

George had made some valid points in his letters to Ruth. And he had no reason to lie — except that he was clearly in love with Ruth. But even she had questioned Claude's motives and been struck by his forwardness with her.

Millie sighed as she slipped on clean clothes and deposited her costume into the bin to be picked up by the cleaners.

It wasn't that Claude was a bad man. Ruth wouldn't have fallen for someone like that. But maybe he didn't know her. Maybe he didn't really know her at all.

And if he didn't know Ruth, Millie wasn't sure she wanted to risk their last chance on him.

Like a woodpecker trying to get her attention, a memory kept pushing at her. Grandma Joy had said that her mom's favorite spot was on the south end of the property. But there wasn't a creek there or the copse of trees she'd mentioned. That couldn't be it.

As she bent to tie her shoes, careful of her ankle that was still a little swollen, her brain kept going through everything she knew about Ruth's summer at the Chateau. There was that night with Claude on the beach, but that was too broad of a location. And there was the picnic with George at Christ Church of Frederica. George had said it was his favorite place in all of St. Simons. And Ruth had said . . . what? That she loved it too? That it might be her favorite spot too?

But it wasn't on the Chateau's property. And she wouldn't have stashed her diary so far away. Would she? No. No way would she have moved it from the hidden hole in her guest room to a church more than two miles away.

Then another memory struck Millie so hard that she nearly fell off the bench.

The gazebo. Ruth had said she loved the gazebo.

If Millie was going to stake their last chance on anything, she'd rather it be Ruth's own words.

Grabbing her bag, she slung it over her shoulder and slammed her locker shut. She took two quick steps toward the door before her ankle yelled at her, and she had to slow to an easier amble.

When she made it back to Ben, he'd all but blended into the surrounding coverage. The lights had been turned down — standard after-hours protocol — and his dark uniform disappeared into the green leaves. It took her two visual passes of the spot where she'd left him to recognize his shape.

"You ready?" she asked.

He reached for her hand, and she slid her fingers between his without thinking. It wasn't a big deal. They'd touched a hundred times before. But she couldn't ignore the bolt of lightning that zipped up her arm.

Tugging her toward a side entrance, he led the way, but she pulled back and said, "Where are we going?"

"The billiard room."

Millie cringed. "I'm not sure I trust Claude Devereaux's assumption about Ruth's favorite spot. Besides, that seems like such a strange place to be her favorite."

His eyebrows dipped low. "You think he's wrong?"

"What do you think? You read the letters from Claude. Do you think he knew her well enough to know where she'd hide something so precious to her?"

Ben chuckled, running his free hand down his face. "I think Claude Devereaux was generally a good guy."

"And?"

"And I think he was arrogant and self-centered. And a terrible poet."

Millie let out a short burst of laughter. "And?"

"And I think he knew her about as well as he knew any woman."

She gasped. He didn't really think that Claude was Ruth's soul mate, did he?

He held up his hand as though he could ward off her panic. "I don't think he knew any woman very well. It's hard to when you're so focused on yourself."

Millie couldn't contain her smile. "Way to give me a heart attack."

Between snickers, a question began to

ease its way across his face. "I thought you wanted him to be your great-grandfather."

That tug-of-war she'd felt earlier was back. Last time it had felt like a tug on her heart. This time it felt more like a war. "I . . . I do." She paused. "But I . . . want to know that Ruth was happy. You know what I mean. That she was with someone who loved her, not just someone who could give her a fancy life. You know?"

"I get it." He glanced in the direction they'd been headed. "But if Claude was clueless, where would it be?"

"Early on in Ruth's journal, she said something about the gazebo."

"The one on the north lawn?"

She shrugged. "It's the only one I know of. And I think it has benches."

"And you think the journal could be stored in there?"

Millie didn't have much more than another shrug and a whole lot of speculation to offer. "I think that if she was looking for a private place to write her thoughts, the north lawn first thing in the morning might have been just about perfect."

Ben didn't say anything, but the line of his jaw worked back and forth several times. She couldn't read his expression in the light, and her brain tried to backpedal as fast as she could. "You think this is a ridiculous idea."

He squeezed her hand. "Not at all. Let's go to the gazebo."

He took off at a quick pace, and she tried to keep up, but her legs were decidedly shorter than his, and her ankle gave out on the third step. Squeaking like a chipmunk, she jerked her hand free and hopped on her good leg as she tried to massage the pain away.

"Millie," he said on a breath, kneeling on the ground by her feet. "I'm sorry. I forgot. Are you all right?" All puppy-dog eyes and regret, he reached for her waist to steady her.

Not that touching her was exactly the way to keep her on her feet. His fingers were warm and firm, but they set off an earthquake in her middle that threatened her bare knees, tight chest, and everything in between.

"Fine." Grabbing his hands, she wasn't sure if she wanted to hold them in place or push them away. But when her fingers brushed his, she knew. Definitely the first option.

"Can you walk? I could give you a piggyback ride or something." There was a note of humor in his voice, but it was laced with something else that she couldn't quite identify.

Suddenly this Ben disappeared, Sir Robert-Ben taking his place. Decked out in armor and wielding a sword with a silly name, he looked ready to face whatever battle was to come.

And she had absolutely nothing to say to him. Not a single syllable.

"Millie?" He still knelt, still knightly, his voice dropping with concern. "Do you need me to carry you?"

Yes. Definitely yes.

But she closed her eyes and shook her head, praying the motion would dislodge whatever daydream she'd conjured. She blinked slowly and sighed when Ben was back to only Ben. Her Ben.

"All right." He stood. "Want to try this again?"

She could only manage a nod, traipsing after him at a much slower pace.

The lawn was nearly black as they shuffled across it. The deep red wood of the gazebo didn't differentiate itself from the rest of the night until they were nearly upon it.

Ben helped her up the steps, and she dipped her head in a quick thank-you, her breath suddenly too shallow to get the words out. The lawn wasn't that expansive, but taking extra care with her ankle had drained her. She wanted nothing more than to sink onto the closest bench, its wooden seat worn smooth by decades of wind and rain. But they didn't have time for that.

Falling to her knees, she pressed at the lip of one of the benches. It didn't budge. It didn't even pretend to.

She strained harder, pressing her palms beneath the lip and putting all of her weight into it. Still nothing.

She shot Ben a look as he pulled out his flashlight. The beam illuminated first the top of the seats and then the underside. He said nothing as he ran his fingers along the bottom of the lip of the bench beside hers. And then he stopped. With a wink he reached to the back of the seat and pulled it straight up.

She jumped up and did the same to the bench before her. "How'd you know to do that?"

"Hinges." His smirk said so much more than that one word, a subtle reminder that she should be glad he was there. And she was. Not just because he'd figured out how to open the bench seats.

There were so many things she wanted to say to him. Like how glad she was that he hadn't run when he'd discovered the truth.

Like how glad she was that for the first time in a long time, she wasn't alone. Like how his touch made her want to melt.

Okay, maybe that last one could wait a little while. But still, it was true.

Ben shined his light into the box in front of her. It was empty except for a few beetles that had found a safe spot inside. Then he moved onto his. Also empty.

They worked their way around the eight seats one at a time. She held her breath and prayed this would be the one as he opened each lid. And let it out on a sigh with each reveal. Her heart beat harder, her hands clenched into fists at her stomach.

Seven empty benches, save for a few spiders unhappy to be disturbed.

That left one. Millie's fists shook and she tried to swallow, but her mouth was far too dry. "I don't know if I should be hopeful or just admit defeat."

Ben looked up from where his beam rested on top of the last bench. "Always hope."

"Easy for you to say."

He grinned. "Sure. But don't forget, my financial future is riding on the treasure map in that diary too."

"Oh. Right." She'd nearly forgotten that he was in this for the money. She'd promised him half of whatever she found. Even if it was just a finder's fee. Amid everything with Grandma Joy, she'd nearly forgotten that he needed money almost as much as she did. But he'd never exactly told her why.

Maybe that was the secret he'd been keeping.

"You ready?"

She pressed a hand to her thundering heart, took a gulp of air, leaned in closer to his shoulder, and nodded. "Do it."

He pulled the bench open, the hinges squealing their unhappiness at being disturbed after nearly a century. But open they did.

When his flashlight beam swung into the open box, it was as empty as all the rest. Her stomach fell, and the back of her eyes burned. She'd wasted their last shot. "I'm sorry." It was all she could muster, but not nearly enough.

Ben didn't appear to be listening. His swung the flashlight beam back and forth over the bottom of the box, his head cocked to the side. "You see that?"

No. But she leaned over his shoulder anyway, seeking out whatever had caught his eye.

"They don't line up."

She frowned and shook her head, still not

seeing what he had focused on, until he reached out and ran his finger along a seam between two boards at the bottom of the box. She gasped. The boards didn't line up. They didn't match. One rested on top of the other. With a small grunt, Ben pulled the top one away.

Suddenly his light swung over something brown. Her heart nearly stopped. And then she lunged for it. It was some sort of thick leather cloth that had been fashioned into a drawstring bag. She flicked away an angry beetle and stared at the package in her hands, which were suddenly trembling.

"Aren't you going to open it?"

She nodded. But she didn't really need to. "This is it." She could feel the sharp corners of a book beneath the case, its covers unbending, and ran her fingers along the book's spine. She didn't need to open it to know that she finally held what they'd been looking for. But whether it contained the map they needed wasn't as clear.

Tugging at the drawstring, she pulled it open, and he lent his light to the process.

"Hey! Is someone out there?"

Millie jumped, her gaze crashing into Ben's and her heart pounding in her throat. Immediately he turned off his light, and beneath the roof of the gazebo it was pitch-black. No moon. No stars. Just darkness.

Another light, bright and long, played across the grass a hundred yards away, but the sweeping motion of the beam was growing closer.

"Theo." Ben whispered it so low that it was more a rumble than a word. But she knew what it meant. If they were found, they'd both lose their jobs, probably be fined, and absolutely lose the journal.

"What are we go-oing to do?" She hated how her voice quaked, but there was no getting around it.

He grabbed her hand and pressed it against his chest, which rose and fell in rapid succession. "We have to run."

She began to nod, then stopped before she remembered that not only could he not see her but she also couldn't run. "My ankle."

He paused. The beam of light grew closer to them. Theo called again, and Ben's heart pounded beneath her hand.

She had to do something. But there was only one thing to do.

She shoved the journal against his chest. "Take it. Run. Hide."

"I'm not leaving you, Millie."

"Do it. You have to. It's the only hope we have of keeping the journal."

He shook his head, but she felt it more than saw it.

"Quit being so stubborn. If you wait, he'll see you. Go." She pushed the package against him again. "Just go. Take it."

His head turned this way and that, but it wasn't the emphatic shake of before. It was like he was looking for something. And not quickly.

"What are you doing?" She managed to hold back the last two words, but her tone definitely implied *you idiot.* "Run."

"All right. But you're coming with me."

"I can —"

Before she could finish the statement, he'd grabbed her arm and swung her around to his back. "Hold on."

She didn't have much choice, so she wrapped her arms over his shoulders and squeezed her knees around his sides as he took off, racing across the grass, racing for the house. But there was nowhere to hide, nowhere that Theo wouldn't find them.

"Hey, hey, you! Stop!" Theo's voice was high and whining, and his light was still yards away from them. But not for long. Not when they reached the lit aurora of the house. He'd know. He'd see them.

Her heart slammed into her breastbone. There was no way this would end well.

SEVENTEEN

Ben gasped, straining for air as the darkness surrounded them. He'd thought chasing Billy earlier that night had been difficult, but running from Theo while carrying Millie was liable to put him in the ground. Quite literally. If he stumbled, they'd both be up to their necks in mud.

Stay on your feet. Stay on your feet. Stay on your feet.

He chanted that to himself over and over in his mind. He didn't have enough oxygen to utter a word.

Besides, his ears were focused on listening for the other set of footfalls. Theo didn't look like he worked out a bunch, and Ben was pretty sure his longer legs could win a fair footrace. But this wasn't fair. So Ben had to use any advantage he could think of. And the only thing he could think of was a secret. A secret passage, to be exact.

Carl had said there was an entrance on

the north side. Past the main entrance. Down three steps and behind a shrub.

Theo shouted again, but his light didn't reach them. Not yet anyway. But it was close. And getting closer.

Ben's foot slammed against a stone paver, and Millie bounced hard against his back. She grunted but said nothing else, then she readjusted her clasped hands in front of his throat. No wonder he couldn't breathe. But there was no air to tell her she was strangling him.

Almost there. Almost there. Go. Go. Go.

He wanted to jump down the steps in one leap but couldn't risk it with Millie in tow, his center of balance way off. Slowing just enough to take them carefully, he gasped for whatever breath he could find.

"What are you doing?" Millie whispered in his ear, sending a full-body shiver through him. "The door is right —" Her body stiffened, and he smiled — even though she couldn't see it — when he knew she'd picked up on his plan.

"Come back . . . here!" Theo shouted, but he was clearly winded too. And too far behind.

Ben looped around the palm tree, reached for the wall, and ran his hand along it in the darkness. The handle was supposed to be at waist height, a sun in all its radiant glory.

And it was right where Carl had said it would be. Ben pushed his palm against the sun's face, and a tiny portion of the wall sank in with a groan. It wasn't a wide gap, and he had to set Millie down to squeeze through. But he kept her hand in his, pulling her into the darkness.

Spinning her into his arms, he moved her against the cool stone wall, his arms around her, shielding her. Her face was pressed into his chest. He could feel her gasps.

"Why are you out of breath?" He kept his voice low but couldn't keep the humor from it. "You didn't have to run."

She pressed a hand flat against the front of his shirt and pushed. It wasn't hard enough to say that she wanted him to back off. Which was good, because he didn't want to.

His heart should have been slowing, but its wild tattoo only increased as he leaned his nose into her hair. In a room that smelled of wet rocks and stale air, she smelled of soap and woman. Clean and fresh.

He jerked back only when Theo's cry echoed around them. "Where are you? I'm going to call the cops!"

"Will he see the opening?" Her question

was more breath than words, and there was a quiver in it that made his chest ache. Where her breath hit him was warm and sweet and unlike anything he could ever remember.

When he laid his hands on her shoulders, he discovered that her voice wasn't the only thing shaking. Her whole body trembled, and he wanted to make it stop. Not because she couldn't handle it but because she shouldn't have to.

There wasn't room at her back to slide his arm around her. And he couldn't possibly pull her any closer than they already were, chest to chest, nose to nose, breath to breath. But doing nothing wasn't an option.

He couldn't see her in the darkness. He couldn't read her expression or guess at her thoughts. But he could hear her. Beneath Theo's continued calls and ongoing threats, he could hear Millie's tiny gulp, and it tied his insides into a knot.

He didn't know what to do with that knowledge, but his hands seemed to have a mind of their own. Dragging so slowly over her silky skin, he walked his fingers down her arms. At her elbows, she gasped. At her forearms, she gave a full-body quiver. At her fingers, she sighed.

It was hard to tell who made the move,

but suddenly their hands were linked, palms flush and pulses throbbing against one another.

He should have stepped away. He should have given her breathing room. As it was, they were sharing oxygen. There was no way to cool down this close.

But he didn't want to. He wanted his heart to pound this hard for as long as it could. He wanted to feel this alive every second of every day. And deep in his gut, he knew it wasn't because Theo had been chasing them — his threats had disappeared into the night. Ben knew his best chance at this feeling was with Millie. Perhaps his only chance was with Millie.

And that nearly knocked him over.

He stumbled forward, which was rather awkward given that there was no more space to move forward. He was already as close as he could be, but there was no denying the urge deep inside. He could be closer.

He could kiss her.

Releasing her hands, he skimmed her arms once again, this time up to her shoulders and then to her neck. Her pulse skittered beneath his fingers, and her skin was like satin, beyond smooth. Beyond perfection.

He let his thumb fall into the curve where

her neck met her shoulder, and she leaned into it, leaned into him.

And that was his undoing.

He took a shot in the dark and captured the corner of her mouth with his. It wasn't perfect, but it was like lightning. Millie froze, and he pulled back, staring hard into the darkness and wishing he could see any of her. But it was all black and the color of regret. He had no doubt he'd read the whole situation wrong.

"I . . ." He should apologize, but he wasn't really sorry. At least not about the kiss. "I shouldn't have presumed . . ."

And then from the darkness, the sweetest words he'd ever heard. "Would you mind trying that again?"

"Excuse me?"

"I wasn't ready." There was a smile in her voice. "And I can't see you."

"All right." There was a frog in his throat, and he couldn't pinpoint why. Maybe it was the unsteady motion in his stomach or the hope that flickered with her invitation. Either way, he cleared his throat, cupped her cheeks, and tried again, this time framing her smile with a thumb on each side.

Her lips were firm, still, hesitant.

At first.

And then she fell into him, melting against

him, her arms wrapping around his waist, and she clung to his shirt with both fists. She was soft and pliant and fierce all at the same time, giving as much as he gave.

The whole Chateau could have crumbled around them and he wouldn't have noticed. The bottom of his stomach dropped out, and he couldn't be bothered to care. In this tiny passage there was only Millie and him.

And that was all he needed.

He was a really good kisser. Millie didn't need to have anyone else to compare it to. She could have kissed a million other guys and she'd still know the truth, plain and simple. Ben was better than great at kissing.

She felt it clear down in her toes. The tingling that had started in her chest had spread everywhere else, and she had to hang on to him for fear her knees would buckle and her heart would explode. She'd thought it had pounded when Theo chased them, but this was entirely new. It was a rhythm so wild she was sure her heart had stopped beating altogether before it slammed against her breastbone to jump-start itself. She lurched and he pulled back, and she was empty.

Please. No. That couldn't be it.

It was wonderful. But she needed more.

Just a little bit more. And then she'd be satisfied.

Liar.

Put a sock in it.

There wasn't time to argue with herself. There was only time to kiss him again.

But he hadn't leaned back in. At least, she didn't think so. She could hear his breathing, ragged and loud, but he was too far away.

Was it bad form to ask a man to kiss you twice in a row? If he'd started it, could she pick it up right where they'd left off?

Her hands fluttered at her sides, so empty without him to hold on to. She wasn't sure when she'd let go of his shirt, but now she was adrift in an ocean of ink and didn't even know if she could call out for rescue. She only knew he was right in front of her. And if he was right there, then she was a fool if she didn't reach out.

Like a drowning woman grabbing for a float, she pulled him to her.

Their lips crashed together. It was lightning and thunder in one, the shock echoing in all of her senses, leaving her so stunned that she was nearly paralyzed.

Maybe this was normal. Maybe it was always like this.

Unlikely.

If every kiss was like this, nothing else would get done.

Oh, shut up.

Her generally annoying inner voice had a point. Why was she assessing the electricity that shot through her with his every touch? He was still kissing her, and she didn't want to miss a second more.

Turning off her inner dialogue, she leaned in. Their hearts pounded against each other until she couldn't tell which one was hers. They both sounded in her ears, steady and in concert.

She quit thinking long enough to cherish the moment. Long enough to wind her fingers into the silky strands of his hair. Long enough to let him fall into her too.

It might have been a minute. It might have been an hour. She didn't know or care. Until he pulled back. Not all the way — just his lips, really. His hands still rested at her sides, their foreheads still pressed together.

On a haggard breath he said, "Wow."

"Pretty good?" She wanted to take those words right back, but it was too late.

He jerked away, still keeping his hold on her waist but putting decidedly more distance between them. Without his warmth the chill of the stone wall at her back made her shiver.

"Only 'pretty good'?"

"No! I mean, it was great. Really great." She swallowed the lump in her throat and tried again, this time with more conviction. "I liked it. It was wonderful. You! You're great too, and . . ."

Oh, be quiet.

Gladly.

This is not how it went in the books. The characters were always cool about a kiss, and they knew exactly what to say after a romantic interlude. They didn't stumble over their words or fight a storm in their stomach. But this was real life, and only a complete romantic novice called them *romantic interludes.*

Millie dropped her head into her hands, fire flickering up her cheeks, even if he couldn't see it.

And then he chuckled. From somewhere deep in his chest, the laughter rumbled, and she could only shake her head. In all the times she'd pictured her first kiss, it had never ended with the guy laughing at her. With Ben laughing at her.

Sir Robert never laughed at Gennie.

But before her heart could take a good stomping, Ben took her face in his hands, pushing her own fingers out of the way.

"Millie, you don't have to describe it. I was here for it."

"But . . . I liked it. A lot. I've just never . . ."

"It's never been like that for me either."

That was good. She guessed so, anyway. But that hadn't been what she was going to say, and if she was going to fulfill her promise to be honest with him, she'd have to tell him the whole truth.

Squaring her shaking shoulders, she gave a quick nod that didn't come close to dislodging his hold on her. "It's not that it's never been like that for me. It's just that . . . um . . . I'm twenty-four years old, and I've never been kissed."

His breathing stopped, and the space was too silent save for the pounding in her ears as she waited for him to say something. Anything.

He didn't.

So she reverted to filling the space with anything else. "My grandpa died when I was younger, and I started working young. I had a boyfriend in high school, but it was really more of a group-of-friends thing. And then my grandma got sick and I didn't have time to think about that. And I've never really —"

He ran his thumbs across her cheeks, and

she gasped when he caught a tear. She could just break away, make a run for it, and be done with this whole mortifying moment. Maybe Theo would catch her and throw her off the property, and she'd never have to see Ben again.

Sure. That sounded like a reasonable response.

And then suddenly his lips pressed to hers again. This wasn't a storm over the ocean. It was like butterfly wings, gone in a moment.

When his chuckle returned, it wrapped around her, warmer than a hug. "I'm surprised you didn't have guys knocking down the door to be with you. But I'm glad you didn't have time for them. I'd have hated to fight them all off, but I would have."

Heat washed over her, and she bit her bottom lip. "Really? You don't seem like a fighter."

"I'd have gone to the gym or something." He laughed again before tucking a strand of her hair behind her ear. "Whatever it took. You're worth it."

That wiped every thought from her mind, and she full-on sighed against him. "I don't know what to say. Thank you?"

"Ha!" It was a burst of humor that seemed to escape untamed. "How about we just have a look at that diary?" His hand dropped from around her waist, and suddenly a light filled the space. He pointed his flashlight at the floor, but she still blinked furiously against it after so long in the dark.

She quickly scanned the space. It was much smaller than she'd suspected, and fully enclosed. It was less passageway and more earthy closet. The coolness made it feel like an underground cave, but the other stone wall was nearly at Ben's back.

An image of her pressing Ben against the wall instead of the other way around suddenly flashed across her mind's eye. And with it came another rush of blood to her face.

Ben's grin dipped a smidge, and she wasn't at all sure she liked being able to see him. Except for his beautiful smile. And the firm line of his jaw. And the perfect slope of his nose. But those eyes — they saw too much. It had been so much easier in the dark.

Funny. Her books never talked about that.

"Are you all right? I didn't mean to . . . I didn't know it was your . . ."

She nodded and ducked her head to avoid his hand, which reached for her cheek. Because she wanted him to hold her again. Maybe too much.

But he was right. They had a diary to look at.

"I'm really fine," she said as she pulled the leather bag from the waistband of her shorts. When she reached inside, he shined his light onto it, and they both held their breath.

The book was thin, barely half the pages of the first volume, and the casing had taken a few hits, especially at the corners. But the words scratched onto the yellow paper were as clear as ever. It began on August 14. And there was no map in it.

She flipped gently through each page, and Ben's light bobbed quickly, a silent acknowledgment that they still didn't know the location of the treasure.

"What's that?" He pointed at the last page, shining his light directly into the fold where the pages met, and she saw that the final page had been ripped almost halfway down.

"It's a letter to George. But it was never sent." She pinched the covers between her fingers, longing to scan it, to read the last line at least. She ought to know how this ended. She should know if this was Ruth's final dismissal. It was what she wanted.

Is it really?

Of course. What would she be looking for,

if not proof of her Devereaux heritage? Without that name she was worth exactly the $5.89 in her checking account.

Her hold on the back cover felt off, and she had to readjust it, but she couldn't tear her gaze away from the top of the page.

My dearest George . . .

No date. No tears that indicated a terrible breakup. No red-lipstick kisses.

Only the certainty that this was the last thing of Ruth's that Millie would ever read. And it was going to either change her life forever or crush every hope she'd ever had.

"I guess we better read this."

"Together?" His question didn't suggest that he wanted to, but as soon as he said it, she knew she needed him by her side to face whatever was in there.

"Meet me at my place?"

"I'll follow you home."

August 14, 1929

I screamed at him. How could I not after that letter he wrote to me?

George doesn't even know Claude, and he had no right to say such things. I told him that as I waved that scrap of paper under his nose, nearly pressing mine to his.

He gently tugged the paper out of my fist and glanced at it, as cool as if he hadn't written such incendiary words about Claude with his own hand.

"I am sorry if I have offended you, Miss Holiday." His words were deferential, but his eyes sparked with something that promised he still believed what he had written to be true. And always with the "Miss Holiday."

He was not really sorry, and I told him I did not believe him. I told him he was probably glad to have the words off his chest. And I shoved at just that spot.

I have never pushed a man before in my life, except for my little brothers. And this was quite unlike that. He did not budge. His chest was like a wall, hard from years of manual labor. But even though I knew it to be useless, I pushed again.

He did nothing to stop me. He only stood there, looking at me like he felt sorry for me. As though I was the one being attacked. That made me even angrier. Everything inside me felt too tight, like my insides had outgrown my skin, like a foot wedged in a shoe two sizes too small.

I yelled at him that he had called himself my friend, yet he spouted such drivel and spread such terrible rumors. A friend would not do that. I yelled it at him until I was nearly out of breath.

He just waited until I had to pause before coming to his own defense. He said that I had asked for his honest opinion. I had. But it did not mean that I wanted it.

I stumbled to find an appropriate retort. We were all alone by his shed, and I could have sworn and gotten away with it. I nearly did. I wanted to. I had heard men on the farm say such things my whole life, and this seemed just the right time to unleash a string of words that would make my mother blush. But before I could, he kept going, asking me if I was unhappy that he had told me the truth about my love.

"He's not my love!" I yelled those exact words, but they popped out before I even realized what I was saying. I had not meant to say any such thing. It was just that George made me spitting mad.

Of course I love Claude. I mean, I think I do. I have never actually been in love before, but this must be what it's like. And I was not about to have George speaking ill of him.

I demanded he take back his words. But he said the most shocking thing. He said that I deserve someone who will care for me more than he cares about his money.

The bottom of my stomach dropped out. I don't know why exactly. Except that there was an implied promise in every one of his words. A suggestion that he is the one who could care for me so.

I went to push him again, but this time he grabbed my wrist and held it there. I tried to yank it back, but the harder I pulled, the tighter his grip became. And the more I wanted to kick him in the shin.

In a low voice I demanded that he let go of me. I wasn't afraid of him. George would never hurt me. But I was terrified of what he was making me feel. All of these emotions. They were so new and strong, and I just wanted to get away.

He dropped my hand and made a snide remark about getting my head out of the clouds.

Ooooooh. I stamped my foot in the grass, and it gave a very unsatisfying thump.

He snorted, and I wanted to scream at the top of my lungs. I had thought about this. I had. I knew what I felt for Claude. And I did not need George's condescending snorts trying to sour my feelings.

I swung my arm back, ready to give him another hard push. But before I could touch him, he grabbed my arms, both of them, and pulled me straight up against him. He did not say a word, but I could feel his chest rising and falling in rapid succession beneath my hands. And his eyes were brighter than the lighthouse, so intense and staring right through me.

I thought he was going to shove me away and storm off. There was thunder in his expression, and I deserved all of it.

And then suddenly his lips were pressed to mine. I froze up, sure that I should push away from him. Only I did not. I melted right there on the spot. I melted into him, letting his lips move against mine in gentle strokes.

When he pulled his hands away from my arms, I thought he might be done, and I did not want to be done. I wanted to be . . . well, I did not want it to end, and I clutched his shirt with both of my fists.

I needn't have worried. He slipped his arms around my waist, holding me even closer. I could not imagine that was even possible, but it must have been. Suddenly our hearts were beating at the same tempo, racing faster than mine ever had before. I could hear them like the thunder of horse hooves at the end of a race.

My entire body tingled as his hands squeezed against my back. He was like granite, and I knew I was safe inside the wall of his embrace. I forgot everything in that moment. Claude. Jane. My mama's warnings. I had nothing to fear from George, so I kissed him back. He made a little noise of surprise, and it was followed by a groan from the back of his throat.

If I could cause him to make that noise every day for the rest of my life . . . Well, that is far beyond any discussion we have had. But I could be happy to the tips of my toes to hear that.

Just when I thought my heart would burst, he pulled back, gasping for breath and pressing his forehead to mine. And then he called me Ruthie, the sweetest name I have ever heard. He told me he was certain he had crossed a line, but he could find not an ounce of regret.

My insides had taken a ride up and down the washboard and been wrung out to dry, and I could offer only a mumbled agreement.

And then he said the words I had been waiting for all summer, words I had expected to hear from another. He said that he could not promise me the world, but he could give me a good life. And he would gladly spend every minute of it making me smile.

How could I not smile at such an offer?

But my head swirled, and I could not let go of him or I would surely stumble to the ground. These were the words I'd been waiting to hear from Claude. These were the words I'd expected after every late-night beach stroll and secret rendezvous. Yet they were coming from George.

So I fled.

I fear that I left him without an answer. How could I give him one when I clearly do not know my own feelings? George is perhaps the best man I know, and I fear that I must break his heart.

But oh, when he speaks my name, it is

better than hearing angels sing.

August 15, 1929

I think I might have seen something I was not supposed to. Oh, I am certain I have seen more than I should have here at the Chateau. And I can never forget the breathless shock of finding Willa's body, something I never want to experience again.

But this time it was dark. I had gotten lost and ended up in the wrong corridor again. It is so easy to do, and only that much more so when I have been able to think of nothing but George and his kiss.

When the rest of the party had retired to the parlor after dinner, I claimed a headache and left for my room. However, I had missed a turn and ended up in a hallway near the kitchens. I could hear the cook and maids singing, but all I could think of was the first time I had gotten lost in this house and George had so kindly walked me back to the front entrance.

I took a handful of other turns and a flight of stairs up before finally reaching a hallway that I had been to only once before. Lucille had taken Jane and me down this hall once and pointed out Mr. Dawkins's private study. She said he did not allow anyone else inside.

But tonight I saw someone exiting the room. The shadows were so thick that I could only see an outline, but I know it was not Mr. Dawkins. It was not any man.

Perhaps I should have shouted or drawn attention. But I was frozen in place and could only think of poor Jenny, who lost her job when she was accused of theft. What if this woman was only a maid cleaning up while Mr. Dawkins was out of his office?

But something in my stomach is so unsettled that I cannot fathom that it could be so innocent.

August 16, 1929

I should have said something last night. Instead I went to bed and tossed and turned all night while someone took off with Mr. Dawkins's stock certificates, ones he had recently acquired for a company right here in Georgia. He was nearly purple this morning at breakfast, his fists shaking and his voice loud enough to take the roof off. I have never seen him so riled, and I think maybe Claude has not either. He sat by my side at our morning meal and held my hand. He looked strained. Almost nervous.

But it was hard to focus on Claude when Mr. Dawkins was yelling. Lucille tried to calm him down, but he brushed her off — I think rather too roughly. She stumbled to her knees, but as Jane and I got up to check on her, she waved us off.

Claude pulled me back to my seat, but I did not particularly want to stay. I really just wanted to be in George's shed. Safe. Peaceful. Quiet. And in his arms.

The realization hit me so hard that I dropped Claude's hand and did not allow him to pick mine back up.

What was I supposed to do? What does one do when she's been determined to marry one man and realizes she's in love with another? What does she do when she realizes she's done things for which the man she loves may never be able to forgive her?

I felt like the piano was sitting on my chest, and I could not swallow a bite.

No one ate during Mr. Dawkins's tirade. He demanded that every room be searched for the certificates. He offered a reward for anyone with information.

Yet I sat there mute. I had some information, but it is still only an inkling. And I daren't begin spreading rumors when I know that doing so could only cause more pain if I am mistaken.

I thought about it through every sleepless hour last night. I do not think the woman I saw was a maid. I am almost certain I recognized her as one of the guests. So I am going to follow her. But I dare not reveal anything until I am certain. It should only drive a wedge in the relationships I have forged here.

In the dim light of this lamp, I do find myself longing for simpler times. There was not so much intrigue or scandal on the farm or even at school. Certainly there were no stolen kisses in a stairwell or a secret rendezvous with a millionaire. And when I came here, that is what I longed for. It was what I had spent my life wishing for — excitement and passion.

And now I long for a simple life, secure in the arms of the man I love. I do not need to see the lights of Paris or to dine in the best restaurants. I do not need to sit at concerts with wealthy men and dance with millionaires.

I do not believe Mr. Dawkins to be a bad man, although I must question some of his choices. Most of all I question whether he cares for his money and his stolen certificates more than those he claims to love.

And I have no doubt that Claude would be the same.

Never once in all my time with Claude has he made me feel more than I did the first time I met George. Mama always says that feelings are just feelings. Perhaps it is true, but perhaps it is not. Perhaps feelings are an indication, not of love or commitment, but of that still small voice the pastor talked about on Sunday last. George had taken me again to his favorite spot, to Christ Church of Frederica. The pastor preached with such conviction of God speaking to us. Not audibly, but silently in the quiet of our hearts. And I wondered if I had ever heard God speak to me even once.

Now I wonder if sometimes that voice is the tug on my heart, a feeling I cannot deny.

Of course, this was before George kissed me. And certainly before I was sure that Claude is not the man for me.

But before I find my way back to that simpler life, I must do what I can to restore what has been taken. And I am almost certain that she will act tonight.

August 17, 1929

I write tonight with a trembling hand as someone who almost did not survive. I would not have, save for the intercession of one man. But I find I must chronicle tonight's events while they are fresh. Jane continues to ask me for details, and I can speak none of them. It is far too difficult to explain all that happened. Perhaps if I write it down, I will show Jane my book, even though I have found her looking for and reading it on two occasions and had to move it.

But this time I may share it with her so that I do not have to relive the moments again. Each time I close my eyes I see that shovel bearing down on me, and I know that I am so close to the end. All I could think about was how much I would miss having a future with George.

It was foolish, really, to follow Angelique last night. I should have told Jane where I was going. Perhaps I should have told Claude or Lucille. Even Mr. Dawkins had calmed down by the evening enough for me to tell him that I had seen someone leaving his study, and I had a pretty good idea of who it could be. But they are all crazy about Angelique, and I was nearly certain that they would try to convince me that I had not seen her head of wild curls exiting the study, or that it had all been entirely innocent.

But the feeling that seemed like so much more than a feeling compelled me to follow her. So I did. I waited in the shadows at the south exit closest to her guest room. I hid behind the trunk of a palm tree and tried to keep my breathing shallow, silent. It was much harder than I thought it should be as my heart pounded in my ears.

Then she appeared. Her hair was tied back and she was wearing trousers, but I could not mistake her porcelain skin or the almond shape of her eyes, so exotic and so secretive.

I stayed back, hoping I wouldn't lose sight of her in the night. Even the moon seemed to be on her side, hidden behind a cloud, blanketing the night in ink. I nearly did miss her turn toward George's small shed, and when she disappeared I had nowhere to hide. So I squatted behind a rosebush and prayed that she could not see my pale shirt. How silly of me to wear such light colors. In my defense, this was the first time I had ever gone sneaking around in the night — except with Claude. And that had been less about sneaking and more about scandal.

When Angelique reappeared, she was carrying a rather large shovel. I thought perhaps it would be awkward in her hands, but she carried it as though she had dug a thousand garden beds, and she set off for the beach. When she was far enough ahead of me, I followed her yet again. The crashing of the waves and the wind covered the sound of my footsteps and, I hoped, the thunder of my heart.

Near the beach, before the grass fully turned to sand, she made her way south. We'd long since abandoned any foliage I might hide behind, and my stomach was in a knot the size of the Chateau itself. But I continued on. It was far too late to abandon my plan now. And if I went for help, I could not possibly find her again.

When she picked up her speed, I did

too. Especially when I saw what was ahead. A copse of trees reached right up to the beach, their long arms black against the deep blue sky. I knew immediately that if she reached the trees, I would lose sight of her and lose any proof I might have.

I began to run, but the grass was slippery, and I was losing ground with each step. She seemed to be flying by now, her hair a trail of wild abandon in her wake. I must have been gasping for breath by the time I reached the tree line. But it was no use. She was gone.

I fell to my knees, sucking in the thick air and praying that I might see a glimpse of her among the trees. I did not. I only felt fire in my shoulder.

The pain came first. And then I heard the clang of metal against something solid. It happened so quickly and yet seemed to drag on for hours. Twisting to cradle my injured arm with my other hand, I caught a glimpse of the edge of the shovel blade, and I knew. I had not found Angelique. She had found me.

"You silly little girl," she cried as the tip of the shovel sliced across my arm. And then she said I was just like Willa, always in the way.

Willa? I could hardly believe what she said, but I knew immediately that she had killed her friend. Why? Because she was going to steal some stock certificates?

Then I suddenly realized the terrible truth. Angelique hadn't only stolen some stock certificates. She was behind all of the disappearances — the brooches and necklaces, silver and diamonds. She'd taken all of it, but why? I could not make sense of it. She is a wealthy woman, and her father and brothers have more money than I could even conceive of. Could they not care for her? Surely they would make certain that she did not go without.

But there was no time for me to parse the facts and come to any sort of conclusion.

I ducked as the shovel scraped my ear, and I lifted my arm only to find that it was nearly useless. Blood dripped from my shoulder, and immediately my head began to spin. But I refused to give in. Pushing to my feet, I tried to look her in the eye and make her see me. Her eyes were cold, like there was no soul behind them, only hatred. Why did she hate me? I have not even refused Claude yet.

I begged her to tell me as I lifted my other arm to deflect another pass of her shovel. But my question went ignored. I tried again, reminding her that we were friends.

The head of her shovel dropped to the ground, and her eyes narrowed. She laughed as though it was quite the joke before spitting out that I had no idea what her life has been like.

I knew that I could not possibly best her in a fight, so I tried to reason with her. I tried to keep her talking, asking her to tell me, to explain it to me.

She did pause then, leaning against the shovel handle. Her eyes stared over my shoulder, maybe seeing the whitecaps of the open ocean. But she looked as though she was seeing something much farther away. And then her voice broke as she explained that her father is forcing her to marry a man she does not love because the one she cares for is not acceptable. He is not wealthy. He does not come from means. Her father believes him to be after her money.

She was silent for a long moment before her gaze returned to me, and she said I knew about that. I tried to assure her that I was not after her brother's wealth, yet my insistence fell on deaf ears.

But for me, speaking the truth was like being released from prison. It was true, and I was suddenly free to love the man I did for the rest of my life, no matter how short it was.

I closed my eyes and prayed that George would have a life filled with joy and love, even though I could not be there to see it. I opened them just in time to see Angelique swing the shovel, and it was almost to my head. I was nearly to heaven when the shovel stopped quite suddenly, and she cried out.

Then George was there, stripping the tool from her hands, and she screamed as loud as the seagulls that he had ruined everything. She went on and on about his roses and how they were too close. Too close. Too close.

She made no sense at all, but her words rang inside of me over and over again as though I should understand them.

I still do not, hours later. But her words are not what haunts me. Nor the vision I see behind my closed eyes.

What haunts me is that I may have

missed my final opportunity to tell George how I feel.

Mr. Dawkins has declared that he is closing the Chateau for the rest of the year, and we must all go home tomorrow. Angelique refuses to reveal where she has hidden the stock certificates, even after the deputies questioned her.

They have taken her away, but Jane is certain she will be released. The Devereaux name holds sway anywhere in the South, and a small-town judge will not be able to hold her, even for Willa's death. She never truly confessed it to me, and they have found no other evidence.

But I'm not afraid of her. She tried to kill me to keep her secret from being revealed. Now the whole world knows.

Claude was beyond apologetic. It was clear that he was appalled by his sister's behavior, all of it. He tried to comfort me, but I had to be honest with him. Despite the exhaustion that had settled over me as soon as George escorted us back to the Chateau, I pulled Claude to the side. His hands were on my face and around my waist, and my skin crawled. Not because he reminded me of Angelique but because for the rest of my life I only want one man to touch me. And I told him as much.

Well, I did not tell him there was another man but rather that I was certain we would not be the right match and we should not spend time together any longer. He did not seem particularly disturbed by it, but for me it was like the last chain had been broken.

Jane insisted I be seen by a doctor, and Mr. Dawkins called for one. The doctor bandaged my arm and assured me it will heal with a minimal scar. Lucille was quite kind to bring me a warm cup of chocolate. They sat with me for hours no matter how many times I assured them I was fine. But I could not tell them what I really wanted, which was to see George.

Jane and I are on the first train to Atlanta tomorrow. I fear I may never see his green eyes and kind smile again.

I am not sure I am ready to live the rest of my life without air.

August 18, 1929

My dearest George,

Do you think it possible that you could still love a fool? For that is certainly what I have been. I should have seen you from the beginning and recognized your kind heart. You have been saving my life from that moment by the pool and through the rest of this summer.

You have made me see a love I could not have imagined possible. I thought that love was about committing to a man no matter how he treated me. But you have shown me tenderness that makes my heart soar. I could not have imagined how this love I feel for you makes me want to care for you in the same way. Could I possibly make you as happy as you have made me?

I leave for Atlanta this morning — Jane and I are off in only a few minutes — but I long for the opportunity to try. I want to try to make you happy. I want to cook for you and care for you and wash your clothes after you jump into a swimming pool to rescue a silly girl.

And I have been silly. I thought that money and wealth and traveling the world would make me happy. I thought that I could belong at fancy house parties and dress in the finest gowns. I thought that my education should afford me a position in a brick house in the best neighborhoods of New York and Chicago.

Now I know none of that matters. None of it makes anyone else happy. Why should I be any different?

I want only the opportunity to be with you. That would make me happy.

You said that day that you loved me. You said you wanted to take me away from here. You said you would like to marry me.

Please, tell me I am not too late to accept.

Yours forever,
Ruthie

Eighteen

Millie looked up from the last page of the diary, her eyes glassy and filled with a sadness Ben hadn't seen there before.

"The letter is still here." She pressed her finger to the final page, her other hand flat against her chest. "Why didn't she give it to him?" There was a strange tremor in her voice, and she blinked hard and fast as a single tear made its way down her cheek.

Ben leaned across her table, the one that looked like it belonged on a front porch between two Adirondack chairs, the one she'd cleared of books and set with coffee mugs when he arrived at her apartment the night before. They'd read until the sun's morning light broke over the horizon, taking only a short nap to see them through.

Swiping his thumb across her cheek, he gave her a gentle smile. "You okay?"

She shook her head, covering her face with both of her hands, her elbows leaning on the edge of the table. "I don't know. I'm just . . . I know that she married Henry and they were happy. But what about George? What if she never got to tell him that she loved him?"

She was a hopeless romantic, his Millie, and it made him chuckle. It also made his heart beat just a little faster.

"I thought you wanted to be a Devereaux."

She dropped her hands and glared at him, her lips pursed to the side, showing off the dimple he hadn't bothered to notice before because he'd been too busy trying not to notice her at all. Until the night before, that is. Somehow a kiss in the dark had suddenly freed him to see what he'd been missing out on.

"I did." She huffed, clearly not satisfied with her answer. "I do. I mean, I need to be. But . . ." Jabbing her fingers through the long hair of her ponytail, she sighed again. "But I want Ruth to get what she wanted."

She shoved back her metal folding chair and picked up her coffee mug. It took all of two strides to get to the other side of the kitchen, where she clunked her mug on the counter with a bit of extra force. It rang in the silence, and she flexed her neck and shoulders several times before picking up the coffeepot and pouring its contents, which were certainly room temperature by now.

"Why did she run off and marry Henry when she was clearly in love with George? You don't just love someone and then run off with someone else." She spun around, a drop of coffee sloshing over the lip of her mug.

"And you have a lot of experience with that kind of thing?"

She shot him a hostile glare, her nostrils flaring and her eyebrows turning into thunderclouds. That just made him laugh harder. Perhaps it was a low blow given that she'd only had her first kiss several hours before. Then her second, third, and fourth. And her fifth when he arrived. And if he didn't mess this up in the next hour, he was hoping she had her sixth before he left.

"You can't read fifty romance novels a year without learning a thing or two."

He eyed the stack of books she'd set on the floor by her chair. White tags on each spine identified them as library loaners, and he raised his eyebrows in question. "All right then. What have you learned?"

"Well." She swung her hand toward the pile and dipped her chin. "I've learned that you don't give up on love. Ruth wouldn't have given up on George. Unless . . ."

He didn't know where she was going exactly, but she seemed to need a nudge. "Uh-huh. Unless what?"

"Unless she was expecting another man's child?" She fell into her chair, setting her cup on the table so hard that coffee splashed across onto the metal top. She mopped it up before it could mar the diary, but the glare she gave the book indicated she wouldn't have cared if it had been tarred and feathered.

"We don't know that she was."

"We don't know that she wasn't. There was the night on the beach. She alluded to a scandal, and that perhaps George would have to forgive her."

"There's not enough here to convict her."

She took a sip of her coffee, cringed, and put it back down. "Says you."

"Yes, says me. And I think you should give her the benefit of the doubt."

"But there are too many unanswered questions. If Henry isn't my great-grandfather, then who is? Ruth didn't tell us. And why would she tell Grandma Joy there was a treasure map in these old diaries? There obviously isn't. I've read every page, and it's useless." She threw up her hands and let out a short breath.

"Grandma Joy is going to be homeless in seventeen days, and I've spent the last month on a wild goose chase for nothing."

Ben reached for her hand and gave it a gentle squeeze. He wasn't certain he could take away her frustration. But he could try. "Maybe it's not for nothing. Ruth did tell us where Angelique buried her treasure."

She let out a little puff of air that sent her bangs flying. "I think I'd have noticed if she did."

"Or maybe you were too focused on Ruth falling in love with George."

She opened her mouth, sure to argue her case, and he held up a finger to hold her off.

"Hear me out." She nodded, and he caught and held her gaze for a long second. "Angelique did not have the stock certificates on her when she was arrested, right? I mean, if she had them on her person, they would have been found by the police when she was booked at the jail. And word would definitely have gotten back to Dawkins before Ruth left that last morning. So if she didn't have the certificates, then she had to have hidden them before she was found out."

Millie's pale eyebrows drew so tight that they almost appeared to be one line, but she nodded a slow concession.

"So then why did she take a shovel with her that night?"

"Because . . ." She bit her lips until they nearly disappeared. "I have no idea."

"I think she took it with her to dig up the treasure and move it."

Her eyes got round, and he could almost see the moment she reached the same conclusion he had.

"When she said that George's roses were too close."

He nodded.

"He was planting new roses too close to where she'd buried it."

He sat back and crossed his arms. "If I were a betting man, I'd put good odds on that."

She flashed him a broad smile, all straight white teeth and sass. But when she lifted her cup to her lips and swallowed, the smile was gone, replaced by a frown that didn't go away. "But that was ninety years ago. It must be long gone by now."

"Why would it?"

"Well, Angelique . . ."

"Went to Europe and died there."

She drummed her fingers against the table, her eyes shifting back and forth. "Her dad's lawyers must have gotten her off the charges or at least free on bail. Just like Jane said he would. And then she fled."

"Probably with that gold digger that her dad didn't want her to marry." His mind raced for the next steps, organizing them like a term paper. Somehow it helped to say things aloud, and Millie's agreement kept him going. "So she never had a chance to go back for it. At least as far as we know. And Ruth never went back for it, or she wouldn't have told Joy that there was a treasure and a map."

"But why not? Why didn't she go back? That doesn't make sense."

Why, indeed. He flipped it over and over in his mind, trying to put together everything he knew to be true about Ruth Holiday. "Well, she didn't forget about it."

Millie shook her head in agreement.

"She might not have known exactly where it was."

"But as far as we know, Ruth never even looked for it," Millie said. She chewed on her thumbnail, her eyes a window to the same mental acrobatics he was performing.

"So what did she do? She got married to Henry, had a baby, and weathered the Great Depression."

They both slammed their hands down on the table at the same time, making the open diary jump.

"Of course." Millie got back on her feet and marched the length of the kitchen. "Just two months later the stock market crashed, and those certificates would have been next to worthless."

"Dawkins never came back to look for them because he was hit so hard. He knew they couldn't save him. Whatever Georgia company he had bought stock in would have tanked too." Ben tapped his foot in time with Millie's stride. Bouncing his fist against his leg, he tried to make the next logical step. But there wasn't much to go on.

"So why didn't Ruth come back for it after the Depression?" His question was meant to be rhetorical.

Millie didn't settle for that. "She told us why in her diary."

He stared at the open pages, gently flipping back a day or two. He let the words roll across his mind. They'd spent an hour reading and talking, and he was certain — never once had Ruth said she didn't want the money. "No she didn't."

Millie leaned against his back, her arm stretched out over his shoulder, and for a moment he forgot to care about the diary and the treasure. He couldn't follow the line of her finger, not when he looked up at the underside of her chin and all the smooth skin of her neck. He remembered how sweet she tasted, like sunshine and strawberries. And he didn't want to argue with her. He didn't care about being right. But she didn't know that.

"Yes, she did. Remember?" She looked down, and their eyes locked.

Sparks shot through him, lighting a fire that burned somewhere deep in his chest. Would it always be like this with her? Could it always be like this?

Always. That wasn't something he'd ever thought about before. Not when his childhood had been nomadic at best. But with Millie, it didn't seem far-fetched. It seemed right. It was right.

Because he had gone and fallen in love with her.

Forget the spark. That fire inside him turned into a raging inferno. And only one thing could quench his thirst.

Stretching his neck up, he kissed her chin. Just a peck. Plenty to get her attention.

"Nice try, bucko. You're trying to distract me because you know you're wrong." But her giggle betrayed that his kiss wasn't unwelcome.

He knew no such thing. He couldn't even

remember what they were disagreeing about.

"It's not going to work." She ran a finger along his jaw, her eyes tracing the movement as she bit her lip.

Oh, those lips. He could practically feel them against his own even now.

"Ruth said it clear as day. She said that Dawkins loved his money more than he cared about people. And Claude would do the same. Why should George or Henry or anyone else be different?"

He tore his gaze away from the pink bow of her mouth just long enough to look into her eyes and hear the truth of her words.

"Maybe Ruth didn't want the money," Millie said. "And maybe she never told another soul about it."

"Which means it's right where Angelique left it."

"Too close to George's rosebushes, where the trees reach the beach."

He couldn't not kiss her again after such a brilliant announcement. "You're smart. You know that, Millie Sullivan?"

She shook her head, her cheeks turning pink, that blush all too familiar and beyond pretty.

"It's true." He pressed his lips to hers again, and she let out a low giggle.

"You really think so?"

"I know so. After all, you chose me to be your partner."

She rolled her eyes and pushed away from him. "I don't recall having much choice in the matter."

"Well, you were smart enough to trust me."

She considered it for a long moment, her hands on her hips and her head tilted. "I suppose that's true. Now let's go find Ruth's treasure."

Millie could hardly breathe. Not because of the long walk from the car to the beach, or because she was carrying a shovel that weighed more than a beluga whale. Not even because the July air was thicker than water.

She couldn't breathe because her heart was in her throat, beating a million times a minute.

And that was because Ben had stopped and pointed. He'd said nothing, but a muscle in his jaw twitched. His knuckles turned white on the handle of his own shovel, and his eyebrows had risen almost to his hairline.

Now she couldn't look away from the row of bushes in front of them. Roses. Pink and white and blooming.

"I'm not sure I really thought those would be here." She choked out the words around her heart.

Ben stabbed his blade into the soil and leaned over the flowers. Pressing his nose against the petals, he took a deep breath and sighed. "George sure knew what he was doing."

"Uh-huh." But Millie didn't stop to literally smell the roses. Her gaze landed on the rock wall to their north, the Chateau's southern property line. "How did they get down here, off the grounds?"

"The wall is relatively new, within the last thirty years or so. Maybe this land was sold off by Dawkins's nephew at some point. We know for sure that the land the museum occupies ends at the wall."

Millie dug the toe of her tennis shoe into the soft soil. It was rich and black, protected from the sun by the canopy of trees above. A small creek trickled along ten yards away, its bubbling a soundtrack of tranquility. "So who owns it now?"

"I don't know. I didn't see any 'No Trespassing' signs on our way. Did you?"

She shook her head.

"But one thing's for sure. If we find a treasure on this land, whoever owns it won't stay silent for long."

With a chuckle, she stepped toward the end of the row of roses. "I'm pretty sure you're right about that. So, where do you want to start?"

Ben surveyed the ground around them, a clearing not more than five feet. The place where Ruth had been nearly killed and George had rescued her. And Angelique had cried out that he was getting too close.

"I mean, it's pretty clear that the treasure isn't under the roses, right?" She didn't really need his agreement. She knew her argument was solid. "Otherwise George would have found it when he was planting them."

"Makes sense." He picked up his shovel again and dragged the point along the ground, seeming to test how hard the dirt had been packed. "And she would have wanted to make sure there was a marker, something that would help her identify the spot."

Millie's eyes roamed the clearing. What would Angelique do? Nothing too brazen or obvious. After all, she'd kept the entire house party in the dark about her thefts for months. She knew how to be low-key, to fly under the radar. So what would that look like here?

She turned a slow circle, surveying every tree and root and fallen twig. But the ground cover wouldn't have been there — at least not as it was now — ninety years ago. She turned again, trying to see what would have been there then. The trees would have grown wider, taller. The branches were thicker now, and they let in only patches of light through the leaves.

And then she saw it. It wasn't remarkable at all — not really. But it made her stomach flip and her heart leap at its spot in the base of her throat.

It was a simple mark on the birch tree. Its white trunk had been marred with a single line longer than an axe head. It was almost at shoulder height now, but ninety years ago it would have been at her shin perhaps. Just right for slamming a shovel through the bark.

"That's it."

Ben stopped his own survey and followed the line of her finger. And when he gasped, she knew he realized it too.

Without any more conversation they began to dig. Their shovels took turns sliding into the earth and tossing it aside. The damp dirt thumped as it landed in the ever-growing piles behind them. The air filled with the scents of dirt and leaves and the outdoors. And sweat.

In a matter of minutes Millie had to stop to wipe the drops from her forehead. When she missed one, it rolled into her eye, the salt stinging. She winced and blinked and wiped her face with her sleeve.

That's when she saw Ben watching her.

Perfect. The man who was used to seeing her in all of her Gilded Age glory now saw her for what she really was. Her silks were gone, her pearls forgotten. Her hair, always so carefully arranged and sprayed permanently into place, ran stringy and wild down her back. And she undoubtedly had sweat marks around her neck and down her back.

Nothing said "kiss me again" like sweat dripping off her nose.

But Ben didn't look away. And he didn't look disgusted. Instead he gave her a smile. It wasn't mocking or filled with pity. It was gentle and sweet, and it promised that they would do the tough things together.

And somehow that hit her harder than the roses or the tree trunk or Ruth's unmailed letter to George. Because this was real life. It was her life. For the first time in almost eight years, she wasn't alone. And more than that, she didn't want to be alone.

Her heart slammed into the back of her throat, and she tried to smile back at him.

But she knew it came out shaky and uncertain at best. He didn't seem to care. He just kept right on shoveling and smiling at her. Shoveling and smiling.

And then he struck something.

It echoed through the clearing and across the grounds, and Millie didn't know if she should fall to her knees or make sure that no one else had heard their discovery. Her stomach dropped, and she followed it, hitting the dirt with a quiet thud. Ben knelt on the far side of the shallow hole, his shovel abandoned and his hands clawing through the mud.

They brushed and scraped at the black earth until it revealed a pale blue metal box. Its corners had rusted over the years, and the silver buckle closure had certainly seen better days — probably right around 1929.

Ben dug his hand down the sides and pulled the box free of its burial place. And there, engraved in the metal below the buckle, were two little letters.

AD.

NINETEEN

Ben tried to pry the metal open with his bare hands, but the rust wasn't going along with his plan. It squealed and groaned and didn't budge at all. "Come on," he mumbled.

"Come on," Millie joined in.

It didn't help.

He was breathing hard by the time he set the box back down. It wasn't particularly heavy, but it was sturdy and built to last. That boded well for whatever was inside it. Not so much for the people trying to crack it open.

He looked at Millie, and she put her hands on her hips, her eyebrows forming an angry V. "We need some sort of leverage. You know, fulcrums and force and all that."

He quickly agreed. Setting the box on its back and wedging it securely between two tree roots, the buckle facing the sky, she shoved the tip of her shovel beneath the lip of the lid. Then she leaned on the handle.

Nothing happened.

She scowled and leaned harder, up on her tiptoes, hips wiggling and body shaking. Still nothing.

He wanted to laugh at her antics, but more than that, he wanted to know what was in that box. So he joined her, adding his weight to the pressure of the handle. The wood in their hands groaned, and he cringed, expecting it to splinter.

And then with no warning, the buckle popped and pieces flew at them. He ducked as his heart skipped a beat and the box clattered end over end.

They raced to it, kneeling on either side. He prayed this was what they'd been looking for, what they needed. He prayed that what they found would let him finally lay his mother's sins to rest.

Millie reached for the lid, but her hand stilled just before opening it. She looked up through thick lashes, and he could read the question in her eyes. Was it going to be enough?

And maybe that was the real question. Could it ever be enough? There was only one way to know.

"Open it," he said.

Squaring her shoulders and sucking in a

quick breath, she gave a dip of her chin and popped the lid open.

His mind couldn't make sense of what was inside. Sunlight sparkled off of a chain of silver like nothing he'd ever seen. And beside it sat a ring with a glowing red ruby the size of the moon. Gold necklaces had tangled together, and strings of pearls pooled in a corner. The missing brooch lay over it all, pink and green gemstones outlining the wings of a butterfly. It was everything Ruth had written about and so much more.

Millie gasped, but Ben didn't have any air to do so. This was beyond what he could have imagined. And it was theirs. All theirs.

Or at least theirs to turn in to the authorities. And then, if unclaimed, unlooked for, unwanted, it could be theirs. Even a fraction. A finder's fee, as Millie had put it, would change their lives. His mom's debts could be paid. Every person he knew she'd swindled would be restored. Grandma Joy would receive the best care money could buy.

Because — for the first time in his life — money wasn't the issue.

Millie squealed as she pressed her hands to her face, then threw her arms around his neck. "We found it! This is really it!" She pressed a wild kiss to his lips and then leaned back on her heels, hands covering her face. Her shoulders shook. He couldn't tell if she was crying or laughing or both. It didn't matter.

His cheeks ached from smiling so hard, and there was a lump in his chest that he couldn't name. It was all so much.

Forcing himself to find out what filled the rest of the box, he pushed the glittering pieces to the side. Paper crinkled beneath his fingers, and his stomach did a full barrel roll, the pressure on his chest suddenly making it hard to breathe.

The stocks. Angelique's final theft was right here with the other things she'd stolen.

He pulled the papers free and read the heading. Across the top in bold letters was a word he knew well. *Coca-Cola*.

A chuckle broke free. Then a full-on laugh. And then his shoulders hunched and his whole body shook with mirth.

"What's so funny?" Millie asked.

It took him two tries to get the words out. "You know — that Georgia company — the one that Dawkins bought shares in?"

She nodded.

"It was Coca-Cola."

"Are you serious?"

He showed her the documents, ten pages of them, all with the same company name emblazoned across the top.

"What are these worth?"

"I don't know exactly. But if they're real, millions."

Her eyes welled with tears as laughter spilled out of her. And he could do nothing but hold her close.

"Can you even imagine? What would you do with this kind of money?" Millie couldn't hold back another giggle as Ben pulled his car into a parking spot in front of the sheriff's office. She hugged Angelique's box to her chest, her head still spinning with the possibilities.

It wasn't theirs yet. But maybe some of it would be.

He chuckled and seemed to think about it for a moment.

She didn't have to. "Of course, I'd find the very best home for Grandma Joy, some-where I could visit her all the time, and when I couldn't be there, I'd be sure that they were taking the best care of her. I'd know she was happy and not scared when she forgot. I'd know it was clean and her sheets would get washed every week. And they'd never make her move again."

"That's a good dream. But nothing for you?"

"Oh, for me? I'd buy a car that always runs. I'd buy a house with real air-conditioning. No more of that useless window unit for me. And I'd buy myself a steak. A real steak — that someone else cooked. And I'd buy bookcases and fill them with books. Books that *I* owned!" She straightened in the passenger seat. "Definitely the books before the steak."

Ben laughed, his gaze off somewhere beyond the brick building before them.

"What about you? What will you do with your half?"

His gaze dropped, and his eyes drooped at the corners. "I'd try to make things right."

His words were vague, but they struck a memory in her, something that reminded her of all the times she'd thought he was holding back.

"Seriously, Ben. What would you do?"

"That's what I'd do. I'd make things right." He stared straight ahead, and his fingers gripped the steering wheel so hard that his knuckles turned pale.

"What things?"

Silence hung between them for so long that she thought he hadn't heard her, until his chin fell to his chest. He took a deep breath and kept his gaze somewhere near his feet. "All of them. As many as I could."

She pressed her hand against his arm. "What's the first one?"

He looked at her out of the corner of his eye. "Who?"

"Who, what?" She squinted at him, but while his face was in focus, his words were as obtuse as ever.

"Cora Aguilar."

She racked her brain for any memory of the name, but it didn't fit in Ruth's journals or their talk of treasure or anything that Ben had said to her. "Who's Cora?"

"My mom's first mark." When he was silent for too long, she squeezed his shoulder to keep him going. "I wasn't quite ten. I didn't understand how life worked. I didn't know where money came from. I just knew that the kids in my class sometimes made fun of me because my clothes had holes or my lunch was a can of sardines. And then one day there would be new shoes, the two-hundred-dollar ones that everyone wanted. I hadn't had three meals a day in two weeks, and suddenly I was wearing brand-new clothes. There were packed lunches and cookies when I got home from school. And then a few days later we had to move, sometimes sleeping in our car until my mom could find us an apartment."

Millie rubbed her eyes, which burned as

he recounted his childhood. She hadn't always had much, but she'd had Grandma Joy and Grandpa Zeke. She'd had a home she didn't have to leave. "I'm sorry."

But he didn't seem to hear her. "I should have asked where the money was coming from."

A fist tightened around her stomach.

"But I didn't. If I wondered, I never asked. I couldn't. Not when whatever money was coming in was the difference between sleeping in our car and having a roof over our heads and a real shower. And you know the worst thing about being a homeless twelve-year-old boy?"

She shook her head. There was no way she could get a word around the lump in her throat, the weight on her chest.

"The other kids always make fun of the smelly one."

"Oh, Ben. I didn't know." She couldn't fuse the image of the clean-cut man before her with the picture in her mind of a little boy in need of a simple shower.

"So I didn't ask. I didn't question. I only wanted to survive. It wasn't until I was a sophomore in high school and I had this history teacher. I was only at that school in Jacksonville for a semester, but this teacher, Mr. Cunningham, made me fall in love with history. He made it so interesting, and I wanted to be just like him — to make students care about the past because it informs our future."

Whatever she'd felt for Ben before grew new blooms. She'd cared about him, really liked him. And now . . . well, she wasn't sure what this was. But it was special. Different. And it swirled inside her, wiping out every doubt that might have stood between them.

"That was the first year I heard Cora's name."

Oh, right. There was more to Ben's story, and she leaned into it, into him.

"One day my mom said that the money had run out. We had to move. She needed another mark, and she had a tip from a friend at a retirement home near Nashville."

The twister inside picked up and took her stomach with it. "A tip?"

"I didn't ask her. I couldn't. I finally had a dream, and I wasn't about to lose out on it because my mom might have been doing something underhanded. But I knew she was."

Bile rose in the back of her throat, and she had to swallow convulsively to keep it down. She knew the type of person his mother was. She knew the damage that

418

person could bring to a family. Damage it had brought to her family.

Ben let go of the wheel long enough to stab his fingers through his hair, rearranging the already wild style. "We were only there for a few months. But within weeks, money was rolling in. We had a new car, then two cars, one for each of us. It was luxury I had never known. I was in town long enough to get decent grades. I had a guidance counselor who convinced me I could go to college, so I weaseled away every dime I could. When Mom would leave me twenty bucks for pizza while she went out on the town with her boyfriend of the week, I would eat tuna sandwiches and tuck that twenty into a box under my bed."

"And that's how you paid for college? With other people's money?" Her voice rose with each word, anger bubbling low inside her like a geyser searching for release.

He nodded. "And I regret it every day. Which is why I —"

"Which is why you want the money."

Again he gave her a nod, but he still didn't look in her direction. His shoulders slumped a little more with each word.

Everything inside her longed to fling open the car door and march into the sheriff's office, turn in the treasure, and hear that they

419

could keep even a fraction of what it was worth. But something inside her had to dig deeper. It demanded to know the rest of his story. He'd given her clues along the way — just like Ruth had — and now she knew she was missing a key piece of the puzzle.

"And now your mom is in prison?"

"Yeah."

"How was she caught?"

His swallow filled the whole coupe. "About eight years ago she started a fake investment firm. She promised big returns on midsize investments, and she targeted retirees, mostly between here and the Florida state line."

"And she took their money and ran?"

She didn't really need to ask the question. The truth was right in front of her, and she could see it like it had been printed on the cover of a book.

And she was going to be sick.

He scrubbed his face with his palms. "When she was convicted, she was ordered to pay restitution, but her lawyers found a loophole. She filed for bankruptcy, and now she'll never pay a dime."

"So that's what you're doing? That's why you're working three jobs? To pay back those people?"

He looked at her then, his head still bent

forward but a question in his eyes. Maybe her words should have been — if not pleased — at least accepting. But she couldn't keep the venom from filling every syllable.

"I am. At least the ones who were named in the court case. As many names as I can find, I'll make it right for them."

"And what about the years that they've lost? What about the ones that were homeless because of her? What about the ones who lost everything, who lost all hope? What about the ones who wouldn't have had to suffer at all if you'd just spoken up when you were a kid?"

He leaned his head back against his seat. "You think I don't think about that? I wish I'd made another choice. But at the time, it didn't feel like I had one. It was my mom or foster care. It was my mom or sleeping on the street. What kind of choice is that?"

Her fists shook in her lap so hard that the metal box rattled, and he looked from it to her face and back, his eyebrows raised with more questions.

But how could she explain? How could she tell him about the war inside her when it stole her breath? Every single thought was replaced with one word. When she closed her eyes, she saw it in the letterhead on her grandma's table like it had been emblazoned across the sky.

Aspire.

Her throat constricted, and she doubled over as tears filled her eyes.

"Millie? I'm sorry." He touched her back, but she couldn't bear it. Flinching away, she hugged the door and the box to her chest.

"I should have told you," he said. "I know it's a lot to ask you — to ask any woman — to deal with."

Yes. He should have told her. He should have told her when she offered him half of the treasure. He should have told her before she took him to see Grandma Joy. He should have told her before he kissed her.

He should have told her before he made her go and fall in love with him.

Stupid Ben.

Stupid Millie.

"Millie? Millie? What is it? I'm going to make it right. I'm doing everything I can to make up for it."

"It's not enough. It'll never be enough."

He blinked hard, jerking back in the tight confines. "What's that supposed to mean?"

But she answered him with a question of her own. "What's the name of the investment company that your mom set up?"

"What? Why?"

"*What* was it?"

Please, please, please. Let him say any other word. Let this all be a hoax, some sick joke. Let the ache in her stomach that threatened to tear her in half be from a misunderstanding.

Please, God. Let me be wrong. Let every coincidence be just that.

But she wasn't wrong. And she knew it from the tips of her toes to the top of her head. She'd followed that case from the jump, and there was no way his mom wasn't the woman she thought she was.

He frowned. "Aspire."

She flung her door open and vomited on the ground. Her stomach rolled and rolled, and she hugged what had been her hope while her insides emptied.

"Millie?" Suddenly Ben was by her side, helping her up, but his touch burned, and she ripped herself out of his grasp.

"Stay. Away. From. Me."

"What is going on?" He tossed up his hands and took a couple steps back. "I don't understand why you're so upset."

"Because." She walked away and then back to him and poked him in the chest. "Your mom. Your mom — who you could have stopped — she stole everything! She took every penny that Grandma Joy ever earned!"

His jaw dropped open, his eyes wider than she'd ever seen them. "Grandma Joy. But she's not on my list. She's not — she wasn't named in the case."

"She didn't want to press charges. She said that justice was going to be done, and she didn't need to have her name on that list. She said . . . she said she could forgive that woman."

She spun and marched away, but she wasn't done. Flinging herself back around, she wagged her finger at him again. "But I can't. I won't!"

"I don't know what to say. I'm so sorry."

She snorted at him, derision dripping from her every cell. "Like that could begin to help." She pivoted and marched away, blind and uncertain where she was going.

"What about the money?"

"The money? Is that what you care about? Then keep it!" She flung the box in his general direction, her vision blurred and her lips trembling. "Keep your stupid money. I don't want it! I don't want you!"

And then she ran.

TWENTY

"You look like someone ran over your dog."

Ben looked up from the keyboard at his desk with no idea how long he'd been staring at his motionless fingers. He was supposed to be responding to an online request for information. Instead he was stuck in a parking lot in front of the sheriff's office, the weight of the box landing in his arms as Millie took off like an Olympic sprinter.

She hadn't returned a single one of his phone calls. And there had been more than several.

He tried to smile at Carl's remark, but it took far too much effort. He managed only to lift one corner of his mouth, and it dropped immediately back to the frown.

Carl pulled on a pair of white cotton gloves and began to open a journal twice as old as Ruth's. "What's wrong? Treasure hunt not going well?"

"No. I mean, it's fine." He shook his head,

trying to focus on Carl and not on the image of Millie's sweet lips as he saw them every time he closed his eyes.

One of Carl's bushy eyebrows raised, clearly doubtful.

Ben blurted out the first thing he thought of. "I mean, we found it. We found the treasure."

"Sure. That's why you look like a kid that got left at Mount Rushmore."

"Really." Ben turned back to his computer screen, his back to Carl. But he could still feel the other man's eyes on him. "We found it. It was south of the security wall — off the property."

"You don't say." Carl abandoned his project and sidled up to Ben's desk. "What'd you find?"

Ben shrugged, unable to muster any enthusiasm for their discovery. It didn't matter that he'd invested a month in trying to locate the treasure. It didn't matter what it contained.

None of it mattered without Millie.

"Well, it has to be better than sweet potato pie," Carl prodded. "If not, no one would bother looking for it. And those treasure hunters are still calling. Fewer than before the Chateau beefed up its security, but still, they're looking. So what was it? Worth the hubbub?"

"If any one of those hunters had found it, they wouldn't have been disappointed."

Carl gave a low grunt. "Uh-huh."

"More jewels than I've ever seen in one place. A handful of silver and gold necklaces, diamond pins, ruby rings."

Shaking his head, Carl let out a long whistle.

"And that's not the most valuable stuff." Carl raised his eyebrows, and Ben gave in. "Stock certificates from Coke."

Carl's jaw dropped. "From 1929? For *the* Coca-Cola Company?"

Ben nodded.

"Those are worth a fortune. Millions maybe."

"I know."

Clapping him on the back, Carl laughed. "So what'd you do with it? Put it in the bank? Does your girlfriend have it?"

"She's not my girlfriend." He snapped the words so quickly that even he wondered why he'd been so sharp. Carl assumed they were a couple. Ben only wished it were true.

He took a deep breath and tried to wipe Millie from his thoughts. Carl hadn't really been asking about his relationship status. Rubbing his hands over his knees, Ben shook his head. "I turned it in to the sheriff."

"I suppose you would have to. And they're going to track down the rightful owners?"

Ben shrugged. "I guess so. They're going to try anyway."

Carl tapped his toe on the ground, uncrossing and then recrossing his arms. "So do you know whose property it was found on? If it's not the museum's, it must belong to someone other than the Dawkins family. Maybe they have a claim to it."

"I don't know. And I don't really care at the moment."

He couldn't believe those words had just come out of his mouth. Even if they were true.

The money didn't matter without Millie. He'd work a dozen jobs to take care of her and Grandma Joy and to repay what his mother had stolen.

But Millie had been right. He couldn't give back the years. He couldn't erase the heartache or stress or give them back that time free of worry and fear. He could never make it right. So why should she forgive him?

Carl gave another long, low whistle. "Tell me what's going on in that head of yours, boy. No man alive would give up a treasure like that. Not without a fight. Or not unless he knew he was beaten."

It didn't take him even a split second to know the truth. "I'm beaten."

"What'd she do to you?"

"Nothing." Oh man. He sounded like a petulant teenager now. He rolled his eyes at himself and leaned back in his chair — the same one Millie had sat in when she'd sprained her ankle. The ankle that had hurt too badly for her to run, so he'd carried her to make sure they were both safe. Which was why he'd arrived at the secret passage out of breath and feeling far too warm. And probably why he'd kissed her like a lunatic.

But being out of breath and overly warm did not explain why he'd enjoyed the kiss so much. Or why he'd thought about a repeat performance every day since. Which was why knowing she didn't want to be any part of his life ever again made his heart feel like it had gone twelve rounds with a meat tenderizer and lost.

Yep. He'd been beaten.

"I'm going to need more than that," Carl said.

"More than what? More than 'nothing'?"

Carl nodded, kindly ignoring what a jerk Ben was being to his own boss.

Ben leaned forward, resting his elbows on

his knees and his face in his palms. "What do you need to know? That Millie and her grandmother are broke because of me?"

All pretense of good humor vanished in an instant. "You best start talking. Right now. That girl was sweet as sugar and put a light in your eyes like I've never seen. And if you treated her badly, then we're going to have words."

"I didn't mean to. I didn't even know I had." And then it all spilled out. About his childhood and his mother and how he was trying to pay them all back. And how he had discovered that Grandma Joy had been swindled but wasn't listed in the court files.

"She's never going to forgive me. And I can't blame her. I've made her life miserable."

Carl sniffed, folding his gloved hands in front of him. "Seems like you weren't really to blame. You were just a kid."

"Well, it might sound that way to you. Millie doesn't agree." Ben sighed into his palms. "And she's not wrong. I messed up. Badly. I thought I could make up for not doing anything. I didn't even realize — until I talked with her — just what my actions had cost my mom's victims."

"The sin of inaction," Carl mused.

Ben sat up enough to see Carl's face. His

430

eyes had taken on a distant look, and there was a pain in the set of his jaw.

"I think maybe we all have regrets. I've read enough letters and journals and newspapers from the last two centuries to know. It isn't a new affliction. People have been struggling with it for years. Good intentions but bad results."

"Yes. But she can't see past the results."

Carl strolled across the room, back to his worktable, his hands moving around the papers in front of him. "Here's what I know for sure. People have been messing up for centuries, millennia. We've been ruining relationships, hurting others, seeking only what's best for ourselves. It's human nature. It's what we do. We're imperfect people."

"Is that supposed to be a pep talk?"

Shooting him a scowl, Carl kept going. "But it's the imperfect — the broken — who need mercy. The perfect don't need anything. But you and me and the rest of the world, we need mercy. We need forgiveness. Even someone like your mom."

Oh man. That was a knife to the heart.

He clutched at his chest and tried to take a deep breath. But there was no air.

"You're more than that, you know."

Ben tried to look up at Carl, but he couldn't lift his chin.

"You know that, right? You're not what your mom did. You're not the bad choices you may have made. You're who you are right now, and you're the next decision you make."

"How can I be who I want to be if Millie can't ever forgive me?" Ben asked.

Carl huffed like he was getting frustrated. "Millie's forgiveness doesn't define you. God's forgiveness takes care of that."

Had he been defined by God's mercy or his mother's scandal? Had he been characterized by grace or by making it right on his own?

Well, now he knew. He could never make it right. There was nothing he could do that would be good enough to wipe it away. There were consequences for his actions.

But there could be forgiveness too.

"Why's it so important to you what Millie thinks of you?"

Ben threw his hands up and groaned. "Because I'm in love with her. I think I am anyway. I never have been before, but when I'm with Millie, I see a different future. It's not about my past. It's about what we could be — together."

Carl nodded like he found the response satisfactory. "And what is it that she wants?"

"To never see me again?" He managed to

quirk the corner of his mouth and let out a half chuckle, half groan.

"Or . . . to know who she is?"

"How'd you know about that?"

Carl shrugged. "She doesn't seem the kind to be consumed by money, so when you said her great-grandmother had been at the Chateau, I figured there was more to her story than all that treasure hunting. So I did a little digging."

Ben pushed himself out of his chair, marching to the worktable and forcing Carl to look at him. "What did you find?"

"Oh, this and that."

Pressing his hand to the tabletop, Ben leaned in closer.

Carl chuckled. "Only that Ruth Holiday was married."

"Right. To Henry Jefferson."

Carl's lips twisted with a Cheshire grin. "To someone else. Before Henry."

"And I kissed him. A lot!" Millie flung her arm across her face. Somehow admitting to the last was so much worse than everything else that she'd just told her grandma. Worse than not knowing where her grandma was going to move. Worse than discovering Ben was the son of the woman who had made their lives miserable. Worse than throwing away the treasure in a fit of anger.

The only thing worse was that she really wanted to kiss him again.

Not that she'd admitted that to Grandma Joy. She had no intention of ever doing such a thing. She'd never tell another soul for the rest of her life.

And maybe by then she'd have stopped thinking about Ben altogether.

Dreamer.

Oh, knock it off. That's what readers did. They dreamed. She dreamed. And if she wanted to dream that she'd someday forget Ben, then she was going to do it.

From her favorite chair, Grandma Joy rocked forward to reach for her hand, and Millie rolled to her side. Lying on her grandma's bed, she was nearly eye to eye with the woman who had raised her.

Gnarled fingers moved to her hair and combed through the strands over and over again. For a second Millie was once again a child. Comforted and cared for. She wasn't the one in charge, and she certainly wasn't responsible for someone she couldn't support.

"I'm sorry," Millie said.

"Whatever for?"

Her stomach swooped, and tears burned

at the back of her eyes. Millie had lost her again.

But then her grandma continued. "You have nothing to be sorry for. You couldn't have known Ben's role in his mother's scheme. And you couldn't have known who his mother is."

"But now I've given away any chance —"

Suddenly her purse vibrated on the tile floor. It rattled and shook her keys. But she didn't get up to answer her phone.

Grandma Joy gave her a hard look that traveled to the bag and back. "Going to get that?"

"No, ma'am."

"You know that every single one of us is more than the worst thing we've done. All of us. We bear the image of our Maker. Even Ben."

Millie stiffened, and perhaps her grandma could feel her trying to pull away. Her hand grew heavier, keeping her in place.

"And we're surely more than the worst thing someone in our family has done."

"But . . . but his mother is the reason we're in this situation. Because of her, I can't afford to take care of you. And Ben was complicit in all of it."

"My dear, he was a child. And there is so much more to life than money."

"But she stole those years from us."

"She stole no such thing. That's life. The struggle and scraping. The figuring out how to find joy in the midst of pain. That's the good stuff." Grandma Joy took a deep breath and closed her eyes, rocking back and forth for a long second. "For as long as the good Lord has us here on earth, that's what we'll keep doing. Can you find happiness, my sweet girl?"

Millie shook her head, not sure she could give the Sunday school answer.

"Losing the money means so much to you. And not being a Devereaux?"

She sat up then, pulling her hand out of her grandmother's grasp, leaning against the wall, and looking her in the eye. "Do you really think I only care about money? I'm doing all of this to care for you. I just want you to be safe and taken care of." Suddenly her grandmother's form swam before her eyes, her dear face wrinkling with concern.

"Honey, you know that money is never going to be enough."

She looked toward the ceiling in an attempt to keep the burning in her eyes from turning into a full-on flood. It was easy for Grandma Joy to say that money wasn't important. She didn't have any idea how much it would cost to put her in a new home. Or how hard Millie had worked to make sure they had all they needed.

"I wish it was that easy, Grandma."

A gentle pat on her hand followed a low hum. "Oh, I never said anything about it being easy. There were times when your grandfather and I thought we'd have to sell the house and every acre we had. But it was never about how many nickels were in our savings account."

"Then what?" Millie threw up her hands. "How can we survive without enough money?" She hated how petulant she sounded, but her grandma was off on another fantasy. Maybe her memories were lucid, but her problem-solving skills left something to be desired.

Grandma Joy patted her hand. "You're looking for money to be your provider."

Millie began to nod, and her grandma cut her off quickly. "Money isn't what provides for you. Money is a tool. God —" She paused and looked hard at her granddaughter. "God is the one who provides. Let him take care of you."

The tears began to leak in earnest then, rolling to her chin and dropping to the front of her shirt. "It's not that easy. How can I trust him when he's taken everything from you? What that woman didn't steal, God has. What's to say he won't take everything from me?"

"And what if he does? Will you fault him for that?"

Honestly? Probably, yes.

"Who am I to question God's ways?" Grandma Joy's smile was filled with concern but as radiant as ever.

Millie wanted to punch a wall. "But he took your memories." As sure as Ben's mother had stolen Grandma Joy's retirement, God had left her a mere shell of the woman she had been.

"Oh, he didn't take my memories."

Millie let out a low snort. Easy to say but contrary to every piece of evidence.

"Sometimes they may not be easy for me to retrieve, but that doesn't make them any less mine. The experiences — those years raising your dad with my Zeke, then a chance to raise a little girl like I'd always wanted, all those years farming and serving my community and my church — those are my story. And even if *I* can't remember them, God hasn't stolen them. Every little face I taught in Sunday school. Every woman I brought a care package to after she gave birth. And every time I look at your face, I'm reminded that my story lives on in all of you. God used me then, and maybe he'll use me now. No check or dollar amount can take that from me. No matter if I forget, I know there are those who remember that I was there during a hard time or brought a measure of comfort in a difficult season or helped to raise a young woman who can change the world."

Millie's chest ached, and she'd entirely given up on trying to stem the flow of tears.

Could it be true? Could all that her grandmother said be true? Maybe a person's story wasn't like a book that became useless after the pages were too worn to read. It wasn't about how much that person could remember. It was about how many lives they had touched. It was about making a difference in the little ways.

"Sometimes I can't remember his face — your grandfather's. And sometimes it is so clear that I think he might be sitting on the bed next to me."

"Oh, Grandma."

"No, no, dear." Her grandma patted her arm. "It's not sad. I love thinking that he's right by my side. Even if I'm mistaken, I know that we were together. I know we shared a life that mattered. Even when I can't remember the details, I'm sure of that. Because even the hard times are manageable when you have someone to share the pain with."

"You have me. I'm right here."

With a laugh and a sigh, Grandma Joy shook her head. "I do love you, my sweet girl. But you need more than me. You need someone to lean on, someone to lean on you. Life is so much sweeter when you're not in it alone. Why do you think God gave Eve to Adam?"

"But she betrayed him." She spit the words out much more vehemently than she'd planned, the story far too close to the one she was currently living.

"Oh, Adam didn't need any help finding sin. He needed someone to be with him after the garden. He needed someone who understood everything he'd lost and could walk by his side anyway."

Someone who could understand loss. Ben had lost his parents. Not exactly like she had, but the result was the same — a life of trying to pick up the pieces all alone. A life of failing to make good out of the pain of the past.

She hiccupped on a restrained sob as another rush of tears covered her cheeks, and she pressed her forehead to her grandma's hand. Had she missed out on her chance to be with someone who could truly understand? Someone who not only cared about her but also cared *for* her?

"But even if he cares for me, how can I forgive him?" She couldn't. It wasn't that simple.

Grandma Joy's eyes turned sad. "All of us are more than the worst thing we've ever done. All of us. Your dad is more than running off and leaving you behind. Because in his selfishness he gave me a gift — you. And that handsome young man of yours is more than failing to turn in his mother."

"You sure about that?"

"What is he?"

"What do you mean?" Millie rubbed her head, trying to push away the pain behind her eyes. "He's a history professor and a security guard and an archivist."

"So, a hard worker?" Grandma Joy looked rather smug, and Millie wanted to contradict her, but she couldn't. He *was* a hard worker. "And what did he do when you told him you'd been hiding your real reasons for looking for the treasure?"

Millie scowled. She hadn't told Grandma Joy that so she would use it as ammunition. "I suppose he forgave me."

"Not only did he forgive you, he did it quickly. On the spot."

"Yes. And he's loyal. And he works at a

library."

Grandma Joy's smile turned even more smug. "He likes books, does he?"

"Well, not novels so much. But yes."

This was not good. Grandma Joy was making far too much sense, and Millie didn't want sense. She wanted to be angry. She wanted to hang on to a grudge. She didn't want to put herself out there and risk being hurt again. Because she knew how badly it could hurt. Because she was just protecting herself. Because . . .

Because you're an idiot.

Yeah, she deserved that.

"I don't know what to do. It's too late." Her heart had been shattered, and it was too late to put the pieces back together again.

"Oh my, no. It's never too late for love. It's never too late for forgiveness. Tell him how you feel."

A line from Ruth's diary jumped to her mind, and she shook her head. "Ruth's mama used to tell her that feelings were just feelings. Maybe it doesn't matter what I feel. Especially if he doesn't feel the same."

Grandma Joy clucked like an old hen. "You've piled those excuses higher than cow patties. And that's all they're worth — a load of manure."

"But —"

"You're sure quick to give up on love for someone who reads so many romance novels. Don't you believe in what you're reading? Don't you think that true love is patient and kind and it doesn't hold a grudge? What kind of drivel is in those books you read if they're not showing that kind of love? Real love isn't love because it's easy or always feels good. It's love because you choose not to be self-serving."

"But . . ." Her mouth flapped like a fish out of water.

"But what? You know I'm right, and you'll never know what he's thinking if you don't return his phone calls."

She glanced at her purse, which had vibrated at least three times since she arrived. "How do you know he's been calling?"

"Because he's followed you on a hunt with no promise of riches, except your time. Because I saw the way he looked at you on that first visit. Because he's a good man who won't let you run off without trying to win you back." She pushed her rocker, setting off the squeaks. "He cares for you the way that George cared for Ruth. And I'd wager a week's worth of pudding that you care for him too. And that you'd like to kiss him again."

Millie dropped her gaze and pressed a hand to her neck, trying to cover the flames that were already rising toward her ears. How did her grandma know her so well?

"I'll take that as a confirmation. Was it nice?"

Nice? A glass of milk was *nice.* A warm shower was *nice.* Finding a new pair of shoes at the thrift store was *nice.*

Ben's kiss had been like fire and ice in one. It had been a choir of angels singing. It had been forget-everything-but-his-lips-on-hers fantastic.

And if she didn't do something about it, she would never have another kiss from him. Ever.

There were things she could live without. Financial security. A two-bedroom home. A purse that had never been owned by someone else.

Ben was not one of those things.

Grandma Joy leaned over and cupped Millie's face with her hands, her skin as smooth as butter. "He's so much more than the mistakes he's made. He knows he was wrong, and he's a history professor."

Millie's eyebrows bunched together.

"Studying history is all about learning

444

from our past so we don't repeat mistakes in the future." Grandma Joy leaned in until their foreheads nearly touched. "Ruth may have missed out on the love of her life because she didn't tell him how she felt. Don't make her mistake."

Millie let out a dry chuckle devoid of any humor. It was true. If she didn't learn from Ruth's mistakes, she was bound to repeat them. And Ruth may have chosen love over money, but if she never told George, what good was it?

Millie might never know how it all ended.

Grandma Joy leaned back in her chair, picking up the old diary once again. She flipped through the pages, landing on the final letter to George. "Imagine missing out on true love by half a page. That's all that connects this letter to the journal."

Millie cringed. Imagine missing out on love because she held on to a grudge.

The thought made her stomach ache, and she doubled over as Grandma Joy studied the back cover of the diary.

"Well, I'll be."

Millie didn't have the wherewithal to ask what had caught her grandma's attention.

Suddenly Grandma Joy howled with delight. "Will you look at that?"

Twenty-One

Millie clutched the folded pieces of paper in her hands, trying not to wrinkle them, but shaking so much she thought she might drop them if she wasn't careful. She wasn't sure if it was what she was holding that had her shaking or the man she hoped to find.

Well, actually, there was a good chunk of her hoping not to find him, even though she really needed to. If anyone could help her make sense of the diary's biggest secret, it was Ben Thornton.

She was fully capable of asking for his help without throwing herself into his arms and begging him to kiss her again. Although that had worked well for Gennie and Sir Robert. Just when it had seemed that all hope was lost and her father would never allow them to find happiness together after Sir Robert swam across the moat, Gennie had climbed out of her bedroom window on a rope of bedsheets and run to the stables, where he was preparing his horse for a midnight ride. She'd flung her arms around him, buried her face in his chest, and whispered the words she'd been holding back for so long. "I love you, Robert. I always have."

Not that Millie would say that to Ben. She wouldn't. Not even anything remotely related to that. She would remain professional and poised. She'd ignore every moment that they'd shared and forget the gentle rasping of his whiskers against her skin or how he'd refused to leave her behind at the gazebo. Or the way he'd forgiven her when she'd been a little less than honest with him about her interest in the Devereaux family. Or the way he'd been so incredible with Grandma Joy.

Or the way his face had melted with heartbreak when he realized that Grandma Joy had suffered at his mother's hand.

Tears began to pool at the corners of her eyes as she marched across the crisp green grass, and she rolled her eyes to keep them at bay. As she walked through the library's sliding glass door, she took a deep breath. It didn't help. Everything inside her was wound as tight as a spool of thread.

The librarian behind the front desk greeted her by name, but Millie could only wave in response. A lump was growing in the base of her throat, and it took everything inside her not to turn around and run. Because she didn't know what she'd say to him. Because she wasn't sure she could be in the same room with him. Because she was a big old chicken.

Only one thing kept her weaving through the stacks of books and refraining from disappearing between the rows of fiction titles. The name on the paper in her hand.

George Whitman.

She paused in front of the closed door at the back corner. Maybe Ben wouldn't be here. Maybe he'd be teaching a class. But that wasn't probable unless he'd changed his schedule in the last three days.

Or unless he was avoiding anywhere she might be looking for him.

It was possible but not likely, given the myriad of messages he'd left on her voice-mail. Not that she'd listened to them. But the calls had come more frequently in the last day and a half, and she couldn't help but wonder if she'd left a void in his chest half the size of the one he'd left in hers.

Raising a trembling hand, she formed a fist and knocked twice. The door swung open before she could strike it a third time.

Suddenly face-to-face with Ben, she took an unsteady step back. His eyes lit with something she couldn't name, and a tentative smile spread across his lips. Oh, those lips. Full and pink and as firm as she remembered.

"Hi." His voice sounded like it had gone through a meat grinder. "Did you get my message?"

"You mean, all seventeen of them?"

If he'd had any proclivity toward it, she was certain he would have blushed in that moment. But her cheeks burned instead.

"I got them."

His entire face transformed from uncertainty to pure joy. "So you know!"

"Know what? I got them . . . but I didn't listen to them."

His eyebrows dipped low again, his voice holding her at bay as much as his arm that kept the door from fully opening. "Then why are you here?"

She shouldn't have come. This was a terrible idea.

Oh, shut up.

No. She would not shut up. She'd let Grandma Joy talk her into coming to see him after her shift at the diner, still smelling of grease and syrup. She'd told herself some story about how they could go back to how it was before she'd known the truth.

But she wasn't sure she could. Because

when she saw him, she saw his mom. She saw the face of the woman with no heart and less conscience.

But that's not Ben. You know it's not.

As if he could hear her internal dialogue, his features softened again. "I'm glad you're here. I'm so glad." He swung the door open into the archivist room. "Carl's at lunch. But we found something."

She shouldn't do it. This couldn't end well.

You can trust him.

She took a step in, then leaned away. Finally she held up the paper in her hand, waving it at him. "I really only came to ask if you could help with this."

Ben held out his hand. "I'll try. What do you have?"

She lowered it onto his palm, keeping her hold on it for a long second.

Let go!

She released it with a sudden jerk, and he opened it up, his eyes scanning the page. With no choice but to follow him inside, she slipped in before the door could close her out.

"This is a property deed. And it belongs to George Whitman."

"I know." She stopped at that, but the silent *I'm not an idiot* was more than implied.

He looked up with a smile. "Of course. Where did you find it?"

"It was hidden in the back cover of Ruth's diary. The second one."

Ben snorted. "Why am I not surprised?"

"What's that supposed to mean?" Millie wrapped her arms around her stomach. It was more of a settling hug than a barrier between them.

"I'll tell you in a minute." Ben plopped down in the chair in front of his computer. "Do you know where this plot is located?"

"That's what I was hoping you could help me with. Do you have access to the county records that far back?"

He nodded, already clacking away at the keys. Suddenly a map appeared on his screen, the land divider a clean white line across a sea of green trees. It was a relatively small plot of land, especially compared to its northern neighbor. But Millie gasped all the same.

"Is that . . ." She pointed at a pale blue line that wiggled its way toward the clearly defined beach. "Is that the creek? The one by where we found the treasure? And that's the . . ." Well, there was no use pointing it out, really. The giant white structure in the adjoining piece of land could only be the Chateau.

"Yep."

"So George owned the land. That land. Where we found the treasure." Her words weren't making a whole lot of sense even to herself, and she leaned over his shoulder to get closer to the truth.

"He owned the property, all right. And if this is still accurate" — he waved his hand toward the screen — "it still belongs to his family. The treasure, even though it was on his land, probably still belongs to the family of the original owner. The sheriff's office will track down Dawkins's heirs and return the certificates and probably the jewelry too."

Millie sagged against his desk, her heart thundering. She'd known that would be the case for the treasure, but it still didn't explain one thing. "Then why did Ruth have it? She never told him how she felt, so why would he have given her the deed to a plot of land worth thousands?"

"Well, that's not exactly right."

Millie's gaze snapped toward him, but she couldn't find the words to formulate a complete question.

Ben pushed back his chair, and with a quick tilt of his head he invited her to follow him to the adjacent table. "I found something. I mean, really Carl did. But he thought it might help."

"Help what?" As soon as they were out there, she wished she could reel her words back in. She knew what. But for a split second she'd forgotten. She'd forgotten that she had to remember that he was more than the worst thing he'd done.

He just was. He was more than the boy who hadn't known how to turn in his mother. He was more than the son of the woman who had conned Grandma Joy. He was more than she'd given him credit for.

He was a child of God, created in his image. Infinitely lovable. And she did love him.

"I'm sorry. I'm so sorry." The words flew out of her mouth of their own accord, but she meant them from the very depths of her soul. "I shouldn't have yelled at you. I shouldn't have thrown the box at you and run away. I was shocked. I was hurt. It just all hit me at once, and I couldn't see past my own past."

Her breaths came in short gasps, and her cheeks were suddenly wet with tears. "I was heartbroken and I was scared — I am scared. I don't know how I'm going to take care of my grandma, and I've blamed your mom for so long. Suddenly I had someone else to blame, and I hated it. Because — because —" She tossed her hands up in the air, fighting for the words she wanted to say and the ones she knew she couldn't.

Just say it, you chicken.

Yes, she was a big chicken. So what?

So, are you going to make the same mistake Ruth made?

"Because I think I'm falling in love with you, and I don't know how to do that and blame you too. I just want —"

She didn't have time to tell him what she wanted because suddenly his hands cupped her cheeks and he pressed his lips to hers. Her stomach tanked, swooping low and fast, and she grabbed at his forearms to stay on her feet.

An electrical current raced down her spine, sweeter than syrup.

And then she was too far away from him. Grabbing his sides, she pulled him against her and wrapped her arms around his waist. He was trembling. Or maybe that was her. It was hard to tell this close, but somehow it didn't matter.

His thumb brushed a tear off her cheek, its path warm and tender. "Sweet Millie. I'd do anything to make it right." His words were little more than warm breath against her skin, his thumb dragging across the bottom of her lip. It built something inside her that she couldn't name, something that burned and churned and begged for more. His gaze followed the same path, and it was more tangible than even his touch, setting her entire being on fire.

"I didn't know how much I needed someone in my life until I met you." He cleared his throat. "I was so used to doing it on my own, and then you showed up in my life, a means to an end. I thought the money might . . . I thought it would help me make up for my regrets. But then, all of a sudden, I couldn't imagine my life without you. I didn't realize just how empty it had been until I lost you. And now I have nothing to offer. Nothing to give. I can only beg for your mercy."

Her lips trembled until she thought she'd never be able to respond, and even as she began, the words were uneven and stuttered. "Grandma Joy always said that those who have been shown mercy give mercy."

His breath hitched, and suddenly his whole face swam before her.

"I forgive you, Ben Thornton. Will you forgive me?"

He tugged on her hand, pulling her into his side and wrapping one arm around her waist. "I'll do you one better."

"Always trying to one-up me, huh?"

He chuckled. "You're going to like this one."

"Better than that last kiss? Doubtful."

He gave her a full belly laugh at that. "Okay, maybe it's not that good. But it's close."

"I might need another example just to make sure."

Leaning over, he obliged her. This one wasn't quite as urgent, not quite as fierce. It was gentle and sweet and as tender as any touch she'd ever known. She could stay in his embrace for the rest of her life.

And she might have if Carl hadn't barged in on them.

Millie jumped back, but Ben didn't let her go completely, even though he couldn't miss the flames licking up her neck.

"Ah, I see you told her then."

Ben shook his head. "I was just about to get to it."

"Get to what?"

Ben's grin made her knees tremble. "We found a picture of your grandma."

"Grandma Joy?" She squinted at him, then at the newspaper clippings printed out and scattered across the work-table. "What do you mean?" She felt like an idiot but she couldn't put any of these pieces together.

"Well, actually, we found a picture of Ruth

— clearly pregnant — in *The Herald.*" Ben looked at Carl as though waiting for approval to continue, but Millie could only push at his chest.

"Was there an article? What did it say?"

"Her loving parents were enjoying a church picnic and eagerly awaiting the arrival of their baby."

She gasped, searching for a full breath and knowing it wouldn't come until he confirmed what she already knew somewhere deep within.

Ben rubbed his hand up and down the full length of her bare arm. "Her loving parents, George and Ruth Whitman."

The tears didn't bother with an introduction. They just poured out of her eyes, down her cheeks, and rolled off her chin. "They —" She hiccupped loudly, slapping a hand over her mouth. "They were married?"

"Carl was the one who found their wedding announcement. It was a small one in their local paper, but as soon as he had George's last name, he was like a hound on a scent."

She turned to the grizzled archivist and reached out to him with both hands. "Thank you. Thank you for finding my heritage."

Carl tried to pull away, but she wouldn't be denied a full hug.

"And he found a building permit request in the county archives," Ben said. "George was going to build her a home on their property, a gift from Howard Dawkins."

"The property." She squeezed Carl again.

Ben swallowed audibly. "There was an obituary only a few weeks after the picnic. George died in a farming accident before he could build her that house, and Ruth remarried."

"They were hard times," Carl said. "It wasn't unusual for a man and woman to marry because they simply needed a partner."

"Henry." She whispered the name, sending up a quick prayer of gratitude that he'd loved Ruth well and Joy as his own all those years. He might not have been the love of Ruth's life, but at least she'd had a short time with George and a constant reminder of him in Joy's smile.

"So, you're definitely not a Devereaux." There was an implied question in Ben's words, and Millie mulled it over, letting the truth fully form before she responded.

"No. I'm not. And I'm good with that. I'm . . . I'm actually really happy about it." Which was true but made no sense considering that she was crying again. Not loud sobs or uncontrollable tears. But her eyes kept filling and leaking with every rapid blink.

Ben reached over and brushed her cheeks dry. Then he leaned in and kissed away one tear that he'd missed. She nearly melted into a puddle at his feet.

Who did that kind of thing? Who was so tender and kind even when she was falling apart for no identifiable reason?

Sir Robert? Probably.

Dan Thornton? Apparently so.

And she'd rather have Ben any day of the week.

But that didn't change the truth. She wasn't a Devereaux, so there would be no money from them. She and Ben had no claim on the treasure — even if it had been found on Ruth and George's property. And Grandma Joy was still about to be kicked out of her room at the home.

All this time. All this effort. All this energy she'd put into finding the diaries and the treasure. It was all a waste. She was no closer to being able to care for Grandma Joy.

But at least you don't have to do it alone.

For once she didn't want to argue with the voice in her head. Instead she leaned against Ben's side, thankful. Maybe everything they'd been through over the summer was for that only — for the certainty that she had a partner. In treasure hunting. And in real life.

"I don't know what I'm going to do with Grandma Joy." Taking a deep breath, she stepped out in faith. "Maybe we can figure it out together?"

He squeezed her, and it was better than all the century-old stock certificates in the world. "As it turns out, Joy happens to be a very wealthy landowner."

"No. She sold her house, and the money . . ."

Ben picked up the deed to the property. "She's the sole heir to George Whitman's estate, which happens to include almost half an acre of beachfront property on St. Simons Island. Do you know what that's worth?"

Millie shook her head and tried to ignore the bells ringing in her head.

"Only about a million and a half or so."

"Dollars?" What a stupid question. Yes, of course, dollars. American dollars. More than a million of them.

Something inside her chest filled to bursting and then exploded with joy and hope and pure relief. She flung her arms around Ben's neck and let all those pesky tears make a pool right on the front of his shirt.

"Unless you want to keep the land. You know, for sentimental purposes."

She chewed on her bottom lip for a long moment. "I guess property is nice. I've never owned any before. But how could a patch of land compare to knowing that Grandma Joy is safe and cared for? With that kind of money, I could get her a spot in a home right on the beach. Can you imagine?"

He chuckled. "She could have any room she wanted. She's a millionaire now."

Millie shook her head, her face still pressed against his chest. "Not quite. Half of it is yours."

He stiffened, his lean body turning immobile. She couldn't manage to look into his face.

"I can't take that money," he said.

"Can't take the treasure?" Carl's voice boomed. "What kind of idiocy is that?" He shook his head and strolled toward the door, mumbling something about being as silly as some woman.

It seemed to shock Ben from his stupor. "Oh, I almost forgot. Sam, Sam Williams. The woman that bought your grandma's house. She's the one who was looking for the treasure and told that crazy website. She's the reason all those treasure hunters visited the Chateau."

Millie nearly had whiplash from the change in topic, and she scrambled to catch up. "How do you know?"

"She showed up here at the library. She was looking for information on the Chateau's history, and when I asked her one question, she folded. Confessed the whole thing. She overheard us talking about it when we went to the farmhouse, and then when she contacted that treasure-hunting website for help, they published the rumors."

Her laugh was little more than a dry cough. "Some people will do anything for a treasure. But you don't seem to want the half I promised you."

His heartbeat picked up speed beneath her ear. "I turned in the treasure to the authorities. All of it. Your land isn't part of that. It's not what we agreed on. Besides, if it hadn't been for me and my mother, you never would have needed it in the first place."

"Um . . . technically that's true. But here's the thing." She risked a quick peek at his lips, which were pursed to the side, his jaw tight. "I think Grandma Joy likes having you around. She's asked about you — at least, I

462

think 'that handsome fellow' is referring to you."

His laughter reverberated in his chest, and it echoed inside her too.

"I think she'd like to have you around some more. I think I'd like that too. And maybe if I could get a good home for her and you could repay the money your mom stole — well, we might only have to work one job apiece. Maybe then we would get to spend some time together."

"And maybe we could see where this thing leads?"

Those bubbles were back in her chest, better than sweet tea on a sunny day. She felt strange and new all over. And she was pretty sure it was almost entirely Ben's fault.

She didn't really need the money. Maybe she never had. She just needed him.

He hooked his finger under her chin and lifted it up, forcing her to meet his gaze. "Is that something you'd be open to?"

"Seeing where this thing" — she thumped his chest and then her own — "goes?" She pretended to think about it, but there was no thinking required.

He squeezed her until she squealed with laughter.

"Yes. I think I'd rather enjoy that."

"Good. Because otherwise I was going to

have to study every one of your books to figure out how the guy woos the girl so I could win your heart."

"You'd be willing to read a romance novel to do that?"

He shrugged, whispering against the corner of her mouth. "Whatever it takes."

"You don't have to try too hard. You already did."

Then he kissed her again, full and strong, a road of possibilities they had yet to explore.

This was so much better than the happily ever afters in her books. Because it was real. And it was only the beginning.

EPILOGUE

Six Months Later

"Ben! Are you here?" Millie burst into his home without an invitation. They'd pretty much given up on those after about a month. Millie wasn't great with waiting to be let in, and Ben didn't much care, as long as she kept coming back. Which she did with appealing regularity.

After all, they both had a lot more time on their hands since Juliet had fired them when the truth came out that they'd taken two antique books from the Chateau. That the diaries belonged to Millie's great-grandmother didn't sway the historical preservation society. When local reporters caught wind that a ninety-year-old treasure had been unearthed, it didn't take long for the *hows* to quickly follow.

The head of the historical preservation society had made a few threats. The sheriff, on the other hand, was so impressed that

Ben and Millie had turned over such a lucrative treasure that he persuaded the society to let the missing diaries pass with nothing more than a pink slip for each of them.

In all honesty, Ben was relieved that the truth had been laid bare. Insurance companies with long memories had quickly claimed the jewelry from the box, and the stocks had been returned to Howard Dawkins's family. With half the earnings from the sale of Joy's property — which Millie insisted he keep — he'd paid back all twenty-three people on the list. And he'd begun searching for the others who hadn't been named.

Ben finally had nothing to hide and plenty of time to spend with Millie. He couldn't ask for anything more.

"Ben! Get down here." She raised her voice to make sure it reached to every corner of his two-story craftsman home, a gift for himself when every debt had been repaid and Grandma Joy had been secured in a room with an ocean view, safe and cared for.

Ben patted his pocket as he loped down the wooden stairs, an odd knot forming in his stomach. He hadn't expected to be nervous. He was pretty sure they were on the same page. They had been since that day at the library. Every step, every task, they'd tackled together. The only thing they'd argued about was that hideous rug she'd wanted to put in his living room. And now he kind of liked it there.

But still. She was clearly more than a little excitable today, so maybe he should wait.

This could be good news or terrible news. Either way, they'd figure it out together. Which was absolutely the best thing about being with Millie Sullivan. He'd never thought he minded being alone. Until he wasn't. And he didn't plan on doing that again.

When he reached the turn in the stairs, he caught Millie's gaze and held it. Her cheeks were flushed, and she waved an envelope in her hand.

"What is it?" he asked.

"It's a letter."

Hustling down the last eight steps, he stopped in front of her, only then seeing the shimmer in her eyes. "Who's it from?" He reached for her arm and gave it a gentle squeeze.

With a trembling lower lip, she sucked in a quick breath. "It's a message from the Dawkins family. They . . . they're so thankful we returned the stocks, they decided to give us a finder's fee."

He laughed. "You always did say that's all we could claim. So, what is it?"

Her lip trembled again, and he bent his knees to look directly into her eyes. "Millie? What does the letter say?"

"They want to give us ten percent."

His insides did a swift barrel roll, and he blinked twice. "Ten percent of how much?"

She swallowed. "Seventy-three million."

"They're going to give us seven million dollars?"

"Seven point three." She pulled a slip of paper from the envelope and held it out to him. "And they already gave it to us."

The multicolored background of the certified check danced in the light, but the zeroes could not be denied. He let out a breathless laugh, scooped her up in his arms, and spun around the entryway.

"You can buy a whole library of books with that. You can go back to school. Or just never have to work again. Or you could give it all away."

When he finally stopped spinning her, she wrapped her arms around his neck. "What are you going to do with your half?"

Well, he wasn't going to get a better lead-in than that. Taking a deep breath, he looked her square in the face. "I think I'd like to take a vacation."

She smiled. "That sounds wonderful. You should take a break. You've earned it. You work so hard."

"I was thinking we should go together."

She nodded quickly. "Where would you like to go?"

He swallowed the lump in his throat and steeled everything inside of him. "I was thinking more about when I'd like to go."

"Okay, when do you want to go?"

"After we get married."

"Okay — wait. What? You want to . . ." Her eyes grew big and round and as blue as the ocean, and he wanted to set her down, but he never wanted to let go of her again in his life. "You want to marry me?"

He nodded very slowly, holding her gaze as he set her back on the floor. "I do."

"You know you can have the money. I already promised it to you." Her voice kept dropping, each word softer than the one before, and he couldn't tell if she was trying to talk herself into believing this was happening or talk him out of proposing.

He reached into his pocket and pulled out the velvet box, then dropped to one knee. "I don't need money or treasure or Coca-Cola stocks. I just need you, Millie Sullivan. Forever."

"You and me forever?" Her smile eclipsed her face before she leaned forward and pressed her lips to his. "That's the greatest treasure I could ever imagine."

ACKNOWLEDGMENTS

Daughter. Sister. Writer. Friend. These are some of the names I'm called, identities I'm known for. And the people who call me by them are the reason you're holding this book in your hands. I owe an enormous debt of gratitude to them.

To my mom and dad, who call me daughter and let me disappear for months at a time to write a book they won't get to read for many more. Your love story might not have come from the pages of a novel, but it is stable and steady and has given me wings to dream.

To Micah and Beth and Hannah and John and their families, who call me sister and Auntie E. You're the best encouragers around. I love being part of this family.

To the team at Revell — Vicki, Karen, Hannah, Michele, Jessica, and so many more — who call me writer and friend. Thank you for cheering me on. Thank you for believing in my stories and helping them become the best versions of themselves. What a privilege and a joy to work with this team.

To Rachel Kent, who calls me writer, client, and friend. Knowing you has been one of the great joys of my writing journey. I could not ask for a better agent.

To Amy Haddock, who calls me friend and willingly reads my very first drafts, red pen in hand. As always, your feedback is invaluable. Your friendship more so.

To Jessica Patch and Jill Kemerer, who call me friend. Your encouragement is such a boost, especially when I hit a rough writing patch. I look forward to each and every Vox from you both, knowing you'll have wise words and so much laughter to share.

To my heavenly Father, who calls me his own. The name you've given me is the one I cling to. Thank you for inviting me to join you on this creative journey.

ABOUT THE AUTHOR

Liz Johnson loves stories about true love. When she's not writing her next book, she works in marketing. She is the author of more than a dozen novels — including *The Red Door Inn, Where Two Hearts Meet,* and *On Love's Gentle Shore* — a *New York Times* bestselling novella, and a handful of short stories. She makes her home in Arizona, where she dotes on her five nieces and nephews.

ECONOMICS
OF AGRICULTURE

ECONOMICS
OF AGRICULTURE

HAROLD G. HALCROW

Professor of Agricultural Economics
University of Illinois at Urbana-Champaign

McGRAW-HILL BOOK COMPANY

New York□St. Louis□San Francisco□Auckland□Bogotá□Hamburg□Johannesburg
London□Madrid□Mexico□Montreal□New Delhi□Panama□Paris□São Paulo
Singapore□Sydney□Tokyo□Toronto

ECONOMICS OF AGRICULTURE

1234567890 DODO 89876543210
This book was set in Helvetica by University Graphics, Inc. The editors were Carol Napier, Micki Laiken, and Susan Gamer; the designer was Anne Canevari Green; the production supervisor was John Mancia.
The drawings were done by Fine Line Illustrations, Inc.
The cover photograph was taken by Barrie Rokeach.
R. R. Donnelley & Sons Company was printer and binder.

Library of Congress Cataloging in Publication Data

Halcrow, Harold G
    Economics of agriculture.

    Bibliography: p.
    Includes index.
    1. Agriculture—Economic aspects. I. Title.
HD1411.H353   338.1   79-20529
ISBN 0-07-025556-3

CONTENTS

PREFACE

Economics of Agriculture is a text for a foundation course applying principles of economics to agricultural production, marketing, and public policy. It begins with the basic concepts of economics and agriculture, develops a broad view of the central economic problems of agriculture, and applies the concepts and principles to show how these problems are solved. There are no prerequisites at the college or university level.

This book presents a basic outline for studying the economic organization of agriculture. It is an introduction to more advanced courses in agricultural economics and may also be used by agricultural students in the physical and biological sciences who require an understanding of the major economic problems of agriculture. Others may wish to read it to supplement their study of economics, sociology, and other social sciences.

A general hypothesis underlying *Economics of Agriculture* is that efficient learning requires orderly loss of unnecessary information. The study emphasizes definitions and the generalizations of economic theory, using only enough detail from the real world to illustrate the given point. The objective is to build a broad, imaginative vision of reality, and to begin to teach the rigor of economic analysis that applies.

The economics of agriculture is a broad and expanding subject that should be of interest to people almost everywhere. The great advances in agricultural production and trade have been nearly matched by growth of the world's population. The greatly accelerating need for more food to meet current and future nutritional goals is evident on every hand. The economic problems of agriculture are large indeed, and growing in importance.

The history of scientific and social progress clearly reveals, however, that well-stated problems yield to appropriate solutions. It is this thought that we carry with us as we proceed through the book. Study of our subject—we may all hope—will whet our appetites for more knowledge and accomplishment, to more nearly reach our own personal goals, and help to improve the society in which we live.

Acknowledgments

Many writers, teachers, and students have contributed to this work. Although none is accountable for my shortcomings, many are worthy of acknowledgment and appreciation. I wish to thank especially my associates at the University of Illinois: S. W. Williams, L. P. Fettig, S. C. Schmidt, and M. M. Wagner, with whom I have shared the teaching of the course on which *Economics of Agriculture* is based; D. I. Padberg, who encouraged me to reenter this area of teaching; and S. W. Williams, L. P. Fettig, and E. R. Swanson, who aided in the review of parts of the manuscript. Much appreciation is also due to my secretary, G. J. Metheny, who competently typed the manuscripts and helped me in other ways.

A major part of the current literature related to this study is listed in the Bibliography. In addition, a large number of journal articles have served as indispensable background, and liberal use has been made of public documents. Publications of the United States Department of Agriculture have been especially helpful. The Department's annual *Handbook of Agricultural Charts* has provided a convenient model for several of the statistical figures, and I am deeply indebted to the Department's Chartbook Committee and its associates for the accuracy and abundance of this material. We should all benefit from the richness of data with which this area of study is endowed.

Photographs in the text that are not otherwise credited have been supplied by University of Illinois photographers, Paul Hixson and Larry Baker. My colleague Franklin J. Reiss supplied the photographs on pages 23, 197, 296, 297, and 320. The chapter-opening photographs for Chapters 2, 5, and 9 are by Marilyn L. Schrut, New York City; the other chapter-opening photographs are from the University of Illinois.

I will appreciate hearing from readers who have suggestions for improvement of future editions of this book.

Harold G. Halcrow

ECONOMICS OF AGRICULTURE

1. SCOPE AND METHOD

"The central idea of economics, even when its Foundations alone are under discussion, must be that of living force and movement."

Alfred Marshall

Alfred Marshall (1842–1924), Cambridge University's great economist at the turn of this century, laid the foundation for a large part of current economic analysis. The central method in his work was partial analysis, involving specific parts of an economic system, from which more general results could be derived. His influence was so enormous that the first 25 years of this century are sometimes called the "age of Marshall," and his *Principles of Economics* still provides the central core of analysis for modern textbooks on economics.

The principles of economics applied generally to agriculture are the essence of our study. It is appropriate, therefore, to start with a statement on the scope of our subject and the methods that apply. We shall begin with three questions: What is economics? What is agriculture? How is economics applied to agriculture?

IN THIS CHAPTER

1. You will learn some of the basic concepts and uses of economics.
2. You will be able to visualize the economic scope and organization of agriculture.
3. You will see how economics is applied to agriculture.

WHAT IS ECONOMICS?

Definition: Economics is a scientific discipline concerned with the allocation of limited resources to satisfy unlimited wants.

The study of economics deals with *what* shall be produced, *how* it shall be produced, and *for whom* it shall be produced. Thus it deals with the principles of production and allocation of resources, the rules that producers must follow in organizing and managing resources. It involves prices because prices allocate resources and distribute incomes. If you want more of something, you offer a higher price. If you raise the price of something high enough, people will find a substitute for it.

Economics deals with marketing because things must get to where they are wanted, when they are wanted, and in the form that is desired before they can satisfy wants. The study of economics involves questions of income distribution: Who shall get what, and how much? It includes the influence of government on what shall be produced, how, and for whom. In short, economics deals with the human condition and how it can be improved. Economics is a system of study showing how the efficiency of our economic system can be improved, and how a person may find the best place in it.

Why study economics?

There are many reasons. Perhaps the most immediate is the idea of personal interest. Everyone makes economic decisions, and few if any of us can avoid making some important ones. How to allocate our scarce resources of time, talent, and money is a crucial part of economics. The study of economics helps us make more rational decisions about earning a living, saving and spending money, the costs and uses of our time, the allocation of our talents between work and play, and the development of our talents for the life ahead. In fact, the functioning of our entire economic system and society depends on the degree to which we as citizens and responsible people are economically literate, interested, and well informed.

Economic decision making

Economics, as has been noted, is concerned with the allocation of scarce resources to maximize benefits, choosing among competing wants. There are a few basic concepts, such as allocation, scarcity, goals, and time.

ALLOCATION

Allocation comprises the idea of putting resources and products to their best use. Economists tend to call anything that satisfies economic wants a *good.* Free goods are things that do not command a price. Economic goods are things that have value in exchange or may be obtained for a price. Prices, then, allocate these goods.

SCARCITY

There simply are not enough resources or goods to satisfy all the desires that people may have. The idea of scarcity enters into practically all economic decisions.

DELIBERATELY ESTABLISHED GOALS

Wants compete for the scarce resources. Economics provides tools to help us decide what kinds of resources and how much to use, even though the establishment of goals takes us beyond economics, into value judgments of what we want to be and do.

TIME

All goods have a time dimension. Individuals must choose, and a society must choose, between consumption and saving, and determine the investment of savings for future use. The more we save now, the more we should have for later. What is "rational" is what maximizes satisfaction over time.

The economizing process

Economists sometimes call the resources used in production *inputs* and the products of production *outputs.* The economizing process, then, involves three categories of decision making in regard to inputs and outputs:

1. *Getting more output from a given total amount of inputs.* Example: To get the most corn for a given total expenditure, we must allocate our money for seed, fertilizer, land, labor, cultivation, chemicals, etc., on the principle that the last dollar spent on each item will add as much to the total output as a dollar spent anywhere else.
2. *Getting the same amount of total output by using fewer inputs.* Example: To produce a given amount of corn, we will want to cut down on inputs that are not very productive and add more that are until the net addition to output from each additional unit of input used in each category is the same.
3. *Getting more output by increasing output relatively more than inputs.* Example: We add more inputs of fertilizer in the production of corn as long as the last unit added contributes enough to the total output to cover the added cost of that unit. When we see that the next unit that could be added will not "pay its way," we don't add it.

These three types of decisions are the essence of the economizing process. They are universal in their application. We will apply them to agriculture.

WHAT IS AGRICULTURE?

Definition

The word *agriculture* has long been associated with the growth of civilization. Originally it applied to the growing of crops and the raising of livestock. As economic systems have developed, it has taken on a broader meaning. The word still applies to growing crops and raising livestock, and the organization and management of farming and ranching. But now it also extends to firms and industries that manufacture farm machinery, produce fertilizer, market farm chemicals—all the services and supplies used in modern farming. It also covers the industries that process and market farm products: the huge grain firms, meat packers, cotton mills, fruit and vegetable dealers and processors, wholesale food firms, and retail supermarkets. It includes a publicly supported sector of government services and regulations, scientific research and education, experiment stations and educational extension services, and market news and economic analysis.

Definition: Agriculture is an industry covering the organization of resources—such as land and minerals, capital in a wide variety of forms, and management and labor—for the production and marketing of food and fiber.

Economic sectors of agriculture

Modern agriculture is organized in three economic sectors, which we identify primarily by function. When we study the economics of agriculture, these sectors must be related to each other. Economics is an organizing and managing discipline, and we must organize our thoughts to integrate, or coordinate, the economics of the system. The economic sectors are farming, agribusiness, and the publicly supported sector.

FARMING

Definition: A farm is an economic unit—a business firm—organized to produce crops or raise livestock. It involves land, capital resources in addition to land, management, and labor.

A farm in the midwestern United States with a concentrated livestock enterprise and land for growing grain. Note the field layout, which involves contour farming to reduce or control soil erosion.

Farming alone is a large and expanding industry, requiring continually increasing amounts of capital, advancing technology, and more high-level management. The capital requirements of modern farming are continuing to rise. Indeed, they are expanding at a rapid pace. But as the efficiency of scientific farming increases and management improves, fewer and fewer operators are needed to run farms. This has led some people to refer to farming as a declining industry, but that is not quite so.

The productivity per farm worker in countries where farming is most advanced is now several times as high as it was a short while ago. Continuing increases in the productivity of farm workers result in more food being raised on a given amount of land with less labor. Modern farming is therefore dynamic and growing, and it requires people with scientific training, management training and capability, ambition, and skill. Knowledge of economics must be combined with chemistry, engineering, pathology, agronomy, entomology, genetics, nutrition, and animal and soil science.

The successful farmer is a broad-ranging person. The successful farm family generally has a good life, with opportunities for contact with nature and outdoor living to an extent that relatively few can enjoy. But farming is also an occupation with many economic pitfalls. Severe penalties are in store for the unwary, inefficient, or poorly trained farm manager. Mistakes in economic judgment have forced many to fail. As farming has developed, both the penalties for poor economics and the rewards for good economics have become larger. You can learn a great deal about economics by a study of the farm sector. Regardless of whether you are a farmer, the farm sector is a useful model for the study of economics.

AGRIBUSINESS

In all countries, the development of agriculture is characterized by relatively rapid growth in businesses that provide farm services and supplies, as well as businesses that process and market farm products. These businesses have grown so rapidly in the United States that a new name has been developed to describe them: *agribusiness.*

Definition: Agribusiness includes firms and economic enterprises organized to produce and sell services and supplies to farmers for use in farm production and farm living; it includes firms and industries that buy and process farm products and distribute them through wholesale and retail markets. The first groups are called

farm service supply industries, and the second *agricultural processing-marketing industries*

Farm service supply industries   The farm service supply industries
transform minerals and other raw materials into farm machinery, fertilizer and other farm chemicals, and a variety of other commodities
and services used in growing crops and raising livestock. In less
developed countries this industry is generally small or poorly developed. But as countries develop, this industry also develops and
grows because it delivers farm services and supplies—farm inputs,
for short—to farmers at a cost or price that is attractive to them. The
new products either complement or displace other inputs when
farmers find that it is economical or profitable to use them. Thus,
tractors displace horses or other work animals when it is found that
costs can be reduced, or that the work can be done faster and more
efficiently. Fertilizer comes into use when it is discovered that the
added output is worth more than the added cost of the fertilizer.
Farm chemicals are used to reduce the amount of cultivation when
it is found that the chemicals control weeds at less cost, or more
completely, than alternative systems. The new innovations are either
cost-reducing or output-increasing; they may be both when inputs

One of the products of agribusiness in farm service supply. Large tractors such as
this have greatly increased the amount of land that can be farmed by a single farm
family. This heavy soil is being worked with a chisel plow, which leaves the land
rough and helps to retard erosion. Liquid nitrogen, with or without some additional
fertilizer ingredients in solution, is being forced under pressure into the soil.

that are complemented or displaced become available for other uses.

The growth of farm service supply industries is one of the important indicators of a country's stage of economic development. The products of these industries are used to increase the yield of crops and livestock and reduce the amount of land required to grow feed for work animals. This brings about other changes in economic organization and management, on farms and elsewhere, that save resources and release them for other uses. Labor requirements for farm production are reduced. As a general rule, firms increase in size and scale as farming becomes a growing market for the products of the farm service supply industries.

A major result is the production of more farm products at a relative decline in the total resources used or employed. The farm sector tends to shrink in relative economic terms as the farm service supply industries grow, to the extent that the value of the products of farm service supply may greatly exceed the value added in farm production. In 1977, for example, American gross farm income after inventory adjustment was $118.5 billion. Total farm production expenses (Figure 1-1) were $97.9 billion. This left a net farm income of $20.6 billion as a return for the labor, capital, and management of operators' families. Not all the farm production expenses went to the service supply industries, but a large part did.

These industries, now include seed, feed, and fertilizer companies; manufacturers of chemical pesticides, pharmaceuticals, farm machinery, and equipment; and professional management, banking, and credit services. A government-sponsored credit system, commercial banks and insurance companies, and individuals and others lend money to farmers and agribusiness firms. Thus credit institutions, or financial intermediaries as they are sometimes called, are part of the agribusiness complex. The service supply industries employ two or three times as many people in service to agriculture as now work on farms, and employment in these businesses continues to expand. The study of these industries must be included in the economics of agriculture.

Agricultural processing-marketing industries   The modern industrial economy is also characterized by a substantial development and growth of these industries, which in essence buy farm products and transform them into commodities suitable for consumption. In fact, the kind and amount of services added by these industries is also an indicator of a country's development and growth. In primitive or less-developed countries much of agriculture is devoted to subsistence, and few services are added to farm products. The bulk

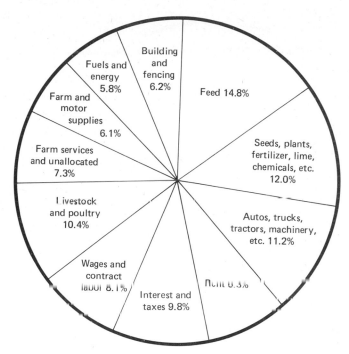

Figure 1-1   Distribution of farm production expenditures in the United States, 1977. The total expenditure of $97.9 billion resulted in an average expenditure per farm of $36,238. (Compare this figure with total farm family income: $20.6 billion net farm income + $31.4 billion off-farm income = about $52 billion.)

of farm produce is delivered to consumers as unrefined food and fiber, unprocessed grain or livestock, or raw fruits and vegetables. As an economy develops, consumers demand more and more refinements in their food supply. They are willing to pay for more processing; increased convenience in terms of packaging, preserving, and freezing; and enrichment of the product by various additives. Agricultural processing-marketing industries grow because people are willing to pay for the services that are added. The modern supermarket offers a testimonial to the level of development or degree of affluence achieved in an economy.

The agribusinesses that process and market farm products are important features in any economic picture of agriculture. Approximately two-thirds of the money that American consumers spend on farm food products goes to these industries (see Figure 1-2). They include grain mills, meat packing, dairy plants, food-freezing firms, food drying and canning, manufacturing of fats and oils, lumber milling, grain barge lines, trucking firms, and railroad services.

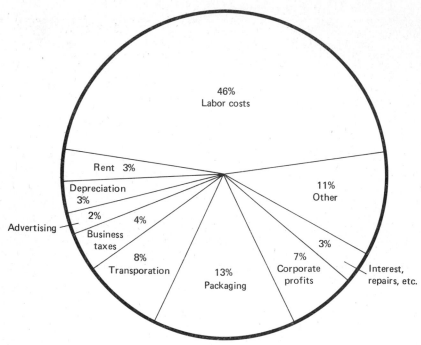

Figure 1-2   Farm food marketing bill in the United States, 1977. This is an estimate of charges by agribusiness processing-marketing firms for transporting, processing, and distributing foods originating on American farms. In 1977 the bill was $129 billion, or about two-thirds of consumer expenditures for farm foods. (*Note:* "Transportation" is intercity rail and truck; "corporate profits" are before taxes; "other" includes utilities, fuel, promotion, local hired transportation, insurance, etc.)

Every type of business or firm that processes or helps market farm food products is included in this category. These agribusinesses now employ four or five times as many people as are on the farm, and employment in these industries is still expanding.

THE PUBLICLY SUPPORTED SECTOR

The development and growth of agriculture in the modern industrial economy is also marked by advances in a wide array of publicly supported services: scientific research; education, including elementary and secondary education, vocational agriculture, agricultural colleges and universities, and cooperative extension services; government services such as food inspection, market news, and sanitary regulations; market supervision; prevention or regulation of monopoly; and government farm price and income programs.

The buildings of the college of agriculture on this large university campus are part of the publicly supported sector of agriculture. The research and education accomplished in facilities such as these have helped to revolutionize agriculture.

Although the farm sector is often cited as the classic example of relatively unregulated free enterprise, it must be evident that farming and the two agribusiness sectors require a great amount of publicly supported services to achieve a high level of efficiency. Investment in the farm sector grows as a result of publicly supported services, which reduce costs or spread the costs over a wider area. These services stimulate economic development, change the allocation of resources between farming and agribusiness, and influence the distribution of income between agriculture and the rest of the economy and within agriculture itself. Employment does not appear to be growing as rapidly in the public sector as in agribusiness; in some areas it is declining. But the sector has a continuing requirement for people with skill and ambition, frequently to play an expanding role in the economic system. The economics of the public sector as it applies to agriculture is certainly part of our study of the conomics of agriculture.

HOW IS ECONOMICS
APPLIED TO AGRICULTURE?

Development of the economics of agriculture has been molded by two major forces: a rapidly changing economic environment and an unfolding economic science. The early work began as applied economics rather than as a new science, and the economics of agriculture has continued to develop in the same vein. It applied then and still applies to the practical problems of farm organization and management. The principles of the economics of production are indispensable to the successful farm manager. Economics was first applied to solving problems in land tenure, or the renting of land, and to growing crops and raising livestock.

Over several decades, the economics of agriculture has broadened in scope while becoming more precise as an analytical tool. In the 1920s, the depressed state of agriculture brought many new problems centering on the relatively low prices of farm products, or the disparity between prices of farm and nonfarm products, and the overexpanded agricultural production in relation to domestic and export markets. Increasing attention was given to the economic problems of reducing the costs of production on farms and finding ways to improve markets for farm products. Farm management, cost accounting, and farm business management were emphasized. Then more attention was given to marketing, both to help individual farmers learn more about the economics of marketing and to help the nation create a more efficient marketing system. Staff members of the United States Department of Agriculture and economists in colleges and universities began to work together on problems of agricultural production and marketing, prices and trade, and transportation, among others.

The Great Depression of the 1930s, with its still lower prices for farm products, brought a new urgency to the solution of these problems. The nation adopted a sweeping new farm program, designed by agricultural economists, to hold down farm production and raise prices. A new era in economic planning had begun. The Second World War brought renewed emphasis on the application of economics to the improvement of farm production. Finally, the increasingly rapid development of agriculture has helped define a broader and more secure base for the application of economic principles to all phases of agriculture.

This has given the economics of agriculture a broader scope now, while our methods of analysis have grown more precise and therefore more practical in their application. People with training in agricultural economics now work in a variety of careers: (1) in farming, as farm owners, operators, or professional farm managers or appraisers; (2) in all phases of farm service supply industries, as economic analysts, planners, and managers; (3) in agricultural processing-marketing firms and related businesses; and (4) in universities, government, and other public agencies, as teachers, researchers, program leaders, and extension workers. Not everyone who works in these occupations is an agricultural economist or is regarded as one. Indeed, perhaps most are not, and should not be. But nearly everyone who works on problems related to the economics of agriculture can benefit from study of the subject. This fact is recognized in the organization of programs of study in colleges and universities.

Agricultural economics includes a variety of subjects and courses of study, generally beginning with an introductory course in the economics of agriculture. This is intended to cover the economics of agricultural production and marketing, and to review the major economic problems of agriculture and related industries. It can or should cover the basic economics of the farm firm as an introduction to farm management and production economics. It should give a perspective on marketing, showing how economic principles apply not only to the marketing and processing of farm products but to the farm service supply industries. It should help us understand some of the broad issues in public policy, such as the role of economic growth in an economy, the effects of selected government programs, and the role of international trade.

After the basic course, agricultural economists tend to pursue more specific in-depth study of all aspects of the economics of agriculture. This requires a number of courses dealing more specifically with the farm firm: organization and management, taxation, finance, appraisals, professional farm management, and advanced problems in farm management.

Several courses in the marketing of agricultural products complement the courses in farm-firm production. These courses may be organized along commodity lines: grain, livestock, dairy, fruit, and vegetable marketing. Such courses may also be organized more according to function, covering the general principles of marketing, agricultural business or agribusiness management, cooperative marketing, futures markets and trading, retail food marketing, agricultural statistics, and agricultural-price analysis.

Courses in agricultural economics include the economics of development, agricultural history, food, and agricultural policy. The subject has a strong tie to the parent discipline of economics and to related social sciences such as sociology, history, and geography. Thus students must complement this program of study with courses in economics and mathematics, physical and biological sciences, language and communication, history, and geography, among others. A one-semester course, which is the basis for this book, is not intended to displace these other courses. Rather it is designed to present a foundation for a general understanding and for further study, while broadening your vision in economics and agriculture and presenting some of the basic analytical concepts that are useful in further studies.

SUMMARY

Economics has been defined as a scientific discipline concerned with allocating limited resources to satisfy unlimited wants. It deals with *what* shall be produced, *how*, and *for whom*. Considerations of both efficiency and equity are involved: how goods and services can be produced more efficiently, and how a society can achieve the desired standards of equity in distribution of them. The economizing process has three categories: (1) how to get more output from a given total amount of inputs, (2) how to get the same amount of total output by using fewer inputs, and (3) how to get more output by increasing output more than inputs.

Agriculture includes farming and ranching; agribusinesses that produce and sell services and supplies to farmers; agribusinesses that buy, process, and distribute farm products; and a publicly supported sector. Transformation of traditional agriculture in a developing economy generally involves integration of farms and ranches into fewer and larger units, relatively rapid growth of agribusiness, and increased output from the publicly supported sector. Agriculture in a developed economy is generally highly industrialized; uses advanced science, management, and technology, with more total capital; and increases output with a long-term decline in the prices of farm products relative to the prices of inputs.

The application of economics to agriculture has been molded by a rapidly changing economic environment and an unfolding economic science. The economics of agriculture has broadened in scope while becoming more precise as an analytical tool and more useful in solving practical problems of organization and management. Advanced study in the economics of agriculture involves a wide and varied array of courses. People with training in the subject also work in a variety of occupations, with generally expanding challenges and opportunities. This book is designed to serve as a foundation for studying the economics of agriculture.

IMPORTANT TERMS
AND CONCEPTS

   Economics
      Allocation
      Scarcity

Economic goods
Economic decision making
The economizing process
Inputs and outputs
Agriculture
Farming
Agribusiness
The public sector
Economics applied to agriculture

LOOKING AHEAD

In our study we shall identify and classify the central economic problems of every agricultural economy and develop the principles or theories by which they may be solved. We shall look at the resources that are used in producing and marketing agricultural produoto in light of the economic problems and potentials in future development and use. We shall study costs of production, principles of resource allocation, and the various effects of competition in production and marketing.

QUESTIONS AND EXERCISES

1. What is economics? With what questions does it deal? Why study economics?
2. What are the basic ideas in economic decision making? Why are they important?
3. What is meant by the economizing process? What is an input? An output? What are the three categories of decision making in the economizing process? State the rules that apply, and illustrate each with an example.
4. What is agriculture? What are the main economic sectors of agriculture? How are they defined? What is accomplished in each? Do the rules of the economizing process apply? If so, how?
5. Characterize the development of the economics of agriculture. Why did people start to work on the topic? What were the main problems? How have these problems developed?
6. What are the main topics of study in or related to the economics of agriculture?

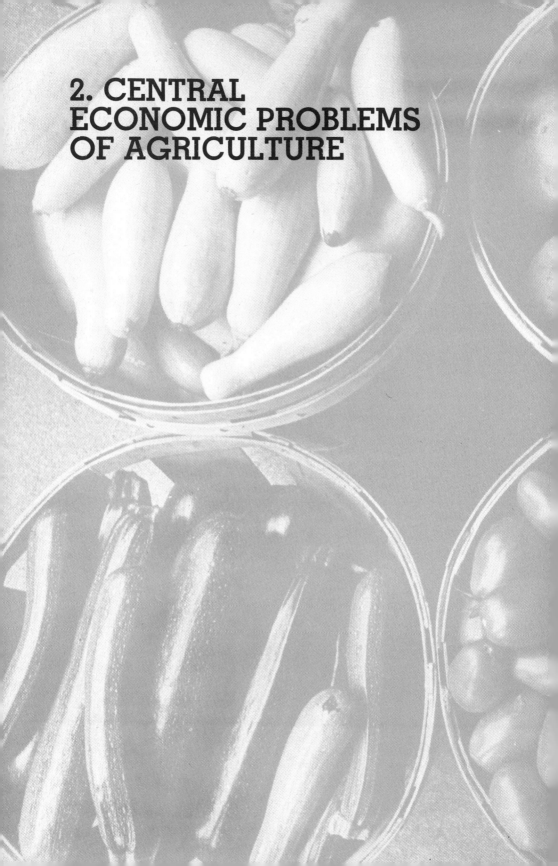

2. CENTRAL ECONOMIC PROBLEMS OF AGRICULTURE

❚❚The problem in life is to use resources 'economically,' to make them go as far as possible in the production of the desired results. The general theory of economics is, therefore, simply the rationale of life.**❚❚**

Frank H. Knight

Frank Hyneman Knight (1885–1972), whose professional career in economics spanned more than half a centruy, the last half of which was at the University of Chicago, will continue to have a deep and broadening influence on economic thought. No social reformer in the ordinary sense of the term, he believed that reform and improvement in the social order could come only through acquisition of ability and willingness to use our minds. He taught that all principles have their limits—most of them are both right and wrong, they hold more or less, and the need for judgment can never be denied. He related profit to uncertainty, which he distinguished sharply from risk, and he stated that where there is no genuine uncertainty, there are no decisions. Economics, then, is a discipline for dealing with uncertainty.

We learned in Chapter 1 about the organization of agriculture and how agriculture and the study of economics are related. Now let us discuss the central problems of every economy and consider how they may be solved. A problem is a situation with alternative solutions, and any problem in economics may be defined in terms of the various alternative courses of action open to society. What are the central economic problems of agriculture, and how are they solved?

IN THIS CHAPTER

1. You will see how the problems of agriculture may be defined, and observe the values and goals that are generally taken into account in defining them.
2. You will see how the law of increasing (relative) costs enters into the determination of production possibilities.
3. You will learn the relationship between the law of diminishing returns and economic growth.

GOALS

Every society faces three fundamental questions: (1) What amounts of the various possible services and products—wheat, beef, cotton, and so on—shall be produced? (2) How shall the various services and products be produced? By small farms or large farms? By corporations or cooperatives? By private industry or government? (3) For whom shall these goods be produced? Who shall get the income? Farmers or agribusiness? Big farmers or little farmers? Workers or financiers? Shall the government intervene to support and stabilize farm prices or let the free market work? How far must farm income drop before the government intervenes? How much higher do the prices of food products have to go before the government intervenes on the other side?

All these questions are related to the central problems of what, how, and for whom to produce. How they are answered depends primarily on our values, expressed as goals—that is, on how important we hold a particular result to be and what we will give up (or ask someone else to give up) in order to get it. The goals are the combination of things that can be achieved, or achieved to some degree, by limiting one to get more of another. We must be explicit about this and state some goals in specific terms. The following goals are suggested: economic progress and growth, stability, justice or equity, freedom, and security.

Economic progress and growth

Definition: Economic progress is an increase in the total amount of goods and services available per capita.

For example, if the output of goods and services increases by 3 percent annually and the population grows by 1 percent, the rate of economic progress is 2 percent annually.

Economic *growth* is not necessarily the same as economic *progress,* because growth may be measured either as a rate of increase in goods and services per capita or as a rate of increase in the national output of goods and services, ignoring population growth. Economic statements on growth are—somewhat confusingly—not entirely consistent, being expressed sometimes as one rate and sometimes as the other. When you are concerned with growth, it is important to know which measure is being used (see pages 00 16).

Economic progress may be taken as a general goal, not just a goal for agriculture. You may wish to think about what you want: the opportunity for a good job, a rewarding career; a good home; a pleasant community; good family life; more recreation. What else?

It took about 40 years to change from one of these tractors to another. How would this change in technology tend to affect the organization of farms? The number of farms? The distribution of the farm labor force?

No economy on earth can provide everything everybody wants. Economic progress is a goal not just for the general society but for individual industries such as agriculture, firms, and families as well.

Economic stability

Stability can be measured in a number of ways: prices, production, income, consumption, saving, investment, and earnings on investment. A stable economy is generally desired; economic judgments can be made more accurately, producers can be more certain about their decisions concerning what and how to produce, and public affairs can be managed more efficiently.

Agriculture is unusual among the major industries in regard to its problem with stability. For American agriculture, the total output is very stable from year to year. Generally, it varies only a percentage point or two from the long-term trend. Even the very bad crop year of 1974 did not reduce the index of output very much because livestock producers, reacting to the high feed prices, sold more livestock than they would normally sell. Stability of output is not the major problem of agriculture.

Stability of prices and incomes is quite another matter. Many farm prices are very unstable, and so farm incomes are unstable. How to achieve more stable prices is one of the most important economic problems of agriculture. When prices are unstable or hard to predict, farm producers cannot be efficient in deciding what and how to produce, and their incomes will be unstable. Although it is possible for some consumers to gain by price instability—say, by filling the freezer when prices are low—price changes are generally irritating to consumers. For one thing, it becomes harder and harder to buy efficiently. Unstable prices reduce the efficiency of the economy and create unearned windfall gains and losses. How much and what kind of intervention there should be in agricultural markets in order to achieve greater price stability is a central problem in our study of the economics of agriculture.

Economic justice or equity

Economic justice deals most specifically with answers to the question: For whom? A just society, according to the work ethic, will strive to reward its members according to their productivity, or contribution to society. But a just society will also try to provide its members an equal opportunity to be productive. When these concepts are applied to agriculture, the first leads to the idea of a fair price, or fair return, while the second leads to help for the poor both at home and abroad.

What methods shall be used, and how far shall a society go in trying to provide economic justice? The concept of a fair price is fundamental in most legislation establishing supports for farm prices. But what constitutes a fair price is not easy to decide. Any effective program of price supports will have serious consequences for farm production, storage programs, domestic markets, and international trade. We will study some of the alternatives and their consequences after we have developed theories of production costs, prices, and determination of output.

The second concept—an equal opportunity to be productive— leads to the establishment of free public schools, special programs for the disadvantaged or underprivileged, aid to the handicapped and indigent, and progressive income and inheritance taxes. The difficult questions concern both what methods to use and how far to go in trying to provide equal opportunity. For whom to produce is—in a broad economic context—the most difficult question.

The concept of equal opportunity has a uniquely important application to agriculture. The American concept of the family farm as the fundamental organization of the firm in farming comes from the idea of providing equal opportunity for families to be productive. But as farming has become more what economists call *capital-intensive*—that is, as it uses more capital per farm worker—equal

Field workers on American farms have had the lowest average annual income of any major sector of the labor force of the United States. Is this economically just? Why, or why not? If not, what would be required to achieve economic justice for them?

opportunity becomes more difficult to provide. A relatively large amount of capital is required now to establish a person in farming. But more help from the government or elsewhere to get more young people started in farming will inflate land prices and other assets and contribute to other broad price and income problems. A large investment in both physical goods and education is a requirement for becoming a successful farmer. The basic agricultural philosophy gives considerable attention to equal opportunity, difficult as its actual achievement may be.

Economic freedom

Economic freedom also has various implications. It may mean simply the opportunity to take a job of your choice, prepare for a career of your choice, and move when or where an opportunity occurs. It involves flexibility but implies something more. The absence of government constraints, or a minimum of constraining rules and regulations, is generally considered important. In a still broader context, however, freedom means open public debate, an uncensored press, the option to form political groups, and the power to dissent.

Traditionally, farming has been considered among the most free of economic enterprises. On a family farm you can be your own boss, even though you must respond to prices and markets, the changing of the seasons, and the rhythm of production. The farmer need not punch a time clock or be subject to the criticism of a manager or supervisor. Freedom is an important tradition in agriculture, with important economic implications.

Economic security

Finally, we must recognize that people want economic security. If you are fired from a job without cause or go broke in business, the fact that your country has economic progress, stability, justice, and freedom will give you little satisfaction. Consequently people try to set up a system that provides economic security. Professors want tenure so that they can discuss controversial questions without fear of repercussions; people in labor unions want job security; bankers want security for loans; farmers want price supports or income supplements, readily available credit, and adequate crop insurance.

Security is never absolute, however, and it is the degree and condition of security that is important in economics. One major problem in agriculture is that managers must continually adapt or adjust to new circumstances and conditions. They must take

Notice the organization and variety of jobs that can be done in this well-equipped farm machinery repair shop. What are the implications for economic freedom? For economic security?

chances, and the only prudent thing to do is balance the opportunities for gain against the risks and uncertainties of possible loss. Dealing with uncertainty is the essence of management. Economic mistakes in agriculture can be reduced by a system that provides more security, but a completely secure system cannot be established without discarding the efficiencies of making economic judgments and taking risks. How far to go in providing security for people in agriculture is an important central economic problem of our study.

PRODUCTION POSSIBILITIES

As was discussed earlier, economics must constantly contend with scarcity as a basic fact of life. The idea is that at any time, or in any given condition, there exists only a finite amount of human and non-human resources. Even with the best technical knowledge, only a limited maximum amount of individual goods and services can be produced. Limited resources and technology mean limited output, and these limitations necessitate a choice between alternative production possibilities. To establish this all-important principle, let us illustrate it with arithmetic examples and geometric diagrams.

Let us assume that there is just so much land available for grow-

Table 2-1   Selected production possibilities for feed grains and soybeans in the United States

Production possibilities	Soybeans, million tons	Feed grains, million tons
A	0	280
B	25	257
C	50	225
D	75	180
E	100	115
F	125	0

Note: Hypothetical data.

ing feed grains and soybeans in the United States. Assume also that the state of technology is fixed, but farmers can shift readily back and forth between feed grains (corn, barley, oats, and grain sorghum) and soybeans. Hypothetical production possibilities can be presented as in Table 2-1.

The critical point, as demonstrated in Table 2-1, is that to get more soybeans with known technology and full use of all the available land, a certain quantity of feed grains must be given up, or sacrificed. In going from 0 to 25 million tons[1] of soybeans, for example, 23 million tons of feed grains is sacrificed. As we go down the table from A to B and eventually to F, more and more feed grains must be given up, or sacrificed, to get a certain additional quantity of soybeans. Similarly, if we go up the table from F to E to A, each successive sacrifice of 25 million tons of soybeans results in lower and lower increases in feed grains. This demonstrates the law of increasing (relative) costs, which is discussed below.

Production-possibilities curve: p-p curve, or p-p frontier

To understand the production possibilities in Table 2-1, let us view these data in a diagram. A simple two-dimensional diagram puts the output of feed grains on the vertical (or y) axis and the output of soybeans on the horizontal (or x) axis, as in Figure 2-1.

Each point on the diagram represents a production possibility for feed grains and soybeans. Point *D,* for example, represents 180

[1]In this text, all references to *tons* mean *metric tons*. The metric unit is used here to reflect its common use throughout the United States.

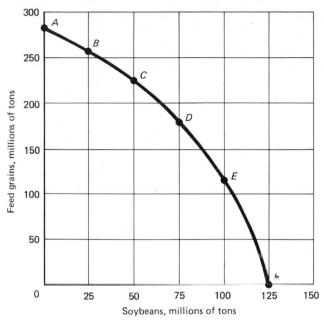

Figure 2-1 Production-possibilities curve, or p-p frontier. Each point on the p-p curve represents a *maximum output* of any two products, such as feed grains and soybeans—hence, a *frontier*. It is also a *transformation curve*, because in moving from one point to another, one product is in a sense "transformed" into another.

million tons of feed grains and 75 million tons of soybeans. By connecting these points, we form what is called a *production-possibilities curve* or sometimes a *production-possibilities frontier.* The term *frontier* is used on the assumption that with the resource limitations that have been imposed, production cannot extend outward or beyond the designated line—the *frontier.* This is also sometimes called a *transformation curve* because in moving from one alternative to another, say from *C* to *D,* feed grains are in a sense "transformed" into soybeans.

The production-possibilities (or p-p) frontier represents a fundamental fact that we can use over and over as it appears and reappears in a variety of forms: When we have reached the limit of available resources, or the resources are fully employed, some amount of one good must be given up to produce more of another. From a reading of the p-p frontier, we may determine between any two points just how much of one good must be given up to obtain a specified amount of another.

Law of increasing (relative) costs

The last column in Table 2-2 shows the amount of feed grains that must be given up, or sacrificed, between any two points on the p-p frontier to produce an additional 25 million tons of soybeans. As we proceed from A to B to F, however, more and more feed grains must be given up, or sacrificed.

The production possibilities in Table 2-2 are based on the assumption that the resources and technologies are not completely flexible, or equally adaptable to use in producing both feed grains and soybeans. If soybeans had not been discovered or developed, the nation might have produced 280 million tons of feed grains. Then, as soon as soybeans were developed for commercial use, it became possible to produce 25 million tons of soybeans while sacrificing only 23 million tons of feed grains. This is because—let us say—soybeans can be fitted into a rotation, making use of previously unused farm labor, spreading out the seeding and harvest seasons, using land especially adaptable to soybeans, and so on. These advantages diminish progressively, however, as more soybeans are produced, until to get the last 25 million tons of soybeans it is necessary to sacrifice 115 million tons of feed grains. Some land may have to be kept idle to control diseases that affect soybeans, and some land that is productive for growing feed grains is not so adaptable for soybeans.

Table 2-2   Selected production possibilities for feed grains and soybeans in the United States

Production possibilities	Soybeans, million tons	Feed grains, million tons	Feed grains sacrificed to produce 25 million tons of soybeans
A	0	280	
			23
B	25	257	
			32
C	50	225	
			55
D	75	180	
			65
E	100	115	
			115
F	125	0	

Note: Hypothetical data.

This lack of perfect flexibility, or complete interchangeability among resources, accounts for the bowed-out, concave shape (from below) of the p-p frontier. The resulting increases in the amount of one product that is sacrificed to produce a given amount of another is expressed as the law of increasing (relative) costs, in which case the costs are expressed in terms of the product that is sacrificed, rather than in money terms as dollars and cents.

Definition: The law of increasing (relative) costs states that to produce equal extra amounts of a certain service or product, an ever-increasing amount of another service or product must be sacrificed.

P-p frontier
and opportunity cost

Movement from point to point on the p-p frontier means that the opportunity to produce something must be sacrificed to produce something else. In the illustration, the opportunity to produce some feed grains is given up in order to produce more soybeans, and vice versa. This is a general, or universal, proposition. To go to college, for example, you must give up the opportunity to do something else—earn income or enjoy more leisure. In addition to the cash outlay, you give up another opportunity, and this may be expressed as a cost.

Definition: Opportunity cost is the value of services or products (goods and services, commodities, leisure, and so on) that must be given up or sacrificed to obtain an additional amount of any service or product.

The last column in Table 2-2 shows the amount of feed grains that must be sacrificed in each case to produce an additional 25 million tons of soybeans. The sacrifice of not growing feed grains is, in this case, the *opportunity cost* of growing soybeans. To use the farm resources in growing soybeans means that the opportunity of growing feed grains is forgone. This illustrates the general proposition in economics that costs have to do with missed opportunities or forgone alternatives. Note that in this case the farmer does not have to pay out any money for just giving up the opportunity to grow feed grains, but the opportunity cost is nevertheless an implicit cost that must be taken into account.

Although the terminology of economists is not always uniform in dealing with opportunity costs, the concept is so important that we shall run into it again and again. You should not have much trouble with it if you just think of the value to you of an opportunity that is forgone. A student who loves football, for example, may have a higher opportunity cost for studying on an autumn afternoon than one who does not. The opportunity cost of writing this book is much higher on a pleasant summer afternoon than it is on a blustery winter day. The concept of opportunity cost is indeed universal.

There are many reasons why agricultural production may not come up to the p-p frontier. Poor weather may cause bad crops. There are diseases of both crops and animals with which to contend. Low prices may discourage a farmer from doing certain things. For instance, low prices may make it unprofitable for a farmer to put on a full dose of fertilizer and other farm chemicals. In some cases a grain farmer may not even cover the current out-of-pocket costs; then it would not pay to plant any crop. There may be government programs to control supply or retire land from crops. Point *U* in Figure 2-2 represents production below the p-p frontier. Point *W* is unattainable with the limited resources and technologies.

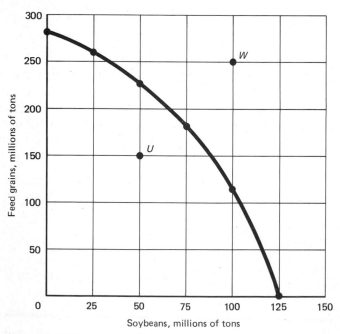

Figure 2-2   Production-possibilities curve, or p-p frontier. Point *U*, which is below the p-p frontier, represents a restriction in production. Point *W*, beyond the frontier, is unattainable with the limited resources and technologies.

PRODUCTION POSSIBILITIES
WITH EXPANDING RESOURCES
AND ADVANCING TECHNOLOGIES

Definition: Economic growth can be defined as an outward shift of the production-possibilities curve as a result of expanding resources and advancing technologies. (Although this does not *require* an increase in goods and services per capita, economic growth more often than not implies this.)

The p-p frontier shifts outward, or to the right and upward, when there are expanding resources and advancing technologies. How it shifts—how much and how fast—depends on all the circumstances that affect production, such as the availability of new resources or the efficiency with which new technologies can be applied. When hybrid corn was developed, for example, the p-p frontier shifted outward as the new technology for production of corn was applied to the other limited resources. In effect, the new technology became a resource. The total resources available for production of corn expanded as technology advanced, and economic growth occurred.

Food and nonfood production

To illustrate economic growth and progress let us shift from grains and soybeans to a concept of food and nonfood, with the latter including everything that a society produces except food. In Figure 2-3, with food products on the x axis and nonfood products on the y axis, we may visualize a as a poor country before economic growth or development and b as a developed country both before and after growth or development—that is, where progress has occurred.

Before economic development and progress production in the poor country (Figure 2-3a) is at point A. Most of its resources must go into food production, and there is little left over to produce other things. In poor countries it is no accident that a large part of the total population is in agriculture, primarily in the farm sector.

With economic development or growth the p-p frontier moves outward as in Figure 2-3b. Because of economic progress—an increase in total goods and services per capita—the society's position on the new p-p frontier shifts upward, resulting in a relatively greater increase in nonfood than in food. With economic development and progress the shift goes from A to B.

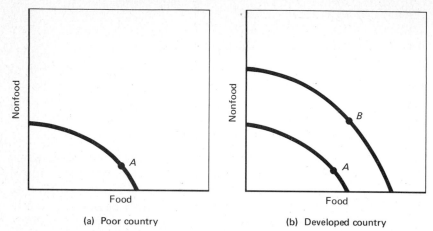

(a) Poor country   (b) Developed country

Figure 2-3   Economic growth and development shift the p-p frontier outward. (a) Before development, the poor country with a p-p frontier at A must use most of its resources to produce food, with little left for nonfood. (b) With economic growth and development, the country shifts from A to B, with relatively more expansion in nonfood than food production.

Capital formation and current consumption of food and nonfood products

An economy must save and invest if economic growth is to occur. Although it is possible to base some growth on borrowing, in the end growth depends on saving and investment. If an economy can produce just enough for current consumption, it will have no saving and investment, and no growth. Figure 2-4 illustrates how different countries may choose between capital formation and current consumption of food and nonfood.

Before growth, as shown in Figure 2-4a, the three countries differ in the ratio of capital formation to current consumption. After growth, as shown in Figure 2-4b, the difference still exists. The third country still has the highest ratio of capital formation to current consumption. Figure 2-4, however, does not indicate the allocation of current production and consumption between food and nonfood. But the implication, carried over from Figure 2-3, is that as the countries develop and economic progress occurs, an increasing percentage of their total current production and consumption is allocated to nonfood products.

Figure 2-4 illustrates the most dramatic feature of the economies of the modern developed countries: the unprecedented vigor

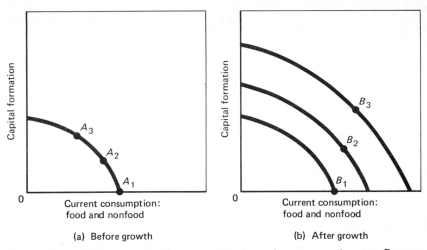

Figure 8-1 (*a*) Before growth, three countries have the same p-p frontier. Country 1, which does not save and invest, puts all its resources into goods for current consumption. Hence it has no capital formation. Country 2, which has some savings and investment, produces less for current consumption, and has some capital formation. Country 3, which saves and invests more, produces least for current consumption and has the highest rate of capital formation. (*b*) After growth, the three countries have different p-p frontiers. Country 1, which did not save and invest, has the same p-p frontier as before; no capital was formed. Country 2, which saved and invested some of its production, has a new p-p frontier, higher than its original one. Country 3, which saves and invests most, has the highest p-p frontier. Capital formation permits countries 2 and 3 to have more capital formation and more for current consumption.

of the sustained economic growth that has occurred and continues to occur. Saving and investment account for more current consumption and more growth. But the lesson that is being applied to agriculture is one of the most important for all countries. *Capital formation is required for the economic growth of agriculture.* Farmers must be able to earn enough to exceed the immediate requirements of the family for current consumption, and the country must provide capital goods for agricultural production at prices that are competitive or attractive enough for farmers to benefit from the purchase and use of these goods. The cheaper these goods are produced relative to the prices of farm products, the faster economic growth will occur in agriculture.

Holding farm product prices below competitive levels, maintaining high interest rates on farm credit, or failing to encourage efficient agribusiness will retard agricultural growth. Many governments have learned this lesson. Those which have not have committed their agricultural economies to slower rates of growth, while the others are prospering with more capital formation and more current consumption of both food and nonfood.

Law of diminishing returns

The p-p curves, or frontiers, may be used to illustrate a famous and widely applied relationship generally known as the *law of diminishing returns.* This law deals with the relation not between two goods or products (such as feed grains and soybeans, or food and nonfood), but between an *input* of production (such as labor) and the *output* that it helps produce (such as food).

Definition: The law of diminishing returns states that diminishing returns occur when with each successive input added to a fixed amount of other inputs, the output is increased less than it was from the immediately preceding added input.

EXAMINING OPTIONS

Imagine that a rich, somewhat eccentric relative has died and left you a section of good farmland. The will provides that you cannot sell it for a certain period of time, cannot lease or buy more land to add to it, and can grow only corn or soybeans on it. However, you have unlimited capital in the sense that you either have or can borrow all that it is prudent to invest. Also, you have the options of (1) letting the land lie idle, (2) trying to farm as much as you can by yourself, (3) hiring one additional person, or (4) hiring two additional persons to farm with you. You want to know what the result will be if you try to grow (a) continuous corn, (b) continuous soybeans, or (c) some combination of corn and soybeans.

Table 2-3 gives the options. Part *a* shows what happens if you try to grow continuous corn. The first worker adds 1,500 tons of corn, the second adds 900, and the third 400. There are diminishing returns with the second and the third added worker. In part *b,* the soybean alternative, the first worker adds 500 tons of soybeans, the second 150, and the third 50. Part *c* gives one alternative in a rotation of corn and soybeans. There are of course an indefinitely large number of possible combinations, any of which could be used to illustrate the law of diminishing returns.

A demonstration of the law of diminishing returns such as this does not by itself tell you what to grow. You will need to know the annual salary or total wages to be paid to each worker, the price of

Table 2-3 Illustration of diminishing returns in corn and soybean production on a section (640 acres) of good farmland

(a) Continuous corn

Number of farm workers	Total corn produced, tons	Extra corn produced, tons
0	0	
		1,500
1	1,500	
		900
2	2,400	
		400
3	2,800	

(b) Continuous soybeans

Number of farm workers	Total soybeans produced, tons	Extra soybeans produced, tons
0	0	
		500
1	500	
		150
2	650	
		50
3	700	

(c) Rotation of corn and soybeans

Number of farm workers	Corn produced Total, tons	Corn produced Extra, tons	Soybeans produced Total, tons	Soybeans produced Extra, tons
0	0		0	
		700		375
1	700		375	
		300		125
2	1,000		500	
		200		50
3	1,200		550	

Note: Hypothetical data.

corn, and the price of soybeans. With this information you can tell whether you should produce at all. The value of the corn or soybeans produced by the first worker (you) will have to be at least enough to cover your opportunity cost, or it will not pay to produce at all. If it is sufficient to cover this cost, you can go on to see if it

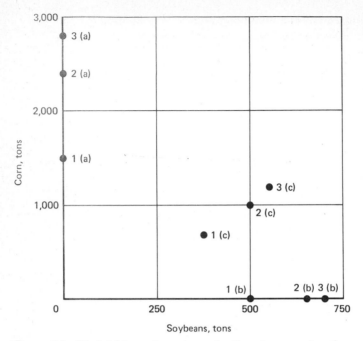

Figure 2-5   Diminishing returns in production of corn and soybeans on a section of good farmland, with 1, 2, or 3 farm workers. Option *a* on the *y* axis is continuous corn. Option *b* on the *x* axis is continuous soybeans. Option *c* is a rotation of corn and soybeans. The data are from Table 2-3.

will pay to hire the second worker, or the third. Figures 2-5 and 2-6 use the data from Table 2-3 to illustrate how diminishing returns may be shown in a diagram.

COMPARING BALANCED GROWTH
WITH FIXITY OF LAND

Figure 2-7, which is purely hypothetical, illustrates conceptually the difference between (*a*) balanced growth in food and nonfood pro-duction, and (*b*) unbalanced growth arising out of a limitation on land, or fixity of land. In (*b*) it is assumed that the fixity of land affects the production of food more than nonfood so that the extra output from each additional application of capital and labor dimin-ishes more rapidly in food production than in nonfood production.

In Figure 2-7*a* there is *balanced growth* between the resources used to produce food and nonfood. The resources of land, labor, and capital are equally available and expandable. Advancing tech-nologies apply with equal productivity to both food and nonfood

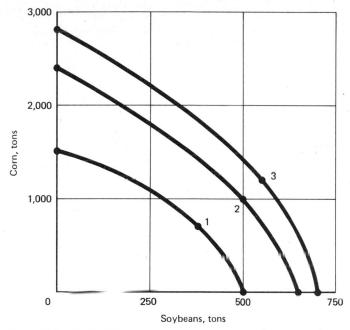

Figure 2-6   Diminishing returns in production of corn and soybeans on a section of good farmland, with 1, 2, or 3 farm workers. The p-p curves, or frontiers, are interpolated from the data of Figure 2-5.

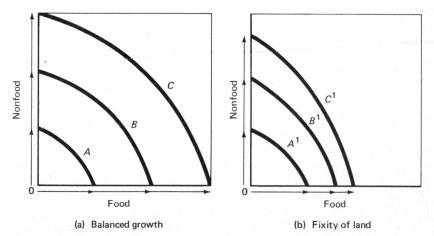

(a) Balanced growth   (b) Fixity of land

Figure 2-7   Growth in food and nonfood production, comparing (a) *balanced growth* of resources and technologies, with (b) *fixity of land,* which makes returns from the other resources and technologies diminish more rapidly in production of food than nonfood.

production. With expanding resources and advancing technologies, the p-p frontier moves outward in a symmetrical fashion, as from *A* to *B* and *B* to *C*. The population spreads out uniformly over the land because there is no unique constraint on land for the production of either food or nonfood.

In Figure 2-7*b* there is limited land, or fixity of land, and this affects the production of food more than nonfood. The population cannot spread out uniformly over more and more land. Diminishing returns due to the fixity of land are more restraining, or serious, in food production than in nonfood production.

IN CONCLUSION: DIMINISHING RETURNS

Diminishing returns are an important central economic problem of agriculture. Although every country in the world can expand its land for agriculture, the amount of good farmland is relatively fixed: additional crop land can be developed only at increasing (relative) cost. This means that crop and livestock production is generally subject to diminishing returns. Although capital resources and advancing technologies can continue to shift the p-p frontier outward for food and nonfood, inevitably there comes a time when the outward-shifting frontiers are restrained more and more by diminishing returns.

MEASUREMENT OF ECONOMIC GROWTH

In connection with the subject of economic growth and production possibilities, it is important to develop a technique for measuring growth and consider some further implications. Thus, it is desirable for us to consider economic growth in further detail, distinguishing between the two definitions that have been implied, which relate to national and per capita output, or growth.

Definition 1: Real national output or real national income

Economic growth may be defined as an increase in the economy's *real* gross national product, or *real* national income. The gross national product (*GNP*) is the total market value of all *final* goods and services produced in a given year. It can be determined by (1) adding up all that is spent on this year's total output, or (2) adding up the incomes derived from this year's output. The results are identical because what is spent on goods and services by a buyer is income to the seller. So the expenditure and the income approaches to *GNP* are always equal to each other, or an identity.

REFINEMENTS OF *GNP*

There are a number of refinements that must be made, however, to get an accurate picture of growth. First, note that the definition of *GNP* hinges on *real* output, not *money* output. Thus, the production of a larger amount of goods and services constitutes growth; paying more dollars for the same or a smaller amount does not. Second, note that the definition of *GNP* emphasizes *final* goods and services, which means that it excludes intermediate products that are used in production or simply transferred from one owner to another in the process of producing and marketing. It generally excludes secondhand sales and like transfers because these do not reflect current production and their inclusion would involve double counting. Finally, it excludes many financial transactions in both the private and public sectors, which are merely transfers of income or wealth.

FROM *GNP* TO *NNP*

The measurement of change in *GNP* gives a somewhat inaccurate picture of growth, however, because *GNP* fails to allow for the capital goods used in current production. A figure for net national product (*NNP*) can be derived by subtracting from *GNP* the estimated value of capital used up or consumed in the year's production. In 1976, for example, *GNP* of the United States was estimated at $1,692 billion. The capital consumption allowance was $190 billion, leaving *NNP* of $1,512 billion. *NNP,* then, is *GNP* adjusted for depreciation charges in plant and equipment, natural-resource depletion, and so on. *NNP* is the amount that can be consumed by the nation's economy—firms, households, and government itself—without impairing the nation's capacity to produce in succeeding years and indefinitely into the future.

FROM *NNP* TO *NI*

NNP includes indirect business taxes, and these must be subtracted from the *NNP* to get national income (*NI*). *NI,* then, is the total wage, rent, interest, and profit incomes earned from the production of the year's output. Measured from the viewpoint of resource suppliers, it is the income the suppliers have earned from their contributions to the year's production. From the viewpoint of business costs, national income is the factor or resource costs of all the inputs that have gone into the creation of the year's output. For example, in the United States in 1976, indirect business taxes of $163 billion, subtracted from $1,512 billion *NNP,* left a national income of $1,349 billion. This is generally the best measure of national economic growth. We shall use it in another example to illustrate how to measure growth under definition 1 by comparing change in *NI* with change in the consumer price index.

ESTIMATING GROWTH BY DEFINITION 1

The economy of Japan provides the most dramatic example of growth in a modern industrial state. Let us measure its growth, using selected data from *Statistical Survey of Japan's Economy 1970* and *Japan Economic Yearbook 1974.* Basic data relating to 1961, 1966, and 1971 are as follows:

Year	NI, trillions of yen	Consumers price index (1970 = 100)
1961	15.2	59.7
1965	29.2	80.6
1971	65.6	106.1

From 1961 to 1971 the exchange rate between Japan and the United States was fixed at 360 yen to $1. Japan's *NI* was increasing rapidly, and so was the consumer price index (*CPI*). What was the real rate of growth according to definition 1? Two steps must be undertaken to determine this.

Step 1: Deflating *NI* for change in *CPI*   In the first step we have the following calculations;

For 1961: 15.2/59.7% = 25.5 trillion, the 1961 *NI* in 1970 yen
For 1965: 29.2/80.6% = 36.2 trillion, the 1965 *NI* in 1970 yen
For 1971: 65.6/106.1% = 61.8 trillion, the 1971 *NI* in 1970 yen

Step 2: Estimating annual rate of growth   In the second step we have the following calculations:

α.   Between 1961 and 1966:

$$\frac{36.2}{25.5} = 1.42 \qquad \text{or } 142\%$$

142% − 100% = 42%   or   42%/5 = 8.4% annual rate

b. Between 1966 and 1971:

$$\frac{61.8}{36.2} = 1.71 \qquad \text{or } 171\%$$

171% − 100% = 71%   or   71%/5 = 14.2% annual rate

c. Between 1961 and 1971:

$$\frac{61.8}{25.5} = 2.42 \qquad \text{or } 242\%$$

242% − 100% = 142%   or   142%/10 = 14.2% annual rate

The rate of economic growth is frequently expressed as an annual rate, and changes in the rate are watched closely because small changes often have broad implications. The rate of growth, when combined with changes in other indicators—such as housing starts, wholesale inventories, railroad-car loadings, nonfarm employment levels, industrial production, and others—tells a great deal about the current performance and future of the economy. For many purposes, however, a more refined definition of growth is desired that relates to *real* output, or *real* income, per capita.

Definition 2: Real output or real income per capita

Economic growth may be defined as an increase in the total amount of goods and services per capita or total real income per capita. This definition correctly recognizes that the level of living in an economy is best measured in terms of the goods and services available for each person. *NI* in real terms must increase at a faster rate than the rate of increase in population if the average level of living is to rise. That is, the level of living in an economy can fall if the population increases at a faster rate than real *NI*. To learn what happened in the example of Japan, we must undertake two more steps.

ESTIMATING GROWTH BY DEFINITION 2

Step 3: Estimating real *NI* per capita   Real *NI* per capita is equal to real *NI* divided by the total domestic population. That is, the *NI* figures derived in step 1 for 1970 yen are divided by the total population for the same year to get real *NI* per capita, as follows:

Year	NI, 1970 yen	Population, millions	Real NI per capita, thousands of 1970 yen
1961	25.5	94.3	270
1966	36.2	99.0	366
1971	61.8	105.3	587

This suggests that in 1966, for example, with an exchange rate of 360 yen to $1, the average income in Japan was a little more than $1,000 per capita. By 1971, it had risen to about $1,631 per capita (587,000 ÷ 360), which is of course a remarkable demonstration of growth. What was the annual rate of growth per capita?

Step 4: Estimating real rate of growth per capita   In the fourth step we have the following calculations:

a.   Between 1961 and 1966:

$$\frac{366}{270} = 136\%$$

136% − 100% = 36%   or   36%/5 = 7.2% annual rate

b.   Between 1966 and 1971:

$$\frac{587}{366} = 160\%$$

160% − 100% = 60%   or   60%/5 = 12% annual rate

c.   Between 1961 and 1971:

$$\frac{587}{270} = 217\%$$

217% − 100% = 117%   or   117%/10 = 11.7% annual rate

Using the two measures of growth

The two measures of growth—real NI and real NI per capita—are both used in economics to measure the performance of an economy. Which is preferred depends on the problem and the purpose to be served. The concepts of real national output and income are usually employed in analyzing short-term changes in economic performance, such as changes in military expenditures, automobile production, steel output, or crop production. The concepts of real income per capita are more meaningfully applied to the longer term, and to changes in real income or wealth arising out of the performance of a given economic sector. Let us illustrate by reference to American agriculture.

EXAMPLE: ECONOMIC GROWTH OF
AGRICULTURE IN THE UNITED STATES

Between 1970 and 1977 the total marketing receipts of American farmers increased from $50.5 billion to $96.1 billion, and the index of farm-product prices rose from 112 to 183, with 1967 − 100. What was the rate of growth? Under the first definition we have the following.

Step 1: Estimating marketing receipts in 1967 prices   The first step has these calculations:

In 1970: $50.5 billion/112% = $45.1 billion, for 1970 output in 1967 prices
In 1977: $96.1 billion/183% = $52.5 billion, for 1977 output in 1967 prices

Step 2: Estimating annual rate of growth in farm marketings in the United States   The second step has these calculations:

$$\frac{\$52.5 \text{ billion}}{\$45.1 \text{ billion}} = 1.164 \quad \text{or } 116.4\%$$

116.4% − 100% = 16.4%   or   16.4%/7 = 2.34% annually

How did this growth compare with the growth in American population, or what was the rate of growth in terms of product per capita? Between similar dates in 1970 and 1977 the total American population increased from 203.2 million to 215.9 million. Then, we have the following.

Step 3: Estimating the value of farm marketings in the United States per capita in 1967 prices   The third step has these calculations:

In 1970: $45.1 billion/203.2 million = $222, the value of 1970 American farm marketings per capita in 1967 prices
In 1977: $52.5 billion/215.9 million = $243, the value of 1977 American farm marketings per capita in 1967 prices

Step 4: Estimating the rate of growth of farm marketings in the United States per capita   The fourth step has these calculations:

$$\frac{\$243}{\$222} = 1.095 \qquad \text{or } 109.5\%$$

$$109.5\% - 100\% = 9.5\% \qquad \text{or} \qquad 9.5\%/7 = 1.36\% \text{ annually}$$

The rate of increase in American farm marketings per capita gives us an idea of how much per capita consumption of farm products could increase, assuming no change in net exports; how much net exports could increase, assuming no change in per capita consumption; or how much both per capita consumption and exports could increase. As a matter of fact, between 1970 and 1977 the average American per capita consumption of farm products increased by only a little more than 2 percent, and for a few years around the mid 1970s per capita consumption was lower than in 1970. Exports of American farm products, which in the late 1960s had absorbed about one-sixth of farm marketings, increased in volume from 1970 to 1977 by about 70 percent. Thus the rapidly increasing export markets—Japan, for example—were the major factors in the economic growth of American agriculture, influencing farm food prices in all markets and providing dollar earnings for increased imports of other products.

SUMMARY

The central economic problems of agriculture have been grouped around three questions: *What* shall be produced? *How?* And *for whom?* Although the problems must be confronted in every society, various societies answer them in different ways. All societies use prices to allocate resources and distribute incomes. But every society has its own economic tradition or heritage, and different rules and regulations are imposed by the various governments around the world. The western democracies, for example, generally rely most on private enterprise, emphasizing the family farm in agriculture. Centrally planned societies such as the Soviet Union assign a larger role to government planning and administration.

Important economic values and goals have been identified, such as economic growth and development, economic stability, economic justice or equity, and economic freedom and security. How we formulate these values and goals, and what priorities we put on each, has a great deal to do with how the basic questions are answered. Such goals are the combination of things that can be achieved, or achieved to some degree, by limiting one to get more of another.

Production possibilities—the p-p curve or frontier—is a basic technique for thinking about economic alternatives. The basic p-p frontier has been used to help define and illustrate the law of increasing (relative) costs. This law prevails when an ever-increasing amount of a good or service must be sacrificed to produce equal extra amounts of another good or service. The value of goods and services that must be given up or sacrificed to obtain an additional amount of any other good or service is the opportunity cost of that good or service.

Economic growth involves an outward shift of p-p frontiers as a result of expanding resources and advancing technologies. Outward-shifting p-p frontiers provide a basis for increasing capital formation and the consumption of food and nonfood. Capital formation is required for the economic growth of agriculture, which produces under the condition of diminishing returns. The law of diminishing returns refers specifically to the extra output that is produced when equal extra units of a varying input are successively added to a fixed amount of some other input or inputs. Increases in agricultural output are specifically subject to diminishing returns as a result of the relative fixity of land and some other natural resources.

The measurement of economic growth helps us visualize the central economic problems of agriculture. Specifically, it has been noted that economic growth can be measured in terms of gross national product (*GNP*), net national product (*NNP*), or national income (*NI*). Our illustration was in terms of *NI* and *NI* per capita. The economic growth of agriculture can be measured in terms of the value of farm marketings in constant prices, expressed as total farm marketings or farm marketings per capita. The growth of American agriculture has become more and more dependent on export markets.

IMPORTANT TERMS
AND CONCEPTS

Economic problem
Economic problems of agriculture
Economic values and goals
    Economic growth and development
    Economic stability for agriculture

Economic justice and equity, the "work ethic"
Economic freedom and security
Production possibilities
   p-p curve
   p-p frontier
Economic growth as a shift in production possibilities
Capital formation and consumption
Balanced and unbalanced growth
Measurement of economic growth
   GNP, NNP, and *NI*
   NI per capita
Economic growth of agriculture
   Total farm marketings
   Farm marketings per capita

LOOKING AHEAD

Chapter 3 will consider alternative solutions to problems of world population and production. An attempt will be made to outline some of the present realities in regard to population and production possibilities, and to look at these realities in light of the past for purposes of the future. It is especially important to be able to coordinate the major economic theories relating to population and production possibilities. Such an understanding provides a foundation for the proceeding chapters dealing with production costs and related topics.

QUESTIONS AND EXERCISES

1. What are the three fundamental problems that every society must confront? How are they confronted?
2. What are the two functions of prices in confronting these problems? Give an example.
3. How have governments used prices to distort agricultural-resource allocation and income distribution?
4. What are the major economic values and goals that tend to guide the solutions to the central economic problems of agriculture? Is any one of these more important or crucial to society than another? Is it prudent to try to rank them in order of importance? Why, or why not?

5. What is economic growth? What are the benefits of the economic growth of agriculture? Is the economic stability of agriculture a problem, a value, or a goal? Why is economic justice or equity important? Freedom and security?

6. What does a p-p curve show? Why do we call it a frontier? Why is it sometimes called a transformation curve?

7. State the law of increasing (relative) costs. Illustrate it by means of a p-p curve. How are costs measured in this case?

8. What is opportunity cost? Give an example. What is an implicit cost?

9. Give reasons and at least one example to explain why a farmer may produce below the p-p frontier. Is it possible to produce beyond the frontier? Why, or why not?

10. What is the law of diminishing returns? Does the law apply to agriculture? Why, or why not?

11. What are the ways to measure economic growth? Give one illustration for the national economy and one for agriculture.

3. POPULATION AND PRODUCTION POTENTIALS

■■To get land's fruit in quantity
Takes jolts of labor evermore,
Hence food will grow like one, two, three . . .
While numbers grow like one, two, four . . .**■■**

Anonymous, "Song of Malthus:
A Ballad of Diminishing Returns"

Thomas Robert Malthus (1766–1834), an English clergyman, saw overpopulation as a great threat to the welfare of the human race. In his *Essay on the Principle of Population* (1798), he expounded the view that population when unchecked increases in a geometric ratio, while food supply at best increases in an arithmetic ratio. Hence, population tends to increase up to the limits of "the means of subsistence." These views were not original, even at the time, but his exposition had profound effects. It strengthened beliefs that the poor could not be helped because they would just produce more children, labor unions would be worse than useless, and efforts at social reform would be self-defeating. These views, dominant throughout the nineteenth and early twentieth centuries, are now giving way to an alternative view of economic progress, which is the essence of our study.

N ow that we have studied the law of diminishing returns, let us put it to work. The world's growing population depends for food and nonfood on production-possibilities frontiers that are always shifting outward. But agricultural production especially is faced with diminishing returns as some of the important resources such as land—economically speaking—are fixed. People want more food, not just in total but per capita. This is especially true in the developing countries where diets are poor and sometimes very deficient. The question is not whether agricultural production *can* be increased. The question is: How can it be increased so as to result in economic progress, which in this case means more food per capita?

This chapter covers comparative trends in agricultural production, in total and per capita; a short review of population growth and some principles or theories relating to population; observations on relationships between economic progress and food consumption, with implications for agriculture; and some comments on the long-term outlook for agricultural productivity. The chapter closes with an explanation of equal-product curves and their use in discussing substitutability among the resources used in food and agricultural production.

IN THIS CHAPTER

1. You will gain a broader vision of the trends in agricultural production in developed and developing countries.
2. You will learn more about population growth and factors influencing growth.
3. You will see the connection between economic progress and food consumption, and some of the implications for agriculture.
4. You will learn how to draw equal-product curves and how to use them in the analysis of agricultural production. The discussion of these curves also serves as an introduction to the analysis of agricultural production and cost functions in Chapter 4.

TRENDS IN AGRICULTURAL PRODUCTION: TOTAL AND PER CAPITA

Barbara Ward, the noted British political economist, began her book *The Rich Nations and the Poor Nations* with the observation that "we live in the most catastrophically revolutionary age that men

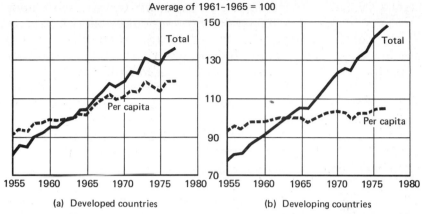

Average of 1961–1965 = 100

(a) Developed countries   (b) Developing countries

Figure 3-1   Agricultural production in (a) developed and (b) developing countries. Total agricultural production is increasing at a combined annual rate of 2.9 percent in developing countries and 2.4 percent in developed countries. On a per-capita basis, however, the rate is 1.3 percent for the developed countries and 0.4 percent for developing countries. Population has continued to increase at a faster rate in the developing countries than in the developed countries. [*Note:* Developed countries include United States, Canada, Europe, U.S.S.R., Japan, Republic of South Africa, Australia, and New Zealand. Developing countries include South and Central America, Africa (except Republic of South Africa), and Asia (except Japan, People's Republic of China, and Vietnam).]

have ever faced."[1] In fact there are several revolutions, all going at the same time—in politics, economics, social customs, religious concepts, length of life, and other human activities. Most of them are still accelerating. The future is coming at us faster and faster. In few major industries is this more true than in agriculture. What are the basic trends?

Agricultural production in developed and developing countries

Economics is a comparative study, and it is most useful to compare agriculture in developed and developing countries (Figure 3-1). From 1955 to 1977, total agricultural production in the developed countries increased by a compound annual rate of 2.4 percent, and increased by 2.9 percent in the developing countries. However, per

[1]Barbara Ward, *The Rich Nations and the Poor Nations,* W. W. Norton & Company, Inc., New York, 1962, p. 13.

capita production in the developed countries increased by 1.3 percent, and increased in the developing countries by only 0.4 percent.

The difference between total and per capita production in Figure 3-1 is, of course, due to differences in the rates of population growth. In the developed countries the rate was 1.2 percent, while in the developing countries it was nearly 2.5 percent. The difference was primarily due to much higher birthrates in the developing countries, rather than lower death rates. Although birthrates have been falling almost everywhere, most of these differences in rates of population growth will continue for many years. This difference will continue and perhaps widen the disparity in per capita food supplies.

Consequences of different rates of growth

The relatively high rate of population growth in the developing countries means that people are eating up the additional food that is produced without having much of anything to add to their generally low and poorly balanced diets. After 1960 in these countries as a whole—whether in Asia, Africa, or Latin America—the per capita food supply changed scarcely at all. In some countries per capita food supplies decreased, sometimes to a large degree. Moreover, we know from historical studies (and economic theory tells us the same) that in a given society economic growth under these circumstances helps the more efficient, higher-income people more than the poorer groups.[2]

Studies by the United Nations have revealed that as many as 500 million people, some 12 to 15 percent of the population in developing regions, are suffering from various degrees of *undernourishment* (generally defined as a deficiency in total caloric intake such that a person cannot maintain normal bodily activity without losing weight and eventually dying). A much larger number of people—children especially—are suffering from *malnutrition* (a lack or deficiency of one or more of the protective nutrients: proteins, vitamins, and minerals). Care, Inc., the worldwide food relief agency, says that half the world's children suffer from malnutrition. The vast majority of these children are in the developing regions.

This all means that the disparity between the affluent and the poor tends to widen as the various countries, especially the developing countries, grind out the day-to-day and year-to-year answers

[2]Irma Adelman and Cynthia Taft Morris, *Economic Growth and Social Equity in Developing Countries,* Stanford University Press, Stanford, Calif., 1973.

to the question: "For whom to produce?" The increases in total agricultural production, essential as they are, do not provide a complete or even good index of human well-being. What to do about this is surely one of the most persistent central economic problems of agriculture. We will try to provide answers, but let us not imagine that the problem in all its many aspects will be simple to solve.

Production in the United States and other developed countries

A comparison between the United States and other developed countries (Figure 3-2) is crucial because the United States supplies well over half of all food exports for these countries, or more than one-sixth of the total world agricultural trade. What happens here affects the national well-being, and affects all other exporting and importing countries as well.

From 1955 to 1977, the rate of increase in total agricultural production was slightly lower in the United States than in other developed countries. The rate of increase per capita was only 0.7 percent in the United States, and 1.4 percent in other developed countries.

Average of 1961-1965 = 100

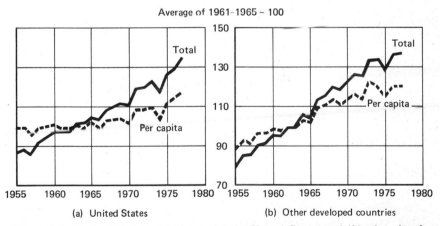

(a) United States   (b) Other developed countries

Figure 3-2 Agricultural production in (a) the United States and (b) other developed countries. Until 1973, total agricultural production in the United States was restrained by relatively low farm product prices and government production-control programs. From 1955 to 1977, production per capita increased at a compound annual rate of 0.7 percent in the United States and 1.4 percent in other developed countries. [Note: Other developed countries include Canada, Europe, Japan, U.S.S.R., Republic of South Africa, Australia, and New Zealand. Developing countries include South and Central America, Africa (except Republic of South Africa), and Asia (except Japan, the People's Republic of China, and Vietnam).]

A slightly higher rate of population growth in the United States accounted for some of the difference.

The relatively slower growth of production in the United States is only partly due to diminishing returns. From 1955 to 1973, growth was retarded by low farm product prices—much lower than in Europe and Japan, the regular major food importers. After 1956, the Soil Bank Program idled some 25 to 30 million acres of good cropland. Beginning in 1961, the Emergency Feed Grain Program kept considerably more good cropland out of production. Wheat and cotton were curtailed, especially after the Wheat-Cotton Act of 1964. Release from these programs came in 1973. But it must be clear that if there had been higher farm product prices and none of these programs, American farm production would have increased much more.

The potential for increasing production is much larger in the United States than in other developed countries. There is comparatively very little good farmland in either Europe and Japan that is not being cropped. Agriculture in Canada, Australia, and New Zealand— the other major developed food exporters—appears to be pressed nearer to the limits of their climatic margins. If economic progress in developing countries provides a larger and larger market for agri-

Increasing the production potential of agriculture includes major improvements in marketing. This picture shows an ocean-going vessel being loaded with grain for shipment overseas. This grain may be consumed directly, or used to increase livestock production in the importing countries. (*The Andersons, Maumee, Ohio.*)

cultural exports from the developed countries, the increase in exports from the United States will be larger than the increase from all other developed countries combined. What are some of the implications of this to agriculture in the United States and the world?

The well-being of humanity in the future depends to a great extent on what happens to population in the developing countries and on what kind of economic transition they can make or what rate of economic progress they can sustain. It is important, therefore, to examine the relation between agriculture and population growth. This can help us visualize the major production-population problems and their possible solutions.

WORLD POPULATION GROWTH: TRENDS, PRINCIPLES, AND PROJECTIONS

There are three questions to keep in mind: What has happened? What are the basic underlying principles and theories? What are the projections for the future?

Trends in world population growth: A short review

In 1975, world population reached 4 billion persons; it is expected that this figure will be 5 billion in the mid-1980s. From then on the rate of growth is more conjectural. The numbers are very large by historical standards, however, and even a slight change in the rate of growth will make a tremendous difference in the requirements for food and the future of agriculture. A study of the present, in the light of the past, can tell us a great deal about the future.

BEGINNINGS OF GROWTH

Although precursors of the human race existed some 3 to 4 million years ago, it was only in the time between the two continental glaciers, some 150,000 to 50,000 years ago, that modern *Homo sapiens* appeared. The features characteristic of modern humans include chins, small brow ridges, delicate facial skeletons, and high flat-sided skulls.

TRANSITIONAL GROWTH

From a relatively few individuals in the interglacial period, the human race grew to some 4 to 5 million by about 15,000 years ago. Then, in the Thai region of southeast Asia, a primitive agricultural

Hereford cattle on productive rangeland on a ranch in the western United States. The steep slope of this land makes it unsuitable for heavy crop production. To control soil erosion, it is kept in grass and pasture crops most of the time.

revolution began. This was followed about 5,000 years later, or 10,000 years ago, by the beginnings of agriculture in Mesopotamia, "the land between the rivers," the Tigris-Euphrates valley in what is now Iraq. About 5000 B.C. or possibly 4000 B.C., people began to move down from higher ground onto the plain; by about 2400 B.C., an imaginative and successful irrigation system was established, largely fed by the Tigris and drained by the Euphrates.

This system was maintained for some 4,000 years, to about A.D. 1600. Then misuse of the land—overgrazing in the headwaters of the rivers and failure to clear the increasingly heavy silt blocking the irrigation channels—led to the breakdown of the system and its abandonment.

The story of the Tigris-Euphrates valley is of more than historic interest—it has much relevance for today. Overgrazing, too intensive or continuous cultivation, and failure to maintain vegetative cover have brought a reduction in productivity on many hundreds of millions—in fact, billions—of acres of agricultural lands. The struggle for conservation, or the problem of achieving an optimum balance of use and conservation, is one of the continuing central economic problems of agriculture. It is, in fact, a problem in all countries, in all stages of economic development.

ACCELERATING GROWTH

By A.D. 1600, the human race—living largely in Europe, Asia, and Africa, with a relatively few in the Americas, Australia, New Zealand,

and the islands of the Pacific—had increased to 450 million or so. The foundation was laid for a short, but historically astounding, period of rapidly accelerating growth. Rudimentary advances in medicine and health care were necessary conditions for this growth to begin.

The industrial revolution and the spread of agricultural improvements soon provided the necessities of life for more and more people. By 1830, world population reached the first billion mark, with more people added in 200 years than in the previous 3 or 4 million. By 1930, in just 100 years, the second billion was added. In another 30 years, by 1960, the third billion was added. In 15 years, by 1975, the fourth billion appeared. The fifth should take about another 10 years (see Figure 3-3).

IMPLICATIONS

Population has tended to follow a geometric pattern of growth, with more persons being added each year than the year before, even though the annual percentage rate of growth is now stabilizing, or in fact falling. The specter of this pattern is alarming. It suggests that with continuation of a nearly constant rate of growth, or even a slightly falling rate of growth, within a few more years the resources

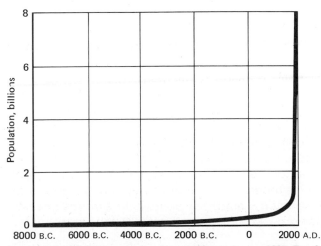

Figure 3-3   World population from 8000 B.C. to A.D. 2000. For the last few centuries, the growth of world population has followed a geometric, or exponential, pattern. More than 2.4 billion was *added* between 1930 and 1980, as compared with the *total* world population of 2.0 billion in 1930. (*Source:* Edward S. Deevey, Jr., "The Human Population," *Scientific American,* September 1960, p. 198.)

might not be adequate to maintain per capita food supplies. Diminishing returns might be carried to the point where millions, indeed billions, could starve.

Population:
Principles and theories of growth

The problem of food production and population growth has been on the minds of many people for a long time. Many alarming prophecies have been made, many solutions suggested, and many alternatives considered.

PRINCIPLE OF POPULATION
ACCORDING TO MALTHUS

A little before 1800, when population growth was accelerating rapidly, a young English clergyman named Thomas Robert Malthus began to argue with his father about the latter's view that the human race would get ever better and better. Finally, he became so agitated that he wrote a book, the famous *Essay on the Principle of Population* (1798). In this essay he expounded on the ultimate danger of uncontrolled population growth and the human tragedies that could result. The book quickly became a best-seller. Six editions were published during his lifetime, and a seventh was published posthumously; the book is a living document today.[3]

The *principle of population,* according to Malthus, is found in this proposition: "The power of population is infinitely greater than the power in the earth to produce subsistence for men." This rests on two postulates. First, food and sexual passion are both essential to human life. Second, while food increases only in arithmetic ratio, population when unchecked tends to increase in geometric ratio.

Malthus started with an observation by Benjamin Franklin that in the American colonies where food was abundant and population unchecked, the population tended to double every 25 years or so. Malthus did not say that a population would necessarily double every 25 years, but the tendency was there. Therefore, he postulated that there is a *universal tendency for population—unless checked by food supply—to grow at a geometric ratio.* It follows, then, that

[3]Thomas Robert Malthus, *On Population,* edited and introduced by Gertrude Himmelfarb, Modern Library, Inc., New York, 1960.

food production, which is inevitably subject to the law of diminishing returns, cannot keep pace with population growth.

According to this principle, growth of the human population must be controlled to prevent human beings from sinking to the minimum levels of subsistence. The first edition of Malthus's book placed emphasis on positive measures that would increase death rates, such as pestilence, famine, and war. The later editions backed away from this gloomy view, emphasizing instead preventive checks on population growth, moral restraint, sexual abstinence before marriage and restraint thereafter, and prudent postponement of marriage until a family could be adequately supported.

For more than 180 years the Malthusian doctrines have had widespread repercussions. They were used, for example, to support a stern revision of the English poor laws, under which destitution was regarded as a result of laziness, failure to pay a bill on time could send a person to jail, and unemployment was made as uncomfortable as possible. These laws were widely copied. The Malthusian ideas were used to support arguments that trade or labor unions could not improve the lot of working people because higher wages would merely permit them to have more babies and larger families. The fact that working people did have large families and were poor was merely the working of the principle. Aid to the poor would simply magnify the problem. Charities were not encouraged, and Malthus himself preached that poverty was just punishment for failure to practice restraint. This view widely influenced people in all walks of life, including writers, politicans, and religious leaders.

ALTERNATIVE PATTERNS AND
PROJECTIONS OF GROWTH

Modern societies are not following the growth patterns of the *principle of population*. Population growth is being deliberately checked. For 100 years or more the trend of birthrates in developed countries has been downward. Increases in birthrates, such as occurred after most major wars, have subsided in a few years. In recent years, birthrates have been falling almost everywhere, in developing as well as developed countries. Population growth rates are leveling off, coming closer and closer to zero population growth.

The pattern of growth suggested in Figure 3-4 has tremendous implications, and projections of population are changing to conform to it. Some population experts have projected for the year 2000 a *medium* estimate for world population of 6.7 billion and a *high*

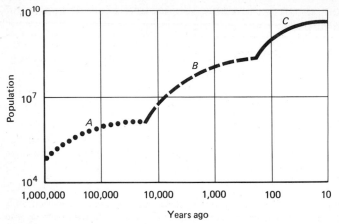

Figure 3-4 Growth of human population in logarithmic scale. Growth curve A covers the period from 3 to 4 million years ago to the time between the two continental glaciers, from 150,000 to 50,000 years ago. Growth curve B covers the interglacial period to about 250 years ago. Growth curve C covers about 250 years, from 1730 to 1980. During this time the world's population grew ninefold, from 0.5 billion to 4.5 billion. This growth curve now appears to be leveling off, with a slower rate of increase than was the case just a few years ago. (*Note:* $10^4 = 10,000$; $10^7 = 10,000,000$; and $10^{10} = 10,000,000,000$. *Source:* Adapted from Edward S. Deevey, Jr., "The Human Population," *Scientific American*, September 1960, p. 198.)

estimate of 7.5 billion, as compared with 3.7 billion in 1970 (Table 3-1).

The high estimate in Table 3-1 implied a very small decline in birthrates and slightly lower death rates in each of the world regions, while the medium estimate assumed a continuing decline in birthrates. But events moved even faster than the experts assumed (as events frequently have a habit of doing). Continuing studies in the United Nations soon developed a medium projection of 6.3 billion, which was used as the base for a broad study of *The Future of the World Economy* begun in 1973.[4] The World Bank began to use a projection of 6 billion as a basis for its planning and operations. In 1978 another study, based on census data and estimates of current trends in countries where census data were not available, predicted a total world population of 5.8 billion by the year 2000.[5] These lower population projections opened up an increas-

[4]Wassily Leontief, Anne P. Carter, and Peter A. Petri, *The Future of the World Economy: A United Nations Study,* Oxford University Press, New York, 1977.

[5]Amy Ong Tsui and Donald J. Bogue, "Declining World Fertility: Trends, Causes, Implications," *Population Bulletin*, vol. 33, no. 4, 1978.

Table 3-1   World population in 1970, year 2000 estimates, and potential
under assumed conditions

	Population, millions			Potential under assumed conditions,[a] millions		
		2000[c]				
	1970[b]	Medium estimate	High estimate	Present diet	Better diet	Adequate diet
Less-developed regions	1,749	3,523	3,936	4,378	4,180	3,825
Communist Asia	879	1,761[d]	1,986[d]	1,354	1,127	952
Developed regions	1,073	1,441	1,574	1,441[e]	1,441[e]	1,441
World	3,701	6,725	7,496	7,178	6,748	6,218

[a]Present diet is that projected for 1970 in the World Food Budget: 1970; better diet assumes a minimum adequate caloric level; adequate diet assumes minimum adequate calories and proteins.

[b]Estimates from the A.I.D.-U.S.D.A. Demand Studies.

[c]Estimates by F. W. Notestein based on United Nations 1963 and 1966 projections in *Overcoming World Hunger*, American Assembly. Medium estimates assume some success in population control measures; high estimates assume straight-line growth rates at current levels.

[d]Estimates by F. W. Notestein, ibid; assuming a population growth rate projected for South Asia, 2.3 percent per year to 2000 (medium projection).

[e]These estimates are the same as United Nations figures for year 2000; a much larger population could be supported by food production capacity now available in these countries.

Source: U.S.D.A., Foreign Economic Development Service, cooperating with the Agency for International Development, *World Food-Population Levels,* Report to the President, April 9, 1970. U.S. Department of State, April 1970, table 1, p. 3.

ingly optimistic view of the possibilities for economic progress and per capita food supplies.

The prediction of 5.8 billion by the year 2000 assumed that family-planning programs would be supported and continued to the end of the century. These programs have grown rapidly in both developed and developing countries, with the support of governments, foundations, and charities. Generally, they include family counseling and information about birth control, plus some financial support for the medical birth control technologies approved by national governments. Chiefly as a result of these programs, the world's total fertility rate (*TFR*) dropped from 4.6 in 1968 to 4.1 in 1975. (*TFR* is the average number of births of women in a given population during a lifetime.) Between 1968 and 1975, the most significant drop occurred among women 20 to 24 years old, which suggests that the decline was of more than temporary character.

The broader trend of reducing the average number of children per family arises out of the many economic and social factors that tend to change as economic progress occurs. An economic explanation is that children become less important in contributing to the economic welfare of the family, and less critical for the support of parents in their old age. But they become relatively more expensive to raise and educate as economic progress occurs. In other words, investment in the human resource becomes more and more necessary, or profitable, as an economy becomes more and more sophisticated. This seems to be true even though a developed country generally has a large number of jobs that require very little training or little more than narrowly specialized skills. The general result is that the children become more expensive to raise and contribute less to the family's budget, and the birthrate tends to drop. Practically all developed countries have exhibited this trend, many of them for the last 100 years or more. The developing countries apparently are in earlier stages of similar trends.

Since the time of Malthus, technological innovation has shifted production-possibilities curves rapidly outward. This has made a higher level of living possible for many more people. At the same time, advances in medicine and health care have greatly lessened the positive checks on population growth and have prolonged human life. As economic progress has occurred, parents have tended to have fewer children on the average. This trend is apparently desired by parents as a result of their changing circumstances, and most governments have encouraged this trend through family-planning programs. For most of the world's population, lower growth rates are not being forced by *stringencies* in the necessities of life, as postulated by Malthus. Although there are many poor families, especially in developing countries, who have just enough food to sustain life, most of the world's population has moved away from the more alarming projections that come from the Malthusian principle of population. Birthrates fall as economic progress occurs. But people strive to enrich their diets with a broader variety of foods, more animal products, and higher-quality and more plentiful food. Let us consider the implications for agriculture.

IMPLICATIONS OF
ECONOMIC PROGRESS

Modern societies demonstrate that as income per person increases, people improve their diets with a broader variety of foods and, especially, an increasing use of animal products. People in developed countries use much more grain per person than people in developing countries. This means that the per capita demands for agricultural products increase greatly as economic progress occurs, and

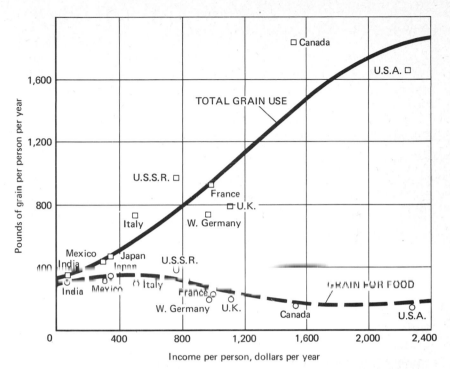

Figure 3-5   General relationship between income per person and pounds of grain per person per year in selected countries. As income per person increases, smaller and smaller amounts are consumed directly as human food, and more is consumed in the form of animal and other products. (*Source:* Orville L. Freeman, "Malthus, Marx, and the North American Bread Basket," *Foreign Affairs,* July 1967, p. 582; copyright 1967 by the Council on Foreign Relations, Inc.)

agricultural production must expand both in total and per capita if these demands are to be satisfied. How much it must expand depends on the rate of population growth and the rate of economic progress as reflected in people's level of living.

Figure 3-5 gives typical relationships between income per person and pounds of grain used per person per year. Note especially the high per capita use of grain in Canada and the United States. This reflects both the high average income per person and the relatively low cost of food. France, the United Kingdom, and West Germany had, at this stage of development, a per capita grain consumption about half as high, reflecting both their lower average real income per person and the relatively higher cost of food, especially livestock products. India, the poorest country in Figure 3-5, has the

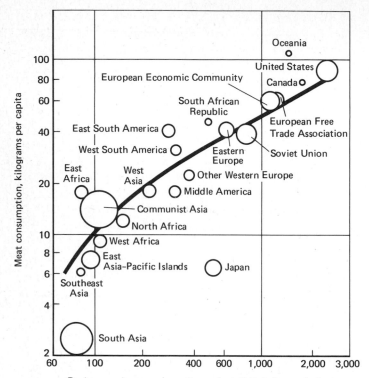

Figure 3-6   Meat consumption in kilograms per capita related to income and population. Note that in these logarithmic scales, this relationship—with the exception of a few countries, such as Japan—appears as a rather smooth curve. This chart, however, also reflects the mixtures of resources available for food production in various countries. East Africa, for example, has a set of resources favorable to livestock production. Japan has just the opposite. (*Note:* Areas of circles are proportioned to population. *Source:* U. S. Department of Agriculture, Economic Research Service.)

lowest per capita consumption of grain, with as much as 90 percent being used directly for human consumption.

Figure 3-6 gives another typical relationship between income and meat consumption per capita. South Asia—with the lowest income per capita and with major religions that prohibit the use of meat—has very low per capita consumption. Meat consumption is also low in Japan, compared with per capita income. Little meat is produced in Japan, imports are strictly controlled by the government, and meat prices are comparatively very high. Figure 3-6 also reflects the relatively high consumption of meat in areas such as east Africa and east South America, where the mix of agricultural resources is relatively favorable for meat production and the population has traditionally depended on meat as a major staple in the diet.

Figures 3-5 and 3-6 tell a story that have very important implications for future agricultural markets. If the lower rates of population growth contribute importantly to greater economic progress, the per capita demands for agricultural products will rise very significantly, and this will be especially important in currently developing countries. The market for food will grow relatively more slowly in the developed countries, especially in countries with high rates of grain consumption such as Canada and the United States. The major food-exporting countries, the United States especially, must look to the currently developing countries for the major expansion of their agricultural markets. What are the production potentials for serving future world markets?

PRODUCTION POTENTIALS: LAND AND NONLAND RESOURCES

The production potentials for agriculture depend on the comparative costs of land and nonland resources. Agricultural production can be expanded by the use of more land, the use of more of the other resources that can be applied to land, or both. In the nineteenth century, for example, agricultural production in the United States increased about 19 to 20 times, almost entirely by the addition of more and more land, livestock, and labor. In the first two or three decades of the twentieth century the use of land for agriculture reached a plateau, and from then on the increases in agricultural production were largely a result of substituting mechanical power for animal and human power, increasing yields of crops, and improving livestock productivity. Although the United States has some 260 million acres of uncropped land that is arable (capable of being plowed, or fit for tillage; the opposite of pasture or woodland), very little of this land is being brought into production. The reason, of course, is not a lack of physical availability, but the costs of bringing this land into use for crops, as compared with its potential productivity. The total cropland in the world might be increased about fourfold if all arable land were used for crops and if multiple cropping were practiced everywhere that physical conditions would permit. Under any foreseeable circumstance of the next few decades, however, it would not pay to do this.

Alternatives indicated
by equal-product curves

At any time, a given level of agricultural production can be achieved with various combinations of land and nonland resources. For the last half century or so, the increases in total agricultural production have been more attributable to rising crop yields and improving livestock productivity than to an increase in the total area of land in crops. It has already been mentioned that in the last half century the increases in agricultural production in the United States have been achieved without much increase in the total land in crops. The same is as true in other developed countries, especially western Europe and Japan, if not more so. In the developing countries the increase in land in crops has been relatively more significant, but even there the main increase has been due to rising yields and improving livestock productivity.

CHANGES IN CROP AREA AND YIELDS

Since 1955, world production of agricultural commodities has increased at an annual compound rate of 2.5 percent (compare Figures 3-1 and 3-2), or by about 60 percent in 25 years. But the total area used for crops has increased by only 12 or 13 percent. In the 20 years between 1957 and 1976, world production of coarse grains (corn, grain sorghums, oats, barley, and rye) increased by about 50 percent (from 443 million tons in 1957–1958 to 662 million tons in 1976–1977). But the area of land harvested increased by only 5.7 percent. Average yields increased by more than 40 percent; a small part of the increase in yield was due to substitution of corn for the other coarse grains.

Between the crop years 1960–1961 and 1977–1978 world production of wheat increased by 58 percent (from about 240 million tons to 380 million tons). Yields increased by 41 percent, while the area harvested increased by only 11 percent.

EQUAL-PRODUCT CURVES

A certain amount of agricultural commodities can be produced in any given crop season with various alternative combinations of land and nonland resources. The 380 million tons of wheat produced in 1977–1978, for example, was produced on 562 million acres. An equal amount of the commodity—or an equal product—could have been produced on, say 100 million acres less land by substituting

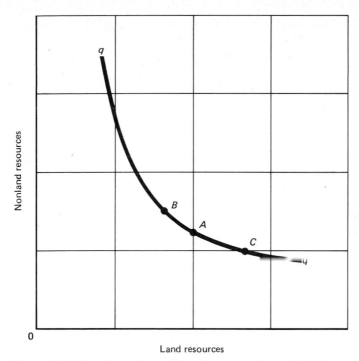

Figure 3-7 Hypothetical equal-product curve for world wheat production. It is assumed that the same amount of wheat, or an equal amount of product, can be produced by any combination of land and nonland resources at any point on this curve, such as *A*, *B*, or *C*.

more fertilizer, adding irrigation water, using more farm chemicals, and so on. Or the crop could have been spread over 100 million acres more, and an equal product produced with less fertilizer, less irrigation water, and fewer farm chemicals.

The basic idea is illustrated in Figure 3-7. Let us say that point *A* represents 562 million acres of land and whatever amounts of nonland resources were used for wheat production in 1977–1978. Then point *B* represents less land and more nonland resources, and point *C* represents more land and less nonland resources.

Definition: An equal-product curve shows the alternative combinations of two sets of resources that will produce the same amount of total product.

Notice that in this case the curve is *bowed in* rather than *bowed out,* as was the case with the production-possibilities curve. Now we have resources rather than products on the *x* and *y* axes. The curve cannot touch either axis without one of the sets of resources going to zero. Thus, the equal-product curve is bowed in for the same reason that the p-p curve is bowed out: *the law of diminishing returns.* As we try to cut down on land resources, for example, it takes more and more nonland resources to obtain the same product. As we cut down on the nonland resources, it takes more and more land resources to obtain the same or an equal amount of the product.

CHANGE IN TOTAL PRODUCT

The equal-product curve must shift outward to show an increase in total product. Figure 3-8 shows the curve shifting from *qq* to *q'q'*. Point *A* shows how much land and nonland resources were used before the shift occurred. Point *B* is located to suggest that there

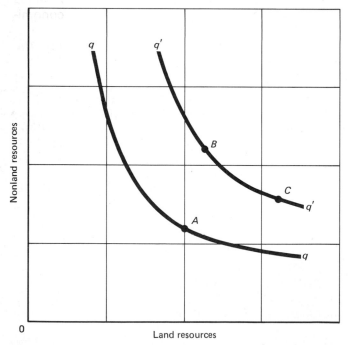

Figure 3-8   Shifting the equal-product curve to show change, or increase in product. The curve is assumed to shift from *qq* to *q'q'* as a result of increasing land resources, nonland resources, or both. In going from point *A* to point *B*, for example, a relatively greater increase occurs in the use of nonland than land resources. In going from point *A* to point *C*, there is a relatively greater increase in use of land.

was a smaller increase in the quantity of land than in the quantity of nonland resources when production increased. This might be visualized as what happened between 1955 and 1977 in the production of coarse grains and wheat. Alternatively, if the increased product used a combination such as at point C, this would imply the use of much more land. This has not been characteristic of recent trends.

Future production goals and resource requirements

The United Nations General Assembly has set a goal for the economic growth of agriculture in developing countries of about 5 percent annually for the rest of this century, as compared with the 2.9 percent annual increase from 1955 to 1977. This assumes that the dependence of developing regions on food exports from developed countries will not increase.[6] This would be an increase of 4.3 times from 1970 to 2000, as compared with an increase of about 1.75 times from 1955 to 1977. Is the goal technically possible? Is it economically feasible?

These are quite different questions. A United Nations study, *The Future of the World Economy,* by Professor Wassily Leontief of Harvard University and others, concluded that the higher rates of growth are technically attainable with known resources and technology.[7] They would require, however, that all, or practically all, the arable land in the developing countries be used for crops. Productivity—measured in terms of crop yields and cattle productivity—would have to increase about threefold. A more modest goal of a 4 percent annual growth rate would still require an increase in crop yields of 200 to 250 percent. These goals are technically attainable.

Are they economically feasible? The investment in land improvements—such as clearing, leveling and terracing, and irrigation and drainage—necessary to raise yields to this level would be immense. It has been suggested that an investment of about $60 billion in land improvements, machinery, transport, and the like would be required to bring the average crop yield in Asia up to 1.6 tons per acre.[8] This is about half of the current maximum yields in many developed

[6]*International Development Strategy: Action Programme of the General Assembly for the Second United Nations Development Decade,* United Nations Publication, Sales No. E.71 II. A, 2, paras. 13–15; and General Assembly resolution 3362 (s-VII) of 19 September 1975, preamble.

[7]Leontief, Carter, and Petri, op. cit., pp. 4, 5.

[8]*Far Eastern Economic Review,* January 23, 1975.

countries. It also represents about half of the estimated maximum for Asia, counting the potentials for multiple cropping, irrigation, and so on. Because of diminishing returns, however, it would require a very much larger investment to raise yields from the 1.6-ton average to the current maximum potential of 3.3 tons per acre.

In addition to the large investments related to land, agribusiness in all its many phases would have to grow rapidly. Farmers would have to have prices for their products that would permit them to save and invest at a much higher rate, and the prices of farm inputs produced by farm service supply industries would have to be low enough to make purchases of these inputs more profitable to the farmer. We may infer that there is serious question about the economic feasibility of these goals for the developing countries even though the potential suggested in the goal is technically attainable.

The broad implication is that the solution to the problem of meeting the goals for economic progress and standard of living is to look to a broader expansion of world trade and a greater reliance on competitive pricing. This means less government interference in world trade and less protection for high-cost industries, including agriculture. In short, it means letting markets work. It also entails more attention to problems of conservation, education, and other aids in the development of resources. We have learned that the costs of converting new lands to crops are very high, including the social costs of erosion—flooding, siltation, and the like. These costs are of major concern, for example, in the Himalayan foothills and the northern plains of India, in the east African highlands, in the plateaus of the Andes in South America, and in the western corn belt and the Great Plains of the United States. The problem of erosion is particularly difficult because the costs to society—especially costs external to the farm operation—are usually much higher than the costs to the farmer.

The question of economic development, particularly the economic development of agriculture, is broad and complicated. No simple solutions are in sight, but there are many important principles. Let us close this chapter on a more optimistic note, with consideration of one of these principles.

Principle of infinite substitutability

Over the very long range, society will subsist on resources that are renewable, such as soil, rainfall, and the energy of the sun, and on elements—such as iron and aluminum—that are practically inexhaustible. After going through stages in which certain nonrenewable resources, such as certain high-grade minerals, are exhausted, society turns to lower-grade inexhaustible resources; this brings it to a steady state of substitution and recycling. This state comes on gradually over several generations, centuries, or millenia (one millenium is 1,000 years), although it is also conceived as developing all the time. Through exploration and advances in technology, society learns to substitute one thing for another, either making or not making economic progress all the while. At some stage or given time, it reaches what is called the *age of substitutability*—a characteristic related to our concepts of the equal-product curve.

H. E. Goeller, of the Oak Ridge National Laboratory, and Alvin M. Weinberg, of the Institute for Energy Analysis, Oak Ridge, have propounded the *principle of infinite substitutability,* applying it to the age of substitutability.[9] The main point of this principle is: *"With the exception of phosphorous and some trace elements for agriculture, mainly cobalt, copper and zinc, and finally the CH_x (coal, oil and gas), society can exist on nearly inexhaustible resources for an indefinite period."*[10] The logic of this principle leads to the technical conclusion that "dwindling mineral resources in the aggregate, with the exception of reduced carbon and hydrogen [coal, oil and gas], are per se unlikely to produce Malthusian catastrophe . . ."[11] But the development of economical alternative sources of energy is critical. This is, however, a task that (according to this principle) can be accomplished over time. In fact, it is possible that in the age of substitutability energy can become cheaper than it has been. The potentials for natural gas, for example, the cleanest and most environmentally acceptable of all fossil fuels, are possibly immense.[12] And other sources of energy such as solar energy, algae, and others, which are practically inexhaustible, may become economically feasible in the age of substitutability.

The implication is that although the social and economic problems of society are very great, the human race need not necessarily face Malthusian catastrophes. The potential exists for higher levels of living for many more people. At some stage society could move off of the growth curve C shown in Figure 3-4 to a new exponential

[9]H. E. Goeller and Alvin M. Weinberg, "The Age of Substitutability," *The American Economic Review,* vol. 68, no. 6, December 1978, pp. 1–11.

[10]T. C. Koopmans, introduction to "The Age of Substitutability," op. cit., p. 1.

[11]Ibid., p. 10.

[12]Bryson Hodgson, photographs by Lowell Georgia, "Natural Gas: The Search Goes On," *National Geographic,* vol. 154, no. 5, November 1978, pp. 632–651.

growth curve. This, however, is a matter for future speculation. Here it is concluded—because of diminishing returns and limited substitutability in the short range of the next generation or so—that increases in agricultural production are limited. The crucial question is not the physical availability of resources, or what is technically attainable. The question is one of economic feasibility, which means costs and the possible returns. Therefore, let us turn in Chapter 4 to a study of production and cost functions.

SUMMARY

Agricultural production in the past quarter century has been increasing at a compound annual rate of about 2.4 percent in developed countries and 2.9 percent in developing countries. But production per capita has increased at an annual rate of about 1.3 percent in developed countries and only 0.4 percent in developing countries. Higher rates of population growth in the developing countries have prevented much, if any, improvement in their per capita food supplies, which are very low and unequally distributed.

World population growth is—for the great majority of people— not following the Malthusian pattern of uncontrolled birthrates. Advances in medicine and health care have greatly lessened the positive checks on population growth and have greatly extended the average length of life in almost all parts of the world. However, the average length of life is still much lower in developing countries, and a higher percentage of the people in these countries suffer from diet deficiencies such as undernourishment and malnutrition. Economic progress is needed to improve this situation.

Economic progress has profound implications for agriculture because it brings expansion in agricultural markets from increasing per capita food consumption. Economic development of the currently developing countries will have the greatest impact. Markets will grow relatively slowly in countries with high rates of grain consumption such as Canada and the United States. There is somewhat more room for growth in Europe and Japan, but large exporting countries such as the United States and others must look to developing regions for the greatest potential market growth.

Agricultural production can be expanded through the growth of either land or nonland resources, or both. The greatest source of expansion in the past half century has been nonland resources. The expansion of nonland resources will be relatively even more important in the future. As a general rule or principle, substitutability becomes more and more important as technology advances and productivity rises, until in the long range we may visualize the operation of the principle of infinite substitutability.

IMPORTANT TERMS
AND CONCEPTS

Total production
Production per capita
Undernourishment
Malnutrition
Population growth
Principle of population
Population projections
Total fertility rate (*TFR*)
Income and food consumption
Equal-product curves
Technical potentials and economic feasibility
Resource substitution
Age of substitutability
Principle of infinite substitutability

LOOKING AHEAD

A real understanding of cost in all its aspects is essential for students of the economics of agriculture, and in Chapter 4 we will study production and cost functions as a foundation for this understanding. This will lead us into general theories of profit maximizing, supply and demand, and market organization, which will be taken up in succeeding chapters.

QUESTIONS AND EXERCISES

1. What are the basic trends in agricultural production in developed and developing countries? Comment on the differences between total and per capita production. What are the implications for the future?
2. What is the difference between undernourishment and malnutrition? How extensive is each among populations in developed and developing countries?

3. What factors have retarded the growth of agricultural production in the United States? What are the implications for production in the future?

4. How long has the human race been on earth? What was the world population in 10,000 B.C.? In A.D. 1600? In 1830? In 1930? In 1960? In 1975?

5. What is the principle of population, according to Malthus? What are the basic postulates on which it rests? What were the implications of this principle in respect to problems of economic progress? Have birthrates been following this principle? Why, or why not?

6. What has changed in respect to the projections of future world population? What are the implications of the lower population projections? What factors account for the declines in birthrates?

7. What are the implications of economic progress for food consumption? For the growth of agricultural markets in developed and developing countries?

8. What is an equal-product curve? What is implied by an outward shift of the curve? What comparative changes in the use of land and nonland resources have taken place since 1955? What does this imply? Does this mean that land is playing a relatively *less* important or *more* important role in agricultural production?

9. What are the general goals that have been established in the United Nations for agricultural production in the developing regions? Are these goals technically attainable? Economically feasible? Explain your answer.

10. What is the principle of infinite substitutability? What are the major exceptions that apply to agriculture? What are the long-range implications for economic progress? For economic progress in respect to agriculture?

4. PRODUCTION FUNCTIONS AND COSTS

4. PRODUCTION FUNCTIONS AND COSTS

❚❚A class in economics would be a real
success if the students gained from it a
real understanding of the meaning of cost
in all its many aspects.**❚❚**

J. M. Clark

John Maurice Clark (1884–1963), professor of economics at the University of
Chicago (1915–1926) and Columbia University (1926–1957), made major
professional contributions to the analysis of production costs. His *Studies
in the Economics of Overhead Costs* (University of Chicago Press, 1923 and
1962) was the standard reference on costs for more than 40 years.

ow that we have studied production-possibilities and equal-product curves, let us use these concepts to develop more understanding about the relationships between production and costs in agriculture. Economics—as was mentioned—is a comparative study, and it is essential to be able to compare the meanings of cost in all its many aspects. Costs, as compared with market prices, determine for agriculture (as well as for other industries) what will be produced, how, and for whom.

Using examples from agriculture, this chapter develops the basic physical relationships between the inputs used in production and the resulting output, and the economic relationships between the costs incurred in production and the resulting products. What are the physical and economic principles that apply?

IN THIS CHAPTER

1. You will learn how to define and construct a production function (the physical relationship between inputs and the resulting outputs).
2. You will learn how production functions and costs are related, and how to solve problems relating to production and costs.
3. You will learn how to distinguish between the short run and the long run as used in economics and see the importance of this distinction, using examples from agriculture.

PRODUCTION FUNCTIONS

Definition: Production is the process of creating an economic good or service from two or more other goods or services.

The basic idea is that it always takes two or more sets of resources, or factors of production such as capital and labor, to create another product, or commodity. Products such as wheat, corn, milk, or cotton are forthcoming only as a number of resources, or factors, are combined. Nothing is produced from a single resource such as soil alone, rain without sunshine, or sun without rain. Even the process of "cloning" requires more than the parent stock to produce another individual. Crops and livestock are biologically oriented—generally male and female. Agricultural crops generally require land, management and labor, and other forms of capital such as seed, fertilizer, machinery, and so on. Livestock require feed, shelter, and care.

General theory of production

The general theory of production starts with the idea that you must have a certain amount of land (or space), management or labor, and other forms of capital. At any time or in any circumstance, *there is a certain maximum amount of output—for any given combination of inputs, or factors of production—that can be created.* This technical law relating inputs to outputs is so important that economists have given it a special name: the *production function.*

Definition: The production function is the technical relationship between inputs and outputs, indicating the maximum amount of output that can be produced with each and every set or combination of the specified inputs.

A given state of knowledge and technology is assumed when the inputs are specified, or identified. There is a specified, or functional, relationship between inputs and outputs, hence the term *production function.*

There are countless production functions in the world. Almost every firm (such as a farm firm) has many production functions, and there are innumerable firms, or productive units. But we need not think about complications in the world. We want to understand the principle. Let us consider the general idea.

TOTAL PHYSICAL PRODUCT (TPP):
THE GENERAL EQUATION

Definition: Total physical product (*TPP*) is the maximum amount that can be produced with any given combination of fixed and variable inputs.

Definition: A fixed input is a factor of production that does not change as the level of output is changed.

Definition: A variable input is a factor of production that changes in such a way as to change the level of output.

TPP generally changes directly, but usually not in direct proportion to the change in a variable input. For example, a 10 percent increase in a variable input generally increases the total product, but seldom by just 10 percent. The exact relationship between inputs and outputs—most important, between the variable input or

The total physical product in this production unit includes eggs, broilers, and cull hens from the producing flock. Which inputs are fixed and which are variable?

inputs and a specified output—is expressed by an equation generally having the following form:

$$Y = X_1 \mid X_2, X_3, \ldots, X_n$$

Where:

Y denotes total physical product (TPP)

X_1 denotes the variable input or group of variable inputs

X_2 denotes a fixed input such as total land in a given crop season

X_3 denotes a second fixed input—such as family farm labor— having in this instance no alternative use

X_n denotes other unidentified fixed inputs, or inputs assumed to be given, such as a given state of nature, rainfall and its distribution, the condition of the soil, and so on

The vertical bar between X_1 and X_2 indicates that all inputs to the left of the bar are variable and all inputs to the right are fixed, or assumed to be fixed, as either a specific datum or a specified range of data. A farmer, for example, may assume a certain amount and distribution of rainfall within a given range of precipitation during a forthcoming crop season, and make decisions concerning the variable inputs, based on this assumption.

Example: *TPP*   A farm has one section (640 acres) of good cropland suitable for continuous corn and three person-years of family labor—no more and no less. The farmer has sufficient capital to buy up to eight units of variable inputs to go with the fixed land and labor. The farmer visualizes a production function based on knowledge of crop responses to the inputs, as shown in Table 4-1, assuming that the variable inputs are purchased one unit at a time. (We will assume later for purposes of illustration that each unit of variable input costs $20,000, but this information is not needed to develop the production function.)

Figure 4-1 is drawn to illustrate the data from Table 4-1; each specific combination of variable inputs and *TPP* appears as a point on the diagram. Notice that *TPP* rises very little as the first unit of variable input is added. It rises more as the second unit is added, and still more as the third unit is added. Then it rises less and less as each successive unit is added until it reaches its zenith, or maximum level, after which it turns down.

Table 4-1   **Example of a production function: A farm firm with variable inputs purchased, fixed inputs consisting of one section of good cropland, and three units of family labor**

Variable inputs purchased for production (X_1)	Fixed input: one section of good cropland[a] (X_2)	Fixed input: three units of family labor[b] (X_3)	Total physical product (*TPP*), tons of corn[c] (Y)
0	1	3	0
1	1	3	100
2	1	3	600
3	1	3	1,500
4	1	3	2,000
5	1	3	2,300
6	1	3	2,450
7	1	3	2,400
8	1	3	2,000

[a]One section of land is 640 acres.

[b]The units of labor are not necessarily identical, but are fixed in total for purposes of illustration. Three adults are assumed to be retained on this farm.

[c]All references to tons are in terms of metric tons (1 metric ton = 2,240 pounds), rather than "short" tons (see also page 26). A ton of corn is the standard equivalent of 40 bushels of no. 2 yellow corn, which is approximately 56 pounds per bushel. Thus: 40 × 56 = 2,240.

Note: Hypothetical data.

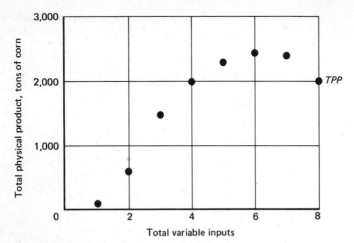

Figure 4-1   Production function expressed as points on a schedule. This is a farm firm growing corn with fixed inputs consisting of 1 section (640 acres) of good cropland, 3 units of labor, and purchased variable inputs (hypothetical data).

Economists often interpolate between the points on a diagram such as Figure 4-1 to produce a continuous curve, as shown in Figure 4-2. This drops the assumption that investments in the variable input must be added in discrete units. The new curve is based on the assumption that the variable inputs can be purchased in various amounts at the same unit price. It is drawn with the aid of a French curve.

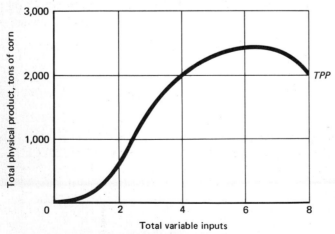

Figure 4-2   Production function as a continuous schedule. A farm firm growing corn.

Table 4-2 A production function and some of its derivatives: a farm firm growing corn

Variable inputs, units (X_1)	Total physical product (*TPP*), tons (*Y* or *Q*)	Marginal physical product (*MPP*), tons [$(Y+1) - Y$]	Average physical product (*APP*), tons (Y/X_1)
0	0		0
		100	
1	100		100
		500	
2	600		300
		900	
3	1,500		500
		500	
4	2,000		500
		300	
5	2,300		460
		100	
6	2,400		400⅓
		50	
7	2,400		342⁶⁄₇
		−400	
8	2,000		250

Note: Hypothetical data.

MARGINAL PHYSICAL PRODUCT (*MPP*):
DERIVATION FROM *TPP*

Definition: Marginal physical product (*MPP*) at each level of output is the net addition to total physical product from adding an additional unit of variable input.

In Table 4-2, *MPP* from the first unit of variable input is 100 tons of corn. The second unit adds 500 tons, the third 900 tons, the fourth 500 tons, and so on. There are increasing returns up to the third unit of variable input. From there on diminishing returns occur.

AVERAGE PHYSICAL PRODUCT (*APP*):
TPP DIVIDED BY UNITS OF VARIABLE INPUT

Definition: Average physical product (*APP*) per unit of variable input is the total physical product divided by the number of variable units at each level of input.

The fixed inputs are not included in Table 4-2; they are not required for purposes of the current illustration, and learning

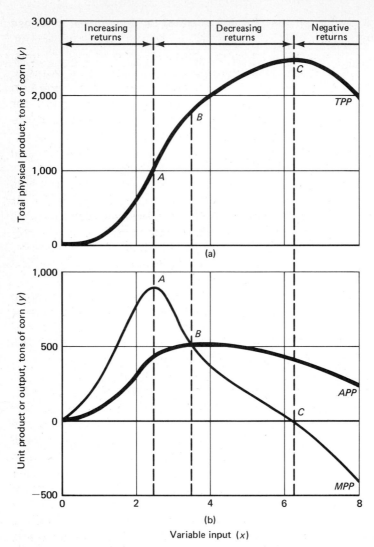

Figure 4-3 Production function with total, marginal, and average products. This illustrates increasing, decreasing, and negative returns. Note that the vertical scale of (b) differs from that of (a), the horizontal scales are the same, and (b) is directly below (a).

requires the orderly loss of unnecessary information. We may include these data again when they will be useful to us.

Example: Increasing and diminishing returns   Figure 4-3, which is based on Table 4-2, illustrates the relationship between *TPP* and its derivatives, *MPP* and *APP*.

The general shape of *TPP* is like a small hill, which in this case has been chopped off after adding the eighth unit of variable inputs. Increasing returns at an increasing rate occur up to point *A*. That is, the slope of *TPP* becomes steeper as we add more of the variable input. Each successive unit of the variable input (or given fraction thereof) adds more to *TPP* than was added by the previous unit (or given fraction). From *A* to *C,* total product is increasing, but the increase from each successive unit is becoming smaller. That is, *TPP* is increasing at a decreasing rate. Beyond *C, TPP* turns down because of the harmful effects of additional inputs.

The purpose of Figure 4-3 is to demonstrate the relationships between *MPP* and *APP* as well as their relationship to *TPP.* At *A*, the point on the *TPP* curve where returns to the variable input shift from increasing at an increasing rate to increasing at a decreasing rate (also called the *inflection point*), *MPP* is at its maximum. Beyond *A*, diminishing returns occur. decreasing from *A* to *C*, and negative beyond *C*.

How typical is this illustration? Most agricultural production functions relating to crop and livestock production have a narrow range of increasing marginal productivity and a wide range of diminishing marginal productivity. In livestock feeding, for example, an increasing marginal productivity of feeds exists when the ration is below the level required for maintenance of body weight. In this case, an increase in the amount of feed by 10, 20, or 30 percent, which carries the ration out of the maintenance range, will usually increase the gain by more than 10, 20, or 30 percent. Beyond this range—that is, beyond point *A*—the relationship is mainly one of diminishing marginal feed productivity; beyond point *C*, it is also one of negative marginal returns. On the one hand, beyond *C* the daily input of concentrates can be so high that the animal is thrown off feed, and the total output of livestock declines. On the other hand, the animal can be fed to such great weights and for such long periods that it finally dies of old age. The total and average products then fall to zero. This, of course, would not be rational for the profit-seeking farmer, and it raises the question: What is rational in production?

Rational and irrational stages of production

Production functions of the classical type—which include ranges of increasing, decreasing, and negative marginal returns—can be divided into three segments, denoted as the three stages of production. Figure 4-4, which is similar to Figure 4-3 in its general relation-

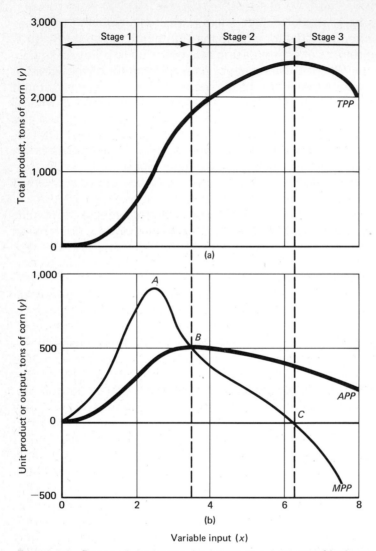

Figure 4-4   Stages of production for a farm firm with variable inputs purchased, and fixed inputs of land and labor (hypothetical data).

ships, illustrates these stages. Stage 1 extends from zero up to the point where the average productivity of the variable factor is at its maximum (point *B* in Figure 4-3). That is, the maximum point on the *APP* curve defines the end of stage 1. Stage 2 extends from this point to the point of maximum *TPP*, or where *MPP* is zero (point *C* in Figure 4-3). Stage 3 includes all inputs that have a negative marginal product, and it extends over the entire range of declining *TPP*. A production function that has only increasing marginal returns would be entirely within stage 1. A function characterized by diminishing marginal returns from the outset would be limited to stages 2 and 3.

IRRATIONAL PRODUCTION: STAGE 1

For the producer to limit resource use to stage 1 is uneconomical. As production is increased from zero to the end of stage 1, the average productivity of all previous inputs of the variable resource increases continuously as more inputs are added. As shown in Figure 4-4*b, MPP* is above *APP* throughout this stage. With each additional unit of input, more is being added to the total output than was added *on the average* by the previous inputs. Therefore, if it pays to produce at all, it will pay to produce up to the end of stage 1 at least, where *APP* is at its maximum point. We can know this without knowing anything about the prices of inputs or outputs, as long as both are positive.

Sometimes, however, a manager may not be able to push production to the end of stage 1 because of limited resources. What then? As production is pushed toward the limits of stage 1, a greater product is forthcoming from the fixed factors as well as from each unit of the variable factor. When there is an upper limit on the amount of the variable factor that is available, a greater product can be obtained by leaving idle or discarding part of the factor that was considered fixed. In our example, for instance, if the farmer cannot find any additional help and must operate the farm alone, the farmer should leave part of the farm idle rather than try to seed the whole thing. If the farmer cannot buy all the fertilizer needed to reach crop yields at least as high as *B*, the total product will be increased by concentrating the fertilizer on only part of the farm for as long as increasing average returns from fertilizer per unit of land are thought to prevail. The alternative of spreading the fertilizer more thinly over the entire crop will not add as much of the total product.

IRRATIONAL PRODUCTION: STAGE 3

Stage 3 is also a level of resource use that is irrational; resources can be cut back or left idle, with the effect of increasing the total output. The only difference is that now the variable resource rather than the fixed resource is withdrawn from use. In the example in Table 4-2, as the variable inputs are cut back from 8 to 7 to 6, the total product increases from 2,000 to 2,400 to 2,450 tons of corn. If the product has any value or price whatsoever, a greater economic return can be obtained by using less of the variable factor even if it is free. If the total product just stays the same and the variable inputs are not free, the net return will be increased by using less of them.

In either stage 1 or stage 3 it can be said that irrational production exists if resources can be rearranged (increased or decreased) in any way that will (1) give a greater product from the same amount of resources, or (2) give the same product with a smaller aggregate outlay on the total fixed and variable resources. Even without knowledge of prices, we can say that production is irrational, or uneconomic, if resources can be recombined to yield more of the product from the same resources or yield the same product from fewer resources.

RATIONAL PRODUCTION: STAGE 2

Now it is evident that stage 2 is the only rational stage of production. The rate at which variable inputs are applied to fixed inputs cannot fall outside this range if the economic return is to be maximized. But we cannot tell where production should fall within this stage until we know something about prices of factors and products: the costs of production associated with each level of output as well as the value of the output.

Before taking up this question, it will be beneficial to consider a number of other important topics related to production functions. These include the effects of advancing technology on production functions, a classification of the types of production decisions that a manager must make, and a statement of the law of comparative advantage as it relates to production functions.

Effects of advances in technology: production innovations

Advances in technology either (1) raise the production function so that more is produced from a given level of resource use, or (2) shift it to the left so that the same amount can be produced with fewer resources. These alternatives are illustrated in Figure 4-5a and b. Generally speaking, in either case more output is produced from each unit of input; to use our earlier terminology, there is an

Figure 4-5 Effects of advancing technology on the production function. The new technology is visualized in (a) as primarily output-increasing, in (b) as primarily resource-saving, and in (c) as output-increasing, favoring the large farm.

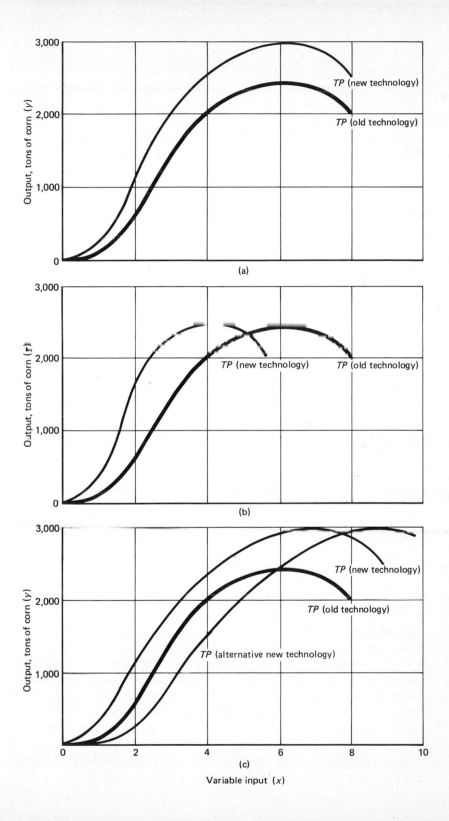

(a)

(b)

(c)

Variable input (x)

increase in productivity. The increase is generally thought of as quantitative, but qualitative factors are also involved in new factors or products. The changes in quality are measured through the price system, or through the construction of indexes of output, taking account of both quantity and quality. Alternatively the new technology may tend to favor the larger farm, moving the production function as indicated in Figure 4-5c. The function for the new technology may be above that of the old at all input levels. Alternatively, more typically, it may be below the old function at low levels of input use and above it at high input levels. This implies that the new technology is disadvantageous for the small farm, giving both relative and absolute advantages to the large farm.

In either the quantitative or the qualitative case an advance in technology changes the production function, and this changes the most profitable level for use of the various resources. Rational production will still be found in stage 2, but it is important to realize that a given advance will be either output-increasing as implied in Figure 4-5a or resource-saving as implied in Figure 4-5b. Fertilizer, for example, or a technological improvement in fertilizer, tends to be primarily output-increasing, and its use may call for either more or less of other inputs such as cultivation, irrigation, or pesticide controls. Generally speaking, technological advances tend to "go together" as "packages" of new technology. The so-called "green revolution" in developing countries, for instance, is usually based on a combination of new or improved crop varieties, more fertilizer, sometimes more irrigation, and more farm chemicals for control of weeds, insects, and crop diseases. Although each new technology may tend to displace a more traditional practice, a given innovation tends to increase the productivity of another, and so the total package is output-increasing. We must not forget, however, that any new technology must be profitable for the farmer, or it will not "pay" to use it.

The new technologies that seem to be primarily resource-saving are also generally output-increasing in practice. Where farm tractors displace horses and mules or other types of animal and human power, the effect—which may be thought of as primarily labor-saving—is to increase output. In the United States, when tractors became profitable for farmers to use, the horse and mule population dropped sharply; the number of workers on farms also began to drop, although more slowly. Since a good farmer could get yields just about as high by farming with horses or with a tractor, however, the farmer generally did not buy a tractor just to get higher yields, although a better job of plowing and cultivating as well as more timely operations could have produced this effect. Primarily the tractor saved resources, but the effect was also to increase output, both for farming and for nonfarm industries. The land that had been used to grow feed for horses and mules was largely converted to cash grain and other crops. Agricultural output expanded as a result of the saving of this resource; of course, over time the net reduction of some 4 million farm families increased the nonfarm labor force.

In summary, although we may think of an advance in technology as primarily tending to save resources, in the end it tends to increase output. The resources saved are likely to become available for other uses. The total output increases as technological advance in one sector of the economy releases, or frees, more resources for use in other sectors. This has been the general experience with technological advances in agriculture, and this has widespread implications not only for agriculture but for other economic sectors as well. Some of these implications relate directly to the types of decisions that must be made.

Decisions in agricultural production

TYPES OF DECISIONS

Products such as wheat, corn, milk, and cotton are forthcoming only as a number of resources are combined in response to three specific types of decisions. These are generally designated (1) factor-product decisions, (2) factor-factor decisions, and (3) product-product decisions.

Factor-product decisions   The basis for factor-product decisions was outlined in the discussion of the production function. Output is dependent on the amount of a single resource that is combined with the fixed resources. In this sense, the single variable resource may contain a wide variety of inputs or factors, and we need to consider how choices are made among these inputs, or factors—this is a factor-factor decision.

Factor-factor decisions   If it has been decided which product shall be produced, decisions must be made about how much of each input, or factor, to use. The rational answer depends on the prices of the factors and how well one substitutes for another, or how the marginal productivity of each factor compares with its cost or price. Generally, as may be inferred from our study of the production function, if capital is unlimited each factor will be used at least up through the end of stage 1. But in choosing among substitutable inputs—such as different kinds of fertilizers, different types and sizes of tractors, or different lines of machinery—the rational manager will pay attention to costs as well as to production functions. Choices will be made among the substitute factors according to their respective costs or prices and their comparative marginal productivities. Rationally, the profit-minded manager will want to use as much of the factor as it pays to use, but no more; the basis for this is the analysis of cost and return as more or less of each factor is used.

Product-product decisions   Product-product decisions require judgments about how many enterprises to have on a farm, or how many lines of a product to produce in a plant, and how many resources to allocate to each enterprise. Suppose a farmer has a certain amount of land that is available for grain production, a hog enterprise, and a cattle-feeding operation. Choices will have to be made about how many cattle and hogs can be managed with the available labor and how these operations will fit with the production of grain. Perhaps an enterprise should be added or dropped. Certain resources, such as labor or available capital, place a limit or restraint on the amount of livestock that can be managed without giving up some of the crop production. The decision depends in part on the degree of competition that exists among the enterprises, the degree of complementarity among them, or the extent to which one enterprise tends to supplement another. These considerations, and the matter of diversification versus specialization, are discussed below.

CONSIDERATIONS IN
PRODUCTION DECISIONS

Competitive, supplementary, and complementary enterprises
    Competitive enterprise   Competitive enterprise is defined as follows:

Definition: Competition exists among enterprises when the output of one can be increased only by reducing the output of another.

Crop and livestock operations that require the same resources at the same time are competitive when one can be increased only at the expense of another. A flock of sheep in the northern Great Plains is competitive with spring wheat production, for example, if the ewes are bred to begin lambing at about the same time the farmer expects to start the spring field work. This is about the optimum time for lambing because the weather has begun to warm. The lambs will not be exposed to as much cold as they would have been earlier. Soon they will be strong enough to enjoy the early green pastures, and they will be ready for market in the early fall. But competition for labor in the early spring planting season may force the farmer to adopt an earlier or later lambing schedule or even discontinue the sheep enterprise.

A change in technology tends to change the competitive relationships among products. Thus, sheep compete for feed with other livestock, especially range cattle. A change in technology that favors range cattle may tend to be disadvantageous to sheep. On the other hand, quite apart from this, the development of substitute products for wool is disadvantageous to sheep. The farm manager's choices between two competitive products, or among several, must be based on the technological relationships as well as a knowledge of markets. Over the past several years, changes in the technologies of production and relative market prices have resulted in a sharp drop in the American sheep population.

Supplementary enterprise   Supplementary enterprise is defined as follows:

Definition: Enterprises are supplementary to each other when they use different resources, or the same resources at different times.

In some of the northern Great Plains, sheep and winter wheat tend to be supplementary enterprises because both the harvest of the winter wheat crop and the seeding of a new crop come at a time when little labor is required for sheep. But although they are supplementary in the use of labor, they may be directly competitive in the use of land. This will be the case unless the farmer has some rough, poorly drained, hilly, or wooded land that is not suitable for wheat or other crops. The point is that some products that are supplementary to each other in the use of some resources tend to be competitive in the use of others, and the manager must consider the effect of the product-product decision on all the resources involved.

In most countries, there is much grazing or pasture land not suitable for crops, and so to some extent livestock are supplementary to crops. The United States, for example, has some 2,264 million acres of land. About 58 percent of that land is forest, grassland pasture, and range, generally not suitable for production of crops (Fig-

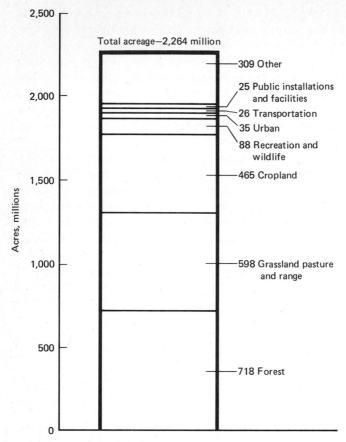

Figure 4-6 Major uses of land in the United States. The United States has a land area of 2,264 million acres. Of the total land area, about one-fifth is cropland; more than one-fourth is permanent grassland pasture and range; nearly one-third is forest land; and one-fifth is in a variety of uses, or unclassified. (*Note:* 1974 data.)

ure 4-6). The total land harvested has tended to be around 350 million acres or less (Figure 4-7). Thus, there is wide latitude in the United States for supplementary crop and livestock enterprises. These enterprises not only tend to use different land resources but are also supplementary to a degree in the use of labor. Cattle may be raised on pasture during the summer when other farm work is at its peak. Also, additional feeder stock may be bought to feed throughout the winter months when the farmer is not working in the fields. Livestock and crops are supplementary in their use of some resources, while they are directly competitive in their use of others.

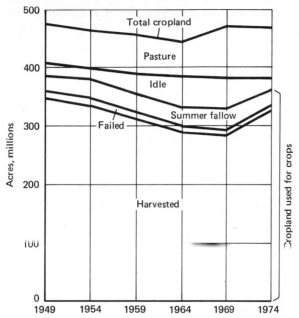

Figure 4-7 Major uses of cropland in the United States. The United States has some 465 million acres of land classified as cropland. Each year part of the cropland is used for crops, part is used for pasture, and part is idle. The proportions vary significantly from year to year.

Complementary enterprise   Complementary enterprise is defined as follows:

Definition: Enterprises are complementary if increasing the production of one automatically increases the output of another.

The production of beef and dairy products is complementary to the production of cattle hides. The growing of range cattle is complementary to the production of grain-fattened cattle. The growing of legumes such as alfalfa and sweet clover is—up to a point—complementary to the production of small grains such as wheat, oats, and barley. But we must emphasize that this is true only up to a point. In a rotation of sweet clover with wheat, oats, and barley, the legume will tend to increase the yield of the crop that follows it because the legume fixes nitrogen in the soil. Thus, the crops are complementary in terms of annual yield. But they are also competitive; beyond a point, an increase in the production of one will cut down the total output of another. To make the matter more complicated, clover is also supplementary to small grains in the use of labor because the two crops use labor resources at different times of the year.

Specialization and diversification   The farm manager must make judgments about what to produce and how much, based on considerations of cost and return: how much of one product must be given up to get so much of another, and how much the cost will be increased or decreased in going from one to another. Many things must be taken into account in deciding whether to specialize in the production of one or two crops or a single livestock enterprise, or whether to diversify by producing a number of products. What are the relative advantages of specializing and diversifying?

The distinction between a *specialized* and a *diversified* farm is one of degree, or common acceptance of the terms. Common usage suggests that a specialized farm is one in which the major part, if not practically all, of the farm income is derived from one or two enterprises. Examples are a wheat farm in Kansas, a large broiler unit in Georgia, a cash corn and soybean farm in the corn belt, a peach orchard in California, and so on. Specialization is easy to see, but diversification is more complicated. A diversified farm may take one of several forms: combining crop and livestock enterprises; growing different types of crops such as cotton, sugarcane, soybeans, and alfalfa; or producing a number of animal or poultry products such as milk, pork, wool, eggs, and broilers.

In any large country such as the United States there is a wide range of farm firms, varying from highly specialized to widely diversified. One of the most important jobs of the farm manager is to appraise the advantages and disadvantages of each and decide whether to specialize in a given situation or tend toward more diversification. On a farm of a given size, specialization has the advantages of producing in large volume and concentrating management decisions on a small number of things. One can become more expert, or professional, by concentrating on one or two enterprises. Feed, fertilizer, and other farm supplies may be bought at a lower unit cost for a large enterprise on a specialized farm. Buying supplies for several enterprises on a farm of the same size may result in higher unit costs. Also, specialized farmers tend to gain a higher price or premium by selling in large volume, and some also become highly proficient in hitting the peaks of market prices. Some, in addition, prearrange their terms of sale by using the commodity-futures markets, contracting ahead, or combining or integrating their business with a marketing firm.

Specialization, however, tends to expose the farmer to greater risks as regards market uncertainty and crop failure, and this makes income uncertain. Also, specialization in a single crop or two often places excessive burdens on farm labor within a few months of the year. This not only creates strain but also tends to reduce family income from farming. On the other hand, specialization in a live-stock enterprise such as dairy or hog production tends to tie the family down, sometimes creating a life of drudgery.

The two main reasons why farm families diversify are (1) to uti-lize more fully the total resources of the farm unit, especially labor, and (2) to reduce or avoid the risk of financial failure. Generally, the farm work load can be spread more uniformly over the year in a greater variety of jobs, fuller use can be made of machinery and equipment, and the smaller-size enterprises can be increased or decreased to take advantage of changing market conditions. On the other hand, the diversified farm generally fails to capture the cost advantages of large-volume production and marketing. There are many more management decisions to make, and a relatively large investment in various types of machines and equipment is some-times required.

In general, technological advance in farming has provided more cost advantages for specialization and for larger-size farms and agribusiness firms. Also, as labor requirements on individual farms of a given size have continued to decline, members of the farm fam-ily have been released from some farm work to enter an off-farm occupation. Thus, the general trend has been for more specializa-tion in farming, combined with a diversification of the income of the farm family between farm and nonfarm sources. Indeed, according to the law of comparative advantage, this is what we should expect from technological advance in agriculture.

Law of comparative advantage

Definition: The law of comparative advantage states that the total output of goods and services can be increased by having firms (or people, industries, countries, etc.) do what they do best, or most efficiently, and by letting the market work as freely as possible to distribute the total goods and services.

The law of comparative advantage is universal in its application. How it works can be illustrated with an example from agriculture. Figure 4-8 is a picture of the major types of farming in the United

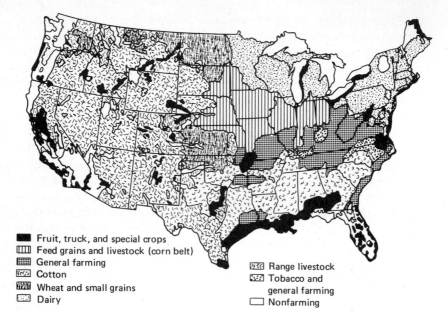

Fruit, truck, and special crops
Feed grains and livestock (corn belt)
General farming
Cotton
Wheat and small grains
Dairy

Range livestock
Tobacco and
general farming
Nonfarming

Figure 4-8   Major types of farming in the United States.

States according to the dominant specialty in each region. This type of regional specialization of production is defined very broadly, and the individual farms in each region are by no means limited to the products indicated for each region. Some regions and some farms within each region of course specialize more than others, while overall the climate, soils, topography, markets, and institutional patterns of development provide certain areas with certain advantages in the production of crops and livestock.

Although the specialization implied in Figure 4-8 is heavily influenced by climate, soils, and topography, economic aspects must be included to get a true picture. The corn belt produces more than most other regions in many crop enterprises, including corn, soybeans, wheat, and many vegetables and fruits. The part of the Great Plains including eastern Colorado, most of Kansas, western Oklahoma, and northern Texas tends to specialize in winter wheat, with some feed grains and livestock, fruits, vegetables, and other commodities. How much each farmer within a region tends to specialize depends on both the physical and the economic relations embodied in the law of comparative advantage, which says in effect that: *To maximize profits, each producer should produce those products—*

considering yields, costs, and returns—from which the percentage return above cost is the greatest.

Let us consider an example. Table 4-3 presents hypothetical yield data for corn and wheat for two types of farm: a cash-grain farm in the corn belt and a wheat farm in the part of the Great Plains mentioned above. The farm in the corn belt, as may be seen, has an absolute advantage in both corn and wheat yields—yields per acre are higher in each case.

Now let us suppose that each farmer in Table 4-3 requires 100 tons of corn and 100 tons of wheat to carry out the individual farm plan of grain and livestock sales. What will be the more economical way to get it? Table 4-3 shows that if each farmer tries to provide the farm's own requirements, a total of 300 acres must be used in production. If the farm in the corn belt specializes in corn and the Great Plains farm specializes in wheat, however, a total of only 266⅔ acres is required and 33⅓ acres is saved. Although the farm in the corn belt has an absolute advantage in both corn and wheat, it has a comparative advantage in corn, and the farm in the Great Plains has a comparative advantage in wheat. Note that we do not need to know anything about the production costs or prices of the two products to see that the exploitation of comparative advantages saves resources. Or it can be said that the total product can be increased from a given total amount of resources by the exploitation of comparative advantages. What is true within an industry or a country is also true between and among countries. This explains why trade is profitable between and among economic units with various levels of efficiency: among developed countries as well as developing countries, between rich nations and poor nations, and so on.

Table 4-3   Comparative advantage in producing corn and wheat

Type of farm	Yields, tons per acre Corn	Wheat	Acres required to produce 100 tons of wheat and 100 tons of corn on each farm Corn	Wheat	Total	Acres required to produce the same total amount of corn and wheat using comparative advantage Corn	Wheat	Total
Corn belt	3	1½	33⅓	66⅔	100	66⅔	None	66⅔
Great Plains	1	1	100	100	200	None	200	200
Total acres required			133⅓	166⅔	300	66⅔	200	266⅔

Note: Hypothetical data.

A logical question arises, however, as to the extent to which each economic unit will want to exploit its own comparative advantage. We can imagine that if the price of wheat rises high enough relative to corn, the farmer in the corn belt will grow some wheat. Also, farmers in the specialty wheat areas of the southern Great Plains often grow some corn. Why? This is because of increasing (relative) costs, the primary effect of which is to make specialization less than complete. Table 4-3 is based on the simplifying assumption of constant costs, which tends to result in complete specialization. But constant costs are the exception rather than the rule in agriculture. Application of the law of increasing (relative) costs, as discussed in Chapter 2 and illustrated in Table 2-2, tends to introduce diversification, even in situations where strong comparative advantages prevail.

This suggests that it is time to turn our attention to the anlaysis of production costs, taking account of the principles of production that have been discussed. The following discussion will be divided into (1) the short run, where some costs are fixed and some are variable, and (2) the long run, where all costs are variable.

PRODUCTION COSTS

Opportunity cost

The economist's concepts of costs are based on the fact that resources are scarce and have alternative uses. Thus, to use a combination of resources in the production of a particular good means that certain alternative products must be forgone. This does not rule out using the same resource, such as a tractor or farm labor, in various lines of production, however. It simply says that production of one product entails giving up so much of the opportunity to produce something else. Thus, production involves what economists call an *opportunity cost.*

Definition: The opportunity cost of producing a certain amount of a good or service is the value of the same resources in an alternative use.

If you were a farmer who owned your own land, for example, the cost to you of using that land in the production of wheat or corn is the net return it might yield in the production of some other product, or what the land would return if you rented it out on the open market. In other words, the cost of using the land for a particular purpose is the value of the opportunity that is forgone. This applies to the land, to your own time, and to any other resource that is used in production. There is always an opportunity cost for everything, whether or not a specific payment is made. The concept applies to leisure and recreation as well as to the production of goods and services. It is a universal phenomenon.

Explicit and implicit costs

Given this notion of opportunity costs and alternative costs, it can be said that economic costs are payments that a firm must make, or incomes it must provide, to attract and keep resources away from alternative lines of production. These payments or incomes may be either explicit or implicit.

Explicit costs are payments made for such things as hired labor, rented land, and industrial commodities or materials bought for the production of farm commodities.

In addition, a firm or family may use certain resources that it owns and controls. Our notion of opportunity costs tells us that regardless of whether the resource is owned, rented, or hired, there is a cost involved in using that resource in production. The costs of resources that are owned—as well as one's own time, which may

Here are some farmers attending an agronomy field day. What are their explicit and implicit costs in attending? What is their opportunity cost?

not involve a current expenditure—are *implicit costs.* To the firm or family, these implicit costs are the money payments that the self-employed resources could have earned in the best alternative employments. A farm that is operated by the owner costs that owner the money that could be received by renting it to another. The opportunity cost of the family staying on the farm is what the family members could earn in their best alternative employments plus the other net advantages or disadvantages of the alternative living conditions. In addition, the implicit costs include a minimum payment, sometimes called a *normal profit,* which is the return necessary to offset the management costs of uncertainty and risk taking. If the farmer cannot make at least a minimum normal profit, it may not be prudent or rational for the family to continue in farming. On the other hand, over and beyond the normal profit, the family may make an additional *pure profit,* which might appear as a windfall gain in excess of the minimum normal profit required to keep them in business.

Both explicit and implicit costs must be taken into account. This may be made more clear by thinking of resources and services as stocks and flows. *Stock services* such as fertilizer and feed may be entirely used up in the production process and must be replaced. If they are not used today, they can be saved for tomorrow or next year. The costs are generally explicit. *Flow services* such as labor or a barn may be used again and again. If they are not used today, the productivity that might have been forthcoming is lost and cannot be regained. The cost of not using them is implicit until the resource is exhausted. Nevertheless, over time the cost of the flow resource is a real cost because resources or commodities involving stocks and flows are used to produce other products, or commodities. Both explicit and implicit costs are included in the firm's costs of production.

The short run and the long run

Think of production as a continuous flow that can be marked off into various kinds of periods. The costs incurred in production depend on the types of adjustments that can be made within a given period. Some resources can be adjusted quickly, such as expenditures on soil fertility, some hired labor, and some machinery repairs, fuel, and hire. Others are very difficult to adjust, such as annual salaries and long-term labor contracts, mortgage interest, property taxes, and other land costs. Some of these may take years to adjust.

These differences make it essential to distinguish between the short run and the long run.

Definition: The short run is a production and market period within which there are both fixed and variable costs.

The short run refers to a period too brief to change the capacity of a firm such as a farm or an agribusiness, yet long enough to permit changes in the level at which the fixed resources are used. The short run might be a single crop season, or two or three seasons, in which the quantity and cost of land have been fixed. Or it might be several years, such as the life cycle of an orange grove, during which time there is no attractive opportunity for buying or leasing more land or for disposing of some of the land being used. But the existing fixed resources can be used more or less intensively in the short run.

Definition: The long run is a production and market period within which all costs are variable.

The long run refers to a period of time which is extensive enough, from the veiwpoint of existing firms, to permit them to change all the resources employed, including the production capacity of the firm. Also, from the viewpoint of an industry the long run permits existing firms to go out of business and new firms to enter the market. For example, the long run permits all farmers who are not making a normal profit to quit farming. It allows all farms that can be profitably combined, or integrated, to do so. It allows farmers to change from one enterprise to another in whatever way might be profitable, and it permits all new farmers who may be attracted to agriculture to enter farming.

Let us turn now to the analysis of short-run costs and then consider long-run costs. The difference is that one includes fixed costs and the other does not.

Production costs
in the short run

FIXED, VARIABLE, AND TOTAL COSTS

Table 4-4 has been designed to compare all the production costs for the hypothetical farm presented in Table 4-1. Columns (2), (3), and (4) give the fixed cost, variable cost, and total cost for the total product given in column (1).

Table 4-4 Production costs of a farm firm

| | Total-cost data, per year | | | Unit-cost data, per year | | | |
| (1) | (2) | (3) | (4) | (5) | (6) | (7) | (8) |
Total product, corn, tons (Y or Q)	Fixed cost (FC)	Variable cost (VC)	Total cost (TC = FC + VC)	Average fixed cost per unit (AFC = TFC/Q)	Average variable cost per unit (AVC = TVC/Q)	Average cost per unit (AC = TC/Q)	Marginal cost (MC = change in TC / change in Q)
0	$120,000	0	$120,000	Infinity	0	Infinity	
							$200.00
100	120,000	$20,000	140,000	$1,200.00	$200.00	$1,400.00	
							40.00
600	120,000	40,000	160,000	200.00	66.67	266.67	
							22.22
1,500	120,000	60,000	180,000	80.00	40.00	120.00	
							40.00
2,000	120,000	80,000	200,000	60.00	40.00	100.00	
							66.67
2,300	120,000	100,000	220,000	52.17	43.48	95.65	
							133.33
2,450	120,000	120,000	240,000	48.98	48.98	97.96	
2,400	120,000	140,000	260,000	50.00	58.33	108.33	

Note: Hypothetical data.

Fixed cost   Fixed costs are defined as follows:

Definition: Fixed costs are costs which do not change in total with changes in output.

Fixed costs—$120,000 for a year in our example—do not change regardless of the stage of production within which the firm operates. We might assume that this total includes the explicit costs of property taxes, interest on farm mortgages and other debt contracts, and contract payments for year-round labor. It also includes implicit charges, which are assumed to be fixed, such as a return on the owner's equity, an allowance for depreciation, and perhaps an additional budget item for the living expenses of the farm operator's family. Notice that the fixed costs are the same at all levels, even when the firm is at zero output. Figure 4-9a shows the fixed cost as a horizontal straight line.

Variable costs   Variable costs are defined as follows:

Definition: Variable costs are costs which change in total with changes in output, starting at zero when output is zero, increasing as output increases up to the end of stage 2 of the production function, and continuing to increase if production continues into stage 3.

Figure 4-9a shows the variable cost starting at zero, curving upward, and then curving back. The variable costs set at $20,000 per unit include explicit outlays for soil fertility, chemicals for control of crop pests and disease, cultivating, harvesting, drying, etc. Also, they will include implicit costs such as wear and tear on farm machinery and equipment, the work of farm animals, or unpaid family labor. Notice that the variable cost is zero when output is zero, increases as output increases up to the end of stage 2, and continues to increase if production continues into stage 3.

Total cost   Total cost is defined as follows:

Definition: Total cost is the sum of fixed and variable costs at each level of output.

Figure 4-9a shows that a zero output fixed cost and total cost are the same. Everything between the horizontal fixed-cost line and the total cost is actually variable cost. Thus, it is not necessary to have another curved line to show the variable cost. On the other hand, another line may be used to show the variable cost, as indicated by the dotted line in Figure 4-9a. This falls below the total cost

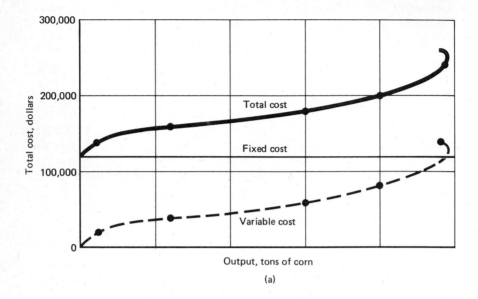

(a)

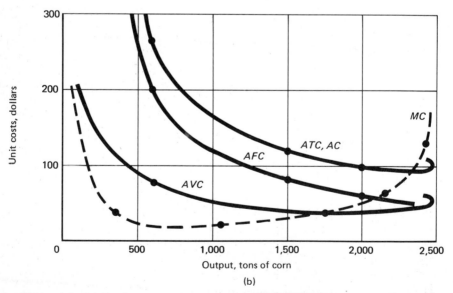

(b)

Figure 4-9 (a) Total cost, total fixed cost, and total variable cost. (b) Marginal
cost, and average cost curves.

by the exact amount of the fixed cost. Adding the fixed and variable costs vertically gives the total cost.

AVERAGE UNIT COSTS OF PRODUCTION

In Table 4-4, columns (5) to (7), the average costs are computed simply by dividing each of the total costs by the number of units produced at each level.

Definition: Average fixed cost (AFC) is total fixed cost (TFC) divided by the corresponding output (Q).

$$AFC = \frac{TFC}{Q}$$

AFC declines as output increases, falling very rapidly at first and then more slowly as the product of the quantity (Q) times *AFC* remains a constant. Fixed costs are sometimes called *overhead costs,* and farm managers or other businesspeople sometimes refer to declining *AFC* when output increases as *spreading the overhead.* Graphically, *AFC* appears as a portion of a rectangular hyperbola in Figure 4-9*b*.

Definition: Average variable cost (AVC) is total variable cost (TVC) divided by the corresponding output (Q).

$$AVC = \frac{TVC}{Q}$$

AVC declines initially, reaches a minimum, and then increases. This gives a typical U-shaped curve, often tending to be flat on the bottom like a saucer or pan as in Figure 4-9*b*. Because of increasing returns, it takes fewer and fewer of the variable resources to produce each additional ton of the first 1,500 tons of corn as the *AVC* declines to $40 per ton. Between 1,500 and 2,000 tons the *AVC* tends to level out. After 2,000 tons it rises rapidly as diminishing returns necessitate the use of more and more of the variable resources to produce each additional ton of corn. In stage 3, when the *MPP* has become negative, *AVC* curls back as the seventh and eighth units of variable input are added.

Definition: Average total cost (ATC) is total cost (TC) divided by the corresponding output (Q); more simply, it is the total of AFC and AVC at each level of output: ATC = TC/Q or AFC + AVC.

Graphically, *ATC,* or *AC,* is found by adding the *AFC* and *AVC* curves vertically as in Figure 4-9*b.* Thus the vertical distance between the *ATC* and *AVC* curves is the same as *AFC* at any level of output. As the output of the firm expands, *ATC* tends to come closer and closer to *AVC* because *AFC* continues to decline until the maximum ouput of the firm is reached.

MARGINAL COST

There remains one final cost concept in Table 4-4: marginal cost (*MC*). This is most critical because it deals with the immediate questions of how much must be added to the variable cost (or to the total cost) to get an additional unit of the product at each level of output.

Definition: Marginal cost (*MC*) is the extra, or additional, cost of producing one more unit of output.

MC may be computed at each level of output simply by dividing the change in the total cost by the change in the quantity produced (*Q*), or by the additional number of units produced.

$$MC = \frac{\text{change in } TC}{\text{change in } Q}$$

In Table 4-4, it may be seen that to produce the first 100 tons of corn it is necessary to spend $20,000 on variable inputs, which of course increases the total cost by just $20,000. *MC* is then $20,000 ÷ 100, or $200 per ton. When the second $20,000 of variable cost is added, output increases by 500 tons. Thus, *MC* is $20,000 ÷ 500, or $40 per ton. When the third $20,000 is added we get 900 tons more; *MC* is $20,000 ÷ 900, or $22.22 per ton, and so on.

MC can also be calculated from the change in total variable cost because the only difference between the total cost and the total variable cost is the total fixed cost. Since the latter is a constant, the changes in total cost and total variable cost for each additional unit of output are the same.

The actual figures for *MC* given in Table 4-4 are, of course, the average *MC* per ton of corn from moving from one level of output to another. The specific *MC* for any given ton of corn cannot be determined from the table. *MC* has been located between the lines of Table 4-4 to indicate that it is the average added cost of moving from one level of output to another. Also, in Figure 4-9*b* the points for *MC* have been plotted midway horizontally between the corresponding points for *AVC*. But we don't really know if *MC* should be exactly midway horizontally between the points for *AVC,* or a little to the right or the left. The shape of the *MC* curve between the points of *AVC* is in this case interpolated visually. The curve does, however, give us an idea of how *MC* tends to change between each level of output in the figure, and we can approximate *MC* for each ton of corn at any point on the curve.

Marginal cost and marginal product   Marginal cost is a concept of great strategic importance because it deals with resources over which the manager of the firm has the most direct control. It always tells how much must be added to the total cost in order to get a certain additional quantity of the product. A study of average costs cannot provide this information. Thus, an efficient manager must always be aware of the marginal cost and try to develop some measure of it at each level of output, as well as its direction of change. What determines its shape, or rate, and direction of change?

The shape of the marginal-cost curve is a reflection of and a direct consequence of increasing and diminishing returns. This may be seen by comparing it with the marginal-product curve. Figure 4-10 has been developed to illustrate the mathematical relationships. We compare points *A, B,* and *C* on the production function in Figure 4-10*a* and *b in relation to the output* or vertical scales, with the corresponding *output scale of the cost curves on the horizontal axis* in Figure 10-10*c.* First, so long as the marginal product is rising to 900 tons at *A* in Figure 4-10*b,* the marginal cost is falling, reaching its minimum point at 900 tons at *A* in 4-10*c,* or $22.22 per ton. But as diminishing returns set in, the marginal product falls and the marginal cost rises. When the marginal product reaches zero at *C,* the marginal cost shoots upward toward infinity. The general rule is: *As long as the price or cost per unit of the variable input is given, increasing returns (or a rising marginal product) will be reflected in a decreasing marginal cost, and diminishing returns (or a falling marginal product) will be reflected in an increasing marginal cost.*

Relation of MC to AVC and ATC   The most important point to note is that the marginal-cost curve cuts both *AVC* and *ATC* curves from below at their respective minimum points.

This is a mathematical relationship to which there are no exceptions, and it may be observed in any number of illustrations. In Figure 4-10*c,* so long as *MC* is below *AVC* and *ATC,* both of these

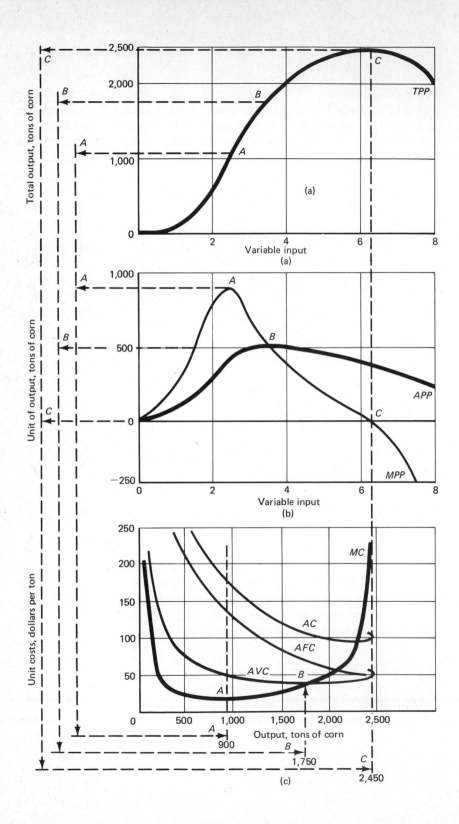

curves must be falling because less is being added to the total cost for each successive unit of output than was added on the average for all the previous units. As soon as the *MC* curve cuts the *AVC* and *ATC* curves from below, each of these curves must begin to rise. Point *B*, remember, which is at 1,750 tons in Figure 4-10*a* and *c*, also marks the beginning of stage 2, when *APP* is at its maximum and *AVC* is at its minimum. If it is profitable to produce at all, it will be profitable to produce at least up to the point where *AVC* is at its minimum. We need not be concerned about the fixed costs at this point because there is no relationship between *MC* and *AFC*.

Note that *B* in Figure 4-10*c* does not fall directly below *B* in Figure 4-10*a* or *b*. In fact, it is mathematically impossible for it do so. The fact that *A* in Figure 4-10*c* appears to fall directly below *A* in Figure 4-10*a* and *b* is coincidental. Point *C* in all three diagrams is directly in line, marking the end of stage 2 and the beginning of stage 3.

Let us turn now to consideration of unit costs in the long run, in which there are no fixed costs and all costs are variable.

Production costs in the long run

In the long run all costs are variable (*AVC* – *ATC*) and all desired resource adjustments can be made. Individual firms can alter the size of their plants and change the mix of inputs and products in any way that seems advantageous. The industry can also increase or decrease in size and change in other ways. As new firms enter and old ones leave, the continuing firms also change.

Since there are no fixed resources or fixed costs, the law of diminishing returns does not apply. The individual firm's long-run cost curve is U shaped, however, not because of increasing and diminishing returns but rather what economists call the *economies and diseconomies of scale*.

ECONOMIES AND DISECONOMIES
OF SCALE

These terms refer to the fact that there are *technical* relationships among resources which cause the average product to increase or decrease as the size of the plant changes, and the fact that there are

Figure 4-10   Comparison of unit cost curves with *TPP, APP*, and *MPP*. Note that *MC* reaches its minimum point when *MPP* is at its maximum; and *MC* intersects both *AVC* and *ATC* at their minimum points.

also financial, or *pecuniary,* advantages and disadvantages related to large size or scale. Different sizes of the corn-soybean combine provide a convenient example.

Figure 4-11 compares the actual *ATC* per acre of a two-row, four-row, and six-row combine used in harvesting corn in Illinois. The three individual curves represent short-run costs because some resources are fixed. In each case, *ATC* declines at first because of the spreading of fixed costs over more units of the product. In this case the subsequent rise in costs is due to increasing field losses resulting from a lack of timeliness in harvest—farmers extend the harvesting season in trying to cover a larger and larger acreage with their fixed harvesting equipment. Even if there were not more field losses, costs would eventually turn up because of such factors as increasing repairs.

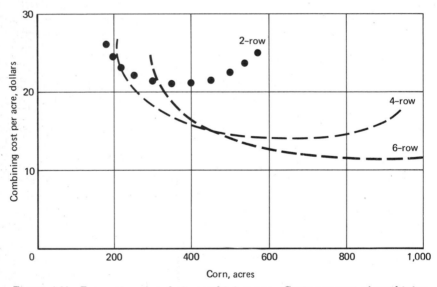

Figure 4-11   Economies of scale in combining corn. Costs per acre of combining corn with 2-row, 4-row, and 6-row combines, 38-inch rows, for selected acreages.

Size	Acres per hour	Combine cost, dollars
2-row, 38-inch	1.6	25,800
4-row, 38-inch	3.2	37,600
6-row, 38-inch	4.8	44,100

(*Source:* R.B. Schwart, *Farm Machinery Economic Decisions,* Illinois Cooperative Extension Service, Circular 1065, revised 1978, p. 18.)

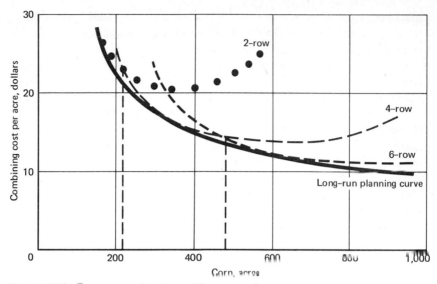

Figure 4-12   Economies of scale and long-run planning curve for combining corn. Note that the cost-conscious farmer should shift from a 2-row to a 4-row combine at about 220 acres, and from a 4-row to a 6-row combine at about 480 acres. An 8-row combine might become cost-reducing at about 1,000 acres; but note that the long-run planning curve is beginning to level out. At some point beyond 1,000 acres we should expect the cost of combining with a single large combine to rise. (*Source:* R. B. Schwart, *Farm Machinery Economic Decisions,* Illinois Cooperative Extension Service, Circular 1065, revised 1978, p. 18.)

Over time, farmers buy new combines and make other investments that permit them to increase the size of the farm. In this case, as the farmer tries to reduce the average costs, the farmer shifts from a two-row to a four-row and then to a six-row combine. This shift over time traces out what economists call the *long-run planning curve.* It is tangent to the individual short-run cost curves as in Figure 4-12. In this case, economies of scale refer to economies obtained by increasing the size of machine. They do not refer to savings from using a given size of machine more fully. Although it is anticipated that costs will go even lower with a still larger combine, eventually costs will rise because of the unwieldiness or other costs related to a still larger-sized machine.

Technical advantages and disadvantages of large scale   The technical advantages of large scale come from a saving in labor, fuel, or other material per acre as the size of the machine and the farm increases. The records show that in the corn belt it does not take twice as much labor to run an 800-acre farm as a 400-acre farm. In growing wheat in the Great Plains, it does not take twice as much labor to farm two sections of land as it does to farm one section. After a certain size of farm is reached, the larger size of machines generally makes the difference rather than the fuller use of a given size of machine. On cash-grain farms in central and northern Illinois, increasing the size of the farm up to about 600 acres generally reduces the labor and machinery costs per acre. But beyond this size generally only very small savings in costs—about $3 to $4 per acre of corn—can be achieved by further increasing the size of the farm by another 200 or 300 acres.[1] This is related to the leveling out of costs as the machines tend to reach the optimum size for field operations (Figure 4-12).

Generally speaking, it has been found that the large family farm tends to combine most of the technical efficiencies found in American agriculture. Thus, over a wide range of crop and livestock enterprises the family farm may be as technically efficient as a larger farm.[2] There are of course many exceptions, especially where very large machines are technically the most efficient or where a given resource can cover a wide range of other inputs. Examples are found in fruit and vegetable production, where some very large machines are technically efficient; in cattle ranching, where a very large herd of cattle may be supervised by a ranch hand or two; and in cattle feeding and hog and broiler production, where large-scale feed-handling equipment is technically efficient.

Apart from such examples, however, there are technical disadvantages to large scale, which arise out of management's inability to coordinate more resources within a single unit. The problems of both production and financial management tend to increase in difficulty as farms and agribusinesses become larger. Also, as has been noted, beyond a certain size any machine tends to become less technically efficient. The multiplication of such problems tends

[1]D. F. Wilken, "Costs, Investments, and Earnings by Size and Type of Farm, 1971–73," in *Economics for Agriculture*, rev. ed., University of Illinois, Department of Agricultural Economics, Urbana, September 1974; and A. G. Mueller and R. A. Hinton, "Farmers Production Costs and Soybeans by Unit Size," *American Journal of Agricultural Economics*, vol. 57, no. 5, December 1975, pp. 934–939.

[2]Angus McDonald, "The Family Farm is the Most Efficient Unit of Agricultural Production," *Farmworkers in Rural America, 1971–1972, Hearings before the Subcommittee on Migratory Labor of the Committee on Labor and Public Welfare, United States Senate, 92d Cong., 1st and 2d Sess.,* January 13, 1972, part 3c, pp. 2067–2073.

to offset other technical advantages so that beyond a certain size the main advantages of large scale tend to be pecuniary rather than technological in nature.

Pecuniary advantages and disadvantages of large scale Some studies show that pecuniary advantages rather than technical advantages tend to predominate among large farms and agribusiness firms.[3] For example, one study in the corn belt found that a 5,000-acre cash-grain farm had a net cost advantage of $7.30 per acre over a 500-acre farm. The larger farm was able to save $14.04 per acre in purchasing farm supplies and services. This was the result of getting quantity discounts, bargaining with suppliers, using contract purchases, leasing rather than buying farm tractors and machinery, and so on. The larger farm was able to gain an advantage of $5.72 per acre in marketing, either by lower marketing costs or by price premiums. This was due to selling in large volume, contracting and scheduling future deliveries and sales, and using the grain-futures market to advantage. On the other hand, there was a pecuniary disadvantage for the large farm in paying $3.82 more per acre for labor and management and $8.64 more per acre in federal and state income taxes. The net pecuniary advantage for the 5,000-acre farm was $14.04 + $5.72, or $19.76, minus $3.82 + $8.64, or $12.46. Then, $19.76 - $12.46 = $7.30—the net pecuniary advantage for the 5,000-acre farm.[4]

SIGNIFICANCE OF ECONOMIES
AND DISECONOMIES OF SCALE

Economies and diseconomies of scale are important in all phases of agriculture. Indeed, firms and economic sectors that have been able to expand their scale of operations to realize the major cost advantages of large-scale machines and equipment have survived and prospered. Farmers and agribusinesses that have been unable to achieve comparable scale advantages have generally found themselves in one of two unenviable positions: producing at high cost or

[3]Harold G. Halcrow, *Food Policy for America,* McGraw-Hill Book Company, New York, 1977, pp. 91–102, 176–187, 346–351, 465–489.

[4]Kenneth R. Krause and Leonard R. Kyle, "Economic Factors Underlying the Incidence of Large Farming Units, the Current Situation and Probable Trends," *American Journal of Agricultural Economics,* vol. 52, no. 5, December 1970, p. 755. See also Leonard R. Kyle, "Who Will Make the Decisions in the Future?" *Illinois Banker,* vol. 22, no. 4, October 1970.

earning a family income so low as to entail a marginal existence and possibly ultimate insolvency and exit from agriculture. This problem of entry and exit will be examined in Chapter 5, and related to production costs in the long run after we have studied the basic theory related to competition and output determination in the short run.

SUMMARY

Production has been defined as the process of creating an economic good or service from two or more other goods or services. The production function is the technical relationship between inputs and outputs, indicating the maximum amount of output that can be produced with each and every set or combination of the specified inputs. Given the total physical product (*TPP*) that can be produced from specified combinations of fixed and variable inputs, all the other significant relationships between inputs and outputs can be derived. The rational range of production under conditions of diminishing returns is in stage 2, between the point of maximum *APP* and zero *MPP*.

The economist's concept of costs is based on the fact that resources are limited and have alternative uses, and costs are measured in terms of opportunities missed and alternatives forgone. Costs are either explicit or implicit. The short run includes both fixed and variable costs, which accounts for the typical U shape of short-run cost curves. Average and marginal cost can be derived from total costs. The *MC* curve pierces the *AVC* and *ATC* curves from below at the minimum point of each curve.

Production costs in the long run are all variable. The U shape of the long-run *ATC* curve is due to the economies and diseconomies of large scale. It envelops the short-run *ATC* curves of individual firms, which are tangent to it. Typically, the long-run *ATC* curve at first declines sharply as the scale of production increases and then tends to decline more slowly or level off.

Agriculture tends to experience important net internal economies of large scale which are both technical and pecuniary in nature. But the prevalence of the one-family farm implies that in general most of the net internal economies are experienced by large one-family farms. With important exceptions, some of which were noted, very large farms tend to experience technical diseconomies of large scale. Some of these are offset or more than offset by the pecuniary advantages of large scale, demonstrated by the example of the 5,000-acre corn farm.

The questions of entry and exit of firms were not taken up. These questions are also related to production adjustments in the long run, and they are discussed in Chapter 5 after the discussion of the basic theory of competition and output determination.

**IMPORTANT TERMS
AND CONCEPTS**

    Production
    Factors of production
    Production function
    Output and input
    Total physical product
    Fixed input
    Variable input
    Marginal physical product
    Average physical product
    Stages of production: 1, 2, and 3
    Diminishing returns
    Production costs: short run
        Fixed costs
        Variable costs
        Total costs
        Marginal costs
        Average total cost
        Average fixed cost
        Average variable cost
    Production costs: long run
        Economies and diseconomies of large-scale production
        Technical and pecuniary economies of large scale

LOOKING AHEAD

The study of costs provides a foundation for studying competition and determination of output. Chapter 5 takes up the case of the farm sector, where it is assumed that the individual firm has no influence on the market price. Succeeding chapters will discuss other forms of competition found in the agribusiness sectors. This will help us move further into studies of allocation of resources and distribution of income, including problems of economic development and progress.

QUESTIONS AND EXERCISES

1. What is production? What is a production function? A fixed input? A variable input?

2. Write the general formula for a production function and explain what it means. Is it necessary to know anything about prices in order to develop a production function? Why, or why not?

3. Define marginal physical product (MPP) and explain how it is derived from total physical product (TPP). How is average physical product (APP) derived?

4. By use of a graph of TPP, locate the range of increasing returns and the range of diminishing returns. Identify stage 1, stage 2, and stage 3. Why is it said that stage 2 is the only rational range for production?

5. Explain how the economist measures costs. What is the difference between an explicit cost and an implicit cost?

6. What is the essential difference between the short run and the long run in economics? Give an illustration of the short run.

7. What is marginal cost? How is MC derived? Illustrate by means of a simple table.

8. Explain why average fixed cost (AFC) is graphed as a rectangular hyperbola. Explain why the short-run average-variable-cost (AVC) and marginal-cost (MC) curves both take a U shape. Why does the MC curve pierce the AVC curve from below at the minimum point of the AVC curve? Is this also the point of maximum APP?

9. Describe the relationship between the long-run ATC curve and the short-run ATC curves of individual firms. Are these curves ever tangent? Why do we call the long-run ATC curve a planning curve? Why does the long-run ATC curve take a U shape?

10. What is an internal economy of large scale? A technical economy? A pecuniary economy? Give an example of each that is related to agriculture.

5. COMPETITION AND DETERMINATION OF OUTPUT

5. COMPETITION AND DETERMINATION OF OUTPUT

❚❚ . . . He [the self-interested person] intends only his own gain, and he is in this . . . led by an invisible hand to promote an end which was no part of his intention. . . . By pursuing his own interest he frequently promotes that of the society more effectually than when he really intends to promote it. **❚❚**

Adam Smith

Adam Smith (1723–1790), author of *The Theory of Moral Sentiments* (1759) and *An Inquiry Into the Nature of Causes of the Wealth of Nations* (1776), wrote the first comprehensive study of economics as applied to a "capitalistic," or predominantly "individualistic," or "competitive market" economy. Smith's work has had more influence than that of any other economist on the development and social history of the western world. It emphasizes economic freedom as a "natural right"; the benefits to be had from specialization, or "the division of labor"; the advantages of "free enterprise," free trade, and the noninterference of government in the individual's choice of occupation, residence, and investment; and the freedom of the individual to make economic decisions of all kinds in response to the price movements of free and fully competitive markets.

Now that we have learned something about agricultural production functions and production costs, let us apply this knowledge to problems of economic organization and determination of output. How is the production and marketing system organized in agriculture? What is the role of government, and how do firms compete? Under what conditions will firms produce, how much will they produce, and what profit or loss will there be?

These are fundamental questions for the economics of agriculture. Let us develop our answers by discussing some of the alternative economic systems that various societies have established, the models for production and marketing, and the principles of output determination, using the farm firm as an initial basic model. This introduces the fundamental concepts of economic organization and output determination, and constructs a foundation for the succeeding chapters.

IN THIS CHAPTER

1. You will learn to identify the basic economic organization and market models that exist in a competitive society and the position of these models in agriculture.

2. You will learn to determine the relationships between prices, costs, and the equilibrium output of purely competitive firms in the short run. You will learn to distinguish between the profit-maximizing case and the loss-minimizing case, and between these and the close-down case. You will learn why the marginal cost above the average variable cost is the supply curve of the firm and how this relates to the supply curve of the industry.

3. You will see how purely competitive firms adjust in the long run to market prices.

ECONOMIC ORGANIZATION
AND MARKET MODELS

We must be aware that various societies have established different goals for outputs and use different methods or systems for organizing their resources in trying to fulfill these goals. Generally speaking, a survey of modern industrialized economies reveals that there are two fundamentally different philosophies concerning the answers to the fundamental questions: What, how, and for whom to produce? At one extreme, as expounded by Adam Smith and practiced in much of the western world, emphasis is put on private ownership of resources, freedom of individual economic units to make the choices that they feel will be in their best interest, and use of a largely profit-motivated marketing system as a coordinating mechanism. At the other extreme, emphasis is put on public ownership of most resources, central economic planning by the government as the coordinating mechanism, and greater exercise of the authority of the state as opposed to the freedom of the individual. Between these extremes there are an unlimited number of hybrid forms in which some resources are owned by the state and some are not, some economic activities are centrally planned and some are not, and individuals enjoy various degrees of freedom in regard to economics, politics, religion, social organization, and so on. Generally speaking, the first extreme comes under the heading of *capitalism.* In between there is what is sometimes called liberal, or democratic, *socialism.* Finally, the other extreme is generally called *communism,* or *authoritarian socialism.*

No economy is purely capitalistic, communistic, or socialistic. The United States, Canada, Australia, and some other advanced countries typify the first extreme. But in these countries many basic resources are publicly owned or controlled by the state, and there are various degrees of central planning. The United Kingdom, Sweden, and other countries in western Europe tend to typify the countries in between. Finally, the Soviet Union, China, and some of the Soviet "satellites" of eastern Europe represent the other extreme. But in all of these countries there is an area of private enterprise, not everything is covered by a central plan, and the authority of the state is not always complete or absolute. A core of basic market models applies broadly throughout the different systems. Let us use these models to generalize about economic organization and output determination, applying the results to agriculture in general.

The models to which we first refer come under the general heading of *pure competition, monopolistic competition, oligopoly,* and *monopoly.* These terms all refer to sellers. The first term—*pure competition*—is sometimes called *perfect competition,* and the last three terms are special cases of a more general term—*imperfect competition.* In addition, other terms are sometimes used to describe the buyers' side of the market. Let us begin by developing our understanding of the first term, the conditions of *pure competition.*

Pure competition

Pure competition is identified by four or five basic market characteristics. The following are the most important:

1. There are a large number of independently acting sellers each of whom generally offers a product for sale in a highly organized, or structured market. Farming is often cited as the classic example.

2. The competing firms offer a standardized product for sale, or one that is standardized in terms of specific market grades or classes. Grain and livestock, for example, are traded in terms of specific classes or grades. Most other farm products can be identified by class or grade, color, texture, or some other characterisitc. Within a specific class or grade, buyers do not discriminate among sellers.

3. Each individual producer exerts little or no influence on the market price. This follows from having a large number of producers and a standardized product. Farming generally meets this condition. Exceptions occur when farmers also perform a marketing function such as operating a roadside fruit and vegetable market or supplying an egg route. More important exceptions occur when farms (usually large-scale farms) combine or integrate with marketing-processing firms, which in turn may sell products by brand name or by contract, bypassing the purely competitively structured market.

4. New firms are free to enter and existing firms are free to leave the industry. That is, there are no restrictions such as licenses, review boards, or entry quotas. Existing firms are free to sell out without getting approval from a government commission or other body. Farming in all capitilistic countries, in most democratic-socialistic countries, and in some communistic countries generally meets this condition.

5. Since by definition each purely competitive firm is producing an identical product, or a product that can be marketed as a particular class or grade, the firms generally do not resort to nonprice competition such as advertising or other sales-promotion activities. The farmers' markets for grains, livestock, and many other farm products generally fit this model of a purely competitive market.

Monopolistic competion

In contrast to pure competition, monopolistic competition involves product differences, what economists call *product differentiation.* This includes not only physical differences in the products of sellers but certain identifying differences such as brand names and claims

Fruit and vegetable markets tend to be purely competitive in the sense that buyers may make their decisions without discriminating among growers and marketing firms; but retail pricing may conform to monopolistic competition, or oligopoly, as supermarket chains differentiate their services from those of their competitors. *(Marilyn L. Schrut, New York City.)*

to superiority over the products of other sellers. Some farm products that are sold initially in purely competitive markets often end up in markets characterized by monopolistic competition. When you go to a grocery store you may notice the brand name of various products, the different prices attached to the products, and some of the differences among them. Do the differences in prices reflect real differences in quality, or do they tend to reflect merely the identity of the manufacturer?

Monopolistic competition differs from pure competition in the following ways:

1. There may be a large number of firms nationally or as few as 25 or 30. Each firm has only a small share of the total market. Food marketing-processing firms provide a number of examples.

2. The firms differentiate their individual products as has just been noted. These differences may be real or imaginary. The important point is that the differences exist, or are made to exist, in the mind of the buyer. Notice the product differentiation in food markets.

3. Firms in monopolistic competition have only limited control over the prices of their products, but they do have some control. There may be significant differences among the products, but the prices of one producer cannot get very far out of line before consumers will shift to another brand or product. In this instance, how far is far? This is a crucial point in economics.

4. Entry into an industry that is monopolistically competitive is generally more difficult than entry into a purely competitive industry. Product differentiation is the general reason. Considerable advertising may be required to establish a brand name. This can be expensive. The outcome is uncertain; it cannot be taken for granted. Manufactured food products illustrate the difficulty of entry for new marketing firms.

5. Because products are differentiated, competition among firms is often vigorous in areas other than price. Such rivalry includes product quality and the conditions for sale of the product as well as advertising and price. Firms that supply supermarkets vie for preferred store locations and more shelf space, which permit them to make a more attractive display. Supermarkets go to considerable expense in advertising and sales promotion, trying to convince the consumer that the products they sell are superior to those of their rivals.

The expense of advertising and sales promotion must be passed on in the price the consumer pays. This is reflected in the price spread between the farmer and the consumer. Monopolistic competition provides a variety of differences in food and other agricultural products, and the emphasis on brand names generally assures a high degree of quality in processing and manufacturing. How to retain these desirable features along with greater market efficiency is one of the central economic problems of agriculture and the food industry.

Oligopoly

Oligopoly—from the Greek *olig,* "few," and *polist,* "seller"—means "few sellers." Some of the agribusinesses in farm services and supplies—such as the major farm-machinery companies, farm-chemical companies, and others—may qualify under the definition of oligopoly. Some of the processing-marketing firms—the producers of breakfast cereals, the major meat packers, the large dairy manufacturing firms, the major supermarket food chains—tend to exhibit the basic elements of oligopoly. The most distinguishing characteristic is interdependence in pricing and market practices.

The following are characteristics of oligopolies:

1. Oligopoly exists whenever a few firms dominate the market for a product. Six firms in the United States, for example, supply 90 percent or more of the total farm-machinery market, about ten or fifteen firms dominate the fertilizer industry, and even fewer firms supply the major portion of other farm chemicals. There are many firms in food marketing, but in many big cities four or five large companies have 50 percent or more of the total market for retail food. Each of the major firms has a large enough share of the market for its actions and policies to have an effect on its rivals. The major firms are mutually interdependent. How they solve their problems of price and quantity is of major concern to all participants, including farmers and consumers as well as other marketing firms.

2. Oligopolists may produce either virtually standardized or highly differentiated products. Those furnishing raw materials generally offer a product that is highly standardized by class and grade, while those appealing directly to the consumer generally try to differentiate their product. The degree of standardization or differentiation affects the prices and market practices of the competing firms.

3. The degree of control over price is limited or circumscribed by the mutual interdependence of firms. Oligopolists generally try to avoid aggressive price competition, which may degenerate into a *price war.* Thus, the prices charged by oligopolists tend to be "rigid," or "sticky." This has wide repercussions for agri-

culture. Farmers often complain about the rigid or sticky prices for machinery and farm chemicals, for example. Consumers complain about high grocery prices whether farm prices are high or low.

4. Obstacles to entry are generally very effective, which is why an industry characterized by oligopoly tends to remain that way. Consider, for example, the difficulty of a small firm trying to

A few very large firms give international grain markets the economic structure of oligopsony-oligopoly; but standardized grading and alternatives in supply result in openly competitive markets, instant price determination, and rather uniform charges for marketing services.

enter the national market for farm machinery in competition with the giant firms such as Deere and Company, International Harvester Co., and Allis-Chalmers. Or consider the problem of an independent grocery store trying to break into regional or national competition. The possibility for the entry and growth of small firms tends, however, to put some limit on the prices oligopolists can charge. Also, the Sherman Act of 1890 and the Clayton Act of 1914 were the first of a number of acts attempting to prevent collusive pricing and restrictive trade practices by oligopolists.

5. Expenses for advertising and sales promotion are generally high among oligopolists who sell a differentiated product. Beer, cigarettes, and soft drinks as well as a number of food products are good examples of advertising and sales promotion by oligopolists in processing and marketing farm products. The heavy advertising of farm chemicals and farm machinery in the major farming areas of the United States attests to the presence of oligopoly. Quality competition may be intense among all these differentiated products and among oligopolists such as steel manufacturers, for example, who sell a standardized product.

Monopoly

Strictly speaking, a pure monoply—a one-firm industry—is exceedingly rare indeed. But monopoly-like conditions are of great importance in agriculture. The measures that may be taken to regulate or control some of the monopoly-like conditions are among the most sensitive issues in our study.

Characteristics of monopolies are as follows:

1. The concept of pure monopoly is important theoretically, and for agriculture the condition of monopoly, or near monopoly, is important in many areas such as transportation, public power, and communication. Farmers who have only one railroad on which to ship their grain or livestock may be faced with a monopoly-like situation even though there are alternatives such as trucks and barges.

2. The monoplist's product is unique in the sense that there are no good, or close, substitutes. What is good or close is not easy to define. Although monopoly is imposed by the seller, not all buyers are affected in the same way. One farmer may have no real alternative to the railroad. To this farmer the railroad is a monopolist. Another farmer may have a good big truck, and so there is

no monopoly for that farmer. The monopoly-like condition depends on both the seller and the buyer. But to protect some buyers there is the Interstate Commerce Commission to regulate transportation; the Federal Communications Commission to regulate telephone rates, television, radio, etc.; a public power commission to regulate public power companies; and so on.

3. The monopolist is the price maker unless the price is regulated by a public commission or other device. The monopolist controls the amount to be offered for sale and the conditions of sale. Thus, the closer the market situation approaches a monopoly-like condition, the more need there is to regulate the monopoly-type firm, even though it may be said that there is hardly ever a pure monopoly in the strict meaning of the term.

4. The existence of monopoly depends on having a barrier to the entry of other firms. The barrier may be economic, legal, or technical. A railroad may decline to build a line close to a line that is already established because there would not be enough business to make it pay. The Interstate Commerce Commission might not grant the second railroad a charter and right of way, or there might not be an acceptable route available for it to use.

5. A firm that enjoys a monopoly-type situation may or may not engage in advertising and sales promotion. It all depends on the market situation and whether advertising and sales promotion will pay. Much depends on how closely the firm approaches a monoploy-type situation, how much it wishes to increase its sales, and how it is regulated. The monopoly-type firm might not charge the highest price permitted. How the firm is regulated is an important problem in most parts of the economy. How a railroad is to be regulated—or whether it should be regulated—is an important issue in agriculture. When railroads were the only means of shipping farm products, the case for regulation of rates and practices was strong, but now certain studies suggest that less regulation would be beneficial.

Imperfect competition: Buyers

We may refer to monopolistic competition, oligopoly, or monopoly as representing some variant of *imperfect competition,* contrasting one or more of these with *pure competition.* These specific terms all refer to sellers. Their counterparts on the buyers' side are known as *monopsonistic competition, oligopsony,* and *monopsony.* Monopsonistic competition designates the existence of a fairly large

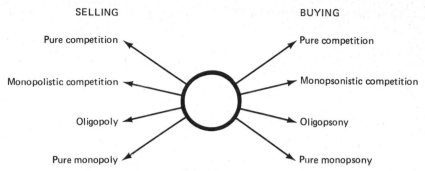

SELLING   BUYING

Pure competition   Pure competition

Monopolistic competition   Monopsonistic competition

Oligopoly   Oligopsony

Pure monopoly   Pure monopsony

Figure 5-1 Basic competitive market relationships. Four basic models are characteristic of both the selling side and the buying side of competitive markets, and
this suggests that there are a very large number of buying and selling relationships in most economic systems.

number of buyers such as might exist in an auction market for farm
products. Oligopsony refers to few buyers. Livestock markets, for
example, tend to link a large number of purely competitive farmers
with a very few large meat-packing companies. Livestock farmers
and ranchers sometimes complain that this market structure does
not result in a "fair" price because the buyers drive down the price
by holding back on bids when the market is weak. One of the functions of farmers' cooperatives is to establish a bargaining power that
will enable farmers to grapple with the concentrated market power
of oligopsonists. Figure 5-1 presents a summary of the basic market
relationships.

THE PURELY COMPETITVE FARM FIRM
IN THE SHORT RUN

The purely competitive farm firm acting alone is a price taker rather
than a price maker. The individual farmer develops production plans
based on the prices that exist or are expected some time in the
future. The farmer adjusts to the market price. The individual may
sell for cash or sell a contract for future delivery without having any
measurable effect on the price.

The first question is: How does the purely competitive firm
adjust to the market price in the short run? There are essentially two
methods for answering this question. One method compares total
costs and total revenues, and the other compares marginal cost and
marginal revenue.

Total-cost–total-revenue approach

The farmer is faced with three related questions in the short run: Shall I produce? If so, how much? What will be the maximum profit, or the minimum loss?

The answer to the first question does not depend simply on whether there will be a profit or not. There are costs in the short run whether the firm produces or not. Although it may not be possible for the firm to make a profit no matter how much it tries to produce, it may still produce, provided it loses less money than it would by closing down. In other words, the correct answer is: *The firm should produce in the short run if it can make an economic profit, or if it loses less than its fixed costs.* This also means that it must produce enough total product for sale or use which, when valued at the market price or other appropriate price, at least covers its variable costs.

The answer to the second question—How much to produce?— is equally specific: *In the short run the firm should produce an output at which it maximizes profits, or minimizes losses.* Let us demonstrate this, using the example developed in Chapter 4, by showing four cases: profit-maximizing, break-even, loss-minimizing, and close-down.

PROFIT-MAXIMIZING CASE

Table 5-1 uses the first four columns of Table 4-4, to which are added columns for total revenue and profit or loss, based on an arbitrarily selected price for corn of $120 per ton. Since this is higher than the minimum average total cost of $95.65, we should expect the farmer to make money, in fact a substantial pure profit. The highest profit in the table is $56,000 at 2,300 tons of corn. Thus, the farmer should produce.

How much should be produced? Should it be just 2,300 tons? Some more? Or less? Figure 5-2 gives us a picture that may be helpful. The logic is that so long as the total cost is increasing less than the total revenue, it will pay to increase production. As soon as the total cost increases just as much as the total revenue, it will pay to go no further. This is at a point on the total-cost schedule where a line drawn tangent to the point is parallel to the total revenue. At this point each added ton is adding just as much to the total cost as to the total revenue. Any additional product beyond this point will add more to the total cost than to the total revenue. The profit-maximizing point appears to be a little less than 2,400 tons.

Table 5-1   Profit-maximizing equilibrium output for a purely competitive farm firm; total-cost–total-revenue approach when corn is $120 per ton

(1) Quantity, corn, tons	(2) Fixed cost (FC)	(3) Variable cost (VC)	(4) Total cost (TC)	(5) Total revenue (TR)	(6) Profit (+) or loss (−) = (5) − (4)
0	$120,000	$ 0	$120,000	$ 0	$−120,000
100	120,000	20,000	140,000	12,000	−128,000
600	120,000	40,000	160,000	72,000	−88,000
1,500	120,000	60,000	.180,000	180,000	0
2,000	120,000	80,000	200,000	240,000	+40,000
2,300	120,000	100,000	220,000	276,000	+56,000
2,450	120,000	120,000	240,000	294,000	+54,000
2,400	120,000	140,000	260,000	288,000	+28,000

Note: Hypothetical data.

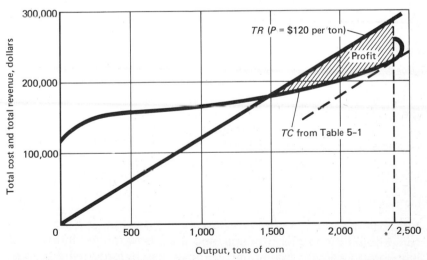

Figure 5-2   A farmer's total cost and total revenue in a profit-maximizing case. The price of corn is $120 per ton (about $3 per bushel). Profits are maximized when a little less than 2,400 tons of corn is produced (asterisk). The farmer just breaks even at about 1,500 tons. A line drawn tangent to curve *TC*, and parallel to *TR*, is tangent at the point, or level of output, where profit is maximized.

Table 5-2 Break-even equilibrium output for a purely competitive farm firm: total-cost–total-revenue approach when corn is $95.65 per ton

(1) Quantity, corn, tons	(2) Fixed cost (FC)	(3) Variable cost (VC)	(4) Total cost (TC)	(5) Total revenue (TR)	(6) Profit (+) or loss (−) = (5)−(4)
0	$120,000	$ 0	$120,000	$ 0	$−120,000
100	120,000	20,000	140,000	9,565	−130,435
600	120,000	40,000	160,000	57,390	−102,610
1,500	120,000	60,000	180,000	143,475	−36,525
2,000	120,000	80,000	200,000	191,300	−8,700
2,300	120,000	100,000	220,000	219,995	−5 (or 0)
2,450	120,000	120,000	240,000	234,342	−5,658
2,400	120,000	140,000	260,000	229,560	−30,440

Note: Hypothetical data.

BREAK-EVEN CASE

This occurs when the minimum average total cost is just equal to the market price. This cost was identified in Table 4-4 as $95.65 per ton. At this price the farmer will just cover both the fixed and the variable total costs. Should the farmer produce, and if so, how much? Again we repeat the first four columns, adding new total-revenue and profit-loss columns as in Table 5-2.

Should the farmer produce? Yes, because all costs can be covered, including a normal profit. If the farm were closed down, all the fixed cost, or $120,000, would be lost. But the farmer does not produce as much as when the price is $120 per ton. Both Table 5-2 and Figure 5-3 suggest that production should be just 2,300 tons instead of about 2,400 tons as in the profit-maximizing case. (More precise estimates of equilibrium output will be made later.)

LOSS-MINIMIZING CASE

Suppose the price of corn is below $95.65 per ton, say, $60.00 per ton. Should the farmer produce, and if so, how much? In this case we want to know if the farmer will lose less by producing than by leaving the farm idle. Table 5-3 shows that the smallest loss is $80,-000 when 2,000 tons is produced. This is $40,000 less than the fixed cost. Therefore the farmer should produce since the farmer can cover all the variable cost, including a normal profit, and have $40,-000 to apply against the fixed cost.

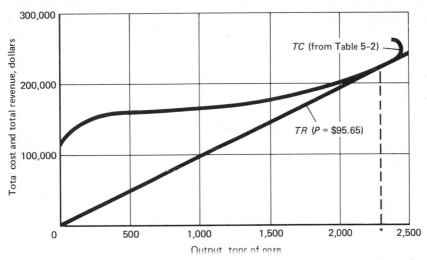

Figure 5-0 A farmer's total cost and total revenue in a break-even case. When the price of corn is $95.65 per ton, the farmer covers the total cost by producing 2,300 tons, which is the break-even point (asterisk). Notice that curve *TR* is tangent to curve *TC* at this level of output.

Table 5-3 Loss-minimizing equilibrium output for a purely competitive farm firm; total-cost–total-revenue approach when corn is $60 per ton

(1) Quantity, corn, tons	(2) Fixed cost (FC)	(3) Variable cost (VC)	(4) Total cost (TC)	(5) Total revenue (TR)	(6) Profit (+) or loss (−) = (5)−(4)
0	$120,000	$ 0	$120,000	$ 0	$−120,000
100	120,000	20,000	140,000	6,000	−134,000
600	120,000	40,000	160,000	36,000	−124,000
1,500	120,000	60,000	180,000	90,000	−90,000
2,000	120,000	80,000	200,000	120,000	−80,000
2,300	120,000	100,000	220,000	138,000	−82,000
2,450	120,000	120,000	240,000	147,000	−93,000

Note: Hypothetical data.

Figure 5-4 shows that the point of tangency of the *TC* curve for a line drawn parallel to the total revenue is about 2,050 tons or a little more. This is the point at which the farmer should attempt to produce in order to minimize the total loss.

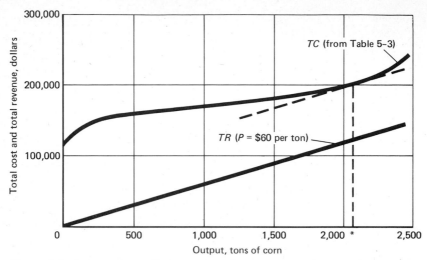

Figure 5-4 A farmer's total cost and total revenue in a loss-minimizing case. When the price of corn is $60 per ton, the smallest loss, about $80,000, will be at 2,050 tons, which is the short-run equilibrium point (asterisk). Notice that the line drawn tangent to TC and parallel to TR is tangent at this level of output.

CLOSE-DOWN CASE

How low must the price of corn fall before this farmer should close down in the short run? We continue to assume that corn is the only crop to be grown, because other crops are less attractive. It was said that the farmer should produce so long as the total loss is less than the fixed cost, or the minimum variable cost is covered.

Table 4-4 showed that the average variable cost was $40 per ton at both 1,500 and 2,000 tons, and Figure 4-5 suggested that AVC dropped below this at the point where MC crosses AVC. This might be around $38 or $39 per ton. Therefore, we might assume that the price would have to drop to around this level or lower before it would be advantageous for the farmer to close down. Table 5-4 suggests that when the selling price is $40 per ton, the farmer just covers the variable cost at 1,500 or 2,000 tons. The loss is the same as the fixed cost. Figure 5-5 gives us a somewhat more precise answer, suggesting that at about 1,750 tons the close-down case will occur at a price slightly below $40.

IMPLICATIONS

These cases illustrate a number of important central economic problems of agriculture. Under a given cost situation, a profit

Table 5-4   Close-down equilibrium output for a purely competitive farm firm; total-cost−total-revenue approach when corn is $40 per ton

(1) Quantity corn, tons	(2) Fixed cost (FC)	(3) Variable cost (VC)	(4) Total cost (TC)	(5) Total revenue (TR)	(6) Profit (+) or loss (−) = (5)−(4)
0	$120,000	$ 0	$120,000	$ 0	$−120,000
100	120,000	20,000	140,000	4,000	−136,000
600	120,000	40,000	160,000	24,000	−136,000
1,500	120,000	60,000	180,000	60,000	−120,000
2,000	120,000	80,000	200,000	80,000	−120,000
2,300	120,000	100,000	220,000	92,000	−128,000
2,450	120,000	120,000	240,000	98,000	−142,000

Note: Hypothetical data.

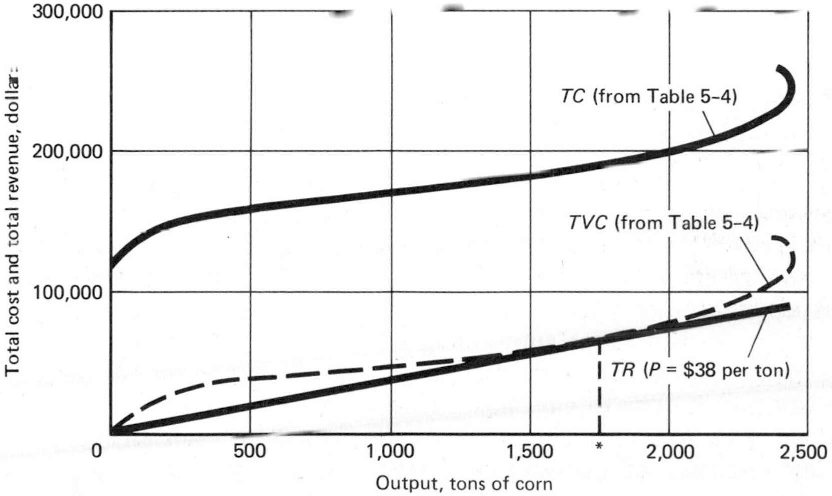

Figure 5-5   A farmer's total cost and total revenue in a close-down case. In this case *TR* is drawn tangent to curve *TVC* (not intersecting *TVC* at 1,500 and 2,000 tons, which would be the case if the price were $40 per ton). The close-down price will therefore be something less than $40 per ton. In this case, we have assumed it to be $38, which means that at any price below $38 the farmer is in a situation where less will be lost by closing down than by trying to produce a crop. The asterisk marks the only point at which *TVC* is covered.

depends on the price of the farm product being above the lowest point of the average-total-cost curve. But in the loss-minimizing case, even though the price goes down to a level that means disaster in a matter of very few years, the individual farmer cannot afford to let the farm lie idle. The family may subsist at a very low income level, hoping for better times. Alternatively, it may go broke or sell out at a sacrifice before this happens. Some farmers may be able to survive or even make money at a price that will force others into bankruptcy. Not all farmers reach the close-down case at the same price. But they all want a higher price, and it should be clear why this is so.

Marginal-cost–marginal-revenue approach

An alternative approach for determining how much the farmer will produce and offer for sale at all possible prices is to determine and compare the amounts that each *additional* unit of output will add to the total cost on the one hand and to the total revenue on the other. The amount added to the total cost by each additional unit of output is called the *marginal cost,* as was discussed in Chapter 4. The definition of *marginal revenue* is similar.

Definition: Marginal revenue is the net addition to total revenue from adding one more unit of output.

We can find the point of maximum profit or minimum loss by simply comparing *MC* and *MR.* Any unit of output where *MC* is less than *MR* should be produced, assuming the firm is not in a close-down situation. Why? On each such unit the amount added to cost is less than the amount added to revenue. Each successive unit is adding to profits, or subtracting from losses. Similarly, any unit where marginal cost exceeds marginal revenue should not be produced. It will pay to cut back because such a unit will not "pay its way." Production managers make decisions in terms of marginal cost and revenue because they need only consider the net gain or net loss from *each added unit* of output rather than continually appraise and reappraise the entire production plan. What rule will they follow to know when they are at the point of maximum profit, or minimum loss?

MC = *MR* (OR *MR* = *MC*) RULE

The discussion in Chapter 4 showed that the *MC* curve declines to a minimum point and then rises. If it falls below the *MR* curve it will eventually rise to intersect, or pierce, the *MR* curve from below. The intersection of *MC* and *MR* establishes a unique point, which is the basis for the general *MR* = *MC* rule: *The firm will maximize profits or minimize losses by producing at the level of output where marginal revenue equals marginal cost (MR = MC).*

FOUR CHARACTERISTICS

Four characteristics or assumptions concerning the *MR = MC* rule merit our attention. First, it is assumed that the firm is in a producing situation and not a close-down situation. For this to be the case, as has just been shown, the selling price cannot be below the minimum *AVC*.

Second, the rule is an accurate guide to profit for all firms whether purely competitive, monopolistically competitive, oligopolistic, or monopolistic. It is not limited to the case of pure competition.

Third, the rule can be expressed in a unique way for the purely competitive firm by substituting price for marginal revenue because the firm can sell all its output at the same price. Generally, this is not the case with imperfectly competitive firms. In pure competition—and theoretically only in pure competition—the marginal revenue, average revenue, and market price are all the same thing. Thus, the rule can be restated as a special case applying to pure competition: *The purely competitive firm will maximize profits or minimize losses by producing at the level of output where price equals marginal cost (P = MC).*

Fourth, in stating the *MR = MC* rule, it is assumed that the firm can obtain all the resources it can profitably employ. If the firm cannot buy, rent, or borrow this much, it will have to stop short of the point where *MR = MC*. That is, a firm with limited capital will not be able to reach the point where *MR = MC* although it will still wish to allocate the resources it has in the most economical manner. This is not a qualification of the general rule, but it is an important point to be observed. It has many applications throughout any society, and it applies to all sectors of agriculture. Farmers especially are often unable to borrow or get control of as much land or other capital as they can profitably employ.

Determining equilibrium output

Now let us use the *MR = MC* rule to determine equilibrium output in the four cases that were just discussed: profit-maximizing, break-even with normal profit, loss-minimizing, and close-down. Price may be substituted for marginal revenue so long as the illustration is limited to pure competition.

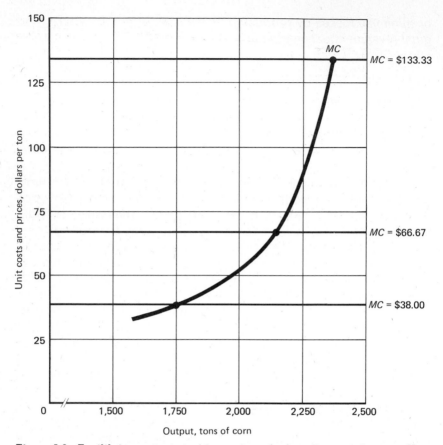

Figure 5-6 Equilibrium output at various prices of a farm firm growing corn. Note that the following points have been identified on *MC:* when *P* = $38, *Q* = 1,750 tons; when *P* = $66.67, *Q* = 2,150 tons; when *P* = $133.33, *Q* = 2,375 tons.

Since we know that the farmer will not produce at less than $38 per ton (or less than 1,750 tons in the close-down case) and cannot produce more than about 2,450 tons under any circumstance, no matter how high the price of corn goes, the scales of the basic diagram may be redrawn as in Figure 5-6. This gives us more space to illustrate the points to be made.

Figure 5-6 presents the same *MC* curve shown in previous figures but with both the vertical and horizontal scales doubled in length. Let us identify three points on the *MC* curve: $38, which is the point at which the *MC* pierces the *AVC* curve below at its minimum point; $66.67, which locates the *MC* midway between outputs of 2,000 and 2,300 tons of corn; and $133.33, which is the *MC* mid-way between the outputs of 2,300 and 2,450 tons of corn (see Table 4-4 and Figure 4-9*b*).

After interpolating and drawing the curve, we may locate the equilibrium output for any given price, or the equilibrium price for any given output, either of which must fall on the *MC* curve. Thus, as in Figure 5-7 we may locate the equilibrium outputs for the prices used to illustrate maximizing profit at $120; breaking even, including a normal profit, at $95.65; minimizing loss at $60; and closing down at $38 per ton. The corresponding equilibrium outputs are 2,350, 2,275, 2,807½, and 1,750 tons, respectively. These equilibrium prices and quantities are examples of the general rule for equilibrium that applies to the purely competitive firm: *A purely competitive firm will maximize profits or minimize losses in the short run by*

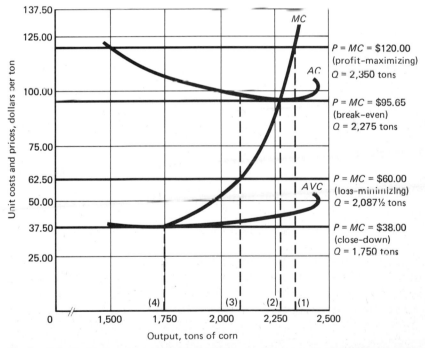

Figure 5-7 Examples of profit-maximizing, break-even, loss-minimizing, and close-down equilibrium prices and outputs. (1) At $120, total profit is ($120 − $96.00) × 2,350 = $56,400. (2) At $95.65, $P = AC = MC$, and the firm breaks even. (3) At $60, total loss is ($97.50 − $60.00) × 2,087½ = $78,281.25. (4) At $38, total loss is ($106.50 − $38) × 1,750 = $119,975. (*Note:* These estimates of equilibrium output, based on *MR/MC* analysis, are more precise than those based on *TR/TC* analysis.)

producting at the point of P = MC, provided the price is greater than the minimum average variable cost.

We may use a diagram such as Figure 5-7 to compute the respective amounts of profit and loss at various prices. When the price is $120, for instance, the *MC* curve intersects the price line at about 2,350 tons. *AC* has begun to rise a little at this point from its minimum of $95.65, say, to about $96. We compute the net profit as $24 × 2,350 = $56,400. At the other end of the *MC* curve, when *P* = *MC* = $38, *AC* is about $106.50 according to the curve drawn on the diagram. Thus, we compute the net loss as ($106.50 − $38) × 1,750, or $68.50 × 1,750 = $119,975. Notice that we do not extend the *MC* curve below $38 because this is the close-down case and production does not occur.

MC above AVC
is the purely competitive supply

We may now use the information that has been developed to state a generalization concerning the purely competitive firm operating in the short run: The portion of the firm's marginal-cost curve that is above the average-variable-cost curve is the firm's short-run supply curve.

Definition: Supply may be defined as a schedule showing the various amounts of the product that a producer is willing and able to produce and offer for sale at each price in a set of possible prices in some specified period of time.

Notice that this definition applies to the entire *MC* curve above *AVC*. Thus, when we speak of the *supply* in economics, we generally have a schedule in mind. We may speak of the *quantity supplied* at a particular price, which would be a point on the supply schedule. Or we can speak about the *change in the quantity supplied* as we move from one price to another on the schedule. In general, on a given supply schedule we may think about a relationship between price and quantity supplied which has been generalized into what is called the *law of supply.*

Law of supply

From the definition of supply, and from relationships that have been observed, economists have developed the so-called *law of supply,* which may be stated generally as follows: *On a given supply schedule, there is a direct relationship between the price and the quantity supplied. As the price rises, the quantity supplied increases. As the price falls, the quantity supplied decreases.*

The law is a commonsense matter, which is demonstrated in most of our examples, and it has an infinite number of applications. There is an exception to the law when higher prices tend to bring forth a smaller quantity. This may occur, for example, when an increase in wages causes the wage earner to want to work fewer hours. But this does not nullify the law, which is used not only to view quantities supplied from the vantage point of price but also to determine what price is required to get a certain quantity supplied, or delivered in a given market. Thus, if a government, firm, or individual wants more of a certain good, commodity, or service, the way to get it is to offer a higher price, other things being equal. This generalization applies to an industry as well as to an individual, a firm, or a group of firms.

Supply of the firm and the industry

Imagine a large number of farm firms each with its own supply curve. As the quantity supplied by each firm at each price is added to the quantities supplied by all other firms at that price, we get the total quantity supplied by the industry at that price. The total quantity supplied will vary directly with the price, and we have a supply curve for the industry. Thus, the law of supply may be applied to the relationship between price and the quantity supplied by a single firm or to price and the quantity supplied by an industry. The law applies equally well to a single commodity, a group of commodities, or the total quantity supplied, such as the total output of agriculture. It is a basic law with an infinite number of applications.

Generalizations about the purely competitive farm firm in the short run provide a background for discussing the long run. How does the purely competitive firm adjust to prices and costs in the long run?

THE PURELY COMPETITIVE FIRM IN THE LONG RUN

As was discussed in Chapter 4, the long run permits firms to make adjustments that cannot be accomplished in the short run. Firms can alter the capacity of a plant, buy and sell resources such as land and other capital inputs, merge and grow, cut down, or close down and eventually go out of business. The number of firms in the industry may either increase or decrease as new firms enter or old firms leave. We want to discover how these long-run adjustments are made and establish the equilibrium position of firms in the long run.

Simplifying assumption

We can simplify our analysis without impairing the validity of our conclusions by using three specific assumptions.

First, all firms in the industry have identical cost curves. This permits use of a "representative" or "typical" firm such as the farm firm in our example to demonstrate what happens in an industry.

Second, the entire long-run adjustment is made by the entry and exodus of firms. This permits us to ignore the short-run adjustments of the firm and concentrate on what happens in the long run.

Third, the analysis is initially limited to the special case of a constant-cost industry, which means that the prices of resources are not affected by the entry and exodus of firms. The unit-cost schedules of the representative firm, or of any firm, are not affected by what happens to other firms.

Long-run equilibrium

Definition: The long-run equilibrium of the purely competitive firm is achieved when the price of the product is exactly equal to the minimum average total cost of the firm and production is at the point where the price, the marginal cost, and the average total cost are equal ($P = MC = ATC$, or AC).

What applies to the representative firm applies to all firms, and these results follow from two considerations: (1) All firms seek profits and shun losses, and (2) all firms are free to enter or leave the industry. According to the assumptions stated above, if the price of the product initially exceeds the minimum point of the average total cost, the resulting profits will attract new firms into the industry until the increase in the quantity supplied brings the price of the product back down to equality with the average total cost. Conversely, if the initial product price is below the minimum average total cost, the resulting losses will drive firms out of the industry. As they leave, the total quantity supplied will decline until the price of the product comes back up to equality with the average total cost. This can be illustrated as in Figure 5-8 by dropping the assumption that all firms in the industry have identical short-run cost curves.

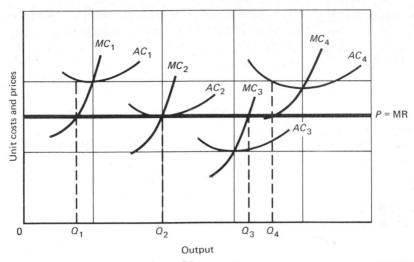

Figure 5-6   Alternative short-run AC and MC curves of four firms compared with a long-run market price of P. Q_1 to Q_4 mark the short-run equilibrium output of each firm. Firm 1 and firm 4 will be losing money in the short run, since AC is above P. They may be covering their AVCs, however. In the long run they must adjust their ACs downward to reach tangency with P, or enough other firms must leave the industry to bring P up to the minimum AC of the firms that stay. Firm 2 is in both short-run and long-run equilibrium, assuming that a normal profit is included. Firm 3 is making a pure profit in the short run, which will disappear in the long run as the assets of the firm—such as real estate and management—appreciate, or are valued upward according to their opportunity cost. Other firms, attracted by the possibilities of such pure profits, will seek to enter the industry. This will tend to increase costs or lower prices in the long run, until profit returns to the long-run normal level.

Market price equals
cost of production

The market price equals the cost of production in the long run. The entry of new firms eliminates profits, and the exodus of old firms eliminates losses. The long-run supply curve of a constant-cost industry is a horizontal straight line at the price established in the market. The price of $95.65 in Figure 5-7 is the long-run equilibrium price for the representative firm in our example. This is also the long-run equilibrium price for all other firms according to the sim-plifying assumptions stated above.

This concept has a number of important applications. If a certain figure is stated as the cost of production for a farm product, for example, and the government sets the price support in a farm program at that level, that price will in the long run become the actual cost of production for the product. The entry and exodus of firms will assure that this is so. The action of the government establishes what is in effect a self-fulfilling prophecy, provided the government support is equal to the actual market price.

Strictly speaking, in the real world the long run never really happens, but firms and industries are constantly adjusting toward a long-run equilibrium position. Agriculture provides many illustrations of this principle in operation. In the early 1970s, for example, high grain prices in the United States brought high profits to most cash-grain farmers. The efforts of farmers and other investors to acquire more land caused land prices to rise very rapidly. The implicit opportunity costs of using land went up accordingly, and some explicit costs such as property taxes began to rise as well. The average-total-cost curves of grain farmers, including both explicit and implicit costs, were adjusted to the market situation, while the increase in grain output tended to force grain prices back down into equality with the average total cost. By the late 1970s, many farmers were claiming that the price of grain had fallen below their cost of production, meaning that the price was below their minimum average total cost. The farmers in this position were in a either a loss-minimizing situation or a close-down situation. In the meantime, livestock prices had tended to move in a direction opposite to that of grain prices, as we should expect, because grain is a major cost in production of livestock.

Agriculture is constantly adjusting toward a long-run equilibrium, but it is not a constant-cost industry. To develop our analysis in a still broader direction, let us turn next to a study of market supply and demand.

SUMMARY

There are four major types of competition—pure competition, monopolistic competition, oligopoly, and monopoly—applying to the sellers' side of the market. Each has its own set of specifications, which are related to questions about the number of firms, types of products, influences on market price, conditions of entry or exit, and use or nonuse of nonprice competition. Monopolistic competition, oligopoly, and monopoly are types of imperfect competition. The comparable classification on the buyers' side is pure competition, monopsonistic competition, oligopsony, and monopsony.

The purely competitive firm is in equilibrium in the short run when it maximizes profits, or minimizes losses, which occurs at the point where marginal revenue equals marginal cost. If the firm's total revenue does not exceed its total variable costs, the firm should close down. The marginal-cost curve always intersects, or pierces from below, the average-variable-cost and average-total-cost curves at their minimum points. The short-run supply curve of the purely competitive firm is the part of its marginal-cost curve which is above the average-variable-cost curve.

The purely competitive firm is not limited in regard to the adjustments it may make in the long run. All costs are variable. Equilibrium is determined by the entry and exit of firms as discussed in this chapter, and such entry and exit is supplemented by the adjustment of individual firms along their long-run planning curves as discussed in Chapter 4.

IMPORTANT TERMS
AND CONCEPTS

Competitive market models (selling)
Pure competition
Monopolistic competition
Oligopoly
Monopoly
Imperfect competition
Competitive market models (buying)
Pure competition
Monopsonistic competition
Oligopsony
Monopsony
Total revenue
Short run
Profit-maximizing case
Loss-minimizing case
Close-down case
$MR = MC$ rule
Limited and unlimited capital
Short-run equilibrium
Short-run supply
Law of supply

Long run
Long-run equilibrium
Long-run cost of production
Average revenue
Marginal revenue
Market price and cost of production

LOOKING AHEAD

The principles of competition and output determination are used in Chapter 6 to develop new concepts and a new understanding of market supply and demand. Laws of supply and laws of demand will be developed and applied to various situations to broaden and deepen our understanding of the economics of agriculture.

QUESTIONS AND EXERCISES

1. What are the conditions for pure or perfect competition? In what parts of an economy are these conditions most prevalent? Does the concept apply to both buying and selling? If not, why not? If so, in what markets?
2. What is a purely competitive firm? Does any such firm really exist? Explain your answer.
3. Define total, average, and marginal revenue. How is average revenue derived from total revenue? How is marginal revenue determined? Give examples of each.
4. Distinguish between the concepts of limited and unlimited capital. Can each exist within the same industry at the same time? Why, or why not?
5. What is the equilibrium level of output of the firm in the short run (a) when capital is unlimited and (b) when it is limited? What is the equilibrium level of output in the long run? Explain how this differs from the short run.
6. Should a farmer continue to produce if average variable costs are not covered? In the short run? In the long run? Explain each of your answers.
7. Theoretically, can excess profits or windfall gains be made by the purely competitive firm in the short run? In the long run? Explain your answers and give an illustration other than the illustration in the text.

8. Define *cost of production.* Do firms necessarily have the same cost of production in the short run? In the long run? Explain.

9. Explain why market price determines the cost of production in long-run equilibrium of the purely competitive firm.

6. SUPPLY AND DEMAND

"Market price, regardless of the character of the market, is always determined by demand and supply, i.e., by the willingness of buyers to buy and sellers to sell. . . . The market price tends to settle at that point at which all buyers will be able to buy all they are willing to buy at that price, and all sellers are able to sell all they are willing to sell at that price. Any change in the demand or the supply, however, will change the location of this point of equilibrium. . . .**"

Jacob Viner

From *The Long View and the Short: Studies in Economic Theory and Policy* (The Free Press of Glencoe, Inc., New York, 1958, pp. 3 and 4). Jacob Viner taught economics at the University of Chicago and Princeton University. During the half century beginning in 1917 he established a preeminent position among scholars in economic theory, the history of economic thought, and economic policy.

This   chapter builds on the concepts of production functions, production costs, and pure or perfect competition to develop ideas concerning market supply. Next it discusses demand, including the law of demand and concepts of utility as related to demand. Finally, it brings supply and demand together to show how prices and quantities are determined for both inputs and outputs. How do we define supply and demand and make use of these concepts in our study of the economics of agriculture?

IN THIS CHAPTER

1. You will learn to identify factors that determine agricultural supply curves and cause these curves to change.
2. You will learn to recognize the major determinants of demand for both the resources and the products of agriculture and the factors that influence demand.
3. You will see how supply and demand interact to determine prices and quantities in both the resource markets and the product markets of agriculture.

SUPPLY

Concepts of the relationship between price and quantity supplied, identified as the law of supply, can be applied to a single producer as in Chapter 5, to any product such as corn, or to the total production of agriculture in any or all markets. A market is defined as any arrangement by which exchange takes place. In constructing a supply curve for a market, the economist assumes that price is the most significant determinant of the quantity supplied of the product or products. The supply curve is drawn on the assumption that certain nonprice determinants are given and do not change.

Definition: Supply may be defined as a schedule showing the various amounts of a product that producers are willing and able to produce and make available in a market, under given conditions, at each specific price in a set of possible prices during a specified time period.

Example of a supply curve

Figure 6-1 is an example of a hypothetical supply curve for the American corn crop. An initial supply curve, drawn as a heavy line and labeled $S_1 S_1$, shows that the price of corn may range from $80

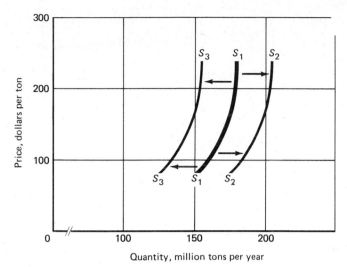

Figure 6-1   Changes in the supply of corn in the United States (hypothetical data). The shift from S_1S_1 to S_2S_2 represents an increase in supply; the shift from S_1S_1 to S_3S_3 represents a decrease in supply. Selected points on the supply curves:

Price per ton, dollars	Quantity supplied, million tons per year		
	S_1S_1	S_2S_2	S_3S_3
80	150	175	125
160	175	200	150
240	180	205	155

to \$240 per ton, while the corresponding quantity supplied ranges from 150 to 180 million tons. The curve is drawn under given conditions where nothing changes except the price of corn and the quantity supplied. The data are equivalent to a price of \$2 to \$6 per bushel and a production of 6 to 7.2 billion bushels.

The concept of supply applies to the products of an industry as well as to the resources supplied for use in production. But the qualifications given in the definition are crucial and must be observed. *The curve refers to given or specified conditions in a specific market and a specified period of time.* According to the law of supply, as the price changes and everything else remains the same, we move from one point to another on the supply schedule. This implies that there can be a change in the quantity supplied without there being any change in the supply itself. If the price of corn rises and everything else remains the same, there can be an increase in the quantity of corn supplied without any change in the supply curve for corn.

Changes in supply

By definition, a change in supply involves a shift in the supply curve itself—to the right for an increase in supply and to the left for a decrease. In Figure 6-1, $S_2 S_2$ designates an increase because producers are willing and able to offer more at each price. $S_3 S_3$ designates a decrease because producers are now offering less at each possible price. Apart from weather and related factors, what determines the location of the curve and causes it to change?

Determinants of supply

The basic factors that determine the location of the supply curve and whether it will change are (1) technologies of production, (2) prices of resources used in production, (3) prices of other products that may be substituted for the given product, (4) expectations about prices, (5) number of sellers in a market, and (6) taxes and subsidies related to the product. A change in any one of these determinants will cause the supply curve for a product to change, or shift to the right or the left. Let us consider the effect on supply of changes in any one of these determinants.

1. TECHNOLOGIES OF PRODUCTION

From the discussion of the production function in Chapter 4, we may derive the basic concept that an advance in technology means an *upward* shift in the production function and a *downward* shift in the related cost curves. This is equivalent to a shift to the *right* of the upward-sloping portions of the average-variable-cost and average-total-cost curves as well as the marginal cost, or the firm's supply curve.

The effect of an advance in technology on the supply curve may be shown by using some of the data from Tables 4-2 and 4-3, applying an advance in technology, say, equivalent to a 50 percent increase in output relative to input. We may confine our interest to stage 2 of the production function and summarize the results as in Table 6-1, Figure 6-2, and Figure 6-3.

We may assume in this case that what is true for the individual firm is true for the industry, in this case a constant-cost industry. With other things remaining the same, any advance in technology, or any increase in supply of resources, will increase the supply of the product for which these resources are used. With other things

Table 6-1   Effects of an advance in technology on the production function and costs of a farm firm with fixed costs of $120,000 and variable costs of $20,000 per unit

Variable input	Corn, tons[a]				Total cost[b]	Unit cost		Marginal cost	
	TPP_1	TPP_2	MPP_1	MPP_2	TC_1 or TC_2	AC_1	AC_2	MC_1	MC_2
3	1,500	2,250			$180,000	$120.00	$80.00		
			500	750				$ 40.00	$26.67
4	2,000	3,000			200,000	100.00	66.67		
			300	450				66.67	44.44
5	2,300	3,450			220,000	95.65	63.77		
			150	225				133.33	88.89
6	2,450	3,675			240,000	97.96	65.31		

[a]The change from TPP_1 to TPP_2 and from MPP_1 to MPP_2 represents the advance in technology.

[b]Total cost does not change, and so TC_1 is the same as TC_2.

Note: Hypothetical data.

remaining the same, any deterioration in technology, or decrease in supply of resources, will result in a decrease in supply.

2. PRICES OF RESOURCES

Since marginal cost and supply are synonymous, any reduction in marginal cost will increase supply, and any increase in marginal cost will decrease supply. Therefore, declines in the prices of resources will have the same effect on increasing supply as advances in technology. Advances in the technologies of agricultural production have been equivalent to declines in resource prices, and this has brought increasing supply for agricultural products.

A deterioration of technology is not characteristic of agriculture in modern society. But increases in the prices of resources are a pronounced phenomenon, and this tends to decrease supply. Rising resource prices have tended in many instances to offset the advances in technologies, and this has tended to obscure the net effect on supply of simultaneous changes in technologies and prices of resources. An advance in fertilizer technology and a rise in the price of fertilizer tend to be offsetting, for example.

3. PRICES OF OTHER PRODUCTS

Changes in the prices of other products that can be substituted in production may change the supply for a given product. An increase

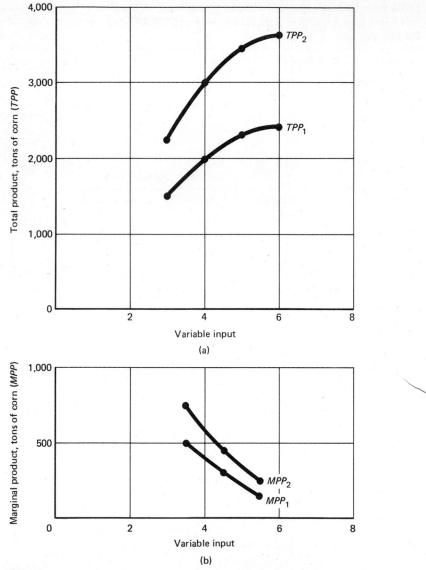

Figure 6-2 Effects of an advance in technology on the production function and marginal physical product of a farm firm (hypothetical data). The shifts from TPP_1 to TPP_2 and from MPP_1 to MPP_2 represent the advance in technology.

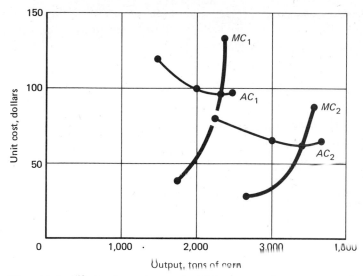

Figure 6-3   Effects of an advance in technology on the average cost and marginal cost of a farm firm (hypothetical data). The shifts from AC_1 to AC_2 and from MC_1 to MC_2 represent the advance in technology. That portion of MC_1 above AVC_1 is S_1S_1; and that portion of MC_2 above AVC_2 is S_2S_2.

in the price of soybeans, for example, may cause a farmer to shift some land from corn to soybeans, thus reducing the supply of corn. Conversely, a decrease in the price of soybeans, with other things remaining the same, will tend to increase the supply of corn.

4. EXPECTATIONS ABOUT PRICES

Expectations about the future price of a product may affect the current supply. Here, however, it is difficult to generalize. The expectation of a higher price for corn may induce farmers to withhold some of their current harvest from market, thus reducing the current supply of the day or week. Or it may induce some livestock feeders to reduce their herds, thus increasing the current supply of livestock. Conversely, the expectation of a higher price may cause farmers to plant more corn, and in anticipation of a larger crop they may reduce the amount of corn held in storage, thus increasing the current supply of the day or week. The anticipation of a higher price for beef cattle may induce cattle producers to keep more heifers and cows for breeding, thus reducing the current supply, but the eventual increase in cattle herds will increase the supply. Reactions such as this set up cycles of increases and decreases in the supply of agricultural products. These vary in length and magnitude, depending on the product and other matters.

5. NUMBER OF SELLERS

Given the scale of operation of each firm, the larger the number of producers, the greater the market supply. As more producers enter an industry, the supply curve will shift to the right. High profits, as was noticed in Chapter 5, will draw firms into an industry, thus increasing the supply. Conversely, the smaller the number of producers, the smaller the market supply. Again, as in Chapter 5, losses will cause firms to leave an industry, thus decreasing supply.

6. TAXES AND SUBSIDIES

Finally, as has been implied—or as we may infer from Chapter 4— an increase in a tax that is related to output, such as a sales tax, will increase variable and marginal costs and therefore decrease supply. You should note, however, that a tax which appears as a fixed cost, such as the farm property tax or any property tax, does not affect marginal cost, or change the short-run supply. Increasing the tax does not decrease the supply, and cutting the property tax does not increase it in the short run.

A government subsidy may or may not increase supply. A subsidy that reduces the cost of a variable input—such as the rebate of sales taxes on tractor fuel or cost-sharing payments on conservation materials—will tend to increase supply either currently or in the future. A government production payment that supplements the price of a farm product, however, will tend to increase the quantity supplied rather than change the supply curve itself. In this instance, the subsidy is simply equivalent to a higher price; unless it is accompanied by a program to restrict production or there is some other restriction, production occurs at a higher point on the supply curve rather than being located on a new or increased supply curve. Considerable attention is given to the effects of taxes and subsidies on agriculture because of the immense importance of this topic to the economic organization and performance of agriculture.

DEMAND

Like supply, the term *demand* has a very definite meaning in economics. What is the meaning, and how does it apply?

Definition: Demand may be defined as a schedule showing the various amounts of a product that will be bought, under given conditions, at each specific price in a set of possible prices during a specified period of time.

Example of a demand curve

Figure 6-4 is an example of a hypothetical demand curve for corn (and also a change in demand). The initial demand curve, drawn as a heavy line and labeled D_1D_1, shows that the price of corn may range from $80 to $240 per ton, while the corresponding quantity demanded ranges from 210 to 165 million tons. The curve is drawn under assumed conditions where nothing changes except the price of corn and the quantity demanded.

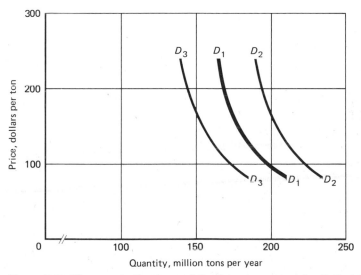

Figure 6-4 Changes in the demand for the corn crop of the United States (hypothetical data). The shift from D_1D_1 to D_2D_2 represents an increase in demand; the shift from D_1D_1 to D_3D_3 represents a decrease in demand. Selected points on the demand curves:

Price per ton, dollars	Quantity demanded, million tons per year		
	D_1D_1	D_2D_2	D_3D_3
240	165	190	140
160	175	200	150
80	220	235	185

As in the case of supply, the concept of demand applies equally to the products of an industry, such as agriculture, and the resources used in production. Again, the qualifications given in the definition are crucial and must be observed. The demand curve refers to the quantity demanded at specified prices, under given conditions, in a specified period of time. As in the case of supply, there can be a change in the quantity demanded when there is a change in price without any change in demand, or the determinants of demand. The change in price and quantity demanded can be explained in terms of the law of demand.

Law of demand

Definition: The law of demand states that there is an inverse relationship between the price and the quantity demanded. As the price falls, the quantity demanded increases; alternatively, as the price rises, the quantity demanded decreases, assuming that other things remain the same.

The law of demand rests on two fundamental propositions, the first being embodied in common sense and the simple observation that people do buy less of a product as the price rises, other things remaining the same. To producers and consumers alike, price is an obstacle that may deter them from buying. The higher the price of a product rises relative to other prices, the more they will try to substitute other things for the product or service that has risen in price. This is known in economics as the *substitution effect.* In addition, the higher the price of a product rises, the less the total quantity that can be bought with a given income. This is known as the *income effect.* If the price of a product such as food that is important in the household budget goes up, this will have an important income effect on the household, reducing the real income of the household without perhaps having so much substitution effect. If the product or service is relatively unimportant, there may be a significant substitution effect without much income effect.

Law of
diminishing marginal utility

The second proposition underlying the law of demand is found in what economists call the law of *diminishing marginal utility.* This law rests on the idea that although wants in general may be insatiable, wants for specific products can be fulfilled. After a certain amount of a product has been obtained, a consumer or producer is less eager to obtain more of it. A family's desire for an automobile, for example, may be very strong when the family doesn't have one. After one is obtained, the desire for a second automobile is usually much less intense, and the desire for a third may be very weak indeed. A farmer may have to have at least one tractor to farm at all. The need for a second is not so strong, and a third may not serve any useful purpose. The power of a specific unit of a product to satisfy a want is measured in terms of utility.

Utility is the ability or power to satisfy a want or wants. It is not the same as *usefulness,* speaking in a practical sense. A family heirloom, for example, may have no practical use. But if the family is sentimentally attached to it, its power to satisfy a want—its utility—may be very great. This suggests that utility involves subjective values that differ from person to person, as well as practical down-to-earth or common values involving products that everyone wants, such as the necessities of life.

Marginal utility simply means the net addition to total utility, or the net additional power to satisfy wants of one more unit of a given product.

Definition: The law of diminishing marginal utility states that at any given time during which a consumer's tastes do not change, after a certain number of units of a product have been obtained, the marginal utility derived from successive units of the given product will decline, or diminish.

Utility-maximizing rule

Utility diminishes with each successive unit acquired because the consumer becomes satiated with it—the consumer has enough of that particular product. The consumer may not be able to measure specifically how fast the utility of a particular product diminishes as more and more of it is acquired, but the rational consumer will compare the cost of acquiring successive units of a particular product with the cost of acquiring other products and services.

Definition: The utility-maximizing rule states that the consumer should allocate the available income or money so that the last unit of expenditure—such as 1 dollar, 100 dollars, or whatever—on each product purchased has the same net additional amount of power to satisfy wants (utility) as the equivalent amount spent on something else.

When the utility-maximizing rule is satisfied, the consumer will be allocating the available income in such a way that no change can be made in the *relative* amounts spent on various products without reducing the total utility. This means that the unit prices of the various products in the consumer's budget will be proportional to the marginal utilities of the respective products to that consumer. If a unit of product A costs as much as a unit of product B, the last unit of each product that is acquired should have the same utility to the consumer. If the price of product A rises relative to the price of product B, the consumer should use less of product A relative to product B. *When the income is all spent, the marginal utilities of all the products or services acquired should be proportional to their specific unit prices.*

The utility-maximizing rule is a universal proposition applying to any specific set of circumstances. If the amount of income changes, however, the relative marginal utilities are apt to change. A consumer at different levels of income, in other words, is not expected to maximize utility at each level by not changing the relative amounts spent on various products, or categories of products. This is simply because the marginal utility of some products—for example, some necessities—diminishes more rapidly than the marginal utility of others—such as luxuries. Also, since utility is subjective,

A utility-maximizing consumer will allocate the food budget so that the unit prices of the available products are proportional to the marginal utilities of those products to that consumer.

we should not ordinarily expect two consumers who have the same total income to buy exactly the same proportions of products and services. The utility-maximizing rule covers all situations, however, and is therefore universally valid.

Individual and market demand

The concept of demand, like that of supply, applies to a single individual or firm as well as to any number of buyers in a market. The transition from an individual to a market demand schedule is accomplished by summing the quantities demanded by each buyer at the various possible prices. The schedule shown in Figure 6-4 is a market demand composed of the aggregate purchases of corn by all kinds of buyers in both the domestic market and the foreign market, plus the quantities fed or used on the farms where the corn was raised. Corn, like most products, has many uses; the total market demand is the sum of the demands for each of these uses by all buyers and users whether the corn moves through a specific market or not. The market demand curve is the sum of all the individual demand curves.

Determinants of demand

The initial demand curve in Figure 6-4, or $D_1 D_1$, is drawn under the condition that a change in the price of the product is the only thing that can cause a change in the quantity demanded because none of the other determinants are allowed to change. When one or more of the nonprice determinants does change, the demand curve will shift to the right or the left. Figure 6-4 shows an increase in demand as a shift from $D_1 D_1$ to $D_2 D_2$ and a decrease as a shift from $D_1 D_1$ to $D_3 D_3$

What are the basic nonprice determinants of demand? The main ones are (1) tastes or preferences of consumers, (2) number of consumers in the market, (3) money incomes or wealth or consumers, (4) the prices of related goods, and (5) the expectations of consumers with respect to future prices and incomes.

1. TASTES

A change in consumers' tastes favorable to a product—possibly prompted by advertising, new information, or a new style—will mean that more is demanded at each price, or that demand increases. Farm food products sold under monopolistic competition or oligopoly are often highly advertised, generally by brand name, as a means of differentiating the product of the processing-marketing firm. This tends to increase the demand for the brand that is advertised. An unfavorable change in consumers' tastes will cause the demand to decrease, shifting the curve to the left.

2. NUMBER OF BUYERS

The growth of population provides the basis for a general increase in the demand for agricultural products around the world, provided per capita income does not fall or other adverse consequences do not occur. It was noted in Chapter 3 that the greatest increases in population, both in percentage terms and in aggregate, are expected in the currently developing countries. This is where the greatest increase in demand for food will occur so long as per capita incomes can be increased or at least do not fall. Improvements in transportation and elimination of the impediments to trade, such as tariffs and import quotas, will expand the demand for products that are exported, such as the grains and oilseeds produced on the farms of the United States.

3. INCOME

The relationships between changes in income and changes in demand are somewhat more complex. An increase in income will increase the demand for most agricultural products. Consumers typically buy more meat and other animal products as their incomes increase. Figure 3-5, for instance, indicated the direct relationship between income per person and pounds of grain used per person per year in selected countries. In Figure 3-6 a close, direct relationship was shown between income per capita and meat consumption per capita in selected countries. *Goods, or commodities, whose demand varies directly with money income are called normal, or superior, goods.* Economic progress in currently developing countries will greatly increase the demand for such products. American farmers thus have a direct interest in encouraging economic progress in other countries.

Although most products including farm food products are normal goods, there are some exceptions. Economic studies generally reveal that as incomes increase beyond some point, the amount of cereals, or baking products, purchased at each price does not increase. The higher incomes permit consumers to buy more of the prepared bakery products and—of greater importance—more high-protein meats, poultry, fish, and dairy products. In addition, rising incomes tend to cause the demands for the cheaper cuts of meat to decline as consumers switch preferences to higher-priced steaks, prime ribs, and the like. *Goods whose demand varies inversely with a change in money income are sometimes called inferior goods.*

The relationship between income and quantity purchased is measured by a coefficient called *income elasticity of demand.* With no change in relative prices, if the percentage of disposable income after taxes spent on a good or service stays the same as real income increases, income elasticity is equal to 1.0. If the percentage spent increases only half as much, income elasticity is 0.5. If it increases one-fourth as much, income elasticity is 0.25, and so on.

A number of studies have revealed that income elasticity in relation to total food is very low in the United States, around 2.5 or there abouts, and generally lower among people with high incomes than among people with low incomes. Also, income elasticities are generally very low, 0.25 or less, for commodities such as lard, margarine, evaporated milk, sweet potatoes, beans, and bread. They are about 0.6, or more, for frozen vegetables; about 0.5 to 0.6 for individual meats such as lamb, beef, veal, and turkey; and around or below 0.4 for pork, chicken, ice cream, all fruit, and cheese.

4. PRICES OF RELATED PRODUCTS

Whether the demand for a given product will be increased or decreased by a change in the price of a related product depends on whether the latter is a substitute for, or a complement to, the product under consideration. Beef and pork, for example, are competing, or substitute, products. When the price of beef rises, consumers will purchase less beef, and this will cause the demand for pork to increase. Similarly, as the price of beef falls, the demand for pork will decrease. *When two products are substitutes, a change in the price of one is directly related to the demand for the other.* This is the case with beef and pork, butter and oleomargarine, tea and coffee, oranges and grapefruit, and so on.

When two products are used together—such as beer and pretzels, bacon and eggs, bread and butter, or milk and cereal—they are complements. A rise in the price of one will decrease the demand for the other, and vice versa. *Two commodities are complements if an inverse relationship exists between the price of one and the demand for the other.*

When two products are not related at all in terms of price and quantity demanded, they are said to be independent. The relationships between some food and nonfood products sometimes fall in this category. We should expect the price of one to have little effect on the demand for the other.

5. EXPECTATIONS

The expectation of higher prices in the future may cause consumers to increase their demand, to buy now to "beat" the expected rise in price, even to borrow more money to "buy now and pay later." Similarly, the expectation of higher incomes may cause people to go into debt with the thought that they will have more money later. Expectations of higher prices and higher incomes—which may be accepted as a definition of inflation—sometimes work together to encourage people to go into debt in order to buy, thus increasing the current demand for various kinds of products and services. An expectation of lower prices will tend to decrease current demand.

Law of demand applied to resources

When the law of demand is applied to resources, we should first recognize this most crucial point: *The demand for resources is a derived demand; it is derived from the demand for the finished products and services that these resources help produce.* Most resources do not satisfy consumers' wants directly. No one consumes an acre of land, a gallon of diesel fuel, or a tractor. But people do consume the commodities that these resources help produce.

The demand for a resource depends on (1) the capability of the resource in production, and (2) the value of the good being produced. That is, the demand for a resource is based on the additional value or revenue that it will produce. This net addition to total revenue for each added unit of input is called the *marginal revenue product (MRP).*

Definition: Marginal revenue product (MRP) is the increase in total revenue resulting from the use of each additional unit of a variable input.

To maximize profits or minimize losses (assuming that the firm is not in a close-down situation), a firm should buy or use additional units of each variable resource so long as each successive unit adds more to the firm's total revenue than to the firm's total cost. The amount that each additional unit adds to the firm's total (resource) cost is called the *marginal resource cost (MRC)*.

Definition: Marginal resource cost (MRC) is the increase in total (resource) cost resulting from the use of each additional unit of a variable input.

Now it can be said that it will be profitable for a firm to buy or use additional units of a resource up to the point where the *MRP* of that resource is equal to its *MRC*. This relationship, which is called the *MRP = MRC* rule, is very similar to the *MR = MC* rule that has been employed up to this point. The rationale of the two rules is the same, but now the point of reference is *inputs* of resources, not *outputs* of products, or services.

MRP IS A DEMAND SCHEDULE

The rational firm which is not in a close-down situation will buy or use each resource up to the point where the *MRC* of the firm is equal to its *MRP*. *Then each point on a MRP schedule indicates the number of units of a variable input that will be demanded at each price within a set of possible prices.* In other words, the *MRP* schedule is the demand for inputs. Table 6-2 has been constructed to provide an example.

The first two columns in Table 6-2 cover stage 2 of our familiar production function, and column (3) is *MPP*. The price of $100 per ton is chosen for convenience, and the total revenue shown in col-

Table 6-2   Demand of the purely competitive farm firm for a variable resource

(1)	(2)	(3)	(4)	(5)	(6)
	Corn, tons		Product	Total	MRP equals
Units of			price	revenue,	demand
resource	TPP	MPP	per ton	(2) × (4)	(3) × $100
3	1,500		$100	$150,000	
		500			$50,000
4	2,000		100	200,000	
		300			30,000
5	2,300		100	230,000	
		150			15,000
6	2,450		100	245,000	

Note: Hypothetical data.

umn (5) is the number of tons produced, multiplied by this price. The crucial step illustrated in column (6) is the derivation of the marginal revenue product (*MRP*). At each point on the schedule, *MRP* is the amount added to total revenue by each added unit of input. Column (6) is column (3) multiplied by $100. At the beginning of stage 2, it can be seen that the fourth unit of the resource adds $50,000 to the total revenue. The fifth adds $30,000, and the sixth adds $15,000.

Table 6-2 can tell us several things. First, it can be seen that if the price of a unit of the variable resource is $50,000 and corn is $100 per ton, the producer is on the verge of closing down at either 1,500 or 2,000 tons. There may be some point between these two levels of output where there will be some surplus revenue above the variable cost. But if the units are indivisible, the producer will be indifferent about adding the fourth unit. Second, if the price is $30,000 the producer will be indifferent about adding the fifth unit. Finally, if the price is $15,000, the fifth unit will be employed, but the producer will be indifferent about adding the sixth. We can think more precisely about the possible solution by transferring the information pertaining to *MRP* and demand to Figure 6-5.

Figure 6-5 may be used to tell us more precisely just how much of the variable input will be demanded at each price, assuming that

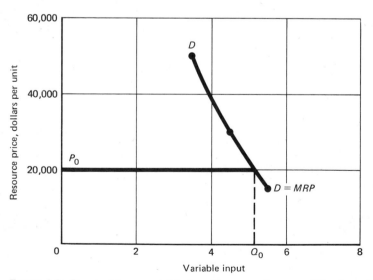

Figure 6-5   Demand for a variable input by a purely competitive farm firm.

the inputs are divisible. At a price of $20,000, the manager will use almost $5\frac{1}{5}$ (P_o and Q_o in Figure 6-5). At $30,000, about $4\frac{1}{2}$ units will be used, at $40,000 almost exactly 4, and at $50,000, about $3\frac{1}{2}$. You can test this by dropping perpendiculars at each price from DD to the x axis.

Thus, MRP is the demand schedule for a single resource. How shall we apply this to the demand for several resources?

FIRM'S DEMAND FOR SEVERAL RESOURCES: UNLIMITED CAPITAL

A firm having unlimited capital will find that it maximizes profits, or minimizes losses, by employing each and every resource up to the point where $MRP = MRC$. That is, MRP will be equated for each resource according to the $MRP = MRC$ rule. We may understand this further by making another assumption about the example in Table 6-2 and Figure 6-5. So far we have thought of the land and the number of workers as fixed for this farm, the units of other resources being variable. Now let us make the alternative assumption that labor is the only variable resource and each unit represents a year of labor. We can see that the same principle will apply. If the price of labor is $20,000 for one person in a year, we will have an answer to how many should be employed. It is about $5\frac{1}{5}$, say five workers hired for the year and one extra worker hired for 10 weeks during harvest. If the price (annual wage) is $30,000, the manager will want about $4\frac{1}{2}$, say four workers full-time and one half-time, three full-time and three half-time, or some other combination, depending on the availability of workers, and the work schedule.

Similar reasoning can apply to land or to any other resource. Thus, we have a general solution. If we assume perfect markets— where the action of the buyer does not affect the market price, or the going wage—the profit-maximizing, or loss-minimizing, amount of any input to buy is the quantity at which the price of the input (which is its MRC) is equal to its MRP. Thus, if we limit this to capital and labor, it can be said that the quantity of capital inputs to buy is the quantity at which the price of capital (P_C) equals its marginal revenue product (MRP_C). The quantity of labor to hire is the quantity at which the price (wage rate) of labor (P_L) equals its marginal revenue product (MRP_L). Or more simply:

$$P_C = MRP_C$$
$$P_L = MRP_L$$

This rule is sometimes alternatively expressed as

$$\frac{MRP_C}{P_C} = \frac{MRP_L}{P_L} = 1$$

Two points should be noted for a correct interpretation of this rule. First, in this instance we are considering a firm that is able to acquire all the resources that it can profitably employ. It is not sufficient that the *MRP*s of the resources be proportionate to their prices; they must be equal. The ratio must be equal to 1. For example, if P_C = \$20,000 and MRP_C = \$30,000, and P_L = \$20,000 and MRP_L = \$30,000, the firm will be underemploying both capital and labor even though the ratios of *MRP* to *P* are the same for both resources. In this case, to reach an equilibrium the farmer would move down the downward-sloping *MRP* curve, increasing the quantity of each resource demanded until each *MRP* was equal to \$20,-000 and the ratios were then equal to 1.

Second, the problem faced by the producer is similar to that faced by the consumer. In achieving the combination of goods that will yield the maximum utility for a given money income, the consuming family or household considers its preferences in terms of diminishing marginal utility and the prices of the various products. Similarly, the producer in attempting to achieve the maximum profit, or minimum loss, must consider both the productivity of the resource as reflected in diminishing marginal physical productivity and the prices (marginal resource costs) of the various inputs. If the price of labor (MRC_L) is very high, for example, only a relatively small amount of labor will be employed and MRP_L will also be high. Conversely, if P_L or MRC_L is low, MRP_L will be low and a large amount of labor will be hired. The same can be said about any other resource in order to reach equilibrium with unlimited resources. What rule applies when resources (capital) are limited?

LEAST-COST COMBINATION
WITH LIMITED CAPITAL

A firm with limited capital cannot employ every resource up to the point where *MRP* = *MRC*. In this case the various possible outputs can be profit-maximizing, or loss-minimizing, only if each is produced in the least costly way. When does this occur? The answer is: When the last dollar spent on each resource entails the same marginal physical product. That is, the cost of any output is minimized when *MPP* per dollar's worth of each resource used is the same. Thus,

$$\frac{MPP \text{ of capital}}{\text{price of capital}} = \frac{MPP \text{ of labor}}{\text{price of labor}} \quad \text{or} \quad \frac{MPP_C}{P_C} = \frac{MPP_L}{P_L}$$

This equation means that the cost of any output is minimized when *MPP* per dollar's worth of resource used is the same for each resource.

We can see why this is so by first assuming the opposite, that they are not the same. Suppose, for example, that the farmer in our illustration has *MPP* of 3 bushels of corn for each $1 spent on capital (fertilizer), but only 2 bushels for each $1 spent on labor (cultivating). Our equation tells us that this is not the least costly combination: $MPP_o/P_o = 3/1$ and $MPP_l/P_l = 2/1$. If the farmer spends $1 less on labor (cultivating) and $1 more on capital (fertilizer), the output of corn will increase by 1 bushel. If diminishing returns prevail, this will push the farmer down the *MPP* curve for capital (fertilizer) and back up the *MPP* curve for labor (cultivating), moving toward the condition where $MPP_C/P_C = MPP_L/P_L$. So long as the condition of limited capital prevails, however, this equation cannot equal unity, although the farmer does move toward the condition of equalizing returns at the margin.

PRINCIPLE OF
EQUAL MARGINAL RETURNS

The basic peculiarity or distinction of the demand for inputs stems from the technological fact that factors do not work alone. The demand for each input depends on the prices, or opportunity costs, of all inputs, not the price of that input alone. That is, the interdependence of the productivities of agricultural land, management and labor, and all the other forms of capital makes the problem of selection and allocation of inputs, and the distribution of returns to inputs, complex. It is a remarkable achievement to reduce this complexity to a single rule.

Appropriate use of the *MRP* = *MRC* rule tells us not only how much of a single resource to employ but how much of each and every resource to use. Furthermore, if capital is limited and the firm cannot obtain all the resources that it can profitably employ, the rule tells us that the ratio of *MRP* to *MRC*—in perfect markets, *MRP* to price—should be the same for all the resources that are employed.

Economists have a term for this, sometimes calling it the *principle of equal marginal returns* or the *equal-marginal-returns principle*. It means that to get the lowest total cost at each point on a total-cost schedule, a rational firm will hire factors until it has equalized the marginal physical product per last dollar spent on each factor of production. At this point *MRP* of resource A is to *MRC* of resource A as the *MRP* of B is to *MRC* of B, as *MRP* of C is to *MRC* of C, and so on.

The principle of equal marginal returns also applies to the choices to be made among products, or to what economists call *product-product decisions*. The rule is essentially the same. The rational firm will allocate resources among products until the *MRP* of a unit of a given resource is equalized among its possible products. This means that at some point a given resource cannot yield a larger *MRP* by being further shifted from one product to another.

PARTIAL BUDGETING: APPLYING THE *MRP* = *MRC* RULE
TO CHOICE OF PRODUCT

Partial budgeting is a technique commonly used for allocating resources among products, and it may be used in applying the *MRP* = *MRC* rule to choices among products. Partial budgeting requires data on production costs, product prices, and yields. Table 6-3 presents actual production costs for corn and soybeans on a selected group of farms in central Illinois. Let us use these data to illustrate the process or technique of partial budgeting.

For 1977, let us select a farm that has the same average total costs as those given in Table 6-3. The farmer wants to decide whether to shift an 80-acre field from corn to soybeans. It will be necessary to know: (1) *MRP* that is lost by not growing the 80 acres of corn, (2) *MRC* that is saved by not growing corn on this land, (3) estimated *MRP* from 80 acres of soybeans, and (4) *MRC* of growing soybeans. Since the fixed costs are not the same for both corn and soybeans, these also must be taken into account. The results of the partial budgeting are shown in Table 6-4. Let us assume an expected yield of 120 bushels per acre (or 3 tons) and a price of $2.50 per bushel (or $100 per ton) for corn. For soybeans, let us plan on a yield of 37 bushels per acre (or 1 ton) and a price of $6 per bushel (or $222 per ton). What are the results?

Table 6-4 shows that with the yields and prices expected, the farmer will lose $2,080 by shifting 80 acres from corn to soybeans. How much will the prices or yields have to change in order to make

Table 6-3 Average production costs per tillable acre to grow corn and soybeans on central Illinois farms with no livestock[a]

	Corn		Soybeans	
	1977	1976	1977	1976
Number of farms	436	447	436	447
Acres grown per farm	305	327	229	201
Yield per acre, bushels	121	143	46	42
Nonland costs				
Variable costs				
Soil fertility	$ 40	$ 46	$ 12	$ 12
Seed, crop, and drying	32	30	21	20
Repairs, fuel, and hire	19	19	17	16
Total, variable costs	$ 91	$ 95	$ 50	$ 48
Other nonland costs				
Labor	$ 25	$ 24	$ 24	$ 23
Buildings and storage	8	7	4	1
Machinery depreciation	26	24	22	20
Nonland interest	31	20	29	27
Overhead	9	8	9	8
Total, other costs	$ 99	$ 92	$ 88	$ 82
Total, nonland costs	$190	$187	$138	$130
Land costs				
Taxes	$ 16	$ 14	$ 16	$ 14
Adjusted net rent	94	87	94	87
Total land cost	$110	$101	$110	$101
Total, all cost per acre	$300	$288	$248	$231
Total, all cost per hectare[b]	$741	$712	$613	$571
Nonland cost per bushel	$ 1.57	$ 1.31	$ 3.00	$ 3.10
Total, all cost per bushel	$ 2.48	$ 2.02	$ 5.39	$ 5.50
Total, all cost per ton[c]	$ 99	$ 80	$199	$203

[a] Including summaries of total costs per tillable acre, per tillable hectare, per bushel, and per ton.

[b] 1 hectare = 2.471 acres

[c] 1 ton = 39.3682 bushels corn and 36.7437 bushels soybeans. Conversion used is 40 bushels corn and 37 bushels soybeans.

Source: 53rd Annual Summary of Illinois Farm Business Records, 1977, Commercial Farms: Production/Costs/Income/Investments, University of Illinois at Urbana-Champaign/College of Agriculture/Cooperative Extension Service, Circular 1162, August 1978, p. 3. Prepared by D. F. Wilken and R. P. Kesler of the Department of Agricultural Economics.

the change profitable? Suppose the expected price for soybeans is $7 per bushel, with no change in anything else. MRP for 80 acres of soybeans will be 80 × 37 × $7 = $20,720. Then, $20,720 − $19,840 = $880, which is what the farmer will gain by shifting the 80 acres to soybeans.

Table 6-4   Partial budgeting approach to choices between growing corn and growing soybeans

(a)   Income lost by not growing corn

1. Gross marketing receipts from 80 acres of corn (*MRP*)
    Assume average yield of 120 bushels (3 tons) per acre
    Assume price of $2.50 per bushel ($100 per ton)
    Then, 80 × 120 × $2.50 = $24,000
2. Cost of growing 80 acres of corn (*MRC*)
    80 × $300 = $24,000
3. Net profit or loss from growing corn (*MRP - MRC*),
    $24,000 − $24,000 = 0 (break-even situation covering all cost)

(b)   Income from growing soybeans

1. Gross marketing receipts from 80 acres of soybeans (*MRP*)
    Assume average yield of 37 bushels (1 ton) per acre
    Assume price of $6 per bushel ($222 per ton)
    Then, 80 × 37 × $6 = $17,760
    Or, 80 × 1 × $222 = $17,760
2. Costs of growing 80 acres of soybeans (*MRC*)
    80 × $248 = $19,840
3. Net profit or loss from growing soybeans (*MRP - MRC*)
    $17,760 − $19,840 = $ −2,080 (net loss in growing 80 acres of soybeans, or shifting 80 acres from corn to soybeans)

Note: Cost data for 1977 from Table 6-3.

We should remember, however, that there are four general classes of items that can change in the partial budget: *MRP* and *MRC* for corn, and *MRP* and *MRC* for soybeans. Within each of these four classes there are subitems that can change: prices and yields for each of the crops, and any item of costs for either crop. Suppose, for example, that the spring is wet and late so that the farmer cannot work the field until late May, and the expected yield on corn drops to 110 bushels per acre. In this area, as a rule of thumb, the yield drops by 2 bushels per acre for each day that planting is delayed beyond a certain critical date. At 100 bushels per acre, *MRP* from the 80 acres of corn is 80 × 100 × $2.50 = $22,000. On the basis of the original data with soybeans at $6 a bushel, the farmer will still be $80 ahead by continuing with corn, even though the normal profit is cut by $2,000. However, if the expected yield were to drop by another 2 bushels as a result of seeding being delayed just one more day, it will pay to shift to soybeans.

We might include any number of changes in costs, yields, and prices to illustrate the flexibilities of partial budgeting. But perhaps enough has been said to support the general statement that applies to its use: *Managers of farms and other businesses must have accurate knowledge of their individual costs, expected yields, and prices in order to most successfully apply the MRP = MRC rule with unlimited capital, or the $MPP_C/P_C = MPP_L/P_L$ rule with limited capital.*

However, the rule or the general statement is not rejected on the grounds that managers do not always have accurate data on costs or are not able to form very firm expectations on yields and prices. This merely points to the uncertainties that the manager must face. The rule still applies, but accurate data on costs and firm expectations on yields and prices are preferred, and one of the jobs of the manager is to develop as accurate a set of data as possible. After that, management must take its chances, for which it expects a normal profit over time.

Determinants of the demand for resources

Discussion of the *MRP = MRC* rule (and partial budgeting as a way of implementing it) provides a background for discussion of the determinants of the demand for resources. What determines the location of the demand curve for a resource? What causes it to change? Since *MRP* is the demand curve for a given resource, we may see the answer more clearly by thinking about the factors that determine the location of *MRP* and cause it to change. These can be limited to three things: (1) the demand for the product, (2) the productivity of the resource, and (3) the prices of other resources in relation to their productivities.

1. DEMAND FOR THE PRODUCT

Generally speaking, if the demand for a product increases (*DD* shifts to the right), we should expect the price to rise, assuming that other things in the market for that product do not change. This will increase the demand for the resources used to produce that product. For example, as in our previous illustration, when the price of soybeans changes from $6 to $7 per bushel, it becomes profitable to shift to soybeans. This will mean an increase in the demand for soybean seed, farm chemicals used on soybeans, and soybean-processing facilities. It also will decrease the demand for seed corn, fertilizer used on corn but not soybeans, preemergence herbicide, insecticides, and other pesticides used on corn. It also might decrease the demand for crop-drying, storage, and transportation facilities. Thus, the demand for the resources used to produce a particular commodity is related to the price of that commodity as well as to the prices of alternative competing commodities.

2. PRODUCTIVITY OF THE RESOURCE

In our example, when the spring is wet and late, the productivity of the resources used to grow corn will decline relative to the productivity of the resources used to grow soybeans. This decline, if continued beyond a certain point, will reduce and eventually eliminate the demand for the resources specifically used to grow corn. Also, the decline may reduce the demand for land and labor, but it will not eliminate the demand so long as there is an alternative that will cover the variable costs.

Speaking more broadly, the marginal physical productivity of any resource depends on the productivity and amount of other resources with which it is combined. *MPP* per worker has traditionally been higher in American agriculture than in European agriculture, in large part because of the high productivity and large amount of land and other resources that American farmers have had available for use. That is, the *MRP* curve per farm worker has been located farther to the right in the United States than in Europe. In recent years, however, the increased protection for agriculture provided by the European Economic Community (E.E.C.) may have shifted the *MRP* curves to the right. If true, in the longer run this of course results in a higher *MRC* for European agriculture.

3. PRICES OF OTHER RESOURCES

Just as the demand for a given product is changed by changes in the prices of other products, so the demand for a given resource is changed by changes in the prices of other resources. Again, the relationship is affected by the existence of substitutes and complements. Typically, within limits any resource is a substitute for some other resource or resources—tractors for horses, farm chemicals for cultivators, trucks for railroad cars, diesel fuel for gasoline, and so on. Typically, a decrease in the price of a given resource will reduce the demand for resources that are close substitutes. A decline in the price of diesel fuel without any change in other prices, or relative to other prices, will reduce the demand for gasoline, as diesel motors are substituted for gasoline motors.

Resources that are used together are jointly demanded; they are called *complements.* In this case, an increase in the price of one tends to decrease the demand for the other. If the price of tractor fuel rises relative to all other prices, this tends to decrease the demand for tractors. Farmers may put on more farm chemicals to control weeds, for example, cutting down on cultivating and the use of farm tractors. Thus, the chemicals substitute for both tractors and cultivators.

But you must be careful in attempting to identify resources that are complements. Tractors and tractor fuel tend to go together, and we may say they are complements. But an increase in the price of tractor fuel may also encourage farmers to buy new tractors that use fuel more efficiently. The new tractors substitute for some of the fuel. An increase in the price of fuel may increase the demand for newer, more fuel-efficient tractors, while an increase in the price of new tractors can also increase the demand for fuel as farmers continue to use their old, less fuel-efficient tractors.

MARKET EQUILIBRIUM

We may now bring the concepts of supply and demand together to see how buying and selling decisions interact to determine the prices and quantities traded in both resource and product markets. Table 6-5 summarizes some of the data on supply and demand for corn from Figures 6-1 and 6-4. There are, of course, a very large number of buyers and sellers and many possible prices, but these three prices illustrate the principle in which we are interested, and we need not be concerned about the number of traders in the market.

It is enough to know—starting at the top of the table—that when the price is $240 per ton, producers will supply 180 million tons, but

Table 6-5   Market supply and demand for corn

(1) Total quantity supplied in a year, million tons	(2) Price per ton	(3) Total quantity demanded in a year, million tons	(4) Surplus (+) or shortage (−), million tons (arrows indicate effect on price)
180	$240	165	+15 ↓
175	160	175	0
150	80	210	−60 ↑

Note: Hypothetical data.

buyers will demand only 165 million tons. At the botton of the table, when the price is $80 per ton, producers will supply only 150 million tons, but buyers will demand 210 million tons. In the first instance, there is a surplus of 15 million tons. What will happen to it? Producers will want to get rid of it. They will offer to sell at a lower and lower price until it is taken off their hands. In the second instance, when the price is $80 per ton, buyers will want more than is supplied. They will compete with each other, offering more and more until they get as much as they are willing to buy at a given price.

The balance between the quantity supplied and the quantity demanded occurs at the price of $160 per ton, which is equivalent to $4 per bushel. There is neither a surplus nor a shortage at this price, and there is no reason for the price of corn to move away from it. The market is in balance at this price, or what economists call *equilibrium.* There is, then, both an *equilibrium price and an equilibrium quantity.*

Definition: Market equilibrium occurs at the price at which the quantity supplied is equal to the quantity demanded.

EFFECTS OF CHANGES
IN SUPPLY AND DEMAND

Now we may observe the effects of changes in supply and demand on the prices and quantities traded. Figure 6-6 shows the effect of a change in supply. An increase in supply causes a decrease in the equilibrium price and an increase in the equilibrium quantity. A decrease in supply has the opposite effect.

A change in demand causes a shift in the same direction for both price and quantity. Figure 6-7 shows that an increase in demand causes an increase in both price and quantity. A decrease in demand causes a decrease in both price and quantity.

Figures 6-6 and 6-7 may look a little strange. In Figure 6-6 it takes a very large increase in supply to push the price of corn down from $160 to $80 per ton, but only a small decrease in supply to cause it to rise to $240 per ton. Also, in Figure 6-7 it takes only a small increase in demand to cause the price to rise from $160 to $240 per ton, but a large decrease in demand to push the price down to $80 per ton. Why is this? It might be said that it is because of the shape of the supply and demand curves as they have been constructed. But economists have another word for it, a word that we have carefully avoided so far. This word is *elasticity,* and it will be taken up in Chapter 7.

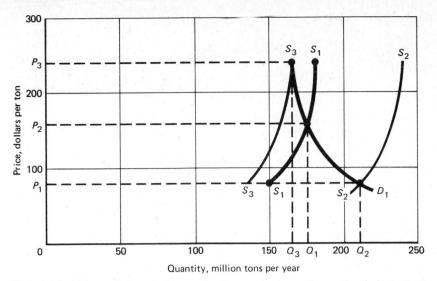

Figure 6-6 Effects of changes in supply of corn on price and quantity (hypothetical data). The shift from S_1S_1 to S_2S_2 is an increase in supply. The shift from S_1S_1 to S_3S_3 is a decrease in supply. Equilibrium prices and quantities are P_1 and Q_1 with S_1S_1, P_2 and Q_2 with S_2S_2, and P_3 and Q_0 with S_3S_3.

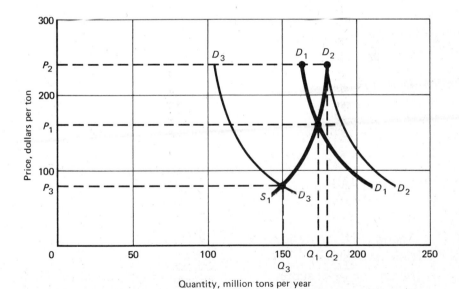

Figure 6-7 Effects of changes in demand for corn on price and quantity (hypothetical data). The shift from D_1D_1 to D_2D_2 is an increase in demand. The shift from D_1D_1 to D_3D_3 is a decrease in demand. Equilibrium prices and quantities are P_1 and Q_1 with D_1D_1, P_2 and Q_2 with D_2D_2, and P_3 and Q_3 with D_3D_3.

SUMMARY

Supply has been defined as a schedule showing the various amounts of a product that will be made available in a market, under given conditions, at each price in a set of possible prices during a specified period of time. A change in supply involves a shift in the schedule. The determinants of supply include the technologies of production, prices of resources, prices of other products, expectation about prices, number of sellers, taxes, and subsidies.

Demand has been defined as a schedule showing the various amounts of a product that will be bought, under given conditions, at each specific price in a set of possible prices during a specified period of time. The law of demand states that there is an inverse relationship between price and quantity demanded. The law rests on two fundamental propositions, one involving substitution and income effects and the other involving the law of diminishing marginal utility. The utility-maximizing rule involves the equalization of marginal utilities with prices. The determinants of demand are the tastes and preferences of consumers, number of buyers, income, prices of related products, and expectations.

The demand for inputs is based on the productivity and value of products produced by the inputs. The demand for inputs is the same as the schedule of marginal revenue product. Equilibrium in the demand for resources occurs when $MRP = MRC$. The main determinants of the demand for resources are demand for the product, productivity of the resource, and prices of other resources.

Market equilibrium occurs at the point at which the quantity supplied is equal to the quantity demanded. At the equilibrium price the quantities supplied and demanded are the same. A change in supply or demand *usually* causes both price and quantity to change.

IMPORTANT TERMS
AND CONCEPTS

Supply
Change in quantity supplied
Change in supply
Determinants of supply
Demand
    Change in quantity demanded
    Change in demand
    Determinants of demand

Law of demand
Law of diminishing marginal utility
Utility-maximizing rule
Individual and market demand
Determinants of demand
Demand for inputs and marginal revenue product
Equal marginal returns
Determinants of demand for resources
Market equilibrium
Effects of changes in supply and demand on market equilibrium.

LOOKING AHEAD

The relationships between the changes in the prices and the quantities supplied (demanded) when there is a change in demand (supply) are determined by what economists call *elasticity*. The concept of elasticity is absolutely crucial in understanding the organization and operation of an economic system. Let us turn to this topic in Chapter 7.

QUESTIONS AND EXERCISES

1. Define supply. What is the law of supply? What is the basic proposition on which this law is based? In what ways does this proposition differ from the proposition underlying the law of demand? In what ways are the propositions similar?
2. What is change in supply? What are the major factors that account for changes in the supply of agricultural inputs? Agricultural products or outputs? How does a change in price expectations influence supply? Give an example.
3. What is the relationship between the marginal-cost curves of firms and the supply curve for an agricultural commodity or the agricultural industry? Illustrate.
4. Define demand. What is the law of demand? On what general proposition does this law rest?
5. What is a change in demand? Is a change in demand the same as a change in quantity demanded? Can there be a change in demand without a change in quantity demanded? A change in quantity demanded without a change in demand? Why, or why not? Illustrate.

6. What major factors account for a change in demand for agricultural inputs? For agricultural products? What is a derived demand?

7. Define income elasticity. What factors account for differences in income elasticities for agricultural products?

8. Define and illustrate market equilibrium. What is market equilibrium price? Market equilibrium quantity? What happens if the price for an agricultural commodity is supported above the market equilibrium price? What happens if the support price is below the equilibrium price?

9. How do market equilibrium price and the quantity demanded or supplied change when there is an increase in demand with no change in supply? A decrease in demand? An increase in supply with no change in demand? A decrease in supply?

10. What happens if there is a change in both demand and supply in the same direction? In opposite directions?

7. ELASTICITY OF DEMAND AND SUPPLY

7. ELASTICITY OF DEMAND AND SUPPLY

// . . . The province of economics . . . is to work out, on the basis of the general principles of conduct and the fundamental facts of social situation, the laws which determine prices of commodities and the direction of the social economic process. . . .**//**

Frank H. Knight

The laws which determine the prices of commodities and the direction of change are universal in their application. As viewed by Frank H. Knight, the exact structure of the economic system varies from society to society, but every society must answer basic questions about what goods and services to produce, how to produce them, and how to distribute them among the members of the society, providing for the present as well as the future. (See Don Patinkin, "Frank Knight as Teacher," *The American Economic Review*, vol. 63, no. 5, December 1973, pp. 787–810.)

Now that we have considered some of the fundamental concepts of supply and demand, let us turn our attention to one concept that is crucial throughout economics: *elasticity*. On a given demand (or supply) curve, elasticity refers to the percentage change in quantity demanded (or supplied) relative to the percentage change in price as we move from one point to another. This rather simple concept is indispensable in understanding the economic organization and functioning of agriculture. What must we know about it?

IN THIS CHAPTER

1. You will learn the basic concepts and determinants of the elasticity of demand.
2. You will learn how to apply the concept of elasticity to agricultural supply.
3. You will learn how to use elasticity in the analysis of economic data on production and consumption, and prices and incomes.

CONCEPTS AND DETERMINANTS OF ELASTICITY OF DEMAND

Individual farmers always strive to produce as much as they can with a given set of resources even though they are well aware that a generally good crop for most farmers will sell for less in the aggregate than a generally poor crop. The fact that high aggregate farm output is associated with low national farm income is one of the basic propositions in understanding the *farm problem,* sometimes called the *agricultural problem.* It is grounded in the fundamental concept of *elasticity of demand.*

Basic concept of elasticity of demand

The law of demand tells us that producers and consumers will respond to a decline in price by buying more of a product. But the degree of responsiveness varies from product to product, and the response to a decline in price is generally not the same at all points on the demand schedule. Economists refer to and measure the response in terms of the concept of *elasticity.*

Definition: Elasticity of demand is the percentage change in the quantity demanded of a product or service in response to a given

percentage change in the price of that product or service, other things being equal. It depends primarily on percentage changes and is independent of the units used to measure quantities and prices.

Categories of elasticity of demand

There are three general categories of elasticity of demand, based on the responsiveness of the quantity demanded to a change in the price, as follows:

1. *Inelastic demand.* When a decline in P brings a smaller percentage increase in Q so that total revenue ($P \times Q$) declines, the demand is inelastic. That is, E_d is between 0 and -1. Note that E_d denotes *elasticity of demand.*
2. *Unitary elasticity of demand.* When a decline in P results in an exactly compensating percentage increase in Q so that total revenue ($P \times Q$) is left exactly unchanged, there is unitary elasticity of demand. That is, $E_d - -1$.
3. *Elastic demand.* When a decline in P increases Q so that total revenue ($P \times Q$) increases, the demand is elastic. That is, E_d is more negative than -1, such as -1.5, -2, and so on.

Figure 7-1 illustrates these three cases. In each case P is arbitrarily cut in half going from A to B, while the percentage change in quantity is different in each case. It occurs arbitrarily, which can be illustrated by changing the price by any other percentage such as 10 or 25 percent. The important thing to note is the change in total revenue ($P \times Q$). Since the curves in Figure 7-1 are proportional, the elastic curve shows more change in Q than in P, and the inelastic curve shows less. Often in the real world, however, scales are not proportional, and we should not get in the habit of trying to judge the degree of elasticity by the slope of the curve.

With scales that are proportional, however, we can learn about elasticity by comparing the rectangles of $P \times Q$. In Figure 7-1b, the cutting of P in half results in a doubling of Q, and so the total revenue (the product of $P \times Q$) is unchanged. In Figure 7-1a, the total revenue decreases from A to B because the percentage change (increase) in Q is less than the percentage change (decrease) in the price. In Figure 7-1c, the total revenue increases from A to B because the percentage change in quantity is more than the percentage change in price.

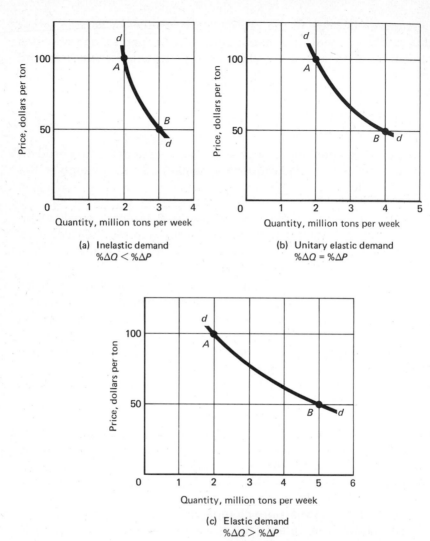

(a) Inelastic demand
%ΔQ < %ΔP

(b) Unitary elastic demand
%ΔQ = %ΔP

(c) Elastic demand
%ΔQ > %ΔP

Figure 7-1   The three cases of elasticity of demand: (a) inelastic, (b) unitary elastic, (c) elastic.

Measurement of elasticity of demand

The three cases of elasticity of demand are illustrated in Table 7-1
for the American crop of feed grain, using imaginary or hypothetical
data. In part a, the quantity demanded increases from 3.5 to 3.6 million tons per week when the price drops from $130 to $120 per ton.
Since total revenue drops from $455 million to $432 million per

Table 7-1 Elasticity of demand for American feed grains

(a) Basic data

Q, Million tons per week	Price per ton	TR, millions per week	E_d
3.5	$130	$455	
			Inelastic
3.6	120	432	
			Unitary elastic
4.0	108	432	
			Elastic
5.0	100	500	

(b) Numerical calculation of elasticity coefficient, E_d

Q, Million tons per week	ΔQ Million tons per week	Price per ton	Δ Price per ton	$\dfrac{Q_1 + Q_2}{2}$	$\dfrac{P_1 + P_2}{2}$	$E_d = \dfrac{\Delta Q}{(Q_1 + Q_2)/2} \div \dfrac{\Delta P}{(P_1 + P_2)/2}$
0.5		$130				
	0.1		−$10	3.55	$125	$\dfrac{0.1}{3.55} \div \dfrac{-10}{125} = -0.35$
3.6		120				
	0.4		− 12	3.80	114	$\dfrac{0.4}{3.8} \div \dfrac{-12}{114} = -1.00$
4.0		108				
	1.0		− 8	4.50	104	$\dfrac{1.0}{4.5} \div \dfrac{-8}{104} = -2.88$
5.0		100				

Note: Hypothetical data.

week, the demand is inelastic. When the price drops again to $108 per ton, total revenue stays the same. Therefore, between $108 and $120 per ton the demand has an elasticity of unity. When the price drops again to $100 per ton, total revenue increases and demand is elastic.

Table 7-1, part b, presents a general numerical method for calculating the elasticity of demand of an arc of a curve between any two points of a demand schedule. The number that is derived is called the *coefficient* of the elasticity of demand. It may be defined as follows:

Definition: The coefficient of the elasticity of demand (E_d) is the percentage change in quantity demanded when there is a 1 percent change in price, assuming no change in demand.

Then,

$$E_d = \frac{\text{percentage change in quantity demanded}}{\text{percentage change in price}}$$

or

$$E_d = \frac{\text{change in quantity demanded}}{\text{original quantity demanded}} \Big/ \frac{\text{change in price}}{\text{original price}}$$

This formula may be accurate enough to measure the elasticity of very small arcs of a demand schedule. But if the arc covers a considerable range, such as the example given in Table 7-1, the answer will be entirely different depending on which end of the arc represents the original price and quantity.

To overcome this difficulty, we may use the average of the two prices and quantities demanded at each end of the arc and then divide by 2. The formula is then

$$E_d = \frac{\text{change in quantity demanded}}{\text{sum of 2 quantitites demanded/2}} \Big/ \frac{\text{change in price}}{\text{sum of 2 prices/2}}$$

or, using the notation shown in Table 7-1 part b,

$$E_d = \frac{\Delta Q}{(Q_1 + Q_2)/2} \div \frac{-\Delta P}{(P_1 + P_2)/2}$$

With the aid of this formula, you can derive the coefficient for individual arcs of the curve as in Table 7-1, part b, or a coefficient for the entire arc of the demand curve, as follows:

$$E_d = \frac{5.0 - 3.5}{(3.5 + 5.0)/2} \div \frac{\$100 - \$130}{(\$130 + \$100)/2}$$

or

$$E_d = \frac{1.5}{4.25} \div \frac{-30}{115}$$

or

$$E_d = \frac{1.5}{4.25} \times \frac{-115}{30} = \frac{-172.5}{127.5}$$

and

$$E_d = -1.35$$

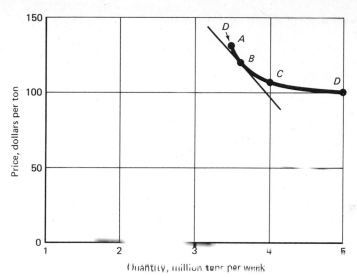

Figure 7-2   Demand for American feed grains (hypothetical data from Table 7-1). In Table 7-1b, we calculated the elasticity of the arcs of this curve labeled A, B, and C. We may also calculate the elasticity at any point on the curve, such as the elasticity at the point of tangency for the straight line added to the diagram above. E_d at this point can be shown to be mathematically equivalent to the following limit:

$$-\frac{\Delta Q}{Q} \Big/ \frac{\Delta P}{P} = -\frac{P}{Q}\frac{\Delta Q}{\Delta P} \rightarrow -\frac{P}{Q}\frac{dQ}{dP}$$

as ΔP goes to zero, ΔQ also goes to zero, making it immaterial which of the P's and Q's or their averages are used to compute percentage changes.

Note that we can measure from either end of an arc or a curve, that is, for a price increase and quantity decrease as well as for a price decrease and quantity increase. We can also measure the coefficient of elasticity for a point on a curve as in Figure 7-2.

The elasticity coefficients are all negative because of the inverse relationship between change in price and change in the quantity demanded, as stated in the law of demand. Economists usually drop the negative sign, however, because this relationship is so universally understood.

The answers will be the same when measured from either end of the arcs, or either end of the entire curve. Elasticity is not the same from arc to arc, however, suggesting that any figure that is quoted as *the* elasticity of demand for a commodity can actually apply, or be valid, only within certain assumed or prescribed limits, or conditions.

Two special cases

INFINITELY ELASTIC DEMAND

One of the basic conditions of pure competition is the fact that a purely competitive individual firm cannot influence the market price. The total output of the firm or any portion of it can be sold at the market price existing at the time of sale. If the firm tries to get a higher price, nobody will buy, and there is no point in selling at less than the competitive price. Thus, the purely competitive individual firm faces a perfectly elastic demand curve. This, however, has nothing to do with the elasticity of demand for the output of the industry, or for the output of a given commodity or group of commodities. The perfectly elastic demand curve is a horizontal straight line. The coefficient of the elasticity of demand would be infinity ($E_d = \infty$).

The situation is not quite comparable in regard to the individual farmer's demand for resources. There is scarcely any input for which there is not some substitute, and farmers can choose among different sellers. The farmer's purchases, however, may not affect any publicly quoted market price. If there are no "quantity discounts," or "bargaining" does not occur, the individual's demand for a specific resource may be perfectly elastic at the price asked. On the other hand, the farmer may bargain or obtain a quantity discount, and demand would not be perfectly elastic. Whatever happens in the case of the individual, the demand of the industry for resources is not, of course, perfectly elastic.

INFINITELY INELASTIC DEMAND

Sometimes a certain quantity may be demanded in a market regardless of price; demand will then be infinitely, or perfectly, inelastic. For example, in the case of a market contract where the buyer agrees to buy a specific amount of a product or service without stipulating the price, the buyer's demand in respect to that contract could be said to be *infinitely inelastic.* The price might be set on the day of delivery, for instance, according to the market price existing at that time. The demand would appear in a diagram as a vertical straight line. The coefficient of the elasticity of demand would be zero ($E_d = 0$). The demand for the output of the industry may be elastic or inelastic, however, without regard to the conditions of demand faced by an individual firm.

Determinants of elasticity of demand

There are no generalizations about the determinants of elasticity of demand that are universally valid or do not have some exceptions. A number of points are extremely important, however, and must be understood.

SUBSTITUTABILITY

Generally speaking, the larger the number of good substitute products available, the greater the elasticity of demand. The demand for the product of the purely competitive firm is infinitely elastic because there is an indefinitely large (not an infinitely large) number of perfect substitutes for that firm's product. If one farmer tries to raise the price for the product raised on the family farm, buyers will turn readily to the product of other farmers.

Somewhat more generally, elasticity depends on how narrowly the product is defined. The demand for aggregate farm output in the domestic market is generally very inelastic, presumably about -0.2. The demand for meat is somewhat more elastic because there are substitutes such as poultry, fish, eggs, and dairy products. The demand for an individual kind of meat such as pork is even more elastic. And the demand for a specific cut of pork such as pork chops is still more elastic. Table 7-2 presents a few typical examples of the elasticity of demand for various farm food commodities.

RELATIVE PRICE LEVELS
IN RELATED MARKETS

Commonly, price elasticity of demand for farm food products is greater at the retail level than at the farm level (Table 7-2). This difference is largely due to the differences in the relative level of prices between the two markets or to the value added to the product between the two markets.

On the average, from year to year the amount received by farmers for all farm products is about 40 percent of the value of the farm (food) products sold through stores. About 40 percent of the farm food dollar is accounted for as *farm value,* while the other 60 percent is the return to *marketing,* which is sometimes called the *marketing bill* or the *marketing spread* (Figure 7-3).

The relative shares do not stay constant from year to year, from month to month, or even from day to day because the prices in each market are almost constantly changing in response to shifts in the

Table 7-2   Selected elasticities of demand for agricultural commodities in the United States at the retail and the farm price level

Commodity	Retail price level (E_d)	Farm price level (E_d)
Lamb and mutton	− 2.35	− 1.78 (sheep)
Veal	− 1.60	− 1.08 (calves)
Turkey	− 1.40	− 0.92
Chicken	− 1.16	− 0.74
Beef	− 0.95	− 0.68 (cattle)
Pork	− 0.75	− 0.46 (hogs)
Butter	− 0.85	− 0.66
Cheese	−0.70	− 0.53
Ice cream	− 0.55	− 0.11
Fluid milk and cream	− 0.28	− 0.14
Eggs	− 0.30	− 0.23
Corn, wheat, barley (farm cash and futures markets)		− 0.02 to − 0.07
Fruit	− 0.60	− 0.36
Beverages	− 0.36	Not available
Sugar and syrups	− 0.30	− 0.18
Vegetables	− 0.30	− 0.10
Dry beans, peas, nuts	− 0.25	− 0.23
Cereals, baking products	− 0.15	Not comparable

Source: George Brandow, *Interrelationships among Demand for Farm Products and Implications for Control of Market Supply,* University Park, Pennsylvania State University, Agricultural Experiment Station Bulletin 680, 1961.

supply and demand in each market. You may assume, as was previously discussed, that if the marketing spread widens, established processing-marketing firms will increase their supply of processing-marketing services, and in the long run new firms will be attracted into the industry. If the spread narrows, some firms will reduce their services, and in the long run there will be a reduction in the total number of firms. The farm sector works the same way. The competitive relationships among the purely competitive farm firms and the imperfectly competitive processing-marketing firms tend to keep the respective shares in rough proportion to each other even though the shares must fluctuate according to the respective changes in supply and demand.

Figure 7-3   Allocation of the farm food dollar between farming and marketing in the United States, 1967 to 1978. (*Note:* Share of dollar consumers spent in retail stores for market basket of domestic farm-food products; 1978 preliminary. *Source: 1978 Handbook of Agricultural Charts,* United States Department of Agriculture, Agriculture Handbook No. 551, November 1978, p. 51.)

What is also called the *farmer's share of the market-basket dollar* is not the same from commodity to commodity. Primarily, this is because different commodities require or absorb different types and amounts of processing, packaging, and other services as they pass through the marketing system. In 1977, for example, the farmer received only 13 percent of the market-basket dollar for bakery and cereal products, while 55 percent of the dollar spent on meat products and 60 percent of the dollar spent on eggs went to the farmer (Figures 7-4 and 7-5).

Under conditions of market equilibrium, when there is a change in the supply of a given commodity with no change in the demand, the percentage change in the quantity demanded of that commodity will be roughly the same in both the farm and retail markets. The percentage change in price, however (not the absolute change), will be greater in the farm market, with the relative change being inversely proportional to the farmer's percentage share of the market-basket dollar.

The demand at the farm level is derived from the demand at the retail level. In general, the differences in the elasticities of demand between the farm and retail markets, as shown in Table 7-2, account

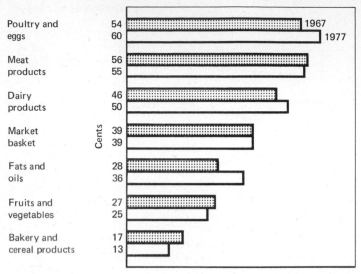

Figure 7-4 The farmer's share of the market-basket dollar in 1967 and 1977 for selected farm food products in the United States.

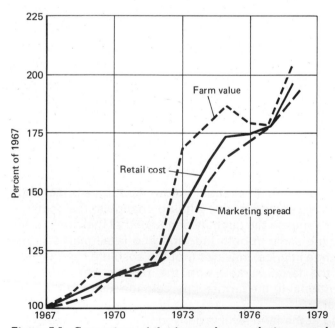

Figure 7-5 Comparison of the farm value, marketing spread, and retail cost of food in the United States, 1967 to 1978. (*Note:* For a market basket of farm foods; 1978 preliminary. *Source: 1978 Handbook of Agricultural Charts,* United States Department of Agriculture, Agriculture Handbook No. 551, November 1978, p. 51.)

for a large part of the relatively greater fluctuations in the prices received by farmers compared with the prices paid by consumers. There are other factors involved—such as the monopolistic competition and oligopoly of the marketing system—which tends to make the retail prices of food more resistant to change. This means that elasticities of supply are also involved, and these must be taken into account along with the differing elasticities of demand.

SUBSTITUTABILITY IN THE
DOMESTIC AND EXPORT MARKETS

Table 7-3 lists some elasticities of demand for American farm output sold in domestic and foreign markets. The large differences in elasticity between the markets are due to the fact that although the demand for total farm output is highly inelastic in the domestic market, American exports compete directly with domestic farm production in the importing country and with alternative sources of farm products from other exporting countries. Because of the availability of substitutes, a small change in the price asked for the American product will make a large difference in the quantity demanded from the United States. In the international grain markets, for example, a difference of a few cents per ton may make the difference between a sale and no sale. Buyers in foreign markets are not necessarily

Standardized agricultural products in export markets generally face a highly elastic demand because of the close substitutes available from other suppliers.

Table 7-3 Elasticities of demand for American farm output sold in domestic and foreign markets

Market	Food and feed		Cotton		Tobacco	
	Three-year	Long-run	Three-year	Long-run	Three-year	Long-run
Domestic	−0.18[a]	−0.10	−0.65	−1.8	−0.10	[b]
Foreign	−1.91	−6.42	−1.84	−3.7	−0.50	[b]

[a]The short-run elasticity is −0.25; the long-run elasticity is −0.10. With 20 percent of the adjustment completed each year, approximately 50 percent of the adjustment is completed in an intermediate run of three years.

[b]No estimate available.

Source: Luther G. Tweeten, "The Demand for United States Farm Output," *Food Research Institute Studies* (Stanford), vol. 7, no. 3, 1967, pp. 343–369.

more sensitive to market prices than their counterparts in the United States. Rather, American exports are only one of several sources of supply, and substitution among these sources makes the demand much more elastic for the products of any single exporting country.

The aggregate demand for imports by an individual country may be very inelastic, however, especially if the total imports are controlled by government action. The countries of the European Community, for example, use a variable tariff duty, or variable import levy, which widens or narrows as required to compensate for the difference between the price of farm products on board a ship at Rotterdam and the level of price support, or internal target price, within the E.C. The levy is varied as needed to keep the internal prices stable even though the competitive market price outside the European Community varies widely. The Japanese government controls most of its imports of farm food products by quotas and tariffs. Despite such controls on total imports by a given country, the demand for American farm food exports is very elastic for any product that is in direct competition with a product produced in other exporting countries.

These results depend, however, on whether the prices of exporters are reflected in the prices paid by importers. Where a single exporting country provides the greater part of total imports by a given country, such as the exports of American grain to Japan or the E.C., the prices of exporters may be only partly reflected in prices paid by importers, because imports and internal prices may be controlled by quota or by the variable import levy. In this case there is less than complete price transfer. What is called the *elasticity of price transfer* may actually vary from 1 to 0, being 1 when there is perfect transfer and 0 when there is none. To the extent that prices are not transferred from exporters to importers, the elasticity of import demand faced by the exporting country will be reduced. The general conclusions about the high elasticity of import demand need not be rejected. Rather, they sould be modified in given short-run situations.

The data given in Table 7-3 may be combined into an estimate of the aggregate elasticity of demand for all American farm output by multiplying the elasticity of each component group by its respective market share. This gives a measure of the contribution of each component to the total elasticity of demand. This procedure is valid only when there is little or no possibility for substitution between or among the component groups. The results of adding the contribution of each component are given in Table 7-4.

The data in Table 7-4 may be interpreted in various ways. The estimate of −0.46 for the elasticity of demand in the three-year term means, for example, that a decrease of 1 percent in the quantity supplied will result in little more than a 2 percent increase in price (−0.01 ÷ −0.46 − 0.022). The elasticity of demand of −1.1 for the

Table 7-4 Estimation of aggregate elasticity of demand from price elasticities of major components in Table 7-3

Markets and components	Market share of each component, percent	Contribution of each component to total elasticity of demand[a]	
		Three-year term	Long-run
Domestic			
Food and feed	76.2	−0.137	−0.078
Cotton	4.8	−0.031	−0.088
Tobacco	2.5	−0.002	−0.012
Foreign			
Food and feed	13.1	−0.250	−0.841
Cotton	2.4	−0.043	−0.089
Tobacco	1.0	[b]	[b]
Total	100.0	−0.463	−1.106

[a]Multiply elasticity from Table 7-3 by the corresponding market share. Thus, for example:

$$-0.18 \times 76.2\% = -0.137$$
$$-0.65 \times 4.8\% = -0.031$$

and so on

[b]The weight is so small for this category that its omission has little impact on the total elasticity.

Source: Luther G. Tweeten, "The Demand for United States Farm Output," in Stanford University, *Food Research Institute Studies* (*Stanford*), vol. 7, no. 3, 1967, pp. 343–369.

long run means that a 1 percent change in the quantity supplied will bring slightly less than a 1 percent change in price in the opposite direction ($+0.01 \div -1.1 = -0.009$). The elasticity of demand for total American farm output in the long run is close to unity according to the data used in this problem.

SUBSTITUTES AND COMPLEMENTS

Since elasticity of demand is affected by the availability of substitutes, it is also affected in both input and product markets by the existence of complements—commodities or services that tend to be used together. In the farm resource or input markets, for example, tractors and tractor fuel, hybrid corn and fertilizers, and soybeans and farm chemicals for control of soybean diseases tend to function as complements. In farm food markets, bread and butter, and pancakes and syrup are examples of complements.

Economists measure complementarity by the percentage change in the quantity of a commodity demanded that is associated with a 1 percent change in the price of another related commodity. For any given commodity, if there is an increase in the quantity demanded when the price of another commodity falls, the two commodities are complements. The degree of complementarity may be measured by what economists call the *coefficient of the cross-price elasticity,* or simply *cross-elasticity of demand* (E_c). If there are two commodities or services with Q referring to the quantity of one and P to the price of the other, then with everything else assumed to be constant,

$$E_c = \frac{Q_1 - Q_2}{(Q_1 + Q_2)/2} \div \frac{P_1 - P_2}{(P_1 + P_2)/2}$$

Let us designate Q as the hours of tractor use in American agriculture in a crop season, for example, and P as the price of tractor fuel, and then set Q_1 and P_1 each equal to 100. Then if the hours of tractor use drop by 5 percent when the price of tractor fuel increases by 10 percent, with no change in other things, the cross-elasticity of demand for tractor use in relation to tractor fuel is

$$E_c = \frac{-5.0}{(100 - 95)/2} \div \frac{+10}{(100 + 110)/2}$$

$$= \frac{-5.0}{97.5} \div \frac{10}{105}$$

or

$$E_c = \frac{-5.0}{97.5} \times \frac{105}{10} = \frac{525}{975} = -.54, \text{ approximately}$$

Commodities or services that are complementary to each other have negative cross-elasticities, while commodities that are substitutes have positive cross-elasticities. If the price of pork goes up, for example, we would expect the quantity of beef demanded to go up, provided there is no change in other things, because pork and beef are substitutes.

Just as substitutability increases the elasticity of demand, complementarity tends to decrease it. The demand for tractor fuel is more inelastic, for instance, than it would be if tractors were not such a close complement. When the price of tractor fuel went up as it did in the early 1970s, it probably had little effect on the amount of tractor time demanded by farmers. The very high cross-elasticity of demand between tractors and tractor fuel makes the demand for each product more inelastic than it would be otherwise.

You must always be careful, however, about generalizations in economics. The inelastic demand for tractor fuel is also related to the fact that there is no good substitute, at least in the short run. Or let us consider another example, such as the individual demands for the three main ingredients of fertilizer—ammonia, phosphate, and potash—which apparently are very inelastic. In the 1970s, there were very large changes in the prices of ammonia and concentrated superphosphate without much apparent change in the quantities demanded. The inelasticity would be related to the fact that neither ingredient has a close substitute. In addition, they are complements for biological reasons, tending to be used in relatively constant proportions. Complementarity does influence the elasticity of demand for both resources and products, but generalizations about complementarity and substitutability must be handled with great perception and care.

IMPORTANCE IN RESPECT
TO INCOME AND COSTS

Other things being equal, the greater the importance of a product or service in a family's budget, the greater the tendency for demand to be elastic. A 50 percent increase in the price of a particular spice or seasoning or a certain dried fruit will have very little effect on the quantity demanded even though there may be close substitutes. But in the United States or Canada a 50 percent increase in the price of beef, other things being equal, should bring a relatively large change in the quantity of beef demanded.

Similarly, in production the size of the expenditure has something to do with elasticity. A 50 percent increase in the price of a pitchfork is likely to have little effect on the number demanded. But a 50 percent increase in the price of a hay baler will tend to make the farmer look for alternatives.

NECESSITIES VERSUS LUXURIES

Demand tends to be inelastic for necessities and elastic for luxuries. Bread tends to be regarded as a necessity, and the demand for bread is generally inelastic. An increase in the price of bread will not have much effect on the quantity demanded. The demand for salt tends to be highly inelastic for a number of reasons. A certain amount of salt is necessary for health and to make food palatable. But nutritionists and doctors of medicine tell us that Americans on the average consume several times as much salt as they need, and much more than is normally advised for good health. This seems to be habitual. Also, salt is a negligible item in the family budget. In contrast, the demand for luxuries tends to be elastic. High-priced liquor, for example, is a luxury, and one can get along without it if the price goes high enough.

TIME

Generally speaking, the longer the time allowed for adjustment to a change in price, the more elastic the demand, other things being equal. This is due in part to the fact that people are creatures of habit, and it takes time for habits to change. Also, it sometimes takes time to find and get used to acceptable substitutes. But at least in a few cases time can work in the opposite direction as well. People may have an immediate reaction to a sharp increase in price for a given product and then become accustomed to the price over a longer period of time. In this case the short-run demand will be more elastic than the long-run demand. Or people may react to a price decline by building inventories, or stocking up. In general, however, we may assume that the longer the time allowed, the greater the elasticity of demand for products and services, both in production and in consumption.

Elasticity of demand for resources

The references to tractor use and tractor fuel, and pitchforks and hay balers tend to suggest that we should note briefly the major points concerning the elasticity of demand for resources. We do not refer to a shift in demand, but to the change in quantity relative to a change in price on a given demand curve. What determines the sensitivity of producers to changes in the prices of resources?

RATE OF DECLINE OF *MRP*

If the marginal product of a variable resource declines rapidly as more of it is added, *MRP* will also decline rapidly, and demand will be highly inelastic. The marginal returns to fertilizer, for example, decline rapidly after a certain point is reached on the production function. Consequently, or as a result, the demand for fertilizer tends to be higher inelastic, as is the demand for many other inputs used in farm production.

EASE OF SUBSTITUTION OF INPUTS

Where there is no input or resource that serves as a close substitute for a given input such as fertilizer, the demand for that particular input tends to be inelastic. However, the larger the number of available substitutes for a given input, the more elastic the demand. If there is little difference for choice among the major lines of farm tractors and machinery, for example, a small change in the prices of one manufacturer without any changes in the prices of the others will cause a sharp drop in the sales of that company. On the other hand, if a manufacturer can convince farmers that its line of machinery is superior, or has unique advantages in service and performance, the demand for its product will be more inelastic. It may be able to raise its price without experiencing a decline in total revenue. The great emphasis on advertising farm machinery, fertilizer, pesticides, certified seeds, etc., indicates the importance to the manufacturer of establishing a unique position for its differentiated product.

Economists refer to the rate at which one resource can be substituted for another as the *marginal rate of substitution*. With a constant total product, this refers to the amount (rate) by which one resource is decreased as the input of another resource is increased by one unit. At some stages in the production function this rate may be nearly constant. For example, in a well-balanced ration we might substitute one grain for another at a constant rate without any change in an animal's rate of gain. But beyond a certain point, as this substitution continues, the marginal rate of substitution falls, or diminishes, according to the law of diminishing returns. The statistic for expressing this relationship is called the *elasticity of substitution.* It refers to the percentage or relative change by which factors combine in producing a constant output.

The elasticity of substitution (E_s) is always negative for substitute resources. For a constant output, as one resource declines the other must increase, with E_s indicating just how rapidly the marginal rate of substitution declines. Where resources exist that are close substitutes, the marginal rate of substitution in production may be a constant, and substitution might be relatively easy. But as a given resource becomes relatively scarce, the marginal rate of substitution declines, and the demand for that resource tends to become less elastic. Thus, as the world population grows, accompanied by technological advance with limited resources of land, the marginal rate of substitution of a given technology for land tends to decline, and the demand for land becomes more inelastic. Increases in the demand for land, assuming a relatively fixed supply, tend to bring sharp increases in land prices. Additional new advances in technology could reverse this in the future and again raise the marginal rate of substitution, thus making the demand for land more elastic. Thus, the elasticity of demand for resources depends on the ease of substitution of inputs.

ELASTICITY OF DEMAND FOR PRODUCTS

The elasticity of demand for any resource also depends on the elasticity of demand for the product it helps produce. The more inelastic the demand for the product, the more inelastic the demand for the resource. The demand for tobacco in the domestic market is very inelastic, for example, so that the demand for the land used to grow tobacco for the domestic market is also very inelastic. Tobacco producers are well aware of this. To get a higher price, they constantly support a farm program to limit the amount of land that can be planted to tobacco. Federal programs for land retirement are generally based on the proposition that the demand for the commodity is inelastic. The elasticity of substitution of other inputs for land is generally low. Thus, land retirement will restrict supply, and raise prices in the domestic market.

IMPORTANCE OF THE
RESOURCE IN PRODUCTION

An increase in the price of pitchforks is not likely to make much change in the number of pitchforks a farmer buys, while an increase in the price of hay balers is likely to prompt a search for another system of handling hay. The less important the resource is in production, the more inelastic its resource demand. The more Important it is, the more elastic its demand will be. For pitchforks, it can also be said that the elasticity of substitution is generally low and that the elasticity of demand is low.

The four factors—rate of *MRP* decline, ease of substitution of inputs, elasticity of demand for the product, and importance of the input in production—all influence the elasticity of the demand for resources, Intermediate courses in production economics go into thooo topics in greater detail. Perhaps enough has boon said to bring out the major points. Let us now link this with a discussion of the elasticity of supply.

CONCEPTS AND DETERMINANTS
OF ELASTICITY OF SUPPLY

Definition: Elasticity of supply is the percentage change in the quantity supplied of a product or service in response to a given percentage change in its price, other things being equal.

The relationship between change in price and quantity on a typical supply curve is generally direct and positive—as indicated by the law of supply—rather than inverse or negative as in the elasticity of demand. The elasticity formula is pertinent In determining the degree of elasticity or inelasticity. It is applied to measure the elasticity of supply by substituting the *percentage change in quantity supplied* for the *percentage change in quantity demanded,* as in the formula to measure elasticity of demand.

Definition: The coefficient of supply elasticity, E_s, is the percentage change in quantity supplied related to a 1 percent change in price, assuming no change in supply.

Determinants of
elasticity of supply

TIME

The main determinant of the elasticity of supply is the *time* that a producer has to respond to a given change in price. The supply may be perfectly inelastic in a momentary period if the total quantity delivered is fixed and must be sold. Fresh produce delivered in the morning to be sold on the same day is an example. The price depends on the location of the demand curve. At the other extreme, a constant-cost industry will have a perfectly elastic curve in the long run. The average cost will equal the price, and the quantity supplied depends on the location of demand. Between these two extremes there are all degrees of elasticity from zero to infinity. In addition, in some special circumstances there is a backward-sloping supply curve where a higher price actually results in a smaller quantity supplied, other things being equal. Generally, however, the supply curve slopes upward and forward, and we may generalize in respect to time.

Alfred Marshall, the great economist who was quoted at the beginning of Chapter 1, distinguished three general cases of elasticity of supply, with a concept of market equilibrium related to each: (1) *momentary equilibrium,* which applies to the *immediate market supply* when the quantity supplied is fixed, (2) *short-run equilibrium,* which applies to firms that can produce either more or less with the existing plant and equipment, and (3) *long-run equilibrium,* which covers a time sufficient for firms to abandon old plants or build new ones and for all firms that wish to enter or leave to do so.

These concepts do not relate to any specific time in the sense of a day or year. They relate to the conditions of supply and to change in the quantity supplied in response to a change in price, other things being equal. The first concept—a fixed quantity supplied and momentary equilibrium—can apply to the one-day fish market or the harvest of a farm food product that has a one-year storage limit, or what the grocery merchants would call a one-year *shelf life.* When the harvest is complete, there is just so much, or we may assume that there just isn't any more. This is what we mean by the immediate market supply. At the other extreme, the concept of long-run supply applies to the situation where all costs are variable, which might represent a few months or many years.

By using Marshall's three time periods for supply, we can visualize the effect of a change in demand on the market equilibrium price and quantity. Figure 7-6 presents the three cases.

Immediate market period   Figure 7-6a illustrates the concept of the immediate market period in which the quantity supplied is fixed. The supply curve is infinitely inelastic. The increase in demand from D_1 to D_2 causes the market equilibrium price to rise from P_o to P_m. But Q_o and Q_m are the same.

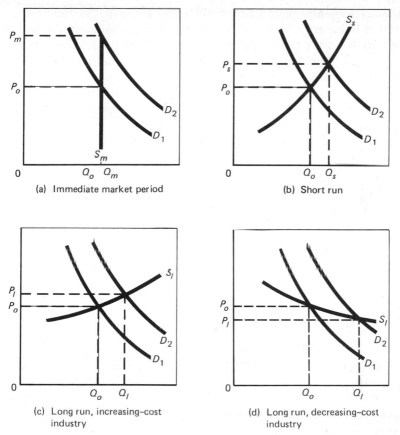

Figure 7-6 Effect of increase in demand on equilibrium price and quantity in three time periods. The longer the time for adjustment to a given increase in demand, the greater the elasticity of supply and output response, and the less the rise in price. (a) In the immediate market period there is no time to increase output, and so the supply is perfectly inelastic. (b) In the short run the rise in price is less than in a and the quantity supplied increases from Q_o to Q_s. (c) The long-run supply S_l implies that this is an increasing-cost industry. The price rises less than in the short run, and output increases from Q_o to Q_l. (d) The supply curve S_l implies that this is a decreasing-cost industry. The price will fall to P_l as quantity increases from Q_o to Q_l. A constant-cost industry, which is not shown in this illustration, would have a horizontal or perfectly elastic, long-run supply curve.

An immediate market period with an infinitely inelastic supply is functionally important in food and agriculture. Any perishable commodity must be sold and consumed within a certain period or it may spoil and go to waste. Fresh fish, for example, generally must be sold the same day or it will begin to spoil. Sweet corn on the cob is best if consumed within a few hours after picking. Such produce may be processed, of course, but this involves additional expense, and the commodity may sharply deteriorate in value. The immediate market period is characteristic of many fresh or perishable agricultural commodities.

The immediate market period is not confined to any specific time or commodity. It may stretch over a complete production period or more. The quantity of broilers that will be supplied is generally known for the next few months, for example, including the broilers in cold storage. A change in price will not affect the total very much if at all. The quantity of hogs that will come to market in the next year or so depends on current farrowings. Except for small changes in average market weights and the number of sows coming to market, the quantity to be supplied is just about fixed. Even the grain market sometimes follows the concept of the immediate market period. In 1972, when the Soviet Union began to buy wheat and feed grains on a large scale, world storage stocks were not large. For several months the world supply was definitely fixed. Prices rose sharply in the United States and in other free markets around the world. The adjustment is suggested in the diagram of the immediate market period.

Short-run market period   Output can be increased in the short run by increasing the variable inputs with the existing plant and equipment. In Figure 7-6b, an increase in demand from D_1 to D_2 causes the equilibrium price to rise from P_o to P_s and the quantity to increase from Q_o to Q_s. In 1973, after there was an increase in demand for exports of grain, farmers increased the quantity of wheat supplied by seeding more land to wheat, applying more fertilizer, and so on. They moved upward on their marginal-cost schedules to reach an equilibrium such as P_s. In 1974, a bad crop year thwarted many farmers' plans to increase grain production, but eventually the quantity of grain supplied increased substantially.

In addition, livestock feeders in the United States and some other countries cut back their operations and reduced their herds under the influence of the higher prices for feed grains, soybean meal, and feed supplements. According to the United States Department of Agriculture's *1976 Handbook of Agricultural Charts* (p. 124), the domestic use of corn in the United States dropped from 4.7 billion bushels in the year beginning October 1, 1972, to 4.6 billion bushels in 1973 and 3.6 billion in 1974 (the equivalent of about 118, 116, and 91 million tons, respectively). Thus, the short-run adjustment to the increase in demand for exports for grains and oilseeds actually reduced the supply of livestock for sale on the domestic market in subsequent years.

Long-run market period   The long-run market period may involve either a constant-cost, increasing-cost, or decreasing-cost supply curve. Figure 7-6c illustrates increasing long-run cost. The long-run supply S_l is more elastic than the short-run supply curve in Figure 7-6b. The price rises from P_o to P_l as the quantity increases from Q_o to Q_l. Figure 7-6d illustrates decreasing cost. Price falls from P_o to P_l as the quantity increases from Q_o to Q_l. The long-run supply for a constant-cost industry (not shown in Figure 7-6) is inflnitely elastic, with price tending to remain the same as demand increases.

Agriculture may exhibit characteristics of either constant, increasing, or decreasing long-run costs. From the mid-1940s to the end of the 1970s decreasing costs prevailed as farm prices had a downward trend relative to the prices paid by farmers. This suggests that over this period at least, American agriculture was a decreasing-cost industry (in terms of constant dollars). Growing shortages, if any, in resource inputs tended to be overbalanced by advances in technology. On the other hand, if increased demand for inputs increases production costs, agriculture may be an increasing-cost industry. It will be, that is, unless advancing technolgy offsets the effects of increased demand for resources. One cannot say that agriculture by virtue of its organization, or stage of economic development, is either an increasing-cost or a decreasing-cost industry. It depends entirely on the circumstances to which the theory is applied.

We can say, however, that agricultural supply is more elastic in the long run than in the short run. The short run is more elastic than the immediate market period. Also, because of the circumstances of production, agricultural supply is more elastic in periods of rising prices for products than it is when prices are depressed.

OTHER DETERMINANTS
OF ELASTICITY OF SUPPLY

Because it takes time to make adjustments in resources, it is of course correct to emphasize the importance of time in determining elasticity of supply. But even allowing for this, it must be evident that other considerations also must be taken into account, especially in dealing with the short run. Let us consider several points somewhat similar to those discussed in respect to demand: (1) shape and location of *MC* curves of individual firms in relation to product price, (2) ease of substitution of one product for another in production plans, (3) elasticity of supply of resources, and (4) time in reference to increasing and decreasing product prices.

1. Shape and location of *MC* curves   As was discussed in Chapter 4, the typical *MC* curve takes a U shape, is often rather flat on the bottom, and rises at an increasingly rapid rate to the end of stage 2 of the typical production function. That is, as prices move up to intercept the *MC* curve at higher and higher levels, with other things remaining constant, the supply curve of the typical firm becomes less and less elastic. This is consistent with the law of diminishing returns as discussed in Chapter 5.

2. Ease of substitution of products   It is a well-known fact in economic studies, however, that farmers place considerable emphasis on relative product prices in determining what acreages of each crop to plant, but that the elasticities are comparatively low for aggregate crop acreage, or total farm output in respect to price. This is because it is easy to shift from one crop to another crop that uses similar resources, such as from spring wheat to oats, barley, or sorghum. But generally, the total acreage cannot be expanded very much in response to high prices, and prices must drop very low before it will be advantageous to let much land lie idle. The total supply of grain tends to be much more inelastic than the supply of individual commodities.

Livestock present a somewhat different picture. In comparison with grains, of course, it is much more difficult and takes longer to shift from one kind of livestock to another. Although single herds can be sold quickly when an operation becomes unprofitable, usually the sale of breeding stock involves some sacrifice. Generally, farmers are reluctant to reduce their herds, and it takes much longer to increase numbers of livestock. In addition, in the beginning of a period of expansion one of the first steps is to keep more breeding stock instead of selling it. This not only reduces the elasticity of supply in the short run but also tends to reduce the total supply in the immediate market period.

3. Elasticity of supply of resources   The elasticity of supply for any product will depend on the elasticity of the supply for the resources used to produce it. Where important resources are relatively fixed in the short run—such as the supply of good farmland—the supply of products produced from the land will tend to be inelastic. Under modern advances in technology, however, the declining importance of agricultural land relative to other inputs used in farm production tends to make the total-supply curve for agriculture more elastic both in the short run and the long run. This assumes, of course, that the supply of the other major inputs—such as farm labor and management, machinery, fuel, fertilizer, and farm chemicals—is more elastic than the supply of farm land.

4. Time in reference to increasing and decreasing prices of products A number of economic studies have shown that the elasticity of aggregate agricultural supply is very low in the short run and that a market period of several years is required to reach an elasticity as high as unity. Moreover, these studies show that the aggregate supply is significantly more elastic in years of rising prices of farm products than in years of falling prices. For instance, one study concluded that in a two-year market period the elasticity of supply is about 0.25 when prices are rising and about 0.10 when they are falling. In a 12-year market period, the corresponding figures are about 1.5 for rising prices and 0.8 for falling prices.[1]

One word of caution seems appropriate, however. Our discussion has tended to imply that no single figure can be used indiscriminately as *the* elasticity of agricultural supply. This caution applies to the total output of agriculture as well as to the supply of a single commodity such as corn. Not only is the elasticity different at various points on a given curve, the concepts of supply are constantly dealing with dynamic, changing conditions. People are constantly making decisions about what to do in various anticipated situations, and it is the results of these decisions, as modified by weather and a host of other factors, that finally determine the elasticity of supply.

Measurement of elasticity of supply

A standard procedure for computing the elasticity coefficient is given in Table 7-5, and this curve is illustrated in Figure 7-7. Unlike demand, there is no test for elasticity equivalent to the total revenue test for distinguishing between an elastic and inelastic curve. As shown in Figure 7-7, however, elasticity at a point on a supply curve is elastic, if a line drawn tangent to the curve at that point intersects the price axis; and inelastic, if a line drawn tangent to the curve at

[1]Luther G. Tweeten and C. Leroy Quance, "Positivistic Measures of Aggregate Supply Elasticities: Some New Approaches," *American Journal of Agricultural Economics,* vol. 51, no. 2, May 1969, pp. 342–352.

Table 7-5   Elasticity of supply for American feed grains
(a) Basic data

Q, million tons per week	Price per ton	TR, millions per week	E_s
2.5	$ 95	$237 .5	
			Elastic
3.0	100	300	
			Unitary elastic
3.6	120	432	
			Inelastic
3.8	140	532	

(b) Numerical calculation of elasticity coefficient, E_s

Q, million tons per week	ΔQ, tons per week	Price per ton	ΔP per ton	$\dfrac{Q_1 + Q_2}{2}$	$\dfrac{P_1 + P_2}{2}$	$E_s = \dfrac{\Delta Q}{(Q_1 + Q_2)/2} \Big/ \dfrac{\Delta P}{(P_1 + P_2)/2}$
2.5		$ 95				
	0.5		$ 5	2.75	$ 97.50	$\dfrac{0.5}{2.75} \div \dfrac{5.}{97.5} = 3.55$
3.0		100				
	0.6		20	3.3	110	$\dfrac{0.6}{3.3} \div \dfrac{20}{110} = 1.0$
3.6		120				
	0.2		20	3.7	130	$\dfrac{0.2}{3.7} \div \dfrac{20}{130} = 0.35$
3.8		140				

Note: Hypothetical data.

that point intersects the quantity axis. Note that a supply curve is typically more elastic at low prices than at high prices, which is consistent with the shape of the typical *MC* curve.

Persistence of low farm income related to inelastic supply with falling farm prices

The general figures on elasticity of supply imply that total farm output declines very little, if at all, in periods of declining farm-product prices. This suggests that farm people do not leave agriculture as quickly as they enter it. Farmers do not liquidate productive resources as quickly as they acquire them. They cannot sell unprofitable machinery and equipment without losing a considerable part of their investment, and so they tend to stay in production. This can be explained in terms of the *MRP* = *MRC* rule, as illustrated in Figure 7-8.

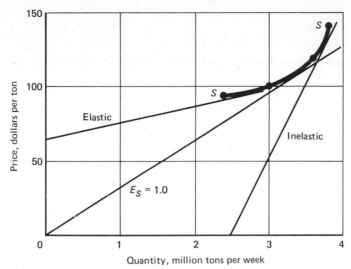

Figure 7-7 Supply of American feed grains (hypothetical data from Table 7-5). Three straight lines have been drawn, each tangent to the supply curve constructed from Table 7-4. The line marked $E_s = 1$, which intersects the origin, has a constant unitary elasticity. It is tangent to SS at the point of unitary elasticity. The steeper line, which intercepts the Q axis, is tangent at a point of inelasticity ($E_s < 1$). The third line, which intercepts the P axis, is tangent at a point of elasticity greater than 1 ($E_s > 1$). Neither of the latter two straight lines has constant elasticity, however. When $E_s < 1$, the line becomes infinitely inelastic as it approaches the Q axis. When $E_s > 1$, the line becomes infinitely elastic as it approaches the P axis.

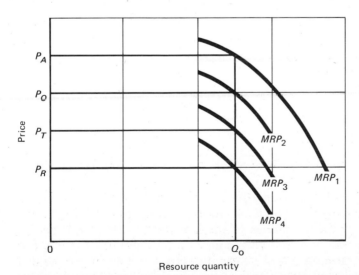

Figure 7-8 Alternative marginal revenue product (MRP) curves representing the demand for resources in agriculture. When P_A is the buying, or acquisition, price, the market-equilibrium quantity demanded is Q_O. P_O, P_T, and P_R represent alternative exit or liquidation prices for quantity Q_O under alternative downward-shifting demand (MRP) curves.

In Figure 7-8, let us assume that MRP_1 is the demand curve for management and labor in farming and P_A is the income level or price for farm labor that is required to attract a number of families into farming equal to Q_O. Or let us assumue that P_A is an acquisition price—the price that must be paid to get a number of families in farming equal to Q_O. When the demand is MRP_1, the quantity of farm families demanded at this price is Q_O.

Now let us assume that P_O is the opportunity cost for families to remain in farming, which is the going wage or price for their services in a nonfarm occupation. The demand for their services in farming will have to fall at least to MRP_2 for outmigration to occur. That is, once established in farming, a number of families equal to Q_O are willing to stay in farming at any price above P_O.

In addition, if the cost of transferring to another occupation—including education, training, and other transfer costs—is equal to the difference between P_O and P_T, the demand would have to fall at least to MRP_3 for outmigration to occur or for there to be a reduction in the number of families to less than Q_O. Thus, P_T is the transfer price for a net reduction in the number of families in farming.

Finally, if people have a strong preference for country living equal to the difference between P_T and P_R and can have this only by farming, the demand will have to drop to MRP_4 and their farm income to P_R before the number of farm families will fall below Q_O.

The locations of P_O, P_T, and P_R are related to the opportunities in nonfarm occupations. If nonfarm employment opportunities improve, P_O, P_T, and P_R will rise, and farm incomes will not have to be so low for outmigration to occur. When the opportunities are declining or the level of unemployment is rising, however, these prices will fall, and farm incomes will have to fall still lower before outmigration will occur. The actual experience in the United States conforms to this hypothesis. That is, migration out of farming rises when the nation's employment is at a high level. It slows down, almost regardless of the level of farm income, when unemployment is high in nonfarm occupations.

This hypothesis not only helps account for the inelasticity of supply of management and labor during periods of declining prices of products, but also extends to other resources. P_A might be the acquisition price of farm tractors and P_O the liquidation price in a going-out-of-farming sale, for example. The net return from the use of a tractor may be below a normal rate of return based on the acquisition price, P_A, but well above the liquidation price, P_O. Many farmers who bought tractors and equipment in 1973–1975, for example, when grain prices were high, were able to justify their purchases on the basis of those prices. But in the late 1970s when grain prices were lower, those farmers were unable to make a normal profit, based on P_A, although the price of grain was well above their close-down level. Thus, farmers have a more elastic short-run supply curve in a period of rising prices than in a period of falling prices.

The concept of acquisition and liquidation prices thus helps to explain why downward-shifting *MRP* curves, or downward-shifting demands for resources, tend to result in little or no decline in the total output of farms. In addition, there are physical and biological conditions in agricultural production that tend to create cycles in production and prices. These also involve concepts of elasticity of both supply and demand.

Periodic cycles in production and prices

Periodic cycles in production and prices are characteristic of several farm food products. These have important implications for all agricultural producers and marketing firms, and for consumers as well. Although the cycles are sometimes magnified or otherwise altered by random disturbances such as unusually good or bad weather or a change in demand for exports, they can be predicted with some degree of success. It is important for us to understand their general causes and consequences.

BASIC CONDITIONS

Four conditions are generally necessary for a commodity to develop a periodic cyclical pattern. First, the commodity must have a standard production period so that once plans are made, production tends to occur at a definite time in the future. Second, storage stocks must not be increased or decreased on a scale sufficient to greatly alter the flow of the commodity to market. Third, producers must be so numerous that an individual firm has little influence on the total output. Fourth, producers must operate to some degree on the assumption that current costs and prices are an acceptable basis for planning future production.

Livestock products and some fruits and vegetables conform most closely to these conditions. Storable commodities for which no large-scale storage program exists sometimes exhibit cyclical pattens. But a government program of price supports that includes control of production, storage, and subsidy of exports tends to eliminate such cycles. Figure 7-9 shows price fluctuations for wheat,

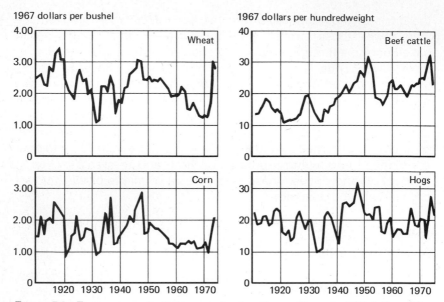

Figure 7-9   Farm prices of wheat, corn, beef cattle, and hogs in 1967 dollars. The periodic cycles in prices are related to lags in production relative to changes in price. The fluctuations in prices of wheat and corn between 1950 and 1970 were moderated by government programs.

corn, beef cattle, and hogs from 1910 to the late 1970s. It may be observed that these prices tend to follow rough periodic patterns, which vary in magnitude and duration from commodity to commodity. The prices of both wheat and corn were more stable from 1950 to 1972 because of government price-support, storage, and production-control programs. These programs were, of course, attempts at holding prices and returns to farmers above the free-market equilibrium levels. Beef cattle and hogs were not affected as directly by the government programs, and these products as well as eggs and broilers may be used to illustrate the economics of cycles.

EXAMPLES

Eggs and broilers   The periodic cycles for eggs and broilers tend to occur at rather regular intervals, with prices and production fluctuating in a strongly inverse fashion. Intervals from peak to peak and trough to trough average about three to four years for eggs and two to three years for broilers, with cycles tending to shorten in the 1970s as more violent price fluctuations occur (Figure 7-10).

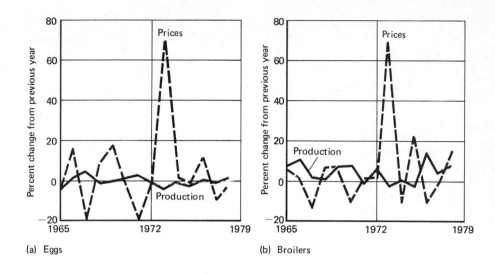

(a) Eggs

(b) Broilers

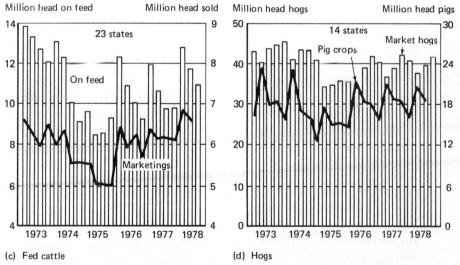

(c) Fed cattle

(d) Hogs

Figure 7-10   Changes in production and farm prices, 1965–1978: (*a*) for eggs, (*b*) for broilers (1978 forecast). Changes in production and marketings, 1973–1978: (*c*) of fed cattle (quarterly data), (*d*) of hogs (pig crops—Dec.–Feb., Mar.–May, June–Aug., Sept.–Nov.; market hogs on farms—Dec. 1 previous year, March 1, June 1, Sept. 1, Dec. 1.). (*Source:* U.S. Department of Agriculture, *1978 Agricultural Outlook Charts*, pp. 80, 88, 89.)

The data in Figure 7-10 suggest that supply and demand are inelastic in the short run for both eggs and broilers. While producers respond to high prices by increasing production and to low prices by cutting production, the percentage change in production is much less than the percentage change in price. Since storage stocks are generally relatively small for both eggs and broilers, the percentage changes in consumption will also be less than the percentage changes in price. Although some producers may gain by anticipating the peaks and troughs in prices and scheduling their production somewhat differently from the production of the industry, the predominant response of the industry is to have low production at a time of high prices and vice versa.

Hog cycle   For many years it was meaningful to relate the output of hogs to the ratio of hog and corn prices some 18 to 24 months earlier. When the price of hogs was high relative to corn, this encoraged hog producers to breed more sows and increase farrowings. This would increase the demand for corn and the supply of market hogs, causing the price of hogs to drop relative to corn. Then producers would want to cut back, cull the excess sows, and reduce farrowings. Therefore, the supply of hogs would decrease, the demand for corn would fall, and the price of hogs would rise relative to corn, thus beginning a new cycle.

Although the general relationship between prices of hogs and corn is still meaningful, many additional factors have been added to influence the hog cycle. Government price supports and production controls have at times diminished the price cycles for corn and other feed grains. The increasing importance of exports of feed grains has magnified the influence of demand for exports as a price-making factor in domestic grain markets. The long-run growth of cattle feeding relative to hogs has lessened the relative influence of hog cycles on prices of feed grains. Thus, changes in prices of hogs at farmers' wholesale markets appear to be the major factor in determining the hog cycle.

Cattle cycle   The cattle cycle is longer than either the hog cycle or the egg and broiler cycles, with the number of cattle tending to reach a peak at approximately 10-year intervals. Typically, relatively high cattle prices bring an increase in numbers of cattle because cattle growers find it profitable to expand their herds. The increased numbers of cattle bring increased production and less favorable prices. This then causes a reduction in cattle herds until the lower production brings higher prices, and again increased numbers.

Cattle cycles are not fully explained until we relate changes in beef production to changes in numbers of cattle. The changes in beef production, which ultimately turn the market around, tend to lag some three years or more behind the changes in numbers of cattle. That is, when prices first turn favorable for cattle growers, the numbers of cattle must be built up before increased production can occur. In the beginning the rapid increase in herds results in reduced production, and it may be three years or more before the increased numbers result in increased production. After numbers have been built up to a peak and prices begin to turn down, production stays up because liquidation of herds adds to the regular market supply.

Rapid increases in cattle herds immediately reduce production of beef and vice versa. A rapid increase in numbers of cattle in 1951 was accompanied by a drop in production, and a decline in numbers five years later brought a rise in production. During the 1960s, it was almost eight years before increased production caught up with the rise in numbers of cattle. But the cycles of the 1970s, unlike the long swings of the 1960s, were unusually violent. The sharp rise in numbers to 1975 as a result of a peak in the cattle cycle led to peak production in 1976 and a sharp break in prices for cattle. High levels of production held in 1977 and 1978 as herds declined. Then production dropped in 1979 and 1980 as favorable prices again brought the beginning of a sharp increase in numbers of cattle. Typically, in the early 1980s, as beef production lags behind the increasing numbers of cattle, favorable prices will be experienced by producers of calves. Cattle feeders, responding to the favorable market prices by attempting to expand production, will bid aggressively for feeder animals. However, consumers facing increased supplies of pork and poultry may tend to moderate the cattle cycle, depending on how much or to what extent they substitute one meat product for another.

COBWEB THEOREM

A general theoretical explanation or rationale for periodic cycles in prices and production may be presented by letting the short-run supply curve represent the quantity produced in a given period in response to the price at the beginning of that period or at some earlier date. That is, production is in response to the initial price as viewed by the producer. Although the lag differs among commodities and is not exactly the same from time to time for any given commodity, the general idea may be seen in a diagram that traces out

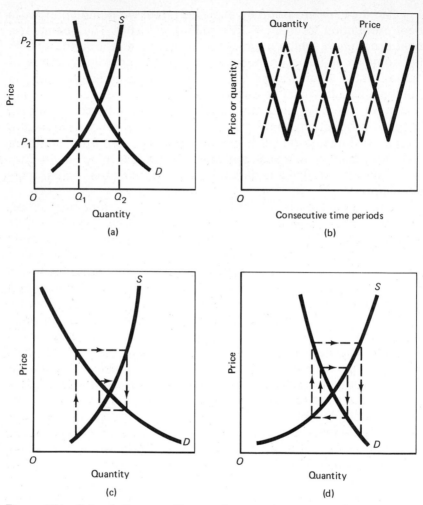

Figure 7-11　Cobweb theorem. The supply curve for a commodity is—in this case—the quantity supplied in a given period in response to a specific price in some previous period, or specific time. The necessary conditions involve a specific time period for production, relatively minor storage stocks, and production that, once under way, is not terminated prematurely. Generally, in addition, producers may assume that their own output does not affect market price, and that current prices are an indicator of the prices that will be received for the product.

the configuration of a cobweb—hence the *cobweb theorem* (Figure 7-11).

In Figure 7-11*a*, let us suppose that farmers expect a price of P_1. Then Q_1 is produced. But if Q_1 is produced, consumers are willing to pay a price equal to P_2. If this is the price, farmers will follow with production of Q_2. If this is the quantity supplied, the price will drop to P_1, and the cycle is ready to repeat. Figure 7-11b shows the production and prices in consecutive time periods.

Whether the cobweb diagram follows a regular pattern as in (a) and (b), a converging pattern as in (c), or an exploding pattern as in (d) depends on the comparative elasticities of supply and demand. When the elasticities are the same, as in (a), the pattern tends to repeat. When demand is more elastic, as in (c), the pattern converges. When supply is more elastic, as in (d), the pattern explodes. The fluctuations that were observed in Figures 7-9 and 7-10 are not dependent on the inelasticity of supply alone, therefore, but on the relative elasticities of supply and demand as well as the biology and technology of production.

SUMMARY

Elasticity of demand has been defined as the percentage change in the quantity demanded in response to a given percentage change in price, other things being equal. The coefficient of the elasticity of demand E_d, is the percentage change in quantity demanded when there is a 1 percent change in price, assuming no change in demand. There are three general cases of elasticity, which can be distinguished by the effect of a change in price on total revenue—elastic, unitary elastic, and inelastic. Infinitely elastic or inelastic demands are special cases of elastic or inelastic demands.

The elasticity of demand for agricultural products and resources is determined by (1) substitutability, (2) levels of prices in related markets, (3) relationships between domestic and export markets, (4) substitutes and complements, (5) importance in respect to income and costs, (6) necessities versus luxuries, and (7) time.

Elasticity of supply has been defined as the percentage change in the quantity supplied in response to a given percentage change in price, other things being equal. The coefficient of supply elasticity, E_s, is the percentage change in quantity supplied related to a 1 percent change in price, assuming no change in supply.

Time is the main determinant of the elasticity of supply, being perfectly or infinitely inelastic in the immediate market period, elastic or inelastic in the short run, and very elastic or perfectly elastic in the long run. The procedure for measuring the elasticity of supply is the same as the procedure for measuring the elasticity of demand except that *change in quantity supplied* is substituted for *change in quantity demanded.* Within a given time period the elasticity of supply is influenced by the ease or difficulty of substituting resources and products.

The analysis of elasticity has many applications in agriculture. Elasticity of supply and demand is important, for example, in planning production, projecting future prices, and estimating production of crops and livestock. The inelasticity of supply in periods of falling prices for products helps account for the persistence of low farm incomes. Lags in the responses of production to changes in prices helps account for the instability in farm prices and incomes and for the periodic cycles in prices and production that are characterisitic of many products.

IMPORTANT TERMS
AND CONCEPTS

Elasticity of demand (supply)
Elastic, unitary elastic, and inelastic demand (supply)
Coefficient of elasticity of demand (supply)
Infinitely elastic demand (supply)
Infinitely inelastic demand (supply)
Determinants of elasticity of demand (supply)
Immediate market period
Short-run supply
Long-run supply
Cobweb theorem

LOOKING AHEAD

Knowledge about supply and demand, including the concepts of change and elasticity, equips us with the tools to proceed further in the analysis of markets and the forms of competition. In Chapter 8 let us consider aspects of organization and competition in agribusiness. This in turn will help us to further define the economic problems of agriculture and their possible solutions.

QUESTIONS AND EXERCISES

1. Define elasticity of demand. What is an elastic demand? Unitary elastic demand? Inelastic demand?
2. What is the coefficient of elasticity of demand? What does it measure? How is it determined? Give an example.
3. What are the determinants of the elasticity of demand?
4. What is an infinitely elastic demand? Where might one be found? Give an example.

5. What is an infinitely inelastic demand? Where might one be found?

6. What is a complement? How is the cross-elasticity of demand determined?

7. Define elasticity of supply. What is an elastic supply? Unitary elastic supply? Inelastic supply?

8. What is measured by the coefficient of elasticity of supply? Give an example.

9. How does time influence the elasticity of supply? Give examples of the elasticity of supply in the immediate market period, the short run, and the long run.

10. Within a given time period, how does the ease or difficulty of substitution among resources or products influence the elasticity of supply?

11. Is the elasticity of aggregate agricultural supply more inelastic in the short run or the long run? In periods of falling or rising farm-product prices? Why?

12. How does inelasticity of supply account for the persistence of low farm income? What is the cobweb theorem? Explain how it may be used to account for cycles in farm prices and incomes.

8. AGRIBUSINESS COMPETITION IN PRODUCTION AND MARKETING

❚❚Both monopolistic and competitive forces combine in the determination of most prices.❚❚

Edward H. Chamberlin

Edward H. Chamberlin, professor of economics at Harvard University, wrote the first of two standard studies of imperfect competition, *The Theory of Monopolistic Competition* (Harvard University Press, Cambridge, Mass., 1933). The other, *Economics of Imperfect Competition*, published almost simultaneously, was written by the British economist Joan Robinson (The MacMillan Company, New York, 1933). Since 1933, the theories of imperfect competition have been extensively applied and have spread widely throughout economic literature. These concepts and theories are important in the economics of agriculture.

Our study of production functions and costs, and supply and demand, which has been applied mainly to farming under pure competition, can now be applied to agribusiness production and marketing, where imperfect competition is the rule rather than the exception. How does this competitive structure affect the economic organization and performance of agriculture?

IN THIS CHAPTER

1. You will learn the basic theory that applies to the determination of price and output under conditions of imperfect competition.
2. You will broaden your understanding of agribusiness, its organization and degree of concentration, and its determination of price and output.
3. You will improve your understanding of the production and marketing strategies of agribusiness as influenced by the economics of imperfect competition.

BASIC THEORY OF IMPERFECT COMPETITION

You may recall that in the first section of Chapter 5 we outlined the four basic forms of competition—pure competition, monopolistic competition, oligopoly, and monopoly—and discussed some examples in agriculture. It was said that the last three—including the buying counterparts of monopsonistic competition, oligopsony, and monopsony (see Figure 5-1)—can be grouped under the more general term *imperfect competition.* Now let us consider a definition and basic model that may apply to all forms of imperfect competition.

Definition: Imperfect competition prevails in an industry, or group of industries, whenever the individual sellers face nonhorizontal, downward-sloping demand curves for their individual products and thereby have some measure of control over price. Imperfect competition prevails among buyers whenever they individually exert a measure of control over the price that they and other competitors pay.

The key phrase in the definition is the individual firm's *measure of control over price.* The term *measure* is used because the control is seldom if ever absolute. Individual firms generally cannot ignore their competitors. But sellers can raise or lower their prices within limits and thereby reduce or expand their sales. First, they can move up or down on their own demand curves, assuming no change in demand. Second, through advertising and sales promotion they can change the location of the demand curve that they face as individual competitors. They may also see their own individual demand curve shift up or down as a result of the actions of their competitors. Figure 8-1 presents the basic models.

On the buying side, imperfectly competitive firms influence the market price largely through the strategies that they pursue individually. A large meat-packing firm can influence the market price, at least temporarily, by its decisions concerning how many and what kind of livestock to buy of each class and grade. That is, the firm can change the market demand by increasing or decreasing its own orders. If it does, this also changes the supply available to other buyers. This change in supply will affect the prices other buyers pay, assuming there is no change in their individual demands. The purely competitive firm, in contrast, cannot affect the market price because, by definition, its role in the market is too small.

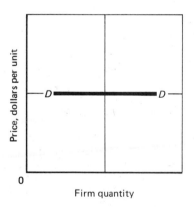
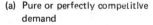

(a) Pure or perfectly competitive demand

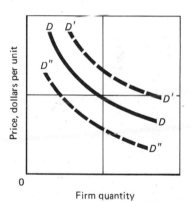

(b) Imperfectly competitive demand

Figure 8-1   Demand faced by the firm under (a) pure, or perfect, competition is infinitely elastic, while demand faced under (b) imperfect competition is downward-sloping. The purely competitive firm cannot influence its own demand curve DD. In contrast, the firm in imperfect competition can increase its demand from DD to D'D' by advertising or sales promotion. Also, by actions of its competitors, the imperfectly competitive firm can see its demand curve increase as to D'D', or decrease as to D''D''. In addition, by raising or lowering its prices, the imperfectly competitive firm can move from one point to another on its demand curve DD, assuming no change in demand.

How much an imperfectly competitive firm can influence or change the market price depends on its position in the market—how large it is, what share of the market it has, and what strategies it follows in buying and selling. Its influence also depends on the market itself, the actions of other competitors, the firm's customers or clients, and the general strength or weakness of market conditions. Let us consider a basic model.

Determination of price and output: A basic model

Let us develop a hypothetical model for determination of price and output of the tractor division of a certain manufacturer of farm machinery. The manufacturer produces a tractor that sells within a range of $44,000 to $52,000, and it estimates that within this price range its sales will vary from 9,900 to 7,100 per year. The alternative prices, quantities demanded, and total revenues are shown in the first three columns of Table 8-1.

The first three columns of Table 8-1 are familiar. Price times quantity sold equals total revenue, or (1) × (2) = (3). This is the familiar demand curve, in this case the demand curve faced by the firm. It is elastic, of course, since the total revenue increases each time the price is reduced by $2,000 per tractor and an additional 700 tractors are produced and sold. The increase in total revenue shown in column (4) is the marginal revenue product obtained by use of

Table 8-1   Price, quantity, and revenue relationships of the tractor division of an imperfectly competitive farm-machinery firm

(1) Price per tractor	(2) Quantity demanded annually	(3) Total revenue per year (1)×(2)	(4) Marginal revenue product	(5) Marginal physical product	(6) Marginal revenue (4)/(5)
$52,000	7,100	$369,200,000			
			$20,800,000	700	$29,714
50,000	7,800	390,000,000			
			18,000,000	700	25,714
48,000	8,500	408,000,000			
			15,200,000	700	. 21,714
46,000	9,200	423,200,000			
			12,400,000	700	17,714
44,000	9,900	435,600,000			

Note: Hypothetical data.

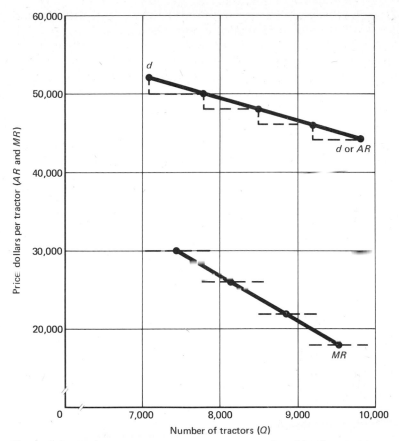

Figure 8-2 Average and marginal revenue curves faced by the manufacturer of a large tractor. The broken lines or "stair steps" indicate an assumption that the price of the tractor is changed in increments of $2,000. The heavy straight line suggests a much smaller incremental change, such as $100 per tractor.

the additional resources required to produce each additional 700 tractors. We may assume that capital and labor, or additional variable inputs, must be added each time production is increased. Marginal revenue is then simply MRP divided by the additional units produced, or $MRP/MPP = MR$, which is (4) ÷ (5) = (6). If the firm changes the prices of its tractors in increments of $2,000, its demand curve, or average revenue (AR) curve, and its marginal revenue (MR) curve will appear in a diagram as a series of steps such as the broken lines in Figure 8-2.

If the firm is more precise or discriminating in its pricing policy and changes the price in increments of $100 or less, the demand curve may be simulated by use of a continuous line such as AR in Figure 8-2. Then MR, bearing a specific relationship to AR, may also be shown as an unbroken line. Note that the slope of MR is steeper than the slope of AR. If projected downward, the MR curve will intersect the x axis at the point where the elasticity of AR is unity.

Elasticity of demand

The straight-line demand curve shown in Figure 8-2 does not have constant elasticity. This is because with each reduction in price the relative change in price becomes larger and larger and the relative change in quantity becomes smaller and smaller. We may confirm this in the following equations:

$$E_d = \frac{7,100 - 7,800}{(7,100 + 7,800)/2} \div \frac{52,000 - 50,000}{(52,000 + 50,000)/2}$$

$$= \frac{-700}{7,450} \div \frac{2,000}{51,000} = -2.4$$

$$E_d = \frac{7,800 - 8,500}{(7,800 + 8,500)/2} \div \frac{50,000 - 48,000}{(50,000 + 48,000)/2}$$

$$= \frac{-700}{8,150} \div \frac{2,000}{49,000} = -2.1$$

$$E_d = \frac{8,500 - 9,200}{(8,500 + 9,200)/2} \div \frac{48,000 - 46,000}{(48,000 + 46,000)/2}$$

$$= \frac{-700}{8,850} \div \frac{2,000}{47,000} = -1.9$$

$$E_d = \frac{9,200 - 9,900}{(9,200 + 9,900)/2} \div \frac{46,000 - 44,000}{(46,000 + 44,000)/2}$$

$$= \frac{-700}{9,550} \div \frac{2,000}{45,000} = -1.6$$

with all elasticities of demand being approximate.

The elasticity of the demand curve may change, of course, when there is an increase or decrease in demand. The firm normally will react to a change in demand by changing either its price, its equilibrium output, or both.

Table 8-2   Total, average, and marginal costs faced by
the manufacturer of a farm tractor

Tractors produced in a year	TFC[a]	TVC[a]	TC[a]	AFC[b]	AVC[b]	ATC[b]	MC[b]
7,000	200	120	320	29	17	46	
							25
8,000	200	145	345	25	18	43	
							35
9,000	200	180	380	22	20	42	
							50
10,000	200	230	430	20	23	43	

[a]Dollars, millions.
[b]Dollars, thousands.
Note: Hypothetical data.

Determination of output

Let us assume that this firm has the capacity to produce 10,000 tractors per year, and for each level of output from 7,000 to 10,000 the
costs are as shown in Table 8-2. What will be the firm's equilibrium
output?

As in pure competition, where capital is unlimited, the equilibrium output of the firm is at the point where the MC curve intersects
the MR curve from below. This is at the point of 7,800 tractors. If this
number of tractors is produced or supplied, it can be seen that the
selling price will be $50,000 per tractor with total average costs of
about $43,500. Thus, the firm will make a profit of about $6,500 per
tractor before income taxes. The total profit before income taxes
will be $6,500 times 7,800 = $53,950,000 (Figure 8-3).

Social cost of imperfect competition

Under given cost conditions, the firm in imperfect competition will
produce less and charge a higher price than the purely competitive
firm. Let us assume for purposes of comparison that a purely competitive firm faces a perfectly elastic demand set at the point where
MC intersects AR, which is at a price of about $46,000 per tractor.
The equilibrium output will be 9,300 tractors. ATC is about $42,000,
with profits before income taxes of about $4,000 per tractor. The

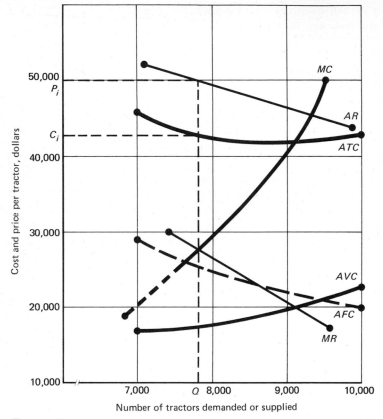

Figure 8-3   Costs, revenues, and equilibrium of the firm in imperfect competition.

total profit is $4,000 times 9,300 = $37,200,000, or $16,750,000 less than under imperfect competition. This difference, which is an additional cost to buyers of the product, is sometimes called the *social cost, or costs of imperfect competition* (Figure 8-4).

DISTRIBUTION OF THE SOCIAL COST

How are the social costs of imperfect competition distributed? The actual distribution of money income or profits does not capture the effects of imperfect competition on economic welfare. Having 1,500 fewer tractors each year will reduce aggregate farm output, or the aggregate amount of farm products supplied. In the short run, since aggregate demand is inelastic (−0.46 in Table 7-4), aggregate

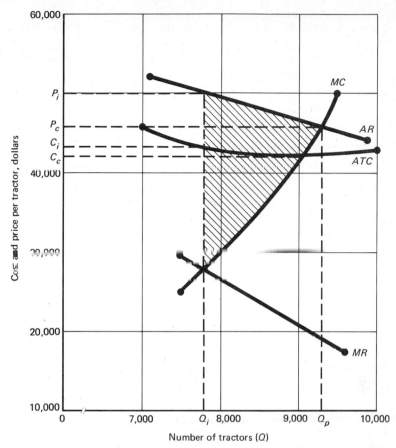

Figure 8-4   Comparative equilibrium of a purely competitive firm (Q_p) and a firm in imperfect competition (Q_i). Given identical costs, the imperfectly competitive firm will find it profitable to charge a higher price and produce a smaller output than a purely competitive firm. The difference in cost and return, or profit, is some-times called the *social cost of imperfect competition*.

receipts from farm marketings will increase. At least some and per-haps all—or more than all—of the cost will be transferred forward to consumers. How net farm income will be affected—whether it will be higher or lower and by how much—depends on how much the supply is restricted as well as the elasticity of demand.

In the long run, however, since the demand for total American farm output is about unitary elastic (−1.1 in Table 7-4), the aggre-gate gross farm-marketing receipts will be about the same under either perfect or imperfect competition in the farm input industries. This implies that the higher payment to the firm in imperfect competition will come out of the gross farm income. Also, because demand is less elastic in the domestic market than in the foreign market, under imperfect competition the domestic consumer will pay more, and the export market return less, than would be the case under pure competition.

DISTRIBUTION OF THE BENEFIT

The additional profits of $16,750,00 a year for the firm in imperfect competition can be paid to employees in the form of higher wages or salaries, or other perquisites; returned to stockholders or other claimants; kept by the firm for capital investment in development and growth; or paid to state and federal governments in the form of higher corporate income taxes. It is estimated that about 75 to 90 percent of the gross capital investment in manufacturing industries in the United States is financed from retained profits. Therefore, after allowing for a competitive return to stockholders and others, we may assume that the amount of money available for capital investment will be directly related to the net profits after taxes. The level of profits, in other words, will help determine how much and how rapidly the firm increases its productive capacity. The other factor, of course, is the cost structure of the firm and the industry—whether the firm has economies of large scale and whether the industry is one of increasing, constant, or decreasing costs.

Although the major social costs of imperfect competition within agricultural industries may be passed on to consumers through higher prices for farm products, the immediate impact of these costs generally is felt more directly and strongly by farmers. The possible benefits to farmers of lower farm output from this source are not generally evident, at least to the farmers. Consequently, farmers have almost universally fought against the concentration of economic power within agricultural industries arising out of imperfect competition. American farm organizations have not only supported federal and state regulation of railroads, power companies, meat-packing companies, warehouses, and other agriculturally related businesses, but have often led the fight for regulations, or the breaking up of monopolies and oligopolies. They have fashioned a number of market strategies to counteract the effects on farm incomes of imperfect competition within agricultural industries. This chapter concludes with a discussion of some of these strategies, but first it seems desirable to broaden our vision concerning the structure of competition and the size and concentration of firms in various parts of agribusiness.

COMPETITIVE STRUCTURE
OF AGRIBUSINESS

It is not possible to judge the effects of imperfect competition on prices and production simply by looking at the number of firms operating in a market. Competitive behavior depends on the elasticity of demand faced by each firm and the possible effects of actions the firm may take to increase the demand for its product or change the elasticity of demand in ways that are favorable to it. In cases where the market structure is oligopolistic, the firm's decisions on pricing are influenced importantly by consideration of how its competitors will react to a particular price policy by its management. Where an individual firm (or very few firms) has a large share of the market, as in soft drinks, soups, and breakfast foods, for example, the larger firms may follow a very rigid price policy. They will tend to advertise if advertising will increase the demand they face, but they will tend not to cut prices because other firms may do the same, leaving them perhaps worse off than before. What they do depends on their judgments concerning the elasticity of their own demand curves, and how the demand for their product can be increased or otherwise changed.

What individual firms will do also depends on their own cost structures and the cost structures of the industry. An aggressive expansion policy by a large firm may push up the prices of resources in general use by all firms. For this reason alone, a large firm may have a less aggressive growth policy than a small firm. All this will affect how imperfectly competitive firms compete, especially in oligopoly.

Somewhat similar considerations may prevail on the buying side of the market, especially in oligopsony. Where three or four meat-packing firms, for example, dominate a market, it has often been contended by farmers that prices are kept down because the firms follow a nonaggressive buying policy. That is, the meat-packing firms have tended to maintain a rather constant share of the total market, instead of individual firms trying to increase their share from time to time by more aggressive bidding and buying. Representatives of the meat-packing industry, on the other hand, contend that retail prices of meat are set at equilibrium levels in retail markets by the interaction of supply and demand. The demand is set by consumers, and the quantity supplied is directly related to the amount of livestock delivered to market by farmers. The demand at the level of the packers, then, is derived from the demand of consumers. Packers contend that they play a very passive role in the market, with their long-run profits set at a normal level by the entry and exit of other meat-packing and marketing firms.

Short-run profits and losses and long-run equilibrium

Figure 8-5 presents an example of the short-run profits, short-run losses, and long-run equilibrium of an imperfectly competitive firm. Generally speaking, in the short run any firm in imperfect competition can experience profits or losses, or break even, including the competitive returns for risk and management. This is the same as in pure competition except that the downward-sloping demand curve causes the firm in all three cases to reach equilibrium at a lower level of output and a higher price than in pure competition. This represents the social costs of imperfect competition.

Generally speaking, imperfectly competitive firms tend to realize a normal profit in the long run. But an oligopoly may realize excess profits for a very long time either nationally or in any local market. When this happens it is generally the result of restrictions on entry. Such restrictions can be strictly pecuniary, relating to the large costs of getting established in some markets. They can be legal, relating to licenses or the meeting of sanitary and environmental standards, for example. Or they can be political, relating to a favored priority position of an established firm in a given market. How important are such situations in agribusiness?

Oligopoly and monopolistic competition in processing-marketing

Table 8-3 presents a summary of examples of concentration in agricultural processing-marketing industries according to the percentage of the value of shipments by the 4 largest and the 20 largest companies in selected food-product industries. On this national basis the degree of concentration is generally not high according to the usual standards of American industries and manufacturing firms. In most cases the four largest firms have less than 50 percent of the total market. But in nearly all cases the 20 largest firms have 50 to 100 percent of the total market.

On a local basis, however, the concentration of major food firms in selected cities and metropolitan areas is much higher. In 30 large

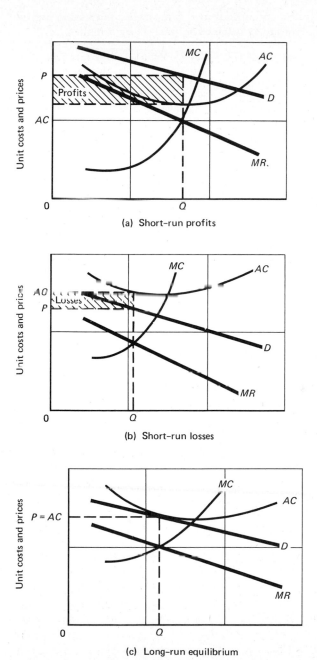

(a) Short-run profits

(b) Short-run losses

(c) Long-run equilibrium

Figure 8-5   Short-run profits and losses and long-run equilibrium of an imperfectly competitive firm. (a) In the short run, profits will attract firms into the industry, causing profits to be competed away, as a result of rising costs or falling demand for the products of the firm. (b) Losses will cause firms to leave the industry until a normal profit occurs, as a result of increasing demand or falling costs. (c) A monopolistically competitive firm tends to realize a normal profit in the long run.

Table 8-3 Concentration in agricultural processing-marketing industries according to percentage of value of shipments by firms

| | Value of shipments accounted for by | | | |
| | Four largest companies | | Twenty largest companies | |
Industry or product market	1963	1972	1963	1972
Grains and cereals				
Flour and other grain mill products	35	33	71	75
Blended and prepared flour	70	68	92	92
Wet corn milling	71	63	99	99
Rice milling	44	43	86	92
Cereal breakfast foods	86	90	99	99
Bread, cake, and related products	23	29	45	50
Cookies and crackers	59	59	80	83
Macaroni and spaghetti	31	38	71	76
Meats and poultry products				
Meatpacking[a]	31	22	54	51
Sausages and other prepared meats[a]	16	19	35	38
Poultry dressing	—	17	—	42
Poultry and egg processing	—	23	—	65
Milk and dairy products				
Fluid milk	23	18	40	42
Creamery butter	11	45	31	78
Cheese	44	42	59	65
Concentrated milk	40	39	71	76
Ice cream and frozen desserts	37	29	64	58
Processed fruits, vegetables, and specialties				
Frozen fruits and vegetables[b]	24	29	54	69
Frozen specialties	—	42	—	70
Canned fruits and vegetables[b]	24	20	50	53
Canned specialties[b]	67	67	94	94
Dehydrated foods	37	33	80	76
Pickles, sauces, and salad dressing[b]	36	33	64	62
Sugars and confectionary products				
Raw cane sugar	47	44	82	84
Cane sugar refining	63	59	100	99
Beet sugar	66	66	100	100
Confectionary products	15	32	45	59
Oils and oil products				
Cottonseed oil	41	43	72	80
Soybean oil	50	54	88	92
Vegetable oil	58	70	99	99
Shortening and cooking oils	42	44	92	93
Other food preparations	24	26	48	51

[a]Percentages based on value added by manufacture.

[b]Percentages computed on value of production.

Source: United States Bureau of the Census, "Concentration Ratios in Manufacturing," *1972 Census of Manufacturers,* MC72(SR)2, pp. 6–10.

Table 8-4 Average net profits after taxes of 85 food firms by degree of market concentration

| Group | Concentration range (4 firms), percent | Number of firms | Net profits as a percentage of stockholders' equity | |
			Simple average, percent	Weighted average,[a] percent
I	Below 40	21	7.5	6.2
II	40–49	32	9.5	9.2
III	50–59	15	13.2	12.9
IV	60 and above	17	14.2	15.1

[a]Weighted by company sales.

Source: Federal Trade Commission, The Structure of Food Manufacturing, National Commission on Food Marketing, Technical Study No. 8, June 1966, p. 204.

American cities, the four top grocery retailers handle from 50 per-cent to more than 90 percent of the volume of the total area.[1] Fur-thermore, much more than 50 percent of the total volume is gener-ally handled by the four largest supermarket chains, who at times have held more than 80 percent of the positions of market control. In some areas of the largest cities, downtown Washington, D.C., for example, one or two supermarkets have a virtual monopoly of the grocery business.

Effects of concentration on net profits of food firms

Table 8-4 shows that the average net profits of food firms are directly correlated—one may say very strongly correlated—with the firms' degree of market concentration in city and metropolitan markets. Where the four top firms have less then 40 percent of the market, net profits averaged only 6.2 percent of the aggregated stockhold-ers' equity. When the top four firms had 60 percent or more of the market, the weighted average of profits was 15.1 percent. The differ-ences between 6.2 percent and 15.1 percent would tend to be reflected in the prices of the food firms, that is, the spread between the prices of the foods bought at wholesale and the prices of the foods sold at retail.

[1]1973 Grocery Distribution Guide, Metro Market Studies Inc., Greenwich, Conn., 1973.

Table 8-5 Profit rates of food-manufacturing firms related to concentration and advertising-to-sales ratios

Advertising-to-sales ratio, percent	1.0	2.0	3.0	4.0	5.0
Four-firm concentration[b]	Associated net firm profit rates as a percentage of stockholders' equity[a]				
40	6.3	7.4	8.5	9.6	10.7
45	8.0	9.1	10.2	11.3	12.4
50	9.3	10.4	11.5	12.6	13.7
55	10.3	11.4	12.5	13.6	14.7
60	11.0	12.1	13.2	14.3	15.4
65	11.4	12.5	13.6	14.7	15.8
70	11.5	12.6	13.7	14.8	15.9

[a]Other variables influencing company profitability were held constant at their respective means. These variables were the firm's relative market share, growth in industry demand, firm diversification, and absolute firm size. Profit rates are averages for the years 1949–1952.

[b]The average concentration ratio (weighted by the company's value of shipments) of the product classes the company operated in 1950.

Source: Federal Trade Commission, Bureau of Economics, Economic Report on the Influence of Market Structure on the Profit Performance of Food Manufacturing Companies, September 1969, p. 7.

Profit rates of food-manufacturing firms related to concentration and advertising-to-sales ratios

Table 8-5 shows that the profit rates of food-manufacturing firms are directly correlated with concentration and with advertising as a percentage of total sales. With an advertising-to-sales ratio of 1 percent when the four-firm concentration was 40 percent or less of the market, their profit rate was only 6.3 percent of the stockholders' equity. When this concentration was 70 percent or more, the profit rate was 11.5 percent. When the advertising-to-sales ratio was 5 percent, the comparable profit rates were 10.7 and 15.9 percent, respectively.[2]

[2]For further discussion, see Harold G. Halcrow, Food Policy for America, McGraw-Hill Book Company, New York, 1977, pages 187–192.

Oligopoly and monopolistic competition in farm machinery and equipment

Among the agribusinesses in farm services and supply, the competitive structure of the farm machinery and equipment industry is perhaps the most revealing in respect to oligopoly and monopolistic competition. In general it may be said that the industry has the structure of oligopoly, with a few very large firms offering a full line of machinery and equipment and supplying the major share of the market. These firms are both price leaders and service leaders, differentiating their products through research, new inventions and patents, nationwide and regionally concentrated advertising, and company service. The major core of their market is the large family farm and the larger-than-family corporations in the production of both crops and livestock. Operators of these large farms buy most of the new tractors and tractor-powered or self-propelled machines and implements. The smaller farms, including part-time farms, provide a market for generally lower-powered tractors and equipment. The small-farm market has continued to shrink, which means that the external economies of large-scale production in farm machinery and equipment are concentrated more among the large-size farms.

The technologically advanced farm machinery and equipment industry is a major, essential factor in the economic development of agriculture. The industry is clearly oligopolistic in organization, especially in regard to the larger-size tractors and equipment. Prices have changed very little from year to year except for the general upward spiral associated with inflation. Pricing is generally not collusive, at least to the extent of being in violation of the antitrust laws. But the oligopoly structure of competition makes prices very inflexible, at least on the down side. When the farmers' demand for new tractors and equipment falters, as it must when there is a downward shift in *MRP* curves, the major companies do not follow the downturn with reduced prices. They maintain their pricing structure and reduce the quantity supplied at the relatively fixed price levels. Farmers have a hard time reducing costs even though their demand for these inputs decreases. The fluctuations in net farm income are thereby accentuated.

Concentration in fertilizers and chemical pesticides

Monopolistic competition and oligopoly are also characteristic of the fertilizer and pesticide industries. Growth in the fertilizer industry has resulted from a technological revolution in commercial production, which has been accompanied by a dramatic expansion in the size of individual firms and a reduction in the total number of firms. Between 1950 and 1980, production in the United States of the major plant nutrients—nitrogen, phosphate, and potash—increased from 4 million tons to more than 25 million tons. Manufacturers have largely gained control of the major sources of raw materials and have integrated production of raw materials with manufacture and sale of the finished product. In most areas of the country no more than three or four firms account for the major part of the total supply, if not all of the total quantity supplied. The pesticide industry has followed a similar pattern of development, with a very small number of firms developing a large volume of standard-formula products that are identified or differentiated by company brand or name. This is the essence of oligopoly.

Analytical complexities of oligopoly: Mutual interdependence

The concept of mutual interdependence among a small number of firms introduces a number of complexities into economic analysis. An individual firm cannot make a rational judgment about prices and outputs without taking into account the effects of its decisions on the prices and outputs of its rivals, and then, in turn, the effects of the rivals' decisions on its own demand curves. Specifically, an oligopoly firm may hesitate to cut its own prices even if this would at first appear to maximize its profits because other firms may do the same, and then the first firm to cut prices, which might not have much increase in sales, may be worse off than before.

The options of the oligopoly firm are illustrated theoretically in Figure 8-6 and 8-7.

Figure 8-6a shows the oligopoly firm in short-run equilibrium with profits related to the firm's share of the market. The typical oligopolist estimates the firm's demand curve by assuming that other firms will be charging similar prices, but not prices so high that they encourage the entry of new oligopoly firms. The firm's demand curve shown in Figure 8-6a is not drawn up, however, on the assumption of *other things being equal*. On the contrary, it is assumed that—if the firm could reduce its marginal cost, shifting it downward by technological advance such as from MC to MC'—a downward move on the given demand curve achieved by cutting its prices will be followed by retaliation from its rivals. This might be in the form of increased advertising or price cutting by its rivals to

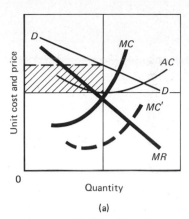
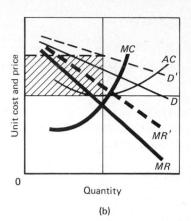

(a)   (b)

Figure 8-6 (a) The oligopolistic short-run equilibrium output allows for oligopoly profits, as indicated by the shaded rectangle. (b) When demand increases as a result of advertising and sales promotion, however, as from DD to D'D', the marginal revenue curve also shifts, as from MR to MR'. But the oligopolist does not expand output, as indicated by the intersection of MR' and MC, because this might bring retaliation by its rivals, such as increased advertising or possibly price cutting. Instead, the oligopolist tends to be content with the same share of the market as in a, but higher prices and higher profits, as indicated by the shaded area in b.

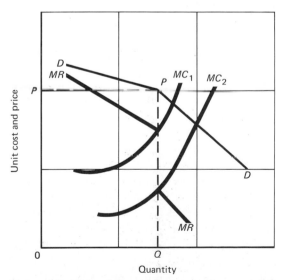

Figure 8-7 Technological advance and price stability under oligopoly. When the marginal cost curve shifts from MC₁ to MC₂, the oligopolist does not increase output or reduce price. Demand curve DD is kinked because a cut in the price of the original oligopolistic firm brings retaliation by its rivals.

maintain their accustomed share of the market. Either action could shift the initial demand curve of the oligopolist downward, leaving it worse off than before, and so the firm contents itself with its oligopoly profit and given share of the market. If it experiences technological advance with downward-shifting marginal-cost curves, this will enable it to make more profit per unit while not increasing its output.

Alternatively, in Figure 8-6b if the original oligopoly firm is able to shift its demand curve outward by advertising and sales promotion, say, from D to D', it may not try to expand production and the quantity supplied as indicated by the new point of intersection of MR' and MC—this also will bring retaliation by its rivals. In this case the increased demand permits the firm to increase its price and profit per unit as indicated by the larger rectangle in Figure 8-6b, again without increasing its output.

There is in effect a "kinked" demand curve faced by the individual oligopolist, which results in a constant output by the firm even under technological advance. Figure 8-7 illustrates this point. The kinked demand curve DD causes a "break" in the MR curve at output Q. If technological advance causes the marginal-cost curve to drop from MC_1 to MC_2, the firm will not find it profitable to drop its price and increase the quantity supplied. This is because the marginal revenue curve to the right of Q is below MC_2, indicating that it will not be profitable to expand output beyond Q.

Development and growth
of oligopoly-type firms

In a given static, or nongrowing, market situation, oligopoly-type firms develop and grow primarily by merging and integrating or buying out or taking over the plants of their rivals rather than by increasing their individual share of the market by cutting prices. The individual firms tend to experience internal economies of scale as technological advance occurs. So there are cost advantages in merging and combining, or taking over the plant and facilities of a rival. The progressive oligopoly expands in scale as it experiences cost reductions; the more it succeeds in cutting costs, the greater the incentive to buy out and take over the plants of its rivals. The concept of growing oligopoly firms with reductions in the total number of firms is compatible with technological advance in a static market that is not growing.

As technological advance takes place, however, the demand increases relatively for the products that are improving the most in quality or design. Quality and design improvements in farm tractors, for example, without any change in relative price, increase the demand and the quantity demanded at that price. The profits of the progressive oligopolist tend to increase, and more funds are then available for further modernization and expansion of the plant.

In a dynamic market where demand curves are shifting to the right, there is more and more room for additional output to be supplied without depressing the market price. The progressive oligopolists can grow relatively more rapidly than the total market as long as they experience internal economies of large scale. When they reach the point of experiencing diseconomies of large scale, their rate of growth will tend to slow down relative to the rates of growth of their smaller rivals. Thus, oligopoly firms do not grow indefinitely in size even though the smaller firms tend to get crowded out as technology advances and the total industry develops and grows.

PRODUCTION AND MARKETING STRATEGIES OF AGRIBUSINESS

The above view of monopolistic competition and oligopoly seems to be compatible with the historical facts of the development and growth of agribusiness. There has been a strong tendency for the development of fewer and larger firms during some stages of growth, after which the agribusiness industries tend to stabilize at some later stage in terms of numbers of firms and shares of the market. This has been the experience generally in food processing-marketing industries including the retail chains of food stores. It has also been the case in most of the agribusiness farm service supply industries. But there are some exceptions to be noted, and it is important to close with a more general comment on the strategies of agribusiness, including the organization and role of farmers' cooperatives.

Meats and poultry products

Technological advances in the meat-packing industry, for example, have tended to make the industry less concentrated and more dispersed geographically. Improvements in highways and the trucking industry, including the development of refrigeration technology adaptable to trucks, have caused meat-packing firms to move their plants out of the great central markets such as Chicago, South St. Paul, Omaha, and East St. Louis in order to develop more-automated, smaller country plants closer to the main sources of supply. The earlier concentrated oligopoly of 30 or 40 years ago that was dominated by four or five very large meat-packing firms has tended to be displaced by a much larger number of more widely dispersed firms, or companies. Table 8-3 shows that the four largest meat-packing companies handle less than one-fourth of the total product. Poultry dressing and poultry and egg processing never experienced the degree of oligopoly, or concentration, that was experienced in meat packing, except sometimes in individual markets.

Grains and cereals

About three-fourths of the flour and other grain-mill products are processed by the 20 largest companies, but the 4 largest companies handle only about one-third of the total. Ninety percent of the market for cereal breakfast foods, however, is supplied by the four largest companies. Oligopoly pricing seems to be clearly evident in regard to the breakfast cereals, while quality improvement has also clearly advanced to a high level. Oligopoly is characteristic of cookies and crackers, with somewhat similar implications for pricing, product quality, and determination of output.

Milk and dairy products

Table 8-3 suggests that only about one-fifth of fluid milk is handled by the four largest dairy companies. But this statistic is misleading because individual city and metropolitan markets are generally supplied almost entirely by only three or four companies at the most. The effects of market concentration are modified, however, by two facts: the use of federal milk-marketing orders, which specify the minimum prices that must be paid to producers for milk that goes into fluid uses, and federal price supports for milk that is used in manufacturing cheese, butter, ice cream, and other dairy products. The dairy farmer is paid a *blend* price, which is a weighted average of the two prices in a given market. Manufactured dairy products are then sold at the retail level as differentiated products, distinguished by company name or brand. Oligopoly pricing comes in at the retail level. Thus, federal regulations and price supports, combined with this oligopoly retail market structure, result in prices for dairy products that adhere closely to the oligopoly model.

Processed fruits, vegetables, and specialities

These commodities present a mixed picture. A large percentage of the total crop is sold off the farm under conditions of pure compe-

Raw fruits and vegetables unidentified by producer or wholesale firm tend to follow the pricing model of pure competition; while some that are packaged and identified by company label tend toward that of oligopoly or monopolistic competition.

tition. Also, marketing agreements and orders are used, especially for fruits, to regulate the grade, or quality, of part or all of the crop. Some of the fruits and vegetables are sold in raw form in retail markets, unidentified by producer or marketing firm, while some are packaged and differentiated by grade or company label. When the commodities are frozen, canned, or dehydrated, they are nearly always identified by brand and company name, with prices and marketing strategies following the oligopoly model. The crucial questions seem to center not entirely on the national market shares of the individual firms but on local and regional markets as well as the services provided to the supermarket chains and their services to the consumer.

Sugars and confectionary; oils and oil products

The four largest companies generally handle 40 percent or more of each product nationally, and the 20 largest companies handle 80 percent or more of each product, except for confectionary products. Market concentration is high, therefore, and pricing tends to follow the oligopoly model as the products move through wholesale and retail markets. Products are differentiated by brand or company name as they appear at retail even though they are sold off the farm by purely competitive firms. How much oligopoly adds to the marketing spread cannot be determined except by a careful step-by-step analysis of the entire processing-marketing system.

Role of farmers' cooperatives in agribusiness

Any study of agribusiness competition would be incomplete without some reference to the special role of farmers' cooperatives. They have a significant share of the market both in processing-marketing services and in farm service supply (Table 8-6). Their effect on determination of prices and outputs cannot be judged simply by looking at the market shares, however. Judgment must involve other matters such as the principles of organization, the system of governance or control, and the strategies used in pricing and determination of output.

The principles of cooperative business enterprise have been known and practiced on a limited scale for two or three centuries or more, but the rapid growth of farmers' cooperatives in the United

Table 8-6 Market shares of farmers' cooperatives in agricultural industries

	1950	1960	1970	1975
Processing-marketing cooperatives: percent of cash farm receipts				
Grain	29	38	32	40
Livestock	16	14	11	10
Dairy	53	61	73	75
Cotton	12	22	26	26
Fruits and vegetables	20	21	27	25
Farm service supply cooperatives: percent of total farmer expenditures				
Feed	19	18	18	17
Fertilizers	15	24	32	36
Petroleum	19	24	26	30
Farm chemicals	11	18	18	29

Source: Farmer Cooperative Service, *Cooperative Growth,* Information Circular 87.

States dates only from the passage of the Capper-Volstead Act of 1922. This made it legal for farmers' cooperatives to participate in interstate commerce by exempting them from certain restraints imposed by the Sherman Antitrust Act of 1890 and the Clayton Act of 1914. This legislation also specified that farmers' cooperatives must conform to one or both of the following requirements:

First. That no member of the association is allowed more than one vote because of the amount of stock or membership capital he may own therein, or,

Second. That the association does not pay dividends on stock membership capital in excess of 8 per centum per annum.

And in any case to the following:

Third. That the association shall not deal in the products of nonmembers to an amount greater in value than such as are handled by it for members. . . . [3]

These requirements have placed the control of farmers' cooperatives largely in the hands of member-users rather than independent investors. This makes cooperatives more directly conscious of the farmers' views on prices and services. The limitation of 8 percent on earnings from dividends assures that earnings in excess of 8 percent will either be kept for reinvestment or returned to member-users as patronage refunds. Such refunds are not taxed as income to the corporate body of the cooperative since, by virtue of the charter of the cooperative, they do not belong to it.

TWO TYPES OF
COOPERATIVE ORGANIZATION

Farmers' cooperatives are generally of either a federated or a centralized type of organization although a few cooperatives are a mixture of both. Under a federated organization, individual cooperatives join together to create a business superstructure for purposes of more coordinated and efficient operation. The individual cooperatives own and control the federated superstructure rather than vice versa. Members elect the board of directors of the federated cooperatives through the local organization. Under a centralized organization, the parent cooperative owns and controls various satellite or

[3]U.S. Department of Agriculture, *Legal Phases of Farmer Cooperatives: Part III, Antitrust Laws.* Farmer Cooperative Service Information Bulletin, no. 70, 1970, pp 29, 31, 32.

local cooperatives. Members vote directly for the board of directors, which controls the total organization.

American farm organizations have been active in sponsoring or developing both types of cooperatives, and much of the success of the American cooperative movement has been the result of this sponsorship. Cooperatives sponsored by the state affiliates of the American Farm Bureau Federation (A.F.B.F.), covering by far the largest volume and variety of the business of farmers' cooperatives in the United States, are spread throughout all the states as largely farmer-patron, business-managed enterprises. Except for instances of dairy cooperatives, and some cooperatives in fruits and vegetables, most individual cooperatives center their business within the state in which they are chartered, although a few spread into neighboring states. The A.F.B.F., the national organization, has the right to audit the books of a state association and some of its sponsored enterprises, but as a matter of policy it does not do so. The cooperatives, generally operating in imperfectly competitive markets, offer their services in competition with other imperfectly competitive firms.

The Farmers' Educational and Cooperative Union of America, or the Farmers' Union as it is generally called, built its organization through cooperative businesses of many kinds—cotton gins, warehouses, grain elevators, fertilizer-buying pools, petroleum cooperatives, and in its early years occasionally a bank, hotel, or livery stable. As early as 1910, its officers claimed to have a system of warehouses in every cotton-growing state in the South. By the 1920s, Farmers' Union cooperatives had become highly successful in Nebraska and successful to a lesser extent in Kansas. Most important, the growth of the Farmers' Union has been based on the strength of its sponsorship of the Farmers' Union Grain Terminal Association. This cooperative, with headquarters in St. Paul, Minnesota, has continued to grow; it owns local grain elevators in more than a dozen states and large terminal elevators on the Great Lakes, the Mississippi, and the west coast. In addition, cooperatives sponsored by the Farmers' Union are important in petroleum, livestock, dairy marketing, and insurance.

Many other farm organizations have been active in the sponsorship of cooperative enterprises. The National Grange of the Patrons of Husbandry—more simply, the National Grange—the first of the national farm organizations of agrarian discontent, favored cooperatives although its interest in their sponsorship was not very widespread. The Missouri Farmers Association, or M.F.A., nearly unique among state organizations in the breadth and scope of its activity, is organized as a centralized cooperative with a broad range of cooperative interests. Since 1955, the National Farmers Organization—or N.F.O. as it is called—has been active in forming cooperatives for the purposes of withholding or managing the sale of farm products and bargaining for higher prices. Over the years, even before 1922, there have been hundreds or thousands of individual cooperatives formed, with or without the support of farm organizations, to process and market farm inputs and farm products or to bargain as cooperative associations with other processing and marketing firms for more favorable prices and terms for farmers.

COOPERATIVE FARMERS' BARGAINING ASSOCIATIONS

Although most of the farmers' cooperatives in the United States have been organized simply to carry out a business operation under the control of members, an element of bargaining is nearly always present, and some farmers' cooperatives have been formed primarily as bargaining associations to negotiate prices and terms of trade collectively for farmers. These have been most active in fruits, vegetables, dairy products, sugar beets, and other specialty crops. A few have been active in poultry. The N.F.O. has attempted to use them in grains and livestock, primarily to withhold products from the market to influence prices and to bargain with oligopsonistic marketing firms for higher prices.

Comparison and contrast with labor unions   Unlike American labor unions, farmers' bargaining associations are voluntary for both sellers and buyers. There is no procedure by which a farmers' bargaining association may win an election to be recognized as the agent with which buyers must deal. California has a law requiring processors of farm products to bargain with "qualified" bargaining associations, and Michigan passed a law in 1973 providing that processors must bargain with "accredited" associations financed by fees for marketing services. But the success of any bargaining association depends on the actions it may take to gain the allegiance of its members and on its ability to control the market supply.

Experience of bargaining associations   Generally, cooperative farmers' associations can attain substantive price goals only when they are able to acquire a large enough amount of the available supply to require buyers to bargain with them collectively. Efforts to develop large regional or national bargaining associations in grains and livestock, such as the attempts of the A.F.B.F. in the early 1920s and the N.F.O. after 1955, have usually had only very limited success. Generally, after some activity, efforts to organize have been discontinued or abandoned.

More limited actions, especially in fruits and nuts in Califorina, have achieved marked success over a number of years, even before 1922. In the early 1970s, about 6,500 fruit farmers in California and other states were marketing more than 1 million tons of fruit a year under contracts, many of which were negotiated through farmers' cooperative bargaining associations. Some 5,000 vegetable farmers were marketing about 2.5 million tons of vegetables under similar arrangements. Some of these were under the American Agricultural Marketing Association (A.A.M.A.), an organization then newly sponsored by the A.F.B.F. to represent farmers through state and local associations in bargaining with agricultural processing-marketing firms, especially in fruits and vegetables and to a lesser degree with livestock and poultry.

Production and Marketing contracts

Generally speaking, 80 to 85 percent of the aggregate output of American farms and ranches is produced and sold without production and marketing contracts, with prices generally determined in purely competitive auction markets. In the early 1970s, some 17 to 18 percent was produced under production contracts, generally between the farmer-producer and the first buyer. But only a portion of these contracts were set through a bargaining association. The others were private, mutually agreed upon contracts between the farmer-producer and the processing-marketing firm to provide greater certainty on terms that were to the advantage of both.

The percentage of farm produce raised or sold under production and marketing contracts varies widely among commodities and groups of commodities. It is very low for grains, oilseeds, tobacco, and miscellaneous crops, and very high for sugar beets, vegetables for processing, and citrus fruits. These contracts are used very little for meat animals except for fed cattle and lambs, but they are used extensively for broilers, turkeys, and fluid-grade milk (Table 8-7).

Vertical integration

Vertical integration has come into use as a term to describe a situation where two or more firms at different stages of production and

Table 8-7   Estimated percentage of agricultural output produced under production and marketing contracts, and vertical integration, in the United States in 1960 and 1970

Product	Contracts		Vertical integration	
	1960, percent	1970, percent	1960, percent	1970, percent
Crop or crop product				
Food grains	1.0	2.0	0.3	0.5
Feed grains	0.1	0.1	0.4	0.5
Oil-bearing crops	1.0	1.0	0.4	0.5
Hay and forage	0.3	0.3		
Cotton	5.0	11.0	3.0	1.0
Tobacco	2.0	2.0	2.0	2.0
Vegetables for fresh market	20.0	21.0	25.0	30.0
Vegetables for processing	67.0	85.0	8.0	10.0
Dry beans and peas	35.0	1.0	1.0	1.0
Potatoes	40.0	45.0	30.0	25.0
Citrus fruits	60.0	55.0	20.0	30.0
Other fruits and nuts	20.0	20.0	15.0	20.0
Sugar beets	98.0	98.0	2.0	2.0
Sugarcane	40.0	40.0	60.0	60.0
Other sugar crops	5.0	5.0	2.0	2.0
Seed crops	80.0	80.0	0.3	0.5
Miscellaneous crops	5.0	5.0	1.0	1.0
Total crops	8.6	9.5	4.3	4.8
Livestock or livestock product				
Hogs	0.7	1.0	0.7	1.0
Sheep and lambs	2.0	7.0	2.0	3.0
Fed cattle	10.0	18.0	3.0	4.0
Broilers	93.0	90.0	5.0	7.0
Turkeys	30.0	42.0	4.0	12.0
Fluid-grade milk	95.0	95.0	3.0	3.0
Manufacturing-grade milk	25.0	25.0	2.0	1.0
Eggs	5.0	20.0	10.0	20.0
Miscellaneous	3.0	3.0	1.0	1.0
Total livestock items[a]	27.2	31.4	3.2	4.8
Total crop and livestock[b]	15.1	17.2	3.9	4.8

[a]The estimates for individual items are based on the informed judgments of a number of production and marketing specialists in the United States Department of Agriculture.

[b]The totals were obtained by weighting the individual items by the relative weights used in computing the ERS index of total farm output.

Source: R. L. Mighell and W. S. Hoofnagle *Contract Production and Vertical Integration in Agriculture*, U.S. Department of Agriculture, Economic Research Service, USDA-ERS-479, April 1972.

processing-marketing combine under a single ownership and management. Examples are a sugarcane plantation having its own sugar-processing plant, and a plant taking over one or more plantations. Other examples are a potato processing-marketing firm acquiring potato farms, a citrus-marketing firm merging with one or more citrus plantations, and a firm that markets fresh vegetables acquiring, or merging with, farms that produce vegetables. In the 1950s the growth of vertical integration aroused fears among farmers that they might be losing their traditional freedoms and that large-scale vertically integrated firms would therefore dominate American agriculture. Although such firms have grown rather rapidly in such areas as sugarcane, fresh vegetables and potatoes, citrus and other fruits and nuts, and eggs and turkeys, by 1970 only 4.8 percent of the total crop and livestock output was under vertical integration, as compared with 3.9 percent in 1960 (Table 8-7). Since 1970, although individual firms continue to grow in size and the number of firms continues to decline in farm service supply and processing-marketing, the growth of vertically integrated firms is not a strong trend.

SUMMARY

Our study of agribusiness competition in production and marketing reveals a broad range and variety of competitive situations, with imperfect competition being the dominant characteristic. Although both monopoly and monopsony are rare, situations resembling one or the other are found to be important. Oligopoly and oligopsony, and monopolistic competition, are typical in both farm service supply and processing-marketing; this contrasts sharply with the general situation of purely competitive firms in the farm sector.

Under given costs, a firm in imperfect competition will produce less and charge more than a firm in pure competition, which results in the social cost of imperfect competition. The distribution of these costs as well as the allocation of benefits cannot be determined solely from either empirical data or a theoretical model. An important consideration is the comparative rates of return on the earnings of the imperfectly competitive firm in the alternative investments that may be made. The ultimate net cost or benefit of imperfect competition within agricultural industries depends on long-range rates of return in investments related to alternatives in development and growth.

Several market strategies have been developed and are used to try to offset some of the short-run costs to the farm sector of imperfect competition within agricultural industries. These include farmers' cooperatives, farmers' cooperative bargaining associations, production and marketing contracts, and vertical integration. The great bulk of total farm output is not first handled through these strategies or systems, however, but through more purely competitive auction markets.

IMPORTANT TERMS AND CONCEPTS

Demand curve faced by the imperfectly competitive firm

How the imperfectly competitive firm can influence the demand curve that it faces

Elasticity of the demand curve faced by the imperfectly competitive firm

Equilibrium of the imperfectly competitive firm

Elasticity of the imperfectly competitive firm's supply curve

Social cost or costs of imperfect competition

Short-run profits and losses of the imperfectly competitive firm

Long-run equilibrium of the imperfectly competitive firm

Effects of concentration on profits of food firms

Concentration in agribusiness service supply industries

Analytical complexities of mutual interdependence

Kinked demand curve of oligopoly

Production and marketing strategies of agribusiness

Special role of farmers' cooperatives in agribusiness

Types of cooperative organization

Cooperative farmers' bargaining associations

Marketing and production contracts

Vertical integration in agriculture

LOOKING AHEAD

To provide greater support for farm prices and incomes, American farmers and farmers' organizations have worked for many years to involve the federal government in actions to strengthen the competitive position of farmers versus both farm service supply and agricultural processing-marketing. The role of government involves a wide range of activities to regulate farm output and the quantity supplied, increase the quantity demanded, supplement farm incomes by direct payments, and encourage agricultural adjustment. Let us consider these activities in Chapter 9, showing how they are based in the development problems of the farm sector.

QUESTIONS AND EXERCISES

1. Distinguish among monopoly, oligopoly, and monopolistic competition. What is the characteristic of demand common to each? In what ways does each differ from the others?

2. What is oligopsony? In what areas of the agricultural industries is it most prevalent?

3. How may an oligopolist manipulate the demand curve for its product? Give an example related to the farm service supply industries; the agricultural processing-marketing industries.

4. What factors account for the apparent inflexibility in prices of oligopolistic firms? Which of these factors do you consider to be most important or influential in the price policies of farm-machinery firms, fertilizer manufacturers, and sellers of cereal breakfast foods?

5. How do farmers' cooperatives differ from other corporations in terms of ownership and control, return on investment, price policies, and tax status?

6. In general, what accounts for the success or failure of cooperative farmers' bargaining associations? In what commodity situations have they been the most successful? The least successful?

7. In what areas are production and marketing contracts most widely used? In what areas are they used the least? What are the reasons for these differences?

8. What is vertical integration? Where is it most prevalent? Account for the fact that vertical integration has not become more widespread.

9. Define what is meant by the social cost of imperfect competition. What must be known in order to determine the distribution of social costs and benefits?

10. Although competition within the farm service supply sector is imperfect, progress in this sector appears to be a major source of development and growth in agriculture. If this is true, what are the major reasons?

9. FARM INCOME: PROBLEMS AND PROGRAMS

9. FARM INCOME: PROBLEMS AND PROGRAMS

"American farm leaders are correct in arguing that our agriculture still must look forward to a definite 'surplus' problem. What they tend to overlook, however, is of what our 'surplus' consists. Fundamentally, America's long-term agricultural problem is not one of 'surplus' cotton, wheat, or grapefruit. Rather it is one of 'surplus' farmers.**"**

William H. Nicholls

William H. Nicholls (1914–1978), a graduate of Harvard University who taught agricultural economics at Iowa State University, the University of Chicago, and Vanderbilt University, wrote the first comprehensive study of imperfect competition in agriculture, *A Theoretical Analysis of Imperfect Competition with Special Application to the Agricultural Industries* (The Iowa State University Press, Ames, 1941). This was followed with a more detailed study of a specific industry, *Price, Policies in the Cigarette Industry* (Nashville University Press, 1951). Also, in a first-prize paper from among 317 papers presented in a contest on the topic "A Price Policy for Agriculture, Consistent with Economic Progress, That will Promote Adequate and More Stable Income from Farming" (*Journal of Farm Economics*, November 1945, pp. 752-756), Nicholls presented a program that has had wide appeal within the profession of agricultural economics. This chapter and Chapter 10 discuss parts of this program and a number of alternatives for raising and stabilizing farm prices and incomes.

O ur studies of agribusiness competition, production functions and costs, and supply and demand may now be related to the major problems of the farm sector regarding income. Contrary to the experience in other sectors, steadily rising productivity in farming has not solved the major problems of income of most farmers. Typically, although some farm families have very favorable incomes, the large majority of farm operators have experienced low rates of return from farming. Consequently, government has intervened in the farm-product markets to raise and stabilize farm family income. What are the dimensions of the problems and the results of government programs?

IN THIS CHAPTER

1. You will see how problems of farm income are related to increasing productivity of farms, relatively declining prices for farm products and competition among farm producers.
2. You will gain an understanding of the three major programs by which the government has intervened in farm-product markets.
3. You may evaluate some of the future alternatives for these programs and their limitations.

DIMENSIONS OF THE PROBLEM

Problems of farm income arise out of (1) relatively declining prices of farm products as the productivity of farms increases, and (2) differences in rates of productivity increase and capital accumulation among farmers. Let us begin by observing the effects of increasing productivity on the relative prices of farm products.

Productivity as output per unit of input

Definition: Productivity is the ratio of total outputs to total inputs used in production.

An index of productivity must include all inputs and outputs weighted according to their relative importance in terms of value in the selected base period. A rise in the index indicates an increase in productivity, and a fall indicates a decrease. Table 9-1 summarizes the changes since 1910.

Table 9-1 emphasizes the relative stagnation in productivity of farms from 1910 to the end of the 1930s. Between 1910 and 1914

Table 9-1   Indexes of total farm output, input, and productivity in the United States, 1910 to 1978 (1967 = 100)

Year	Output	Input	Productivity[a]	Year	Output	Input	Productivity[a]
1910	43	86	50	1945	70	103	68
1911	42	88	48	1946	71	101	71
1912	47	90	53	1947	69	101	68
1913	43	90	47	1948	76	103	74
1914	47	92	51	1949	74	105	71
1915	49	92	53	1950	74	104	71
1916	44	92	48	1951	76	107	71
1917	47	93	51	1952	79	107	74
1918	47	95	49	1953	79	106	75
1919	47	95	50	1954	80	105	76
1920	50	98	52	1955	82	105	78
1921	45	95	47	1956	82	103	80
1922	49	96	51	1957	81	101	80
1923	50	97	51	1958	87	100	87
1924	10	99	50	1959	88	102	87
1925	51	99	51	1960	91	101	90
1926	52	101	52	1961	91	100	91
1927	52	99	52	1962	92	100	92
1928	54	101	53	1963	96	100	96
1929	53	102	52	1964	95	100	95
1930	52	101	51	1965	98	98	100
1931	57	101	56	1966	95	98	97
1932	55	97	57	1967	100	100	100
1933	51	96	53	1968	102	100	102
1934	43	90	48	1969	102	99	103
1935	52	91	57	1970	101	99	102
1936	47	93	50	1971	111	100	111
1937	57	98	59	1972	110	100	110
1938	57	96	60	1973	112	101	111
1939	58	98	59	1974	106	101	105
1940	60	100	60	1975	114	100	115
1941	62	100	62	1976	117	102	115
1942	70	103	68	1977	121	103	118
1943	69	104	66	1978[b]	120	102	118
1944	71	105	67				

[a]Data computed from unrounded index numbers.

[b]Preliminary.

Source: U.S. Department of Agriculture, Economic Research Service, USDA-ERS-241, 1977, pp. 261–496, and U.S. Department of Agriculture, *1978 Handbook of Agricultural Charts,* p. 16.

and 1935 and 1939, the total increase in output was a little more than one-fifth, with total inputs increasing by 7 percent and productivity by 14 percent, as follows (based on 1967 = 100):

Year	Output	Input	Productivity
1910–1914	44.4	89.2	49.8
1935–1939	54.2	95.2	57.0
1910–1914 to 1935–1939, percent increase	22	7	14

The increase in productivity, in other words, averaged about 0.5 percent per year, or less than 5 percent per decade. It should be noted, however, that from 1933 to 1941 the federal government was attempting to restrict total output in order to increase farm prices and incomes. The main results have been very difficult to assess even in retrospect. It may be presumed that productivity was reduced by the program, with the main restriction being the general failure of farm prices to improve.

Table 9-1 also emphasizes the contrasting upward trend in productivity starting about 1942 and continuing with generally increasing force up to the beginning of the 1980s. By 1978, it may be noted, productivity was about double what it had been in 1940, while the index of total output was exactly twice the index for 1940. Correspondingly, the index of total inputs was only 2 or 3 percent higher than in 1940. This is, we may assume, the most dramatic growth in productivity ever to occur on such a sustained and grand scale.

Compared with the 30-year period from 1910 to 1939, the 40-year period from 1940 to 1979 appears as follows (based on 1967 = 100):

Year	Output	Input	Productivity
1940–1944	66.4	102.4	64.6
1975–1978	118.0	101.8	116.5
1940–1944 to 1975–1978, percent increase	78	−0.5	80

Changes in relative prices

The long-term growth in productivity from 1940 to 1978 was accompanied by a long-term decline in the prices received by farmers relative to the prices farmers paid for all inputs used in farm production. Figure 9-1 shows the prices paid and the prices received by farmers from 1910 to 1978 as a percentage of the base period of

Figure 9-1   Prices received and paid by farmers, and the parity ratio. In comparison with the base period, if the change in prices received just matches the change in prices paid, the parity ratio is 100. If prices received are half of what they were in the base period, while prices paid are still at 100, the parity ratio is 50. In the late 1970s, the ratio was between 70 and 75.

1910 to 1914. The vertical scale (which is logarithmic) shows that the prices paid at the end of this period were more than six times as high as the prices paid in 1910–1914. The prices received were about 4½ times the prices of the base period. Thus, the prices received were about three-quarters, or about 75 percent, as high relative to prices paid as they were in the base period. The parity ratio shown in Figure 9-1 is the ratio of prices farmers receive relative to the prices they pay, compared with the base period of 1910 to 1914.

The base period used in Figure 9-1 is actually 1910 to 1914 for prices paid and August 1909 to July 1914 for prices received, the last five years before the outbreak of the First World War. These years marked the end of a 20-year period of upward-trending prices for farm products, which was so favorable to farmers that it has been dubbed the *golden age of American agriculture*. During these 20 years, industrial output in the United States increased by about two and one-half times, and exports of farm products were very stable.

These exports helped to account for a favorable balance of trade for the United States—an excess of exports over imports—which was used in part to pay back some of the capital that had been invested by Europe in the building of the United States. The war in Europe caused the demand for American farm products to skyrocket, and the prices for farm products moved up still more relative to the prices paid by farmers.

But these conditions could not last. The ability of central Europe to buy American farm products was shattered by the terms of the peace treaty, and prices for farm products fell sharply. Figure 9-1 shows that the parity ratio was low throughout the 1920s and 1930s. During the Second World War it rose to a very favorable level for farmers. Beginning about 1948 it began a long-term downward trend. In the 1970s, except for the short boom of 1973–1974, it hovered between 70 and 75 percent of the 1910–1914 base.

Figure 9-2 shows the prices received and paid by farmers as a percentage of 1967 prices, and also shows a comparable price ratio based on 1967. It is noticeable that except for the unusual conditions of 1973–1974, the ratio of prices received to prices paid has tended to slide below the ratio for 1967.

Changes in supply and demand in two markets

Is the continued decline in the parity ratio the logical result of the rising productivity of farming? Or is it merely a coincidence that prices have gone down as productivity has increased? Increasing productivity means that production functions are shifing upward. The demand curves for inputs that are increasing in productivity— or the MRP curves—are shifting to the right, assuming no change in other things. But then the increasing demand for inputs will tend to raise the prices of these inputs, and the increased output will tend to reduce the prices of farm products.

The relative decline in prices of farm products may be visualized in terms of two markets, one for farm products and the other for farm inputs. The farm-product market faces an increasing demand as a result of change in some of the factors mentioned in Chapter 6, especially increases in population and income. Supply increases as a result of advancing technology, or declines in the prices of inputs relative to their productivity. Thus the farm-product market has supply and demand curves that shift constantly to the right.

The market for farm inputs also has its own set of supply and demand curves. The demand is of course derived from the demand

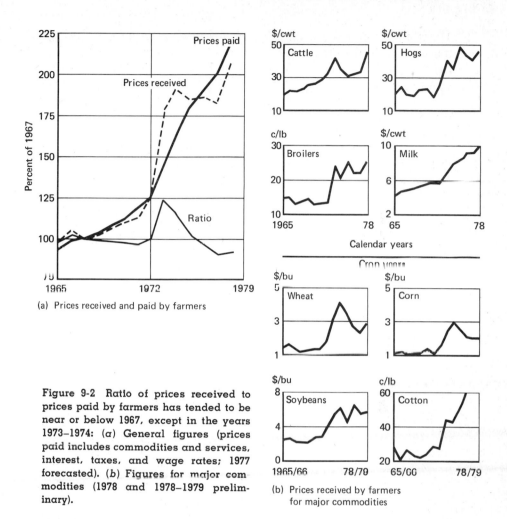

(a) Prices received and paid by farmers

Figure 9-2 Ratio of prices received to prices paid by farmers has tended to be near or below 1967, except in the years 1973–1974: (a) General figures (prices paid includes commodities and services, interest, taxes, and wage rates; 1977 forecasted). (b) Figures for major commodities (1978 and 1978–1979 preliminary).

(b) Prices received by farmers for major commodities

for farm products, and the demands for the individual inputs used in farm production are their own marginal revenue product curves, as was discussed in Chapter 6 (you may wish to refer to Table 6-2 and Figure 6-5). Any advance in the technology of a farm input without a change in the price of the input or a change in farm products, will bring an increase in demand for that input. Farm output will then increase without any change in the prices of inputs or products. If the increase in productivity is great enough, more will be demanded

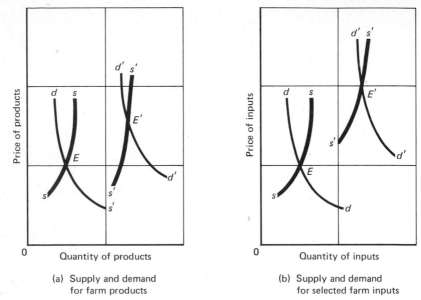

(a) Supply and demand
for farm products

(b) Supply and demand
for selected farm inputs

Figure 9-3   As the years go by, the supply and demand increase from ss to s's' and from dd to d'd' for both (a) farm products and (b) farm inputs. (a) Quantity of farm output increases while price rises from E to E'. (b) Quantity of selected farm inputs increases while price rises from E to E', which is a relatively greater price increase for inputs than for products.

even though prices of these inputs rise relative to the prices of farm products.

Figure 9-3 shows the relative changes in the markets for farm inputs and products. The farm-product market in Figure 9-3a is shown with supply increasing from ss to s's' and demand increasing from dd to d'd'. This allows for an increase in the equilibrium price of farm products from E to E'. The market for inputs that are experiencing relative increases in productivity then shifts as suggested in Figure 9-3b. The shift of the demand curve to the right is a composite of the shifts to the right of individual MRP curves. The supply of certain inputs shifts to the right as technology advances. The suggested shift in Figure 9-3b allows for a greater increase in the price of inputs (from E to E') than in the price of products.

Figure 9-4 illustrates the same changes in terms of the parity ratio. It is drawn on a somewhat different scale, with the price on the vertical axis representing the prices received as a percentage of the prices paid (P_r/P_p). In Figure 9-4 let point E represent the initial equilibrium of supply and demand when the parity ratio is at 100. As

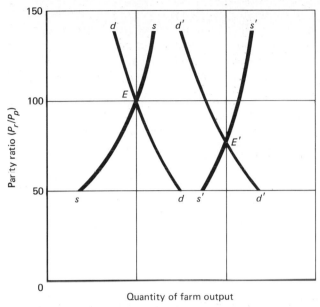

Figure 9-4 Supply and demand for farm products in terms of the parity ratio (prices received divided by prices paid). As the years go by, the increase in demand for farm products generated by population and income growth tends to be less than the increase in supply based on the rising productivity of selected farm inputs. Prices of products fall relative to prices of inputs.

the years go by, the increase in demand generated by growth of population and income tends to be less than the increase in supply based on the rising productivity of selected farm inputs. The parity ratio drops to E'.

Explaining the problem with farm income in terms of productivity and price

The drop in the parity ratio to around 75 in the 1970s does not, however, explain the problem with farm income. How can there be a problem if farmers are buying or using about the same amount of total inputs as in 1940, for example, while the product from these inputs is twice what it was then, and the price of products has dropped by only 25 percent relative to the prices of the inputs? If we select 1940 as a base year for measurement, the value of farm output should be 50 percent greater ($2.00 \times 0.75 = 1.50$) relative to the total expenditure on inputs than it was in 1940. Also, there are fewer than half as many farmers as in 1940 to share the total income.

The answer to the question above is found in the changing mix of inputs, especially the kinds of substitutions that have taken place between and among the inputs of capital and labor in farm production. Most of the inventions have been *labor-saving* according to the following definition:

Definition: An invention is called *labor-saving, capital-saving,* or *neutral* depending on whether it tends to lower the relative share going to labor and management, lower the relative share going to capital inputs and property, or leave the relative shares unchanged.

Figure 9-5 shows the change in the use of selected farm inputs between 1967 and 1978, which is a continuation and in general an acceleration of earlier trends. The decline in the use of real estate or land and the substantial straight-line downward trend in the use of farm labor illustrate the essence of the problem. Increases in the prices of land have not been sufficient to increase the total quantity supplied. The decline in the use of labor means that either (1) the demand for labor, or labor's *MRP*, is shifting to the left as technological advance occurs in other inputs, or (2) *MRC*, or opportunity cost, of labor is rising because of improving opportunities for nonfarm employment, without necessarily any change in the *MRP* curve of labor. If the latter is the case, the problem is well on its way to solution. If the former is the case, a further substantial reduction in "surplus" farm families will be needed to "solve" the problem of farm income. Figure 9-6 suggests that after allowing for inflation, there has been only modest change in *MRC* of farm labor. In other words the major inventions and innovations in farming are still primarily labor-saving, which implies that further reductions in farm labor and management still lie ahead.

Average family income from farming

Figure 9-6 shows the general trend between 1965 and 1978 in disposable income per capita of the farm and nonfarm population as well as the aggregate national net income from farming in current and real (1967) dollars.

This graph "smooths out" the fluctuations in income of individual farm families that are due to the variations in prices and outputs experienced farm by farm. That is, the individual farm family's income will be much more unstable than indicated in Figure 9-6.

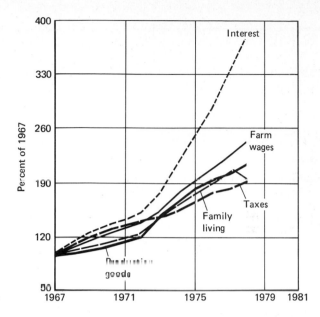

(a) Changes in prices farmers pay

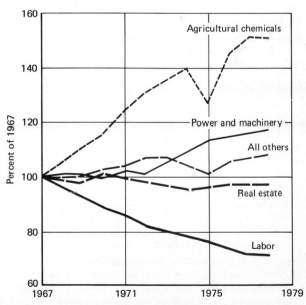

(b) Use of selected farm inputs

Figure 9-5   Trends in use of selected farm inputs from 1967 to 1978. (a) Changes in prices farmers pay (1978 January–June average; taxes include state and local property taxes on farm real estate). (b) Use of selected farm inputs (1978 preliminary).

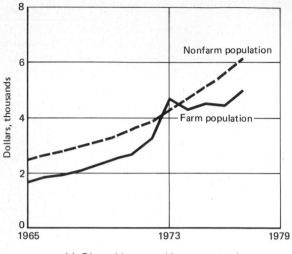

(a) Disposable personal income per capita

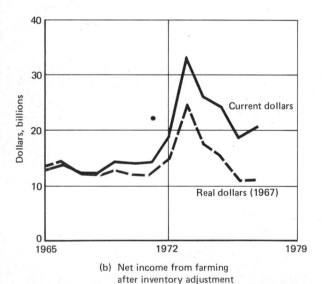

(b) Net income from farming
after inventory adjustment

Figure 9-6   (a) Disposable personal income per capita of the farm and the nonfarm
population has been increasing; but since 1965 there has been little change in the
two categories relative to each other. [*Note:* Disposable personal income represents income from all sources less personal contributions for social insurance and
personal tax and nontax payments. *Source:* Data from *Farm Income Statistics,* July
1978 (ESCS).] (b) Net income from farming (income from all sources) implies an
increase in real income in terms of 1967 dollars because (as shown in Figure 9-5)
the 1977 input of labor was only 71 percent of the 1967 input.

Figure 9-6a tends to suggest that between 1965 and 1977 the disposable personal income per capita of the farm population increased, but not more than the income of the nonfarm population. Figure 9-6b, together with the data from Figure 9-5, indicates that there was a substantial increase in the net income per capita from farming after inventory adjustment in real (1967) dollars. In 1977 the aggregate national income in 1967 dollars was 97 percent of income in 1967, and the 1977 volume of farm labor was only 71 percent of volume in 1967. The net income per capita in real dollars increased by 36 percent (97 ÷ 71 = 136%). This comparison, however, is only part of the story. How was the income distributed among farm families?

Distribution of
farm family income

Figure 9-7 shows the trend in farm family income from all sources, comparing two different sets of farm operators: (1) operators selling $20,000 or more of crops and livestock per year, and (2) operators selling less than $20,000 per year. Perhaps the most important point is the substantial rise in off-farm income of the small-farm group and their low net income from farming.

Figure 9-8 shows the distribution per farm of cash receipts and net income from farming in 1977. In 1977, farms with sales of $200,000 or more represented only 2 percent of all farms but accounted for 35 percent of the total cash receipts and 13 percent of net income. Farms with sales of $40,000 to $99,999 represented 13 percent of all farms and accounted for 26 percent of cash receipts and 13 percent of net income. Farms selling less than $20,000 of farm products represented 69 percent of all farms but accounted for only 11 percent of cash receipts and 21 percent of the total net income from farming.

Profile of a small farm

Table 9-2 gives a more detailed profile of the small farm on the basis of data for 1976. The table emphasizes the very small net income from farming of $2,206, compared with the proprietor's equity per farm of $82,902 and the average income from off-farm sources of $12,963 ($15,169 − $2,206). It must be remembered, however, that the profile of the small farm covers a very wide variety of individual situations, with off-farm income varying very widely from farm to farm.

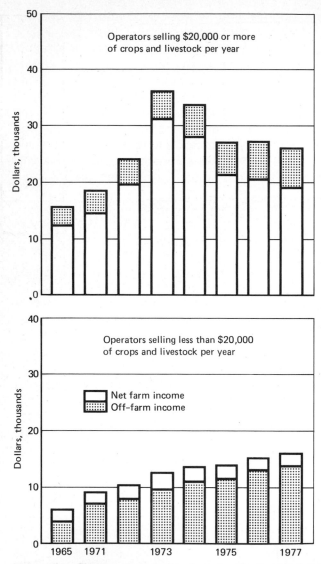

Figure 9-7 Changes in average farm family income (all sources; net income before adjustment for inventory change) from 1965 to 1977. [*Source: Data from Farm Income Statistics, July 1978 (ESCS).*]

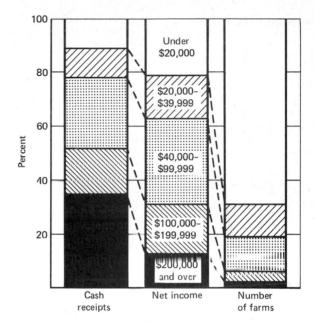

(a) Cash receipts, net income, and farms by sales classes

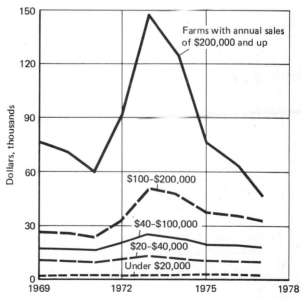

(b) Net income per farm by sales classes

Figure 9-8 (a) Total cash receipts and net income (before adjustment for inventory change) from farming are very unevenly distributed, as is suggested by these data for 1977. (b) Change in net income per farm has tended to fluctuate more widely for the farms in the higher sales classes. [Source: Data from Farm Income Statistics, July 1978 [ESCS].]

Table 9-2   Profile of the small farm. Selected characteristics of farms and farm operators with annual gross sales less than $20,000

Number of farms, 1976	1,917,000
Percent of total number of farms, 1976	71
Percent of total farm assets, 1976	31
Percent of total farm liabilities, 1976	17
Percent of total cash receipts, 1976	11
Percent of total federal payments for farm programs, 1976	25
Average value of cash receipts, 1976, dollars	5,516
Average net income from farming, 1976, dollars	2,206
Proprietor's equity per farm, 1976, dollars	82,902
Average income per farm-operator family, 1976[a], dollars	15,169
Percent of family income from off-farm sources, 1976	85
Percent of families in poverty, 1976	15–20
Average age of operator, 1974	52
Percent of operators under 35 years, 1974	13
Percent of operators 65 years or older, 1974	23
Percent of operators with less than high school education, 1970	67
Percent of operators working off-farm 200 days or more, 1974	40
Percent of operators who are minorities, 1974	4

[a]Estimated by summing realized net income from farming and off-farm income, dividing by the number of farms, and assuming one family per farm.

Source: U.S. Department of Agriculture, Economic Research Service, Farm Income Statistics, July 1978, and Balance Sheet of Farming Sector, September 1977; U.S. Department of Commerce, Bureau of the Census, U.S. Census of Agriculture, 1974, and Current Population Reports, September 1977; and Congressional Budget Office, Public Policy and the Changing Structure of American Agriculture, September 1978.

Summary:
The problem of income

Rising productivity in farming has resulted in a substantial improvement in the incomes of large family farms and larger-than-family farms, even with a continuing decline in the parity ratio. The appreciation of farm real estate has been most pronounced in relation to the restricted supply of land and MRP curves related to land shifting to the right. The return to management and labor has generally increased in real terms on large farms. But many farm firms that have not increased their productivity as much as the average have experienced declining real income from farming as the parity ratio has declined. This has set the stage for continued efforts on the part of some farm groups to involve the federal government in stronger or more effective programs supporting farm prices and incomes. What is the general theory and substance of these programs?

FARM PRICE AND
INCOME PROGRAMS

Intervention by the federal government to raise and stabilize farm prices and incomes has generally not been concentrated on the problems of the small farm, such as by subsidizing their use of inputs or by major aids of an educational or management nature. The federal government has financed special lending programs—sometimes through the Farmers Home Administration—to provide some credit and management help to small farmers who cannot get credit from other sources. It has also provided a number of emergency programs to offset crop failures and other disasters. But these emergency aids are generally available to operators of farms of all sizes, and a relatively small amount of aid has been programmed for the exclusive use of the operators of very small farms.

The reason for this is perhaps not hard to find. Government intervention to raise and stabilize farm prices and incomes is always politically motivated. The record of farmers' movements in the United States in attempting to get help from the government to improve prices and incomes dates back more than 100 years, not counting the long struggles of farm settlers to get free land. The hard times of the 1920s and 1930s brought a great political upheaval as people voted for more government intervention to solve their problems of income. The long downturn in the parity ratio has brought more political agitation and support for programs that could solve price and income problems related to farms.

The potential programs take three general forms: (1) a reduction of the supply of farm products to get higher prices, (2) an increase in the demand by means of more exports of farm products and more food aid to low-income domestic consumers, and (3) direct payments to farmers to supplement their incomes and ensure their compliance with programs to control supply. The three types of programs are generally used together; it is not a question of one or the other, but how much of each. They require, however, separate and distinct analysis.

Option 1:
Reduction and control of supply

The elasticity of demand determines how much the price of a product will increase with a given reduction in supply, or how much supply must be reduced to get a certain price increase. The demand for wheat is very inelastic in the domestic market, while the demand for

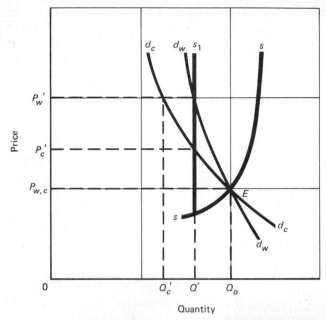

Figure 9-9   Elasticity of demand determines how much output must be reduced to achieve a certain increase in price; or how much a given cut in production will increase price. Curve ss is supply for wheat, corn, or cotton; $d_w d_w$ is demand for wheat; and $d_c d_c$ is the demand for corn, or cotton. (a) A cut in output from Q to Q' will raise the price of wheat from the original equilibrium E to P'_w, while the price of corn or cotton will rise only to P'_c with the same cut in production. (b) Corn or cotton production will have to be cut back to Q'_c to raise the price the equivalent of P'_w.

corn or cotton is not so inelastic (see Tables 7-2 and 7-3). A given reduction in supply will have a greater effect on the price of wheat than on the price of corn or cotton. Or the supply of corn or cotton must be reduced more than the supply of wheat to get the same price increase. This is shown in Figure 9-9.

EXPORT PRODUCTS

The problems of price support are more difficult for a major commodity that is exported—such as wheat, corn, or cotton—than for a commodity that is not. If the price of corn is to be raised from $120 to $160 per ton (from $3 to $4 a bushel), for example, and the United States exports one-quarter of a crop of 160 million tons, or 40 million tons (one-quarter of 6.4 billion bushels, or 1.6 billion bushels), the government will have to provide a subsidy of $1.6 billion in addition to the costs of control of production. If it does not provide such a subsidy, the United States will lose most if not all of its export sales. In that case, the program would fail in its major goal of price support.

Exporters will have to be paid at least the difference between net prices in export markets (dockside prices less marketing and transportation costs) and American support prices in order to maintain exports. Thus, American consumers will have to pay higher prices for the livestock produced with corn, provide the tax money to control the production of corn, and subsidize the exports. The Emergency Feed Grain Program adopted in 1961 and continued until 1973 cost about $1.5 billion per year by the end of the 1960s in price-support payments and land-diversion payments alone, not counting the cost of export subsidies and the efffects of the program on domestic food prices.[1]

Export subsidies have been combined with price supports and production controls to keep American farm products "competitive" in foreign markets. But they have not always been sufficient to stabilize the share of the world market supplied by American agriculture. In the case of cotton, for example, in the four years between 1929 and 1932 just before establishment of production control under the Agricultural Adjustment Act of 1933, exports of cotton averaged 7.6 million bales per year. Total production outside the United States averaged 11.6 million bales. Forty years later, in the early 1970s, exports were averaging less than 5 million bales a year. Total production outside the United States had increased to nearly 50 million bales a year. That is, despite the billions of dollars spent to keep American cotton "competitive" in world markets, the combination of price supports and production controls tended to price it out of world markets. This suggests that there is a delicate balance between price supports and export subsidies that must be maintained if a crop under production control is to maintain its share of the export market.

CROPS OR COMMODITIES
ON AN IMPORT BASIS

For commodities such as sugar and wool, which are both produced domestically and imported, the problem of controlling supply is

[1]Harold G. Halcrow, *Food Policy for America*, McGraw-Hill Book Company, New York, 1977, p. 314.

quite different. Imports occur because American producers do not enjoy a cost advantage over other major producing areas of the world. The government may simply regulate imports by means of a tariff or quota to establish the price it wants. In addition, it can use tariff receipts to finance direct payments to producers, which has been done in the United States since 1934 for sugar and since 1954 for wool.

This type of program can be just as expensive for consumers as the huge subsidies required for the export crops. It has been estimated, for example, that the cost of the sugar program to American consumers has been $500 million to $800 million annually in various selected years, although the benefits to producers are much smaller because most of the subsidy is needed to compensate for their high costs of production.[2] Similarly, in the American wool program the costs to consumers far exceed the demonstrated benefits to American producers of wool. The major costs are hidden in the higher prices paid for sugar and wool products, which are not readily apparent to the consumer.

Option 2:
Supplements to
or subsidization of demand

The government has various ways of supplementing or subsidizing market demand. It may choose to (1) subsidize exports as has just been discussed, which is a way of supplementing or subsidizing demand, (2) subsidize the demand of consumers, such as by food stamps, (3) set loan rates on farm commodities above the equilibrium market price, and move a portion of the crop into storage, or (4) purchase commodities outright and sell them abroad at a discount or give them away as part of an emergency program.

Figure 9-10 illustrates the general principle. The market is in equilibrium initially at E, with price and quantity at P and Q. To get an equilibrium price of P' the government will have to increase demand from dd to $d'd'$ by taking the quantity equal to $Q'' - Q'$ off the market. How much must be taken off the market depends on the elasticity of both demand and supply and whether there is a supply-control program accompanying the program for expansion of demand. In Figure 9-10, if the government controls the quantity sup-

[2]D. Gale Johnson, *The United States Sugar Program: Large Costs and Small Benefits*, The American Enterprise Institute, Washington, D.C., 1974.

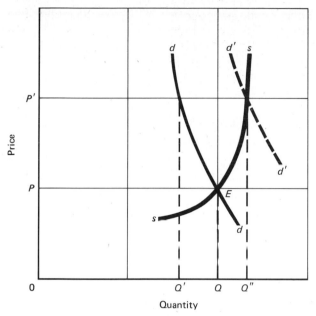

Figure 9-10   When the government attempts to raise prices from *P* to *P'* by supplementing or subsidizing demand, it must take quantity *Q″* − *Q'* off the market. Demand, in effect, increases from *dd* to *d'd'*. This program may also be combined with reduction and control of supply.

plied at *Q* instead of letting it rise to *Q″*, there will be less product to take off the market, equal to *Q* − *Q'*.

Important issues are involved in the question of using a government storage program to stabilize prices. The concept of the *ever-normal granary*—with some supplies moving into storage during years of large crops and moving out during years of small crops—has been an attractive idea for a long time. Planners are also attracted to the concept of using storage in the United States to maintain our normal exports during years of small crops or to increase exports in years of strong foreign demand. Prices can be stabilized to a considerable degree by such a program, and exports can be increased over time. Recent computer-assisted studies have shown that such beneficial results can be achieved, provided the political problems of management of programs are brought under control.[3]

[3]Takashi Takayama, Hideo Hashimoto, and Harold G. Halcrow, *Stabilizing the World Food Economy*, University of Illinois at Urbana-Champaign, manuscript in process.

Public expenditures for food assistance have an important advantage over programs to control supply in that they are more humanitarian. Food is being distributed to people in need rather than being destroyed; on this account such programs have received increasing support (Figure 9-11).

It is important to understand that the criticisms leveled at programs for food assistance or subsidy are generally directed not at the idea or concept but at the problems of administration and management. The public money spent for food stamps, school lunches, and the like apparently has filled an important need. In 1978, the money appropriated for food stamps accounted for about 3 percent of all food expenditures in the United States. Although this did not increase the quantity demanded by as much as 3 percent, it had both an important income effect on recipients and a substitution effect in favor of food (Figure 9-12).

Option 3: Direct payments to farmers, or a producer-consumer price differential

A producer-consumer price differential involves paying an artificially high price to farmers, and reselling the commodity to consumers at whatever lower price the market brings. The government of course loses the difference. In lieu of this, the government may use direct payments to farmers. This method leaves both producers' and consumers' prices where they were but pays farmers directly to bring the return per unit up to the support level. Or the government may pay part of the purchase price of a food stamp program, a school lunch program, or a donation of food in a general relief program.

The options are illustrated in Figure 9-13. Before the beginning of the program the market is in equilibrium at E, or at P and Q. If P' is the target level for compensation, returns may be established at this level by stabilizing the quantity supplied at Q and making payments to farmers equal to (P' minus P) times Q. If the government does not control the quantity supplied, it will have to make much larger payments equal to (P' minus P'') times Q'. This illustrates why a program of direct payments to farmers is normally accompanied by a program to control the quantity supplied.

Direct payments to farmers in lieu of price supports permit the market to clear. There are no "surpluses," farm income is supported, and consumers get the advantage of a low price. But the program can also be very expensive. Under the Wheat-Cotton Act of

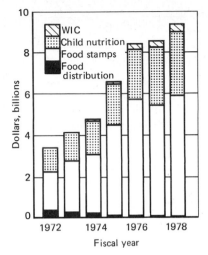

(a) U.S.D.A. funding for food assistance

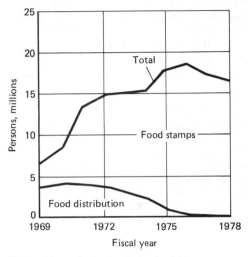

(b) Participants in the family food assistance programs

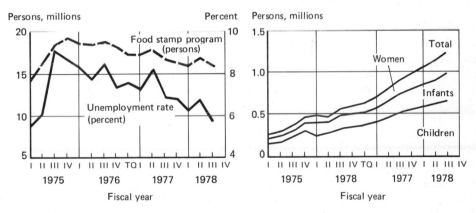

(c) Unemployment rate and participation in the food stamp program

(d) Participants in WIC program

Figure 9-11 Expenditures on food assistance programs in the United States generally grew throughout the 1970s, as the philosophy of supplementing the demand of consumers took precedence over supply control. (*Notes:* 1978 preliminary; *TQ* = transitional quarter; *WIC* = supplemental food program for women, infants, and children.)

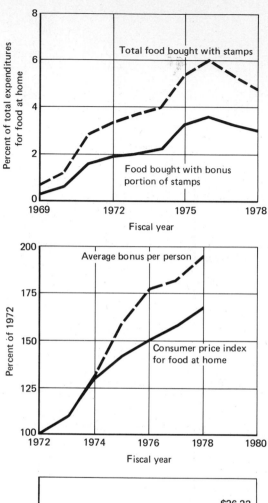

(a) Food at home bought
    with food stamps,
    United States

(b) Changes in food prices
    and food stamp bonus

(c) Average monthly food
    stamp bonus per person

Figure 9-12 By 1978 about 3 percent of the total food bought by American consumers was bought with the bonus portion of food stamps, while from 4 to 5 percent of all food was bought with food stamps. The net increase in demand is less than 3 percent, however, as consumers are not forced to maintain their own cash outlay for food. (*Notes:* 1978 preliminary; *b* is based on July–June average; bonus in *c* is portion of food stamp allotment paid by U.S.D.A.)

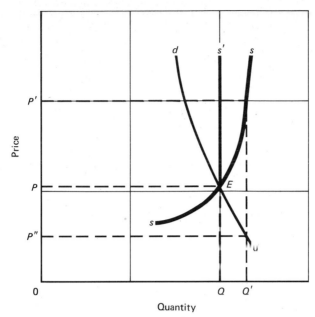

Figure 9-13 Production and level of compensation under a direct-payment program. If the government combines control of supply with direct payments, it must
pay to farmers the difference of $P' - P$ times Q, to raise the level of compensation
from P to P'. If control of supply is not part of the program, then the government
must pay the difference of $P' - P''$ times Q' to raise the level of compensation from
P to P'.

1964, for example, which provided for direct payments in lieu of
price supports combined with control of supply, the direct cost of
the wheat program rose to about $600 million annually by the end
of the 1960s, not counting other smaller payments for related land-
retirement programs. Direct payments under the cotton program
rose to more than $750 million annually. These were neccessary to
get cotton producers to comply with the program. But since payments were distributed to growers in direct proportion to their allot-
ted production, and there are some very large cotton producers,
some of the very large payments to a small number of growers
became the subject of editorial criticism and protest. Succeeding
agricultural acts placed limits on the amount that could be paid to
an individual producer, but the payments could not be limited very
severely without discouraging producers from complying with the
program and reducing their output.

EVALUATION OF PROGRAMS

As the parity ratio declines, the political pressures generally increase for programs to raise and stabilize farm prices and incomes. The first strong surge began in the early 1920s and grew throughout the decade. In 1932, an avalanche of votes for farm relief helped sweep Franklin Roosevelt's New Deal into office to establish programs that have continued to the present day. In the 1950s, the 1960s, and again in the late 1970s declines in the parity ratio brought more political activity and support for new or stronger programs. Generally, these have all involved in one way or another the basic concepts: control of supply, supplements to or subsidization of demand by government, and direct payments to maintain returns to producers at a higher level than the price paid by consumers.

Political successes and failures

The ideas for programs have had varying degrees of acceptance and success or failure. In 1922, as was noted, the Capper-Volstead Act was passed to give a new charter for farmers' cooperatives. Although cooperatives blossomed under this act, efforts to establish cooperatives as strong nationwide bargaining associations were not successful either then or in more recent years. Efforts to subsidize exports were pushed vigorously in the 1920s. Bills to implement a program passed in Congress twice, but they were vetoed by President Coolidge. In the 1930s, programs for control of supply rose to dominate the efforts of government, but efforts to establish subsidy programs for exports were rejected by President Roosevelt largely on the grounds that they would be inconsistent with the broader-based political efforts of the New Deal to revive and expand world trade. During the Second World War and the early postwar years the United States helped finance sales and relief programs abroad, but subsidy of exports did not become a major program until the mid-1950s. Even then it was almost submerged in the continuing conflict over production adjustment, or control of supply through limitation of crops.

Programs for limitation of crops

Beginning with the act of 1933, control of supply through limitation of crops has been emphasized as the major program for supporting farm incomes. Two methods of crop limitation have been used. One

THE MORROW PLOTS
AMERICA'S OLDEST
EXPERIMENT FIELD
ESTABLISHED IN 1876

Public support for experimental work, demonstration, and education has been a vital force in the growth and development of agriculture. The occasion for this picture was the dedication of these plots as a national monument. *Left to right,* M. D. Thorne, Head of Agronomy; J. W. Peltason, Chancellor; and O. G. Bentley, Dean of the College of Agriculture, University of Illinois at Urbana-Champaign.

method is to determine specific allotments on each farm for each crop in the program, such as wheat, corn, cotton, tobacco, and rice. The allotment is set at a specific percentage—such as 80 or 90 percent—of the amount of land determined to be seeded to that crop in a specified base period. A farmer who complies with a program is paid so much per acre—this is sometimes called an *allotment payment*—to compensate for the income lost by reducing the amount of land seeded. The payment is set according to the average yield verified for the farm in the base period. The other method is to base payments on the land that is taken out of production, retired, or set aside, with payments set according to the productivity of the land or the specified conservation practice carried out.

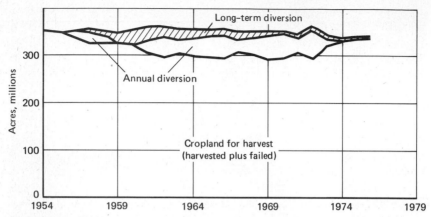

Figure 9-14 The largest land diversion or land retirement since the 1930s was carried out under the Soil Bank Program of 1956, the Emergency Feed Grain Program of 1961, and the Wheat-Cotton Act of 1964. (*Note:* prior to 1956, acreage allotment provisions effectively limited the acreage that could be planted to basic crops, including wheat, corn, and cotton, but they had little effect on total crop acreage. *Source:* 1976 data from June SRS crop report.)

Soil Bank Program

The Agricultural Act of 1956, which established the so-called *Soil Bank*, provided for both of these methods. Under an *acreage reserve* farmers were paid for an annual diversion of part of their land from wheat, cotton, corn, tabacco, peanuts, and rice without increasing the amount of land planted to other crops. Under a *conservation reserve* farmers were paid for a long-term diversion, under contract (usually 5 or 10 years), of a specified amount of cropland to designated soil-conserving uses. Although the Soil Bank Program had been planned in order to divert 60 million acres or more of land from crops each year, it was funded at a much lower level, and the total diversion under the program was correspondingly smaller. The Emergency Feed Grain Act of 1961, designed especially to divert land away from production of feed grains, greatly expanded payments to farmers for taking land out of production. The Wheat-Cotton Act of 1964 accomplished a similar purpose for those crops. The annual appropriations under these and succeeding acts achieved a large diversion of cropland up to 1973 (Figure 9-14).

Nonrecourse loans

Generally, farmers who comply with a program of crop limitation are eligible to apply for a loan on a commodity held in government-approved sealed storage. The maximum loan that may be secured is specified in the act or announced by the Secretary of Agriculture. If the market price falls below the loan level. the farmer may deliver the commodity to the government in full satisfaction of the loan. In such case, there is no recourse by the government for full collection. Hence, this has been called a *nonrecourse loan*. Generally, there have been no specific goals on the part of the government in regard to the magnitude of storage stocks and no specific policy or plan for their management. Stocks have been built up when price supports were at or above market equilibrium levels and have been reduced as the government attempted to reduce its cost of holding stocks (Figure 9-15). Thus, the government has appeared as a reluctant participant in a reserve program by reducing its stocks to nearly zero when the opportunity has occurred. In the Agricultural Act of 1977 however, a modest goal was set for reserves of wheat and feed grains. Apparently the intent of Congress was to use stock accumulation as a specific means for support of prices and to establish emergency minimum stocks to offset years when crops are bad.

· Government storage may be used to (1) stabilize supply by accumulating inventories in years of large crops and reducing inventories in years of poor crops, (2) stabilize prices by accumulating stocks in times of price weakness and liquidating stocks in times of

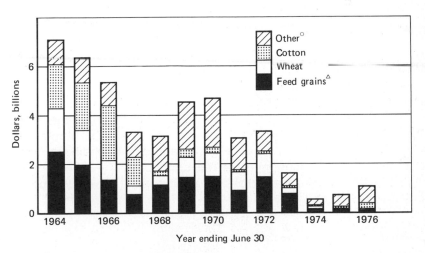

°Primarily dairy products and tobacco.
△Includes corn, barley, grain sorghums, oats, and rye.

Figure 9-15 Value of stocks held by the United States Commodity Credit Corporation (C.C.C), under price-support inventories and loans.

price inflation, or (3) stabilize the flow of commodities for domestic consumption and export. On balance, storage programs can help stabilize farm income if inventories are accumlated in years of large crops and sold in years of small crops. Some of the cost incurred by the government can be offset by accumulating inventories when prices are low and selling when prices are high. The total volume of exports can be increased over time by using storage to maintain an export capability in years of small crops as well as in years of large crops. As a general rule, the government must have a way of marketing accumulated inventories or the reduction of inventories will depress market prices just as acquisition stimulated prices.

Marketing quotas

A marketing quota sets the maximum amount of a commodity that a farmer can sell without incurring a penalty. In 1934, the first marketing quotas were authorized in the Bankhead Cotton Control Act and the Kerr-Smith Act for tobacco. The cotton act required approval by referendum by two-thirds of the producers of cotton before a program of quota allotments could go into effect. The tobacco act required agreement from three-fourths of tobacco growers. In case of an affirmative vote the quota was introduced by allotting to each producer certificates which, when accompanying the crop, would exempt the crop from a sales tax that the Secretary of Agriculture was directed to levy.

Quota programs are generally voluntary in principle and almost compulsory in practice. Under the Bankhead Act, for example, when there was an affirmative vote on the adoption of quotas, a tax of 50 percent ad valorem was placed on all cotton ginned. Certificates of tax exemption were issued to growers to cover each participant's quota. Since 1934, provisions for quotas have been included in each of the general agricultural acts, and the specific requirements have been varied according to circumstances. In all, a large number of commodities have been made eligible, and provisions have been adjusted to fit the economics of the commodity. In spite of their obvious advantages for control of market supply, however, quotas have been used only sparingly.

Federal marketing agreements and orders

Marketing agreements and orders have the general purpose of influencing prices by regulating the timing, volume, and sometimes quality of the commodities marketed. They have been used most for milk, fruits, and vegetables. Although most orders are issued under a federal statute, state laws may also apply. In California, for example, the marketing of milk is regulated under a special state law, while the federal law permits the establishment of minimum prices for producers. Under California statutes any agricultural commodity is eligible to be covered under an order, while the federal statutes exclude some commodities.

Orders are usually written for a single commodity produced in a specific area for either a definite or indefinite period of time, and the orders are subject to amendment, suspension, or termination. Once approved, an order is binding on all firms in an industry, with producers and handlers generally bearing most if not all of the direct operating and administrative costs. The gain to producers in an order program depends on the effectiveness of the regulation and control of supply and the existence of an inelastic demand for the commodity.

MARKETING ORDERS FOR FLUID MILK

Each of the major milk markets in the United States is covered by a marketing order. The portion of grade A milk that is demanded for fluid consumption at the price set and regulated by the order is sold as class I. Milk that is not bought for fluid use is placed in class II or class III for manufacturing butter, cheese, nonfat dry milk powder, and evaporated milk. The price of class II and class III milk is supported by the federal government through purchase of products that are not bought by manufacturers or dealers at the level of price support.

Dairy farmers selling in federal order markets receive a *blend* price, which is the weighted average of the price paid by dairy companies for milk for both fluid and nonfluid uses. The government then purchases and stores the "surplus" that is not bought at the level of the federal price support. From 1949–1950 to 1972–1973, after which the demand temporarily made action unnecessary, total purchases were almost $8 billion, about 5 percent of total milk production. This was diverted into relief programs overseas, domestic school lunch and welfare programs, and American military and veterans' hospitals. This, in essence, involves the government in a producer-consumer price differential program for consumers who are the recipients of the government stocks, while the higher prices resulting from control of supply are passed on directly to the unsubsidized consumers.

MARKETING ORDERS FOR
FRUITS AND VEGETABLES

Agreements and orders have been used extensively to regulate the marketing of fruits and vegetables as a supplement to competitive markets rather than a substitute for them. Generally, an order applies to a specified production or marketing area and, in contrast to an order for fluid milk, is normally covered by a prior voluntary agreement—a contract entered into by the Secretary of Agriculture with the handlers of a particular commodity to regulate the marketing of that commodity. Since an agreement is binding only on those who sign it, an agreement alone is seldom effective and is useful mainly as a basis for promulgating an order. A marketing order is binding on all handlers of a commodity in the specified production and marketing area regardless of whether they have signed an agreement, provided it has been approved in referendum by at least two-thirds of the producers or by those who produce at least two-thirds of the total volume of a commodity. The Secretary may propose an order without a prior agreement, although—for political reasons—this generally is not done.

A federal agreement and order for a fruit or vegetable may permit or provide for any one or all of the following:

1. Specification of grades, size, quality, or maturity of the commodity that handlers may ship to market
2. Allotment of the amount each handler may purchase or handle on behalf of any and all producers
3. Establishment of the quantity of the commodity that may be shipped to market during any specified period
4. Establishment of methods for determining the extent of any surplus in order to control and dispose of the surplus and equalize the burden of elimination of surplus among producers and handlers
5. Establishment of a reserve pool of the product
6. Inspection of the commodity
7. Specification of the size, capacity, weight, dimensions, or pack of the container used in handling the commodity[4]

In addition, miscellaneous provisions may authorize actions to prohibit certain unfair trade practices in interstate commerce or to

[4]U.S. Department of Agriculture, *Self-Help Stabilization Programs with Use of Marketing Agreements and Orders*, Agriculture Stabilization and Conservation Service, PA-479, November 1961, p. 4.

coordinate federal orders with the orders of individual states. Although controls over marketing vary somewhat among the states, states with enabling legislation do not generally attempt to control the volume of supplies going to market, but limit their activity to regulation of quality, size, or pack; control of advertising and sales promotion; and support of research and investigation. The federal legislation is restricted primarily to fruits and vegetables for fresh shipment. Most production for canning or freezing is excluded. Enforcement of sanitary standards and other standards for protection of consumers is not, of course, dependent on the existence of an agreement or order.

In general, it may be said that the wise design of programs for a marketing agreement and order depends on the staff of the Secretary of Agriculture and on the corresponding state officials. Positive benefits must be weighed against the various costs and disruptions that an order imposes. Usually orders are most applicable and most popular where the quantity or quality of a perishable crop varies from season to season, where production is highly localized, where demand is relatively inelastic, where production is not dominated by a few large firms who may continue as oligopolists or may vertically integrate through the marketing chain, or where a strong cooperative has great influence on the marketing of the product and growers thus want the protection of an order. Where surplus diversion is to be undertaken, an order is sometimes helpful for attaining market order and stability.

Although we cannot compare directly the various effects of programs for controlling supply, it may be evident that they tend to complement each other. There are general benefits in obtaining more stable markets, and farmers benefit from increasing stability and higher prices. But there is a waste of resources and a loss in efficiency as resources are withdrawn from production or diverted to a use that does not reflect market supply and demand. Government intervention in product markets must be held to modest levels if agriculture is to grow and prosper in the future.

SUMMARY

As farm productivity has increased, prices received by farmers have followed a downward trend relative to prices paid. Some farmers with a high rate of productivity increase have prospered, while many farm families who have had lower rates of productivity increase have failed or left farming. Many small family farms now get a very small part of their total income from farming; the rates of return as a percentage of farm equity are very low, and the major income gains of such farms in recent years have come from increasing off-farm income. The net income of large farms, measured in real terms, has generally increased. These farms have growing internal economies of large scale. They are in a position to benefit from the external economies of large scale associated with developments in agribusiness, and these benefits may increase in the future.

The three general policy options for dealing with product markets are (1) reduction and control of supply, (2) supplementation or subsidization of demand, and (3) direct payments. Although any one of the programs may be used alone, this is seldom the case, and one type of intervention tends to encourage another. Thus, direct payments are used to implement a program for reduction and control of supply. Also, direct payments to producers in lieu of price supports are a way of keeping consumer prices low, thus increasing the quantity demanded.

The main shortcoming of government policy in the farm-product markets is its direction toward supporting farm prices and incomes in the short run rather than alleviating the problems of allocation of resources that are the fundamental cause of low income. Subsidies are allocated roughly in proportion to farm output rather than proportioned to need criteria or inversely proportional to income. Most of the policy tends to be output-restricting and generally cost-increasing or wasteful of resources. Beyond the strictly short run, if the policy is successful in supporting prices above the competitive market equilibrium, the cost of production will rise to equal the established price. A program of production control that is continued indefinitely without other resource adjustments will in the end fail to improve the net incomes of farmers while representing a continuing cost to consumers.

IMPORTANT TERMS
AND CONCEPTS

Productivity of farm resources

Index of farm productivity

Parity ratio

Labor-saving, capital-saving, and neutral innovations

Disposable income of the farm and nonfarm population

Distribution of farm family income

Profile of a small farm

Farm price and income programs

Option 1: Reduction and control of supply

Option 2: Supplements to or subsidization of demand

Option 3: Direct payments to farmers, or a producer-consumer price differential

Acreage allotment program

Soil Bank Program

Nonrecourse loans

Marketing quota

Federal marketing agreements and orders

LOOKING AHEAD

Chapter 10 will be concerned with exports and the world food economy. Although this deals with the long view rather than the short, it must be recognized that short-term policies dealing with production and trade are crucial. In the long view, policy must move away from restriction of output and other impediments and toward expanded production and trade. This is dictated by the growth of markets for agricultural products around the world and the great benefits to be gained by viewing agriculture in terms of its world potential through development and trade.

QUESTIONS AND EXERCISES

1. Define *productivity*. How fast did the productivity of farming in the United States change between 1910 and 1940? Between 1940 and 1980? In general terms, what are the reasons for these differences in the rates of change?

2. What is the parity ratio? What has been its general direction of change since 1945? What factors would cause it to change in this direction?

3. Explain how some farmers have become more and more prosperous even as the parity ratio has fallen. If all farmers do not experience the same rate of increase in productivity, how will a declining parity ratio affect the distribution of farm income?

4. How does an increase in productivity change the *MRP* curve for an input that is increasing in productivity, assuming no change in other things? How does a "labor-saving" invention change the share of total income that goes to labor?

5. How does an increase in the off-farm income of families on small farms tend to change the *MRC* of their labor in farming? Does it also change the *MRP* of their labor in farming? Why, or why not?

6. What are the three main options for government intervention in farm-product markets? What are the advantages and disadvantages of each (a) to farmers, (b) to government, and (c) to consumers?

7. Why is it more difficult for the government to raise prices for a commodity that is exported than for a commodity that is imported? Give an example. How does the elasticity of demand influence the ease or difficulty of carrying out a program?

8. What are the welfare, or humanitarian, advantages of programs to subsidize food and create demand over programs to control supply?

9. What is the main advantage of using a direct payment in lieu of price support as a means of supplementing farm income? The main disadvantage? Why does control of production tend to be involved in each program?

10. What is a nonrecourse loan? A marketing quota? A marketing order?

10. INTERNATIONAL TRADE AND DEVELOPMENT

10. INTERNATIONAL TRADE AND DEVELOPMENT

> **"The master economist must study the present in the light of the past for the purposes of the future."**

> *John Maynard Keynes*

John Maynard Keynes (1883–1946), whose economic theories on employment, interest, and money are the foundation of the so-called *Keynesian revolution* in economic theory, stressed the fact that competence in economics requires the development of broad vision as well as rigorous analytical ability. This thought dominates Chapter 10 as we study the basis for trade and the implications of international trade in agricultural products for economic progress, stability, and growth.

N ow that we have discussed national problems of farm income and programs supporting farm income, let us turn our attention to international trade and development. This chapter links American agriculture more specifically to the rest of the world, showing how it has become increasingly more dependent on international trade for growth and prosperity. This chapter also shows the United States has become increasingly dependent on the surplus of exports generated by agriculture to settle its international payments accounts. How has all this happened, and what are the implications for the future?

IN THIS CHAPTER

1. You will see the economic basis for international trade and some of the results of trade and development policies.
2. You will learn about efforts being made to expand trade by reduction of tariffs and nontariff barriers to trade.
3. You will be able to relate alternatives in trade in agricultural products to economic progress, market stability, and growth.

ECONOMIC BASIS FOR TRADE

The economic basis for all trade between two states (or individuals, firms, nations, etc.) is embodied in the principle of *comparative advantage*, which states that *whether or not one of two states is absolutely more efficient in the production of every product than the other, if each specializes in the products in which it has the greatest relative efficiency, trade will be mutually beneficial to both states*.

On the basis of this principle, we should expect that technological advance in agriculture would increase the benefits from specialization and trade. Growing world markets for farm food products should greatly increase the importance of trade, other things being equal. We should expect this to be especially true of the United States, where the rapidly advancing productivity of agriculture, combined with the relatively slow growth of domestic demand for farm products, tends to create an ever larger "surplus" for export. Is this what has happened? If so, what are the implications?

Trade transformation of the 1970s

The 1970s witnessed a fundamental transformation in agricultural trade. Up to 1972, American farm exports were less than $7 billion a year. Also, much of this amount was financed by the government, either through the foreign aid programs of Public Law 480 or with the aid of subsidies for *commercial* exports. Beginning in 1961 for feed gains and 1964 for wheat and cotton, the United States shifted from high price supports, which restricted exports, to lower supports and direct payments to farmers.

This was intended to facilitate exports. But even with this change in the law and with substantial subsidies for exports, exports of farm food products largely failed to increase. Instead, they stabilized at around 13 to 14 percent of the total value of farm marketings, which meant that the major part of the product from the rapidly increasing productivity of agriculture had to clear through the domestic market. The prices of farm products continued to drop relatively, as we have seen, and consumer expenditures on food dropped to a historic low, averaging about 16 percent of the total disposable income of consumers nationally.

Starting in 1971, several things began to shift farm food markets away from this stable pattern. First and of more than temporary importance, growing deficits in the American balance of international payments and falling American gold reserves reached crisis proportions. This forced the United States to abandon the gold standard, which fixed the value of the dollar at $35 per ounce of gold. The dollar was devalued—that is, made cheaper—by raising the price of gold. It was devalued by 8 percent in August 1971 and by another 10 percent in February 1973. Finally, it was allowed to float without a fixed price in gold. Subsequently, by the end of the 1970s the price of gold had soared to more than $400 an ounce. There were then upward revaluations of the currencies of other countries in exchange for the dollar, especially among the countries of the European Economic Community and Japan. This tended to reduce the prices of American exports, including American farm food exports, in terms of the importing nations' currency.

Second, in the spring of 1972 the Soviet Union broke its historic policy of not importing grain and began to buy more wheat and feed grains abroad to carry out its policy of improving its supply of food. Back to 1967 at least, wheat production in the Soviet Union had generally held steady in contrast to Soviet plans to increase production. Feed grains also generally failed to increase to the extent called for in Soviet plans. Subsequent Soviet purchases of wheat and feed grains in the United States totaled some 18 million tons in the next 12 to 18 months. Although the Soviet Union did not offer a very stable or reliable market for American farm exports, in this instance and later in the 1970s it added significantly to the American market for farm exports.

Between the fiscal years 1971 and 1973, total American exports of farm products expanded sharply. Exports of wheat and flour in grain equivalent increased from 17 to 32 million tons. Total exports of feed grains increased from 21 to 44 million tons. Soybean exports, which had been running about 11 to 12 million tons, increased to nearly 15 million tons (Figures 10-1, 10-2, and 10-3).

By the end of the 1970s, total American agricultural exports accounted for almost one-third of the total harvested crop area of the United States, including crops and livestock products in terms of crop equivalent (Figure 10-4). Exports accounted for almost three-fourths of the rice crop, more than half of wheat and soybean crops, almost 40 percent of cotton and tobacco crops, and almost 30 percent of the rapidly increasing output of corn (Figure 10-5).

In terms of value, American agricultural exports increased by some five to six times in the 1970s, with the greatest increases occurring in products for which American farmers are presumed to have important comparative advantages in production and marketing (Figure 10-6). By the end of the 1970s, the trade balance of agricultural exports less imports was about $14 billion to $15 billion annually, compared with about $1 billion at the beginning of the decade. This allows for some $6 billion for imports, which are largely not "competitive" with American agriculture, such as coffee, cocoa, rubber, and bananas. If these imports are not counted against the trade balance of agriculture, the net agricultural contribution to the balance of trade would be more than $20 billion annually (Figure 10-7).

So far, the major increases in American exports involve two types of countries. First and by far the greatest in terms of value are exports to the most highly industrialized nations: Japan, West Germany, the Netherlands, Canada, and the United Kingdom. Second are exports to nations that are developing or growing industrially and whose agriculture is relativley limited in terms of technology or natural resources: the Soviet Union, Korea, Italy, Spain, Mexico, Taiwan, Egypt, and Belgium-Luxembourg (Figure 10-8). Exports to the O.P.E.C. nations (not shown in Figure 10-8) were about $2 billion in 1977–1978, compared with $0.4 billion in 1972. This of course reflects dietary improvement and the effects of growing earnings of foreign exchange in these countries.

The historic shift in American exports raises a number of questions. Was the trade transformation of the 1970s merely the result of agricultural productivity in the importing countries lagging behind increases in the productivity of other economic sectors? Or was devaluation of the American dollar and the subsequent changes in

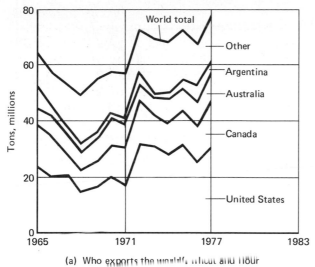

(a) Who exports the world's wheat and flour

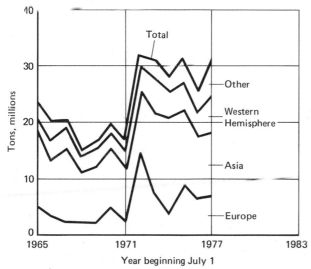

Year beginning July 1

(b) Where United states wheat
and flour exports go

Figure 10-1   Total wheat and flour exports of the United States doubled between
1971 and 1972, and have tended to continue at the new higher level. (a) World
exporters. (*Note:* Year beginning July 1 includes wheat equivalent of flour and
products; 1977 preliminary.) (b) Destinations of United States flour exports. (*Note:*
1977 preliminary.)

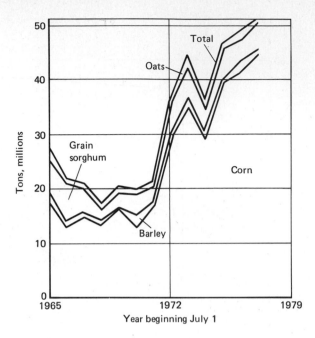

(a) By commodity

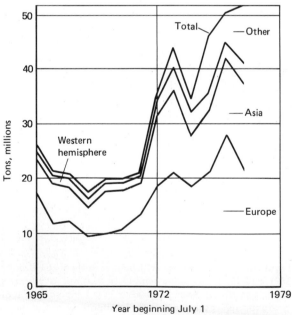

(b) By destination

Figure 10-2 Total exports of feed grains from the United States increased in the 1970s, with corn being the dominant export to all major destinations. (a) By commodity. (*Note:* Includes cornmeal, oatmeal, and barley malt; 1977 preliminary.) (b) By destination.

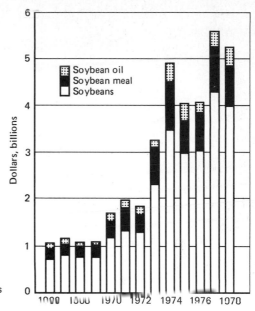

(a) United States exports of soybeans
and products

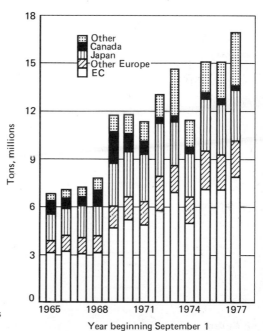

(b) Where the United States exports
its soybeans

Year beginning September 1

Figure 10-3 Increases in exports of soybeans have constituted one of the most
significant growth factors for American agriculture. (*a*) United States exports of
soybeans and soybean products. (*Note:* Fiscal year beginning October 1; 1978,
October–June.) (*b*) Destinations. (*Note:* 1977, September 1–June 30.)

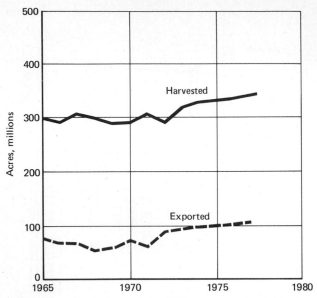

Figure 10-4 By the end of the 1970s, exports of farm food products accounted for almost one-third of the product from harvested acres. (*Note:* "Exported" includes feed required to produce exported livestock products.)

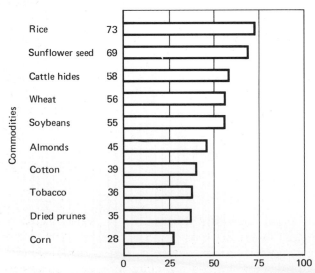

Figure 10-5 Percent of farm production exported by the United States is highest among those commodities where American farmers enjoy comparative advantages in production. (*Note:* Year ending September 30, 1978, partially estimated; soybeans include bean equivalent of meal and oil.)

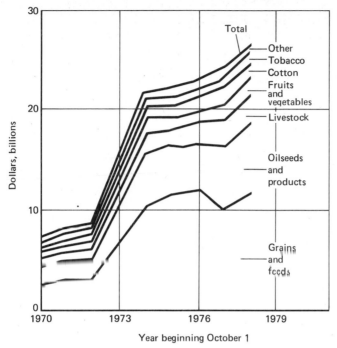

Figure 10-6 By the end of 1970s, the annual value of agricultural exports of the United States was almost six times as large as at the beginning of the decade. (*Note:* 1977–1978 partially estimated.)

trade conditions the ultimate explanation? The answers to these questions are important in judging the future of agricultural trade. Let us consider an economic explanation of the traditional farm problem in the United States before 1972 and the economic conditions pertaining therafter.

Traditional farm problem related to trade

An interpretation of the traditional problem of farm prices and farm income, covering roughly the 50 years from the early 1920s to the early 1970s—with, of course, the exception of World War II—is that rapid technological advance caused agricultural supply curves to forge ahead of demand to push prices of farm products down to levels that were unacceptable to farmers and others with agricultural interests. The politically powerful farm bloc, which was formed

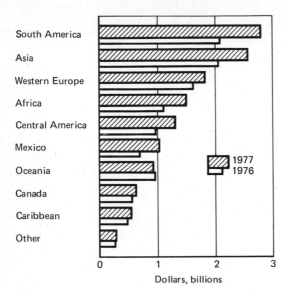

(a) Where we get our agricultural imports

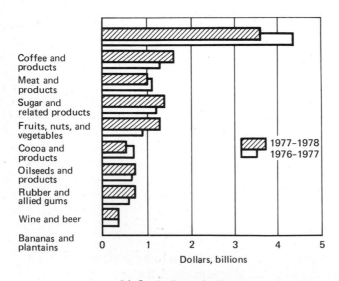

(b) Our leading agricultural imports by value

Figure 10-7   (a) Sources of agricultural imports into the United States. (b) Leading agricultural imports by value. (*Note:* (b), October–September years; 1977–1978 partially estimated.) About half of American agricultural imports by value are products that do not compete directly with American agriculture, while most of the other half are subject to various degrees of tariff and nontariff barriers to trade.

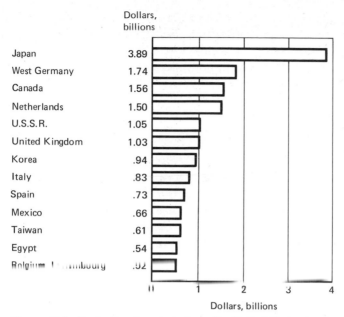

Figure 10-8   Agricultural exports from the United States tend to be concentrated among a small group of countries. (*Note:* 1977 data; adjusted for transshipments through Canada and western Europe.)

in Congress in the 1920s, obtained some of its objectives in the New Deal of the 1930s and continued to influence policy throughout the decades of the 1950s and 1960s. It had some degree of success in establishing price supports for politically important farm products at levels that were generally above equilibrium prices in the world market. This success led to other measures to clear the market, such as the measures discussed in Chapter 9, most but not all of which were supported by the farm bloc. These included control of supply, subsidies for demand, direct payments to farmers, and subsidies to maintain the traditional volume of farm-product exports.

Low farm prices in the 1920s and 1930s were related to the lack of growth in markets for American farm exports. The Versailles treaty, which levied punitive reparations on the defeated nations and more importantly failed to provide for their economic recovery, destroyed the major export market for American farm food products. The Fordney-McCumber tariff of 1922 and the Smoot-Hawley tariff of 1930, which raised duties on many products to record levels, dealt a crippling blow to foreign trade. This helped bring on economic collapse and the Great Depression of the 1930s.

In 1934, the United States embarked on a new program under the Reciprocal Trade Agreements Act. This gave the President the authority to negotiate agreements with individual nations to reduce American tariffs as much as 50 percent, provided the other nations made a reciprocal reduction for American exports. The act also included the so-called *most-favored-nation* clause, which allowed similar tariff reductions for the exports of any other nation to the United States, provided that nation agreed to the same terms as the most favored nation. Although there was a general revival of trade under the 1934 act, agricultural exports continued to drop under the influence of price supports above world price levels until by 1940 the agricultural export trade of the United States was practically zero.

World War II, of course, revived American farm export markets; world prices for food soared above the levels of American support for farm prices, and recovery programs after the war added further support. But some time in the 1950s and 1960s, the American dollar—still tied to a fixed price in gold which permitted it to serve as the common reserve currency in world markets—began to be overvalued in terms of gold and other world currencies. This had the effect of raising the prices of American exports in relation to other nations' currencies. Suggestive evidence of overvaluation is found in declining American gold stocks, which began to fall sharply in the latter half of the 1950s, and rising foreign claims for dollars, or increases in holdings of American dollar assets by foreign investors, which are the means for settling the deficits in the American balance of payments (Figure 10-9).

Deficits in the balance of payments, which are settled by gold outflows and rising foreign claims for dollars, do not give firm evidence of overvaluation, however. This is because the deficits are— or can be—due to a number of other factors. Military expenditures and economic aid can be important factors, provided they are not financed with exports of American products. Favorable opportunities for investment for American businesses abroad add to net outflows of private capital, which in some years have been as high as $20 billion. Increases in foreign productivity of industrial products (such as foreign-made cars, cameras, and television sets) tend to cause these products to be substituted for American products; this increases American imports. Domestic inflation, or rising dollar costs of American-made products, adds to this problem. Finally, increases in the prices of necessary imports—such as oil, natural gas, and a wide array of metals and other minerals—add to the value of imports.

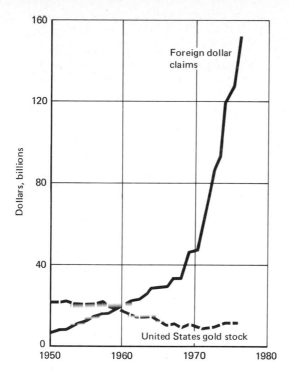

Figure 10-9   Increases in foreign dollar claims and a declining gold stock were the means for settling the chronic deficits in the balance of payments of the United States. The huge deficit of 1971, which brought a sharp rise in foreign dollar claims, forced the United States to abandon the gold standard.

Expanding American agricultural exports have been the most dynamic force in farm food markets, with these exports playing a larger and larger role in settling trade balances for the United States.

The cure for such deficits involves a number of interlacing factors. Getting other nations to share a larger part of costs for mutual defense would be an important step. Improving American productivity in basic industries would be another. Increasing opportunities for profit for business investments in the United States relative to investment opportunities for American businesses abroad would be still another. But not all deficits need be erased, provided foreign investors still find attractive opportunities in the United States. Because of these factors, economists cannot generate very clear evidence of the extent or timing of overvaluation.

But in the period up to 1972 especially, to the extent that American farm products were not increasingly competitive in export markets, American exports were not increasing, and so the increasing output of American agriculture was forced back on the domestic market. As a consequence, the benefits of capital growth and technical change in agriculture were distributed more toward American consumers and away from farm producers who otherwise would have received a larger share of the benefits of technological advance. Under these circumstances, the main beneficiaries of rising American agricultural productivity were domestic consumers, who bought food at low prices; more affluent family farmers, farm corporations, and other agricultural investors, who were able to acquire farmland and real estate at depressed prices; and people in certain foreign countries, who were the recipients of shipments of low-cost or free food. The small-scale farmer was most adversely affected by the combination of rapid technological advance and market restriction, as seen in the statistics on abandonment and consolidation of farms.

After 1972, with devaluation and then floating of the dollar, major American farm food products apparently became a "better buy" in terms of the currencies of other nations. Although the increases in imports of some commodities were limited by tariffs and quotas, especially in the E.E.C. and Japan, important increases in American farm exports did occur. The basis for this may be made more clear by an illustration of the effects on exports of overvaluation and devaluation, other things remaining the same.

Overvaluation and devaluation illustrated

Viewed externally, as in the case of a country importing farm products from the United States, overvaluation of the dollar keeps the prices of the imports high in terms of the currency of the importing nation. If corn is $2.50 per bushel, or $100 per ton, in the United

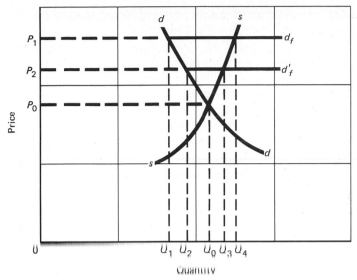

Figure 10-10 Effects of dollar valuation on agriculture. When there is no foreign trade, the market for agricultural products is in equilibrium at P_0 and Q_0. The addition of foreign demand dd_f results in equilibrium price P_1, with Q_1 sold domestically, and exports equal to $Q_4 - Q_1$. An increase in the value of the dollar reduces the foreign demand to dd'_f, resulting in price P_2, with Q_2 sold domestically, and exports equal to $Q_3 - Q_2$. Devaluation restores the original foreign demand at dd_f, raising American prices to P_1 and exports to $Q_4 - Q_1$.

States, for example, and $1 will exchange for 4 German marks—as it did in the early 1970s—it will take 400 marks to buy 1 ton of corn. If the value of the dollar declines so that $1 will exchange for only 2 marks—as it did in the late 1970s—it will take only 200 marks to buy 1 ton of corn. Without any change in the domestic price in the United States, the price of corn to the German importer is cut in half, provided there is no change in other factors. These effects are illustrated in Figure 10-10.[1]

Figure 10-10 compares and contrasts three different situations for an export commodity for which the United States is assumed to have a comparative advantage. First, if there is no foreign trade, market equilibrium is at Q_0 and P_0, assuming that ss and dd repre-

[1]This discussion is based in part on G. Edward Schuh, "The Exchange Rate and U.S. Agriculture," *American Journal of Agricultural Economics*, vol. 56, no. 1, February 1974, pp. 1–13. See also Amalia Vellianitis-Fidas and Schuh in ibid., vol. 57, no. 4, November 1975, pp. 692-700; Thomas Grennes, "The Exchange Rate and U.S. Agriculture: Comment," and G. Edward Schuh, "The Exchange Rate and U.S. Agriculture: Reply," in ibid., vol. 57, no. 1, February 1975, pp. 134–137.

sent the intitial domestic supply and demand. Second, if a foreign demand is added equal to dd_f, the equilibrium market price will rise to P_1, with Q_1 used domestically and exports equal to $Q_4 - Q_1$. The foreign-demand portion of the total demand curve, dd_f, is drawn as perfectly elastic in order to simplify the illustration. We know that foreign demand is very elastic but not perfectly, or infinitely, elastic.

Third, what happens if the dollar is increased in terms of the importing nation's currency? This will be equivalent to an increase in the price of the commodity in the importing nation, other things remaining the same. The foreign demand will fall as from dd_f to dd'_f. The price in the United States will drop from P_1 to P_2. Then Q_2 will be used domestically, and $Q_3 - Q_2$ will be exported. American consumers will benefit from the lower prices (as they apparently did up to 1972), and the income loss to American farmers will be equal to $(P_1 \times Q_4) - (P_2 \times Q_3)$.

American programs to control supply, which tended to cut production back from Q_4 to Q_3, for example, could restore the price to P_1, provided the government subsidized exports by the difference between P_1 and P_2. Alternatively, as in the Wheat-Cotton Act of 1964, the government might make a direct payment to farmers equal to $P_1 - P_2$ and let the price drop to P_2 in the United States. Under either circumstance, however, farm income would be reduced by the reduction of output from Q_4 to Q_3.

When devaluation occurs—or overvaluation ceases—the results will depend first on whether the effects are allowed to run their full course. The effects on farm exports can be offset by the United States through use of export quotas or by an embargo. An embargo was applied to soybeans briefly in 1973 and to sales of grain to the Soviet Union from August to October 1975 to prevent further increases in American food prices, although in both cases this was bitterly opposed by American farm organizations. Much more importantly for American farm exports, however, the effects can be offset by tariffs, quotas, and government control of farm food imports by the importing countries. This is the case in Japan and the European Community especially, with imports controlled in Japan by the use of quotas implemented by a government trading corporation, and in the E.E.C. by use of a variable import levy.

E.C. import levy and its effects

The E.E.C.—or the E.C. as it is identified in American statistics— uses a variable import levy to control imports of grains, meats, poultry, and dairy products. The levy increases or decreases as neces-

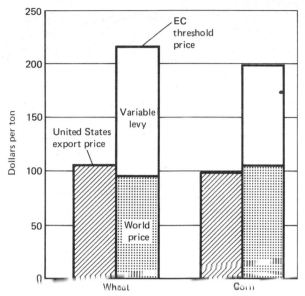

Figure 10-11 Common Market minimum prices. The variable import levy of the E.C. is used to keep farm product prices high in the E.C. relative to American or world prices. In this example the United States might be required to subsidize wheat exports to maintain domestic price-support levels, but not corn exports. (*Note:* 1977; E.C. = European Community; "threshold price" is the minimum import price at which the E.C. allows grain to enter a member country.)

sary to bridge the gap between the E.C.'s supports of farm prices and the competitive market price for these products outside the E.C. Specifically, the levy is the difference between a so-called *threshold* price, which is the minimum import price at which farm products are allowed to enter a member country, and the competitive world preimport price at Rotterdam. In 1977, for example, the minimum import price for wheat in the Common Market was more than double the world price, while the minimum import price for corn was just about double the world price (Figure 10-11).

The basic farm policy of the E.C. has developed around the variable levy, which has been the means of getting political support from farm and rural people for a country's membership in the E.C. Thus, the variable levy is a testament to the political power of farm organizations in the E.C. Its effects are, of course, to keep farm food prices in the E.C. higher than they would be otherwise.This stimulates farm production in the E.C.; somewhat reduces consumption of food in the E.C., depending on the elasticity of demand; and tends

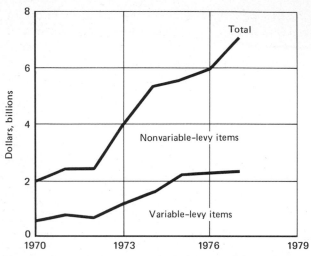

Figure 10-12   Agricultural exports from the United States to the European Community. The variable levy imposed by the E.C. has tended to limit the growth of American agricultural exports to the E.C. in the variable-levy items—grains, meats, poultry, and dairy products. The nonvariable-levy items, especially soybeans, have tended to grow relatively more. (*Note:* Years ending September 30, 1977–1978 partially estimated; data not adjusted for transshipments; variable-import-levy commodities are those regulated by E.C.'s common agricultural policy.)

to limit the growth of imports of products to which the variable import levy applies. Between 1972 and 1977, for example, American agricultural exports to the E.C. of variable-levy items increased relatively less than did exports of nonvariable-levy items (Figure 10-12).

The higher farm prices in the E.C. do not solve its problems of farm income, however, because in the long run, as was discussed in Chapter 4 (see pages 143–146), the costs of production tend to rise to equal the price that is set. In the short term, the higher prices tend to pacify farm organizations in the E.C., and the government in power tends to gain their political support. But food costs are undoubtedly higher for consumers in the E.C., and American farm exports are restricted.

The interest groups that promote tariffs and quotas as well as other restrictions to trade are, of course, not limited to the E.C. or to agriculture. But agriculture has been a particularly significant stumbling block to freer trade because of the political influence of organized producers' groups. The American National Cattlemen's Association and the National Livestock Feeders Association, which generally support restrictions on beef imports, are an important example in the United States. Also, the American sugar program and wool program, both of which limit imports, are examples of protectionist policies. In various countries around the world agricultural imports are limited by tariffs and quotas or by direct control of trade by the national government. But the benefits from freer trade are so evident and so important to economic growth and development that the United States along with many other governments has worked for many years to bring about freer trade. These efforts are so important to the economics of agriculture that they merit our closest attention.

INTERNATIONAL TRADE POLICIES
AND AGRICULTURE

Generally speaking, agricultural protectionism and government intervention in farm food markets distort agricultural incentives, increase production costs in countries where prices are held above the levels of competitive world prices, and retard economic development of agriculture in countries where farm prices are held down or depressed.[2] In general, the highly protected prices of the E.C. and Japan do not bring high profits to farm producers in those countries. High levels of protection by the United States for sugar, wool, peanuts, and a few other products do not in general maintain unusually high profits for American farmers growing those products. Once the high price is established and expectations are based on it, production costs of farms tend to rise to meet it. That is, the high level of price support tends to become a self-fulfilling prophecy in terms of farm costs. Similarly, in countries where certain prices are held below competitive levels by government price boards—rice in India and palm oil in Nigeria, for example—farm firms tend to be retarded in their development, and agricultural output—especially of these products—fails to grow.

Low prices for American farm exports due to trade restrictions in other countries, however, tend to retard farm progress in the United States. The economic problem is to work away from the special interests of individual commodities and groups of producers to a more general solution for expanded world trade. What has been done, and what are the prospects for international trade policy?

[2]See D. Gale Johnson, *World Agriculture in Disarray*, St. Martin's Press, in association with the Trade Policy Research Centre, London, 1973.

Reciprocal trade agreements
and G.A.T.T.

The Reciprocal Trade Agreements Act of 1934, which was the basis for bilateral (two-nation) negotiations, gave way to a broader approach in 1947 when 23 nations, including the United States, signed a General Agreement on Tariffs and Trade (G.A.T.T.) involving three cardinal principles: (1) equal, nondiscriminatory treatment for all member nations, (2) reduction of tariffs by multilateral (several-nation) negotiations, and (3) elimination of quotas for imports, a feature especially important for American agriculture. More than 100 nations now belong to G.A.T.T., and in general it has been an important force for liberalizing international trade. Under its sponsorship, six distinct "rounds" of negotiations to reduce trade barriers have been completed. A seventh, in which the United States has emphasized freer markets for agricultural exports, has become a reality.

E.C.C., or Common Market

The E.E.C., or Common Market—or the E.C., as it tends to be called in the United States—was begun in 1958 under the influence of G.A.T.T., with France, West Germany, Italy, Belgium, the Netherlands, and Luxembourg as members. The United Kingdom, Denmark, and Ireland joined in 1973. These countries constitute the *E.C. 9*. The goals, which have been recognized since 1958, called for (1) the gradual abolition of all tariffs and import quotas on products traded among the members, (2) a common system of tariffs applying to all products imported from outside the E.C., (3) eventual free movement of labor and capital within the E.C., and (4) creation of common policies with respect to matters of joint concern such as agriculture, transportation, and restrictive business practices.

The results of the E.C. are impressive in terms of a relatively rapid high-level rate of economic growth, which is in sharp contrast to the relatively slow growth of these countries previously. Although some countries—such as the United Kingdom—appear to have had difficulty conforming to some of the price conditions of the E.C.— such as higher food prices, for example—it seems clear that the closer economic integration has been a major contributing factor to the economic progress of the E.C. This has promoted a more rational allocation of economic resources within the E.C. according to the principle of comparative advantage, and it has created a larger mass market which has helped each of the member countries benefit from the economies of large-scale production. This has also made producers in the E.C. more competitive in the markets of other countries, generally to the advantage of American consumers and with increased competition for American business firms. The variable import levy of the E.C., however, has been particularly objectionable to the agricultural interests of exporting countries such as the United States, Canada, Australia, and New Zealand. The persistence of this and other trade barriers has been a matter of recurring "rounds" of discussion and bargaining in the interests of reduction of tariffs.

The "Kennedy Round"

In the early 1960s, after several rounds of negotiations it became more evident that if the United States was to avoid further isolation from the E.C., an initiative would have to be undertaken to more generally reduce trade barriers. This resulted in the Trade Expansion Act of 1962, which gave the President broad powers to negotiate reciprocal reduction of tariffs. American negotiators were given the authority to reduce tariffs as much as 50 percent on broad classes of industrial products and to eliminate tariffs where they had been only 5 percent or less. The reductions were on a reciprocal basis, with the reduced rates for the individual *most favored nation* extended automatically to other countries that agreed to similar terms.

The act acknowledged that sweeping tariff reductions leading to a closer trade relationship with the E.C. and other nations would create a disadvantage for certain American business firms in the short run. Therefore, the act provided for *trade adjustment assistance* for the firms or industries that were adversely affected. Individual firms could get tax relief and loans as well as technical assistance for reorganization and modernization of plants. Workers who lost their jobs as a result of the act could get relocation allowances, job training, and cash compensation. The tariff negotiations under the act were called the "Kennedy Round" in honor of President Kennedy, who was responsible for initiating the legislation.

The Kennedy Round achieved tariff cuts averaging more than 35 percent on some $40 billion worth of products that were mostly of industrial origin. The developing countries also benefitted in that efforts were made to reduce tariffs on products of particular interest to these countries without requiring full reciprocity. The main disappointment, however, was in agriculture. The United States, after first proposing a generally more liberal program of freer trade in farm food products which was not acceptable to the E.C., proposed a market-sharing agreement guaranteeing American exports a certain share of the E.C. market. In addition, American negotiators proposed that the E.C. and other countries of western Europe should participate to a greater extent in the costs of holding food stocks and financing aid to developing countries. The E.C., however, proposed that the levels of support of agricultural prices in the United States and other exporting countries should be fixed and that the governments should bind themselves not to raise those levels. This, of course, was not possible within the framework of American policy-making. If it were to be accomplished, the main result as far as the E.C. is concerned would be to make competitive world prices a little more flexible, which then would establish a more prominent role for the E.C.'s variable import levy.

The Kennedy Round ended in May 1967 with an agreement on an international scheme to donate 4.5 million tons of cereals in food aid annually to meet emergencies in the developing countries. The cost would be shared by the developed countries (United States, 42 percent; European Economic Community, 23 percent; Canada, 11 percent; United Kingdom, 5 percent; and so on). An agreement to raise the minimum price under the International Wheat Agreement by 21½ cents to $1.73 for hard winter wheat at Gulf of Mexico ports instead of setting the price in terms of Canadian wheat at Fort William proved to be unimportant. World prices soon lay above this level. From 1967 to 1971, American agricultural exports increased rather slowly, by no more than $1 billion or $2 billion for the entire period, while domestic policy in the United States emphasized control of crop production and limited growth.

The "Tokyo Round"

In September 1973, representatives of 105 nations, including the United States, met in Geneva to begin a new round of negotiations. The reductions of trade barriers negotiated in the Kennedy Round were having some favorable effects on trade, and a new initiative toward freer trade was thought to be worthwhile. The expansion of the Common Market to include the United Kingdom, Denmark, and Ireland opened new possibilities. The shift from the fixed exchange rate in existence up to 1971 to a more flexible international exchange was creating new conditions for expansion in trade. Finally, the general lowering of tariffs as a result of the Kennedy Round, however, was increasing the relative importance of a number of nontariff trade barriers (NTBs) such as import quotas, licensing requirements, and unrealistic health and safety standards for imports. Consequently, the "Tokyo Round" concentrated on the reduction or elimination of *NTBs*.

Reduction or elimination of important *NTBs* is not something that can be handled quickly or easily, however, and very sensitive political problems are often involved. Most European countries and Japan, for example, frequently require importers to obtain licenses. By restricting the issuance of licenses, these countries can effectively control imports. The United Kingdom prevents the importation of coal by this method. The United States has "buy American" legislation which restricts or limits purchases of foreign goods by both military and nonmilitary agencies. Imports of sugar and some other farm products are especially limited by quotas. Finally, unnecessarily complex procedures in the administration of customs regulations can reduce the flow of imports into any country.

The reduction of *NTBs* is often most difficult for agriculture. Negotiations between the United States and Japan were stalled for several months in the Tokyo Round, for example, by the insistence of the United States on increases in Japanese import quotas for American farm products, mainly but not exclusively livestock products. The problems of *NTBs* also involve exports. In 1979, for example, the price of American heavy native cowhides rose to over $1 a pound, almost triple the price just a year earlier. This was the result of lower slaughter of cattle in the United States and strong foreign and domestic demand. American shoemakers sought controls on exports, while the American cattle industry, of course, opposed them. Slaughter of cattle in the United States was expected to be 37 million head in 1979, compared with 39.5 million in 1978 and 41.9 million in 1977. Shoemakers in other countries hoped for an uninterrupted flow of American shipments of hides.

The predominant position of the exporting countries in the Tokyo Round was reduction or elimination of the *NTBs* of the importers, a pressure to which the importing nations tended to yield rather slowly. The United States—American agriculture especially—stood to gain the most from relaxation of *NTBs*, and this will continue to be the case in the future. In the short run of the next few years, the United States can gain the most by freer trade among major developed areas such as the E.C. and Japan. But trade with countries in rather rapid stages of development—such as the O.P.E.C. countries, Taiwan, South Korea, and Mexico—has become relatively much more important, especially for agriculture. Expanding and stabilizing trade between the United States and the Soviet Union has become an important issue. Finally, however, in the longer run trade with and development of the currently less-developed countries will be crucial for economic progress. What are the most important issues in the future?

ECONOMIC PROGRESS, STABILITY, AND GROWTH

Our study of international trade should now help us understand the alternatives for economic progress, stability, and growth, especially as related to agriculture. In the long view, there should be greatly increasing trade between the developed and currently developing countries. The F.A.O. has projected that by 1985 the developing countries will need to have net imports of 80 to 100 million tons of grain annually just to maintain the dietary levels of the 1970s. This compares with 20 to 25 million tons of net imports in the early 1970s. In addition, to raise dietary levels to more acceptable levels, greater increases in agricultural production as well as trade will be required. In the short view, the problems of achieving freer trade among the developed countries are yielding very slowly to the efforts for lower tariffs and the reduction or elimination of *NTBs*.

Still, it is clearly evident that trade is increasing and economic progress is occuring. Basic principles of comparative advantage are receiving increasing attention, and this is of immense importance to agriculture, especially to the agriculture of the world's largest exporter, the United States. However, the magnitude of the effort to increase world food production and trade in line with the broad food goals of the world will be great indeed.

Transforming traditional agriculture is a slow process in many developing countries depending on broader transitions in agribusiness and the economy at large.

World demand for food
in the long view

Total world demand for food by the year 2000 or shortly thereafter could be double what it is in the early 1980s. Whether it will, however, depends on a number of economic factors. The recently lowered projections for growth of population raise expectations of more rapid economic progress, other things being equal. This tends to greatly increase the aggregate demand for farm food products, compounding the effects of population growth and increases in demand per capita. Indications of the growth of demand for food are most evident in the increases of American exports of farm food to rapidly developing areas such as Mexico, South Korea, Taiwan, and the O.P.E.C. countries. Moreover, in the longer view, if the currently developing areas achieve what it is believed should be the minimum average recommended dietary levels, the developing countries will account for as much as three-fourths of the total growth in world demand for food. To achieve those levels of consumption, the developing countries must accelerate the growth of their production of food and, in most cases, increase their imports of food. Expansion of their industrial raw materials and finished products will be required in order to pay for these imports over time. The most rapidly developing countries all exhibit large increases in food demand, which will be satisfied only by increasing production and imports of food.

Economic progress
based on disequilibria

Generally, a major reason for increasing trade as a factor in economic progress is that development and growth constitute a disequilibriating process. Agriculture seldom experiences uniform rates of growth between major regions within a large country and even more rarely between countries. The United States, for example, has not achieved uniform rates of growth between the corn belt and Appalachia, the corn belt and the cotton belt, or the corn belt and the Great Plains. Had it attempted to do so, the government would have restricted the growth of productivity. Similarly, the rates of increase in agricultural productivity or growth are seldom the same between two developing countries or even between two crops within a country.

Certainly, in a developing country the choice of technique for increasing agricultural productivity is an important, often crucial, problem. But the choice is not concerned with the ratio of capital to labor or to output. The problem is to get the optimum allocation of investible resources. To achieve the maximum rate of economic progress, the government of the country should not be concerned with maintaining a specific rate of profit, or rate of return on the preexisting stock of capital within a sector of agriculture, but in equalizing the marginal rates of return in the alternatives that are available for investment. This means that it is generally inappropriate for a government to try to reach a position of self-sufficiency in regard to food, or even to try to reach self-sufficiency in respect to a given agricultural commodity. Certainly it is most inappropriate for a government to try to protect a costly and therefore obsolescent sector of agriculture by means of tariffs or import levies, whether fixed or variable, or by means of NTBs, as has been discussed.

High costs of protecting obsolescence in agriculture

The overwhelming evidence is that the high levels of protection afforded certain sectors of agriculture in various countries—which are considered so politically important by producers' groups in the short run—entail high costs for the society and generally fail to meet the major income objectives applied to agriculture. American tariffs, or import quotas, on sugar, wool, peanuts, and manufactured dairy products, for example, generally do not result in anything more than the usual rates of profit to producers of these commodities. The variable import levies of the Common Market, which may result in a price of corn or wheat double or more than double the competitive prices outside the E.C., do not bring abnormally high incomes to producers of these commodities in the E.C. The Japanese quotas on meats may drive meat prices sky-high in Japan without bringing high incomes to Japanese producers of livestock. The limitations imposed by the government of India on imports of farm machinery, which may or may not help the infant farm-machinery industry in India, tend also to restrict the growth of Indian agriculture without creating abnormally high rates of return for agribusinesses in India.

The attempt to maintain a specific rate of return on preexisting stocks of capital in agriculture, agricultural land, or labor tends to slow down the rates of increase in agricultural productivity and retard agricultural development and growth.[3]

[3]Theodore W. Schultz (ed.), *Distorting of Agricultural Incentives*, Indiana University Press, Bloomington, 1978.

The general theory of investment, which underlies the Keynesian revolution, supports the idea that it is a proper function of government to see that resources are invested where they will yield the highest real rates of return. This means that domestically (within a country) a government should not only attempt to remove the barriers to the free flow of resources but should also step in to provide aids to development, or supplements to investments in resources that will yield a high rate of return, provided these investments would not otherwise be made. This is the case for publicly supported education, federally sponsored programs for farm credits in the United States, development of agricultural cooperatives, and development of rural economic communities. Internationally, however, it means less government intervention involving restraint of trade, and more positive help primarily from the rich nations to the poor nations to develop their agriculture and industry. Where this help should be invested in the recipient country depends of course on that country's comparative advantage in the production of both agricultural and industrial commodities. The free flow of trade combined with government efforts to allocate resources according to their marginal productivities is the optimum guide for economic progress, or growth. Actually, however, governments may exert two positive influences, one dealing with economic stability and the other dealing with optimum economic progress, or growth. These must be treated separately.

Economic stability for agriculture related to trade

As we look at the statistics of trade for the 1970s, it should be evident that the growth in American farm food exports has had two quite different effects on agriculture. One effect is to stimulate growth, as has been observed. The other is to destabilize farm food markets. The increase in demand for exports of the early 1970s brought sharp increases in grain and oilseed prices to the detriment of livestock producers. The subsequent effect in the late 1970s was to greatly increase livestock prices as a result of lowered livestock population. This helped depress grain and oilseed prices despite continued high exports. Other emergencies such as those of the mid-1960s did not have such important destabilizing effects.

Generally speaking, a number of studies have shown that market stability can be increased for farm food products from year to year, provided there are certain specified minimum stocks of grain on hand and these stocks are managed so as to compensate for major changes in supply and demand. The procedure for such a program is to (1) establish a price band for certain grain, oilseed, and livestock products, with prices allowed to move freely only within that price band, and (2) specify a coordinated stocking operation involving timely withdrawals and injections. The price bands must be designed so that they reflect the interactions among various commodity markets over time, and the reserve stock guidelines must be coordinated with the price bands.[4]

Since the United States exports a significant portion of certain major crops, reserve-stock operations within the United States can contribute a great deal to domestic and world price stability even though a coordinated world reserve-stock program may be preferred by the United States government as a means of spreading the costs of program operations. To illustrate the workings of a reserve program, let us consider the implications of four different scenarios where we make different assumptions about stocks and their use in regulating the quantities supplied, as follows:

1. Export demand increases by 25 percent.
2. Before the increase in export demand, 50 percent of the American crop is exported, and the rest is either used or stored in the United States.
3. The elasticity of demand for total American farm output is −0.25.

SCENARIO 1

The United States government has stocks sufficient to offset the increase in demand and chooses to release the stocks at the price existing before the increase in demand. This is similar to having an infinitely elastic supply. As shown in Figure 10-13, the reserve is sufficient to stabilize price; this is a simulation of the global emergency of the mid-1960s.

SCENARIO 2

The United States has no excess grain stocks, or none that the government wishes to release, and buyers must depend solely on the

[4]Harold C. Halcrow and Takashi Takayama, "Dynamic Models for Stabilizing Food Prices," in *Contributed Papers Read at the Seventeenth International Conference of Agricultural Economists*, University of Oxford Institute of Agricultural Economics for the International Association of Agricultural Economists, Oxford, England, 1980.

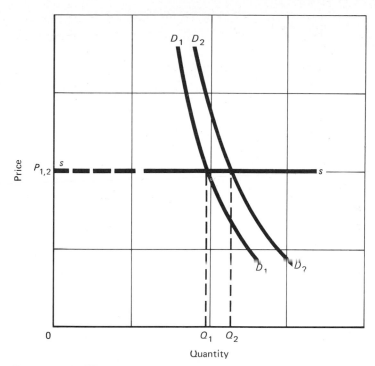

Figure 10-13 When reserve stocks are sufficient to offset an increase in demand, and the government releases stocks at the existing price, there is no change in price and quantity supplied increases from Q_1 to Q_2. In this illustration, the increase in export demand of 25 percent increases total demand by 12.5 percent ($0.25 \times 0.50 = 0.125$). Since supply is infinitely elastic, price does not change, and there is no change in the quantity demanded on the domestic market. The example might apply to the emergency of the mid-1960s.

current crop which is already predetermined. As in Figure 10-14, the supply is infinitely inelastic and does not change, and so the increase in demand of 12.5 percent results in an increase in domestic price of 50 percent.

This example might be used to illustrate a situation such as occurred in 1973–1974, after the United States had sold the stocks formerly held by the C.C.C. Livestock feeders would cut back as they did in response to high prices for feed grains and soybeans, and there would be a decline in grain consumed by cattle and hogs. The high prices for grains and oilseeds and the increased supply of livestock cause depressed incomes for livestock producers in the mid-1970s, and slow growth in livestock numbers brought relatively high prices for livestock—especially cattle—and low prices for feed

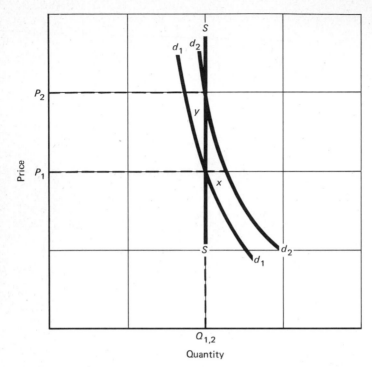

Figure 10-14   When supply is infinitely inelastic, an increase in demand brings an increase in price and no change in quantity supplied. Since $E_D = -0.25$, $y = 4x$. Then, $y = 4(0.125)$, or 0.50. Domestic use will decline by 12.5 percent, so that only 43.75 percent of the total crop will be used domestically [$0.50 \times (-.125) = -0.0625$; and $0.50 - 0.0625 = 0.4375$].

grains in the late-1970s, These situations might have been prevented by a more adequate reserve-stock program.

SCENARIO 3

The United States has reserve stocks sufficient to make the elasticity of supply equal to 0.25. In Figure 10-15, since the elasticity of supply and demand are numerically equal, the 12.5 percent increase in demand increases prices by 25 percent.

This example might apply to a situation such as the summer of 1972, for example, where the stocks of the C.C.C. were used to moderate the price increase. As soon as the stocks of the C.C.C. were exhausted, however, a situation similar to Figure 10-14 tended to develop.

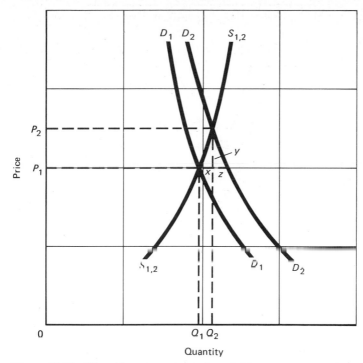

Figure 10-15   When elasticity of supply is 0.25, an increase in demand will bring an increase in price four times greater than the increase in quantity supplied. In this example, $x + z = 12.5$ percent. Since $x = z$, each is equal to 6.25 percent. Since $y = 4x$, or $4z$, $y = 0.25$.

SCENARIO 4

The United States has larger stocks than in Scenario 3, sufficient to make elasticity of supply equal to 1. When demand increases, the increase in price and quantity supplied will be the same in terms of percentage, or 10 percent as in Figure 10-16.

This example may help us visualize how a reserve-stock storage program may be used to moderate the price effects of sudden, or unanticipated, increases or decreases in demand for exports. It should be evident that the program can work either way to strengthen farm-product prices in years of weak demand or large crops, and to prevent large increases in farm food prices during years of unusually strong export demand due to poor crops or world food crises. It need not depress prices in the exporting country over a period of accumulation and depletion of stocks. On the contrary,

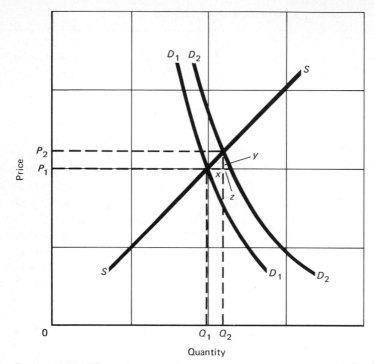

Figure 10-16   When elasticity of supply is unity, an increase in demand will bring equal percentage changes in price and quantity supplied. Let: $x + z = 0.125$; $x/y = 1$, or $x = y$; $z/y = 0.25$, or $z = 0.25 y$. Substitute: $y + 0.25y = 0.125$; $1.25y = 0.125$. Then: $y = 0.10$, or 10 percent. And: $x = 0.10$, or 10 percent.

stabilizing the supply of grains and oilseeds can assure a high level of export capacity in poor crop years in the United States, thus increasing the export potential over time, increasing export earnings, and raising aggregate American farm income without increasing the aggregate domestic expenditure on food. World food crises and price instabilities such as those experienced in the 1970s, which were primarily the result of temporary adverse weather conditions in important world food-producing areas, may not be eliminated by the program of food reserves. But they can be greatly moderated. The results that are achieved depend on how the program is coordinated with the fluctuations in American farm production and export trade, including commercial exports and various food-aid programs.

Government intervention to stabilize supplies can have positive benefits in terms of the aggregate product made available to consumers, other things being equal. It is the opposite of policies of trade restriction, which are generally carried out to protect producers by restricting supplies. It can be supported, in other words, in terms of the general welfare as well as in the interest of maximizing the benefits to agriculture.

In the longer term

Estimates of the availabilities of regional and global resources provide us with little insight about the likely costs of the most desirable patterns of longer-term development and growth. This is because the potentials for economic progress and growth in respect to agriculture tend to outrun most projections, provided there is relatively greater freedom in trade and a balanced application of scientific, technological, and economic knowledge. This has been demonstrated in the progress and growth of agriculture in the United States. Who imagined in 1940, for instance, when American agricultural exports were practically zero, that 40 years later agricultural exports would be almost two-thirds as large as the total output of agriculture in 1940; that relative prices for farm products would be 10 to 15 percent lower than they were in 1940; that indexes of the quality of diet and per capita food consumption would be substantially higher; and that the rate of increase in agricultural productivity would show little sign of slackening? Did we generally foresee or imagine that American corn yields would increase some four to five times in this 40-year period and that many other crops would double and triple their yields?

Economic progress and growth in agriculture tend to come from various combinations or packages of advancing technologies such as developing higher-yielding crop varieties, improving fertilizer efficiency, improving plant and animal nutrition, and reducing losses to weeds, insects, and plant and animal diseases. The potentials for scientific, technological, and managerial advances in overcoming specific limitations of resources and in pushing out the frontiers of diminishing returns in agriculture have been demonstrated not only in the United States but in most other developed countries around the world.

Yet it is important also to recognize the limitations. The distribution of natural resources in relation to population is very uneven. Asia, for example, contains more than 70 percent of the population of the developing countries but only 11 percent of the unutilized cropland potential of the developing areas. Although the development of land for crops in Africa and Latin America is not so constrained, the costs of bringing a significantly larger percentage of these lands into production is generally thought to be high, and there is uncertainty about the most economical technologies. Advances in technology that revolutionize agriculture in one area are seldom directly applicable to another. This is especially the case in attempting to transfer technologies of temperate zones, where the greatest progress has been made in the last few decades, to the tropical zones, where the largest amount of unutilized potential cropland is thought to exist.

The general problem is development of agriculture according to the comparative advantages that exist. This means less government intervention in trade, more positive assistance in research and development to bring down the real costs of agricultural inputs, and more emphasis on helping people adjust to the opportunities that exist or can be created.

SUMMARY

The principle of comparative advantage is the general basis for trade. The 1970s brought a transformation in the conditions for agricultural trade, growing out of increases in the demand for American farm food exports. The traditional farm problem, which was related to lack of growth in these exports, tended to give way to a more dynamic situation where exports tended to dictate the prices of farm food products and American agriculture became more and more dependent on exports for determination of its prices and incomes. Agricultural exports came to play a larger role in the trade balance of the United States.

Agricultural protectionism through tariffs and NTBs has distorted incentives to agricultural production and increased the costs of production in countries where prices are held above competitive levels of world prices. This led to continuing efforts by the major trading nations, including the United States, to reduce tariffs and NTBs. Considerable success has been achieved, but agriculture has tended to remain among the most highly protected major industries. On the other hand, efforts by some countries to hold farm food prices below world market prices have tended to slow agricultural development.

The long-term development of agriculture has been related to the growing world demand and to greater freedom in trade. Although the increasing volume of international trade increases the ability or capacity of agriculture to meet various types of world food crises, the larger relative magnitude of trade also has destabilizing effects on the United States which can be moderated but not eliminated by a reserve program. There is a high potential for growth in the longer term even though important limitations must be observed.

IMPORTANT TERMS AND CONCEPTS

Principle of comparative advantage

Specialization and trade

Trade transformation of American agriculture

Traditional farm problem related to trade

Balance of payments

Curing deficits in the balance of payments

Overvaluation and devaluation effects of

Variable import levy of the E.C.

Reciprocal trade agreements

G.A.T.T.

Tariffs and trade, effects on agriculture

Kennedy Round

Toyko Round

World demand for food in the long view

Conditions of economic progress for agriculture

Costs of protecting obsolescence in agriculture

Economic stability for agriculture related to trade

LOOKING AHEAD

Over the next generation at least, agriculture will become more and more important. The twin effects of economic progress and increasing world population will have multiple, compounding effects on the demand for farm food products. Higher prices for energy will affect costs in almost all areas of agricultural production and marketing. Advancing technology, international trade, and economic development in all parts of the economy will be needed to sustain economic progress.

This means that the economics of agriculture will also become more and more important as a field of study applied primarily to problems of producing and marketing farm food products. The preceding chapters have tried to build a foundation for such study by developing basic theory and giving examples that apply to agriculture. You may continue to build on this foundation by further studies in economics and by more in-depth applications in a range of courses such as those mentioned in Chapter 1.Career planning may be advanced by such study as your interests, aptitudes, and skills develop. In this case, the basic study of the present in the light of the past will be helpful for your future.

QUESTIONS AND EXERCISES

1. State the principle of comparative advantage. How may it be illustrated? Give an example. Why does trade generally rest on this principle?

2. How was American agricultural trade transformed in the 1970s? What might be the role of devaluation of the dollar in this transformation?

3. What countries account for the major export markets of American agriculture? What are the economic characteristics of these countries? What does this trade indicate about the relationship between trade and economic development or progress?

4. What are the conditions associated with the traditional interpretation of the farm problem? How could these conditions have been modified to solve the problem? How was it solved?

5. What is the effect on American farm exports of the variable levy of the E.C.? What is a nontariff trade barrier? What is its economic effect?

6. What was the purpose of G.A.T.T.? What successes have been achieved in respect to this purpose? What failures have occurred?

7. What are the possibilities for world demand for food in the long term? How may these possibilities be modified in the future?

8. How does trade tend to influence the stability of American agricultural markets? How may reserves be used to create greater stability?

9. Why do resource availabilities not give a clear picture of world production potentials?

10. What are the major limiting factors in world agricultural productivity?

APPENDIX: CONVERSIONS

The table on the following page shows conversions from United States units to metric units and vice versa for weight, volume, length, area, pressure, yield or rate, and temperature.

To convert *from United States units to metric units*, find the appropriate unit in column (2) and multiply the measurement by the number in the column to the right of it.

To convert *from metric units to United States units*, find the appropriate unit in column (1) and multiply the measurement by the number in the column to the left of it.

Conversion between United States units and metric units

To convert column (1) to column (2) multiply by:	(1) Metric units	(2) U.S. Units	To convert column (2) to column (1), multiply by:
Weight			
1.102	ton (metric)	ton (U.S.)	0.907
2.205	kilogram, kg	pound, lb	0.454
0.035	gram, g	ounce (avdp), oz	28.349
Volume			
0.264	liter, L or l	gallon (U.S.), gal	3.785
1.057	liter, L or l	quart (fluid), qt	0.946
2.838	hectoliter, hl	bushel, bu	0.352
0.034	milliliter, ml	ounce (fluid), oz	29.573
Length			
0.621	kilometer, km	mile, mi	1.609
1.094	meter, m	yard, yd	0.914
3.281	meter, m	feet, ft	0.305
0.394	centimeter, cm	inch, in	2.540
Area			
2.471	hectare, ha	acre, A	0.405
247.1	$kilometer^2$, km^2	acre, A	0.004
0.386	$kilometer^2$, km^2	$mile^2$, mi^2	2.590
10.765	$meters^2$, m^2	$feet^2$, ft^2	0.093
0.155	$centimeters^2$, cm^2	$inches^2$, in^2	6.452
Pressure			
0.987	bar	atmosphere, atm	1.013
14.504	bar	lb/in^2, psi	0.069
14.223	kg/cm^2	lb/in^2, psi	0.070
14.70	atmosphere, atm	lb/in^2, psi	0.068
0.968	kg/cm^2	atmosphere, atm	1.033
Yield or rate			
0.446	1 ton (metric/hectare)	ton (U.S./acre)	2.242
0.892	kg/ha	lb/A	1.121
1.149	hl/ha	bu/A	0.870
0.107	l/ha	gal/A	9.346
8.347	kg/l	lb/gal	0.120
Temperature			
$1.80° C + 32$	Celsius, ° C	Fahrenheit, ° F	$0.55 (F - 32)$

Source: From R. Gordon Halfacre and John A. Barden, *Horticulture,* McGraw-Hill Book Company, New York, 1979, app. table 2, p. 695.

GLOSSARY: DEFINITIONS OF TERMS, RULES, AND LAWS

Agribusiness

Agribusiness includes firms and economic enterprises organized to produce and sell services and supplies to farmers for use in farm production and living; it includes firms and industries that buy farm products, and process and distribute them through wholesale and retail markets. The first groups are called *farm service supply industries* and the second *agricultural processing-marketing industries*.

Agricultural, or farmers', cooperatives

Agricultural cooperatives—or farmers' cooperatives, as they may be called—are of either a federated or a centralized type of organization although a few cooperatives are a mixture of both. Under a federated organization individual cooperatives join together to create a business superstructure for purposes of more coordinated and efficient operation. The individual cooperatives own and control the federated superstructure rather than vice versa. Members elect the board of directors of the federated cooperatives through the local organizations. Under a centralized organization, the parent cooperative owns or controls various satellite or local cooperatives. Members vote directly for the board of directors, which controls the total organization.

The Capper-Volstead Act of 1922 provided the charter for the modern growth of farmers' cooperatives in the United States. It legalized cooperatives engaged in interstate commerce by exempting them from prosecution under the Sherman Act of 1890 and the Clayton Act of 1914, and by specifying the following:

First: That no member of the association is allowed more than one vote because of the amount of stock or membership capital he may own therein, or,
Second: That the association does not pay dividends on stock membership capital in excess of 8 per centum per annum.

And in any case to the following:

Third: That the association shall not deal in the products of nonmembers to an amount greater in value than such as are handled by it for members.

These requirements have placed the control of farmers' cooperatives largely in the hands of the member-users rather than independent investors. This makes the cooperatives more directly conscious of the farmers' views on prices and services. The limitation of 8 percent on earnings from dividends assures that earnings in excess of 8 percent will either be kept for reinvestment or returned to member-users as patronage refunds. Such refunds are not taxed as income to the corporate body of the cooperative since, by virtue of the charter of the cooperative, they do not belong to it.

Agriculture

Agriculture is an industry involving the organization of resources—such as land and minerals, capital in a wide variety of forms, and management and labor—for the production and marketing of food and fiber.

It includes four major economic sectors: (1) agribusiness farm service supply industries, (2) farms, including livestock ranches, (3) agribusiness agricultural processing-marketing industries, and (4) a publicly supported sector of agricultural research and education that involves government regulation of markets, weights and standards, programs for support of agricultural prices and trade, programs for soil conservation, and so on.

Comparative advantage, law of

The law of comparative advantage states that the total output of goods and services can be increased by having firms (or people, industries, countries, etc.) do what they do best, or most efficiently, and by letting the market work as freely as possible to distribute the total goods and services. To maximize profits, each producer should produce those products—considering yields, costs and returns— from which the percentage return above cost is the greatest.

Comparative advantage, principle of

The economic basis for all trade between two states (or individuals, firms, nations, etc.) is embodied in the principle of comparative advantage, which states that whether or not one of two states is absolutely more efficient in the production of every product than the other, if each specializes in the products in which it has the greatest relative efficiency, trade will be mutually beneficial to both states.

Competition

There are a number of types of competition, including pure or perfect competition and imperfect competition. The latter may be divided on the selling side into monopolistic competition, oligopoly, and monopoly. Imperfect competition on the buying side includes monopsonistic competition, oligopsony, and monopsony. All these are important in the economics of agriculture. A more general decription follows.

IMPERFECT COMPETITION

This is the general term referring to selling under monopolistic competition, oligopoly, or monopoly, and to buying under monopsonistic competition, oligopsony, and monopsony. Four basic models— including also pure competition in selling and buying—are characteristic of both the selling and the buying sides of competitive markets; this suggests that there are a very large number of buying and selling relationships in most economic systems.

Imperfect competition prevails in an industry, or group of industries, wherever the individual sellers face nonhorizontal, downward-sloping demand curves for their individual products and thereby have some measure of control over price. Imperfect competition prevails among buyers whenever they individually exert a measure of control over the price that they and other competitors pay.

Given identical costs, the imperfectly competitive firm will find it profitable to charge a higher price and produce a smaller output than a purely competitive firm. The difference in cost and return, or profit, is sometimes called the *social costs of imperfect competition*.

MONOPOLY

A pure monopoly—a one-firm industry—is rare indeed. But a number of monopoly-like conditions are of importance in agriculture.

1. The concept of pure monopoly is important theoretically. For agriculture, the condition of monopoly, or near monopoly, is important in many areas such as transportation, public power, and communication.
2. The monopolist's product is unique in the sense that there are no good, or close, substitutes. What is good or close is not easy to define.
3. The monopolist is the price maker unless the price is regulated by a public commission or other device. The monopolist tends to control the amount to be offered for sale and the conditions of sale.
4. The existence of monopoly depends on having a barrier to the entry of other firms. The barrier may be economic, legal, or technical.
5. A firm that enjoys a monopoly-type situation may or may not engage in advertising and sales promotion. It all depends on the market situation and whether advertising and sales promotion will pay. Much depends on how closely the firm approaches a monopoly-type situation, how much it wishes to increase its sales, and how it is regulated. The monopoly-type firm may not charge the highest price permitted.

MONOPOLISTIC COMPETITION

In contrast to pure competition, monopolistic competition involves product differences, or what economists call product differentiation. This may include physical differences in products as well as identifying differences such as brand names and claims to superiority over the products of other sellers. Some farm products that are sold initially under pure competition come under monopolistic competition farther along the marketing chain.

1. There may be a large number of firms nationally or as few as 25 or 30. Each firm has only a small share of the total market. Food marketing-processing firms provide a number of examples.
2. The firms differentiate their individual products. These differences may be real or imaginary. The important point is that the differences exist, or are made to exist, in the mind of the buyer. Notice the product differentiation in food markets.
3. Firms in monopolistic competition have only limited control over the prices of their products, but they do have some control. There may be significant differences among the products, but the prices of one producer cannot get very far out of line before consumers will shift to another brand or product. In this instance, how far is far? This is a crucial point in economics.
4. Entry into an industry that is monopolistically competitive is generally more difficult than entry into a purely competitive industry. Product differentiation is the general reason. Considerable advertising may be required to establish a brand name. This can be expensive. The outcome is uncertain; it cannot be taken for granted. Manufactured food products illustrate the difficulty of entry for new marketing firms.
5. Because products are differentiated, competition among firms is often vigorous in areas other then price.

OLIGOPOLY

This word—from the Greek word *olig*, "few," and *polist*, "seller"— means "few sellers."

1. Oligopoly exists whenever a few firms dominate the market for a product. Each of the major firms has a large enough share of the market for its actions and policies to have an effect on its rivals. The major firms are mutually interdependent. How they solve their problems of price and quantity is of major concern to all participants. Oligopoly is important in markets for farm inputs and in many other major markets such as grain and livestock marketing.
2. Oligopolists may produce either virtually standardized or highly differentiated products. Those furnishing raw materials gener-

ally offer a product that is highly standardized by class and grade but which may be differentiated by a brand name. Those appealing directly to the consumer generally try to differentiate their product. The degree of standardization or differentiation affects the prices and market practices of the competing firms.

3. The degree of control over price is limited or circumscribed by the mutual interdependence of firms. Oligopolists generally try to avoid aggressive price competition, which may degenerate into a price war. Thus, the prices charged by oligopolists tend to be "rigid," or "sticky."

4. Obstacles to entry are generally very effective, which is why an industry characterized by oligopoly tends to remain that way. The possibility for the entry and growth of small firms tends, however, to put some limit on the prices oligopolists can charge. Also, the Sherman Act of 1890 and the Clayton Act of 1914 were the first of a number of acts attempting to prevent collusive pricing and restrictive trade practices by oligopolists.

5. Expenses for advertising and sales promotion are generally high among oligopolists who sell a differentiated product. Beer, cigarettes, soft drinks as well as a number of food products are good examples of advertising and sales promotion by oligopolists in processing and marketing farm products. The heavy advertising of farm chemicals and farm machinery in the major farming areas of the United States attests to the presence of oliogopoly.

PURE COMPETITION

The following are the more important general characteristics of pure or perfect competition:

1. There are a large number of independently acting sellers each of whom generally offers a product for sale in a highly organized, or structured, market. Farming is often cited as the classic example.

2. The competing firms offer a standardized product for sale, or one that is standardized in terms of specific market grades or classses.

3. Each individual producer exerts little or no influence on the market price. This follows from having a large number of producers and a standardized product. Farming generally meets this condition.

4. New firms are free to enter and existing firms are free to leave the industry.

5. Since by definition each purely competitive firm is producing an identical product, or a product that can be marketed as a particular class or grade, the firms generally do not resort to nonprice competition such as advertising or other sales-promotion activities.

Costs of production

See *comparative advantage*, *economic costs*, *opportunity costs*.

Demand

Demand may be defined as a schedule showing the various amounts of a resource or product that will be bought, under given conditions, at each specific price in a set of possible prices during a specified period of time.

CHANGES IN DEMAND

By definition, a change in demand involves a shift in the demand curve itself: to the right for an increase in demand and to the left for a decrease.

DEMAND FOR SUBSTITUTES
AND COMPLEMENTS

When two products are substitutes, a change in the price of one is directly related to the demand for the other. When two products are not related at all in terms of price and quantity demanded, they are said to be independent. Two commodities are complements if an inverse relationship exists between the price of one and the demand for the other.

DETERMINANTS OF DEMAND
FOR CONSUMER GOODS

The main determinants are (1) tastes or preferences of consumers, (2) number of consumers in the market, (3) money incomes or wealth of consumers, (4) prices of related goods, and (5) expectations of consumers with respect to future prices and incomes.

DETERMINANTS OF DEMAND
FOR RESOURCES

The demand for resources is derived from the demand for the finished products and services that those resources help produce. The demand for a resource depends on (1) the capability of the resource in production, and (2) the value of the good being produced. That is, the demand for a resource is based on the additional value or revenue that it will produce. The net addition to total revenue from each added unit of input is called the marginal revenue product (*MRP*). Thus, by definition the marginal revenue product (*MRP*) is the increase in total revenue resulting from the use of each additional unit of a variable input. Each point on a *MRP* schedule indicates the number of units of a variable input that will be demanded at each price within a set of possible prices. In other words, the *MRP* schedule is the demand for inputs.

INCOME ELASTICITY OF DEMAND

The coefficient of the relationship between income and expenditure is known as the income elasticity of demand. If the percentage of income spent on a good or service stays the same as real income increases, the income elasticity is equal to 1. If the percentage spent increases only half as much, the income elasticity is 0.5. If it increases one-fourth as much, the income elasticity is 0.25, and so on. This assumes constant relative prices.

A number of studies have revealed that the income elasticity for total food is very low in the United States, while wide variations exist among different food items. The income elasticities are very close to zero for commodities such as lard, margarine, evaporated milk, sweet potatoes, beans, and bread. They are generally more than 0.6 for frozen vegetables; about 0.5 to 0.6 for individual meats such as lamb and mutton, beef and veal, and turkey; and around or below 0.4 for pork, chicken, ice cream, all fruit, and cheese. In general, higher-income groups tend to consume high-quality products insofar as quality can be measured in terms of price. This means that income elasticity can take account of quality as well as quantity in respect to the relationship between income and expenditure on farm food products.

INFERIOR GOODS

Goods or services whose demand varies inversely with a change in real income are called inferior goods.

LAW OF DEMAND

On a given demand schedule, there is normally an inverse relationship between the price and the quantity demanded. As the price
falls, the quantity demanded increases. As the price rises, the quantity demanded decreases, assuming that other things remain the
same.

NORMAL GOODS

Goods or services whose demand varies directly with real income
are called normal, or superior, goods.

PRINCIPLE OF
EQUAL MARGINAL RETURNS

The demand for each input depends on the prices, or opportunity
costs, of all inputs, not its own price alone. The $MRP = MRC$ rule—
that is, marginal revenue product equals marginal resource cost—
states that when capital as a resource is unlimited, a firm will maximize profits or minimize losses by employing each and every
resource up to the point where $MRP = MRC$. When capital is limited
and the firm cannot meet this condition, or cannot obtain all the
resources it can profitably employ, the rule states that the ratio of
MRP to MRC—in perfect markets, MRP to price—should be the
same for all the resources employed. That is, MRP from resource A
is to MRC of resource A as MRP from B is to MRC of B, and as MRP
from C is to MRC of C, and so on.

Economic, or economics

Economics is a scientific discipline concerned with the allocation of
limited resources to satisfy unlimited wants.

Economic ideas generally may be grouped around (1) the idea
of allocation, putting resources and products to their best use, (2)
the idea of scarcity, that goods and services are limited, (3) the idea
of deliberate goals, involving what resources and how much of each
to use, and (4) the idea of time, involving concepts of consumption
and saving. What is rational in economics is what maximizes satisfaction over time.

Economists tend to call what goes into the production of goods
and services an *input*. What comes out as a product—a good or
service—is an *output*. Economic goods or services command a

price, or have value in exchange. Free goods are goods that do not command a price, or have value in exchange.

The economizing process involves three general types of decision making in regard to inputs and outputs: (1) how to get more out of a given amount of inputs, (2) how to get the same total output by using fewer inputs, and (3) how to increase output relatively more than input.

Economic costs

Economic costs are payments that a firm must make, or incomes it must provide, to attract and keep resources away from alternative lines of production. These payments or incomes may be either explicit or implicit.

EXPLICIT COSTS

These involve actual payments such as the money spent for hired labor, rented land, and products obtained from farm service supply industries for farm production.

FLOW SERVICES AS COSTS

Certain resources—such as labor or a barn—may be used again and again. If they are not used today, the productivity that might have been forthcoming is lost and cannot be regained. The cost of not using them is generally implicit until the resource is exhausted.

IMPLICIT COSTS

These generally do not involve money outlay, as with a firm or family using resources that it owns and controls itself. Payments to the manager or entrepreneur for organizing and combining resources in production may be either explicit or implicit.

OPPORTUNITY COST

The value of goods and services that must be given up, or sacrificed, to obtain an additional amount of any other good or service. That is, the opportunity cost of a certain amount of a good or service is the value of those resources in an alternative use. Thus, there is an opportunity cost for everything whether an explicit payment is made or the cost is implicit.

STOCK SERVICES AS COSTS

Certain resources—fertilizer and feed, for example—may be entirely used up in the production process and must be replaced. If they are not used today, they can be saved for tomorrow or next year. The costs are generally explicit.

Economic growth, development, and progress

Economic growth may be defined as an outward shift of production-possibilities curves as a result of expanding resources and advancing technologies. It results in either (1) an increase in total output, without regard to population change, or (2) an increase in output per capita, allowing for population change. Economic development generally implies growth accompanied by significant changes in economic organization, such as changes in sizes and types of farms, substitution of tractors for horses, or change in the marketing system. Economic progress also implies growth with definite improvements in output per capita and definite welfare gains, such as increases in the level of living of certain lower-income groups.

Economic growth involves outward-shifting p-p frontiers which provide a basis for increasing capital formation and consumption of food and nonfood. Capital formation is required for the economic growth of agriculture, which produces under conditions of diminishing returns. The law of diminishing returns refers specifically to the extra output produced when equal units of a varying input are successively added to a fixed amount of some other input, or inputs. Increases in agricultural output are specifically subject to diminishing returns as a result of the relative fixity of land and some other natural resources.

Economic progress related to growth in agriculture tends to come from various combinations or packages of advancing technologies such as developing higher-yielding crop varieties, improving fertilizer efficiency, improving plant and animal nutrition, and reducing losses to weeds, insects, and diseases of plants and animals. The potentials for scientific, technological, and managerial advances in overcoming specific limitations of resources and in pushing out the frontiers of diminishing returns in agriculture have been demonstrated not only in the United States but in most other developed countries.

Economic growth, measurement of

Economic growth can be measured in terms of (1) real national output or income, and (2) real output or income per capita. The following concepts and terms are relevant:

DISPOSABLE INCOME (*DI*)

Disposable income is personal income minus personal taxes such as personal income taxes, personal property taxes, and inheritance taxes. Income taxes are of course by far the most important. The disposable personal income per capita of the farm and the nonfarm population has been increasing, but with very little change relative to each other since 1965 (see Figure 9-6)

GROSS NATIONAL PRODUCT (*GNP*)

The gross national product is the total market value of all final goods and services produced in a given year. It can be determined (1) by adding up all that is spent on the year's total output, or (2) by summing all the incomes derived from the year's output. The results are identical because what is spent on goods and services by a buyer constitutes income to the seller. Thus, the expenditure and the income approaches to *GNP* are always equal to each other, or an identity.

NATIONAL INCOME (*NI*)

National income may be derived from *NNP* by subtracting from *NNP* the indirect business taxes which go to support of government. *NI*, then, is the total wage, rent, interest, and profit incomes earned from the production of the year's output. Measured from the viewpoint of suppliers of resources, it is the income they have earned from their contributions to the year's production. From the viewpoint of business costs, it is the factor or resource costs of all that has gone into the year's production. Growth was measured in terms of national income and, in the case of agriculture, the value of farm marketings, in constant dollars.

NET NATIONAL PRODUCT (*NNP*)

Net national product may be derived from *GNP* by subtracting from *GNP* an allowance for the part of the year's output which is necessary to replace the capital goods used in the year's production. *NNP* is the amount that can be consumed by the nation's economy—firms, households, and government itself—without impairing the nation's capacity to produce in succeeding years and indefinitely into the future.

PERSONAL INCOME (*PI*)

Personal income is *NI* plus transfer payments, minus income earned but not received. Thus, for example, the personal income of families that operate farms might be the value of farm marketings plus transfer (income) payments from government, less farm business expenses and (in the case of farm corporations) undistributed corporate profits.

Economies and diseconomies of scale

These terms refer to the fact that there are technical relationships among resources which cause the average product to increase or decrease as the size of the plant changes, and that there are also financial, or pecuniary, advantages and disadvantages related to large size, or scale.

Farms generally experience technical economies of scale up to the level of a large family farm (see *farm, family farm*). Beyond a certain size—around 600 or 700 hundred acres in the center of the corn belt, for example—further technical economies of scale (increasing output per unit of input) are generally small. However, additional financial or pecuniary advantages sometimes accrue to larger farms due to economies in acquisition of resources for production and in marketing, or sale of farm products.

There are certain disadvantages to large-scale enterprises that are called *diseconomies of scale*. These may be due to the technical problems of efficiently managing larger amounts of resources in production or to financial or pecuniary problems of organization and control, including tax problems.

Elasticity of demand

Elasticity of demand is the percentage change in the quantity demanded of a service or product in response to a given percentage change in its price, other things being equal. It depends primarily on percentage changes and is independent of the units used to measure quantities and prices. There are three general categories:

1. *Inelastic demand.* When a decline in P brings a smaller percentage increase in Q so that total revenue ($P \times Q$) declines, the demand is inelastic. That is, E_d is between 0 and -1. (Note that E_d denotes *elasticity of demand*.)
2. *Unitary elasticity of demand.* When a decline in P results in an exactly compensating percentage increase in Q so that total revenue ($P \times Q$) is left exactly unchanged, there is unitary elasticity of demand. That is, $E_d = -1$.
3. *Elastic demand.* When a decline in P increases Q so that total revenue ($P \times Q$) increases, the demand is elastic. That is, E_d is more negative than -1, such as -1.5, -2, and so on.

COEFFICIENT OF
ELASTICITY OF DEMAND (E_d)

The percentage change in quantity demanded when there is a 1 percent change in price, assuming no change in demand is the coefficient of elasticity of demand.

Then $\quad E_d = \dfrac{\text{percentage change in quantity demanded}}{\text{percentage change in price}}$

or $\quad E_d = \dfrac{\text{change in quantity demand}}{\text{original quantity demanded}} \Big/ \dfrac{\text{change in price}}{\text{original price}}$

The general formula for measuring the elasticity of demand for an arc of a demand curve is:

$$\mathbf{E}_d = \frac{\Delta Q}{(Q_1 + Q_2)/2} \div \frac{-\Delta P}{(P_1 + P_2)/2}$$

Where: ΔQ denotes change in quantity
$-\Delta P$ denotes change in price

Q_1 and P_1 are quantity and price at one end of the arc
Q_2 and P_2 are quantity and price at the other end

DETERMINANTS OF ELASTICITY OF DEMAND

There are no generalizations that are universally valid, or that do not have some exceptions. A number of points are extremely important, however, and must be understood.

1. Substitutability Generally speaking, the larger the number of good substitute products available, the greater the elasticity of demand.

2. Relative price levels in related markets Usually, the elasticity of demand for farm food products is greater at the retail level than at the farm level. This difference is largely due to the differences in the relative level of prices between the two markets or to the value added to products between the two markets.

3. Substitutability in the domestic and export markets For farm food products, large differences in elasticity between the two markets are due to the fact that although the demand for total farm output is highly inelastic in the domestic market, American exports compete directly with domestic farm production in the importing country and with alternative sources of farm products from other exporting countries. Because of the availability of substitutes, a small change in the price asked for the American product will make a large difference in the quantity demanded from the United States in foreign markets. In the international grain markets, for example, a difference of a few cents per ton may make the difference between a sale or no sale.

4. Substitutes and complements Complements are resources or products that tend to be used together. But complementarity is seldom absolute, and resources or products that appear as complements in one stage of production or consumption may appear as substitutes in another. Just as substitutability tends to increase the elasticity of demand, complementarity tends to decrease elasticity.

Economists measure degrees of complementarity or substitutability by the percentage change in the quantity of a commodity demanded that is associated with a 1 percent change in the price of another related commodity. For any given commodity, if there is an increase in the quantity demanded when the price of another commodity falls, the two commodities are complements. The degree of complementarity may be measured by what economists call the *coefficient of the cross-price elasticity* or simply *cross-elasticity of demand* (E_c). If there are two resources, commodities, or services, with Q' referring to the quantity of one and P'' to the the price of the other, then with everything else assumed to be constant:

$$E_c = \frac{\Delta Q'}{(Q'_1 + Q'_2)/2} \div \frac{\Delta P''}{(P''_1 + P''_2)/2}$$

ELASTICITY OF DEMAND FOR RESOURCES

This depends on (1) rate of decline of *MRP*, (2) ease of substitution of inputs, (3) elasticity of demand for products and (4) importance of the resource in production.

1. Rate of decline of *MRP*   If the marginal product of a variable resource declines rapidly as more of it is added, *MRP* will also decline rapidly, and demand will be highly inelastic.

2. Ease of substitution of inputs   Where there is no input or resource that serves as a close substitute for a given resource—fertilizer, for example—the demand for that particular input tends to be inelastic.

Economists refer to the rate at which one resource can be substituted for another as the marginal rate of substitution. The elasticity of substitution (E_s) refers to the percentage, or relative, change by which factors combine in producing a constant output. E_s is always negative for substitute resources. For a constant output as one resource declines the other must increase. E_s will indicate how rapidly the marginal rate of substitution declines as more of one resource is substituted for another.

3. Elasticity of demand for products   The elasticity of demand for any resource depends on the elasticity of demand for the product it helps produce.

4. Importance of the resource in production   The less important a resource is in production, the more inelastic its resource demand.

Elasticity of supply

Elasticity of supply is the percentage change in the quantity supplied of a resource or product in response to a given percentage change in its price, other things being equal. It depends primarily on percentage changes and is independent of the units used to measure quantities and prices. The relationship between change in price and quantity on a typical supply curve is generally direct or positive—as indicated by the law of supply—rather than inverse or negative as in the elasticity of demand.

COBWEB THEOREM

This refers to the periodic cycles in production and prices of several farm food products. The supply curve for a commodity represents— in this case—the quantity supplied in a given period in response to a specific price in some pervious period, or specific time. The necessary conditions involve a specific time period for production, relatively minor storage stocks, and production that once under way is not terminated prematurely. Generally, in addition, producers may assume that their own output does not affect market price and that current prices are an indicator of the prices that will be received for the product.

DETERMINANTS OF
ELASTICITY OF SUPPLY

The main determinant is the time the producer has to respond to a given change in price. The supply may be perfectly inelastic in a momentary period if the total quantity delivered is fixed and must be sold. At the other extreme, a constant-cost industry will have a perfectly elastic curve in the long run. The average cost will equal the price, and the quantity supplied depends on the location of demand. Between these two extremes there are all degrees of elastictiy from zero to infinity. In addition, in some special circumstances there is a backward-sloping supply curve where a higher price actually results in a smaller quantity supplied, other things being equal. Generally, however, the supply curve slopes upward and forward, and one may generalize in respect to time.

Within a given time period the elasticity of supply is determined by (1) shape and location of *MC* curves, (2) ease of substitution of products in the process of production, (3) elasticity of supply of resources, and (4) time in reference to increasing and decreasing prices of products. That is, in agriculture at least, supply is more inelastic in periods of declining prices for products than in periods of rising prices, other things being equal.

Enterprise classification

COMPETITIVE

Competition exists among enterprises when the output of one can be increased only by reducing the output of another.

COMPLEMENTARY

Enterprises are complementary if increasing the production of one automatically increases the output of another.

SUPPLEMENTARY

Enterprises are supplementary to each other when they use different resources, or the same resources at different times.

Equal-product curve

An equal-product curve shows the alternative combinations of two sets of resources that will produce the same amount of total product. *See* production-possibilities, marginal returns, elasticity of resource demand.

Equilibrium
in respect to markets

Market equilibrium occurs at the price at which the quantity supplied is equal to the quantity demanded.

Equilibrium output of the firm
in the long run

IMPERFECT COMPETITION

The long-run equilibrium of the imperfectly competitive firm is achieved when average cost is equal to selling price and a normal profit is realized.

PURE COMPETITION

The long-run equilibrium of the purely competitive firm is achieved when the price of the product is exactly equal to the minimum average total cost of the firm and production is at the point where the firm makes a normal profit.

Equilibrium output of the firm in the short run

Two questions must be answered. Shall the firm produce? And if so, how much?

The general answers are as follows:

1. The firm should produce in the short run if it can make an economic profit or if it loses less than its fixed costs. This also means that it must produce enough total product for sale or use which when valued at the market or other appropriate price at least covers its variable costs.
2. In the short run the firm should produce the output at which it maximizes profits, or minimizes losses.

All competitive firms will maximize profits or minimize losses by producing at the level of output where marginal revenue equals marginal cost ($MR = MC$). A purely competitive firm will maximize profits or minimize losses in the short run by producing at the point of $P = MC$, provided the price is greater than the minimum average variable cost.

Farm, farming

A farm is an economic unit—a business firm—organized to produce crops or raise livestock. It involves land, capital resources in addition to land, and management and labor. Farms vary widely in size and type.

The distinction between a specialized and a diversified farm is one of degree, or common acceptance of the terms. Common usage suggests that a specialized farm is one in which the major part, if not practically all, of the farm income is derived from one or two enterprises. Examples are a wheat farm in Kansas, a big broiler unit in Georgia, a cash corn and soybean farm in the corn belt, a peach orchard in California, and so on. Specialization is easy to see, but diversification is more complicated. A diversified farm may take one of several forms, combining crop and livestock enterprises; growing different types of crops such as cotton, sugarcane, soybeans, and alfalfa; or producing a number of animal or poultry products such as milk, pork, wool, eggs, or broilers.

In a private-enterprise economy the individual farm is generally organized as a profit-maximizing, income-producing unit. In most countries, the farm economy is mixed with varying degrees of individual proprietorships, cooperative enterprises, and types of government ownership and control. The United States, Canada, and a number of other western democracies were founded on the concept of the family farm as an ideal of organization of resources and distribution of income. Generally, a family farm is regarded as a unit that is large enough to provide most if not all of the income for at least an average level of family living and small enough so that the family can do most of the work of farming. This concept was fostered by government policy in the United States, which encouraged settlers to take up farming through grants of land of sufficient size for family farming. Large family farms have been growing in the United States relative to small farms. Some larger-than-family farms have grown also, with some reaching a factory-type size, or scale. The growth of large farms has been encouraged by advancing technology, favorable tax laws which permit the reporting of some income from sales of livestock as capital gain, and laws favoring incorporation of large units.

Farm management

Farm management emphasizes the application of economic principles and skills to the organization and operation of farms. Increasingly, the quantitative concepts of production economics have been applied to management. Farm management is taught in high schools, junior colleges, and university classes and extension programs. The profession of farm management and appraisal has grown rapidly in the United States, based in part on the growth of farm management as a discipline within the field of agricultural economics.

Increasing (relative) costs, law of

The law of increasing (relative) costs prevails when to produce equal extra amounts of a certain good or service, an ever-increasing amount of another good or service must be sacrificed.

See *elasticity of demand for resources*, under *elasticity of demand; principle of equal marginal returns*, and *production possibilities*, under *production*..

Long run

The long run is a production and market period within which all costs are variable. See *production costs in the long run* under *production costs per unit*.

Marketing agreements and orders, federal

Marketing agreements and orders have the general purpose of influencing prices by regulating the timing, volume, and sometimes quality of the commodities marketed. They have been used most for milk, fruits, and vegetables. Although most orders are issued under a federal statute, state laws may also apply. In California, for example, the marketing of milk is regulated under a special state law, while the federal law permits the establishment of minimum prices for producers. Under California statutes any agricultural commodity is eligible to be covered under an order, while the federal statutes exclude some commodities.

Orders are usually written for a single commodity produced in a specific area for either a definite or an indefinite period of time, and the orders are subject to amendment, suspension, or termination. Once approved, an order is binding on all firms in an industry, with producers and handlers generally bearing most if not all of the direct operating and administrative costs.

MARKETING ORDERS FOR FLUID MILK

Each of the major milk markets in the United States is covered by a marketing order. The portion of grade A milk that is demanded for fluid consumption at the price set and regulated by the order is sold as class I. Milk that is not bought for fluid use is placed in class II or class III for manufacturing butter, cheese, nonfat dry milk powder, and evaporated milk. The price of class II and class III milk is supported by the federal government through purchase of products that are not bought by manufacturers or dealers at the level of price support.

Dairy farmers selling in federal order markets receive a *blend* price, which is the weighted average of the price paid by dairy companies for milk for both fluid and nonfluid uses. The government then purchases and stores the "surplus" that is not bought at the level of the federal price support.

MARKETING ORDERS
FOR FRUITS AND VEGETABLES

These have been used extensively to regulate the marketing of fruits and vegetables as a supplement to competitive markets rather than a substitute for them. Generally, an order applies to a specified production or marketing area and, in contrast to an order for fluid milk, is normally covered by a prior voluntary agreement—a contract entered into by the Secretary of Agriculture with the handlers of a particular commodity to regulate the marketing of that commodity. Since an agreement is binding only on those who sign it, however, an agreement alone is seldom effective and is useful mainly as a basis for promulgating an order. A marketing order is binding on all handlers of a commodity in the specified production and marketing area regardless of whether they have signed an agreement, provided it has been approved in referendum by at least two-thirds of the producers or by those who produce at least two-thirds of the total volume of a commodity. The Secretary may propose an order without a prior agreement, although—for political reasons—this generally is not done.

A federal agreement and order for a fruit or vegetable may permit or provide for any one or all of the following:

1. Specification of grades, size, quality, or maturity of the commodity that handlers may ship to market
2. Allotment of the amount each handler may purchase or handle on behalf of any and all producers
3. Establishment of the quantity of the commodity that may be shipped to market during any specified period
4. Establishment of methods for determining the extent of any surplus in order to control and dispose of the surplus and equalize the burden of elimination of surplus among producers and handlers
5. Establishment of a reserve pool of the product
6. Inspection of the commodity
7. Specification of the size, capacity, weight, dimensions, or pack of the container used in handling the commodity

In addition, miscellaneous provisions may authorize actions to prohibit certain unfair trade practices in interstate commerce or to coordinate federal orders with the orders of individual states. Although controls over marketing vary somewhat among the states, the states with enabling legislation do not generally attempt to control the volume of supplies going to market, but limit their activity to regulation of quality, size, or pack; control of advertising and sales promotion; and support of research and investigation. The federal legislation is restricted primarily to fruits and vegetables for fresh shipment. Most production for canning or freezing is excluded. Enforcement of sanitary standards and other standards for protection of consumers is not, of course, dependent on the existence of an agreement or order.

Marketing or production contracts

Generally speaking, 80 to 85 percent of the aggregate output of American farms and ranches is produced and sold without production or marketing contracts, with prices usually determined in competitive markets. In the 1970s, some 17 to 18 percent was produced under production contracts, generally between the farmer-producer and the first buyer. But only a portion of these contracts were set through a bargaining association. The others were private, mutually agreed upon contracts between the farmer-producer and the processing-marketing firm in order to provide greater certainty on terms that were to the advantage of both.

Marketing quotas

A marketing quota sets the maximum amount of a commodity that a farmer can sell without incurring a penalty. In 1934, the first marketing quotas were authorized in the Bankhead Cotton Control Act and the Kerr-Smith Act for tobacco. The cotton act required approval by referendum by two-thirds of the producers of cotton before a program of quota allotments could go into effect. The tobacco act required agreement from three-fourths of tobacco growers. In case of an affirmative vote the quota was introduced by allotting to each producer certificates which, when accompanying the crop, would exempt the crop from a sales tax that the Secretary of Agriculture was directed to levy.

Overvaluation and devaluation

Viewed externally, as in the case of a country importing farm products from the United States, overvaluation of the dollar keeps the prices of the imports high in terms of the currency of the importing nation. If corn is $2.50 per bushel or $100 per ton in the United States, for example, and $1 will exchange for 4 German marks—as it did in the early 1970s—it will take 400 marks to buy 1 ton of corn. If the value of the dollar declines so that $1 will exchange for only 2 marks—as it did in the late 1970s—it will take only 200 marks to buy 1 ton of corn. Without any change in the domestic price in the United States, the price of corn to the German importer is cut in half, provided there is no change in other factors. The effects of devaluation of the dollar on farm exports can be offset by the United States through use of export quotas or by an embargo. An embargo was applied to soybeans briefly in 1973 and to sales of grain to the Soviet Union from August to October 1975, partly to prevent further increases in American food prices although in both cases this was bitterly opposed by American farm organizations. Much more importantly for American farm exports, however, the effects can be offset by tariffs, quotas, and government control of farm food imports by the importing countries. This is the case in Japan and the European Community especially with imports controlled in Japan by use of quotas implemented by a government trading corporation, and in the E.C. by use of a variable import levy.

Production

Production is the process of creating an economic good or service from two or more other goods or services.

PRODUCTION FUNCTION

The production function is the technical relationship between inputs and outputs that indicates the maximum amount of output that can be produced with each and every set or combination of the specified inputs, or factors of production. For production in the short run, a fixed input is a factor of production that does not change as the level of output is changed. A variable input is a factor of production that changes in such a way as to change the level of output.

AVERAGE PRODUCT

The average physical product (*APP*) per unit of variable input is the total physical product divided by the number of variable units at each level of output.

LAW OF DIMINISHING RETURNS

As successive units of a variable resource (say fertilizer) are added to a fixed resource (say a given amount of land), beyond some point the extra, or marginal, product attributable to each additional unit of the variable resource will diminish, or decline. Thus, in general, the law of diminishing returns refers specifically to the extra output produced when equal extra units of a varying input are successively added to a fixed amount of some other input, or inputs.

MARGINAL PRODUCT

The marginal physical product (*MPP*) at each level of output is the net addition to total physical product from adding an additional unit of variable input.

PRODUCTION POSSIBILITIES

Each point on a production-possiblities curve represents the maximum output of any two products, assuming given resources and technologies. With given resources and technologies, production cannot go beyond the p-p curve; hence it is a frontier. The p-p curve, or p-p frontier, may also be called a transformation curve because in moving from one point to another on the curve, one product is in a sense transformed into another.

PRODUCTION STAGES

The typical production function may be divided into three stages. Stage 1 is from zero output up to the point where the average productivity of the variable factor is at its maximum level. That is, the maximum point on the *APP* curve defines the end of stage 1. Stage 2 extends from this point to the point of maximum *TPP*, or where *MPP* is zero. Stage 3 includes all inputs that have a negative marginal product, and it extends over the entire range of declining *TPP*. A production function that has only increasing marginal returns would be entirely within stage 1. A function characterized by diminishing marginal returns from the outset would be limited to stages 2 and 3.

TOTAL PRODUCT

The total physical product (*TPP*) is the maximum amount that can be produced with any given combination of fixed and variable inputs.

Production costs

Production data must be coupled with prices of resources to determine production costs. It has been noted that in the short run some resources—those associated with a firm's plant—are fixed. Others are variable. This correctly suggests that in the short run costs are either fixed or variable.

FIXED COSTS

Costs which do not change in total with changes in output.

TOTAL COSTS

The sum of fixed and variable costs at each level of output.

VARIABLE COSTS

Costs which increase in total with the level of output. They start at zero when output is zero, increase as output increases up to the end of stage 2 of the production function, and continue to increase if production continues into stage 3.

Production costs per unit, average and marginal

These may be derived from the total production costs, as follows:

AVERAGE FIXED COST (*AFC*)

The total fixed cost (*TFC*) divided by the corresponding output (*Q*).

$$AFC = \frac{TFC}{Q}$$

AVERAGE TOTAL COST (*ATC*)

The total cost (*TC*) divided by the corresponding output (*Q*); more simply, the total of *AFC* and *AVC* at each level of output:

$$ATC = \frac{TC}{Q} \quad \text{or} \quad AFC + AVC$$

AVERAGE VARIABLE COST (*AVC*)

The total variable cost (*TVC*) divided by the corresponding output (*Q*).

$$AVC = \frac{TVC}{Q}$$

MARGINAL COST (*MC*)

The extra, or additional, cost of producing one more unit of output.

$$MC = \frac{\text{change in } TC}{\text{change in } Q}$$

MC AND MARGINAL PRODUCT

Given the price (cost) of the variable resource, increasing returns (or a rising marginal product) will be reflected in a decreasing marginal cost, and diminishing returns (or a falling marginal product) will be reflected in an increasing marginal cost.

MC RELATED TO *AVC* AND *ATC*

The *MC* curve cuts both the *AVC* and *ATC* curves at their respective minimum points. As long as the *AVC* or *ATC* curves are falling, the *MC* curve must be below them; when they are rising, the *MC* curve must be above them. No such relationship exists between *MC* and average fixed cost because *MC* deals with costs that change with output.

PRODUCTION COSTS IN THE LONG RUN

The long run is a production or market period in which all costs are variable.

In the long run, all firms that wish to enter or leave an industry may do so. Individual firms adjust their scale of output along a long-run planning curve so that average total cost equals price when the firm is in equilibrium.

See also *economies and diseconomies of scale*.

Productivity

The ratio of total outputs to total inputs used in production. Productivity in American agriculture during the 40-year period from 1940 to 1979 appears as follows (based on 1967 = 100):

Year	Output	Input	Productivity
1940–1944	66 .4	102.4	64 .6
1975–1978	118.0	101.8	116.5
1940–1944 to 1975–1978 percent increase	78	− 0.5	80

In terms of productivity, an innovation (or a new invention) is called *labor-saving*, *capital saving*, or *neutral* depending on whether it tends to lower the relative share of income going to labor and management, lower the relative share going to capital inputs and property, or leave the relative shares unchanged.

Soil Bank Program

The Agricultural Act of 1956, which established the so-called *Soil Bank*, provided for an acreage reserve (under which farmers were paid for an annual diversion of part of their land from certain cash crops without increasing the amount of land planted to other crops) and a conservation reserve (under which farmers were paid for a long-term diversion of a specified amount of cropland to designated soil-conserving uses). Although the Soil Bank Program had been planned in order to divert 60 million acres or more of land from crops each year, it was funded at a much lower level, and the total diversion under the program was correspondingly smaller. The Emergency Feed Grain Act of 1961, designed especially to divert land away from production of feed grains, greatly expanded payments to farmers to take land out of production. The Wheat-Cotton Act of 1964 accomplished a similar purpose for those crops. The annual appropriations under these and succeeding acts achieved a large diversion of cropland up to 1973.

Supply

Supply may be defined as a schedule showing the various amounts of a product that producers will produce and offer for sale in a market, under given conditions, at each specific price in a set of possible prices during a specified time period.

CHANGES IN SUPPLY

By definition, a change in supply involves a shift in the supply curve itself—to the right for an increase in supply and to the left for a decrease.

DETERMINANTS OF SUPPLY

The basic factors that determine the location of the supply curve and whether it will change are (1) technologies of production, (2) prices of resources used in production, (3) prices of other products that may be substituted for the given product, (4) expectations about prices, (5) number of sellers in a market, (6) taxes and subsidies related to the product, and (7) especially in farming, the effects of weather. A change in any one of these determinants will cause the supply curve for a product to change, or shift to the right or the left.

LAW OF SUPPLY

On a given supply schedule, there is normally a direct relationship between the price and the quantity supplied. As the price rises, the quantity supplied increases. As the price falls, the quantity supplied decreases, assuming that other things remain the same.

Trade agreements

In 1934, the United States embarked on a new program under the Reciprocal Trade Agreements Act. This gave the President the authority to negotiate agreements with individual nations in order to reduce American tariffs as much as 50 percent, provided the other nations made a reciprocal reduction for American exports. The act also included the so-called *most-favored-nation* clause, which provided that similar reductions in tariffs could apply to the exports of any other nation to the United States, provided it agreed to the same terms as the most favored nation. Although there was a general revival of trade under the 1934 act, agricultural exports continued to drop under the influence of price supports above world price levels until by 1940 the trade of agricultural exports of the United States was practically zero.

The Reciprocal Trade Agreements Act of 1934, which was the basis for bilateral (two-nation) negotiations, gave way to a broader approach in 1947 when 23 nations, including the United States, signed a General Agreement on Tariffs and Trade (G.A.T.T.) involving three cardinal principles: (1) equal, nondiscriminatory treatment for all member nations, (2) reduction of tariffs by multilateral (several-nation) negotiations, and (3) elimination of quotas for imports, a feature especially important for American agriculture. More than 100 nations now belong to G.A.T.T., and in general it has been an important force for liberalizing international trade. Under its sponsorship, six distinct "rounds" of negotiations to reduce trade barriers have been completed. A seventh, in which the United States has emphasized freer markets for agricultural exports, has become a reality.

Utility

Utility is the ability or power to satisfy a want or wants. In regard to consumer goods, utility involves subjective values that differ from person to person as well as practical down-to-earth or common values involving products that everyone wants, such as the necessities of life.

LAW OF DIMINISHING MARGINAL UTILITY

At any given time during which a consumer's tastes do not change, after a certain number of units of a product have been obtained, the marginal utility derived from successive units of the given product will decline, or diminish.

MARGINAL UTILITY

The net addition to total utility, or the net additional power to satisfy wants, of one more unit of a given product.

UTILITY-MAXIMIZING RULE

To maximize utility, the consumer must allocate the available income or money so that the last unit of expenditure—such as 1 dollar, 100 dollars, or whatever—on each product purchased has the same net additional amount of power to satisfy wants (utility) as the equivalent amount spent on something else.

This means that the unit prices of the various products in the consumer's budget will be proportional to the marginal utilities of the respective products to that consumer.

When the income is all spent, the marginal utilities of all products or services acquired should be proportional to their respective unit prices.

Vertical integration

Vertical integration has come into use as a term to decribe a situation where two or more firms at different stages of production and processing-marketing combine under a single ownership and management. Examples are a sugarcane plantation having its own sugar processing plant, and a plant taking over one or more plantations. Other examples are a potato processing-marketing firm acquiring potato farms, a citrus-marketing firm merging with one or more citrus plantations, and a firm that markets fresh vegetables acquiring, or merging with, farms that produce vegetables.

BIBLIOGRAPHY

Adelman, Irma, and Cynthia Taft Morris: *Economic Growth and Social Equity in Developing Countries*, Stanford University Press, Stanford, Calif., 1973.

Agency for International Development: *War on Hunger*, Washington, D.C., 1975.

Ball, Gordon, and Earl O. Heady (eds.): *Size, Structure, and Future of Farms*, Iowa State University Press, Ames, 1972.

Behan, R. W., and Richard M. Weddle (eds.): *Ecology Economics Environment*, University of Montana, Missoula, 1971.

Bishop, C. E., and W. D. Toussaint: *Agricultural Economic Analysis*, John Wiley & Sons, Inc., New York, 1958.

Black, John D.: *Economics for Agriculture: Selecting Writings of John D. Black*, edited by James P. Cavin, with introductory essays, Harvard University Press, Cambridge, Mass., 1959.

Black, Lloyd D.: *The Strategy of Foreign Aid*, D. Van Nostrand Company, Inc., Princeton, N. J., 1968.

Bogue, Donald J.: *Principles of Demography*, John Wiley & Sons, Inc., New York, 1969.

Brandow, George E.: *Interrelationships among Demand for Farm Products and Implication for Control of Market Supply*, Pennsylvania State University, Agricultural Experiment Station Bulletin no. 680, University Park, 1961.

Breimyer, Harold F.: *Farm Policy: 13 Essays*, The Iowa State University Press, Ames, 1977.

————: *Individual Freedom and the Economic Organization of Agriculture*, The University of Illinois Press, Urbana, 1965.

Bryson, Reid A., and Thomas J. Murray: *Climates of Hunger: Mankind and the World's Changing Weather*, The University of Wisconsin Press, Madison, 1977.

Chrispeels, Maarten, Jr.: *Plants, Food and People*, W. H. Freeman and Company, San Francisco, 1977.

Clarkson, Kenneth W.: *Food Stamps and Nutrition*, American Enterprise Institute for Public Policy Research, Evaluative Study no. 18, Washington, D.C., April 1975.

Cramer, Gail L., and Clarence W. Jensen: *Agricultrual Economics and Agribusiness: An Introduction*, John Wiley & Sons, Inc., New York, 1979.

Crosson, Pierre, and Kenneth D. Frederick: *The World Food Situation*, Resources for tho Future, Washington, D.C., 1977

Davis, Kenneth P.: *Land Use*, McGraw-Hill Book Company, New York, 1976.

Dornbusch, Rudiger, and Stanley Fischer: *Macroeconomics*, McGraw-Hill Book Company, New York, 1978.

Ehrlich, Paul R., with Anne H. Ehrlich: *Population, Resources and Environment, Issues in Human Ecology*, W. H. Freeman and Company, San Francisco, 1970.

Enke, Stephen: *Economics for Development*, Prentice-Hall, Inc., Englewood Cliffs, N. J., 1963.

Ferguson, Elizabeth S.(ed.): *U.S. Trade Policy and Agricultural Exports*, The Iowa State University Press, Ames, 1973.

George, P. S., and G. S. King: *Consumer Demand for Food Commodities in the United States with Projections for 1980*, Giannini Foundation of Agricultural Economics Monograph no. 26, University of California, Davis, 1971.

Goodwin, John W.: *Agricultural Economics*, Reston Publishing Company, Reston, Va, 1977.

Griswold, A. Whitney: *Farming and Democracy*, Harcourt, Brace and Company, Inc., New York, 1948.

Guither, Harold D.: *Heritage of Plenty, A Guide to the Economic History and Development of U.S. Agriculture*, The Interstate Printers & Publishers, Inc., Danville, Ill., 1972.

Halcrow, Harold G.: *Food Policy for America*, McGraw-Hill Book Company, New York, 1977.

Harbison, Frederick, and Charles A. Myers: *Education, Manpower, and Economic Growth: Strategies of Human Resource Development*, McGraw-Hill Book Company, New York, 1964.

Hardin, Charles M.: *Food and Fiber in the Nation's Politics*, National Commission on Food and Fiber, Technical Papers, vol. 3, 1967.

———: *The Politics of Agriculture*, The Free Press of Glencoe, Ill., Chicago, 1952.

Hathaway, Dale E.: *Problems of Progress in the Agricultural Economy*, Scott, Foresman and Company, Glenview, Ill., 1964.

Hayami, Yujiro, and Vernon Ruttan: *Resources, Technology and Agricultural Development: An International Perspective*, The Johns Hopkins Press, Baltimore, 1971.

Headley, J. C., and J. N. Lewis: *The Pesticide Problem: An Economic Approach to Public Policy*, Resources for the Future, Inc., The Johns Hopkins Press, Baltimore, 1967.

Heady, Earl O.: *Economics of Agricultural Production and Resource Use*, Prentice-Hall, Inc., Englewood Cliffs, N.J., 1952.

Hicks, John D.: *The Populist Revolt, A History of the Farmer's Alliance and the People's Party*, University of Nebraska Press, Lincoln, 1968 (first published by University of Minnesota Press, Minneapolis, 1931).

Johnson, D. Gale: *World Agriculture in Disarray*, St. Martin's Press in association with the Trade Policy Research Centre, London, 1973.

Johnston, Bruce F., and Peter Kilby: *Agriculture and Structural Tranformation: Economic Strategies in Late-Developing Countries*, Oxford University Press, New York, 1975.

Kendrick, John W.: *Productivity Trends in the United States*, National Bureau of Economic Research, New York, Princeton University Press, Princeton, N. J., 1961.

———: *Postwar Productivity Trends in the United States, 1948-1969*, National Bureau of Economic Research, New York, Columbia University Press, New York and London, 1973.

Keynes, John Maynard: *The General Theory of Employment, Interest and Money*, Macmillan & Co., Ltd., London, 1936.

Leontief, Wassily, Anne P. Carter, and Peter A. Petri: *The Future of the World Economy: A United Nations Study*, Oxford University Press, New York, 1977.

McConnell, Campbell R.: *Economics: Principles, Problems, Policies*, 7th ed., McGraw-Hill Book Company, New York, 1978.

McKenzie, Richard B., and Gordon Tullock: *Modern Polictical Economy: An Introduction to Economics*, McGraw-Hill Book Company, New York, 1978.

Madden, J. Patrick, and David E. Brewster,(eds.): *A Philosopher Among Economists, Selected Works of John M. Brewster*, J. T. Murphy Co., Inc., Philadelphia, 1970.

Malthus, Thomas Robert: *On Population*, edited and introduced by Gertrude Himmelfarb, Modern Library, Inc., New York, 1960.

Marshall, Ray: *Rural Workers in Rural Labor Markets*, Olympus Publishing Company., Salt Lake City, 1974.

Meadows, Donella H., Dennis L. Meadows, Jørgen Randers, and William W. Behrens III: *The Limits to Growth: A Report for the Club of Rome's Project on the Predicament of Mankind*, Universe Books, New York, 1972.

Mesarovic, Mihajlo, and Edward Pestel: *Mankind at the Crossroads*, Dutton/Readers Digest Press, New York, 1975.

Michael, Robert T.: *The Effect of Education on Efficiency in Consumption*, National Bureau of Economic Research, New York, Occasional Paper no. 116, 1972.

Mosher, Arthur T.: *Getting Agriculture Moving, Essentials for Development and Modernization*, Agricultural Development Council, Frederick A. Praeger, Inc., New York, 1966.

National Advisory Commission on Food and Fiber: *Food and Fiber for the Future*, U.S. Government Printing Office, Washington, D.C., 1967.

National Commission on Food Marketing: *Food from Farmer to Consumer*, U.S. Government Printing Office, Washington, D.C., 1966.

National Farm Institute: *Farmers and a Hungry World*, The Iowa State University Press, Ames, 1967.

National Research Council: *World Food and Nutrition Study: The Potential Contribution of Research*, National Academy of Sciences, Washington, D.C., 1977.

———: *Pest Control: Strategies for the Future*, National Academy of Sciences, Washington, D.C., 1972.

Nicholls, William H.: *A Theoretical Analysis of Imperfect Competition with Special Application to the Agricultural Industries*, The Iowa State University Press, Ames, 1941.

North, Douglass C.: *Growth and Welfare in the American Past: A New Economic History*, Prentice-Hall, Inc., Englewood Cliffs, N. J., 1966.

North Central Regional Research Committee: *Agricultural Cooperatives and the Public Interest*, N. C. Project 117, Monograph no. 4, N.E. Regional Research Publication no. 256, September 1978.

O'Hagen, James P.: *Growth and Adjustment in National Agricultures: Four Case Studies and an Overview*, Food and Agriculture Organization (F.A.O.), Universe Books, New York, 1977.

Ophuls, Willian: *Ecology and the Politics of Scarcity: Prologue to a Political Theory of the Steady State*, W. H. Freeman and Company, San Francisco, 1977.

Padberg, Daniel I.: *Economics of Food Retailing*, Cornell University, Food Distribution Program, Ithaca, N.Y., 1968.

Perelman, Michael: *Farming for Profit in a Hungry World: Capital and the Crisis in Agriculture*, Universe Books, New York, 1978.

Rechcigl, Miloslav, Jr. (ed.): *Man, Food, and Nutrition: Strategies and Technological Measures for Alleviating the World Food Problem*, The Chemical Rubber Co., CRC Press, Inc., Cleveland, 1973.

―――: *World Food Problem: A Selective Bibliography of Reviews*, The Chemical Rubber Company Co., CRC Press, Inc., Cleveland, 1975.

Ricardo, David: *Protection to Agriculture*, John Murray (Publishers), Ltd., London, 1822.

Ritson, Christopher: *Agricultural Economics: Principles and Policy*, St. Martin's Press, Inc., New York, 1977.

Ruttan, Vernon W., Arley D. Waldo, and James P. Houck (eds): *Agricultural Policy in an Affluent Society*, W. W. Norton & Company, Inc., New York, 1969.

Saloutos, Theodore, and John D. Hicks: *Agricultural Discontent in the Middle West, 1900–1939*, The University of Wisconsin Press, Madison, 1951.

Samuelson, Paul A.: *Economics*, tenth ed., McGraw-Hill Book Company, New York, 1976.

Saulnier, R. J., Harold G. Halcrow, and Neil H. Jacoby: *Federal Lending and Loan Insurance*, National Bureau of Economic Research, New York, Princeton University Press, Princeton, N.J., 1968.

Saunderson, Mont H.: *Western Land and Water Use*, University of Oklahoma Press, Norman, 1950.

Schickele, Rainer: *Agrarian Revolution and Economic Progress: A Primer for Development*, Agricultural Development Council, Inc., Frederick A. Praeger, Inc., New York, 1968.

Schultz, T. W. (ed.): *Distortions of Agricultural Incentives*, Indiana University Press, Bloomington, 1978.

―――: *Economic Crises in World Agriculture*, The University of Michigan Press, Ann Arbor, 1965.

―――: *Economic Growth and Agriculture*, McGraw-Hill Book Company, New York, 1968.

―――: *Transforming Traditional Agriculture*, Yale University Press, New Haven, Conn., 1964.

Snodgrass, Milton M., and L. T. Wallace: *Agriculture, Economics, and Resource Management*, Prentice-Hall, Inc., Englewood Cliffs, N.J., 1975.

Steinhart, John S., and Carol E. Steinhart: "Energy Use in the U.S. Food System," in Philip H. Abelson (ed.), *Food: Politics, Economics, Nutrition and Research*, American Association for the Advancement of Science, Washington, D.C., 1975.

Talbot, Ross B., and Don F. Hadwiger: *The Policy Process in American Agriculture*, Chandler Publishing Company, San Francisco, 1968.

Taylor, Henry C., and Anne Dewees Taylor: *The Story of Agricultural Eco-*

nomics in the United States, 1840–1932, The Iowa State University Press, Ames, 1952.

Tinbergen, Jan: *The Design of Development*, The Economic Development Institute, International Bank for Reconstruction and Development, The Johns Hopkins Press, Baltimore, 1958.

Toffler, Alvin: *Future Shock*, Random House, Inc., New York, 1970.

Trans Atlantic Committee on Agricultural Change: "Agricultural Change and Economic Method," *European Review of Agricultural Economics*, vol. 3, nos. 2 and 3, 1976.

Tsui, Amy Ong, and Donald J. Bogue: "Declining World Fertility: Trends, Causes, Implications," *Population Bulletin*, vol. 33, no. 4, 1978.

Tweeten, Luther: *Foundations of Farm Policy*, University of Nebraska Press, Lincoln, 1970.

————: "The Demand for United States Farm Output," *Food Research Institute Studies*, vol. 7, no. 3, Stanford University Press, 1967, pp. 343-369.

U.S. Department of Agriculture and the National Science Foundation. *Policy Analysis of Grain Reserves*, Washington, D.C., 1976.

U.S. General Accounting Office, Comptroller General: *Grain Reserves: A Potential U.S. Food Policy Tool*, Washington, D.C., OSP-76-16, March 1976.

U.S. Senate, Committee on Agriculture and Forestry: *Agriculture, Rural Development, and the Use of Land*, Washington, D.C., 1974.

Viner, Jacob: *The Long View and the Short: Studies in Economic Theory and Policy*, The Free Press of Glencoe, Inc., New York, 1958.

Ward, Barbara: *The Rich Nations and the Poor Nations*, W. W. Norton & Company Inc., New York, 1962.

Wilcox, Walter W., Willard W. Cochrane, and Robert W. Herdt: *Economics of American Agriculture*, 3rd ed., Prentice-Hall, Inc., Englewood Cliffs, N.J., 1974.

Will, Robert E., and Harold G. Vatter (eds.): *Poverty in Affluence: The Social, Political and Economic Dimensions of Poverty in the United States*, Harcourt, Brace & World, Inc., New York, 1970.

Wright, Jim: *The Coming Water Famine*, Coward-McCann, Inc., New York, 1966.

INDEX